INDEX TO FAIRY TALES, 1987–1992

*Including 310 Collections
of Fairy Tales,
Folktales, Myths, and Legends
With Significant pre-1987 Titles
Not Previously Indexed*

compiled by
JOSEPH W. SPRUG

The Scarecrow Press, Inc.
Metuchen, N.J., & London
1994

OTHER SCARECROW TITLES BY NORMA OLIN IRELAND AND/OR JOSEPH W. SPRUG

INDEX TO FAIRY TALES, 1978–1986, INCLUDING FOLKLORE, LEG-
 ENDS, AND MYTHS IN COLLECTIONS. Compiled by Norma Olin
 Ireland and Joseph W. Sprug.
INDEX TO WOMEN OF THE WORLD, FROM ANCIENT TO MODERN
 TIMES: BIOGRAPHIES AND PORTRAITS. Compiled by Norma
 Olin Ireland.
INDEX TO WOMEN OF THE WORLD, FROM ANCIENT TO MODERN
 TIMES: A SUPPLEMENT. Compiled by Norma Olin Ireland.
INDEX TO AMERICA: LIFE AND CUSTOMS—TWENTIETH CEN-
 TURY TO 1986. Compiled by Norma Olin Ireland.
INDEX TO AMERICA: LIFE AND CUSTOMS—NINETEENTH CEN-
 TURY. Compiled by Norma Olin Ireland.
TIME RESEARCH: 1172 STUDIES. Compiled by Irving Zelkind and
 Joseph W. Sprug.
IRELAND'S INDEX TO INSPIRATION: A THESAURUS FOR SPEAK-
 ERS AND WRITERS, CONTINUED THROUGH 1990. Compiled
 by Joseph W. Sprug.

British Library Cataloguing-in-Publication data available

Library of Congress Cataloging-in-Publication Data

Sprug, Joseph W., 1922–
    Index to fairy tales, 1987–1992 : including 310 collections of fairy tales, folktales,
 myths, and legends : with significant pre-1987 titles not previously indexed / compiled
 by Joseph W. Sprug.
        p.   cm.
    Continuation of : Index to fairy tales, 1978–1986 / compiled by Norma Olin Ireland
 and Joseph W. Sprug.
    Includes bibliographical references.
    ISBN 0-8108-2750-6 (acid-free paper)
    1. Fairy tales—Indexes.   2. Mythology—Indexes.   3. Folklore—Indexes.   4.
 Folk literature—Indexes.   I. Ireland, Norma Olin, 1907–   Index to fairy tales, 1978–
 1986.   II. Title.
 Z5983.F17S67   1994
 [GR550]
 016.3982—dc20   93-29709

Index to Fairy Tales
Publishing History

Index to Fairy Tales. Mary Huse Eastman. 1915.

Index to Fairy Tales. 2nd edition revised. Mary Huse Eastman. 1926.

———— *Supplement* / Eastman. 1937.

———— *Second Supplement* / Eastman. 1952.

Index to Fairy Tales, 1949–72. Norma Olin Ireland. 1973.

Index to Fairy Tales, 1973–77. Norma Olin Ireland. 1979.

Index to Fairy Tales, 1978–86. Norma Olin Ireland and Joseph W. Sprug. 1989.

Index to Fairy Tales, 1987–1992. Joseph W. Sprug. 1994.

CONTENTS

v

INTRODUCTION

PURPOSE

This, the seventh compilation in the *Index to Fairy Tales* (IFT) series, retains the fundamental purpose of providing access to the contents of collections of fairy tales (and related titles classified as folktales, fables, legends, or myths); the titles indexed aim at being qualitatively comprehensive for the children's area.

THREE IMPORTANT CHANGES IN THIS IFT COMPILATION

The major change in this compilation is that each entry (whether author, title, or subject) is "complete" in that it gives the location where the tale is to be found.

(Previous volumes had complete citations only under the title; all author and subject entries were cross-references to the title. By far, most usage of the *Index* is by way of the subjects; and formerly each item selected required reference to the title entry.)

The second major change is in the order of elements in the entry. In this compilation of *IFT* the order—location first, followed by title/modifier—replaces the former title-followed-by-location arrangement in subject and author entries. (This is discussed later in this Introduction.)

The third major change is that in the descriptive part of the entry (the modifier), titles are extended, modified, or even replaced for the purpose of making the item more informative.

Prior to implementing these changes, consultations were held with a number of children's librarians and publisher representatives.

SELECTION PROCEDURE

The following activities detail how the titles in this compilation of *IFT* were selected:

—Book-by-book examination of the 398 classification in the (fine) children's collection of the Salem (Oregon) Public Library. The same exercise (but less frequent) in the public libraries of Portland, Vancouver (WA), Eugene, Corvallis, as well as in smaller towns in this area.

—The *Children's Book Review Index* (and other sources) was checked for all titles considered for inclusion.

—Regular reading of *Book Review Digest, Booklist, Library Journal,* and the *New York Times Book Review.*

—Analysis of the *Books in Print* Subject Catalog and also the *Cumulative Book Index.*

—Use of lists of "best books," *e.g.,* The *Reader's Adviser, Public Library Catalog, Junior High School Library Catalog,* and a number of titles from selective bibliographies (identified as "listed in" in the List of Titles Indexed).

—Study of catalogs of the major publishers of children's books, followed by search for book reviews for titles appropriate to the IFT scope.

—On-line search of the Online Computer Library Center (OCLC) database to determine if particular titles were to be found in public libraries *throughout* the country.

—Note that some of the lists of best books are not restricted as to date of publication. If not previously indexed in *IFT,* these titles are selectively included here.

DISTRIBUTION OF 310 TITLES INDEXED, BY DATE

1990–91	44 titles	14%
1987–89	98 titles	32%
1980–86	120 titles	39%
1970–79	41 titles	13%
1960–69	7 titles	02%

ARRANGEMENT OF INDIVIDUAL ENTRIES

The following considerations and observations provide the background for changes in format adopted for this compilation.

Clients are looking for a *particular* title, subject, or author. They need to identify the item, find out which collection contains it, and find a library that has it.

When the search is for a subject, it is more effective to have all material in any one source together; the client can then restrict the initial search to the collections available locally. If dispersed by title, *all* titles have to be looked at to find the locally-available source.

To satisfy these needs, the format is now cast to group subheads (titles of descriptors) first by the collection(s) containing the subject; then alphabetically by title/modifier.

Again: each item, whether author, title, or subject, gives the exact location without having to refer to a "title main entry."

INDEXING LEVEL

This refers to comprehensiveness of indexing for a particular collection. In the list of titles indexed, levels are indicated by the Roman numbers I, II, III, IV—with the lower number being the most comprehensive.

All * (children's books) tend to be in the I (most comprehensive) class.

Indexing level does not correlate with quantity. Hypothetically, a book rated I, containing five stories, might have 25 entries; a book rated III, with 50 stories, might have 75 entries.

The books in the IV class tend to be more specialized, college-level or research works, whose contents are covered generally by library subject-catalog type entries.

READING LEVEL

This is a difficult area in which to be objective. If a review or a publisher's statement indicates a reading level, this is usually followed. A good clue is the public library location of a book: easy reading, children's, young adult, or adult.

Although the number of books indexed totals 310, the Reading Levels (in the table below) total 573; this is because some titles span more than one level. However, books in the * A (All Ages) group are only counted once.

Some books in the * A or * M classes may appear to be too hard. It is assumed that these stories will be read to, or told to, children not sufficiently advanced to read them on their own.

DISTRIBUTION OF 310 TITLES INDEXED, BY READING LEVEL:

* P	Primary; Easy Reading	21 titles	04%
* A	All Ages	58 titles	10%
* M	Middle School	63 titles	11%
J	Junior High School	112 titles	20%
S	Senior High School	139 titles	24%
C	Adult: Public Library; College	126 titles	22%
R	Research; College Graduate	40 titles	07%
IV	"C" books, partially indexed	14 titles	02%

TITLE ENTRIES

Titles (as main entries) in the books indexed are not automatically listed as printed. All the "classics" are entered under "common titles." Determination of common-title wording is based primarily on the "popu-

lar title index" in Clarkson's *World Folktales*. Cross-references are made as needed.

Keywords in titles are often identical to subject headings, and further recognition of a theme wanted can result from reading the modification. (A typical entry is made up of Main Entry, location on the second line, and modification plus page numbers on the third line.)

In many cases the main entry is a keyword from the title, with the title itself as the modification (third line). Other than classics, unique or especially meaningful titles are entered.

Titles appear with the initial word capitalized and the rest in lower case.

AUTHOR ENTRIES

Original authors appear as main entries. However, because of the need to save space, authors of the classics (*e.g.*, Andersen, Grimm, Perrault) have cross references under their names, to the titles of their stories. (Aesop is an exception.)

Author entries appear in capital and lower case. When the author is also a subject, the name is printed in all capital letters.

Illustrators are listed under the heading: ILLUSTRATOR(-s).

SUBJECT ENTRIES

By far, most of the entries in the index are subjects. These entries are printed in all capital letters.

Particular terminology is usually followed; *e.g.*, look for "cat" under CAT and not under ANIMAL. This compilation of *IFT* tries to keep its forms of entry consistent with past volumes.

While direct entry is the norm, in some cases the indirect form is used. Thus animals, gods, etc. are entered specifically. Indirect headings are used notably for birds and snakes. Thus the user will find BIRD: RAVEN and SNAKE: COBRA.

The reason for this is that even though Raven is important in its own right, for the most part bird (or snake) species is arbitrary in the tale. A second reason is that the client is, presumably, more likely to be looking for *any* "bird" tale, rather than a tale about a particular species.

Indians are also collected under one heading; also saints, obscure princes, kings, and queens. Cross-references are made for the more important names. Thus you will find:

> **Eagle,** *see* **BIRD: EAGLE.**
> **George, Saint,** *see* **SAINT GEORGE.**
> **Iroquois,** *see* **INDIANS: IROQUOIS.**

Correlative terms (*e.g.,* good and evil) synonyms and antonyms are problems for both indexers and users. The attempt here is to choose the more common term, and cross-references are made for the more significant headings. Thus, for example, "disobedience" is included under the OBEDIENCE entry.

In modifications (third line under the subject heading) frequently a common noun (usually a bird or animal) is capitalized. This means that in this particular tale, "Rat" (for example) is presented as a person, but with no name other than "Rat."

For many entries, the last symbol (after the page number) is @. The @ sign means that this particular reference is to a *discussion, commentary, or essay* about the subject; and is not a tale as such.

The designation (index) is also often found after a page number; this is a reference to the *book's own* index, in which many more citations may be found.

LOCATIONS (—)

The first line under the heading gives the key to the collection where the tale appears. A dash (em dash) (—) is on the left margin. The location key is made to be as informative as possible. Hence the form varies: in some cases the form is Keyword / Author; in others, it is Author / Keyword.

Thus, names like Aesop, Bierhorst, Hamilton, or Yolen are given first; but terms like Dragons, Giant, Tall Tales, Turkish are sometimes put in the first position because of their informative quality.

TALE MOTIFS

It is quite common for collections of folktales to be analyzed and arranged according to the Stith Thompson *Motif Index.*

To the advantage (hopefully) of *IFT* users, a majority of themes in tales found here have been identified with Thompson *Motif Index* numbers. Greater likelihood of achieving consistency is the expected result of using this system.

The letter-number symbols (less liable to unwanted dispersion) were, in the end, translated into the traditional *IFT* alphabetical format, with much of the Motif phraseology retained.

ACKNOWLEDGMENTS:

—To Mount Angel Abbey Library,
      for office space, computer assistance, interlibrary
      loan service, general interest and support . . .
—To the Chemeketa Regional Library Network,
      for interlibrary loan service, especially by Mount Angel
      Public Library . . .
—To the Salem Public Library, with special thanks to
      Mary Finnegan . . .
—To various publishers, for interest and support,
      especially Anne Okie (Macmillan) and Ghazala Osman
      (Random House) . . .
—To my wife, Joan,
      for reading, summarizing, and applying the Thompson Motifs
      to a majority of these tales; and proofreading each of the fourteen
      installments as this compilation of *IFT* developed . . .
—To Mrs. Norma Olin Ireland,
      for her friendly following of the progress of this work . . .

                                            JWS
                                    Mount Angel, Oregon

LIST OF COLLECTIONS
ANALYZED
AND
KEY TO SYMBOLS USED

Information contained in this list:

—Titles indexed arranged by symbols for the collection.
—Bibliographic citation for each title (title, author, publisher, date, pages).
—Review(s) and/or Resource citation.
—Reading level (RL) and Indexing level (IL).
—The sign * indicating a children's level book.
—Cross references from secondary authors.

Abbreviations

ARBA—*American Reference Books Annual*
BIP—*Books in Print*
BL—*Booklist*
CBRS—*Children's Book Review Service*
CCBB—*Center for Children's Books Bulletin*
Ch Sci Mon—*Christian Science Monitor*
HB—*Horn Book*
IFT—*Index to Fairy Tales*
IL—Indexing Level [see Introduction]
LJ—*Library Journal*
NYTBR—*New York Times Book Review*
PW—*Publishers Weekly*
RL—Reading Level [see Introduction]
RL: * A—All Ages

RL: C—Public Library Adult; College
RL: J—Junior High School
RL: * M—Middle School
RL: * P—Primary; Easy Reading
RL: R—Research; Post-graduate
RL: S—Senior High School
RQ—*Reference Quarterly*
Sat Rev—*Saturday Review*
SLJ—*School Library Journal*
TLS—*Times Literary Supplement*
WLB—*Wilson Library Bulletin*

Abrahams, Roger D., *see* **African / Abrahams**
———— *see* **Afro-American / Abrahams**

Aesop / Alley *
Seven fables from Aesop / retold and illustrated by R.W. Alley. New York: Dodd, Mead, c1986. 32 p.

Resource: Salem (OR) Public Library.
Review: BL 83:404 (Nov '86).
* RL: A / IL: I.

Aesop / Holder *
Aesop's fables / illustrated by Heidi Holder. New York: Viking Kestrel, c1981. 25 p.

Resource: Chemeketa Community College Library.
* RL: A / IL: I.

Aesop / Reeves-Wilson *
Fables from Aesop / retold by James Reeves; illus. by Maurice Wilson. New York: Bedrick/Blackie, 1985, c1961. 123 p.

Review: Book World 16:10 (Feb 9 '86)
* RL: A / IL: I.

Aesop / Zwerger *
Aesop's fables / illustrated by Lisbeth Zwerger. Saxonville, MA: Picture Book Studio, c1989. [26] p.

Resource: Silverton (OR) Public Library.
Review: BL 86:655 (Nov 15 '89); SLJ 35:92 (Dec '89).
* RL: A / IL: I.

Afanasev, Aleksandr, *see* Russian / Afanasev

African / Abrahams
African folktales: traditional stories of the Black world / Roger D. Abrahams. New York: Pantheon, c1983. 354 p.

Reviews: BL 80:453 (Nov '83); NYTBR (Nov 20 '83) p.12.
RL: SC / IL: IV.

Afro-American / Abrahams
Afro-American folktales: stories from Black traditions in the New World / Roger D. Abrahams. New York: Pantheon, c1985. 327 p.

Reviews: Choice 23:106 (Sept '85); LJ 110:177 (Feb 15 '85).
IL: IV.

Aleichem / Holiday *
Holiday tales of Sholom Aleichem / selected and translated by Aliza Shevrin; illus. by Thomas di Grazia. New York: Atheneum, c1979. 145 p.

Reviews: BL 76:234 (Oct '79); SLJ 26:147 (Sept '79).
* RL: MJ / IL: II.

Alley, R.W., *see* Aesop / Alley *

Allison / I'll Tell *
I'll tell you a story, I'll sing you a song / Christine Allison; a parents' guide to the fairy tales, fables, songs, and rhymes of childhood. New York: Delacorte, c1987. 216 p.

Resource: McMinnville (OR) Public Library.
Review: BL 84:812 (Jan '88).
* RL: A / IL: I.

Am Children / Bronner
American children's folklore / compiled and edited by Simon J. Bronner. Little Rock, AR: August House, c1988. 281 p. (American folklore series).

Reviews: Educational Leadership 47:90 (Oct '89); Journal of American
Folklore 101:76 (Jan '88).
RL: CR / IL: II.

Amer Ind / Erdoes
American Indian myths and legends / selected and edited by Richard Erdoes
and Alfonso Ortiz. New York: Pantheon, c1984. 527 p.

Listed: Public Library Catalog 1989; Readers Adviser 1986.
Review: BL 81:171 (Oct 1 '84).
RL: SC / IL: IV.

American / Read Dgst
American folklore and legend. Pleasantville, NY: Reader's Digest Assn,
1985, c1978. 448 p.

Listed in: Mercatante. 1988.
Review: LJ 103:1654 (Sept '78).
RL: JSC / IL: II.

Andersen / Eighty *
Eighty fairy tales / Hans Christian Andersen; trans. by R.P. Keigwin; introd.
by Elias Bredsdorff; illus. by Vilhelm Pedersen and Lorenz Frolich. New
York: Pantheon, 1982, c1976. 483 p.

Listed in Gillespie (1990).
Reviews: BL 79:288, 317 (Oct '82); HB 58:677 (Dec '82).
* RL: A / IL: IV.

Andersen, Johannes C., *see* **Polynesians / Andersen**

Andersen / Lewis *
Hans Andersen's fairy tales; a new translation by Naomi Lewis. New York:
Viking Penguin (Puffin Books), 1981. 175 p.

Twelve tales, with introductions and notes.
* RL: A / IL: I.

Andersen / Raverat *
An anniversary edition of the first four tales from Hans Andersen; illustrated
with woodcuts by Gwen Raverat. New York: Cambridge University Press,
c1986. 76 p.

Review: Book World 17:10 (Apr 12 '87).
* RL: A / IL: I.

Animal Legends / Kerven *
Legends of the animal world / Rosalind Kerven; illus. by Bernard Georges.
New York: Cambridge Univ. Press, c1986. [32] p.

Reviews: CBRS 15:96 (Ap '87); School Librarian 35:136 (May '87).
* RL: MJ / IL: II.

Animals / Rowland
Animals with human faces: a guide to animal symbolism / Beryl Rowland.
Knoxville, TN: University of Tennessee Press, c1973. 192 p.

Resource: Salem (OR) Public Library.
Review: SLJ 35:146 (Aug '89).
RL: SC / IL: II.

Arabian / Lewis
Stories from the Arabian nights / retold by Naomi Lewis; illus. by Anton Pieck.
New York: Holt, c1987. 224 p.

Reviews: Ch Sci Mon (Nov 6 '87)p.B4; SLJ 34:80 (Feb '88).
RL: JSC / IL: II.

Arabian / McCaughrean
One thousand and one Arabian nights / Geraldine McCaughrean; illus. by
Stephen Lavis. New York: Oxford University Press, c1982. 249 p.

Reviews: Economist, 285:103 (Dec 25 '82); HB 59:342 (June '83).
RL: JSC / IL: II.

Arabian / Riordan
Tales from the Arabian nights / James Riordan; illus. by Victor G. Ambrus.
Chicago: Rand McNally, 1985. 125 p.

Resource: Salem (OR) Public Library.
Reviews: Book World, 15:16 (Nov 10 '85); Junior Bookshelf, 47:210 (Oct
'83).
RL: JS / IL: II.

Asbjornsen, Peter Christen, *see* **Norwegian / Asbjornsen**
———— *see* **Trolls / Asbjornsen**

Ashe, Geoffrey, *see* **King Arthur / Ashe**

Ashley, Mike, *see* **Pendragon / Ashley**

Ashliman / Guide
   A guide to folktales in the English language; based on the Aarne-Thompson classification system / D.L. Ashliman. New York: Greenwood, 1987. 368 p.

   A reference book.
   Review: Choice 25:881 (Feb '88).
   RL: CR / IL: III.

Astrology / Gettings
   Dictionary of astrology / Fred Gettings. Boston: Routledge & Kegan Paul, c1985. 365 p.

   Reviews: BL 82:1672 (Aug '86); Choice, 23:1520 (June '86).
   RL: SCR / IL: III.

Aylesworth, Thomas G., *see* **Werewolves / Aylesworth**

Babylonia / Spence
   Myths & legends of Babylonia & Assyria / by Leonard Spence. Detroit: Gale, 1975. 411 p.

   First published: London, Harrap, 1916. Reprinted: Detroit, Omnigraphics, 1990.
   RL: CR / IL: II.

Barber / Anthology
   The Arthurian legends; an illustrated anthology selected and introduced by Richard Barber. New York: Bedrick, c1979. 224 p.

   Selections from classics.
   RL: JS / IL: II.

Baring-Gould / Curious
   Curious myths of the Middle Ages / Sabine Baring-Gould; ed. by Edward Hardy. Illustrated with woodcuts by Albrecht Duerer. London: Jupiter Books, c.1977. 159 p.

   Resource: Seattle Pacific University.
   RL: SCR / IL: II.

Barrick, Mac E., *see* **German-American / Barrick**

Baskin, Leonard, *see* **Dragons / Baskin** *

Beasts / McHargue
The beasts of never: a history natural & unnatural of monsters mythical & magical / Georgess McHargue; illus. by Frank Bozzo. Rev. ed. New York: Delacorte, c1988. 118 p.

Listed in: Children's Catalog 1989.
Review: BL 84:1928 (Aug '88).
RL: JS / IL: II.

Beat / Bryan *
Beat the story-drum, pum-pum / retold and illustrated by Ashley Bryan. New York: Aladdin Books; Atheneum, 1987, c1980. 68 p.

Review: PW 231:81 (May 29 '87)
* RL: PM / IL: II.

Bedtime / Padoan & Smith *
The Macmillan book of 366 bedtime stories / retold by Gianni Padoan; illus. by Sandra Smith; trans. by Colin Clark. New York: Macmillan (Aladdin Books), c1986. 191 p.

Review: PW 232:69 (Oct 30 '87).
* RL: P / IL: IV.

Bell / Classical Dict
Dictionary of classical mythology: symbols, attributes & associations / by Robert E. Bell; illus. by John Schlesinger. Santa Barbara, CA: ABC-CLIO, c1982. 390 p.

Reviews: BL 80:342 (Oct '83); Choice 20:552 (Dec '82).
RL: J-R / IL: II.

Bierhorst, John, *see* Coyote / Bierhorst *

Bierhorst / Mexico
The mythology of Mexico and Central America / John Bierhorst. New York: Morrow, c1990. 239 p.

Reviews: NYTBR (Jan 6 '91) p.28; SLJ 36:142 (Nov '90).
RL: SC / IL: IV.

Bierhorst / Monkey *
The monkey's haircut, and other stories told by the Maya / edited by John
Bierhorst; illustrated by Robert Andrew Parker. New York: Morrow, c1986.
152 p.

Reviews: BL 82:1615 (July '86); HB 62:602 (Sept '86).
* RL: A / IL: I.

Bierhorst / Naked *
The naked bear: folktales of the Iroquois / edited by John Bierhorst; illus. by
Dirk Zimmer. New York: Morrow, c1987. 123 p.

Reviews: Ch Sci Monitor (Aug 14 '87) p.26; SLJ 33:92 (Je-Jl '87)
* RL: MJS / IL: I.

Bierhorst / Sacred
The sacred path: spells, prayers & power songs of the American Indians /
edited by John Bierhorst. New York: Morrow, c1983. 191 p.

Reviews: Choice 21:1609 (Aug '84); HB 59:459 (Aug ' 83).
RL: J-C / IL: II.

Bierhorst / South America
The mythology of South America / John Bierhorst. New York: Morrow, c1988.
269 p.

Reviews: BL 85:145 (Sept 15 '88); NYTBR (Oct 2 '88) p.35; HB 64:794
(Nov '88).
RL: SC / IL: IV.

Bird, Malcolm, *see* Witch Hndbk / Bird *

Bird Symbol / Rowland
Birds with human souls: a guide to bird symbolism / Beryl Rowland. Knoxville:
Univ. of Tennessee Press, c1978. 213 p.

Resource: Salem (OR) Public Library.
Reviews: LJ 103:2096 (Oct 15 '78); Sat Rev 5:46 (Nov 25 '78).
RL: SC / IL: II.

Birds / Carter & Cartwright *
Birds, beasts, and fishes: a selection of animal poems / selected by Anne
Carter; illus. by Reg Cartwright. New York: Macmillan, 1991. 64 p.

* RL: A / IL: III.

Bomans / Wily *

The wily witch, and all the other tales and fables / Godfried Bomans. Illus. by Wouter Hoogendijk; translation by Patricia Crampton. Owings Mills, MD: Stemmer House, c1977 (reprinted 1988). 205 p.

Resource: Grants Pass (OR) County Library.
Reviews: BL 73:1726 (July 15 '77); SLJ 24:121 (Sept '77).
* RL: A / IL: I.

Bosma / Classroom

Fairy tales, fables, legends, and myths: using folk literature in your classroom / Bette Bosma. New York: Teachers College, Columbia University, c1987. 116 p.

Note: this book is for elementary school teachers, and children's librarians (storytellers).
Reviews: Language Arts 64:552 (Sept '87); SLJ 33:118 (Mar '87).
RL: SCR / IL: II.

Bradley, Josephine, *see* Unicorn / Bradley

Briggs, Katharine, *see* British Dict / Briggs
———— *see* British / Briggs *
———— *see* Fairies / Briggs

British / Briggs *

British folktales / Katharine Briggs. New York: Pantheon, c1977. 315 p.

Review: BL 74:729 (Jan '78).
* RL: A / IL: IV.

British Dict / Briggs

A dictionary of British folk-tales in the English language; incorporating the F.J. Norton collection / Katharine M. Briggs. New York: Routledge, 1991. 2 v.

First published: 2 v. in 4, by Routledge (London), and Indiana University Press (Bloomington), 1970–71; reprinted (selections) by Dorset, 1988; reprinted, Routledge, 1991.
Listed in Mercatante, 1988.
Review (original ed.): LJ 95:3263 (Oct 1 '70).
IL: IV.

Bronner, Simon J., *see* **Am Children / Bronner**

Bronner / Piled
  Piled higher and deeper: the folklore of campus life / Simon J. Bronner. Little
    Rock, AR: August House, c1990. 256 p.

  Review: LJ 115:228 (Sept 1 '90).
  RL: SC / IL: III.

Brooke / Telling *
  A telling of the tales; five stories / William J. Brooke; drawings by Richard
    Egielski. New York: Harper & Row, c1990. 132 p.

  Resource: Newberg (OR) Public Library.
  Review: SLJ 36:116 (June '90).
  * RL: MA / IL: I.

Brown / Amer Folklore
  The tall tale in American folklore and literature / Carolyn S. Brown. Knoxville:
    Univ. of Tenn. Press, c1987. 168 p.

  Review: Choice 25:764 (Jan '88).
  RL: SCR / IL: II.

Bruchac / Iroquois
  Iroquois stories: heroes and heroines, monsters and magic / as told by
    Joseph Bruchac; illus. by Daniel Burgevin. Trumansburg, NY: Crossing
    Press, c1985. 198 p.

  Review: SLJ 32:84 (Apr '86).
  * RL: MJ / IL: II.

Bryan, Ashley, *see* **Beat / Bryan ***

Bryan / Lion *
  Lion and the ostrich chicks and other African folk tales / retold and illustrated
    by Ashley Bryan. New York: Atheneum, c1986. 87 p.

  Reviews: BL 83:841 (Feb 1 '87); HB 63:227 (Mar '87); SLJ 33:60 (Ja '87).
  * RL: MJ / IL: I.

Bulfinch / Sewell *
  A book of myths: selections from Bulfinch's Age of fable. With illus. by Helen
    Sewell. New York: Macmillan, 1981, c1942. 126 p.

*   RL:M / IL: III.

Bullchild / Sun
The sun came down / Percy Bullchild. San Francisco: Harper & Row, c1985. 390 p.

Reviews: Choice 23:1106 (Mar '86); LJ 110:102 (Nov 15 '85).
RL: SCR / IL: IV.

Burland, Cottie, *see* Indian Myth / Burland

Bushnaq / Arab
Arab folktales / translated and edited by Inea Bushnaq. New York: Pantheon, c1986. 386 p.

Reference: Public Library Catalog, 1989.
Reviews: Choice 24:133 (Sept '86); LJ 111:158 (Ap 1 '86).
RL: SC / IL: IV.

Caduto / Keepers *
Keepers of the earth: Native American stories and environmental activities for children / Michael J. Caduto and Joseph Bruchac; foreword by N. Scott Momaday; illus. by John Kahionhes Fadden and Carol Wood. Golden, CO: Fulcrum, Inc., c1988. 209 p.

Reviews: Instructor 98:53 (Mar '89); Science Books & Films 24:296 (May '89).
*   RL: PMJ / IL: I.

Calvino / Italian
Italian folktales / selected and retold by Italo Calvino; translated by George Martin. New York: Pantheon, c1980. 763 p.

Reviews: LJ 105:1877 (Sep 15 '80); NYTBR (Oct 12 '80) p.1.
IL: IV.

Cambodian / Carrison
Cambodian folk stories from the Gatiloke / retold by Muriel Paskin Carrison, from a translation by Kong Chhean. Rutland, VT: Tuttle, c1987. 139 p.

Resource: Chemeketa Community College Library.
Reviews: BL 84:472 (Nov '87); SLJ 34:107 (Ap '88).
RL: J / IL: II.

Campbell / West Highlands
Popular tales of the West Highlands, orally collected / edited by J.F. Campbell. First published by A. Gardner, 1890; reissued by Singing Tree Press, Detroit, 1969. 4 vols.

Resource: Gale.
Review: NYTBR (Nov 9 '69), p.54.
RL: CR / IL: III.

Carle / Treasury *
Eric Carle's treasury of classic stories for children / retold and illustrated by Eric Carle. New York: Orchard Books, c1988. 154 p.

Tales by Aesop, Andersen, and Grimm.
Reviews: CCBB 41:200 (June '88); SLJ 34:94 (Apr '88).
* RL: A / IL: I.

Carrison, Muriel Paskin, *see* Cambodian / Carrison

Carter, Angela, *see* Old Wives / Carter

Carter, Anne, *see* Birds / Carter & Cartwright *

Carter / Sleeping *
Sleeping Beauty, & other favourite fairy tales / chosen and translated by Angela Carter; illustrated by Michael Foreman. New York: Schocken, 1984. 128 p.

Resource: Salem (OR) Public Library.
Review: SLJ 30:74 (Nov '83).
* RL: A / IL: I.

Cavendish, Richard, *see* Legends / Cavendish

Celtic / MacCana
Celtic mythology / Proinsias MacCana. New York: Bedrick, 1985. 136 p. (Library of the world's myths and legends)

Reviews: BL 81:1421 (June 15 '85); LJ 110:67 (May 1 '85)
RL: SC / IL: II.

Celts / Hodges *
The other world: myths of the Celts / retold by Margaret Hodges; illus. by Eros Keith. New York: Farrar, Straus and Giroux, c1973. 176 p.

Reviews: HB 49:267 (June '73); LJ 98:2194 (July '73)
* RL: MJ / IL: I.

Chaucer / Cohen *
Canterbury tales / Geoffrey Chaucer; selected, translated, and adapted by Barbara Cohen; illustrated by Trina Schart Hyman. New York: Lothrop, Lee & Shepard, c1988. 87 p.

Listed: Gillespie, 1990.
Reviews: HB 65:214 (Apr '89); NYTBR (Dec 11 '88) p.20.
* RL: MJ / IL: I.

Childcraft 1 / Once *
Childcraft 2 / Time *
Childcraft 3 / Stories *
Childcraft: the how and why library. Chicago: World Book, c1991. 15 volumes (available only as a complete set).

This compilation of IFT covers fairy tales, folk tales, myths, and legends to be found in vols. 1–3 of the 1991 edition of Childcraft.
Resource: Elementary School Library Collection, 1990.
Reviews: ARBA (1990) #47, p.19; BL 86:1032 & 1917 (Jan 15 & June 1 '90)
* RL: P / IL: II.

Chin, Yin-lien C., *see* **Chinese / Chin ***

Chinese / Chin *
Traditional Chinese folktales / Yin-lien C. Chin [and others]. Illus. by Lu Wang. Armonk, NY: M.E. Sharpe, c1989. 180 p.

Review: SLJ 35:146 (Aug '89).
RL: A / IL: I.

Chinese / Christie
Chinese mythology / Anthony Christie. New York: Bedrick, c1983. 144 p. (Library of the world's myths and legends)

Reviews: BL 82:292 (Oct 15 '85); TLS (Jan 11 '85) p.47.
RL: SC / IL: II.

Chorao / Child's *
The child's story book / Kay Chorao. New York: Dutton, c1987. 63 p.

Review: PW 232:85 (Oct 9 '87); SLJ 34:120 (Oct '87).

* RL: A / IL: I.

Chorao / Child's FTB *
The child's fairy tale book / Kay Chorao. New York: Dutton, c1990. 62 p.

Review: PW 237:64 (Aug 31 '90).
* RL: A / IL: I.

Christian, Peggy, *see* **Old Coot / Christian** *

Christian / Every
Christian legends / George Every. New York: Bedrick, c1987. 144 p. (Library of the world's myths and legends)

Reviews: BL 83:1231 (April 15 '87); SLJ 33:102 (Aug '87)
RL: SC / IL: II.

Christie, Anthony, *see* **Chinese / Christie**

Civil War Ghosts
Civil War ghosts / edited by Martin H. Greenberg, F.B. McSherry, Jr., C.G. Waugh. Little Rock, AR: August House, c1991. 205 p.

RL: JSC / IL: IV.

Clarkson / World *
World folktales; a Scribner resource collection / Atelia Clarkson & Gilbert B. Cross. New York: Scribner's, c1980. 450 p.

Listed in: Reader's Adviser, 15th ed., 1986.
Reviews: Choice 17:382 (May '80); Horn Book 56:431 (Aug '80); Scientific American 243:59 (Dec '80).
* RL: A / IL: I.

Classic / Downer
Classic American ghost stories: 200 years of ghost lore from the Great Plains, New England, the South and the Pacific Northwest / ed. by Deborah A. Downer. Little Rock, AR: August House, c1990. 214 p.

Review: Come All Ye 11:1 (Winter '90).
RL: JS / IL: II.

Clouston / Popular
 Popular tales and fictions: their migrations and transformations / Wm. A. Clouston. First published: Edinburgh, 1887; reprinted by Singing Tree Press, Detroit, 1968; reprinted by Omnigraphics, Detroit, 1990. 2 v. (485, 515 p.)

 Resource: St Edward's University Library.
 RL: SCR / IL: II.

Cohen, Barbara, *see* **Chaucer / Cohen** *

Cohen, Daniel, *see* **Ghosts / Cohen**
────── *see* **Monsters / Cohen**
────── *see* **Restless / Cohen** *
────── *see* **Unnatural / Cohen**

Colum / Golden *
 The golden fleece and the heroes who lived before Achilles / by Padraic Colum; illus. by Willy Pogany. New York: Macmillan, 1983, c1921. 316 p.

 First published 1921; reprinted 1949, 1983; in print, 1991.
 Newberry Honor Book. Listed in Reader's Adviser (1988).
 * RL: MJ / IL: IV.

Constellations / Gallant *
 The constellations: how they came to be / by Roy A. Gallant. Revised ed. New York: Four Winds, c1991. 203 p.

 * RL:MJS / IL: II.

Corrin / Eight-Year *
 Stories for eight-year-olds, and other young readers / edited by Sara and Stephen Corrin; illus. by Shirley Hughes. Englewood Cliffs: Prentice-Hall, c1971. 191 p.

 Classics, republished by Faber & Faber, 1984.
 * RL: MJ / IL: I.

Corrin / Favourite *
 The Faber book of favourite fairy tales / edited by Sara and Stephen Corrin; illustrated by Juan Wijngaard. Boston: Faber and Faber, c1988. 243 p.

 Reviews: BL 85:1001 (Feb 15 '89); SLJ 35:78 (Feb '89).
 * RL: A / IL: I.

Corrin / Imagine *
Imagine that! fifteen fantastic tales / Sara and Stephen Corrin; illus. by Jill Bennett. Boston: Faber & Faber, c1986. 175 p.

Reviews: BL 83:648 (Dec '86); SLJ 33:93 (Apr '87).
* RL: M / IL: I.

Corrin / Six-Year *
Stories for 6-year-olds / edited by Sara and Stephen Corrin. Boston: Faber and Faber, 1989, c1967. 198 p.

Traditional, and some modern, tales.
* RL: PM / IL: I.

Cotterell / Encyclopedia
The Macmillan illustrated encyclopedia of myths & legends / Arthur Cotterell. New York: Macmillan, c1989. 260 p.

Reviews: Choice 27:1478 (May '90); LJ 115:78 (Feb 1 '90).
RL: JSC / IL: II.

Coville, Bruce, *see* **Unicorn / Coville ***

Coyote / Bierhorst *
Doctor Coyote: Native American Aesop's fables / retold by John Bierhorst; pictures by Wendy Watson. New York: Macmillan, c1987. [46] p.

Resource: Salem (OR) Public Library.
Reviews: BL 83:1123 (Mar 15 '87); HB 63:348 (May '87).
* RL: A / IL: I.

Coyote / Ramsey
Coyote was going there; Indian literature of the Oregon country / compiled by Jarold Ramsey. Seattle: Univ. of Washington Press, c1977. 295 p.

Reviews: Choice, 15:225 (Ap '78); LJ 103:372 (F 1 '78).
RL: C-R / IL: II.

Crane / Beauty *
Beauty and the beast, and other tales; introduction by Anthony Crane. London: Thames and Hudson and the Metropolitan Museum of Art, c1982. unpaged.

Classics.
* RL: A / IL: I.

Crane / McLean *
The frog prince, and other stories / by Walter Crane; introduction by Ruari McLean. New York: Mayflower, 1980. 38 p.

Resource: McMinnville (OR) Public Library.
* RL: A / IL: I.

Creatures (illus) / Huber *
Treasury of fantastic and mythological creatures: 1,087 renderings from historic sources / by Richard Huber. New York: Dover, c1981. [155] p. (Dover pictorial archive series.)

Resource: Portland State University Library.
* RL: A / IL: II.

Crockett Almanacs
The tall tales of Davy Crockett: the second Nashville series of Crockett almanacs, 1839–1841. Tennesseana editions. An enl. facsimile ed. with an introd. by Michael A. Lofaro. Knoxville: Univ. of Tenn. Press, c1987. 116 p.

RL: SC / IL: III.

Crossley-Holland, Kevin, *see* Norse / Crossley

Crossley / Animal (Grimm) *
The fox and the cat: animal tales from Grimm / Kevin Crossley-Holland ; illus. by Susan Varley. New York: Lothrop, Lee & Shepard, c1985. 58 p.

Reviews: BL 82:1396 (May 15 '86); SLJ 32:90 (May '86)
* RL: M-A / IL: I.

Crossley / British FT *
British folk tales: new versions / by Kevin Crossley-Holland. New York: Orchard Books, c1987. 383 p.

Listed in: Gillespie (1990).
Reviews: BL 84:860 (Jan 15 '88); HB 64:364 (May '88); SLJ 34:72 (Jan '88).
* RL: A / IL: I.

Crossley / British Isles *
Folk-tales of the British Isles / chosen by Kevin Crossley-Holland; wood-engravings by Hannah Firmin. New York: Pantheon, c1988. 393 p.

Review: BL 84:1558 (May 15 '88).
* RL: A / IL: IV.

Crossley / Dead *
The dead moon / edited by Kevin Crossley-Holland; illus. by Shirley Felts. Boston: Faber & Faber, c1986. 104 p.

Review: Junior Bookshelf 47:38 (Feb '83).
* RL: MJ / IL: II.

Cunningham, Keith, *see* **Oral Trad / Cunningham**

Curry /Beforetime *
Back in the beforetime: tales of the California Indians; retold by Jane Louise Curry; illustrated by James Watts. New York: McElderry, c1987. 134 p.

Listed: Gillespie (1990).
Reviews: CCBB 40:165 (May '87); SLJ 33:93 (Apr '87).
* RL: MJ / IL: II.

D'Aulaire / Greek *
Book of Greek myths / Ingri and Edgar Parin D'Aulaire. Garden City, NY: Doubleday, 1986, c1962. 192 p.

Listed in Gillespie, 1990.
Reviews: Chr Sci Monitor (Nov 15 '62) p.8B; LJ 87:4616 (Dec '62)
* RL: MJ / IL: II.

Davidson, H.R. Ellis, *see* **Scandinavian / Davidson**

Davidson / Dictionary
A dictionary of angels: including the fallen angels / Gustave Davidson. New York: Free Press c1980, c1967. 386 p.

Resource: Publisher.
Reviews: LJ 92:4139 (Nov '67); Saturday Review, 50:43 (Nov '67).
RL: JSC / IL: III.

Davy Crockett / Dewey *
The narrow escapes of Davy Crockett / by Ariane Dewey. New York: Greenwillow, c1990. 48 p.

Reviews: BL 86:1339 (Mar 1 '90); SLJ 36:83 (May '90).
* RL: P / IL: II.

DeLarrabeiti, Michael, *see* **Provencal / De Larrabeiti**

Demi / Reflective *
Demi's reflective fables / retold and illustrated by Demi. New York: Grosset & Dunlap, c1988. [27] p.

Resource: Salem (OR) Public Library.
Reviews: CBRS, 17:50 (Jan '89); SLJ 35:69 (Jan '89).
* RL: A / IL: I.

Demons / Gettings
Dictionary of demons: a guide to demons and demonologists in occult lore / Fred Gettings. North Pomfret: Trafalgar Square, c1988. 255 p.

Review: BL 85:689 (Dec 15 '89).
RL: J-C / IL: III.

Dewey, Ariane, *see* **Davy Crockett / Dewey ***
————*see* **Pecos Bill / Dewey ***

Dictionary / Leach
Standard dictionary of folklore, mythology, and legend / ed. by Maria Leach. New York: Funk & Wagnalls, c1972. 1,235 p.

Reprinted by Harper & Row, 1984. In BIP, 1991.
Listed: Mercatante 1988; Reader's Adviser, 15th ed., 1986.
RL: SCR / IL: II.

Douglas / Magic *
The magic carpet, and other tales / retold by Ellen Douglas; with the illus. of Walter Anderson. Jackson: Univ. Press of Mississippi, c1987. 184 p.

Review: NYTBR 92 (Dec 13 '87) p.36.
RL: A / IL: I.

Downer, Deborah A., *see* **Classic / Downer**

Downs, Robert B., *see* **Tall Tales / Downs: Bear**

Dracula / McNally
In search of Dracula: a true history of Dracula and vampire legends / Raymond T. McNally and Radu Florescu. New York: Galahad Books, c1972. 223 p.

Reviews: Choice, 10:275 (Ap '73); LJ 98:422 (Feb '73).
RL: SC / IL: III.

Dragons / Baskin *
A book of dragons / by Hosie and Leonard Baskin. New York: Knopf, 1985.
[47] p.

Resource: Abilene (TX) Public Library.
Reviews: BL 82:807 (Feb 1 '86) & 83:361 (Oct '86); SLJ 32:62 (Jan '86)
* RL: A / IL: II.

Dragons / Hogarth
Dragons / Peter Hogarth with Val Clery. New York: Viking, c1979. 208 p.

Reviews: BL 76:311 (Oct '79); Harper, 259:98 (Nov '79) [Very satiric of the
text].
Included chiefly for illustrations.
RL: S / IL: III.

Dragons / Johnsgard
Dragons and unicorns: a natural history / Paul and Karin Johnsgard. New
York: St Martin's Press, c1982. 163 p.

Review: BL 79:172 (Oct 1 '82).
RL: JSC / IL: III.

Dramatized / Kamerman
Dramatized folk tales of the world: a collection of 50 one-act plays . . . / edited
by Sylvia E. Kamerman. Boston: Plays, Inc., c1971. 575 p.

Review: LJ 97:775 (Feb 15 '72).
RL: JS / IL: II.

Drury / Dictionary
Dictionary of mysticism and the occult / Nevill Drury. San Francisco: Harper &
Row, c1985. 281 p.

Resource: Mount Angel Abbey Library.
Reviews: BL 82:963 (Mar '86); LJ 110:66 (Apr '85).
RL: JSC / IL: III.

Dulac / Fairy *
Edmund Dulac's fairy book: fairy tales of the world. New York: Gallery, 1984.
163 p.

First published in 1916. Reprinted by Portland House (Crown), 1988.
Resource: Salem (OR) Public Library.
* RL: MJ / IL: I.

Dyer, T.F. Thiselton-Dyer, *see* Plants / Dyer
———— *see* Women / Dyer

Earth / Hadley *
Legends of earth, air, fire, and water / by Eric and Tessa Hadley; illus. by Bryna Waldman. New York: Cambridge University Press, 1988, c1985. [32] p.

Reviews: CBRS 14:85 (Mar '86); Junior Books 50:22 (Feb '86).
* RL: M / IL: II.

Earthmaker / Mayo *
Earthmaker tales: North American Indian stories about earth happenings / by Gretchen Will Mayo. New York: Walker, c1989. 89 p.

Resource: Salem (OR) Public Library.
Reviews: BL 85:1194 (Mar 1 '89); SLJ 35:193 (Mar '89).
* RL: MJ / IL: II.

Edens / Glorious ABC *
The glorious ABC / selected by Cooper Edens; with illustrations by the best artists from the past. New York: Atheneum, c1990. 32 p.

Resource: Salem (OR) Public Library.
Review: PW 237:123 (Sept 14 '90).
* RL: A / IL: III.

Egyptian / Harris
Gods & pharaohs from Egyptian mythology / text by Geraldine Harris; illus. by David O'Connor; line drawings by John Sibbick. New York: Schocken, 1983. 132 p. (World mythologies series).

Reviews: BL 80:856 (Feb 15 '84); SLJ 30:82 (Feb /84).
RL: JSC / IL: II.

Egyptian / Ions
Egyptian mythology / Veronica Ions. New York: Bedrick, 1983. 144 p. (Library of the world's myths and legends)

Resource: Klamath County (OR) Library.

Reviews: BL 80:382 (Nov 1 '83); Choice 22:289 (Oct '84).
RL: SC / IL: II.

Egyptian / Mercatante
Who's who in Egyptian mythology / Anthony S. Mercatante. New York: C.N. Potter, c1978. 231 p.

Reviews: Choice, 16:648 (July '79); LJ 103:2506 (Dec 15 '78).
RL: SC / IL: III.

Elijah / Schwartz
Elijah's violin, & other Jewish fairy tales / retold by Howard Schwartz; illus. by Linda Heller. New York: Harper & Row, c1983. 302 p.

Reviews: CCBB 37:36 (Oct '83); LJ 108:598 (Mar '83).
RL: JSC / IL: IV.

Ellis / Dict Irish Myth
A dictionary of Irish mythology / Peter Berresford Ellis. Santa Barbara, CA: ABC-CLIO, c1987. 240 p.

Resource: Mount Angel Abbey Library.
Reviews: BL 86:603 (Nov 1 '89); Choice, 27:284 (Oct '89).
RL: SCR / IL: III.

Erdoes, Richard, *see* **Amer Ind / Erdoes**

Erdoes / Sound *
The sound of flutes, and other Indian legends / told by Lame Deer [etc.]; transcribed and edited by Richard Erdoes; pictures by Paul Goble. New York: Pantheon, c1976. 134 p.

Review: BL 73:664 (Jan '77); HB 53:47 (Feb '77).
* RL: MJ / IL: II.

Every, George, *see* **Christian / Every**

Fahs / Old *
Old tales for a new day: early answers to life's eternal questions / Sophia Lyons Fahs and Alice Cobb. Buffalo, NY: Prometheus, c1980. 201 p.

Resource: Seattle Pacific University.
Review: CCBB 34:169 (May '81).
* RL: MJSC / IL: II.

Fairies / Briggs
An encyclopedia of fairies: hobgoblins, brownies, bogies, and other supernatural creatures / Katharine Briggs. New York: Pantheon, c1976. 481 p.

Reviews: LJ 101:2468 (Dec '76); Newsweek 89:85 (Feb 21 '77).
RL: SCR / IL: II.

Floyd, E. Randall, see Southern / Floyd

Floyd / Gr Am Myst
Great American mysteries / E. Randall Floyd. Little Rock, AR: August House, c1990. 190 p.

Review: BL 87:1304 (Mar 1 '91).
RL: JS / IL: II.

Folk Ballads / McNeil
Southern folk ballads / compiled by W.K. McNeil. Little Rock, AR: August House, 1987–88. v.1 (219 p.), v.2 (223 p.)

Review: Choice, 25:918 (Feb '88).
RL: SCR / IL: III.

Folk-rhymes / Northall
English folk-rhymes; a collection of traditional verses . . . / G.F. Northall. Detroit: Singing Tree Press, 1968. 565 p.

First published in London, 1892. Reprinted by Singing Tree Press. Available (1990–91 Books in Print) from Gordon Press, New York.
RL: SCR / IL: III.

Fox, David Scott, see Saint George / Fox

Frankel, Ellen, see Jewish / Frankel

Frog Rider (Chinese)
The frog rider; folk tales from China (first series). Beijing: Foreign Languages Press, 1980. 140 p.

Resource: Eugene (OR) Public Library.
RL: JS / IL: II.

Gallant, Roy A., see Constellations / Gallant *

Georgia Coast / Jones
  Negro myths from the Georgia coast, told in the vernacular / Charles Colcock
  Jones. Detroit: Singing Tree Press, 1969. 171 p.

  Review: American Book Collector, 21:6 (Oct '70).
  RL: SC / IL: III.

Geras / Grandmother *
  My grandmother's stories; a collection of Jewish folk tales / Adele Geras.
  Illus. by Jael Jordan. New York: Knopf, c1990. 96 p.

  Reviews: HB 67:76 (Feb '91); NYTBR, (Nov 11 '90) p.31.
  * RL: MJ / IL: I.

German-American / Barrick
  German-American folklore / Mac E. Barrick. Little Rock, AR: August House,
  c1987. 264 p.

  Review: Choice 25:1250 (April '88).
  RL: SC / IL: III.

Gettings, Fred, *see* **Astrology / Gettings**
——— *see* **Demons / Gettings**

Ghost (South) / McNeil
  Ghost stories from the American South / compiled by W.K. McNeil. Little
  Rock, AR: August House, c1985. 170 p.

  Reviews: PW 228:49 (July 12 '85); SLJ 32:115 (Dec '85).
  RL: J / IL: III.

Ghost (S'West) / Young
  Ghost stories from the American Southwest / edited by Richard Alan Young
  and Judy Dockery Young. Little Rock, AR: August House, c1991. 192 p.

  RL: JS / IL: II.

Ghosts / Cohen
  The encyclopedia of ghosts / Daniel Cohen. New York: Dodd, Mead, c1984.
  307 p.

  Resource: Salem (OR) Public Library.
  Reviews: BL 81:667 (Jan '85); SLJ 32:114 (Sept '85).
  RL: JS / IL: II.

Ghosts / Starkey
Ghosts and bogles / Dinah Starkey; pictures by Jan Pienkowski. London: Heinemann, 1985, c1978. 123 p.

Reviews: Junior Bookshelf, 42:260 (Oct '78); School Librarian, 34:53 (Mar '86)
RL: JSC / IL: II.

Ghosts / Time-Life
Ghosts / by the editors of Time-Life Books. Distributed by Silver Burdett, Morristown, NJ, c1984. 143 p.

RL: SC / IL: II.

Giant / Harrison *
The book of giant stories / by David L. Harrison; illus. by Philippe Fix. New York: American Heritage Press, 1979, c1972. 44 p.

Resource: Salem (OR) Public Library.
Review: LJ 98:253 (Jan 15 '73).
* RL: PM / IL: I.

Gillespie, Angus K., *see* **Wildlife / Gillespie**

Gillespie / Best Books *
Best books for children: preschool through grade 6. (4th ed.) / John T. Gillespie and Corinne J. Naden, editors. New York: Bowker, c1990. Pages 275–309 list/annotate folk literature.

A reference book. Review: BL: 87:876 (Dec 15 '90).
* RL: A / IL: III.

Glassie, Henry, *see* **Irish / Glassie**

Glooskap / Norman *
How Glooskap outwits the Ice Giants, and other tales of the Maritime Indians / retold by Howard Norman; wood engravings by Michael McCurdy. Boston: Little, Brown, c1989. 60 p.

Resource: Salem (OR) Public Library.
Reviews: BL 86:1007 (Jan 15 '90); SLJ 36:97 (Jan '90).
* RL: MJ / IL: II.

Gobble / Graham-Barber *
Gobble: the complete book of Thanksgiving words / by Lynda Graham-Barber; pictures by Betsy Lewin. New York: Bradbury, c1991. 122 p.

* RL: MJ / IL: III.

Gods / Schwab
Gods & heroes: myths and epics of ancient Greece / Gustav Schwab. New York: Pantheon, c1977, 1946. 764 p.

Reviews: BL 74:730 (Jan '78); NYTBR (Oct 2 '77) p.49.
IL: IV.

Gorion, Micha Joseph bin, *see* **Mimekor / bin-Gorion**

Goss, Linda, *see* **Talk / Goss**

Gould / Mythical
Mythical monsters / Charles Gould. New York: Crescent Books, c1989. 407 p.

Reprint of a work completed in 1884.
Resource: Woodburn (OR) Public Library.
RL: SC / IL: III.

Graham-Barber, Lynda, *see* **Gobble / Graham-Barber ***

Gray / Near East
Near Eastern mythology / John Gray. New York: Bedrick, 1985, c1982. 144 p. (Library of the world's myths and legends)

Reprint, first published 1969.
RL: SC / IL: II.

Greaves / Hippo *
When Hippo was hairy, and other tales from Africa / told by Nick Greaves; illus. by Rod Clement. New York: Barron's, c1988. 143 p.

Review: SLJ 35:94 (Feb '89).
* RL: MJ / IL: I.

Greek / Osborne
Favorite Greek myths / retold by Mary Pope Osborne; illustrated by Troy Howell. New York: Scholastic, c1989. 81 p.

Resource: Salem (OR) Public Library.
Reviews: BL 85:1981 (Aug '89); CCBB 42:261 (June '89); SLJ 35:121 (May '89).
RL: J / IL: II.

Greek / Switzer

Greek myths: gods, heroes, and monsters—their sources, their stories, and their meanings / by Ellen Switzer and Costas. New York: Atheneum, c1988. 208 p.

Resource: Publisher.
Reviews: BL 84:1334 (Ap 1 '88); NYTBR, (Oct 2 '88), p.34; SLJ 34:119 (Apr '88).
RL: JS / IL: II.

Greenberg, Martin H., *see* Civil War Ghosts

Grimal / Concise

A concise dictionary of classical mythology / Pierre Grimal; edited by Stephen Kershaw. Cambridge, MA: Blackwell, c1990. 456 p.

Resource: Silverton (OR) Public Library.
Review: LJ 115:70 (Sept 15 '90).
RL: SC / IL: III.

Grimal / Dictionary

The dictionary of classical mythology / Pierre Grimal. New York: Blackwell, c1986. 603 p.

Reviews: BL 83:113 (Sep 15 '86); LJ 111:73 (Feb 1 '86); SLJ 33:26 (Sept 15 '90).
RL: SCR / IL: II.

Grimm / Complete *

The complete Grimm's fairy tales. New York: Pantheon, c1972. (The Pantheon fairy tale & folklore library). 863 p.

Introd. by Padraic Colum. Folkloristic commentary by Joseph Campbell. Illus. by Josef Scharl.
Listed in: The Reader's Adviser, 1988 ed.
* RL: A / IL: I.

Grimm / Legends (Ward)
The German legends of the Brothers Grimm / edited and translated by Donald Ward. Philadelphia: Institute for the Study of Human Issues, c1981. 2 volumes.

> Reviews: BL 77:1177 (May 1 '81); LJ 106:895 (Ap 15 '81).
> RL: SCR / IL: II.

Grimm / Sixty *
Sixty fairy tales of the Brothers Grimm; illustrated by Arthur Rackham; translated by Mrs Edgar Lucas. New York: Weathervane Books, c1979. 325 p.

> * RL: A / IL: I.

Gross, Gwen, *see* **Knights / Gross ***

Guiley, Rosemary Ellen, *see* **Witch Encyc / Guiley**

Gullible Coyote / Malotki
Gullible coyote: a bilingual collection of Hopi coyote stories / Ekkehart Malotki; Michael Lomatuway'ma, Hopi consultant; Anne-Marie Malotki, illustrator. Tucson: Univ. of Arizona Press, c1985. 180 p.

> Review: Choice 24:123 (Sept '86).
> RL: SC / IL: II.

Haboo / Hilbert
Haboo: Native American stories from Puget Sound / translated and edited by Vi Hilbert; foreword by Thom Hess; drawings by Ron Hilbert Coy. Seattle: Univ. of Washington Press, c1985. 204 p.

> Review: Choice 23:1548 (June '86).
> RL: C / IL: II.

Hadley, Eric, *see* **Earth / Hadley ***

Haile, Berard, *see* **Navajo Coyote / Haile**

Hall, Angus, *see* **Monsters / Hall**

Hall / Treasury *
The Platt & Munk Treasury of stories for children / edited by Nancy Christensen Hall; illustrated by Tasha Tudor, Georgy and Doris Hauman [etc.]. New York: Platt & Munk, c1981. 114 p.

Resource: McMinnville (OR) Public Library.
* RL: A / IL: I.

Halloween ABC / Merriam *
Halloween A B C / poems by Eve Mirriam; illus. by Lane Smith. New York: Macmillan, c1987. [30] p.

Reviews: CCBB 41:72 (Dec '87); HB 63:753 (Dec ' 87).
* RL: A / IL: II.

Hamilton / Dark *
The dark way: stories from the spirit world / told by Virginia Hamilton; illus. by Lambert Davis. San Diego: Harcourt Brace Jovanovich, c1990. 154 p.

Reviews: BL 87:519 (Nov 1 '90); HB 66:753 (Dec '90); NYTBR (Aug 11 '91) p.16.
* RL: MJ / IL: I.

Hamilton / In the Beginning *
In the beginning: creation stories from around the world / told by Virginia Hamilton; illustrated by Barry Moser. New York: Harcourt Brace Jovanovich, c1988. 161 p.

Reviews: Ch Sci Monitor, (Nov 4 '88)p.B4; NYTBR, (Nov 13 '88)p.52; CCBB 42:37 (Oct '88).
* RL: M-A / IL: I.

Hamilton / People *
The people could fly: American Black folktales / told by Virginia Hamilton; illus. by Leo and Diane Dillon. New York: Knopf, 1985. 178 p.

Reviews: NYTBR (Nov 10 '85) p.38; SLJ 32:85 (Nov '85).
* RL: M-C / IL: I.

Harris, Christie, *see* Muddleheads / Harris

Harris, Geraldine, *see* Egyptian / Harris

Harris-Parks / Jump *
Jump! the adventures of Brer Rabbit / by Joel Chandler Harris; adapted by Van Dyke Parks and Malcolm Jones; illustrated by Barry Moser. San Diego: Harcourt Brace Jovanovich, c1986. 40 p.

Resource: Salem (OR) Public Library.

Review: NYTBR, Feb 1 '87, p.29.
* RL: A / IL: I.

Harris-Parks / Jump Again *

Jump again! More adventures of Brer Rabbit / by Joel Chandler Harris; adapted by Van Dyke Parks; illustrated by Barry Moser. San Diego: Harcourt Brace Jovanovich, c1987. 39 p.

Resource: Chemeketa Community College Library.
Reviews: HB 64:76 (Feb '88); NYTBR (Nov 1 '87) p.36; SLJ 34:121 (Oct '87).
* RL: A / IL: II.

Harrison, David L., *see* Giant / Harrison

Hartland / English *

English fairy and other folk tales / edited by Edwin Sidney Hartland. Detroit: Singing Tree Press, 1968. 282 p.

Originally published: London: Walter Scott, 1890.
* RL: A / IL: IV.

Hathaway, Nancy, *see* Unicorn / Hathaway

Headon, Deirdre, *see* Knights / Heller-Headon

Hearne, Michael Patrick, *see* Victorian / Hearne

Hearne / [Bibliog.] *

Choosing books for children: a commonsense guide / Betsy Hearne. Revised ed. New York: Delacorte, c1990. 228 p.

Review: HB 66:474 (Aug '90); NYTBR (Sept 9 '90) p.33.
* RL: A / IL: III.

Hepburn / World *

World of stories: six stories told by Katharine Hepburn. Artists: Brian Lee, Ginny Humphreys, Alison Claire Darke, Christopher Marlowe. New York: Harper & Row, c1983. 128 p.

Resource: Portland (OR) Public Library.
Classic, traditional tales.
* RL: A / IL: I.

High John / Sanfield *
 The adventures of High John the Conqueror / by Steve Sanfield; illus. by
 John Ward. New York: Orchard Books, c1989. 113 p.

 Resource: Corvallis (OR) Public Library.
 Review: BL 85:1656 (May 15 '89); SLJ 35:120 (June '89); WLB 64:52 (Nov
 '89).
 * RL: A / IL: I.

Hilbert, Vi, *see* Haboo / Hilbert

Hinnells, John R., *see* Persian / Hinnells

Hodges, Margaret, *see* Celts / Hodges *

Hodne, Ornulf, *see* Norwegian / Hodne

Hogarth, Peter, *see* Dragons / Hogarth

Hoke / Giants
 Giants! giants! giants! from many lands and many times / selected by Helen
 Hoke; illustrated by Stephen Lavis. New York: F. Watts, c1980. 156 p.

 Reviews: Junior Books, 44:191 (Aug '80); SLJ 27:56 (Aug '81).
 RL: JS / IL: I.

Holder, Heidi, *see* Aesop / Holder *

Hope / Holy Wells
 The legendary lore of the holy wells of England . . . / by Robert Charles Hope.
 Detroit: Singing Tree Press, c1968. 222 p.

 RL: CR / IL: III.

Hopi / Talashoma-Malotki
 Hopitutuwutsi: Hopi tales; a bilingual collection of Hopi Indian stories /
 narrated by Herschel Talashoma; recorded and translated by Ekkehart
 Malotki; illus. by Anne-Marie Malotki. Tucson: Sun Tracks and the Univ. of
 Arizona Press, c1983. 213 p.

 Listed in: Reader's Adviser, 15th ed., 1986.
 Review: Choice 23:1504 (June '86).
 RL: SC / IL: II.

Hopi Coyote / Malotki
Hopi coyote tales: Istutuwutsi [bilingual] / Ekkehart Malotki, Michael Loma-tuway'ma; illus. by Anne-Marie Malotki. Lincoln: Univ. of Nebraska Press, c1984. 343 p.

Review: Choice 23:164 (Sept '85).
RL: CR / IL: II.

Huber, Richard, see Creatures (illus) / Huber *

Humor / Midwest
Midwestern folk humor / compiled by James P. Leary. Little Rock, AR: August House, c1991. 268 p.

RL: JSC / IL: II.

Igloo / Metayer
Tales from the igloo / edited and translated by Maurice Metayer; foreword by Al Purdy; illustrated by Agnes Nanogak. New York: St Martin's Press, 1977, c1972. 127 p.

Reviews: BL 73:1321 (May 1 '77); SLJ 24:132 (S '77).
RL: M / IL: I.

Imaginary / Nigg
A guide to the imaginary birds of the world / by Joe Nigg; featuring woodcuts by David Frampton. Cambridge, MA: Applewood Books, c1984. 160 p.

Reviews: ARBA, 16:p.445 (1985); LJ 109:2118 (Nov 15 '84)
RL: JS / IL: II.

Indian Myth / Burland
North American Indian mythology / Cottie Burland; revised by Marion Wood. New York: P. Bedrick, c1985. 144 p. (Library of the world's myths and legends)

Reviews: BL 82:709 (Ja 15 '86); SLJ 32:31 (My '86).
RL: JC / IL: II.

Indic / Ions
Indian mythology / Veronica Ions. New York: Bedrick, c1983. 144 p. (Library of the world's myths and legends)

Review: TLS (15 June '67) p.545.
RL: JSC / IL: II.

Ions, Veronica, *see* **Egyptian / Ions**
——— *see* **Indic / Ions**

Iosa, Ann, *see* **Witches / Iosa** *

Irish / Glassie
Irish folktales / edited by Henry Glassie. New York: Pantheon, c1985. 353 p.

Reviews: BL 82:174 (Oct 1 '85); LJ 110:108 (Oct 1 '85).
IL: IV.

Ivanits, Linda J., *see* **Russian / Ivanits**

Jaffrey / Seasons
Seasons of splendour: tales, myths & legends of India / Madhur Jaffrey; illus. by Michael Foreman. New York: Atheneum, c1985. 128 p.

Reviews: BL 82:758 (Jan 15 '86); SLJ 32:89 (Dec '85).
RL: J / IL: I.

Jameson / Appalachians
Buried treasures of the Appalachians: legends of homestead caches, Indian mines, and loot from Civil War raids / W.C. Jameson. Little Rock, AR: August House, c1991. 207 p.

IL: IV.

Jameson / Buried
Buried treasures of the American Southwest: legends of lost mines, hidden payrolls and Spanish gold / W.C. Jameson; illus. by Wendell E. Hall. Little Rock, AR: August House, c1989. 220 p.

Reviews: American West 26:S10 (Aug ' 89); Roundup Qtly 2:42 (Spring '90).
RL: JSC / IL: III.

Japanese / Tyler
Japanese tales / ed. and tr. by Royall Tyler. New York: Pantheon, c1987. 340 p.

Reviews: Journal of American Folklore 102:224 (June '89); LJ 112:150 (Apr 1 '87); NYTBR (June 28 '87).
RL: SC / IL: III.

Jewish / Frankel
The classic tales: 4,000 years of Jewish lore / Ellen Frankel. Northvale, NJ: Jason Aronson, c1989. 659 p.

Review: LJ 114:61 (June 15 '89).
RL: JSCR / IL: II.

Jewish / Sadeh
Jewish folktales / selected and retold by Pinhas Sadeh; translated from the Hebrew by Hillel Halkin. New York: Doubleday, c1983. 443 p.

Resource: Salem (OR) Public Library.
RL: CR / IL: I.

Johnsgard, Paul, *see* **Dragons / Johnsgard**

Jones, Charles Colcock, *see* **Georgia Coast / Jones**

Jones / Tales *
Tales to tell: six traditional stories / retold and illustrated by Harold Jones. New York: Greenwillow, c1984. 43 p.

Review: SLJ 31:80 (April '85)
* RL: P / IL: I.

Jonsen / Trolls *
Favorite tales of monsters and trolls / retold by George Jonsen; illustrated by John O'Brien. New York: Random House, c1977. 32 p.

* RL: P / IL: I.

Journey Sun (Chinese)
Journey to the sun: folk tales from China (fourth series). Beijing: Foreign Languages Press, 1981. 140 p.

Resource: Eugene (OR) Public Library.
RL: JS / IL: II.

Journeys / Norris *
Legends of journeys / Olga Norris; illus. by Bryna Waldman. New York: Cambridge University Press, c1988. [32] p.

Review: School Librarian 37:61 (Sept '89).
* RL: M / IL: II.

Kamerman, Sylvia E., *see* **Dramatized / Kamerman**

Kanawa, Kiri Te, *see* **Maori / Kanawa ***

Kellogg, Steven, *see* **Pecos Bill / Kellogg ***

Kerven, Rosalind, *see* **Animal Legends / Kerven ***
————— *see* **Tree / Kerven ***

Kessler / Turtle Knock *
Old turtle's 90 knock-knocks, jokes, and riddles / Leonard Kessler. New York: Greenwillow, c1991. 48 p.

* RL:P / IL: III.

Kessler / Turtle Riddle *
Old turtle's riddle and joke book. New York: Greenwillow, c1986. 47 p.

Review: BL 82:1404 (May 15 '86).
* RL:P / IL:III.

Kimmel / [Bibliog.] *
For reading out loud: a guide to sharing books with children / Margaret Mary Kimmel & Elizabeth Segel; drawings by Michael Hay. Revised ed. New York: Delacorte, c1988. 266 p.

Review: BL 84:1844 (July '88).
* RL: A / IL: III.

King Arthur / Ashe
The landscape of King Arthur / Geoffrey Ashe. New York: Holt, 1988, c1987. 191 p.

Resource: Salem (OR) Public Library.
Review: SLJ 35:178 (Oct '88).
RL: JSC / IL: III.

King Arthur / Senior
Tales of King Arthur / Sir Thomas Malory. Edited and abridged with an introd. by Michael Senior. New York: Schocken, c1980. 321 p.

Classic; with illus. from medieval manuscripts.
Listed in: Public Library Catalog, 1989.
RL: JSC / IL: II.

Klah, Hasteen, *see* **Navajo / Klah**

Knights / Gross *
Knights of the Round Table / adapted by Gwen Gross; illus. by Norman Green. New York: Random House, c1985. 109 p. (Step-up adventures).

Resource: Silverton (OR) Public Library.
Review: SLJ 32:85 (Feb '86).
* RL: M / IL: II.

Knights / Heller-Headon
Knights / text by Deirdre Headon; [illus. by] Julek Heller. New York: Schocken, c1982. 190 p.

Resource: Corvallis (OR) Public Library.
Reviews: LJ 107:2177 (Nov '82); SLJ 29:92 (Jan '83).
RL: J / IL: II.

Kunz, George Frederick, *see* **Precious Stones / Kunz**

Kvideland, Reimund, *see* **Scandinavian / Kvideland**

Lacy / Arth Ency
The Arthurian encyclopedia / Norris J. Lacy [et. al.]. New York: Garland, 1986. 649 p.

Reviews: Choice 23:1367 (May '86); LJ 111:134 (Aug '86).
RL: SCR / IL: III.

Lang / Wilkins
The Andrew Lang fairy tale treasury / edited by Cary Wilkins; with illustrations by H.J. Ford, G.P. Jacomb Hood, and Lancelot Speed. New York: Avenel, c1979. 614 p.

Selections from Lang's nine "color" collections.
RL: JSC / IL: I.

Lankford, George E., *see* **Native American / Lankford**

Leach, Maria, *see* **Dictionary / Leach**

Leary, James P., *see* **Humor / Midwest**

Leete / Golden *
The big Golden Book of fairy tales / retold by Lornie Leete-Hodge; illus. by Beverlie Manson. New York: Western Publ. Co., c1981. 157 p.

  * RL: PM / IL: I.

Legends / Cavendish
Legends of the world / edited by Richard Cavendish; illus. by Eric Fraser. New York: Schocken, c1982. 432 p.

  Listed in: Reader's Adviser, 15th ed., 1986.
  Reviews: Choice 20:1130 (Apr '83); LJ 107:1743 (Sep 15 '82).
  RL: CR / IL: II.

Leonardo / Fables *
Fables of Leonardo da Vinci; interpreted and transcribed by Bruno Nardini; illustrated by Adriana Saviozzi Mazza. Northbrook, IL: Hubbard, c1973. 118 p.

  Listed in: Bosma, 1987.
  Resource: Altadena (CA) Library District.
  Reviews: BL 70:387 (Dec '73); LJ 99:207 (Jan '74).
  * RL: A / IL: II.

Leon-Portilla, Miguel
    see **Mesoamerican / Leon-P.**

Lester / Brer Rabbit *
The tales of Uncle Remus: The adventures of Brer Rabbit / as told by Julius Lester; illustrated by Jerry Pinkney. New York: Dial, c1987. 151 p.

  Resource: Silverton (OR) Public Library. Reviews: BL 83:1290; 84:329 (Ap & Oct '87); HB 63:477 (July '87).
  * RL: A / IL: II.

Lester / Leopard *
How many spots does a leopard have? and other tales / by Julius Lester; illustrated by David Shannon. New York: Scholastic, c1989. 72 p.

Resource: Salem (OR) Public Library.
Reviews: CCBB 43:10 (Sept '89); SLJ 35:99 (Nov '89).
* RL: MJ / IL: I.

Lewis, Naomi, *see* Andersen / Lewis *

Lewis / Proud
Proud knight, fair lady: the twelve lais of Marie de France; translated by Naomi Lewis; illus. by Angela Barrett. New York: Viking Kestrel, c1989. 100 p.

Reviews: HB 65:781 (Dec '89); SLJ 34:80 (Feb '88).
RL: JS / IL: II.

Limburg / Weird *
Weird! : the complete book of Halloween words / Peter R. Limburg; pictures by Betsy Lewin. New York: Bradbury, c1989. 122 p.

Reviews: BL 86:78 (Sept 1 '89); SLJ 35:265 (Sept '89).
* RL: MJ / IL: III.

Lines / Magical *
The Faber book of magical tales / ed. by Kathleen Lines. Boston: Faber & Faber, 1985. 176 p.

Review: Economist 297:91 (Nov 30 '85).
* RL: MJ / IL: I.

Lipson / Best Books *
The New York Times parent's guide to the best books for children / Eden Ross Lipson. New York: Times Books, c1988. 421 p.

Reviews: HB 64:803 (Dec '88); Reading Teacher 44:62 (Sept '90).
* RL: A / IL: III.

Livingston, Myra Cohn, *see* Owl Poems / Livingston

Lofaro, Michael A., *see* Crockett Almanacs

Lopez, Barry Holstun, *see* Wolves / Lopez

Lore of Love
The lore of love / by the editors of Time-Life Books. New York, c1987. 143 p.

Resource: Salem (OR) Public Library.
RL: JSC / IL: II.

Lurker / Dict Gods

Dictionary of gods and goddesses, devils and demons / Manfred Lurker. New York: Routledge, c1987. 451 p.

Reviews: ARBA, 1988, p.529; BL 89:914 (Feb '88); Choice, 25:748 (Jan '88)
RL: SCR / IL: III.

Lycanthropy / Otten

A lycanthropy reader: werewolves in western culture / edited by Charlotte F. Otten. New York: Dorset, 1989; c1986 by Syracuse University Press. 337 p.

Resource: Mt Angel Abbey Library.
Review: NYTBR, 92:33 (Ap 5 '87).
RL: SC / IL: II.

Lynn / Fantasy *

Fantasy literature for children and young adults: an annotated bibliography / Ruth Nadelman Lynn. New York: Bowker, c1989. 771 p.

A reference book.
Review: LJ 114:61 (Feb 1 '89).
* RL: A / IL: II.

MacCana, Proinsias, *see* Celtic / MacCana

McCaughrean, Geraldine, *see* Arabian / McCaughrean

MacDonald / Sourcebook *

The storyteller's sourcebook: a subject, title, and motif index to folklore collections for children / by Margaret Read MacDonald. Detroit: Gale, c1982. 818 p.

A reference book. Listed in: Public Library Catalog, 1989.
Reviews: Choice, 20:244 (Oct '82); LJ 107:1451 (Ag '82).
* RL: A / IL: III.

McGowen / Encyclopedia *

Encyclopedia of legendary creatures / Tom McGowen. Chicago: Rand Mc-Nally, c1981. 64 p.

40

Resource: Austin (TX) Public Library.
Review: BL 78:598 (Jan '82).
* RL: M / IL: II.

McHargue, Georgess, *see* **Beasts / McHargue**

McNally, Raymond T., *see* **Dracula / McNally**

McNally / Clutch
 A clutch of vampires—these being among the best from history and literature / Raymond T. McNally. Greenwich: New York Graphic Society, c1974. 254 p.

Review: Choice 11:1119 (Oct '74).
RL: JSC / IL: III.

McNeil, W.K., *see* **Folk Ballads / McNeil**
———— *see* **Ghost (South) / McNeil**

McSherry, Frank D., *see* **Civil War Ghosts**
———— *see* **Pirate Ghosts / McSherry**

Malotki, Ekkehart, *see* **Gullible Coyote / Malotki**
———— *see* **Hopi Coyote / Malotki**
———— *see* **Hopi / Talashoma-Malotki**

Man Myth & Magic
 Man, myth & magic: the illustrated encyclopedia of mythology, religion, and the unknown / Richard Cavendish, C.A. Burland. New edition edited by Yvonne Deutsch. New York: Marshall Cavendish, 1983. 12 vols.

Listed in The Reader's Adviser, 1986 ed.
Review: ARBA, 1985, p.444–445; BL 80:1238 (May 1 '84); WLB 58:227 (Nov '83).
RL: JSC / IL: II.

Manning / Cats *
 A book of cats and creatures / Ruth Manning-Sanders; illus. by Robin Jacques. New York: Dutton, c1981. 126 p.

Revised indexing of title included in IFT VI.
Resource: McMinnville (OR) Public Library.
Review: SLJ 28:128 (Sept '81).
* RL: MJ / IL: I.

Manning / Cauldron *
A cauldron of witches / Ruth Manning-Sanders; illus by Scoular Anderson.
London: Methuen, c1988. 127 p.

Reviews: Growing Point 27:5016 (July '88); Junior Bookshelf 52:139 (June
'88).
* RL: M / IL: I.

Maori / Kanawa *
Land of the long white cloud: Maori myths, tales and legends / Kiri Te
Kanawa; illus. by Michael Foreman. New York: Arcade (Little, Brown),
c1989. 118 p.

Resource: Salem (OR) Public Library.
Reviews: BL:1807 (May 15 '90); NYTBR (Oct 21 '90)p.40.
* RL: MJ / IL: II.

Mayo, Gretchen Will, *see* **Earthmaker / Mayo ***

Medicine-Plants / Read Dgst
Magic and medicine of plants / Reader's Digest. Pleasantville, NY: R.D.
Assn., c1986. 464 p.

Reviews: BL 83:611 (Dec 15 '86); LJ 111:103 (Oct 1 '86); SLJ 33:123 (May
'87).
RL: SC / IL: III.

Mercatante, Anthony S., *see* **Egyptian / Mercatante**

Mercatante / Encyclopedia
The Facts on File encyclopedia of world mythology and legend /Anthony S.
Mercatante. New York: Facts on File, c1988. 807 p.

Reviews: BL 85:849 (Jan 15 '89); Choice, 26:1308 (Ap '89).
RL: JSC / IL: II.

Mercatante / Good/Evil
Good and evil: mythology and folklore / Anthony S. Mercatante; illustrated by
the author. New York: Harper & Row, c1978. 242 p.

Resource: Salem (OR) Public Library.
Review: Choice, 15:1200 (Nov '78).
RL: SC / IL: II.

Mercer, John, *see* **Vanishing / Mercer ***

Merriam, Eve, *see* **Halloween ABC / Merriam ***

Mesoamerican / Leon-P
Native Mesoamerican spirituality: ancient myths . . . from the Aztec . . . and other sacred traditions / edited by Miguel Leon-Portilla. New York: Paulist, c1980. 300 p.

Review: LJ 107:731 (Mar '80).
RL: SCR / IL: II.

Metayer, Maurice, *see* **Igloo / Metayer**

Mex-Am / West
Mexican-American folklore: legends, songs, festivals, proverbs, crafts, tales of saints . . . / ed. John O. West. Little Rock, AR: August House, c1988. 314 p.

Review: BL 85:528 (Nov 15 '88).
RL: SC / IL: II.

Mimekor / bin-Gorion
Mimekor Yisrael: selected classical Jewish folktales / collected by Micha Joseph bin Gorion. Bloomington: Indiana Univ. Press, c1990. 271 p.

Review: BL: 87:698 (Dec 1 '90).
RL: SC / IL: IV.

Monsters / Cohen
The encyclopedia of monsters / Daniel Cohen. New York: Dodd, Mead, c1982; reprinted by Dorset, 1989. 287 p.

Resource: Monmouth (OR) Public Library.
Review: LJ 107:2162 (Nov 15 '82); WLB 57:786 (Sept '83).
RL: JS / IL: II.

Monsters / Hall
Monsters and mythic beasts / Angus Hall. Garden City, NY: Doubleday, c1975. 144 p.

Resource: Mount Angel Abbey Library.
RL: JS / IL: II.

Muddleheads / Harris
Mouse women and the muddleheads / Christie Harris; drawings by Douglas Tait. New York: Atheneum, c1979. 131 p.

Reviews: Reading Teacher, 33:482 (Jan '80); Scientific American, 241:48 (Dec '79).
RL: J / IL: II.

Muhawi, Ibrahim, *see* **Palestinian / Speak (Muhawi)**

My Mama / Viorst *
My mama says there aren't any zombies, ghosts, vampires, creatures, demons, monsters, fiends, goblins, or things / Judith Viorst; drawings by Kay Chorao. 2nd ed. New York: Aladdin Books, 1988. [45] p.

* RL: P / IL: III.

Native American / Lankford
Native American legends: southeastern legends;—tales from the Natchez, Caddo, Biloxi, Chickasaw, and other nations / comp. by George E. Lankford. Little Rock, AR: August House, 1987. 265 p.

Review: Choice 25:1563 (June '88).
IL: IV.

Native American / Rock
The Native American in American literature / Roger O. Rock. Westport, CT: Greenwood, c1985. 211 p.

A classified, annotated bibliography; detailed indexes; numerous references to tales and myths.
Reviews: BL 82:670 (Jan '86); Choice 23:430 (Nov '85). IL: IV.

Navajo / Klah
Navajo creation myth / by Hasteen Klah; recorded by Mary C. Wheelwright. New York: AMS Press, 1980. 237 p.

Reprint of 1942 ed. published by Museum of Navajo Ceremonial Art, Santa Fe.
RL: CR / IL: III.

Navajo Coyote / Haile
Navajo coyote tales: the Curly To Aheedliinii version / Berard Haile; Navajo orthography by Irvy W. Goossen; edited by Karl W. Luckert. Lincoln: Univ. of Nebraska Press, c1984. 146 p.

Review: Choice, 23:164 (Sept '85).
RL: CR / IL: II.

Nesbit / Fairy *
Fairy stories / E. Nesbit; illustrated by Brian Robb; edited by Naomi Lewis. London: Benn, c1977. 171 p.

Review: Junior Bookshelf, 41:338 (Dec '77).
* RL: M / IL: II.

Nielsen / Old Tales *
Old tales from the north / illustrated by Kay Nielsen. Seattle: Seattle Book Company, c1975. 1 v. (unpaged).

With colored plates and black-and-white illus.
* RL: A / IL: I.

Nigg, Joe, *see* **Imaginary / Nigg**

Norman, Howard, *see* **Glooskap / Norman ***

Norman / Northern
Northern tales: traditional stories of Eskimo and Indian peoples / edited by Howard Norman. New York: Pantheon, c1990. 343 p.

Review: BL 87:399 (Oct 15 '90).
RL: SC / IL: IV.

Norris, Olga, *see* **Journeys / Norris ***

Norse / Crossley
The Norse myths / introduced and retold by Kevin Crossley-Holland. New York: Pantheon, c1980. 276 p.

Reviews: LJ 105:2339 (Nov '80); Scientific American 245:40 (Dec '81). IL: IV.

Northall, G.F., *see* **Folk-rhymes / Northall**

Norwegian / Asbjornsen
Norwegian folk tales, from the collection of Peter Christen Asbjornsen and Jorgen Moe. New York: Pantheon, 1982. 188 p.

Listed: Reader's Adviser, 15th ed., 1986.
Review: HB 58:677 (Dec '82).
IL: IV.

Norwegian / Hodne
The types of the Norwegian folktale / Ornulf Hodne. Oslo: Universitetsforlaget, c1984. 400 p.

A reference book.
RL: CR / IL: III.

O'Brien / Tales *
Tales for the telling: Irish folk & fairy stories / Edna O'Brien; illus. by Michael Foreman. New York: Atheneum, c1986. 127 p.

Reviews: NYTBR 92:31 (Mar 1 '87); SLJ 33:82 (Feb '87).
* RL: MJS / IL: II

Occult & Parapsych / Shephard
Encyclopedia of occultism & parapsychology / edited by Leslie Shephard. Detroit: Gale, c1984–85. 3 v. (1617 p.)

Indexing is applicable to the 3rd ed., 1991.
Review: BL 81:630 (Jan '85).
RL: SCR / IL: III.

Old Coot / Christian *
The old coot / by Peggy Christian. New York: Atheneum, c1991. 58 p.

Resource: Salem (OR) Public Library.
* RL: M / IL: II.

Old Wives / Carter
The old wives' fairy tale book / ed. by Angela Carter; illus. by Corinna Sargood. New York: Pantheon, c1990. 242 p.

Traditional.
RL: SC / IL: II.

Oral Trad / Cunningham
The oral tradition of the American west: adventure, courtship, family, and place—in traditional recitation / editor, Keith Cunningham; introd. by W.K. McNeil. Little Rock, AR: August House, c1990. 264 p.

Review: BL 87:584 (Nov 15 '90).
RL: SC / IL: III.

Osborne, Mary Pope, *see* Greek / Osborne

Otten, Charlotte F., *see* Lycanthropy / Otten

Owl Poems / Livingston
If the owl calls again: a collection of owl poems / selected by Myra Cohn Livingston; woodcuts by Antonio Frasconi. New York: McElderry, c1990. 114 p.

Review: BL 87:328 (Oct 1 '90).
RL: JSC / IL: III.

Padoan, Gianni, *see* Bedtime / Padoan & Smith *

Palestinian / Speak (Muhawi)
Speak, bird, speak again: Palestinian Arab folktales / editors: Ibrahim Muhawi & Sharif Kanaana. Berkeley: Univ. of Calif. Press, c1989. 420 p.

Reviews: Choice 27:639 (Dec '89); Middle East Journal 44:338 (Spring '90).
RL: CR / IL: III.

Parks, Van Dyke, *see* Harris-Parks / Jump *
——— *see* Harris-Parks / Jump Again *

Paxton / Aesop *
Aesop's fables / retold in verse by Tom Paxton; illustrated by Robert Rayevsky. New York: Morrow, c1988. [40] p.

Reviews: CCBB 42:81 (Nov '88); SLJ 35:178 (Sept '88).
* RL: A / IL: I.

Paxton / Belling *
Belling the cat, and other Aesop's fables / retold in verse by Tom Paxton; illustrated by Robert Rayevsky. New York: Morrow, c1990. [40] p.

Reviews: CCBB 43:194 (Apr '90); BL 86:1456 (Mar 15 '90).
* RL: A / IL: I.

Pecos Bill / Dewey *
Pecos Bill / Ariane Dewey. New York: Greenwillow, c1983. 56 p.

Reviews: BL 79:974 (Mar 15 '83); SLJ 29:160 (Mar '83).
* RL: P / IL: III.

Pecos Bill / Kellogg *
Pecos Bill / retold and illustrated by Steven Kellogg. New York: Morrow, c1986. [40] p.

Reviews: BL 83:63 (Sept 1 '86); SLJ 33:123 (Sept '86). *
RL: P / IL: III.

Pellowski / Family *
The family storytelling handbook: how to use stories . . . to enrich your family traditions / Anne Pellowski; illus. by Lynn Sweat. New York: Macmillan, c1987. 150 p.

Reviews: BL 84:327 (Oct 1 '87); SLJ 35:126 (Sept '88).
* RL: PM / IL: II.

Pellowski / Story
The story vine; a source book of unusual and easy-to-tell stories from around the world / Anne Pellowski; illus. by Lynn Sweat. New York: Macmillan, c1984. 116 p.

Resource: Publisher.
Reviews: BL 81:254 (Oct '84); CBRS 13:21 (Oct '84).
RL: P / IL: I.

Pendragon / Ashley
The Pendragon chronicles: heroic fantasy from the time of King Arthur / editor, Mike Ashley. New York: Bedrick, c1989. 417 p.

Reviews: BL 86:1688 (May '90); LJ 115:127 (Ap 15 '90).
RL: SC / IL: II.

Perowne, Stewart, *see* **Roman / Perowne**

Persian / Hinnells
Persian mythology / John R. Hinnells. New York: Bedrick, c1985. 143 p.
(Library of the world's myths and legends)

Reviews: Sci Books & Films, 22:31 (Sept '86); SLJ 32:31 (Sept '86)
RL: SC / IL: II.

Philip, Neil, *see* **Spring / Philip**

Pirate Ghosts / McSherry
Pirate ghosts of the American coast: stories of hauntings at sea / edited by
Frank D. McSherry, Jr., Charles G. Waugh, and Martin H. Greenberg. Little
Rock, AR: August House, c1988. 206 p.

Resource: San Antonio Public Library.
Traditional literary stories.
RL: SC / IL: II.

Plants / Dyer
The folk-lore of plants / T.F. Thiselton-Dyer. Detroit: Singing Tree Press,
1968. 328 p.
First published in London, 1889. Reprinted by Singing Tree Press, Detroit,
1968. Available (1990–91) from Gordon Press, New York, 328 p.

Review: Choice, 6:1044 (Oct '69); listed in Mercatante, 1988.
RL: SC / IL: II.

Polynesians / Andersen
Myths & legends of the Polynesians / by Johannes C. Andersen. Rutland, VT:
Tuttle, 1986, c1969. 513 p.

Review: Best Sellers 29:60 (May 1 '69).
RL: SCR / IL: II.

Pourrat / French
French folktales from the collection of Henri Pourrat / selected by
C.G. Bjurstrom; trans. by Royall Tyler. New York: Pantheon, c1989.
484 p.

Reviews: LJ 114:94 (Oct 1 '89); NYTBR (Dec 24 '89) p.25.
IL: IV.

Precious Stones / Kunz
>*The curious lore of precious stones . . . with information on . . . the protective and preventative functions of amulets and talismans* / George Frederick Kunz. New York: Bell, c1989. 406 p.

>Reprint. Originally published: Philadelphia, 1913; reprint: New York: Dover, 1971.
>RL: JSC / IL: II.

Preston / Dict Classical
>*A dictionary of pictorial subjects from classical literature; a guide to their identification in works of art* / Percy Preston. New York: Scribner's, c1983. 311 p.

>Reviews: BL 81:429 (Nov 15 '84); Choice, 21:956 (March '84); LJ 109:76 (Jan '84).
>RL: SCR / IL: III.

Provencal / De Larrabeiti
>*The Provencal tales* / Michael de Larrabeiti. New York: St. Martin's Press, c1988. 222 p.

>Reviews: LJ 114:79 (July '89); SLJ 35:130 (Dec '89).
>IL: IV.

Quayle / Cornish *
>*The little people's pageant of Cornish legends* / Eric Quayle; [illus. by] Michael Foreman. New York: Simon & Schuster, c1986. 106 p.

>Review: SLJ 34:191 (Sept '87).
>* RL: MJ / IL: I.

Quayle / Shining *
>*The shining princess, and other Japanese legends* / Eric Quayle; illus. by Michael Foreman. New York: Arcade (Little, Brown), c1989. 111 p.

>Resource: Newberg (OR) Public Library.
>Reviews: BL 86:835 (Dec 15 '89); SLJ 35:115 (Dec '89).
>* RL: M / IL: I.

Rabinowitz, Sholom, *see* **Aleichem / Holiday.**

Ramsey, Jarold, *see* **Coyote / Ramsey**

Raverat, Gwen, *see* **Andersen / Raverat** *

Reader's Digest, *see* **American / Read Dgst**

Reeves, James, *see* **Aesop / Reeves-Wilson** *

Reeves / Shadow
   The shadow of the hawk, and other stories by Marie de France / retold by
   James Reeves; pictures by Anne Dalton. New York: Seabury, c1977. 154 p.

   Resource: Salem (OR) Public Library.
   Reviews: HB 54:50 (Feb '78); SLJ 24:96 (Apr '78).
   RL: JSC / IL: II.

Restless / Cohen *
   The restless dead: ghostly tales from around the world / Daniel Cohen; illus.
   with photographs, prints, and drawings. New York: Dodd, Mead, c1984.
   109 p.

   Resource: Woodburn (OR) Public Library.
   Reviews: CCBB 37:183 (June '84); SLJ 31:116 (Sept '84).
   * RL: MJ / IL: II.

Riordan, James, *see* **Arabian / Riordan**

Rock, Roger O., *see* **Native American / Rock**

Rockwell / Puss *
   Puss in Boots, and other stories / told and illustrated by Anne Rockwell. New
   York: Macmillan, c1988. 88 p.

   Review: SLJ 35:175 (Mar '89)
   * RL: A / IL: I.

Roman / Perowne
   Roman mythology / Stewart Perowne. New York: Bedrick, 1969; rev. ed.
   c1983. 144 p. (Library of the world's myths and legends)

   Review: TLS (Jan 8 '70) p.38.
   RL: JSC / IL: III.

Roman / Usher
   Heroes, gods & emperors from Roman mythology / Kerry Usher; illus. by John
   Sibbick. New York: Schocken, c1983. 132 p. (World mythologies series)

Reviews: BL 80:1349 (May 15 '84); SLJ 31:134 (Sept '84).
RL: JS / IL: II.

Room / Classical Dict
Room's classical dictionary: the origins of the names of characters in classical mythology / Adrian Room. Boston: Routledge & Kegan Paul, c1983. 343 p.

Reviews: BL 80:737 (Jan '84); Choice, 21:404 (Nov '83).
RL: J-R / IL: III.

Rovin / Superheroes
The encyclopedia of superheroes / Jeff Rovin. New York: Facts on File, c1985. 443 p.

Resource: Salem (OR) Public Library.
Review: BL 82:356 (Nov 1 '85).
RL: JS / IL: III.

Rowland, Beryl, *see* Animals / Rowland
———— *see* Bird Symbol / Rowland

Russian / Afanasev
Russian fairy tales / trans. by Norbert Guterman from the collections of Aleksandr Afanasev; illus. by Alexander Alexeieff. New York: Pantheon, c1973. 661 p.

Reviews: BL 72:493, 508 (Dec '75); New Republic 173:34 (Nov 1 '75).
IL: IV.

Russian / Ivanits
Russian folk belief / Linda J. Ivanits; design and illustrated by Sophie Schiller. Armonk, NY: M.E. Sharpe, c1989. 257 p.

Reviews: Choice 27:806 (Jan '90); NYTBR (Aug 13 '89) p.18; Russian Review 50:90 (Jan '91).
RL: SCR / IL: II.

Russian Hero / Warner *
Heroes, monsters and other worlds from Russian mythology / text by Elizabeth Warner; illus. by Alexander Koshkin. New York: Schocken Books, c1985. 132 p. (World mythologies series)

Reviews: BL 82:1546 (June 15 '86); SLJ 33:147 (Sept '86).
* RL: SC / IL: II.

Sadeh, Pinhas, *see* **Jewish / Sadeh**

Saint George / Fox
Saint George, the saint with three faces / David Scott Fox. [England] Kensal Press, c1983. 187 p.

Resource: Mt Angel Abbey Library.
RL: SC / IL: III.

Sanfield, Steve, *see* **High John / Sanfield** *

Scandinavian / Davidson
Scandinavian mythology / H.R. Ellis Davidson. New York: Bedrick, 1988, c1982. 143 p. (Library of the world's myths and legends)

Review: TLS (Dec 20 '69) p.1345
RL: SC / IL: II.

Scandinavian / Kvideland
Scandinavian folk belief and legend / Reimund Kvideland, Henning K. Sehmsdorf, editors. Minneapolis: Univ. of Minn. Press, c1988. 429 p.

Resource: Salem (OR) Public Library.
Review: Choice 27:132 (Sept '89).
RL: CR / IL: II.

Scarry's Best *
Richard Scarry's Best Christmas book ever. New York: Random House, c1981. [44] p.

Reviews: BL 78:239 (Oct '81); SLJ 28:156 (Oct '81).
* RL: P / IL: II.

Scary / Young *
Favorite scary stories of American children / Richard and Judy Dockery Young. Little Rock, AR: August House, c1990. 110 p.

Reviews: BL 87:754 (Dec 1 '90); SLJ 37:210 (Mar '91).
* RL: PM / IL: II.

Schwab, Gustav, *see* **Gods / Schwab**

Schwartz / Gates
Gates to the new city: a treasury of modern Jewish tales / ed. by Howard Schwartz. New York: Avon, c1983. 815 p.

Review: LJ 108:1888 (Oct '83).
RL: SCR / IL: II.

Schwartz / Gold
Gold & silver, silver & gold; tales of hidden treasure / collected and retold by Alvin Schwartz; pictures by David Christiana. New York: Farrar Straus Giroux, c1988. 128 p.

Reviews: SLJ 35:107 (Feb '89); Scientific American, 261:149 (Dec '89).
RL: J / IL: III.

Schwartz, Howard, *see* Elijah / Schwartz

Scriven / Full Color *
The full color fairytale book / by R.C. Scriven; illus. by Andrew Skilleter. New York: Derrydale Books, c1974. 92 p.

Contains 20 "classic" tales.
* RL: A / IL: I.

Senior, Michael, *see* King Arthur / Senior

Sewell, Helen, *see* Bulfinch / Sewell *

Shah / Central Asia
Folk tales of central Asia / Amina Shah. London: Octagon Press, c1975. 147 p.

RL:JSC / IL: II.

Shannon / More *
More stories to solve; fifteen folktales from around the world / told by George Shannon; illus. by Peter Sis. New York: Greenwillow, c1990. 64 p.

* RL: P / IL: II.

Shephard, Leslie, *see* Occult & Parapsych / Shephard

Sholem Aleichem, *see* Aleichem / Holiday *

Sioux / Standing Bear *
Stories of the Sioux / by Chief Luther Standing Bear; illus. by Herbert Morton Stoops. Lincoln: Univ. of Nebraska Press, 1988, c1961, c1934. 79 p.

First published 1934; reprinted 1961 and 1988.
* RL: MJ / IL: II.

South / Mythical
Mythical and fabulous creatures: a source book and research guide / edited by Malcolm South. New York: Bedrick, 1987. 393 p.

Contains bibliographic essays; no texts of tales.
Listed in: Public Library Catalog, 1989.
Reviews: ARBA, 19:p.530 (1988); College & Research Libraries, 49:67 (Jan '88).
RL: SCR // IL: II.

Southern / Floyd
Great southern mysteries / E. Randall Floyd. Little Rock, AR: August House, c1989. 177 p.

Resource: Salem (OR) Public Library.
Review: SLJ 36:156 (Apr '90).
RL: JS / IL: II.

Spanish-Am / Van Etten *
Spanish-American folktales: the practical wisdom of Spanish-Americans in 28 eloquent and simple stories. Little Rock, AR: August House, c1990. 127 p.

* RL: M / IL: II.

Speck / New World
Myths and New World explorations / Gordon Speck. Fairfield, WA: Ye Galleon Press, c1979. 531 p.

Resource: Mount Angel Abbey Library.
RL: SC / IL: II.

Spence, Leonard, *see* **Babylonia / Spence**

Spring / Philip
The spring of butterflies, and other folktales of China's minority peoples / translated by He Liyi; ed. by Neil Philip; paintings by Pan Aiqing and Li Zhao. New York: Lothrop, Lee & Shepard, c1985. 144 p.

Reviews: CCBB 40:12 (Sep '86); SLJ 32:98 (May '86).
RL: J+ / IL: II.

Standing Bear, Luther, *see* **Sioux / Standing Bear ***

Starkey, Dinah, *see* **Ghosts / Starkey**

Strauss / Trail
Trail of stones / Gwen Strauss; illustrated by Anthony Browne. New York: Knopf, c1990. 35 p.

Reviews: BL 86:1272 (Mar 1 '90); CCBB 43:200 (Apr '90).
RL: JSC / IL: II.

Switzer, Ellen, *see* **Greek / Switzer**

Switzer / Existential
Existential folktales / Margaret Switzer. Berkeley: Cayuse Press, c1985. 157 p.

Rewritten storylines for traditional tales.
Review: Choice 23:607 (Dec '85).
RL: SC / IL: II.

Talashoma, Herschel, *see* **Hopi / Talashoma-Malotki**

Talk / Goss
Talk that talk: an anthology of African-American storytelling / edited by Linda Goss & Marian E. Barnes. New York: Simon & Shuster, c1989. 521 p.

Resource: Corvallis (OR) Public Library.
Review: Essence 20:48 (Mar '90); LJ 114:122 (Dec '89).
RL: SC / IL: III.

Tall Tales / Downs: Bear
The bear went over the mountain: tall tales of American animals / edited by Robert B. Downs. Detroit: Singing Tree Press, 1971. 358 p.

Listed in: Reader's Adviser, 15th ed., 1986.
Reprinted: Detroit: Omnigraphics, 1990.
RL: SC / IL: II.

Terada, Alice M., *see* **Vietnam / Terada ***

Thompson / NA Indians
Tales of the North American Indians / selected and annotated by Stith
Thompson. Bloomington: Indiana Univ. Press, 1968. 386 p.

First published 1929; in print, 1991. Listed in Mercatante, 1988.
RL: CR / IL: IV.

Tibet / Timpanelli *
Tales from the roof of the world: folktales of Tibet / retold by Gioia Timpanelli; illus. by Elizabeth Kelly Lockwood. New York: Viking, c1984.
53 p.

Reviews: HB 60:602 (Oct '84); SLJ 31:124 (Sept '84).
* RL: MJ / IL: II.

Timpanelli, Gioia, *see* Tibet / Timpanelli *

Tree / Kerven *
The tree in the moon, and other legends of plants and trees / Rosalind
Kerven; illus. by Bryna Waldman. New York: Cambridge University Press,
c1989. [32] p.

Resource: San Bernardino (CA) County Library.
* RL: A / IL: I.

Trolls / Asbjornsen
A time for trolls: fairy tales from Norway / told by Asbjornsen and Moe;
selected and translated by Joan Roll-Hansen; illus. by Hans Gerhard
Shorensen. 3rd ed. Oslo: Tanum-Norli, c1983. 82 p.

Resource: Salem (OR) Public Library.
RL: JS / IL: II.

Turkey / Walker
Tales alive in Turkey / compiled by Warren S. Walker & Ahmet E. Uysal.
Lubbock, TX: Texas Tech Univ. Press, c1990. 310 p.

First published 1966; reprinted 1975, 1990.
RL: CR / IL: IV.

Turkish / Walker
A treasury of Turkish folktales for children / retold by Barbara K. Walker.
Hamden, CT: Linnet, 1988. 155 p.

Resource: Salem (OR) Public Library.
Reviews: CCBB 42:111 (Dec '88); SLJ 35:159 (Oct '88).
RL: JS / IL: I.

Turkish (Art I) / Walker
The art of the Turkish tale / Barbara K. Walker; illus. by Helen Siegl. Lubbock,
TX: Texas Tech Univ., 1990. 249 p.

RL: JSC / IL: II.

Tyler, Royall, *see* Japanese / Tyler

Unicorn / Bradley
In pursuit of the unicorn / Josephine Bradley. Corte Madera, CA: Pomegranate Artbooks, c1980. 1 v. (unpaged)

Resource: Silverton (OR) Public Library.
Chiefly full-page color illustrations.
RL: JS / IL: III.

Unicorn / Coville *
The unicorn treasury / compiled and edited by Bruce Coville; illus. by Tim
Hildebrandt. New York: Doubleday, c1988. 166 p.

Resource: Salem (OR) Public Library.
Reviews: BL 85:943 (Feb 1 '89); SLJ 35:118 (Nov '88).
* RL: MJ / IL: II.

Unicorn / Hathaway
The unicorn / Nancy Hathaway. New York: Viking, c1980. 191 p.

Resource: Chemeketa Community College.
Reviews: BL 77:602 (Jan '81); Choice, 18:934 (Mar '81); Public Library
Catalog, 1989.
RL: JSC / IL: II.

Unnatural / Cohen
A natural history of unnatural things / Daniel Cohen. New York: Dutton,
c1971. 148 p.

Review: LJ 96:2926 (Sept '71).
RL: J / IL: II.

Usher, Kerry, *see* Roman / Usher

Van Etten, *see* Spanish-Am / Van Etten *

Vanishing / Mercer *
The stories of vanishing peoples: a book for children / John Mercer; illustrated by Tony Evora. New York: Allison & Busby, c1982. 128 p.

Review: SLJ 29:180 (March '83).
* RL: MJ / IL: II.

Victorian / Hearne
The Victorian fairy tale book / edited by Michael Patrick Hearne. New York: Pantheon, c1988. 385 p.

Review: English Studies 69:419 (Oct '89).
RL: JSC / IL: II.

Vietnam / Terada *
Under the starfruit tree: folktales from Vietnam / told by Alice M. Terada; illus. by Janet Larsen; introd. and notes by Mary C. Austin. Honolulu: Univ. of Hawaii Press, c1989. 136 p.

Resource: Corvallis (OR) Public Library.
Review: PW 236:71 (Nov 24 '89).
* RL: M / IL: II.

Viorst, Judith, *see* **My Mama / Viorst** *

Walker, Barbara G., *see* **Woman's Encyc / Walker**

Walker, Barbara K., *see* **Turkish (Art I) / Walker.**
—— *see* **Turkish / Walker.**

Walker, Warren S., *see* **Turkey / Walker.**

Warner, Elizabeth, *see* **Russian Hero / Warner** *

Water Buffalo (Chinese)
The water-buffalo and the tiger: folk tales from China (second series). Beijing: Foreign Languages Press, 1980. 115 p.

Resource: St Edward's University Library.
RL: JS / IL: II.

Waters / Encyclopedia
The encyclopedia of magic and magicians / T.A. Waters. New York: Facts on File, c1988. 372 p.

Reviews: BL 84:1720 (June 15 '88); LJ 113:162 (Feb 15 '88).
RL: SC / IL: III.

Weinreich, Beatrice Silverman, *see* **Yiddish / Weinreich**

Weinstein / Owls
Owls, owls, fantastical fowls / compiled by Krystyna Weinstein. New York: Arco, c1985. 144 p.

Resource: Salem (OR) Public Library.
RL: JSC / IL: III.

Werewolves / Aylesworth
Werewolves and other monsters / Thomas G. Aylesworth. Reading: Addison-Wesley, c1971. 127 p.

Resource: Salem (OR) Public Library.
RL: J / IL: II.

West, John O., *see* **Mex-Am / West**

Wheelwright, Mary C., *see* **Navajo / Klah**

Wilde / Happy *
The happy prince, and other stories / Oscar Wilde; illus. by Charles Robinson. New York: Morrow, c1991. 133 p.

* RL: MJ / IL: II.

Wilde / Lynch *
Stories for children / Oscar Wilde; illus. by P.J. Lynch. New York: Macmillan, c1991. 94 p.

* RL: MJ / IL: II.

Wildlife / Gillespie
American wildlife in symbol and story / edited by Angus K. Gillespie and Jay Mechline. Knoxville: Univ. of Tenn. Press, c1987. 251 p.

Review: Choice 25:900 (Feb '88).
RL: SC / IL: II.

Wilkins, Cary, see Lang / Wilkins

Williams-Ellis / Tales *
Tales from the enchanted world / Anabel Williams-Ellis; illus. by Moira Kemp.
Boston: Little, Brown, c1987. 195 p.

Review: NYTBR (June 19 '88) p.28; SLJ 34:98 (Apr '88).
* RL: A / IL: I.

Witch Encyc / Guiley
The encyclopedia of witches and witchcraft / Rosemary Ellen Guiley. New
York: Facts on File, c1989. 421 p.

Review: LJ 114:98 (June 1 '89).
RL: SC / IL: II.

Witch Hndbk / Bird *
The witch's handbook / Malcolm Bird. New York: Aladdin, 1988. 96 p.

Resource: Mt Angel Public Library.
Review: School Librarian 33:134 (June '85).
* RL: A / IL: II.

Witches / Iosa *
Witches / compiled and illustrated by Ann Iosa. New York: Platt & Munk,
c1981. 39 p.

Resource: Silverton (OR) Public Library.
* RL: MJ / IL: I.

Wolkstein / Love
The first love stories, from Isis and Osiris to Tristan and Iseult / Diane
Wolkstein. New York: HarperCollins, c1991. 270 p.

Reviews: BL 87:999 (Jan 15 '91); NYTBR (Feb 17 '91) p.17
RL: SCR / IL: II.

Wolves / Lopez
Of wolves and men / Barry Holstun Lopez; with photographs by John Bau-
guess. New York: Scribner, c1978. 309 p.

Reviews: LJ 103:2123 (Oct '78); NYTBR, (Nov 19 '78) p.44.
RL: SC / IL: III.

Woman's Encyc / Walker

The woman's encyclopedia of myths and secrets / Barbara G. Walker. San Francisco: Harper & Row, c1983. 1,124 p.

Note: reviewers say: "use with caution."
Listed in: Mercatante. 1988.
Reviews: Atlantic, 253:105 (Feb '84); Choice, 21:960 (Mar '84); LJ 109:174 (Feb '84).
RL: C / IL: III.

Women / Dyer

Folk-lore of women, as illustrated by legendary and traditionary tales, folk-rhymes, proverbial sayings, superstitions, etc. / T.F. Thiselton-Dyer. Detroit: Singing Tree Press, 1968; Detroit: Omnigraphics, 1991. 253 p.

First published: Chicago, 1906.
Resource: Corvallis (OR) Public Library.
Review: RQ 8:219 (Spring '69).
RL: SC / IL: II.

Wood, Marion, *see* Indian Myth / Burland

Yep / Rainbow *

The rainbow people / Laurence Yep; illus. by David Wiesner. New York: Harper & Row, c1989. 194 p.

Reviews: BL 85:1393 (Ap 1 '89); HB 65:382 (May '89); SLJ 35:123 (May '89).
* RL: MA / IL: I.

Yiddish / Weinreich

Yiddish folktales / edited by Beatrice Silverman Weinreich. New York: Pantheon, c1988. 413 p.

Review: NYTBR (Mar 5 '89) p.30.
IL: IV.

Yolen / Baby Bear *

Baby Bear's bedtime book / written by Jane Yolen; illustrated by Jane Dyer. New York: Harcourt, Brace, Jovanovich, c1990. [32] p.

Review: SLJ 36:94 (May '90).
* RL: P / IL: II.

Yolen / Faery Flag
The faery flag; stories . . . of fantasy and the supernatural / Jane Yolen. New York: Orchard Books, c1989. 120 p.

Reviews: WLB 64:96 (March '90); HB 66:90 (Feb '90).
RL:JS / IL: II.

Yolen / Shape Shift
Shape shifters: fantasy and science fiction tales about humans who can change their shapes / compiled and introduced by Jane Yolen. New York: Seabury, c1978. 182 p.

[Eight tales, within *IFT* scope, are indexed here.]
Reviews: NYTBR, (Ap 30 '78) p.50; SLJ 25:167 (Sept '78).
RL: JS / IL: II.

Yolen / Werewolves
Werewolves; a collection of original stories / edited by Jane Yolen and Martin H. Greenberg. New York: Harper, c1988. 271 p.

Review: BL 84:1842 (July '88); English Journal, 78:86 (Feb '89).
RL: JS / IL: II.

Young, Richard & Judy Dockery, *see* Scary / Young *

Young, Richard Alan, *see* Ghost (S'West) / Young

Zipes / Beauties *
Beauties, beasts, and enchantment: classic French fairy tales / translated and with an introd. by Jack Zipes. New York: New American Library, c1989. 598 p.

Resource: Salem (OR) Public Library.
Reviews: LJ 114:94 (Oct 1 '89); NYTBR (Dec 24 '89) p.25.
* RL: M-C / IL: II.

Zwerger, Lisbeth, *see* Aesop / Zwerger *

THE INDEX

A (the letter)
—Yolen / Baby Bear *
Arnold the 'gator only likes "A"
things/words, [18–19]
Abandoned children, *see* CHIL-
DREN, ABANDONED.
ABBESS
—Reeves / Shadow
twin girls parted at birth; reunited
at wedding of one, 113–
128
ABC(-s), *see* ALPHABET(-s)
ABDUCTION
see also CHANGELING(-s); KID-
NAPPED
—Bell / Classical Dict, 1–4 @
—Bruchac / Iroquois *
monstrous, two-headed snake a
traitor, 97–102
—Bryan / Lion *
lion steals ostrich chicks, 3–23
—Crossley / British FT *
abductee must tell tale to receive
hospitality, 77–85
Dark Horseman abducts Jemmy
Nowlan, 77–85
—Douglas / Magic *
by frog; Thumbelina, 43–53
—Dulac / Fairy *
Bashtchelik (real steel), 91–113
—Grimm / Complete *
Pink [carnation], The, 355–360
—Grimm / Legends (Ward), II:385 (in-
dex)
—Grimm / Sixty *

prince abducted; The Pink, 171–
176
—Hopi Coyote / Malotki
coyote and Pavayoykyasi, 141–
149
—Jewish / Sadeh
wife abducted; desperate man
and prophet Jonah, 154–
158
—Legends / Cavendish
wife abductions, 407 (index)
—Manning / Cats *
witch abducts king's two children;
Katchen the cat helps escape,
9–15
—Manning / Cauldron *
Elsa, abducted by witch to tend
her baby, escapes aided by
goat, 90–98
—Muddleheads / Harris
Mink Being wants to marry human princess, 5–25
—O'Brien / Tales *
giant Trencross abducts princess; white cat helps rescue,
92–105
—Old Wives / Carter
mother foils attempt to abduct
daughter (girl who stayed in
fork of tree), 33–38
—Scriven / Full Color *
Rapunzel, 9–12
—Shah / Central Asia
Feroz-Shah and the mechanical
flying horse, 131–145

princess imprisoned in mountain of jade, 19–24

—Spring / Philip
girl sheepherder finds water and salt, 98–102
lovers reincarnated as butterflies, 35–41
woman's love: wife rejects series of suitors, 58–74

—Tree / Kerven *
king takes beautiful bride of poor man, [16–19]

—Vanishing / Mercer *
little duck and big water-rat, 54–57
origin: turtles in Aussie creeks, 61–64
quest for wife abducted by giant bird, 42–49

—Vietnam / Terada *
sea snake captures mandarin's wife, 88–94

ABILITY (proper)
—Leonardo / Fables *
peach tree envies walnut tree, 26

ABOMINABLE SNOWMAN
—McGowen / Encyclopedia * 7–8
—Monsters / Cohen, 3–9 @
—Monsters / Hall, 100–115

Aboriginal tales, see AUSTRALIAN ABORIGINAL TALES.

ABRAHAM
—Jewish / Frankel, 653 (index)
—Jewish / Sadeh
appearances; prayer group, etc., 35–38
—Schwartz / Gates, 796 (index)

ABSURDITIES
see also Clever Elsa; DAY-DREAMS; FOOL; Golden goose, The (etc.)
—Childcraft 2 / Time *
absent-mindedness: Abu Ali

counts his donkeys [except one he's riding], 30–32
toad searches for button (Lobel), 44–53

—Crossley / Animal (Grimm) *
fox and geese: one last prayer, 26–28

—Grimm / Complete *
Clever Elsa, 171–174
Lean Lisa: milk of future cow, 696–698

—Grimm / Sixty *
Clever Elsa, 177–181

—Hoke / Giants
short-sightedness: pleasure first (Fiji), 130–132

—Old Wives / Carter
three sillies: crying over imagined harm to unborn child, 104–107

—Rockwell / Puss *
absurd advice: the miller, his son, and the donkey, 27–29
mismanagement: Mr. Vinegar (makes series of bad trades), 60–65
procession: Dummling: The Golden Goose, 30–39

ABSURDITIES: disregard of proper nature
—Bomans / Wily *
king tries to avoid death, 118–120
old man tries to hide from death, 104–107
wings: man tries to fly, 152–155

—Cambodian / Carrison
rider holds rice on head to lighten load for buffalo, 97–99

—Corrin / Six-Year *
snow-man (bully) takes people's clothes; melts, 19–23

—Crossley / British FT *
parrot greets; miner: I thought you were a bird, 293–294

—Grimm / Complete *
Fred and Kate [repeated foolish
acts], 283–289
Mouse, bird, sausage [trade duties = disaster], 131–133
—Grimm / Sixty *
Fred and Kate [as above], 144–
155
Mouse, bird, sausage [as above],
108–110
—Old Wives / Carter
three sillies: cow taken to roof to
graze, 104–107
—Rockwell / Puss *
Miller (The), his son, and the donkey, 27–29
—Russian Hero / Warner *
foolish man exchanges daughter
for help, 57–60
—Switzer / Existential
hen who baked the bread (absurd
cheerfulness), 9–16

ABSURDITIES: *misunderstandings*
—Animal Legends / Kerven *
breadfruit falls: hare heralds
earthquake, [26–27]
—Bruchac / Iroquois *
brave woman and the Flying
Head, 184–187
—Clarkson / World *
bobo (fool) misuses witches'
charm; robbers think he's devil,
173–175
humor: not recognizing selves in
mirror, 367–369
—Crossley / British FT *
man believes vegetable marrow
is mare's egg, 153–154
—Grimm / Complete *
good bargain: peasant thinks
frog and dog are speaking, 51–
55
maid of Brakel, 623
—Hall / Treasury *

Uncle Wiggily and the red spots,
26–31
—Jones / Tales *
misunderstanding: Chicken
Licken (sky falling!), 16–20
—Spanish-Am / Van Etten *
thieves mistake man, board on
head, for monster, 25–28
—Turkish / Walker
boasting mouse misunderstands
natural phenomena, 1–3
mosquito "hurts" water buffalo,
14
—Water Buffalo (Chinese)
plop! spread of unquestioned
danger, 30–32
—Yep / Rainbow *
Eel's disguise, 38–44

ABSURDITIES: *worries: "Clever
Elsa"*
—Grimm / Complete * 171–174
—Grimm / Sixty * 177–181

Abu Ali fools his friends
—Childcraft 2 / Time *

ABUSED CHILD
—Lang / Wilkins
mistreated Tontlawald girl lives
with fairies, 557–570

ACCIDENT(-s) (often unlikely)
see also HERO, UNLIKELY;
LUCKY ACCIDENTS
—Arabian / McCaughrean
miser's everlasting shoes, 58–64
—Jaffrey / Seasons
Shravan Kumar: husband accidently shot by king, 16–20
—Lore of Love
curse causes husband to forget
wife, 26–31
—Water Buffalo (Chinese)
trifles may cause disasters, 13–
17

ACCIDENTAL ENCOUNTERS
—Grimm / Complete *

Man among the thorns, 503–508

—Grimm / Sixty *
Man among the thorns, 182–189

—Lines / Magical *
Cormac Mac Art: actions explained by Manannan Mac Lir, 141–149

—Lore of Love
deity keeps book; all are fore-ordained, 18–23

—Old Wives / Carter
woman questions Sun in behalf of spinsters, cold woman, river, rock, 4–7

—Spring / Philip
golden fish rewards kindness, 103–113

—Turkish / Walker
lazy, bald Keloglan wins sultan's daughter, 20–22

ACCUSATION(-s) (usually false)

—Arabian / Lewis
Attaf's hospitality; Jafar's misfortunes, 199–209

—Bierhorst / Naked *
assault: Quilt of men's eyes, 101–109

—Cambodian / Carrison
Princess Amaradevi: husband accused of treachery, 23–30

—Clouston / Popular
Beryn in Falsetown, II.99–114, 478–480
king's favorite envied and plotted against, II.444–457
Llewellyn and his dog Gellert, II.166–186

—Douglas / Magic *
six swans (enchanted princes saved by their sister), 35–41

—Egyptian / Harris
Anpu and Bata, 77–83

—Erdoes / Sound *
Iktome "made off with the food," 31–32

—Fahs / Old *
daughter saves father from punishment by mutilation, 133–138

—Greaves / Hippo *
hare kills leopard's cubs; blames men, 22–26

—Grimm / Complete *
Six swans: sister faithful to transformed brothers, 232–237

—Grimm / Legends (Ward), II:385 (index)

—Hamilton / Dark *
Joseph Golem: blood accusation against Jews, 87–96

—Jewish / Frankel
Rabbi's mirror allows king to see treachery in his bedroom, 405–409

—Jewish / Sadeh
bride auctioned; bought by prince; chastity test, 332–333
Jewish pope; bastard converts to Catholicism, 195–197
king who couldn't sleep, 208–210
peddler and the woman who lied, 327–328
rabbi Isaac Abrabanel and king's shoe, 222–223
two tailors and wonderful photograph, 204–208
woman who was almost stoned to death, 18–20

—Lang / Wilkins
magic ring: happiness and power if . . . , 220–227

—Lester / Brer Rabbit *
Brer Rabbit eats the butter; accuses Brer Possum, 46–50

—Lewis / Proud
Lanval: Queen Guinivere claims seduction attempt, 26–47

—Lines / Magical *
  birth of Pryderi; Queen accused
  of murder, 116–122
  Joseph (in Egypt) accused by
  master's wife, 149–169
—Maori / Kanawa *
  Hutu accused of killing girl (a suicide), 106–110
—Nielsen / Old Tales *
  wife accused of murdering children, [5–15]
—Reeves / Shadow
  Launfal: secret love for Rosamund, 49–83
—Scriven / Full Color *
  cook eats meal prepared for
  guests, 65–68
—Shah / Central Asia
  nobleman and slave (later king),
  103–108
—Turkish / Walker
  foolish parents give con man gifts
  for dead son, 85–87
—Turkish (Art I) / Walker
  good to the good, and damnation
  to the evil: poor man and grand
  vizier, 204–207
—Vietnam / Terada *
  jealous husband accuses faithful
  wife of infidelity, 10–13

ACHILLES
—Gods / Schwab, 745 (index)
—Greek / Switzer, 203 (index)
—Grimal / Dictionary, 561 (index)
—Mercatante / Encyclopedia, 741 (in-
  dex)

ACHU
—Journey Sun (Chinese)
  qingke (barley) seed stolen from
  snake king, 24–46

ACORN
—Russian Hero / Warner *
  cock and the corn mill; magic
  acorn, 52–53

ACTIVITY PROGRAMS
—Bosma / Classroom
  folk literature, 1–116

ADAM and EVE
—Christian / Every, 142, 143 (index)
—Hamilton / In the Beginning *
  Yahweh the Creator, 120–125
—Jewish / Frankel, 653 (index)
  Eve, 655 (index)
  tempt phoenix; does not eat for-
  bidden fruit; immortal, 15–
  17
—Lester / Leopard *
  why dogs chase cats, 21–26
—Schwartz / Gates, 796, 800 (index)

ADAPTABILITY
—Cambodian / Carrison
  guards propose punishment for
  treacherous prince, 73–76
—Dramatized / Kamerman
  The wise people of Gotham, 88–
  97

ADOLESCENCE
—Bierhorst / Sacred
  Indian youth, 29–43

ADOPTION (child)
—Cambodian / Carrison
  Phnong family murdered; one
  child is saved, 78–85
—Dulac / Fairy *
  serpent-prince: marries, regains
  human form, 29–42
—Yolen / Werewolves
  werewolf's gift, 35–44

ADULTERY
  See also FIDELITY
—Grimm / Complete *
  Old Hildebrand: husband vs.
  adultress, 440–444
—Lewis / Proud
  King Equitan, seducer; dies in
  boiling bathwater, 82–87
—Old Wives / Carter
  hare seduces woman; she tricks,

cooks, feeds him to husband, 47

wife gives rice to lover; tricks husband to accept chaff for grain, 72

ADULTS
—Dramatized / Kamerman
happy adults: children at wishing well, 15–22

ADVENTURE
—Brooke / Telling *
Sleeping Beauty: event after awakening, 3–33

ADVICE (*usually not followed; with bad consequences*)
see also WARNING
—Clarkson / World *
Ivan [trades wages for master's advice], 314–317
—Coyote / Bierhorst *
while coyote gabs, wolf raids his house, [16]
—Frog Rider (Chinese)
questioning God of the West, 92–99
—Grimm / Complete *
catch Golden Bird; warnings repeatedly ignored, 272–279
—Grimm / Sixty *
catch Golden Bird . . . , 1–9
—Jewish / Frankel
bird gives hunter three pieces of wisdom, 378–379
—Jewish / Sadeh
hunter and the bird, 164
—Mex-Am / West
boy gives last three pesos for three counsels, 99
—Rockwell / Puss *
absurd: Miller (The), his son, and the donkey, 27–29
—Spring / Philip
son test's father's advice; cures king, 82–86

—Turkish (Art I) / Walker
laborer purchases four pieces of advice, to his good fortune, 179–183
—Water Buffalo (Chinese)
little camel tests mother's advice, 39–43
—Yep / Rainbow *
compulsive giving: The homecoming, 144–151

AELIAN
—Animals / Rowland, 179 (index)

AENEAS
—Gods / Schwab, 745 (index)
—Grimal / Dictionary, 562 (index)
—Roman / Usher
Dido and Aeneas, 40–45 @
golden bough: Aeneas in the Underworld, 51–57 @
site of Rome, 61–63 @
Trojan war, 32–39 @
war in Italy, 58–60 @

AENEID
—Mercatante / Encyclopedia, 742 (index)

Aesop (*collections of fables by Aesop*)
—Aesop / Reeves-Wilson *
Fifty-one fables by Aesop, 1–123
—Bedtime / Padoan & Smith *
more than fifty fables, 1–191 passim
—Paxton / Aesop *
ten fables, retold in verse, [1–40]
—Paxton / Belling *
ten fables retold in verse, [1–40]
—Wolves / Lopez
eight wolf fables (texts), 254–256
_____ (*individual fables by Aesop*)

Aesop: Ant and the dove
—Childcraft I / Once * 164

Aesop: Ass and the lap dog
—Aesop / Zwerger * 25

Aesop: Ass in lion's skin
—Birds / Carter & Cartwright * 47
Aesop: Bat, bramblebush, and cormorant
—Aesop / Holder, 8–9
Aesop: Belling the cat
—Allison / I'll Tell * 121
—Carle / Treasury * 38–39
—Paxton / Belling * [6–9]
Aesop: Blackbird and the peacocks
—Carle / Treasury * 64–65
Aesop: The boy who cried "Wolf"
—Aesop / Alley * 4–9
—Allison / I'll Tell * 105
—Childcraft I / Once * 162
—Paxton / Aesop * [33–35]
—Rockwell / Puss, 40–41 *
Aesop: Cock and the jewel
—Aesop / Holder * 20–21
Aesop: Crow and the picture
—Childcraft I / Once * 160
Aesop: Dog and his reflection
—Aesop / Alley * 24–25
Aesop: Dog and the bone
—Childcraft I / Once * 165
Aesop: Dog and the sow
—Aesop / Zwerger * 21
Aesop: Dove and the snake
—Aesop / Holder * 2–3
Aesop: Fox and the crow
—Aesop / Zwerger * 19
—Carle / Treasury * 66–67
Aesop: Fox and the grapes
—Aesop / Alley * 14–15
—Aesop / Holder, 14–15
—Aesop / Zwerger * 15
—Paxton / Aesop * [10–13]
Aesop: Frog and the ox,
—Carle / Treasury * 70–71
Aesop: Grasshopper and the ants
—Carle / Treasury * 110–111
—Paxton / Aesop * [36–39]
Aesop: Hare and the tortoise
—Aesop / Alley * 26–31

—Aesop / Holder * 22–23
—Aesop / Reeves-Wilson * 68–75
—Aesop / Zwerger * 17
—Allison / I'll Tell * 102
—Carle / Treasury * 36–37
—Childcraft I / Once * 161
Aesop: Hares and frogs
—Aesop / Zwerger * 11
Aesop: Laden ass and a horse
—Aesop / Holder * 10–13
Aesop: Lion and the mouse
—Aesop / Alley * 16–19
—Allison / I'll Tell * 115
—Childcraft I / Once * 159
—Paxton / Belling * [19–21]
Aesop: Man and the satyr
—Aesop / Zwerger * 7
Aesop: Marriage of the sun
—Aesop / Holder * 16–19
Aesop: Milkmaid and her pail
—Aesop / Alley * 10–13
—Aesop / Zwerger * 5
—Paxton / Belling * [34–37]
Aesop: Monkey and the camel
—Aesop / Zwerger * 13
Aesop: Monkey [as king] and the fox
—Carle / Treasury * 40–41
Aesop: Moon and her mother
—Aesop / Zwerger * 23
Aesop: Shepherd boy and the wolf
—Aesop / Alley * 4–9
—Aesop / Zwerger * 9
Aesop: Stag and the hounds
—Aesop / Holder * 24–25
Aesop: Town mouse and city mouse
—Aesop / Holder * 4–7
—Aesop / Zwerger * 3
—Allison / I'll Tell * 124–125
—Hall / Treasury * 17–21
—Paxton / Belling * [12–15]
Aesop: Wind and the sun
—Aesop / Alley * 20–23

Aesop: Wolf and the dog,
—Carle / Treasury * 104–105
Aesop: Wolf and the lamb
—Carle / Treasury * 108–109
AESOP (*writings about* Aesop)
—Aesop / Alley *
life and fables, 32 @
—Aesop / Reeves-Wilson, 12–13 *
—Coyote / Bierhorst *
Aztec versions, [1–46]
—Mercatante / Encyclopedia, 723 (index)
—Shannon / More *
never seen, never heard: king vs.
Aesop, 35–38
AFRICA (-n; -ans)
—American / Read Dgst
flew like birds, in ancient times,
34–35
—Cotterell / Encyclopedia, 46–47 @
—Creatures (illus) / Huber * 121–
125
—Dictionary / Leach, 1199–1200 (index)
—Greaves / Hippo *
general information, 9–14 @
vegetation zones; map, 11 @
—Legends / Cavendish, 7 (index)
—Man Myth & Magic, 3109 (index)
—Mercatante / Good/Evil
mythology, 145–152 @
AFRICAN TALES
—African / Abrahams
94 tales, 1–354
—Animal Legends / Kerven *
friends ask too much: guinea's
crest feathers; lizard's skin,
[24–25]
matchmaker: boy's dog learns
beloved's secret name, [18–
19]
—Bryan / Lion *
lion, wind, jackal, foolish boy (four
tales), 1–86

—Corrin / Imagine *
Arap Sang and the cranes, 47–
53
Chura and Marwe, 142–150
Onsongo and the Masai cattle,
80–96
—Dramatized / Kamerman
three one-act plays, 3–14
—Fahs / Old *
stolen drum to dance by;
Bakongo tale, 86–90
—Greaves / Hippo, 1–143 *
—Journeys / Norris *
ox-horn magically supplies
needs, [6–9]
—Manning / Cauldron *
Moti-katika and the Water Witch,
118–127
—Mercatante / Encyclopedia, 723 (index)
—Old Wives / Carter
girl who stayed in fork of tree,
33–38
market of the dead, 166–169
—Pellowski / Story *
thumb-piano stories, 103–110
—Tree / Kerven *
drums: unfaithful bride reverts to
thorn tree, [16–19]
—Williams-Ellis / Tales *
magic bird unplows field, gives
milk, lures children, 62–76
AFRO-AMERICAN(-s; -tales)
see also NEGRO; SLAVE
—Afro-American / Abrahams, 1–327
—Clarkson / World *
stolen pig disguised as baby in
crib, 286–288
—Georgia Coast / Jones
sixty-one tales (fox, wolf, owl,
rabbit, etc.) in dialect; with
glossary, 1–171
—Hamilton / People *
animals in, 12 @

celebration of the human spirit,
ix-xii @

voices from slavery past, 1–178

—High John / Sanfield *

High John the Conqueror; sixteen
tales; commentary, 1–113

—Lester / Brer Rabbit * 1–151

Brer Rabbit versions, vii-x @

—Lynn / Fantasy * 746 (index)

—Talk / Goss 1–521

family and home; fourteen tales
and commentary, 217–298

sermons, 183–216

AFTERLIFE

see also HEAVEN; OTHER-
WORLD; UNDERWORLD

—Christian / Every, 106–121, 142 (index)

—Cotterell / Encyclopedia, 251 (index)

—Egyptian / Harris

journey of the soul, 48–50

—Egyptian / Ions, 142 (index)

Osiris cult, 126–139 @

—Fahs / Old *

Brahman, the universal being,
189–192

hunter in Walumbe's country of
Death, 181–184

what kind of life: seed analogy,
185–188

—Hamilton / Dark *

priest denies afterworld, until visited by angel of death, 119–
125

—Jewish / Sadeh

allegory: king for a year (then
banished to desert isle), 379–
381

miser: eternally dirty pastry, 169

—Mesoamerican / Leon-P, 287 (index)

—Persian / Hinnells, 63–70

—Vietnam / Terada *

general's duty re punishing crimi-
nals after death, 78–80

spirits ask man to die and be their
leader (general), 78–80

Afterworld, see AFTERLIFE.

AGAMEMNON

—Gods / Schwab, 746 (index)

—Greek / Switzer, 203 (index)

AGATE

—Precious Stones / Kunz, 393 (index)

AGED

see also OLD . . .

—Bruchac / Iroquois *

respect for elders; boy who lived
with the bears, 24–30

—Crossley / Animal (Grimm) *

Bremen Town musicians [kill the
useless], 54–59

Aged mother, The

—Grimm / Complete * 826–827

AGGADA

—Schwartz / Gates, 1–815

AGING (usually marvelous)

—Bomans / Wily *

Anna: mayfly born, weds, begets,
grows old—all in one day, 43–
46

—Bruchac / Iroquois *

knowledge: gifts of the Little People, 41–44

—Dulac / Fairy *

boy gathers six helpers: the
seven conquerors, 22–28

Urashima Taro; Dragon Sea-
King's palace, 140–152

—Grimm / Complete *

elves: magic aging, 199

—Nesbit / Fairy *

magic apples: age with each
wish, 125–138

—Quayle / Shining *

Urashima opens forbidden box; is
suddenly very old, 57–68

AGNI
—Indic / Ions, 142 (index)
AGRAVAIN, Sir
—King Arthur / Senior, 318 (index)
AGREDA, Maria de (1602–1665)
—American / Read Dgst, 66–67
—Ghost (S'west) / Young
    Lady in Blue, 116–117
AGREEMENT(-s) *(usually broken; often foolish)*
    see also BARGAIN; PROMISE
    (-s)
—Celts / Hodges *
    Lad of Luck [foolish] and monster
    of the loch, 89–103
—Chorao / Child's *
    Pied Piper (rats; children), 51–
    55
—Dramatized / Kamerman
    Pedro and the burro, 458–470
—Hamilton / People *
    alliance: Bruh Alligator and Bruh
    Deer, 26–30
—Leonardo / Fables *
    ant's pact with grain of wheat,
    58–59
—Lore of Love
    Aucassin and Saracen maid, 98–
    106
—MacDonald / Sourcebook *
    deceptive; motif index, 265–271
—Manning / Cats *
    Pussy Cat Twinkle sells fur (life)
    to wizard; saved by female cat,
    19–28
—Williams-Ellis / Tales *
    King O'Toole's goose made
    young by St. Kevin, 37–43
AGRICULTURE
—Bell / Classical Dict, 4–6 @
—Lurker / Dict Gods, 394 (index)
AGROPELTER (mythical beast)
—Hoke / Giants
    Paul Bunyan and Babe, 11–29

AHURA MAZDA (god)
—Persian / Hinnells, 142 (index)
AINU PEOPLE
—Vanishing / Mercer *
    creation myths, 95–98
AIR
—Jewish / Sadeh
    Baal Shem Tov and the imps,
    352–353
Air castle, *see* DAYDREAM.
AIR GODS
—Cotterell / Encyclopedia, 251 (index)
AIRPLANE
—Nesbit / Fairy *
    last dragon; tamed; becomes first
    airplane, 161–171
AJAX
—Gods / Schwab, 746 (index)
Aladdin and the magic lamp
    [*finds, loses, regains*]
—Arabian / Lewis, 153–165
—Arabian / McCaughrean, 153–
    184
—Arabian / Riordan, 12–25
—Bedtime / Padoan & Smith * 145–
    147
—Corrin / Favourite * 61–86
—Crane / McLean * 28-[39]
—Scriven / Full Color * 79–83
ALADDIN STORIES
—Clouston / Popular, I.314–346
    variants, I.470–482
ALAMO
—American / Read Dgst, 172–173
ALASKA
—Wolves / Lopez, 299 (index)
ALATANGANA (god)
—Hamilton / In the Beginning *
    Sa: Kono creation myth, 14–19
ALBANIAN TALES
—Clouston / Popular, II.503 (index)
ALBATROSS
—Bird Symbol / Rowland, 200 (index)

ALCHEMY
—Arabian / Lewis
    Hasan, the alchemist, and the
    Jinn princess, 138–143
—Hamilton / Dark *
    servant opens forbidden book,
    summons devil to work; can't
    stop, 126–131
—Man Myth & Magic, 3110 (index)
    analytics, 3183 (index)
ALDROVANDI
—Animals / Rowland, 179 (index)
ALE
—Crossley / British FT *
    Pict keeps secret of brewing ale
    from Scots, 142–144
ALEXANDER the Great
—Legends / Cavendish, 420 (index)
Algonquin Indians
    see INDIANS: ALGONQUIN
Ali Baba and the forty thieves
—Arabian / Lewis, 188–198
—Arabian / McCaughrean, 108–121
—Arabian / Riordan, 88–99
—Corrin / Eight-Year * 62–74
—Corrin / Favourite * 148–164
—Lines / Magical * 89–105
—Scriven / Full Color * 20–25
ALI NUR
—Arabian / Lewis
    slave girl (Sweet-Friend) and Ali
    Nur, 25–34
ALIBI
—High John / Sanfield *
    slaves forbidden to catch catfish,
    34–39
Alice in Wonderland
—Childcraft 1 / Once *
    down the rabbit-hole, 238–253
ALIENS
—Monsters / Cohen, 189–222 @
ALLAH
—Douglas / Magic *
    fisherman's promise to genie,
    13–19
—Mercatante / Encyclopedia, 743 (index)
—Turkish / Walker
    ruler gives daughter to poor man
    as punishment, 139–147
—Turkish (Art I) / Walker
    Hoca punished for not saying "If
    Allah wills," 51–52
ALLAH: Sinbad's first and last voyage
—Arabian / Lewis , 94–105
—Arabian / McCaughrean, 16–21
—Arabian / Riordan, 38–55
ALLEGORY
—Lycanthropy / Otten
    Housman (Clemence): The werewolf, 281–320
—Lynn / Fantasy *
    annotated bibliography, 3–60
Allerleirauh
—Grimm / Complete * 326–331
ALLIGATOR(-s)
    see also CROCODILE(-s)
—Corrin / Six-Year *
    little jackal tricks alligator into revealing self, 93–97
—Dulac / Fairy *
    Bashtchelik (real steel), 91–113
—Hamilton / People *
    alliance: Bruh Alligator and Bruh
    Deer, 26–30
    Bruh Alligator meets trouble, 35–41
—Wildlife / Gillespie, 237 (index)
—Yolen / Baby Bear *
    Arnold the 'gator only likes "A"
    things/words, [18–19]
Allingham, William (1824–1889)
—Victorian / Hearn
    The fairies [poem], 128–130

ALMANAC
—Folk-rhymes / Northall
England, 430–458
ALMS
—Jewish / Sadeh
accept demon's gift: fall into his
net, 169–172
miser given one hour to repent;
fails, 177
seven good years: now or later,
187–189
ALONE . . .
—Allison / I'll Tell *
bundle of sticks: strength in sticking together, 114
ALPHABET(-s)
—Edens / Glorious ABC *
full-page color illus. by best artists
from the past, 1–32
—Halloween ABC / Merriam *
rhymes, [1–30]
—Jewish / Frankel
recited; God to make it into
prayer, 547–548
—Yolen / Baby Bear *
alligator only likes "A" things/
words, [18–19]
ALS (Armenian creature)
—McGowen / Encyclopedia *
half-human, half-animal, 9–10
ALTAR
—Man Myth & Magic, 3110 (index)
ALTERNATE WORLDS/HISTORIES
—Lynn / Fantasy *
annotated bibliography, 155–
185
AMADA
—O'Brien / Tales *
defeats giants (who daily return
to life), and a series of mon-
sters, 21–30
AMAZONS
—Legends / Cavendish, 255–259
—Speck / New World, 517 (index)

AMBITION
—Fahs / Old *
magic pillow: dream projects van-
ity, 121–124
—Jewish / Frankel
punishment: rabbi to werewolf;
wife to donkey, 450–455
—Shah / Central Asia
punishment: Rustam and the iron
fortress, 25–30
AMEN
—Jewish / Sadeh
Jew executed: failure to say
"Amen," 210–211
AMENDMENT OF LIFE
—Jewish / Frankel
pursuit of gazelle; "60 days" [one
hour] learning common life,
410–414
AMERICA (-s)
—Floyd / Gr Am Myst
pre-Columbus voyagers in the
New World, 142–145
—Legends / Cavendish, 420 (index)
—Speck / New World
early discovery and exploration,
1–531
AMERICANISMS
—American / Read Dgst, 433 (index)
AMON-RA
—Egyptian / Ions, 142 (index)
AMPUTATION
—Hopi Coyote / Malotki
foolish imitation: crow standing
on one leg, 69–75
AMULET(-s)
—Man Myth & Magic, 3110 (index)
—Precious Stones / Kunz, 19–114 @
—Witch Encyc / Guiley, 9–10, 409 (in-
dex)
ANAL HUMOR
—Erdoes / Sound *
dogs electing a leader; satire,
23–24

ANANSI TALES
—Animal Legends / Kerven *
   trickery: how tiger and monkey
   both escaped, [28–29]
—Bryan / Lion *
   Jumoke ("Foolish Boy") outwits
   Ananse, 60–86
—Childcraft 3 / Stories *
   Anansi and the plantains (Sher-
   lock), 108–113
   Anansi plays dead, 259–261
—Hamilton / In the Beginning *
   trickster finds darkness, sun,
   moon, 52–57
—Williams-Ellis / Tales *
   Anansi (death for saying "five"),
   143–150
ANCESTOR(-s)
—Cotterell / Encyclopedia, 251 (index)
—Coyote / Bierhorst *
   crocodile brags; coyote says:
   look at self, not ancestors, [40]
ANCESTOR WORSHIP
—Man Myth & Magic, 3111 (index)
**Andersen, Hans Christian (1805–
1875)**
—Andersen / Eighty *
   eighty fairy tales, 1–483
—Andersen / Raverat *
   first four tales: anniversary edi-
   tion, 1–76
   see individual title entries:
   Evil king
   Little Klaus, Big Klaus
   Magic boots
   Marsh king's daughter
   Traveling companion
   Ugly duckling
   Wild swans
   Winners [rabbit races snail]
ANDERSEN, _____ (as subject)
—Allison / I'll Tell * 32–33 @
—Andersen / Raverat *
   language technique, ix-xiii @

—Lynn / Fantasy *
   bibliography (about the author),
   412–415
Androcles and the lion
—Douglas / Magic * 167–175
ANDROMEDA (Chained Woman)
—Constellations / Gallant * 199 (in-
   dex)
ANECDOTES
—Ashliman / Guide
   titles arranged in Aarne-Thomp-
   son system, 204–309 @
ANGEL(-s)
—Baring-Gould / Curious
   Swan maidens: hearts of seven
   Samoyeds, 140–144
—Bierhorst / Monkey *
   Lord of the Clouds; weather-
   control, 70–71
—Bomans / Wily *
   odyssey of the Christmas tree an-
   gel, 181–185
—Christian / Every, 142 (index)
—Davidson / Dictionary, 1–386
   archangels, 51, 268, 338
   conjurations of, 357–361
   fallen angels, 111–112, 352
   Gabriel, 117–119
   guardian, 127–128
   hierarchy (lists), 336–337
   Israfel, 151–152
   Metatron, 192–193, 347
   Michael, 193–195
   Raphael, 240–242
   Samael, 255
   sarim, 350–351
   script, 335
   tree of life (illus.), 319
   watchers, 311–312, 349
—Demons / Gettings, 32
—Fahs / Old *
   Zoroaster: Mazda vs. Manyu,
   140–147
—Geras / Grandmother *

peddler (angel) takes kvetch to Market of Misery, 66–76
—Grimm / Complete *
  flail from heaven, 514–515
—Grimm / Legends (Ward), II:386 (index)
—Jewish / Frankel, 644, 648 (index)
—Jewish / Sadeh
  fall, 1
  Rabbi Joseph de la Reina; fight against Samael, 233–237
—Lurker / Dict Gods
  divine messengers, 404 (index)
—Man Myth & Magic, 3111 (index)
  analytics, 3184 (index)
—Mercatante / Good/Evil, 233 (index)
  fallen, 236 (index)
—Russian / Ivanits, 245 (index)
—Schwartz / Gates, 797 (index)
ANGEL OF DEATH
—Davidson / Dictionary, 26
—Hamilton / Dark *
  priest becomes proud, denies afterworld, until visited . . . , 119–125
—Jewish / Frankel, 653 (index)
  bride saves husband from death, 600–602
  Elijah in heaven: recording angel, 577–578
  fox escapes from Angel of Death; Leviathan's fish, 11–14
  kamzan: two keys to each coffer, 369–371
  Milham's walled city, barred to Angel of Death, 15–17
—Jewish / Sadeh
  Angel's seven messengers, 180–181
  bride and, 11–13
  master thief, 291–295
ANGER
—Demi / Reflective *
  boar declares war on forest, [10]

—Jewish / Frankel, 648 (index)
—Jewish / Sadeh
  father's advice averts evil, 333–334
ANGRA MAINYU (evil spirit)
—Persian / Hinnells, 142 (index)
ANIAN, STRAIT OF
—Speck / New World, 517 (index)
ANIMAL(-s) (often personified)
  see also FABULOUS ANIMALS; MARRIAGE to ANIMAL in HUMAN FORM; also individual species, e.g., FOX; also particular tales, e.g., Bremen Town musicians
—Amer Ind / Erdoes
  fifteen tales, 387–426
—American / Read Dgst
  trapper tales, 185
—Animal Legends / Kerven *
  native races: twelve legends on origins, [1–32]
—Animals / Rowland
  in fables, 179 (index)
—Ashliman / Guide
  titles arranged in Aarne-Thompson system, 1–50 @
—Babylonia / Spence, 384 (index)
—Beat / Bryan *
  creation; insect pests; get tails, 53–70
  why wild animals always fight in the bush, 14–29
—Bierhorst / Monkey *
  bad compadre oft exploits Juan; animals perform his impossible tasks, 94–106
  Blue Sun: beheads younger brother every day; various origins, 107–112
—Birds / Carter & Cartwright *
  juvenile poetry, 1–64
—Bosma / Classroom
  folk literature, 5–6

—Bruchac / Iroquois *
  boy who lived with the bears
    (save human life), 24–30
—Bryan / Lion *
  legal relations: lion steals ostrich
    chicks, 3–23
—Childcraft 3 / Stories *
  creation: Glooscap vs. Malsum,
    143–151
—Chinese / Chin *
  year of the rat [Chinese calen-
    dar], 157–167
—Clarkson / World *
  cat, etc., attack thieves in dark,
    drive them away, 154–156
—Clouston / Popular
  gold-producing animals, I.123–
    132
  thankful beasts, I.223–242, 314–
    346
  ungrateful, I.262–265
—Corrin / Six-Year *
  fanciful trait: captured field
    mouse escapes with acorn,
    113–115
—Cotterell / Encyclopedia, 251 (in-
    dex)
—Curry / Beforetime *
  before man appeared, animals
    had human characteristics,
    121
  length of bows determine man/
    animal share in ruling, 121–
    127
  war between beasts and birds;
    fickle bat, 68–69
—Douglas / Magic *
  Puss in Boots; helps men acquire
    wealth, 99–107
—Dramatized / Kamerman
  magically grants three wishes;
    capture bandit, 324–333
—Earth / Hadley *
  bear, fawn, panther, and moose

  help control the four winds,
    [11–12]
—Egyptian / Ions
  sacred animals, 120–125 @
—Egyptian / Mercatante
  deities, 9–10
—Fahs / Old *
  make sickness for human enemy,
    71–80
  Prometheus brings fire to man-
    kind, 145–147
—Fairies / Briggs, 134–135
—Geras / Grandmother *
  overcrowded house (move an-
    imals in/out; seems larger),
    77–85
—Ghosts / Cohen
  animal-ghosts, 137–149
—Glooskap / Norman *
  original giant-size reduced by
    Glooskap, 1–10
—Greaves / Hippo *
  African why/how tales, 1–144
  warning: lion's roar means he's
    hunting, 15–18
—Grimm / Complete *
  failing vs. non-failing in feeding
    animals, 698–704
  musician promises to teach wolf,
    fox and hare to play, 56–58
  straw, coal and stone fail as
    bridge for animals, 365–367
—Grimm / Legends (Ward), II:387 (in-
    dex)
—Hall / Treasury *
  wedding: The owl and the pussy-
    cat (Lear), 40–41
—Hamilton / Dark *
  punishment for not heeding truth
    told by, 49–53
—Hamilton / People *
  Black folktales, 12 @
  fear men: He lion, Bruh bear,
    Bruh rabbit, 5–12

—Indic / Ions
  animal deities, 100–107 @
—Jaffrey / Seasons
  animal army aids Ram in battle
  with Ravan, 62–69
—Jewish / Frankel, 645, 648 (index)
—Jewish / Sadeh
  poor brother and three beasts; reveal hidden treasure, 140–143
—Kessler / Turtle Knock *
  humor, 1–48
—Kessler / Turtle Riddle *
  humor, 1–48
—Lang / Wilkins
  magic Nightingale (sings for emperor), 317–326
  queen poisons stepdaughter's
  suitor; animal advises, 460–473
—Legends / Cavendish
  helpful, 402 (index)
—Lester / Brer Rabbit *
  animals with horns vs. animals
  with claws; Brer Wolf exposed,
  122–124
  how animals came to earth (leave
  Sister-Moon), 1–3
—Lurker / Dict Gods, 394 (index)
—Lycanthropy / Otten, 325 (index)
—Lynn / Fantasy *
  annotated bibliography, 61–103
—MacDonald / Sourcebook *
  motif index, 41–87
—Man Myth & Magic, 3111 (index)
  analytics, 3185–87 (index)
—Mex-Am / West
  motif index, 298
  tales and fables, 89–93
—Monsters / Hall
  mythical, 1–144
—Northern / Norman
  thirteen tales, 141–170
—Norwegian / Hodne, 19–53
—Occult & Parapsych / Shepard,
  1577–79 (index)

—Palestinian / Speak (Muhawi)
  motif-index, 387–388
—Pellowski / Story *
  why [Buddhist] years are named
  for, 87–89
—Persian / Hinnells, 142 (index)
—Pourrat / French
  sixteen tales, 335–386
—Scandinavian / Kvideland
  healing, xi (index)
—Schwartz / Gates, 797 (index)
—Shah / Central Asia
  grateful to captor for release (Ahmad), 126–130
  magic: Rustam and the iron fortress, 25–30
—Sioux / Standing Bear *
  buffalo brothers: one aids its
  wounded "brother," 44–47
—Spanish-Am / Van Etten *
  cat/rooster/sheep/ox escape
  from wolves/coyote, 97–100
—Talk / Goss
  twenty-one tales, and commentary, 21–111
—Tall Tales / Downs: Bear, 1–358
—Turkey / Walker
  helpful, 299 (index)
—Unicorn / Hathaway
  false unicorn, 140–149 @
—Vanishing / Mercer *
  Nagas myth: origin of domesti-
  cated animals, 91–94
—Water Buffalo (Chinese)
  plop! spread of unquestioned
  danger, 30–32
—Wildlife / Gillespie, 1–251 @
—Williams-Ellis / Tales *
  magic bird lures children, 62–76
—Yep / Rainbow *
  grateful: "We are all one," 72–
  78

ANIMAL CHARACTERISTICS
(appearance, habits, origin, etc.)

—Aesop / Reeves-Wilson *
Birds, beasts, and bat, 55–56
—Animal Legends / Kerven *
how turtle got her shell, [15–17]
magic song: koalas created by
boy's transformation, [6–7]
Sedna marries seabird; unhappy;
father kills bird, [30–32]
—Beat / Bryan *
how animals, birds, fish got tails,
53–70
—Bierhorst / Monkey *
toad hides/rides in hawk's bag;
tries to float; crashes, 136–137
—Bruchac / Iroquois *
buzzard's feathers, 61–63
chipmunk: origin of stripes, 37–
39
fox trickster: how bear lost his tail,
32–34
origin of plants, 15–17
rabbit's legs, tail, lip, 65–67
turtle's cracked shell, 55–59
turtle's face, 55–59
two brothers: one brings good,
the other evil, 19–23
—Caduto / Keepers *
Four Worlds (Dine); creation of
animal life, 31–34
turtle's cracked shell, 157–158
why buzzard has red skin (head),
49–50
—Childcraft 1 / Once *
how camel got hump (Kipling),
268–271
why bear has stumpy tail 96–97
why mosquitoes buzz in people's
ears, 130–136
—Childcraft 3 / Stories *
why kangaroo hops on two legs,
83–86
—Chinese / Chin *
cat enemy of rat forever, 157–167
—Clarkson / World *

origin of cracks on turtle's shell,
342–347
why buzzard is bald, 332–333
—Corrin / Imagine *
Arap Sang: bald vultures, elephant large head, crane
crowns, 47–53
—Crossley / Animal (Grimm) *
Hedge-king [choosing king of
birds], 15–20
—Crossley / British FT *
magpies set tree afire; fall as
cooked crabs, 247
old Charger sold; sinks with rider,
into ground, 307
—Curry / Beforetime *
coyote rides sun (why his back
and tail are dark), 100–106
Old-Man-Above created animals
from sticks and leaves, 1–4
why dog and man walk together,
128–131
—Erdoes / Sound *
how crows came to be black, 57–
59
—Greaves / Hippo *
Creator permits hippo to live in
water, 67
how buffalo became a grass
eater, 73–77
how cheetah got his speed, 28–
29
how hippo lost his hair, 68–71
how jackal got its markings, 47
how tortoises' eggs are cared for,
134–136
how tsessebe got his horns, 104–
106
how waterbuck got white circle on
rump, 92–95
how zebra got stripes, 99–102
rhino borrows porcupine's, 64–65
waterbuck runs into swamp; escapes lion, 91–92

why cheetah's cheeks are tear-stained, 29–33

why giraffe and oxpecker are friends, 84–86

why giraffe has a long neck, 86–88

why lion does not eat fruit, 18–20

why lion roars, 15–18

why ostrich has a long neck, 128–130

why rhino scatters his dung, 60–64

why wart hog goes on his knees, 108

why wart hog is so ugly, 109–112

zebra and impala, special prey of wild dogs, 35–38

zebra's only choice: striped coat, 97–99

—Grimm / Complete *

cock, hen, et al, attack Herr Korbes, 205–206

God creates animals; devil creates goats with long tails, 642–644

sole (fish) punished: mouth position, 709

three languages [dog, bird, frog], 169–171

—Grimm / Sixty *

three languages [as above], 223–226

—Hamilton / In the Beginning *

Popul Vuh: cannot praise god, 89–90

Raven creates, for humankind, 5

—Hamilton / People *

Alligator: smooth, white hide turns . . . , 35–41

Tappin: how turtle got marks on back, 20–25

—Hoke / Giants

raven characteristics, 150–155

—Hopi / Talashoma-Malotki

game animals (wild) made hard to catch, 50–69

—Jewish / Frankel

mouse: puckers at corner of mouth, 41–42

—Lester / Leopard *

why dogs chase cats, 21–26

why monkeys live in trees; eat pepper, 41–44

—MacDonald / Sourcebook *

motif index, 41–62

—Maori / Kanawa *

how Kaka (parrot) got beautiful feathers, 115

how Toroa came to roam oceans, 113–114

—Unicorn / Hathaway

unicorn: first animal named; Old Testament, 29–39 @

—Vietnam / Terada *

how tiger got its stripes, 7–9

hunter given one wish; origin of the gecko, 69–71

—Water Buffalo (Chinese)

loyalty: origin of horse-headed fiddle, 44–48

white rabbit: origin of long ears, pink eyes, 93–102

—Yep / Rainbow *

cats and dogs as "Natural enemies," 12–18

ANIMAL GHOSTS

—Scary / Young *

Old Raw Head: hillbilly steals/butchers witch's hog, 11–13

white wolf eventually thought to be boy's ghost, 40–42

ANIMAL(-s), GRATEFUL

—Bomans / Wily *

animals save kind girl, 135–137

—Celts / Hodges *

Lad of Luck and monster, 89–103

—Douglas / Magic *

Androcles and the lion, 167–175

—Grimm / Complete *
    brothers: one rescues princess; is
      rescued by other, 290–311
    fisherman and his wife, 103–112
—Grimm / Sixty *
    fisherman and his wife, 47–56
—Russian Hero / Warner *
    Koshchei the Deathless; Bulat
      the Brave; Vasilisa, 96–99
—Shah / Central Asia
    Ahmad and the nagging wife,
      126–130
—Turkish (Art I) / Walker
    death, if shepherd does not keep
      secret his knowing language of
      animals, 190–194
—Yep / Rainbow *
    "We are all one," 72–78
ANIMAL(-s), HELPFUL (*beneficial to
    humans*)
    see also Snow-White and Rose-
      Red (*etc.*)
—Bierhorst / Monkey *
    bird bride: toad helps youngest
      son re oft-ruined cornfield, 25–
      31
—Bierhorst / Naked *
    Porcupine's grandson [aban-
      doned boy], 93–100
—Bomans / Wily *
    animals save kind girl, 135–137
—Bruchac / Iroquois *
    boy who lived with the bears
      (save human life), 24–30
—Caduto / Keepers *
    earth's origin; primal water; tur-
      tle's back, 25–26
    fisher to Skyland: origin of Big
      Dipper, 117–120
    how Raven made the tides, 103
—Celts / Hodges *
    Lad of Luck and monster, 89–
      103
—Chinese / Chin *

    cowherd's marriage to fairy weav-
      ing maid, 113–125
—Clarkson / World *
    gold in chimley; helpful cow,
      sheep, horse, 26–29
—Chorao / Child's FTB *
    ants push sky; rescue Indian from
      tree top, 43–50
    girl given to the Ranee's pet fish
      Muchie Lal, 21–31
—Corrin / Eight-Year *
    Rikki-Tikki-Tavi (mongoose) kills
      cobras, 173–191
—Corrin / Imagine *
    Arion and the dolphin, 161–163
—Douglas / Magic *
    white cat (enchanted princess),
      69–83
—Earth / Hadley *
    muskrat retrieves bit of earth to
      begin rebuilding, [6–7]
—Erdoes / Sound *
    brothers transformed to rattlers;
      snake medicine, 37–42
    eagles save marooned warrior
      (Spotted Eagle), 25–30
    Owl Woman (Hinhan Win) is mes-
      senger; pay attention, 93–
      94
    teaches Indian to make a flute,
      3–9
—Grimm / Complete *
    Queen bee, The, 317–319
    three feathers: youngest prince
      marries toad, 319–322
—Grimm / Sixty *
    Queen bee, The, 206–208
—Hall / Treasury *
    A home for [elf] Tandy, 54–61
—Hamilton / People *
    Talking cooter; master frees
      slave, 155–155
—Hoke / Giants, 93–102
—Igloo / Metayer

protector: dog kills would-be girl-takers, 122–127
—Jaffrey / Seasons
how Ram, son of Dashrat, defeated demon king Ravan, 48–69
—Lang / Wilkins
Fairer-than-a-Fairy, 274–281
—Lester / Leopard *
magic bird makes milk for famine-stricken people, 5–11
—Lines / Magical *
Little Fool Ivan and the little humpback horse, 70–85
—Lore of Love
King Nala and Princess Damayanti, 110–119
—Manning / Cauldron *
Elsa, abducted by witch to tend her baby, escapes aided by goat, 90–98
—Old Coot / Christian *
Coyote promises "gold" (i.e., tales) to Old Coot, 3–13
—Rockwell / Puss *
cat (white bear) on the dovrefell, 71–79
Puss in Boots, 80–88
—Russian Hero / Warner *
captive tricks witch's daughter; geese help escape, 82–85
—Scary / Young *
Hobbyahs scared away by barking dog, 26–30
—Scriven / Full Color *
Babes in the wood, 16–20
—Sioux / Standing Bear *
wolves save woman caught in blizzard, 3–9
—Unicorn / Coville *
task: help young girl regain will to live, 92–104
—Vanishing / Mercer *

beaver saves boy left to die (Blackfeet), 106–111
—Vietnam / Terada *
elder brother inherits all but starfruit tree, 3–6
Mister Thirty: tiger remorseful after killing man, 18–22
—Williams-Ellis / Tales *
trolls driven away by bear ("great white cat"), 17–23
—Yep / Rainbow *
cats and dogs as "Natural enemies," 12–18
ANIMAL-HUMAN COMMUNICATION
[humans understanding animal "speech"]
see also TALKING ANIMALS
—Bomans / Wily *
thrush-girl: learns to understand birds, bees, mole, 135–137
—Bruchac / Iroquois *
dogs who saved their master, 85–91
—Jewish / Sadeh
bread cast upon the water [understood by humans], 28–31
—Shah / Central Asia
Ahmad and the nagging wife, 126–130
—Sioux / Standing Bear *
Horse Dreamer and Singing Colt, 51–54
wolves save woman caught in blizzard, 3–9
—Turkish (Art I) / Walker
death, if shepherd does not keep secret his knowing language of animals, 190–194
—Vietnam / Terada *
Da Trang crab: grateful snake gives magic pearl, 37–41
ANIMAL(-s): HUMAN TRAITS
—Bierhorst / Naked *

turtle and partridge hide bagged elk from wolves, 67–71
—Bomans / Wily *
frog poet, 116–118
human-like hen, 83–86
human-like maybug, 83–86
mayfly with human-like life events, 43–46
—Bruchac / Iroquois *
turtle makes war on men, 55–59
—Childcraft 1 / Once *
Pooh goes visiting (Milne), 201–207
Potter: Tale of Peter Rabbit, 192–196
—Childcraft 3 / Stories *
Toad's escape; addiction to fast cars (Grahame), 6–21
—Corrin / Eight-Year *
Rikki-Tikki-Tavi (mongoose) kills cobras, 173–191
—Corrin / Six-Year *
discontented pig: some unpleasantness in all work, 116–119
farm couple adopt boy-mouse; he seeks a wife, 125–131
pig (Harold Trotter) with human feelings, 62–69
Tim Rabbit uses mushroom as umbrella, 161–165
—Crossley / Animal (Grimm) *
cat/mouse partnership, 21–25
fox and cat; arrogance and modesty, 8–10
fox helps old horse, 34–38
hare and hedgehog race, 39–44
hedge-king (bird) defeats bear, 49–53
kill Old Sultan, faithful dog, 11–14
wolf and seven young goats, 29–34
—Douglas / Magic *
Bremen Town musicians, 123–129

—Erdoes / Sound *
mice powwow in elk skull, 68–70
—Grimm / Complete *
cat (princess) gives horse to miller's apprentice, 482–485
princess marries donkey; it removes animal skin at night, 632–635
—Grimm / Sixty *
Chanticleer and Partlet, 74–79
—Jones / Tales *
Goldilocks and the three bears, 8–15
—Rockwell / Puss *
Puss in Boots, 80–88
—Scriven / Full Color *
Goldilocks and the three bears, 27–28
—Spanish-Am / Van Etten *
cat/rooster/sheep/ox escape from wolves/coyote, 97–100
—Switzer / Existential
hen who baked the bread (existential retelling), 9–16
—Turkish (Art I) / Walker
donkey and camel: irresistible urges, 44–45

ANIMAL KING(-dom)
—Arabian / McCaughrean
animals tell lion of man's cruelty, 51–57
—Clarkson / World *
pet cat disappears; now 'king o' the cats,' 210–211
—Crossley / Animal (Grimm) *
Hedge-king [choosing king of birds], 15–20
—Grimm / Complete *
willow-wren: contest to select king of birds, 705–708

ANIMAL(-s), MYTHICAL
see also particular creatures, e.g., UNICORN
—Beasts / McHargue, 1–118 @

—Childcraft 1 / Once *
 bunyip of Berkeley's Creek, 231–
 235
—Creatures (illus) / Huber * 1–155
—Jaffrey / Seasons
 Krishna defeats five-headed serpent-king, 30–31
—McGowen / Encyclopedia * 1–64
—Maori / Kanawa *
 talking dragon (Taniwah) of Rotorua trapped/killed, 52–60
—Monsters / Cohen
 encyclopedia, 1–287 @
—Nesbit / Fairy *
 last dragon; pet of princess, 161–
 171
—South / Mythical
 sources; bibliographic essays, 1–
 393
—Turkish (Art I) / Walker
 Camesap befriended by padishah of snakes, 218–224
—Unicorn / Coville *
 hunting season: children try to
 save unicorn, 79–89
 king would own unicorns; princess: they must be free, 24–37
 Unicorn in the maze (Lindholm),
 7–22
—Yep / Rainbow *
 "Trouble-snake," 118–123

ANIMAL PARLIAMENT
—Caduto / Keepers *
 Awi Usdi: deer and excessive
 hunting, 173–174
—Erdoes / Sound *
 mice powwow in elk skull, 68–70

**ANIMAL(-s): SALE OF WORTH-
 LESS ANIMALS**
—Bierhorst / Naked *
 quilt of men's eyes, 101–109
—Grimm / Complete *
 master-thief given three tasks,
 773–780

—Turkish (Art I) / Walker
 swindlers swindled: bagged,
 thrown into river to get underwater sheep, 147–153
 swindlers swindled: messenger
 rabbit, 147–153

ANIMAL WARFARE
—Beat / Bryan *
 why bush cow and elephant always fight, 14–29
—Bruchac / Iroquois *
 snakes make war of revenge, 93–
 95
—Curry / Beforetime *
 war between beasts and birds;
 fickle bat, 68–69
—Grimm / Complete *
 Wolf and the man [fox's warning],
 350–351
—Grimm / Sixty *
 Wolf and the man , 211–212
—Hamilton / People *
 alliance: Bruh Alligator and Bruh
 Deer, 26–30
—Water Buffalo (Chinese)
 water-buffalo vs. tiger, 85–88
—Williams-Ellis / Tales *
 mice repel invaders of kingdom of
 friendly humans, 45–54

ANIMAL(-s), WISE (*magic wisdom*)
—Grimm / Complete *
 Goosegirl: servant's imposture of
 princess revealed, 404–411
 twelve huntsmen; lion serves
 prince, 334–336
—Grimm / Sixty *
 Goosegirl (as above), 67–73
 twelve huntsmen (as above),
 271–273
—Lang / Wilkins
 Fairy of the Dawn; magic well
 water, 571–601
 Nightingale sings for emperor,
 317–326

—Rockwell / Puss *
　Puss in Boots, 80–88
—Switzer / Existential
　truth-telling horse: goose girl (*existential retelling*), 1–8
ANISHINABA
—Hamilton / Dark *
　tiny thing: Anishinaba and Boshk-wadosh, 54–59
ANPU and BUTA
—Egyptian / Harris
　two brothers; betrayed by woman, 77–83
—Egyptian / Mercatante
　Anpu and Buta: tale of two brothers, 197–204
ANSWER
—Shannon / More *
　Theseus' ship (not all puzzles have an answer), 61–62
ANT(-s)
　see also Aesop: grasshopper and the ant
—Allison / I'll Tell *
　dove saves ant; ant warns dove of trap, 106
—Bierhorst / Monkey *
　youngest son, lazy Tup, gets ants to clear/plant/harvest cornfield, 44–51
—Carle / Treasury *
　improvident grasshopper plays music for ants (Aesop), 110–111
—Chorao / Child's FTB *
　ants push sky; rescue Indian from tree top, 43–50
—Dramatized / Kamerman
　ant king: quick-witted Jack; suitor test, 400–412
—Grimm / Complete *
　Queen bee, The, 317–319
—Grimm / Sixty *
　Queen bee, The, 206–208

—Gullible Coyote / Malotki
　coyote joins ants in dance, 47–54
—Hamilton / People *
　Anton's shapechange: Beautiful girl of the moon tower, 53–59
—Leonardo / Fables *
　ant's pact with grain of wheat, 58–59
—Lines / Magical *
　Princess Labam, suitor test: Raja's son helped by ants; tiger, 56–66
—MacDonald / Sourcebook *
　motif index, 561
—Spanish-Am / Van Etten *
　ant and (begging) grasshopper visit spider's home, 95–96
　ant, etc., tell suitor drum is made of flea hide, 65–72
—Trolls / Asbjornsen
　boy who became lion, falcon, ant, 64–70
—Yep / Rainbow *
　We are all one, 72–78
Ant and the dove, *see under* Aesop
ANTEATER
—Yolen / Baby Bear *
　Aldo the anteater teaches ants to waltz, [14–15]
ANTELOPE
—Fahs / Old *
　knowledge hoarded by tortoise, shared with all, 29–31
—Greaves / Hippo *
　how cheetah got his speed, 28–29
—Gullible Coyote / Malotki
　Coyote Woman kills woman; tries to get her children, 27–36
ANTICHRIST
—Baring-Gould / Curious
　and Pope Joan, 68–73 @
ANTICIPATION
—Paxton / Belling *

night singer: bat and caged bird
(Aesop), [10–11]
ANTIGONE
—Gods / Schwab, 747 (index)
ANTIHERO
—Coyote / Bierhorst *
coyote eats all his animals; peo-
ple discreetly leave, [8]
ANTIQUITIES
—Man Myth & Magic
analytics: myths and legends,
3194–97 (index)
ANTI-SEMITISM
—Jewish / Frankel, 648 (index)
ANU (god)
—Babylonia / Spence, 384 (index)
ANUBIS
—Egyptian / Ions, 142 (index)
ANZU (Sumerian legendary bird)
—Wolkstein / Love, 236 @
APE
—Animals / Rowland, 180 (index)
—Shannon / More *
firefly defeats 100 club-wielding
apes, 19–22
APHRODITE
—Cotterell / Encyclopedia, 251 (in-
dex)
—D'Aulaire / Greek * 190 (index)
—Gods / Schwab, 747 (index)
—Greek / Switzer, 203 (index)
—Grimal / Dictionary, 565 (index)
—Man Myth & Magic, 3111 (index)
—Mercatante / Encyclopedia, 744 (in-
dex)
—Room / Classical Dict
by-names (list), 319–322 @
APOLLO
—D'Aulaire / Greek * 190 (index)
—Gods / Schwab, 747 (index)
—Greek / Osborne
Cupid's arrows: Daphne and
Apollo, 23–26
—Greek / Switzer, 203 (index)

—Grimal / Dictionary, 565 (index)
—Lore of Love
doomed trysts: Apollo; Pyramus,
77
—Man Myth & Magic, 3112 (index)
—Mercatante / Encyclopedia, 745 (in-
dex)
—Roman / Usher, 131 (index)
—Room / Classical Dict
by-names (list), 323–326 @
APOPHIS
—Hamilton / In the Beginning *
The sun-god and the dragon,
110–115
APOSTLES
—Grimm / Complete *
Twelve Apostles (sleep 300 yrs,
awaiting Redeemer), 818–819
APPALACHIAN REGION
—Jameson / Appalachians
legends: treasure, mines, Civil
War loot, 1–207
APPARITION(-s)
see also GHOST(-s)
—Arabian / Lewis
court singer and beggar-singer
[apparition?], 91–93
—Jewish / Sadeh
King David; healing waters;
Rabbi Reconnati, 41–43
—Occult & Parapsych / Shepard, 52–
53, @ 1588 (index)
—Southern [legends] / Floyd
Virgin Mary in Lubbock (1988),
100–103
—Tree / Kerven *
corn-maiden: love and respect
the earth, [30–32]
mystery man of the peonies, [10–
13]
APPEARANCE(-s)
—Allison / I'll Tell *
value: stag's legs vs. antlers, 100
—Coyote / Bierhorst *

coyote mistakes statue for (brain-less) live person, [42]

—Igloo / Metayer

owl, ridiculed, kills wolf, 55–57

APPEARANCE, DECEIVING

see also Snow-White and Rose-Red

—Crossley / Animal (Grimm) *

wolf and seven young goats, 29–34

—Douglas / Magic *

Beauty and the Beast, 85–97

—Shah / Central Asia

wise man and apprentice, 45–48

APPEASEMENT

—Allison / I'll Tell *

farmer, son, and donkey: attempt to please everyone, 128–129

lion, fox, ass: dividing spoils "equally," 116

APPLE(-s)

—Campbell / West Highlands, IV.429 (index)

—Douglas / Magic *

golden apples of immortality, 177–179

—Greek / Osborne

Atalanta and Hippomenes: golden apples, 51–54

—Imaginary / Nigg

golden apples, the prince, and the firebird, 89–91

—Limburg / Weird , 83–87

—Nesbit / Fairy *

magic apples: age with each wish, 125–138

princesses transformed to golden apples, 141–158

—O'Brien / Tales *

magic apples: red produce horns; golden remove, 31–37

—Pellowski / Family *

paper-cutting story: the apple thieves, 85–91

Apple of contentment, The (Pyle)

—Lines / Magical * 15–23

APPLESEED, Johnny (John Chapman, 1774–1845)

—Dramatized / Kamerman

rescues runaway girl, 537–548

APPRECIATION

—Demi / Reflective *

know/treasure the more valuable, [24]

APSU

—Hamilton / In the Beginning *

Marduk, god of gods, 78–85

AQUARIUS

—Constellations / Gallant * 199 (index)

ARAB TALES

—Bushnaq / Arab

Pantheon fairy tale and folklore library, 1–386

—Clouston / Popular, II.503 (index)

—Dictionary / Leach, 1201 (index)

—Palestinian / Speak (Muhawi), 1–420

ARACHNE

—Greek / Osborne

weaving contest: Arachne and Minerva, 19–21

ARAP (jinn-like)

—Turkish (Art I) / Walker

simpleton receives three magic objects from "Arap," 195–198

Arap Sang and the cranes

—Corrin / Imagine * 47–53

ARCHAEOLOGY

—Floyd / Gr Am Myst

Mystery Hill, NH, 28–32

ARCHERY

—Childcraft 3 / Stories *

shooting match at Nottingham Town (Pyle), 279–295

—Russian Hero / Warner *

Dunai: archery contest ends in death, 37–41

—Turkish / Walker
  boast re archery prowess; the
  third shot, 43–44
ARES
—D'Aulaire / Greek * 32
ARGENTINE TALES
—Dictionary / Leach, 1201 (index)
—Dramatized / Kamerman
  Pedro and the burro, 458–470
ARGONAUTS (Greek mythology)
—Colum / Golden * 1–316
—Gods / Schwab, 86–142
ARIEL
—Jewish / Frankel
  pious man and the lion, 343–344
ARION
—Corrin / Imagine *
  Arion wins prize; is thrown over-
  board; saved by dolphin, 161–
  163
ARISTOCRACY
—Mesoamerican / Leon-P, 287 (in-
  dex)
ARIZONA
—Jameson / Buried
  legendary lost mines, gold, etc.,
  13–32
ARKANSAS
—American / Read Dgst, 158–166
—Jameson / Buried
  legendary lost mines, gold, etc.,
  33–93
ARMADILLO
—Vanishing / Mercer *
  origin of good/bad people, 16–19
—Wildlife / Gillespie, 238 (index)
ARMENIAN MYTH / TALES
—Lore of Love
  sculptor carves palace for prin-
  cess, 79–83
—Mercatante / Good/Evil, 61–66 @
—Old Wives / Carter
  Nourie Hadig, 192–199
Armless maiden

—Old Wives / Carter, 135–139
ARMS and ARMOR
—Bell / Classical Dict, 10–13 @
—Lacy / Arth Ency, 11–17
Arnold, Matthew (1822–1888)
—Barber / Anthology
  Tristram and Iseult, 185–189
ARROGANCE
—Crossley / Animal (Grimm) *
  fox and cat; arrogance and mod-
  esty, 8–10
—Leonardo / Fables *
  arrogant water falls as rain, 72
—Water Buffalo (Chinese)
  arrogant fox pretends to be king,
  36–38
ARROW (*sometimes magic*)
  see also BOW AND ARROW
—Bell / Classical Dict, 13–15 @
—Bierhorst / Naked *
  Mother of Ghosts; life-restored,
  37–43
—Bruchac / Iroquois *
  monstrous, two-headed snake, a
  traitor, 97–102
—Haboo / Hilbert
  stuck in sky to aid climber, 3–5
—Russian Hero / Warner *
  Ivan son of Mare kills his treach-
  erous brothers, 120–124
—Sioux / Standing Bear *
  bow broken, hunter repels enemy
  by throwing arrows, 14–19
ART AND MYTHOLOGY
—Creatures (illus) / Huber * 1–155
—Mesoamerican / Leon-P, 287 (in-
  dex)
—Preston / Dict Classical
  classical subjects in visual art,
  1–311 @
ARTEMIS
—D'Aulaire / Greek * 44
ARTHUR, King
—Barber / Anthology

death of Arthur, 24–32
Geoffrey of Monmouth, 12–28
Welsh tradition, 1–8
—Campbell / West Highlands, IV.429
(index)
—Celtic / MacCana, 141 (index)
—Celts / Hodges *
last battle, 157–169
Merlin: life and magic powers,
117–132
—Cotterell / Encyclopedia, 251 (index)
—Douglas / Magic *
Merlin: Arthur's birth, childhood,
the sword, 141–149
—Dramatized / Kamerman
scenes from his legend, 106–127
—King Arthur / Ashe, 189 (index)
background and photos, 1–191 @
—King Arthur / Senior, 318 (index)
—Knights / Gross *
last battle, 100–110
sword in the stone, 7–25
—Knights / Heller-Headon, 10–19
death of, 186–189
—Lacy / Arth Ency, 1–649
—Legends / Cavendish, 421 (index)
—Lewis / Proud
Lanval: knight boasts, nearly
loses his lady, 26–47
—Lycanthropy / Otten
Gorlagon, 234–255
—Lynn / Fantasy *
adaptations, 760–761 (index)
—Man Myth & Magic, 3112 (index)
—Reeves / Shadow
Launfal: secret love for Ro-
samund, 49–83

ARTHURIAN ROMANCES
—Barber / Anthology
Arnold, Matthew: Tristram and
Iseult, 185–189
Chretien de Troyes: Yvain, or the
Knight with the Lion, 53–71
Gottfried von Strassburg: Tristan,
72–92
Maginogion: Culhweh and
Olwen, 33–43
Marie de France: lay of Sir Laun-
fal, 44–52
Morris, William: Defence of Gue-
nevere, 190–194
Sir Gawain and the Green Knight,
112–134
Sir Thomas Malory: the Morte
Arthur Saunz Guerdon, 135–
150
Swinburne: Tristram of Lyo-
nesse, 195–203
Tennyson: Idylls of the King,
169–184
Victorian images, 165–203
White, T.H.: The once and future
king, 213–220
Wolfram von Eschenbach: Par-
zival, 93–111
—Corrin / Eight-Year *
Sir Gawaine and the Green
Knight, 161–172
—Crossley / British FT *
Welsh boy tries to take gold; King
Arthur's sleeping army, 38–44
—Fairies / Briggs
Matter of Britain, 281–282
Sir Launfal, 366–367
—King Arthur / Ashe, 1–191 @
—King Arthur / Senior, 1–321
Arthur becomes king, 32–39
birth of Arthur, 27–31
death of Arthur, 262–317
Excalibur, 40–41
expedition to Rome, 61–71
Grail, the, 156–213
Guenever, 42–45
Lancelot, 73–81
Lancelot and Elaine, 136–155
Lancelot and Guenever, 214–
261

Malory-Caxton, 9–24 @
Merlin's death, 46–49
Morgan le Fay, 50–59
Tristram, 82–135
—Knights / Gross * 1–109
beautiful witch: Morgan Le Fey,
41–58
kitchen knight: "Big Hands" is Sir
Gareth, 77–99
Lancelot and the Round Table,
26–40
Sir Gawain and the Lady Ragnell,
59–76
sword in the stone, 7–25
—Knights / Heller-Headon, 1–190
—Lacy / Arth Ency, 1–649
bibliographic essay: English and
American, 152–171
bibliographic essay: German,
215–232
heraldry, 278–283
illuminated manuscripts, 359–
374
modern scholarship, 479–494
vulgate cycle, 609–614
—Legends / Cavendish, 6 (index),
235–248
—Pendragon / Ashley
Amros, killed by his father, King
Arthur, 23
Artos, son of Marius (Norton),
344–371
chroniclers: survey, bibliographical essay; bibliog., 402–416 @
Dragon's boy, The / Jane Yolen,
32–48
guide to Arthurian characters, 3–
9 @
Jaufrey (knight) and fair Brunissende, 260–321
Jn Brunner: entry not found in
Domesday Book, 372–384
King's damosel: Lynette
(Chapman), 120–203

King's man: Merlin and Niniane,
78–88
Lady of Belec / P.A. Karr, 344–
353
Lady of the Fountain [Luned =
Lynette] (Mabinogion), 204–
226
Sir Percivale of Wales (R.L.
Green), 89–100
Son of the morning [Mordred],
322–343
survey, by Joy Chant, 10–31
ARTIST(-s)
—Chinese / Chin *
magic brush of artist Ma Liang,
143–153
—Corrin / Eight-Year *
painter (long dead) gives lessons
to servant, 51–61
Artos, son of Marius (Norton)
—Pendragon / Ashley, 344–371
ASCANIUS
—Roman / Usher, 131 (index)
ASCETIC
—Japanese / Tyler, 333 (index)
ASCLEPIUS
—D'Aulaire / Greek * 96
ASDILDA
—Muddleheads / Harris
desecrates Cormorant Hat, 94–
114
ASGARD (kingdom of the gods)
—Scandinavian / Davidson, 142 (in-
dex)
Ash tree
—Reeves / Shadow
twin girls parted at birth; reunited
at wedding of one, 113–128
Ashenputtel, see Cinderella
ASIA MINOR
—Dictionary / Leach, 1201 (index)
Asimov, Isaac (1920-)
—American / Read Dgst
true love, 401–402

ASMODIUS
—Jewish / Sadeh
marriage: merchant's son and
Ashmodai's daughter, 69–76
punishment: Ashmodai rules in
Solomon's place, 58–61
ASP
—Animals / Rowland, 180 (index)
Ass, see DONKEY
Ass in lion's skin
—Birds / Carter & Cartwright * 47
Ass [jealous of] the lap dog
—Aesop / Zwerger, 25
ASSIPATTLE
—Fairies / Briggs, 11
ASSURBANIPAL (king)
—Babylonia / Spence, 385 (index)
ASSYRIA
—Babylonia / Spence
myths and legends, 1–411
—Dictionary / Leach, 1201 (index)
—Mercatante / Good/Evil, 21–30 @
ASTROLOGY(-ers)
—Astrology / Gettings, 365 @
—Lore of Love
enchanter's snare, 121
—Man Myth & Magic, 3113 (index)
—Occult & Parapsych / Shepard,
1493 (index)
—Witch Encyc / Guiley, 409 (index)
ASTRONOMY
—Aesop / Reeves-Wilson *
Zorian the star-gazer, 101–102
—Constellations / Gallant * 199 (index)
—Grimm / Complete *
Four clever brothers, 580–584
—Grimm / Sixty *
Four clever brothers, 220–234
—Indian Myth / Burland, 143 (index)
ASURAS
—Indic / Ions, 142 (index)
ATALANTA
—Greek / Osborne

race: Hippomenes and the
golden apples, 51–54
ATHENA
—D'Aulaire / Greek * 190 (index)
—Gods / Schwab, 748 (index)
—Greek / Switzer, 203 (index)
—Mercatante / Encyclopedia, 746 (index)
—Room / Classical Dict
by-names (list), 327–329 @
ATHLETIC CONTESTS WON by DECEPTION
—Crossley / Animal (Grimm) *
hare and hedgehog race, 39–44
—Greaves / Hippo *
tortoise tricks hare in race, 114–118
tug-of-war: hare vs. hippo and
rhino, 118–120
—Lester / Leopard *
Tug-of-war: turtle cons elephant
and hippo, 17–20
ATLANTIS
—Legends / Cavendish, 262–267
—Pirate Ghosts / McSherry
vintage from Atlantis, 158–165
—Southern [legends] / Floyd, 24–30
—Speck / New World
early exploration, 13–20
ATONEMENT
—Ghosts / Starkey
Tregeagle's ghost, 58–65
—Jewish / Frankel
sin of pride, 516–517
—Jewish / Sadeh
impious tailor trades clothes with
pauper, 337
ATRI
—Corrin / Eight-Year *
Atri: ring bell if wrongly dealt with,
75–78
ATTITUDE(-s)
—Aesop / Reeves-Wilson *
Fox and [sour] grapes, 57–58

—Bomans / Wily *
  echo well: mis-shapen people
    not/aware of defects, 97–
    100
—Jewish / Frankel
  Good Purim, Good Purim! 528–
    530
—Spanish-Am / Van Etten *
  wise woman asks three sisters:
    why do you clear your field?
    52–53
—Strauss / Trail
  princess revolted by frog before it
    turns (poem), 24–26
ATUM
—Egyptian / Ions, 143 (index)
AU (Sumerian Sky God)
—Wolkstein / Love, 235 @
AUCASSIN and NICOLETTE
—Lore of Love
  French soldier and Saracen
    maid, 98–106
Auguring match, The
—Old Coot / Christian *
  talking contest, 41–56
Aulnoy, M-C d,' (1650?-1705)
  see the following title entries:
  Babiole
  Beauty with the golden hair
  Bee and the orange tree, The
  Belle-Belle, or The Chevalier for-
    tune
  Beneficent frog, The
  Blue bird
  Finette Cendron
  Golden branch, The
  Good little mouse
  Green serpent, The
  Island of happiness, The
  Little good mouse
  Princess Mayblossom
  Princess Rosette
  Ram, The
  Story of pretty Goldilocks

  White cat
  Yellow dwarf
AUSTRALIA(-n; -ns)
—Dictionary / Leach, 1201–1202 (in-
  dex)
—Legends / Cavendish, p.7 (index),
  379–389
—Man Myth & Magic, 3114 (index)
—Mercatante / Encyclopedia, 724 (in-
  dex)
AUSTRALIAN ABORIGINAL TALES
—Animal Legends / Kerven *
  kangaroo's first human encoun-
    ter: windstorm, [12–14]
  magic song: koalas created by
    boy's transformation, [6–7]
—Earth / Hadley *
  Baiame sends Yhi to bring earth
    to life, [9–10]
  drought ends when snake makes
    frog laugh, [23–24]
—Fahs / Old *
  unseen Spirit speaks through na-
    ture, 24–28
—Hamilton / In the Beginning *
  Karora: creation myth, 46–51
—Journeys / Norris *
  great chase: Mirragen the Cat-
    man vs. Gurangatch, [10–12]
—Pellowski / Story *
  fire used for cooking; origin; sand
    story, 70–74
—Tree / Kerven *
  creator Baiame gives seeds;
    flower life cycle, [22–25]
  forest spirit imprisons boys in
    tree, [6–7]
—Vanishing / Mercer *
  origin of fishing nets, 58–60
  origin of platypus, 54–57
  owl eyes; hurricane living apart,
    61–64
  turtles in Aussie creeks; origin,
    65–67

AUSTRIAN TALES
—Dramatized / Kamerman
  happy adults: children at wishing
  well, 15–22
—Restless / Cohen *
  fate of George Woodfall, 84–93
AUTHORITARIANISM
—Bomans / Wily *
  Princess Steppie and King's rigid
  "principles," 20–27
AUTHORITY
—Jewish / Frankel
  authority figures, 643 (index)
—Turkish (Art I) / Walker
  host's supreme authority (not to
  be contradicted), 41–44
AUTUMN
—Vanishing / Mercer *
  Ona people: parrot that brought
  autumn, 80–83
AVALON (Happy Isle)
—Baring-Gould / Curious
  Fortunate Isles: Paradise for
  souls of the dead, 134–
  138 @
—Celts / Hodges *
  Arthur's last battle, 157–169
—King Arthur / Ashe, 189 (index)
AVARICE
—Clouston / Popular
  Chaucer's Pardoner's tale,
  II.379–412
—Vietnam / Terada *
  elder brother inherits all but star-
  fruit tree, 3–6
AWL WAY (*rite*)
—Navajo Coyote / Haile, 23–24 @
AXE
—Aesop / Reeves-Wilson *
  trees: handle for woodcutter's
  axe, 112–113
—Paxton / Belling *
  honesty is the best policy
  (Aesop's "lost ax"), [24–27]

AYMAR, JACQUES (17th cent.)
—Baring-Gould / Curious, 36–42 @
AZTEC(-s)
—Cotterell / Encyclopedia, 251 (in-
  dex)
—Creatures (illus) / Huber * 135–
  138
—Hamilton / Dark *
  pretender: sacrificed to Tezcut-
  lipoca after year of high living,
  60–64
—Lore of Love
  Aztec couple: reunion in flames,
  52–57
—Man Myth & Magic, 3114 (index)
—Mercatante / Encyclopedia, 725 (in-
  dex)
—Mesoamerican / Leon-P, 287 (in-
  dex)
—Speck / New World, 518 (index)

BAAL
—Babylonia / Spence, 386 (index)
—Gray / Near East, 143 (index)
—Man Myth & Magic, 3114 (index)
BAAL SHEM TOV
—Jewish / Frankel, xv (index)
  thirteen tales, 473–503
—Jewish / Sadeh
  fifteen tales, 343–361
—Schwartz / Gates, 797 (index)
BABA YAGA TALES
—Childcraft 3 / Stories *
  Baba Yaga's geese abduct girl's
  brother, 114–118
—Clarkson / World * 179–181
—Corrin / Favourite * 93–101
  Baba Yaga, the bony-legged
  witch
—Hamilton / Dark *
  Baba Yaga, Vasilisa, and her
  doll, 14–22

—Manning / Cats *
    chain-tale: boy, hare, fox, wolf,
    bear vs. Baba Yaga, 58–64
—McGowen / Encyclopedia *
    illus., 10, 11
—Old Wives / Carter, 151–154
—Russian / Afanasev, 657 (index)
—Russian Hero / Warner *
    duo: one good, one bad, 85–86 @
    magic doll helps Vasilisa escape,
    86–92
    three princes/brides, one a frog-
    princess, 101–106
—Williams-Ellis / Tales *
    Marusia's kindness helps es-
    cape, 113–124
Babbitt, Ellen C.
—Childcraft 1 / Once *
    The foolish, timid rabbit, 166–168
BABE (Blue Ox)
—Hoke / Giants
    Paul Bunyan, 11–29
Babes in the wood
—Scriven / Full Color * 16–20
Babiole (d'Aulnoy)
—Zipes / Beauties * 438–458
BABOON
—Egyptian / Harris
    Hathor: Thoth transformed to,
    26–33
—Greaves / Hippo * 81–83 @
    fight: how zebra got stripes, 99–
    102
BABY(-ies)
    see also CHILD . . .
—Fahs / Old *
    Glooskap ignored by baby, 153–
    155
—Glooskap / Norman *
    tantrums more powerful than
    Glooskap, 29–37
—MacDonald / Sourcebook *
    motif index, 563
—Spanish-Am / Van Etten *

    evil, elder sisters dispose of
    youngest's infants [rescued],
    78–80
BABYLONIA (-ian myth)
—Babylonia / Spence
    myths and legends, 1–411
—Constellations / Gallant * 199 (in-
    dex)
—Dictionary / Leach, 1202 (index)
—Hamilton / In the Beginning *
    Marduk, god of gods, 78–85
—Man Myth & Magic, 3114 (index)
BACCHUS
—Dramatized / Kamerman
    anything touched, turns to gold,
    177–190
—Greek / Osborne
    golden touch: Bacchus grants
    King Midas' wish, 9–11
Bad luck, see LUCK, BAD.
BADGER
—Chorao / Child's *
    teakettle turns into badger, 21–27
—Curry / Beforetime *
    coyote: many tricks trying to get
    deer meat from badger; fails,
    78–88
    coyote tries badger's hunting
    method; fails because ticklish,
    74–77
—Hopi Coyote / Malotki
    coyote lusts for girl resuscitated
    by badger, 23–41
—Navajo Coyote / Haile
    tingling maiden: coyote as suitor-
    seducer, 15, 69–77
BAG (sack)
—Arabian / McCaughrean
    wonderful bag: claimants make
    impossible list of contents,
    130–132
—MacDonald / Sourcebook *
    motif index, 564
Baher, Constance Whitman

—Dramatized / Kamerman
Robin Hood outwits the sheriff,
61–78

BAKER(-s)

—Arabian / Lewis
merman trades jewels for fruit,
131–137

—Arabian / McCaughrean
merman trades jewels for fruit,
83–96

—Dramatized / Kamerman
Baker would charge man for
smelling bakery, 471–480

BALD

—Nesbit / Fairy *
Melisande [fairy curse], 59–78

—Turkish / Walker
lazy, bald Keloglan wins sultan's
daughter, 20–22

BALDER (god)

—Norse / Crossley, 265 (index)

BALI

—Dictionary / Leach, 1202 (index)

—Indic / Ions, 142 (index)

BALLADS

—Folk Ballads / McNeil, 1–219, 1–
223 p. (2 vols.)

Bandit, see ROBBER; THIEF

BANK(-s; -ers)

—Shannon / More *
banker denies having received
money Brahman entrusted to
him, 39–42

BANSHEE

—Fairies / Briggs, 14–16

—Ghosts / Time-Life, 11

—Hamilton / Dark *
scream; death coming, 1–4

BANTU . . .

—Earth / Hadley *
hideous Kanya, god of fire, tries
in vain to get a wife, [17–18]

—Vanishing / Mercer *
how South Africans came to be

hunters and gatherers, 74–
75

BAPTISM

—Man Myth & Magic, 3115 (index)

—Russian / Ivanits, 245 (index)

BARBER

—Arabian / Lewis
treachery: good barber and evil
dyer, 123–130

—Grimm / Complete *
brothers: barber, blacksmith,
fencing master (most skilled?),
561–562

BARGAIN, see AGREEMENT; DE-
CEPTIVE BARGAIN(-s);
FOOLISH BARGAIN(-s); PRO-
MISE(-es)

BARISAL GUNS

—Floyd / Gr Am Myst, 114–116

Barnard, Catherine

—Zipes / Beauties *
Riquet with the tuft, 95–100

Barrie, J.M. (1860–1937)

—Childcraft 1 / Once *
Come away! (from Peter Pan),
276–295

—Victorian / Hearn
Peter Pan in Kensington Gardens
[excerpt], 358–379

Barrows, Marjorie

—Witches / Iosa
Halloween song (poem) * 1

BASEBALL

—Switzer / Existential
ugly duckling (first woman in major league), 150–157

—Tall Tales / Downs: Bear
horse that played third base for
Brooklyn / W. Schramm, 285–
297
Bash Tshelik, man of steel

—Corrin / Eight-Year * 120–133

Bashtchelik (real steel)

—Dulac / Fairy * 91–113

BASILISK
—Animals / Rowland, 180 (index)
—Beasts / McHargue, 37–43 @; 116
    (index)
—Dragons / Baskin * [20–21]
—McGowen / Encyclopedia *
    illustration, 11
—South / Mythical
    sources; bibliographical essay,
    113–122, 381 (index)
BASKET
—Spring / Philip
    king "never heard of this before,"
    134–139
BASKET OGRESS
—Haboo / Hilbert, 17–22, 42–44,
    108–110, 150
BASQUES
—Dictionary / Leach, 1202 (index)
BASTARD
—Jewish / Sadeh
    Jewish pope; bastard converts to
    Catholicism, 195–197
Bastianelo
—Clarkson / World * 362–364
BAT(-s)
—Aesop / Holder
    bat, bramblebush, and cormo-
    rant, 8–9
—Aesop / Reeves-Wilson *
    origin of characteristics, 55–56
—Bird Symbol / Rowland, 201 (index)
—Curry / Beforetime *
    war between beasts and birds;
    fickle bat punished, 68–69
—Demi / Reflective *
    wit saves itself from weasels, [6]
—Erdoes / Sound *
    contest with birds; for deception,
    bat turned into mouse, 90
—Halloween ABC / Merriam * [7]
—Paxton / Belling *
    night singer: bat and caged bird
    (Aesop), [10–11]

Bata, see ANPU AND BATA.
BATHHOUSE
—Russian / Ivanits, 245 (index)
—Turkey / Walker, 300 (index)
BATTLE(-s)
—Bruchac / Iroquois *
    snakes make war of revenge, 93–
    95
—Chinese / Chin *
    secret of the moon cake [up-
    rising], 171–180
—Douglas / Magic *
    Thumbelina, 43–53
—Erdoes / Sound *
    girl saves brother; battle of the
    Rosebud, 10–15
—Ghosts / Time-Life, 75–81
—Imaginary / Nigg
    golden peacock befriends captor,
    97–99
—Lore of Love
    French soldier and Saracen
    maid, 98–106
    gods/demons; curse causes hus-
    band to forget wife, 26–31
—Manning / Cats *
    kind witch raises foundling to be
    knight; bewitched Cat-Johann
    his aide, 111–117
Battle of the birds
—Old Wives / Carter, 76–85
BAUM, L. Frank (1856–1919)
—Lynn / Fantasy *
    bibliography (about the author),
    422–425
BAY-KOK
—McGowen / Encyclopedia * 12
Be yourself, see CONTENTMENT.
Bealmear, J.H.
—Dramatized / Kamerman
    Covetous councilman, 504–
    513
Beam, The
—Grimm / Complete * 645

BEAN(-s)
—Grimm / Complete *
  personification: straw, coal, and
    bean, 102–103
—Grimm / Sixty *
  personification (as above), 29–30
—Jewish / Sadeh
  old bachelor lost a bean, 22–25
BEANSTALK
see Jack and the Beanstalk.
BEAR(-s)
see also Goldilocks . . .
—Aesop / Reeves-Wilson *
  The two travellers, 103–104
—Allison / I'll Tell *
  bear and travelers: misfortune as
    test of friendship, 117
—American / Read Dgst, 433 (index)
—Animal Legends / Kerven *
  magic song: koalas created by
    boy's transformation, [6–7]
  mother bear adopts abandoned
    boy, [8–9]
—Animals / Rowland, 180 (index)
—Bierhorst / Naked *
  Porcupine's grandson [aban-
    doned boy], 93–100
—Bruchac / Iroquois *
  boy who lived with the bears, 24–
    30
  chipmunk ridicules bear, and
    pays, 37–39
  fox trickster: how bear lost his tail,
    32–34
  hunting of the Great Bear (Big
    Dipper), 189–195
  turtle's race with bear, 51–53
—Childcraft 1 / Once *
  why stumpy tail; fox tricks; frozen
    in ice, 96–97
—Corrin / Favourite *
  taboo: looking at while asleep:
    East of the sun . . . , 1–15
—Corrin / Imagine *

goldsmith steals friend's gold;
  friend "turns" goldsmith's chil-
    dren into bears, 23–46
—Coyote / Ramsey
  swallowing match: coyote/bear,
    118
—Crossley / Animal (Grimm) *
  hedge-king (bird) defeats bear,
    49–53
—Curry / Beforetime *
  grizzley: Old-Man-Above created
    animals from sticks and leaves,
    1–4
—Davy Crockett / Dewey * 8–13, 16–
  19
—Fahs / Old *
  animals make sickness for hu-
    man enemy, 71–80
  grizzly vs. coyote on day/season
    lengths, 96–99
—Grimm / Complete *
  cunning tailor: riddle, bear, prin-
    cess, 525–528
—Haboo / Hilbert
  grizzly and rabbit play on ice-
    covered lake, 155–157
  Yellowhammer and his wives,
    130–136
—Hall / Treasury *
  Little Brown Bear afraid of the
    dark, 22–25
—Hamilton / People *
  He lion, Bruh bear, Bruh rabbit,
    5–12
—Hopi Coyote / Malotki, 287 @
—Igloo / Metayer
  bear kills mother, raises her child,
    118–121
  bear-men: the orphan and the
    bears, 24–31
  Coppermine River legend:
    feigned death, 78–81
  dog kills would-be girl takers,
    122–127

Kajortoq: bears and wolf become fox's food, 19–23

Kautaluk: Great Spirit grants marvelous strength, 35–39

—Jonsen / Trolls *
The trolls and the pussy cat [a white bear, 15–23]

—Lang / Wilkins
Snow White and Rose Red (befriend bear), 99–105

—Lester / Brer Rabbit *
end of Brer Bear; the honey tree, 74–75
steals Brer Fox's peanuts; puts blame on Brer Bear, 71–74
why Brer Rabbit has no tail, 99–101

—Lycanthropy / Otten, 326 (index)

—MacDonald / Sourcebook *
motif index, 567–568

—Man Myth & Magic, 3115 (index)

—Manning / Cats *
chain-tale: boy, hare, fox, wolf, bear vs. Baba Yaga, 58–64
old man: caught cranes carry cart into sky; bear pulls cart, 91–96
rhyming water-nick fries fish; bear and monkeys feast, 97–100

—Navajo Coyote / Haile
Changing Bear Maiden (widow) transformed to monster bear, 16, 82–84
Youngest Brother; Bear Maiden, 16, 22–24 @, 85–88

—Paxton / Aesop *
bear whispers: choose friend who stands by in danger, [31–32]

—Rockwell / Puss *
cat (white bear) on the dovrefell, 71–79

—Russian / Afanasev, 657 (index)

—Russian Hero / Warner *
bear bites off head of woman who cut off its leg, 117–120

captive Mashen'ka tricks bear, 116–117
wondrous animals, 110–111 @

—Shah / Central Asia
charcoal burner and enchanted bear (prince), 92–102

—Sioux / Standing Bear *
grandmother and the bear, 58–60

—Tall Tales / Downs: Bear
bear hunt in reverse / W. Hendricks, 37–39

—Trolls / Asbjornsen
trolls invade each Christmas Eve; mistake white bear for cat, 51–52

—Turkish / Walker
bear tricks (goat) kids; goat gets even, 4–7

—Vanishing / Mercer *
bears' tower: rock "grows," to protect girls, 118–120

—Wildlife / Gillespie, 238 (index)

—Williams-Ellis / Tales *
trolls driven away by bear ("great white cat"), 17–23

BEARD
—Grimm / Legends (Ward), II:389 (index)
—Jewish / Sadeh
rabbi and the beardless rich man, 214
—Turkey / Walker, 300 (index)

Bearskin
—Grimm / Complete * 467–472

Beast, see ANIMAL

BEAST-MEN
—Journey Sun (Chinese)
small yellow dragon defeats big black dragon, 81–89
—South / Mythical
sources; bibliographical essay, 123–239, 371 (index)

BEAUTY
—Aesop / Holder *

stag and hounds: utility (legs) vs.
ornament (antlers), 24–25
—Aesop / Reeves-Wilson *
stag: proud of antlers; ashamed
of legs, 29
—Bell / Classical Dict, 20–24 @
—Carter / Sleeping *
Ricky and twin princesses:
beauty but stupid; ugly but
clever, 93–102
—Demi / Reflective *
eyes (two pair) of beholders, [4]
ugly, jealous cat imitates, [18]
—Geras / Grandmother *
talking plants' contest: olive tree
the winner, 57–65
—Wilde / Lynch *
young king dreams: the poor suf-
fer to provide grandeur, 73–94
—Witch Hndbk / Bird * 56–61
—Women / Dyer
women, 15–33 @
—Zipes / Beauties *
Ricky and twin princesses (as
above), 52–57, 95–100
Beauty and Pock Face
—Old Wives / Carter, 200–204
Beauty and the Beast
[*versions*: Frog prince (Grimm);
Rikki of the Tuft (Perrault); The
well at the end of the road]
—Carter / Sleeping * 45–62
—Corrin / Favourite * 226–244
—Corrin / Six-Year * 151–160
—Crane / Beauty * [7–19]
—Douglas / Magic * 85–97
—Hepburn / World * 110–128
—Lang / Wilkins, 44–63
—Strauss / Trail
beast's thoughts, waiting for be-
loved to return (poem), 30–32
—Zipes / Beauties * 153–245
**Beauty and the Beast (LePrince de
Beaumont)**

—Zipes / Beauties * 233–245
BEAUTY CHANT (Navajo)
—Indian Myth / Burland, 102–104
**Beauty with the golden hair
(d'Aulnoy)**
—Zipes / Beauties * 309–320
BEAVER(-s)
—Animals / Rowland, 180 (index)
—Bruchac / Iroquois *
turtle's race with beaver, 47–49
—Childcraft 3 / Stories *
good and evil: Glooscap vs. Mal-
sum, 143–151
—Earthmaker / Mayo *
brings end of the world, 81 @
—Erdoes / Sound *
remaking of the (third) world,
126–129
—Gullible Coyote / Malotki
Coyote Woman kills Antelope
Woman; tries to get her chil-
dren, 27–36
—Haboo / Hilbert
wolf brothers kill elk and beaver,
10–13
—Navajo Coyote / Haile
beaver and coyote (bet their
"clothes" [skins]), 12, 33–34
—Tree / Kerven *
pines have fire; beaver steals a
coal, [8–9]
—Vanishing / Mercer *
befriends boy left to die by wicked
brother (Blackfeet), 106–111
Bechstein, Ludwig
—Hoke / Giants
Strong Gottlieb, 103–111
BEE(-s)
—Bomans / Wily *
thrush-girl: learns to understand
birds, bees, mole, 135–137
—Cambodian / Carrison
frog boasts to bee: to Himalayas
in one day, 100–101

—Dramatized / Kamerman
bee rewards King Solomon's
kindness, 250–257

—Greaves / Hippo *
why lion roars, 15–18

—Journey Sun (Chinese)
Yangang saves village incinerated by shooting star, 47–60

—MacDonald / Sourcebook *
motif index, 568

—Tibet / Timpanelli *
test of "seer": reputation made by
luck/coincidence, 29–41

**Bee and the orange tree, The
(d'Aulnoy)**

—Zipes / Beauties * 417–437

BEE HIVE

—Lester / Brer Rabbit *
riddle: bee hive in gum tree, 91–95

BEE: The Queen Bee

—Grimm / Complete * 317–319

—Grimm / Sixty * 206–208

**Beebyeebyee marries water god
(fish-man)**

—Earth / Hadley * [25–26]

BEER

—Clarkson / World *
Cluricaune shows hiding place of
treasure, 115–117

—Egyptian / Harris
Ra's anger, 35

BEETLE

—Egyptian / Mercatante
khepera; scarab, 83–84, 137

BEFORETIME

—Curry / Beforetime *
before man appeared, animals
had human characteristics,
121

BEGGAR

—Arabian / Lewis
court singer and beggar-singer
[apparition?], 91–93

—Arabian / McCaughrean

little beggar "killed" over and
over, 97–103

—Arabian / Riordan
little beggar . . . [as above], 122–
124

—Dramatized / Kamerman
The price of eggs, 149–154

—Grimm / Complete *
King Thrushbeard; haughty princess, 244–248

—Grimm / Sixty *
King Thrushbeard; haughty princess, 312–316

—Jewish / Sadeh
charity saves peddler's wife from
foreordained death, 335–336
tailor and Haman: "years" really
only fifteen minutes, 201–204

—O'Brien / Tales *
adventures of Marteen: grateful
beggar gives magic gold-
producing ring, 31–37

—Spanish-Am / Van Etten *
beggar-woman turned away:
curse for not sharing, 50–51

—Tibet / Timpanelli *
hunter's son can't kill animals;
father buries him, 1–13

—Yep / Rainbow *
beggar woman: child of calamity,
46–52

BEHAVIOR
see also COMPULSORY BE-
HAVIOR

—Grimm / Complete *
surgeons; body parts removed;
cat eats; other parts substituted; effects, 535–538

BEHEAD(-ed)(-ing)

—Bell / Classical Dict, 62 @

—Bierhorst / Monkey *
Blue Sun: beheads younger
brother every day; various origins, 107–112

—Bomans / Wily *
  Happy Hughie: head continues to laugh and tell jokes, 62–70
—Corrin / Eight-Year *
  Sir Gawaine and the Green Knight, 161–172
—Douglas / Magic *
  white cat (enchanted princess), 69–83
—Jewish / Sadeh
  princess' head, "to make it an even hundred," 106–111
—Lore of Love
  head of murdered lover buried in pot of basil, 64–65
BEHEMOTH
—Beasts / McHargue, 52–53 @
BEL (god)
—Babylonia / Spence, 387 (index)
BELGIAN TALE
—Dulac / Fairy *
  boy-suitor gathers six helpers: the seven conquerors, 22–28
BELIEF(-s)
—Am Child / Bronner
  customs; mores, 161–174
—Jewish / Sadeh
  whom God loves, 149–152
—Wildlife / Gillespie
  folk belief, 241 (index)
Belinda and Bellamant
—Corrin / Imagine * 54–69
BELL, Mary
—American / Read Dgst
  an overseeing haunt, 134–135
BELL(-s)
—Corrin / Eight-Year *
  Atri: ring bell if wrongly dealt with, 75–78
—Grimm / Legends (Ward), II:389 (index)
—Nesbit / Fairy *
  Belinda & Bellamant; Carillon-Land, 101–122

—Witch Encyc / Guiley, 410 (index)
Belle-Belle, or The Chevalier fortune (d'Aulnoy)
—Zipes / Beauties * 564–598
BELLEROPHON
—D'Aulaire / Greek * 128
Belling the cat, see Aesop: Belling . . .
BELT
—Nielsen / Old Tales *
  blue belt (magic strength), [37–62]
Benedictus le Puncteur
—Jewish / Frankel
  thirteen "fox" fables, 458–469
Beneficent frog, The (d'Aulnoy)
—Zipes / Beauties * 545–563
BENGALI TALES
—Clouston / Popular, II.504 (index)
Bennett, Rowena
—Witches / Iosa * 16–17
  Witch of Willowby Wood (poem)
Benny's luck
—Aleichem / Holiday * 17–44
BEOWULF
—Lines / Magical *
  Beowulf and Grendel [battle], tears off arm, 105–116
BERMUDA TRIANGLE
—Floyd / Gr Am Myst, 169–173
BERYL
—Precious Stones / Kunz, 394 (index)
BERYN
—Clouston / Popular
  Beryn in Falsetown, II.99–114, 478–480
Best books, see BIBLIOGRAPHY; REFERENCE BOOKS.
BESTIARY
—Animals / Rowland, 181 (index)
—Bird Symbol / Rowland, 201 (index)
—Wolves / Lopez, 299 (index)
Bet, see WAGER.
BETROTHAL
—Fahs / Old *

girl chooses death over unfaithfulness, 44–51
—Grimm / Complete *
Sweetheart Roland; girl flees
murderous stepmother, 268–
271
true bride; prince forgets betrothal, 752–760
twelve huntsmen; prince forgets
his betrothed, 334–336
—Grimm / Sixty *
Sweetheart Roland (as above),
156–160
twelve huntsmen (as above),
271–273
—Jewish / Frankel
man who breaks vow punished
by childlessness, 523–527
—Jewish / Sadeh
dead fiancee [apparition], 14–17
sky, rat, and the well, 9–11
—Lang / Wilkins
charm (singing) protects from
yara (fairies), 474–484
—Tree / Kerven *
mystery man of the peonies, [10–
13]
Bewitching, see DISENCHANT-
MENT; SPELL.
BIBLE
—Animals / Rowland, 181 (index)
—Bomans / Wily *
in world-ending flood, clergy argue
about biblical text, 107–108
—Christian / Every, 142 (index)
—Lynn / Fantasy * 746 (index)
—Man Myth & Magic, 3116 (index)
—Schwartz / Gates, 798 (index)
—Unnatural / Cohen, 145 (index)
BIBLE. New Testament
—Christian / Every, 144 (index)
BIBLE. Old Testament
—Babylonia / Spence
Daniel, 390 (index)

—Gray / Near East
myth and history in, 106–116
—Wolkstein / Love
The Song of Songs, 91–109,
265 @
BIBLE. O.T. Genesis
—Hamilton / In the Beginning *
Elohim the Creator, 148–153
Yahweh the Creator, 120–125
BIBLE. O.T. Psalms
—Gray / Near East
myth and poetic imagery, 117–
121
—Jewish / Frankel
foolish imaginings: "what if" dis-
asters as real, 571–573
—Jewish / Sadeh
David and bugle corp at Reb
Yudel's funeral, 43–44
David judge: rich man vs. poor
water drawer, 45–47
BIBLIOGRAPHY (-ies) (*best books*)
—Gillespie / Best Books
folk literature; annotated list,
275–309
—Hearne / [Bibliog.]
Choosing books for children, 1–
228 *
For reading out loud! 1–266
—Lipson / Best Books
New York Times guide, 1–
421 *
—Lynn / Fantasy *
best fantasy literature, 1–771
—Mercatante / Good/Evil
annotated, 183–231 @
—Norwegian / Hodne 1–400
BICYCLE
—Nesbit / Fairy *
Billy and cousin: kite/bicycle, 45–
56
Big Dipper, see STAR(-s).
BIG HENRY
—Hamilton / Dark *

witch takes off skin; as cat, rides
Big Henry, 143–148

Big Klaus . . . *see* Little Klaus . . .
· (Andersen)

BIG SLAT and HIS BROTHERS
—O'Brien / Tales *
Amada defeats giants (who daily
return to life), and series of
monsters, 21–30

BIGAMY
—Arabian / McCaughrean
woman marries (a) robber (b)
pickpocket, 218–224
—Lewis / Proud
Bisclavret: wife keeps husband in
wolf-form, 29–35

BIGFOOT
—Floyd / Gr Am Myst
Northwest phantom and Grover
Krantz, 88–93
—McGowen / Encyclopedia *
illus., 12–13
—Monsters / Cohen, 13–20

Bignon, Jean-Paul
—Zipes / Beauties *
Princess Zeineb and King Leop-
ard, 145–150

BILINGUAL
—Mex-Am / West
anecdotes, 92

Billy goat, *see* GOAT(s).

BILOCATION
—Floyd / Gr Am Myst
prison inmate Ed Morrell, 57–60

BIRD(-s)
—Arabian / Lewis
Princess' dream: all men are
faithless, 52–59
reveals identity of abandoned
children, 166–173
—Arabian / McCaughrean
Voyage of Sinbad [gigantic bird],
10–15
—Arabian / Riordan

reveals identity of abandoned
children, 78–87
—Bierhorst / Naked *
Boy who learned the songs of the
birds, 60–66
—Birds / Carter & Cartwright *
juvenile poetry, 1–64
—Bomans / Wily *
curse: princess' hair; king's cruelty to (transformed) "bird
witch," 165–173
thrush-girl: learns to understand
birds, bees, mole, 135–137
—Campbell / West Highlands
Battle of the birds, I.25–63
—Clouston / Popular
monstrous, I.155–167
secrets learned from birds, I.242–
248
—Corrin / Imagine *
popplesnitch: huntsman's pact
with demon to produce un-
known bird, 70–79
—Creatures (illus) / Huber * 155 (index)
—Curry / Beforetime *
Old-Man-Above (creator) lives in
ice "teepee": Mt. Shasta, 1–4
war between beasts and birds;
fickle bat, 68–69
—Demi / Reflective *
wild bird killed by kindness, [16]
—Erdoes / Sound *
birds have contest: eagle vs. bat,
90
—Folk-rhymes / Northall
England, 267–277
—Frog Rider (Chinese)
Shigar saves birds from python;
shoots down six suns, 60–70
—Glooskap / Norman *
panther-witch and her scissorbill
birds, 39–49
—Grimm / Complete *

juniper tree: murder exposed by
singing bird, 220–229
mouse, bird, sausage [trading
duties ends in disaster], 131–
133
three languages [dog, bird, frog],
169–171
willow-wren: contest to select
king of birds, 705–708
—Grimm / Sixty *
mouse, bird, sausage . . . , 108–
110
three languages . . . , 223–226
—Gullible Coyote / Malotki
coyote swallows birds alive, goes
crazy, predicts flood, 37–45
—Hamilton / People *
wolf insults birds; borrowed feathers taken back, 43–48
—Hopi Coyote / Malotki
Bird Girls, grinding corn, give
feathers to Coyote Girl, 91–97
coyote and bird play: pluck out/
retrieve eyes, 63–67
duped by little bird, coyote kills
his grandmother, 83–89
—Jewish / Frankel, 645, 648 (index)
bird gives hunter three pieces of
wisdom, 378–379
—Lang / Wilkins
Sylvain and Jocosa (befriended
by fairy), 178–185
—Leonardo / Fables *
falcon dives into water after duck;
regret, 83
snake and the birds, 113
—Lester / Brer Rabbit *
Brer Fox would eat Brer Rabbit's
children; bird gives advice on
tasks, 54–56
—Lester / Leopard *
magic bird makes milk for famine-
stricken people, 5–11
—Lurker / Dict Gods, 419–420 (index)

—MacDonald / Sourcebook *
motif index, 570–579
—Man Myth & Magic, 3116 (index)
analytics, 3185–87 (index)
—Manning / Cats *
crocodile would eat girl; hawk,
crow and stork do not help;
Roller Bird saves her, 51–57
old couple: repeated tries to cut
down tree; bird, instead, supplies needs, 101–106
—Monsters / Cohen, 87–96 @
—Muddleheads / Harris
wives: Robin Woman and Sawbill
Duck Woman, 44–59
—Paxton / Belling *
night singer: bat and caged bird
(Aesop), [10–11]
—Pellowski / Story *
finger-play story, 92–93
picture-drawing story, 52–55
—Scary / Young *
boy reincarnated as bird; sings
tale of murder; revenge, 78–83
—Schwartz / Gates, 798 (index)
—Trolls / Asbjornsen
stepsisters: one kind, one cruel;
escape service of witch, 42–
50
BIRD: ALBATROSS
—Maori / Kanawa *
how Toroa came to roam oceans
(contest with parrot), 113–114
BIRD: BLACKBIRD
—Bird Symbol / Rowland, 201 (index)
—Carle / Treasury *
vain blackbird wears peacock
feathers; ridiculed (Aesop),
64–65
—Leonardo / Fables *
bramble: cage for trapped bird,
61
—Scriven / Full Color *
Babes in the wood, 16–20

—Yolen / Shape Shift
shapeshifting into, 77
BIRD: BLUEBIRD
—Curry / Beforetime *
pine-nut thieves: birds put to
sleep by coyote's chant, 90–99
—Dulac / Fairy *
blue bird (prince transformed),
77–90
BIRD: BLUE JAY
—Curry / Beforetime *
mink and bluejay retrieve Little
Weasel, stolen by lizard, 60–
67
—Tall Tales / Downs: Bear
Jim Baker's bluejay yarn / M.
Twain, 181–185
BIRD: BUZZARD
—Bierhorst / Monkey *
lazy farmer trades places with
buzzard; dies foolishly, 37–43
—Bird Symbol / Rowland, 202 (index)
—Bruchac / Iroquois *
how buzzard got his feathers,
61–63
—Caduto / Keepers *
cause of buzzard's red skin:
stealing the sun, 49–50
—Clarkson / World *
why buzzard is bald, 332–333
—Lester / Brer Rabbit *
tricks Brer Buzzard and Brer Fox,
21–23
tries to trick Brer Buzzard out of
his share of garden, 69–71
—Tall Tales / Downs: Bear
how the burro tricked the buzzard / G. Barbera, 103-105
BIRD: CHACHATATUTU
—Water Buffalo (Chinese)
trifles may cause disasters, 13–
17
BIRD: CHICKADEE
—Navajo Coyote / Haile

dupe coyote (pluck out eyes) 12,
35
BIRD: CORMORANT
—Aesop / Holder *
bat, bramblebush, and cormorant, 8–9
BIRD: CRANE
see also Fox and the crane
[Aesop]
—Allison / I'll Tell *
crane's long beak; bone in wolf's
throat (fable), 101
—Bird Symbol / Rowland, 203 (index)
—Corrin / Imagine *
Arap Sang: provide shade, given
crowns, hunted for them, 47–53
—Igloo / Metayer
swan vs. crane: dancing, neck-
wrestling contests, 43–45
—Leonardo / Fables *
cranes guard king's palace, 44
—Manning / Cats *
old man: caught cranes carry cart
into sky; bear pulls cart, 91–96
—Spring / Philip
brothers: one honest, one
greedy, 94–97
BIRD: CROW
see also Aesop: Fox and the crow
—Aesop / Reeves-Wilson *
thirsty crow and pitcher, 99–100
—Allison / I'll Tell *
crow finds way to get to water in
pitcher, 109
falling for fox flattery, crow loses
cheese, 127
—Arabian / McCaughrean
old fox wants crow as hunting
partner, 198–202
—Campbell / West Highlands
tale of the hoodie, I.64–71
—Erdoes / Sound *
how crows came to be black, 57–
59

106

—Greaves / Hippo *
  elephant vs. Rain Spirit: who is
  greater? 53–58
—Hopi Coyote / Malotki, 295 @
  coyotes make chain to try to
  reach crow's nest, 151–159
  foolish imitation: crow standing
  on one leg, 69–75
—Igloo / Metayer
  Kajortoq (fox) outwitted by crow,
  46–48
—Jaffrey / Seasons
  crow drops queen's necklace on
  washerwoman's doorstep, 81–
  84
—Jewish / Sadeh
  king and forty crows; dream, 31–
  34
—Leonardo / Fables *
  sadness, 107
—Old Coot / Christian *
  Old Coot to rustler: crow envies
  hawk, 17–26
—Paxton / Belling *
  crow and the pitcher (Aesop),
  [22–23]
—Water Buffalo (Chinese)
  crow-messenger disobeys God
  of Heaven, 23–29
BIRD: CUCKOO
—Bird Symbol / Rowland, 203 (index)
BIRD: DOVE
  see also Aesop: Ant . . .
—Allison / I'll Tell *
  dove saves ant; ant warns dove
  of trap, 106
—Bierhorst / Monkey *
  Christ chased; birds help/hinder
  his flight, 133–135
—Bird Symbol / Rowland, 203 (index)
—Crane / McLean *
  Princess Belle-Etoile; evil Queen,
  16–27
—Geras / Grandmother *

judge of talking plants' contest:
  which is most beautiful? 57–65
—Grimm / Complete *
  girl lost in wood; witch, ring, and
  dove/prince, 558–560
—Hamilton / People *
  Anton's shapechange: beautiful
  girl of the moon tower, 53–59
—Man Myth & Magic, 3127 (index)
—Williams-Ellis / Tales *
  Anansi (death for saying "five"),
  143–150
BIRD: EAGLE
—Animals / Rowland, 183 (index)
—Bell / Classical Dict, 74–75 @
—Bird Symbol / Rowland, 204 (index)
—Caduto / Keepers *
  Kokopilau, the hump-backed
  flute player, 151
—Cambodian / Carrison
  Siva believes eagle's dreams; owl
  asks equal treatment, 67–72
—Coyote / Ramsey
  land of the dead: coyote and ea-
  gle, 81–84
—Curry / Beforetime *
  animals build mountains, to be rid
  of coyote, 22–25
—Erdoes / Sound *
  how Sioux Nation came into be-
  ing, 72–73
  treachery: two warriors love same
  girl, 25–30
—Fahs / Old *
  Niyak and Umak; condition bro-
  ken, 71–80
—Hamilton / People *
  Anton's shapechange: beautiful
  girl of the moon tower, 53–59
  Tappin: how turtle got marks on
  back, 20–25
—Hopi / Talashoma-Malotki
  Hopi boy and his two pet eagles,
  150–199

—Jewish / Frankel
princess to God: restore my lover
or take my life, 360–365
ruby/serpent: Solomon's daughter shut in tower; power of love,
254–257
—Jewish / Sadeh
eagle takes rabbi's son to Christian palace, 273–275
two shopkeepers, eagle, mountain of gold, 271–273
—Leonardo / Fables *
testament of the eagle: rejuvenation, 118
trapped eagle, and the owl, 96–
97
—Man Myth & Magic, 3128 (index)
—Manning / Cats *
man marries bird-wife; his mother
drives her out, 75–82
—Scandinavian / Davidson, 142 (index)
—Sioux / Standing Bear *
hunter on ledge, saved by young
eagles, 20–25
—Vietnam / Terada *
elder brother inherits all but starfruit tree, 3–6
—Wildlife / Gillespie, 241 (index)
BIRD: FALCON
—Celts / Hodges *
Lad of Luck and monster of the
loch, 89–103
—Lines / Magical *
Ian Direach vs. giant with five
heads, 45–55
—Lurker / Dict Gods, 426 (index)
—Trolls / Asbjornsen
boy who became lion, falcon, ant,
64–70
BIRD FEATHERS
—Bruchac / Iroquois *
wanting best (creation) ends with
worst, 61–63

BIRD: FLICKER
—Bierhorst / Naked *
Animal-Foot hitter kills sorcerer,
24–30
BIRD of FORTUNE
—Turkish / Walker
son "loves father like salt," 108–
113
BIRD: FULMER
—Caduto / Keepers *
Sedna: woman under the sea,
95–97
BIRD, GOLDEN
—Grimm / Complete *
task: catch Golden Bird, the ap-
ple thief, 272–279
—Grimm / Sixty *
task (as above), 1–9
BIRD: GULL
—Hamilton / Dark *
Manabozo: manitou hare swal-
lowed by king of fishes, 27–31
BIRD: HAWK
—Beat / Bryan *
call cat: frog threatens hen; hawk
gets frog, 3–13
—Bierhorst / Monkey *
toad hides/rides in hawk's bag;
tries to float; crashes, 136–
137
—Bird Symbol / Rowland, 205 (index)
—Erdoes / Sound *
gets even for being ridiculed by
Iktome, 60–61
—Lewis / Proud
Yonec: knight/lover killed by jeal-
ous husband's trap, 53–60
—Old Coot / Christian *
Old Coot and rustler: crow envies
hawk, 17–26
—Reeves / Shadow
bride locked in tower; shape-
change knight as lover, 1–48
—Sioux / Standing Bear *

Hawk Dreamer invokes hawk,
leaps to safety, 28–31
BIRD, HELPFUL
—Arabian / Lewis
abandoned children (grown) re-
stored, 166–173
—Arabian / Riordan
abandoned children (as above),
78–87
—Fahs / Old *
Niyak, Umak, and the eagle, 71–
80
—Grimm / Complete *
girl lost in wood; witch, ring, and
dove/prince, 558–560
—Hoke / Giants
helpful birds, 71–78
—Maori / Kanawa *
Maui: how robin got cap of white
feathers, 117
—Scary / Young *
tiger (imposter) eats woman;
robin gets aid for sister, 73–77
—Scriven / Full Color *
Snow Queen [seduces boy; girl
rescues], 35–36
BIRD: HERON
—Russian Hero / Warner *
Ivan son of Mare; herons change
into women, 120–124
Bird, Imaginary
see BIRD(-s), MYTHICAL [after
BIRD: WREN]
BIRD: KERERU
—Fahs / Old *
Maui in bird-shape, goes to Un-
derworld, 37–43
BIRD: KINGFISHER
—Bird Symbol / Rowland, 207 (index)
—Hamilton / Dark *
Manabozo: manitou hare swal-
lowed by king of fishes, 27–31
BIRD: KITE
—Bird Symbol / Rowland, 207 (index)

—Paxton / Belling *
bird who lost his song (Aesop),
[28–31]
BIRD: LARK
—Bird Symbol / Rowland, 207 (index)
BIRD: LOON
—Erdoes / Sound *
remaking of the (third) world,
126–129
—Igloo / Metayer
the ball players [losers die], 32–
34
mother blinds her hunter-son,
92–98
—Vanishing / Mercer *
Eskimo blind boy; origin of loon's
white chest, 36–39
BIRD: MAGPIE
—Bird Symbol / Rowland, 207 (index)
—Crossley / British FT *
magpies set tree afire; fall as
cooked crabs, 247
—Leonardo / Fables *
willow, magpie and pumpkin, 92–
95
—Turkish / Walker
magpie spills milk; loses/regains
tail, 11–13
BIRD-MAIDENS
—Clouston / Popular
transformations, I.182–191
BIRD-MEN
—Arabian / Lewis
Sinbad's first and last voyage,
94–105
—Arabian / McCaughrean (as
above), 16–21
—Arabian / Riordan (as above), 38–
55
—Journeys / Norris *
great chase: Mirragen the Cat-
man vs. Gurangatch, [10–12]
BIRD MIGRATION
—Caduto / Keepers *

how Turtle flew south for the winter, 157–158

BIRD: MUDHEN

—Erdoes / Sound *
why mudhens stay away from ducks, 91–92

BIRD: MUDLARK

—Spanish-Am / Van Etten *
father kills meadowlark, dies; need "spirit of song" to live, 54–56

BIRD: MYNAH

—Animal Legends / Kerven *
commands judge in voice of emperor, [20–21]

Bird(-s), Mythical.
see below, after BIRD: WREN

BIRD: NIGHTINGALE

—Bird Symbol / Rowland, 208 (index)
—Lewis / Proud
Laustic killed by cruel husband, 61–64
—Reeves / Shadow
cruel husband; young wife loves bachelor neighbor, 87–95
—Turkish (Art I) / Walker
youngest son aided in quest by nine-headed female giant, 230–239
—Wilde / Lynch *
nightingale gives life to produce red rose for student-in-love, 14–23

Bird: Ostrich, see OSTRICH.

BIRD: OWL

—Bird Symbol / Rowland, 208 (index)
—Cambodian / Carrison
Siva believes eagle's dreams; owl asks equal treatment, 67–72
—Corrin / Imagine *
Caliph and Vizier into storks; forget magic word; marriage to (enchanted) owl, 164–76
—Davy Crockett / Dewey * 14–15
—Erdoes / Sound *
owl is messenger; pay attention, 93–94
owl saves young warrior, 93–94
—Grimm / Complete *
fear: people burn down barn to kill owl, 711–713
—Gullible Coyote / Malotki
mate dies; Coyote Woman grinds his penis to enjoy sex, 55–67
—Hall / Treasury *
Owl and the pussy-cat (Lear), 40–41
—Igloo / Metayer
owl, ridiculed, kills wolf, 55–57
owl-suitor rejected by ptarmigan, 40–41
—Leonardo / Fables *
trapped eagle and the owl, 96–97
—Man Myth & Magic, 3159 (index)
—Manning / Cats *
small-small cat seeks advice on growing large, 126–127
—Navajo Coyote / Haile
Old Man Owl raised Coyote's son, 13, 53–54
—Owl Poems / Livingston
includes nursery and folk rhymes, Navaho and Chippewa poems, comic verse and tale elements; poets include Carroll, Ciardi, Farjeon, Lear, Tennyson, etc. Author, title, and first-line indexes, 114 p.
—Pellowski / Story *
finger-play story, 96
—Sioux / Standing Bear *
woman kills hooting owl (really an enemy Crow), 55–57
—Spanish-Am / Van Etten *
owl wishes: to lie to a witch means death, 48–49
—Vanishing / Mercer *

why owl has huge eyes; Australian Abo tale, 61–64
—Weinstein / Owls
collection of lore, legends, tales, excerpts, verse, selections from literature, fables, beliefs, superstitions. Heavily illustrated. 144 p.

BIRD: OXPECKER
—Greaves / Hippo *
why giraffe and oxpecker are friends, 84–86

BIRD: PARROT
—Clouston / Popular
parrot tales; wife's fidelity, II.196–211
—Jewish / Sadeh
advice: escape by feigning death, 165–166
—Maori / Kanawa *
how Kaka (parrot) got beautiful feathers, 115
—Turkish (Art I) / Walker
to win beautiful mute, prince must make her speak, 34–41
—Vanishing / Mercer *
Ona people: parrot that brought autumn, 80–83

BIRD: PARTRIDGE
—Bierhorst / Naked *
turtle and partridge hide bagged elk from wolves, 67–71
—Bird Symbol / Rowland, 209 (index)
Bird: Peacock, see PEACOCK.

BIRD: PELICAN
—Bird Symbol / Rowland, 209 (index)
—Vanishing / Mercer *
origin of fishing net (Australian Abo tale), 54–57

BIRD: PHEASANT
—Haboo / Hilbert
hunters, 60–65

BIRD: PIGEON
—Old Wives / Carter
wives cure boastfulness: vulture fights pigeons, 211–212

BIRD: QUAIL
—Bird Symbol / Rowland, 210 (index)

BIRD: RAVEN
—Bird Symbol / Rowland, 210 (index)
—Bomans / Wily *
hunter spares deer, swan, raven; saves man accused of theft, 16–19
—Caduto / Keepers *
how Raven made the tides, 103
—Earthmaker / Mayo *
daylight comes at last (Lillooet tale), 12–16
—Grimm / Complete *
father vows to kill twelve brothers; transformation, 59–64
princess under spell, broken by persistence, 431–436
riddle: raven poisoned by witch, 128–131
sea-hare: suitor must conceal self from princess, 769–772
—Grimm / Sixty *
princess under spell, broken by persistence, 250–256
—Haboo / Hilbert
hunters, 60–65
—Hamilton / In the Beginning *
creates man and animals: The pea pod man, 2–7
—Hoke / Giants
giant, no heart in his body, 93–102
origin of characteristics, 150–155
—Igloo / Metayer
deceives/kills people, for food, 58–60
—Indian Myth / Burland
transformations, 39–40
—Man Myth & Magic, 3164 (index)
—Muddleheads / Harris

seal of Mouse Children recovered
from Big Raven, 60–74
—Russian / Afanasev, 660 (index)
—Russian Hero / Warner *
foolish man exchanges daughter
for help, 57–60
wolf helps quest; warnings ig-
nored, 112–116
—Victorian / Hearn
Melilot (H. Morley), 117–127
BIRD: ROADRUNNER
—Curry / Beforetime *
weasel opens weather-bundles in
roadrunner's pack, 5–9
BIRD: ROBIN
—Bird Symbol / Rowland, 210 (in-
dex)
—Maori / Kanawa *
Maui: how robin got cap of white
feathers, 117
—Scary / Young *
tiger (imposter) eats woman;
robin gets aid for sister, 73–77
Bird: Rooster, see ROOSTER.
BIRD: SEABIRD
—Animal Legends / Kerven *
Sedna marries seabird; unhappy;
father kills bird, [30–32]
BIRD: SEA GULL
—Earthmaker / Mayo *
daylight comes at last (Lillooet
tale), 12–16
BIRD: SHAG
—Vanishing / Mercer *
origin of Rangitoto channel rock,
32–33
BIRD: SPARROW
—Bird Symbol / Rowland, 211 (index)
—Lester / Brer Rabbit *
tattletale: Mr. Jack Sparrow
meets his end, 35–37
—Quayle / Shining *
tongue-cut sparrow: kind hus-
band, cruel wife, 44–56

BIRD: SPARROW HAWK
—Hopi Coyote / Malotki
hawk eats all Cicada's children,
105–111
BIRD: STARLING
—Jewish / Frankel
caged starling and the princess
(fable), 468–469
BIRD: STORK
—Allison / I'll Tell *
fox and stork; dinner invitations;
victim of joke, 110
—Lewis / Proud
Milun/lover wait twenty years to
be wed, 65–75
BIRD: SWALLOW
—Wilde / Happy *
The happy prince [statue sends
swallow with jewels for poor],
15–38
—Wilde / Lynch *
happy prince . . . (as above),
41–54
BIRD: THRUSH
—Bird Symbol / Rowland, 212 (index)
BIRD: TURTLEDOVE
—Bird Symbol / Rowland, 212 (index)
BIRD: VULTURE
—Bell / Classical Dict, 268 @
—Bird Symbol / Rowland, 212 (in-
dex)
—Corrin / Imagine *
Arap Sang: why vultures are bald,
47–53
—Greaves / Hippo *
elephant vs. Rain Spirit: who is
greater, 53–58
—Old Wives / Carter
wives cure boastfulness: vulture
fights pigeons, 211–212
BIRD: WAGTAIL
—Vanishing / Mercer *
Ainu myth: origin of tides,
quakes, hills, etc., 95–98

Bird who lost his song (Aesop)
—Paxton / Belling * [28–31]
BIRD: WOODLARK
—Leonardo / Fables *
    key to life or death, 18–19
BIRD: WOODPECKER
—Bierhorst / Monkey *
    origin of red-head, 52–55
—Bird Symbol / Rowland, 213 (index)
—Erdoes / Sound *
    courtship: origin of use of flute,
    3–9
—Man Myth & Magic, 3180 (index)
—Manning / Cauldron *
    prince and retinue turned into
    trees; girl breaks spell, 39–45
BIRD: WREN
—Bird Symbol / Rowland, 213 (index)
—Grimm / Complete *
    willow-wren: contest to select
    king of birds, 705–708
—Hopi / Talashoma-Malotki
    Hopi boy and his two pet eagles,
    150–199
    Kokosori and his witch wife, 23–
    41
—Hopi Coyote / Malotki
    coyote and wren play hide and
    seek, 57–61
—Manning / Cats *
    baby wrens lie; father wren
    "scares off" King Tiger, 124–
    125
BIRDS: MYTHICAL (or imaginary)
—Arabian / Lewis
    Sinbad's first and last voyage,
    94–105
—Arabian / McCaughrean (as
    above), 16–21
—Arabian / Riordan (as above), 38–
    55
—Imaginary / Nigg, 1–160
    aitvaras, 17–19
    anka, 45–47

basilisk, 29–31
bird of happiness, 81–83
bird-watcher notes, 143–154 @
firebird, 89–91
foster-mother: the alan, 113–115
garuda, 73–75
gillygaloo, 121–123
golden crane; fisherman; em-
    peror, 105–107
golden peacock, 97–99
halcyon, 65–67
kaha, 77–79
kikimora, 33–35
king/queen and the hatthilinga,
    109–111
oshadegea, 133–135
phoenix, 41–43
raven, 125–127
ravens: Hugin and Munin, 37–
    39
roc, 57–59
simurgh, 49–51
tengu, 101–103
thunderbird, 129–131
wizard and the chonchon, 117–
    119
—Manning / Cats *
    king loses sight; cure if washed in
    Katchka's blood, 118–123
—South / Mythical
    sources; bibliographical essay,
    59–74 (D. McMillan), 388 (in-
    dex)
BIRD: BOOBRIE
—Beasts / McHargue, 47 @
BIRD: FIREBIRD
—Dulac / Fairy *
    princess, heart of prince, 153–
    164
—Russian Hero / Warner
    wolf helps quest; warnings ig-
    nored, 112–116
BIRD: MOA
—Monsters / Cohen, 88–90 @

BIRD: PHOENIX
—Beasts / McHargue, 29–35 @, 118 (index)
—Bird Symbol / Rowland, 209 (index)
—Gould / Mythical
Chinese phoenix, 366–374 @
—Jewish / Frankel
Milham does not eat forbidden fruit; immortal, 15–17
—Water Buffalo (Chinese)
trifles may cause disasters, 13–17
BIRD: ROC
—Beasts / McHargue, 45–46 @
—Douglas / Magic *
its egg eaten, roc gets vengeance on Sinbad, 21–25
—Monsters / Cohen, 91 @
—South / Mythical sources; bibliographical essay, 75–83 (D. McMillan), 389 (index)
BIRD: ROC: Sinbad's first and last voyage
—Arabian / Lewis, 94–105
—Arabian / McCaughrean, 16–21
—Arabian / Riordan, 38–55
BIRD: SIMURG
—Beasts / McHargue, 82 @
—Shah / Central Asia
Rustam and the iron fortress, 25–30
BIRD: THUNDERBIRD
—Erdoes / Sound *
giants: when the earth was young, 33–36
—Indian Myth / Burland
color illustration, 42–43
—Monsters / Cohen, 92–95 @
Birth, see CHILDBIRTH.
BIRTHDAY
—Witch Hndbk / Bird *
Monday's witch . . . , 40
BIRTH-STONE
—Precious Stones / Kunz, 307–337 @

Bisclavret, see WEREWOLF.
BISHOP(-s)
—Baring-Gould / Curious
priest (sixth cent.) slandered, deposed, restored, 156–159 @
—Jewish / Sadeh
Abraham ben Ezra and the bishop, 220–221
Bishop of Salzburg converted to Judaism, 225–226
Bittern and the hoopoe, The
—Grimm / Complete * 710–711
Black-American, see AFRO-AMERICAN . . .
Black bull of Norroway
—Crossley / British FT * 59–70
BLACK DEATH
—Scandinavian / Kvideland, xvii, 419, 426 (index)
Black dog of Bungay
—Crossley / Dead * 73–76
BLACK DOGS (*ghosts, fairies, etc.*)
—British / Briggs *
three tales, 115–119
BLACKBEARD (Edward Teach, pirate)
—American / Read Dgst, 76–78
—Southern [legends] / Floyd, 154–161
BLACKFACE
—Jewish / Sadeh
merchant's son in love with princess, 117–121
Blackfeet Indians, see INDIANS: BLACKFEET.
BLACK HUMOR (a sardonic, literary response to meaninglessness)
—Hopi / Talashoma-Malotki
how Palongawhoya killed his grandmother, 42–49
—Yolen / Shape Shift
The wonderful dog suit / D. Hall, 38–41

BLACK MASS
—Witch Encyc / Guiley, 26–27
BLACKS
see also AFRO-AMERICANS;
SLAVERY
—Afro-American / Abrahams
Caribbean, 1–327
—American / Read Dgst, 434 (index)
—Jewish / Frankel
Elijah: soft like reed, not hard like
cedar; race, 583–584
BLACKSMITH
—Grimm / Complete *
brothers: barber, blacksmith,
fencing master (most skilled?),
561–62
BLAKE, William (1757–1827)
—Demons / Gettings, 56–58
BLESS
—Grimm / Complete *
lambkin and the little fish, 625–
627
BLIND (-ed; -ness) (sight usually re-
stored)
—Arabian / Lewis
sea rose; father blinded if he
looks at son, 212–216
—Arabian / McCaughrean
Sinbad's second voyage, 22–28
—Arabian / Riordan
Sinbad's second voyage, 38–55
—Bell / Classical Dict, 27–29 @
—Caduto / Keepers *
how Raven made the tides, 103
—Coyote / Bierhorst *
blind woman cured, but coyote
steals all her possessions, [28]
—Coyote / Ramsey
coyote takes self apart to get
through hole; trickery, 133–134
coyote the eye-juggler, 245–247
—Crossley / British FT *
midwife uses ointment; fairy husband blinds that eye, 287–292
—Egyptian / Harris
brothers (Lies and Truth personified), false accusation, 84–85
—Grimm / Complete *
tailor overcomes evil shoemaker,
386–496
—Hopi Coyote / Malotki
coyote and bird play: pluck out/
retrieve eyes, 63–67
—Igloo / Metayer
mother blinds her hunter-son,
92–98
—Jewish / Frankel
fate: can't change wheel of fortune, 394–395
—Jewish / Sadeh
whom God loves, 149–152
—Lang / Wilkins
Fairy of the Dawn; magic well
water, 571–601
—MacDonald / Sourcebook *
motif index, 580
—Manning / Cats *
king loses sight; cure if washed in
Katchka's blood, 118–123
—Manning / Cauldron *
crusader beaten, robbed by comrades; witches reveal secrets,
46–57
—Nielsen / Old Tales *
blue belt (mother conspires with
troll to kill son), [37–62]
—Scriven / Full Color *
Rapunzel, 9–12
—Turkish (Art I) / Walker
tyrant Bolu Bey blinds man; son
gets revenge, 99–109
unfaithful wife detected by blind
hoca, 89–91
—Vanishing / Mercer *
Eskimo blind boy and the loon,
36–39
—Yep / Rainbow *
restored: We are all one, 72–78

BLIZZARD
—Earthmaker / Mayo *
  Snowmaker torments the people
  (Menominee tale), 48–52
—Sioux / Standing Bear *
  wolves save woman caught in
  blizzard, 3–9
Bloch, Robert
—Pirate Ghosts / McSherry
  The red swimmer, 45–68
BLOOD
—Bell / Classical Dict, 29–30 @
—Grimm / Legends (Ward), II:391 (in-
  dex)
—Man Myth & Magic, 3116 (index)
—Witch Encyc / Guiley, 410 (index)
Bloody Mary (a tale in rhyme)
—Scary / Young * 58–60
BLUBBER
—Old Wives / Carter
  blubber boy: chunk of blubber an-
  imated by being rubbed
  against genitals, 31–32
**Blue Beard (or Bluebeard) (murder-
  ous husband)**
—Carter / Sleeping * 33–40
—Corrin / Favourite * 184–191
—Lang / Wilkins, 110–115
—Strauss / Trail
  reflection on women destroyed
  (poem), 20–21
—Zipes / Beauties * , 31–35
Blue bird [trout-faced stepsister]
—Zipes / Beauties * 321–349
Blue light, The
—Grimm / Complete * 530–534
—Grimm / Sixty * 244–249
Blue spectacles
—Pirate Ghosts / McSherry, 73–
  83
Blue-tail fly (Jimmie crack corn)
—Allison / I'll Tell * 139
BLUFFING
—Clarkson / World *

Brave Kong takes credit for tiger
  killed by wives, 356–361
—Grimm / Complete *
  stupid giant conned by boastful
  tailor's "power," 745–747
—Rockwell / Puss *
  cat (white bear) on the dovrefell,
  71–79
  Nail Soup [series of small lies],
  12–18
—Russian Hero / Warner *
  gypsy cons dragon: he's
  stronger, 71–72
—Williams-Ellis / Tales *
  trolls driven away by bear ("great
  white cat"), 17–23
BLYMIRE, John
—Witch Encyc / Guiley, 30–33
BOAR
—Animals / Rowland, 181 (index)
—Bell / Classical Dict, 30–32 @
—Demi / Reflective *
  boar declares war on forest,
  [10]
—Man Myth & Magic, 3116 (index)
Boasting, see BRAGGART(-s)
BODHISATTVA
—Cambodian / Carrison
  old mother would kill Bodhisattva
  to marry his pupil, 90–94
BODY (*human; body parts*)
—Grimm / Complete *
  surgeons remove; cat eats; other
  body parts substituted; effects,
  535–538
—Jewish / Frankel
  body parts, 645 (index)
—Lester / Leopard *
  body parts argue: which is most
  important, 45–51
—Lycanthropy / Otten, 326 (index)
—Man Myth & Magic, 3116 (index)
BODY AND SOUL
—Fahs / Old *

Buddhism: soul after death of
  body, 178–180
BOG (mire; bogland)
—Dulac / Fairy *
  buried moon (captured by evil
  bog creatures), 7–14
—Ghosts / Starkey
  moon (personified) captured/
  rescued (bogles), 96–101
BOGGART(-s)
—Crossley / British FT *
  farmer and boggart [trick: crop
  above/below ground], 224–227
—Fairies / Briggs, 29–30
—Ghosts / Starkey
  The boggart of Castle Farn, 30–
  35
—McGowen / Encyclopedia * 15
BOGIES / BOGGLES
—British / Briggs *
  five tales, 121–127
—Crossley / Dead *
  dead moon [boggles; marsh folk],
  1–9
—Fairies / Briggs, 30–32 (with illus.)
—Ghosts / Starkey
  moon (personified) captured/
  rescued, 96–101
BOGY (bogey-beast; goblin)
—Fairies / Briggs
  Hedley Kow, 218–219
BOHEMIAN . . .
—Dictionary / Leach, 1203 (index)
—Manning / Cauldron *
  crusader beaten, robbed by com-
  rades; witches reveal secrets,
  46–57
Boiko, Claire
—Dramatized / Kamerman
  Lady Moon and the thief, 23–31
  Pepe and the cornfield bandit,
  324–333
BONE(-s) (often magic)
  see also Aesop: Dog . . .

—Grimm / Complete *
  singing bone: murder revealed,
  148–150
—Hamilton / Dark *
  John (brother) kills Little Tom;
  talking bone reveals murder,
  132–136
  tiny thing: Anishinaba and Boshk-
  wadosh, 54–59
—Hopi Coyote / Malotki
  Coyote Woman and Turkey
  Woman roast their children,
  77–81
—Jewish / Frankel
  dim-witted boy buys box of bones
  (chain tale), 414–418
—Manning / Cauldron *
  Moti-katika to be eaten by Water
  Witch; saving-bones provided,
  118–127
Boo! [*shortest tale?*]
—Crossley / British FT * 338
BOOK, MAGIC
—Arabian / McCaughrean
  keys of destiny; Iram, 65–82
—Bomans / Wily *
  three riddles; wizard can read fu-
  ture, 202–204
—Egyptian / Mercatante
  Setna and the magic book, 145–
  153
Book of the Dead
—Egyptian / Ions, 143 (index)
BOONE, Daniel (1734–1820)
—American / Read Dgst
  legendary backwoodsman, 116–
  120
BOORISHNESS
—Hamilton / People *
  wolf insults birds; steals milk of
  helpful walrus, 43–48
BOOTS
—Carle / Treasury *
  Magic boots (Andersen), 31–35

Boots and his brothers
—Clarkson / World *
   Boots discovers how to do tasks;
     wins princess, 277–281
Boots of buffalo-leather
—Grimm / Complete * 808–811
BORDEN, Lizzie (1860–1927)
—Floyd / Gr Am Myst, 21–25
BOREDOM
—Bomans / Wily *
   king totally bored; has all, = noth-
     ing; learns work, 101–103
BORNEO
—Dictionary / Leach, 1203 (index)
—Fahs / Old *
   struggle: boy half-good, half-bad,
     1–6
BORS de Ganis, Sir
—King Arthur / Senior, 318 (index)
BOSHKWADOSH
—Hamilton / Dark *
   tiny thing: Anishinaba and Boshk-
     wadosh, 54–59
BOTTLE, MAGIC
—O'Brien / Tales *
   poor farmer trades cow for magic
     "do your [whatever] duty" bot-
     tle, 46–52
BOUKI
—Hamilton / Dark *
   free spirits: Bouki and Malice,
     102–107
BOULDER(-s)
—Grimm / Legends (Ward), II:392 (in-
   dex)
BOW AND ARROW
—Curry / Beforetime *
   length of bows determine man/
     animal share in ruling, 121–
     127
—Dulac / Fairy *
   magic: always hits its mark, 114–
     123
—Igloo / Metayer

   child kidnapped by wolf-men, 73–
     77
—Vietnam / Terada *
   magic crossbow used to kill king,
     120–125
BOWL, MAGIC
—Jaffrey / Seasons
   goddess Parvati gives magic
     bowl to old man, 103–109
BOX
—Pellowski / Family *
   origami: Brothers Short and
     Long; treasure box, 79–84
Boy and the north wind
—Hall / Treasury * 32–34
Boy who cried 'Wolf,' *see under*
   Aesop
Boy who drew unicorns (J. Yolen)
—Unicorn / Coville * 157–166
BRAGGART(-s) *(boasting)*
—Bruchac / Iroquois *
   chipmunk ridicules bear, and
     pays, 37–39
   Skunny-Wundy defeats the
     Stone Giants, 161–167
—Cambodian / Carrison
   frog boasts to bee: to Himalayas
     in one day, 100–101
—Coyote / Bierhorst *
   crocodile brags; coyote says:
     look at self, not ancestors,
     [40]
—Greaves / Hippo *
   jackal boast to wildcat: can out-
     run dogs, 45–47
—Grimm / Complete *
   stupid giant conned by boastful
     tailor's "power," 745–747
   three spinners help attain bride's
     mother's boast, 83–86
—Lewis / Proud
   Lanval nearly loses his lady, 26–
     47
—Maori / Kanawa *

totara tree boasts, fails, hides in
forest, 83
—O'Brien / Tales *
Lord Mount Dhraggin: weaver
"kills" three-score and ten;
made Lord, 72–81
—Old Wives / Carter
wives cure boastfulness: vulture
fights pigeons, 211–212
—Turkish / Walker
boast re archery prowess; the
third shot, 43–44
boasting mouse misunderstands
natural phenomena, 1–3
—Yep / Rainbow *
Virtue goes to town, 118–123
BRAHMA(-n; -nism)
—Cotterell / Encyclopedia, 252 (index)
—Dramatized / Kamerman
deception: tiger, brahman, and
jackal, 212–217
—Fahs / Old *
Brahman, the universal being,
189–192
—Indic / Ions, 143 (index)
—Wolkstein / Love, 237 @
Bramblebush, see Aesop: Bat, bram-
ble . . .
BRAN, the Blessed
—Fairies / Briggs, 39–41
BRAVADO
—Manning / Cats *
baby wrens lie; father wren
"scares off" King Tiger, 124–
125
Brave little tailor (Valiant tailor)
—Grimm / Complete * 112–120
—Grimm / Sixty * 88–97
—Lang / Wilkins, 64–72
Bravery, see COURAGE.
BRAZIL
—Bierhorst / So Am
Indian religion and mythology, 1–
269

—Man Myth & Magic, 3117 (index)
—Speck / New World, 518 (index)
—Vanishing / Mercer *
Tupis, Pamaris, Juruna tales, 13–
27
BREAD
—Grimm / Legends (Ward), II:392 (in-
dex)
—Jewish / Sadeh
rabbi scolds poor man offering
bread to God, 238–239
BREASTPLATE
—Precious Stones / Kunz
Jewish high-priest's breastplate,
275–306 @
BREATH
—Jewish / Frankel
Maimonides and the limekiln: bad
breath, 392–394
BREATH OF LIFE
—Hamilton / In the Beginning *
Erlik vs. Ulgen: creation of
woman, 28–33
Bremen Town musicians (Grimm)
—Childcraft 3 / Stories * 88–92
—Crossley / Animal (Grimm) * 54–59
—Douglas / Magic * 123–129
—Dramatized / Kamerman, 155–161
—Grimm / Complete * 144–148
—Grimm / Sixty * 21–25
BRER RABBIT TALES
—American / Read Dgst
tar baby; Brer Fox; the deluge,
260–262
—Childcraft 3 / Stories *
Tony Beaver: how it snowed fur
and rained fry cakes, 199–201
—Clarkson / World *
Buh Fox's number nine shoes,
145–147
Sheer [share] crops, 272–274
—Harris-Parks / Again
Brer Rabbit "fishing" in a well,
2–5

Brer Rabbit's courtship: wins
 Miss Molly Cottontail, 30–39
Brers Mink-Possum-Coon-Fox-
 Bear guard butter, 14–21
Miss Wolf (Brer Wolf's niece) and
 mosquitoes, 22–29
Tar-Baby story, 6–13
—Harris-Parks / Jump *
Brer Fox hunts, Brer Rabbit gets
 the game, 11–16
Brer Rabbit tricks Brer Wolf into
 trunk, 3–8
Brer Rabbit uses Brer Fox as rid-
 ing horse, 27–32
Brer Terrapin "wins" race with
 Brer Rabbit, 19–24
moon in millpond: Brers Rabbit
 and Terrapin play trick, 35–
 38
—Lester / Brer Rabbit *
animals with horns vs. animals
 with claws; Brer Wolf exposed,
 122–124
breaks up party, 134–137
Brer Fox and Brer Rabbit go hunting, 42–43
Brer Fox feigns death; Brer Rabbit tricks him, 29–31
Brer Fox tricked; gets beaten by
 Mr. Man, 75–78
Brer Fox would eat Brer Rabbit's
 children; bird gives advice on
 tasks, 54–56
Brer Lion meets the creature (Ole
 Boy), 65–68
Brer Turtle as traveler, 26–29
Brer Turtle put in sack; replaced
 with hornet's nest, 110–112
Brer Wolf steals Brer Rabbit's
 lucky rabbit foot, 145–151
caught by Brer Wolf; tricks him
 into saying grace, 37–40
cons Brer Wolf into trap built for
 himself, 106–109

consults Aunt Mammy-Bammy
 Big Money, 145–151
courting King Deer's daughter,
 131–134
covered with honey and leaves;
 seen as monster, 127–131
eats the butter; accuses Brer
 Possum, 46–50
end of Brer Bear; the honey tree,
 74–75
goes to Earth in behalf of Sister
 Moon, 1–3
invitation to dinner: Brer Fox
 seeks revenge, 8–10
lettuce patch; Mr. Man's daughter, 78–81
moon in the pond: fishing party,
 96–99
mosquitoes, and Brer Wolf's
 daughter, 124–127
Mr. Man with wagon load of
 money, 104–106
noise in the woods: run! 113–115
origin of popped eyes and split
 lip, 3
outwits Mr. Man, 137–141
race: Brer Turtle beats Brer Rabbit, 31–34
riddle: bee hive in gum tree, 91–95
says that molasses is "fox blood,"
 141–144
steals Brer Fox's peanuts; puts
 blame on Brer Bear, 71–74
steals Brer Wolf's fish; gives cow,
 but ends up with the meat, 51–
 53
talking house: tricks Brer Wolf to
 reveal himself, 68–69
(and the) Tar Baby, 10–16
tattletale: Mr. Jack Sparrow
 meets his end, 35–37
trapped in hollow log; burns up
 Brer Wolf, 117–122
trapped in Mr. Man's garden;

cons Brer Fox to take his place, 81–86

tricked: Brer Possum hears the singing, 87–91

tricks Brer Fox: "Hold'im [horse] down," 6–8

tricks Brer Fox into being his saddle-horse, 16–23

tricks Brer Lion: "hurricane coming," 60–62

tricks Brer Wolf into trunk; kills him with boiling water, 40–42

tricks Sister Cow (horns stuck in tree), 23–26

tries to trick Brer Buzzard out of his share of garden, 69–71

warns Sister Goose re Brer Fox, 4–6

(in the) well: Brer Rabbit tricks Brer Fox, 44–46

Wiley Wolf and Riley Rabbit: play Riding/Tying the Bag, 101–104

with Brer Elephant's help, causes Brer Tiger to leave area, 62–65

with Brer Wolf kills a cow; pretends to be poisoned, 115–117

with Fox, goes inside cow to cut meat; the Man kills fox, 57–60

—Tall Tales / Downs: Bear

why Brer Rabbit doesn't have to work anymore / J. Sale, 87–93

BRETON TALES

—Lewis / Proud, 1–100

Briar patch tale, *see* TAR BABY.

Briar Rose, *see* Sleeping Beauty.

BRICRIU (mischief-maker)

—Celts / Hodges *

Cuchulain: champion of Ireland, 17–31

BRIDE(-s) (*including "bride tests"*)

see also FAIRY BRIDE

—Bierhorst / Monkey *

bird bride: toad helps youngest

son re oft-ruined cornfield, 25–31

—Clarkson / World *

Indian Cinderella: Strong Wind will marry truthful girl, 43–45

most obedient wife, 86–91

—Dramatized / Kamerman

peach tree kingdom; imposter; bride test, 288–305

—Fairies / Briggs

fairy, 135–137

—Geras / Grandmother *

matchmaker: use of messy wool to test brides, 41–48

—Grimm / Complete *

Maid Maleen, in menial disguise, at lover's court, 801–807

shepherd chooses bride who eats properly, 655–656

three spinners help attain bride's mother's boast, 83–86

white bride and black bride, 608–612

—Jaffrey / Seasons

by pretending madness, faithful sister changes brother's fate, 96–101

—Jewish / Frankel

bride saves husband from angel of death, 600–602

—Jewish / Sadeh

bride auctioned; bought by prince; chastity test, 332–333

—Lang / Wilkins

Indian chief goes to lowerworld for dead bride, 282–284

—Old Wives / Carter

for her fidelity, king-robber-ogre absolve woman of promise(s), 13–15

—Reeves / Shadow

given by father to rich, cruel old man, 1–48

locked in tower; hawk (shape-
change knight) as lover, 1–48
—Scary / Young *
bride always wears ribbon around
neck; husband removes; her
head falls off, 61–63
—Spanish-Am / Van Etten *
captive bride in lizard's den, 19–24
—Turkey / Walker
false, 300 (index)
—Turkish (Art I) / Walker
using disguise and bracelet, girl
seeks bride for her widowerfather, 224–230
—Women / Dyer, 206–215 @
BRIDEGROOM
—Grimm / Complete *
Robber bridegroom [witness to
murder], 200–204
—Grimm / Sixty *
Robber . . . (as above), 120–124
—Jewish / Sadeh
finger: she-demon claims, as her
husband, 241–242
BRIDGE(-s)
see also Three billy goats Gruff
—Dramatized / Kamerman
Bridge to Killybog Fair, 227–238
ogre; guess name; carpenter's
ear, 278–287
—Grimm / Complete *
straw, coal and stone fail as
bridge for animals, 365–367
—Grimm / Legends (Ward), II:392 (in-
dex)
—Yep / Rainbow *
Breaker's bridge, 118–123
Bright sun brings it [murder] to light
—Grimm / Complete * 528–529
Britain, see ENGLAND; GREAT
BRITAIN.
BRITISH . . .
—British / Briggs * 1–315
—British Dict / Briggs, 2 v.

—Crossley / British FT * 1–383
—Crossley / British Isles * 1–393
—Dulac / Fairy *
buried moon captured by bog
creatures, 7–14
friar and the boy, 114–123
—Ghosts / Starkey
sixteen tales (British Isles), 1–123
—Hartland / English * 1–282
—Manning / Cauldron *
her cat advises witch (who makes
self invisible), to steal farmer's
eggs, 32–38
—Mercatante / Encyclopedia, 725 (in-
dex)
BRITTANY
—Dictionary / Leach, 1203 (index)
BROCADE
—Spring / Philip
wonderful brocade picture, 23–
34
BRODER MENINE (Irish chieftain)
—Ghosts / Starkey
the buggane and the tailor, 16–23
BROLLACHAN
—Beasts / McHargue, 55 @
BRONZE AGE
—Scandinavian / Davidson, 142 (in-
dex)
Brooke, Maxey
—Pendragon / Ashley
Morte d'Alain, 70–77
BROOM, MAGIC
—Corrin / Six-Year *
taken by mistake, scientist goes
to moon; witch, 87–92
—Witch Encyc / Guiley, 410 (index)
BROOMSTICK, MAGIC
—Quayle / Cornish *
ointment put on eye makes one
invisible, 13–20
BROTHER(-s)
see also YOUNGEST BROTHER
—Bierhorst / Naked *

heroes: Turtle, his sister, and
Great Wind, 110–115
Quilt of men's eyes, 101–109
—Bruchac / Iroquois *
two brothers: one brings good,
the other evil, 19–23
—Coyote / Ramsey
brothers become sun and moon,
78–81
—Egyptian / Harris
Anpu and Bata, 77–83
—Frog Rider (Chinese)
Big Lang (evil) and Little Lang
(good) divide property, 100–110
—Grimm / Complete *
brothers: one rescues princess; is
rescued by other, 290–311
seven ravens [transformed broth-
ers], 137–139
—Grimm / Sixty *
Seven ravens (as above), 284–
287
—Hamilton / Dark *
John kills Little Tom, takes credit
for his feat, 132–136
—Hopi / Talashoma-Malotki
Poqangwhoya, 206 @
—Jewish / Frankel, 648 (index)
—Jewish / Sadeh
poor brother and three beasts,
140–143
whom God loves, 149–152
—Lester / Leopard *
town where snoring was not al-
lowed, 27–30
—MacDonald / Sourcebook *
motif index, 585
—Pellowski / Family *
origami: Brothers Short and
Long; treasure box, 79–84
—Russian / Afanasev, 657 (index)
—Russian Hero / Warner *
Ivan son of Mare kills his treach-
erous brothers, 120–124

—Spring / Philip
wise king exposes gold thief, 50–
57
—Water Buffalo (Chinese)
seven remarkably endowed sons
"reason" with tyrant, 49–54
BROTHER(-s) and SISTER(-s)
—Bierhorst / Naked *
Cannibal Island; rescue; commanding nature, 44–51
—Dulac / Fairy *
Bashtchelik (real steel), 91–
113
—Frog Rider (Chinese)
Big Lang and Little Lang divide
property, 100–110
—Grimm / Complete *
brother transformed to fawn; sister faithful, 67–73
father vows to kill 12 brothers if
daughter is born, 59–64
seven ravens [transformed broth-
ers], 137–139
six swans: sister faithful to trans-
formed brothers, 232–237
—Grimm / Sixty *
seven ravens [transformed broth-
ers], 284–287
—Hoke / Giants
Finlay, the giant killer, 142–149
—Jaffrey / Seasons
by pretending madness, faithful
sister changes brother's fate,
96–101
—Legends / Cavendish
family, 404 (index)
Brother Lustig
—Grimm / Complete * 367–377
Brown owl, The (Ford)
—Victorian / Hearn, 260–316
BROWNIE
—Fairies / Briggs, 45–49
wag-at-the-Wa, 425–426
—McGowen / Encyclopedia * 15

Browning, Robert (1812–1889)
—Victorian / Hearn
   Pied piper of Hamelin, 24–34
BRUNISSENDE
—Pendragon / Ashley
   Jaufrey (knight) and fair Brunis-
   sende, 260–321
Brunner, John
—Pendragon / Ashley
   entry not found in Domesday
   Book, 372–384
BUBER, Martin (1878–1965)
—Schwartz / Gates, 798 (index)
BUDDHA (-ism; -ist tales)
—Cambodian / Carrison
   Gatiloke, 11–18 @
   glossary, 131–135
—Chinese / Christie, 142 (index)
—Clouston / Popular, II.504 (index)
—Cotterell / Encyclopedia, 252 (in-
   dex)
—Dictionary / Leach, 1203 (index)
—Fahs / Old *
   soul after death of body, 178–180
   two kings dispute over land, 101–
   103
—Indic / Ions, 128–141 @
—Legends / Cavendish, 5, 422 (in-
   dex)
—Man Myth & Magic, 3118 (index)
—Mercatante / Encyclopedia, 726,
   750 (index)
—Mercatante / Good/Evil, 117–125 @
—Pellowski / Family *
   the hungry stranger, 126–129
—Pellowski / Story *
   why years are named for animals,
   87–89
—Vietnam / Terada *
   spiritual values, 87 @
BUDDHIST MONK(-s)
—Cambodian / Carrison
   four rogues pretend to be Buddhist monks, 36–48

   greedy for silk robe, monk loses
   robe and money, 52–57
   Phnong family murdered; one
   child is saved, 78–85
   woman tricked by thief in disguise, 31–35
—Chinese / Chin *
   monkey: on road to fetch scriptures, 95–110
—Spring / Philip
   dragon seen by unprotected
   men, 119–133
—Tibet / Timpanelli *
   hunter's son can't kill animals;
   father buries him, 1–13
Buechler, James
—Dramatized / Kamerman
   Stone soup, 381–387
BUFFALO
—Caduto / Keepers *
   gift of the gods, 187–188
—Coyote / Ramsey
   turtle wins swimming race, 22–
   23
—Erdoes / Sound *
   crows warn buffalo about hunters, 57–59
   gives one eye to trickster Veeho,
   86–89
   three brothers transformed to rattlers; remain friendly, 37–42
   White Buffalo Woman (Lakota),
   117–123
—Greaves / Hippo * 78 @
   how buffalo became a grass
   eater, 73–77
—Sioux / Standing Bear *
   buffalo brothers: one aids its
   wounded "brother," 44–47
   year of the buffalo; the Buffalo
   Dreamer, 68–70
**BUFFALO BILL (Wm F. Cody, 1846–
   1917)**
—Erdoes / Sound *

Sitting Bull, his dancing horse, his death, 103–107

BUFFALO DANCERS
—Gullible Coyote / Malotki, 162–164 @

BUGGANE(-s) (vicious, imaginary animal)
—Ghosts / Starkey
Broder Menine and the tailor, 16–23

BULAI (*giant*)
—Hoke / Giants
short-sighted acts, 130–132

BULGARIAN TALE
—Manning / Cauldron *
witch's flute: goatherd can't stop playing; goats and people can't stop dancing, 99–105

BULL(-s)
—Animals / Rowland, 181 (index)
—Babylonia / Spence, 388 (index)
—Bell / Classical Dict, 37–39 @
—Cotterell / Encyclopedia, 252 (index)
—Jewish / Sadeh
Aaron's bull: supports world but sin adds to load, 163–164
—Lurker / Dict Gods, 421 (index)
—Man Myth & Magic, 3118 (index)
—Manning / Cats *
small-small cat seeks advice on growing large, 126–127
—Persian / Hinnells, 142 (index)
Bullfrog, *see* FROG.

BULL-ROARERS
—Hamilton / In the Beginning *
Bandicoot creation myth, 48

BULLOCK
—Journeys / Norris *
road to death: old man takes form of bullock, [16–18]

BULLY
—Corrin / Six-Year *

snow-man, a bully, tricked; melts at stove, 19–23
—Coyote / Ramsey
boy defeats Thunder, 195–200

BUMBUKU
—Hamilton / Dark *
tanuki magic teakettle, 76–81

BUNGLING FOOL(-s)
—Geras / Grandmother *
golden shoes (worn on hands to keep them clean), 21–29
—Grimm / Complete *
Clever Hans, 166–168
Fred and Kate [repeated foolish acts], 283–289
—Grimm / Sixty *
Clever Hans, 217–222
Fred and Kate . . . , 144–155
—Spanish-Am / Van Etten *
start/stop monastery mare; farmer starts, at edge of cliff, 44–47

BUNYAN, Paul (*legendary character*)
—American / Read Dgst, 356
—Brooke / Telling *
acquire wisdom by being taught, 37–48
—Dramatized / Kamerman
Big Paul Bunyan; Babe, the blue ox, 514–525
—Hoke / Giants
his Great Blue Ox, 11–29
How we logged Katahdin Stream (verse), 30–33

BUNYIP
—Beasts / McHargue, 49–50 @
—Childcraft 1 / Once *
Wagner: the bunyip of Berkeley's Creek, 231–235
—McGowen / Encyclopedia * 16

BURD ELLEN
—Hamilton / Dark *
Childe Rowland and Burd Ellen, 65–72

—Williams-Ellis / Tales *
  Childe Rowland rescues sister
  from Elfland, 24–36
BURD JANET
—Celts / Hodges *
  Tam Lin freed from evil spell by
  love, 76–83
BURIAL
  see also GRAVE(-s)
—American / Read Dgst, 434 (index)
—Bruchac / Iroquois *
  origin of customs, 129–133
—Chinese / Chin *
  conscripted husband of Meng-
  Jiang Nyu, 128–139
—Egyptian / Ions
  burial rites, 130–143 @
—Jewish / Frankel
  dim-witted boy buys box of bones
  (chain tale), 414–418
  grateful dead: youth buries Sul-
  tan's accused treasurer, 427–
  430
—Man Myth & Magic, 3118 (index)
BURIED-ALIVE
—Ghosts / Cohen, 206–211
—Spring / Philip
  son tests father's advice; cures
  king, 82–86
—Tibet / Timpanelli *
  hunter's son can't kill animals;
  father buries him, 1–13
Buried silver (Taylor)
—Pendragon / Ashley, 227–259
BURMESE . . .
—Dictionary / Leach, 1204,1212 (index)
—Old Wives / Carter
  promise kept; honor satisfied,
  13–15
Burro, see DONKEY
BUSH COW
—Beat / Bryan *

stronger? why bush cow and ele-
  phant always fight, 14–29
BUSHMEN
—Dictionary / Leach, 1199 (index)
—Vanishing / Mercer *
  how men first got fire; Bushman
  tale, 76–79
  how South Africans came to be
  hunters and gatherers, 74–75
BUSY BODY
—Yep / Rainbow *
  after thousands of years: home-
  coming, 144–151
Buta, see ANPU and BUTA [brothers].
BUTCHER
—Vietnam / Terada *
  chess player dies; enters body of
  newly dead butcher, 75–77
BUTTER
—Harris-Parks / Again
  Brers Mink-Possum-Coon-Fox-
  Bear guard butter, 14–21
—Lester / Brer Rabbit *
  Brer Rabbit eats the butter; accuses Brer Possum, 46–50
—Turkish / Walker
  pretense: three tricksters "steal"
  pot of butter, 88–90
BUTTERFLY
—Crossley / British FT *
  butterfly soul flutters, goes into
  horse skull, 365–367
—Hamilton / Dark *
  origin: souls of the once-alive,
  119–125
—Leonardo / Fables *
  pleasure: butterfly and the flame,
  68
—Spring / Philip
  lovers reincarnated as butterflies,
  35–41
Buzzard, see BIRD: BUZZARD.

CABALA
—Man Myth & Magic, 3119 (index)
—Schwartz / Gates, 1–815
CACTUS CAT
—Beasts / McHargue, 57 @
CADBURY CASTLE
—King Arthur / Ashe, 189 (index)
CAIN
—Schwartz / Gates, 798 (index)
CALAMITIES / CATASTROPHES
see also FIRE (world catastrophes); FLOOD(-s)
—Erdoes / Sound *
Sioux woman works blanket 1,000 years, 124–125
—Journey Sun (Chinese)
Yangang saves village incinerated by shooting star, 47–60
—Yolen / Werewolves
nuclear holocaust, 95–118
CALENDAR
—Chinese / Chin *
year of the rat [etc., Chinese calendar], 157–167
—Constellations / Gallant * 199 (index)
—Coyote / Ramsey
Klamath calendar, 201–202
—Mesoamerican / Leon-P, 287 & 295 (index)
—Plants / Dyer, 216–232
Callow Pit coffer
—Crossley / Dead * 45–54
CAMBODIA
—Cambodian / Carrison
Cambodian tales, 1–139
people, history, customs, 108–130
—Scary / Young *
Ki'in spirits eat souls, take over bodies; boy outwits Ki'in, 52–56
CAMEL
—Aesop / Zwerger
monkey [dances] and camel [envies], 13
—Animals / Rowland, 182 (index)
—Childcraft 1 / Once *
how camel got hump (Kipling), 268–271
—Jewish / Sadeh
marriage: princess to donkey's head, 4–8
singing donkey and dancing camel, 167
—Turkish (Art I) / Walker
donkey and camel: irresistible urges, 44–45
—Water Buffalo (Chinese)
little camel tests mother's advice, 39–43
CAMELOT
see also ARTHURIAN ROMANCES
—King Arthur / Senior, 318 (index)
CAMEROON TALE
—Earth / Hadley *
Beebyeebyee marries water god (fish-man), [25–26]
Campbell, Joseph
—Grimm / Complete *
Work of the Brothers Grimm, 833–864
CAMPCHURCH
—Beasts / McHargue, 49 @
—King Arthur / Ashe, 37–50 @, 189 (index)
CANAAN MYTHS
—Gray / Near East, 77–91
CANADA
—Dict / Leach, 1204 (index)
CANDELABRA
—Corrin / Imagine *
Pari hides in golden candelabra; prince buys, falls in love, 151–160
CANDLE
—Pellowski / Story *
string-story, 16–21
—Russian / Ivanits, 245 (index)

—Turkish / Walker
  survive cold night; candle 100
    meters away, 47–48
—Witch Encyc / Guiley, 410 (index)
CANNIBAL(-ism)
  see also GHOUL; GIANT;
    TROLL
—Arabian / McCaughrean
  Sinbad's second voyage, 22–
    28
—Arabian / Riordan
  Sinbad's second voyage, 38–
    55
—Bell / Classical Dict, 40–41 @
—Bierhorst / Naked *
  Animal-Foot hitter kills sorcerer,
    24–30
  Cannibal Island; rescue; com-
    manding nature, 44–51
—Bomans / Wily *
  city hires wizard to destroy "wily
    witch," 3–8
—Bruchac / Iroquois *
  Stone Coat Woman aids hunters,
    135–144
—Coyote / Ramsey
  arrow-point maker and tobacco-
    hunter, 76–78
  Numuzo'ho plays ball, 248–250
  wild woman ate children, 148–
    150
—Dulac / Fairy *
  Bashtchelik (real steel), 91–113
—Hoke / Giants, 112–118
—Hopi / Talashoma-Malotki
  So'yoko monsters killed by
    Poqangwhoyas, 1–21
—Lang / Wilkins
  prince's mother would eat prin-
    cess and children, 14–17
—Lycanthropy / Otten, 326 (index)
—Maori / Kanawa *
  Putawai: evil wairua carries girl to
    underworld, 92–100

—Old Wives / Carter
  she-ghoul fattens poor woodcut-
    ter, wife, children, to eat them,
    216–220
—Quayle / Shining *
  Rashomon: ogre loses arm, 103–
    111
—Russian Hero / Warner *
  witch (blood sister) and sun's sis-
    ter, 60–61
—Starkey / Ghosts
  cannibalism, 52–57
  Tammy escapes from Lucky Min-
    nie (troll), 110–115
—Turkey / Walker, 300 (index)
—Yep / Rainbow *
  Bedtime snacks, 4–10
CANNIBALISM, UNWILLING
—Bomans / Wily *
  innkeeper feeds guests his own
    leg when famine strikes, 111–
    115
—Grimm / Complete *
  juniper tree: murder exposed by
    singing bird, 220–229
—Scary / Young *
  beheads boy; makes his sister
    think she killed him; cooks boy,
    78–83
CANOE
—Glooskap / Norman *
  panther-witch and her scissorbill
    birds, 39–49
  secluded home found by wolves,
    51–60
CAP, MAGIC
—Grimm / Complete *
  hero must hold crystal ball before
    enchantress to free princess,
    798–801
Cap o' Rushes
—Corrin / Six-Year * 98–103
—Lines / Magical * 23–31
—Williams-Ellis / Tales * 8–16

CAPILANO CANYON
—Fahs / Old *
  daughters bring peace and brotherhood, 104–107
CAPTIVE (-ivity; capture) (*escape or
  rescue is usual*)
—Bierhorst / Naked *
  torture: Boy who learned the
  songs of the birds, 60–66
  Turtle's war party vs. Seven Sisters, 31–36
—Bomans / Wily *
  rescue: lady of the lake, 9–16
—Caduto / Keepers *
  folly: Gluscabi hunting; bag never
  fills, 165–167
—Celts / Hodges *
  freed from evil spell by love, 76–83
—Childcraft 1 / Once *
  turtle "killed" by being thrown into
  water, 172–173
—Childcraft 3 / Stories *
  Baba Yaga's geese abduct girl's
  brother, 114–118
—Corrin / Imagine *
  Sorfarina not sorry for slapping
  prince, as child, 11–22
—Corrin / Six-Year *
  captured field mouse escapes
  with acorn, 113–115
—Crossley / Dead *
  dead moon [boggles; marsh folk],
  1–9
—Douglas / Magic *
  Rapunzel: her daughter promised
  to witch, 27–33
—Dulac / Fairy *
  Finn, and Queen of many-colored
  bedchamber, 69–76
—Egyptian / Harris
  Ra's anger over rebellious man-
  kind, 34–35
—Fairies / Briggs
  in fairyland, 62–66

—Ghosts / Starkey
  moon (personified) captured/
  rescued (bogles), 96–101
—Greaves / Hippo *
  baboon tricks/escapes leopard,
  79–80
  lion steals ostrich chicks, 130–
  132
—Grimm / Complete *
  drummer rescues princess from
  glass mountain, 781–791
  four clever brothers, 580–584
  glass coffin; bewitched maid,
  672–678
  iron stove: princess frees prince;
  breaks tabu, 571–577
  nixie (mill-pond) captures young
  man; wife rescues, 736–742
  Pink [carnation], The, 355–360
  Strong Hans escapes from robber den, 688–695
  wizard captures three sisters;
  Fitcher's bird, 216–220
  youngest huntsman rescues
  princesses from dragon, 420–
  424
—Grimm / Sixty *
  four clever brothers, 220–234
  Pink [carnation], The, 171–176
—Hamilton / People *
  Bruh Fox makes Tar Baby; rabbit
  gets stuck, 13–19
  deception: Wiley triumphs over
  Hairy Man, 90–103
—Jewish / Frankel
  Pope Elhanan: Jewish child,
  raised Christian, returns to Judaism, 395–398
  ruby/serpent: Solomon's daughter shut in tower; power of love,
  254–257
—Journey Sun (Chinese)
  wives in the mirror, 109–124
—Lang / Wilkins

Dwarf Long Nose (boy under
spell), 534–556
enchantment: princess must stay
in tower . . . , 415–431
gnome king Rubezahl captures
princess, 497–512
King Solomon's ring; Dragon of
the North, 285–297
Little good mouse, 116–127
Little King Loc, 441–459
—Lewis / Proud
Yonec: lover killed by jealous
husband's trap, 53–60
—Lore of Love
French soldier and Saracen
maid, 98–106
lovers forced apart; rendezvous
in dreams, 37–49
—MacDonald / Sourcebook *
motif index, 290–293
—Maori / Kanawa *
Kahu rescues wife from dragon
(Taniwah), 52–60
—Pirate Ghosts / McSherry
no ships pass; people cannot die,
13–39
—Russian Hero / Warner *
wolf helps quest; warnings ig-
nored, 112–116
—Old Wives / Carter
princess exposed only to women,
to prevent marriage, 222–224
—Palestinian / Speak (Muhawi), 399–
400
—Russian Hero / Warner *
Dobrynya spares abductor/
dragon, 69–70
three kingdoms: copper, silver,
gold, 53–56
Vasilisa (Golden Braid) and Ivan
the Pea, 63–68
—Scriven / Full Color *
how to catch a leprechaun, 85–87
Rapunzel, 9–12

—Shah / Central Asia
princess imprisoned in mountain
of jade, 19–24
—Turkish / Walker
jackal shows crow: destroy
cheater by trick, 17–19
—Unicorn / Coville *
king would own unicorns; princess: they must be free, 24–37
princess, cat/prince, and conceited unicorn, 120–134
Unicorn in the maze (Lindholm),
7–22
—Williams-Ellis / Tales *
youngest sister saves her two bewitched sisters, 125–130
**CAPTIVE: enticement into volun-
tary captivity**
—Arabian / McCaughrean
animals tell lion of man's cruelty,
51–57
jinni tricked back into bottle by
fisherman, 29–35
—Arabian / Riordan (as above), 26–
37
—Cambodian / Carrison
four rogues pretend to be Buddhist monks, 36–48
woman tricked, endanger baby,
then robbed, 31–35
—Chaucer / Cohen *
Chauntecleer: vanity leads to
capture, 19–31
—Grimm / Complete *
cunning tailor: riddle, bear, princess, 525–528
musician promises to teach animals to play, 56–58
spirit in the bottle, 458–462
Tom Thumb, 187–193
Turnip, The, 637–640
—Grimm / Sixty *
Tom Thumb, 125–132
Turnip, The, 213–216

—Muddleheads / Harris
   Mink Being wants to marry hu-
      man princess, 5–25
—Turkish / Walker
   bear tricks (goat) kids; goat gets
      even, 4–7
   duck as judge: rabbit removed
      stone from wolf's back, 15
—Turkish (Art I) / Walker
   huge man-eating jinn enticed
      back into bottle, 60
CARAVAN
—Shah / Central Asia
   dream of Habeeb, 56–61
CARBUNCLE
—Precious Stones / Kunz, 395 (in-
      dex)
CARE/CARING
—Bomans / Wily *
   chest (casket symbol) and the
      student, 193–196
—Tree / Kerven *
   good sister: brother shares soul
      with mango tree, [20–21]
CARIBBEAN TALES
—Afro-American / Abrahams, 1–327
CARIBOU HOUSE
—Wolves / Lopez, 92–94 @
Carlson, Natalie Savage
—Childcraft 1 / Once *
   sheep with wooden collar, 147–
      157
CARNELIAN
—Precious Stones / Kunz, 395 (index)
CAROLINA BAYS
—Southern [legends] / Floyd, 61–63
Carp, see FISH: CARP.
CARPENTER
—Arabian / McCaughrean
   animals tell lion of man's cruelty,
      51–57
—Dramatized / Kamerman
   covetous councilman (tricked; re-
      turns gold), 504–513

ogre; guess name; carpenter's
      ear, 278–287
Carpet, Flying, see MAGIC TRANS-
      PORT.
CARPET-MAKER
—Shah / Central Asia
   dream of Habeeb, 56–61
Carroll, Lewis (pseud., 1832–1898)
—Childcraft 1 / Once *
   Alice: down the rabbit-hole, 238–
      253
—Lynn / Fantasy *
   bibliography (about the author),
      446–453
CART
—Manning / Cats *
   old man: caught cranes carry cart
      into sky; bear pulls cart, 91–96
CASCADE RANGE
—Earthmaker / Mayo *
   monster overeats and erupts,
      65 @
Casey at the bat (Thayer)
—Childcraft 3 / Stories * 128–130
CASTE
—Fahs / Old *
   Brahman, the universal being,
      189–192
CASTLE(-s)
   see also ARTHURIAN RO-
      MANCES; CADBURY CASTLE
—Crossley / British FT *
   Gruagach, Finn, and the Lady of
      the Green Gown, 228–243
—Ghosts / Cohen
   Glamis Castle, 100–106
—Grimm / Complete *
   goldfish gives magic castle to
      fisherman, 388–393
   hero must hold crystal ball before
      enchantress to free princess,
      798–801
—Knights / Heller-Headon, 70–73
   siege, 72–73

CASTLE DRACULA
—McNally / Dracula, 82–104 @
CASTLE MAIDEN
—Grimm / Legends (Ward), II:394 (index)
CAT(-s)
see also Aesop: Belling the cat
Bremen Town musicians
Puss in Boots
—Aesop / Reeves-Wilson *
cat to woman [per Venus], 61
—Allison / I'll Tell *
mice in council: belling the cat, 121
—Animals / Rowland, 182 (index)
—Beasts / McHargue, 57 @
—Chinese / Chin *
year of the rat [Chinese calendar], 157–167
—Clarkson / World *
cat went a-traveling (joined by other animals), 154–156
eats enormous quantity: animals, people, etc.; all escape, 223–225
how manx cat lost her tail, 329–331
man witnesses funeral of 'king o' the cats,' 210–211
—Clouston / Popular
Whittington; six versions, II.65–78
—Crossley / Animal (Grimm) *
cat/mouse partnership, 21–25
fox and cat; arrogance and modesty, 8–10
—Crossley / British FT *
Dildrum and Doldrum: king of the cats, 55–57
—Demi / Reflective *
ugly, jealous cat imitates beautiful cat, [18]
—Douglas / Magic *
white cat (enchanted princess), 69–83
—Grimm / Complete *

cat (princess) gives horse to miller's apprentice, 482–485
—Gullible Coyote / Malotki
coyote joins cats in dance challenge, 83–93
—Hall / Treasury *
Owl and the pussy-cat (Lear), 40–41
—Hamilton / People *
better "wait till Martin [ghost] comes," 133–137
—Jewish / Frankel
mouse wants not to share food with cat; God punishes, 41–42
—Jonsen / Trolls *
The trolls and the pussy cat [a white bear], 15–23
—Lang / Wilkins
Nunda, eater of people, 602–614
—Lester / Leopard *
why dogs chase cats, 21–26
—MacDonald / Sourcebook *
motif index, 589–590
—Manning / Cats *
imp becomes gigantic when threatened; shifts shape to cat, 16–18
Leeshy Cat saved by Vasily and his magic mirror, 37–50
Pussy Cat Twinkle sells fur (life) to wizard; saved by female cat, 19–28
small-small cat seeks advice on growing large, 126–127
witch abducts king's two children; Katchen the cat helps escape, 9–15
—Manning / Cauldron *
cat advises witch who makes self invisible, to steal farmer's eggs, 32–38
—O'Brien / Tales *
giant Trencross abducts princess; white cat helps rescue, 92–105

—Paxton / Belling *
   belling the cat (Aesop; a verse
      version), [6–9]
—Pellowski / Story *
   picture-drawing story, 48–51
—Rockwell / Puss *
   cat (white bear) on the dovrefell,
      71–79
—Russian / Afanasev, 657 (index)
—Trolls / Asbjornsen
   trolls invade each Christmas Eve;
      mistake white bear for cat, 51–
      52
—Unicorn / Coville *
   princess, cat/prince, and con-
      ceited unicorn, 120–134
—Water Buffalo (Chinese)
   cat teaches tiger, but not how to
      climb trees, 78–81
—Williams-Ellis / Tales *
   mice repel invaders; king ban-
      ishes cats, 45–54
—Witch Encyc / Guiley, 411 (index)
—Witches / Iosa *
   animals help kind children es-
      cape giant witch, 18–22
—Yep / Rainbow *
   cats and dogs as "natural ene-
      mies," 12–18
—Yolen / Shape Shift
   witchcraft; lore; transformations,
      43
—Zipes / Beauties *
   White cat (d'Aulnoy), 515–544
Cat and mouse in partnership
—Crossley / Animal (Grimm), 21
—Grimm / Complete * 21–23
—Grimm / Sixty * 64–66
Cat Johann
—Manning / Cats *
   kind witch raises foundling to be
      knight; cat a bewitched prince,
      111–117
Cat on the dovrefell

—Childcraft 1 / Once * 100–101
Catastrophes, see CALAMITIES.
CATERPILLAR
—Demi / Reflective *
   life a butterfly's dream, [22]
—Dramatized / Kamerman
   fierce creature bluffing, 3–6
—Leonardo / Fables *
   patience, 114
Catfish, see FISH: CATFISH.
CATHAY
—Speck / New World, 519 (index)
CATHOLIC CHURCH
   see also POPE
—Witch Encyc / Guiley, 411 (index)
CAT'S CRADLE
—Navajo Coyote / Haile, 20–21 @
—Pellowski / Story *
   string-story; two versions, 31–40
CATTLE
—Corrin / Imagine *
   Onsongo, lazy artist, steals
      Masai cattle for dowry, 80–96
—Russian / Ivanits, 246 (index)
CAULDRON
—Witch Encyc / Guiley, 411 (index)
CAUSE and EFFECT
—Jewish / Sadeh
   bread cast upon the water, 28–31
—Paxton / Aesop *
   boy who cried wolf, [33–35]
—Turkish / Walker
   boasting mouse misunderstands
      natural phenomena, 1–3
   mosquito "hurts" water buffalo, 14
CAUTION
—Allison / I'll Tell *
   fisherman and little fish (bird in
      hand . . .), 104
—Yep / Rainbow *
   Bedtime snacks, 4–10
CAVE
—Jewish / Sadeh
   Father Abraham, 34–35

—Southern [legends] / Floyd
lost sea (Tenn.), 64–67
Rock Oven (Georgia), 68–71
Caylus, Philippe de (1692–1765)
—Lang / Wilkins
Fairy gifts, 186–189
Heart of ice, 190–219
Sylvain and Jocosa, 178–185
—Zipes / Beauties *
Princess Minute and King Floridor, 253–257
CELTIC MYTH(-s; -ology) / TALES
—Campbell / West Highlands, v.I-IV
—Celtic / MacCana, 1–143
heroic tradition, 94–113
sources, 14–16
—Cotterell / Encyclopedia, 26–27 @
—Dict / Leach, 1204
—Ellis / Dict Irish Myth, 1–240
—Legends / Cavendish, 6 (index)
—Man Myth & Magic, 3120 (index)
—Mercatante / Encyclopedia, 727 (index)
CEMETERY
—High John / Sanfield *
overhears the Lord and Devil "dividing up souls," 44–49
—Turkish / Walker
Deli feigns death, frightens thieves, gets reward, 80–84
Cengidilaver
—Turkish (Art I) / Walker, 1–10
CENTAUR
—Creatures (illus) / Huber * 155 (index)
—South / Mythical
sources; bibliographical essay, 225–239 (Kollmann), 380 (index)
CENTIPEDE
—Yep / Rainbow *
We are all one, 72–78
CENTRAL AMERICA
—Cotterell / Encyclopedia, 42–43 @

CEREMONIES
—Mesoamerican / Leon-P, 288 (index)
CERES
—Douglas / Magic *
Cupid and Psyche, 151–165
—Greek / Osborne
kidnapping: Ceres and Proserpina, 35–39
CHAC (rain-god)
—Bierhorst / Monkey *
Lord Sun courts woman; succeeds over father's objections, 84–91
CHAIN TALE(-s)
see also CUMULATIVE TALES
—Bierhorst / Monkey *
monkey's haircut; steals razor, gives to butcher; takes guitar, 138–143
—Cambodian / Carrison
series of thefts; cheater cheated, 58–64
—Childcraft 1 / Once *
foolish, timid rabbit: "earth breaking up," 166–168
the house that Jack built, 58–59
why mosquitoes buzz in people's ears, 130–136
—Childcraft 2 / Time *
old lady who swallowed a fly (folksong) 206–211
—Childcraft 3 / Stories *
Baba Yaga's geese abduct girl's brother, 114–118
—Clarkson / World *
cat eats enormous quantity: animals, people, etc.; all escape, 223–225
talk (by yam, dog, tree, stone, etc.), 229–232
—Crossley / British FT *
Eagle asks all animals: which one is oldest? 178–181

—Grimm / Complete *
  cock, hen *et al* attack Herr
    Korbes, 205–206
  death of the little hen, 365–367
  louse and the flea, 158–160
—Hopi Coyote / Malotki
  five uncles: Coyote Boy marries
    Musangnuvi Girl, 229–283
—Jewish / Frankel
  dim-witted boy buys box of bones
    (chain tale), 414–418
  foolish imaginings: "what if" dis-
    asters as real, 571–573
  Had Gadya, 387–388
  mouse seeks a wife (fable), 463–
    465
—Manning / Cats *
  water-pool: boy, hare, fox, wolf,
    bear vs. Baba Yaga, 58–64
—Manning / Cauldron *
  witch's flute: goatherd can't stop
    playing; goats and people can't
    stop dancing, 99–105
—Old Wives / Carter
  woman questions Sun in behalf
    of spinsters, cold woman, river,
    rock, 4–7
—Trolls / Asbjornsen
  cock would aid hen with nut stuck
    in throat, 22–24
—Turkish (Art I) / Walker
  community mourning for Brother
    Louse, 58–59
  Tekerleme; a tall tale, 11
—Williams-Ellis / Tales *
  Johnny-Cake runs away from all
    but fox, 96–101
  Little Weasel's series of trades,
    102–112

CHAIR
—Restless / Cohen *
  Holland: death and tragedy fol-
    low haunted hooded-chair, 94–
    102

CHALDEANS
—Babylonia / Spence, 389 (index)
CHAMELEON
—Hamilton / In the Beginning *
  Olorun, sky god, 72–77 (illus. p.
    75)
CHANCE (*motif index*)
—MacDonald / Sourcebook * 328–
  339
—Palestinian / Speak (Muhawi), 398
CHANGE (*often magical*)
—Aesop / Zwerger
  moon [always changing] and her
    [dressmaker] mother, 23
—Celts / Hodges *
  Dermot; ugly woman becomes
    beautiful, 57–73
—Lore of Love
  King Nala and Princess Damay-
    anti, 110–119
—Yep / Rainbow *
  Breaker's bridge, 118–123
CHANGELING(-s)
—Crossley / British FT *
  fairies steal newborn child, leave
    devil in his place, 212–214
—Fairies / Briggs, 69–72
—Grimm / Complete *
  elves: child made to laugh * 200
—Grimm / Legends (Ward), II:395 (in-
  dex)
—Scandinavian / Kvideland, 426 (in-
  dex)
—Scary / Young *
  to steal baby, goblin's arms grow
    longer/longer; cross saves,
    43–46
—Yep / Rainbow *
  husband kidnapped by ghosts,
    162–168
CHANGING-BEAR MAIDEN
—Navajo Coyote / Haile
  Coyote's widow transformed to
    monster bear, 16, 82–84

Chanticleer and Pertelette
—Corrin / Six-Year * 195–198
—Grimm / Sixty * 74–79
CHANTS
—Pellowski / Story *
   picture-drawing story, 56–57
CHANUKAH
—Aleichem / Holiday *
   Benny's luck: boy cheats friends,
   playing with dreydl, 17–44
Chapman, Vera
—Pendragon / Ashley
   The King's damosel: Lynette,
   120–203
CHARACTER (-traits; -types)
—Jewish / Frankel, 643–644 (index)
—MacDonald / Sourcebook *
   motif index, 369–374
—Tibet / Timpanelli *
   girl who was already queen, 43–
   51
CHARACTER: *favorable traits*
—Cambodian / Carrison
   poor cook's helper says he's rich
   as king, 77–78
—Fahs / Old *
   struggle: boy half-good, half-bad,
   1–6
—Hall / Treasury *
   Little Engine that could, 1–9
—Hoke / Giants
   Hercules and the golden apples,
   130–132
—Old Wives / Carter
   Nourie Hadig tells her tragic story
   to Stone of Patience, 192–199
—Spanish-Am / Van Etten *
   wise woman asks three sisters:
   why do you clear your field?
   52–53
—Starkey / Ghosts
   "Dauntless girl," 72–79
—Wilde / Happy *
   happy prince [statue sends swallow with jewels for poor], 15–
   38
—Yep / Rainbow *
   beggar woman: child of calamity,
   46–52
CHARACTER: *unfavorable traits*
—Caduto / Keepers *
   Loo-Wit, the fire-keeper, 41–43
—Curry / Beforetime *
   animals build mountains, to be rid
   of coyote, 22–25
—Geras / Grandmother *
   complainer (kvetch) chooses her
   own misery, 66–76
—Grimm / Complete *
   bittern and the hoopoe, 710–711
—Spanish-Am / Van Etten *
   angry reply: clearing field to
   "grow more stones," 52–53
—Yep / Rainbow *
   The homecoming, 144–151
   "Snake-spoke," 86–95
CHARIOT
—Bell / Classical Dict, 44–47 @
CHARITY
   see also LOVE
—Bomans / Wily *
   evils wanted by four generations
   of wizards; people turn it to
   good, 71–75
—Grimm / Complete *
   star-money: poor girl gives all
   away, 652–654
   three sisters encounter St. Joseph, 815–818
—Jewish / Frankel, 648 (index)
   cast your bread upon the waters,
   385–387
   Elijah: gift of seven years of prosperity, 585–586
   money hidden in tree: Abraham
   the Carpenter, 380–381
   Rabbi Zusya: two kinds of gifts,
   514

Reb Haim and the three lawsuits, 506–509

second chance: wheel of fortune, 492–493

Yossele, the holy miser, gives secretly, as God gives, 557–560

—Jewish / Sadeh

impious tailor trades clothes with pauper, 337

mice that ate the iron, 317–318

miser: eternally dirty pastry, 169

rich man prepared for rainy day, 178–179

saves peddler's wife from foreordained death, 335–336

valuable ring given by mistake, 374

—Turkish (Art I) / Walker

three "reformed" brigands granted wishes; two fail test, 155–159

—Wilde / Lynch *

happy prince: statue persuades swallow to help aid the poor, 41–54

CHARLEMAGNE (742–814)

—Legends / Cavendish, 6 (index)

CHARM(-s) (magic)

—Folk-rhymes / Northall

England, 125–159

—Ghosts / Starkey

hair: Draiglin' Hogney defeated by youngest brother, 80–87

—Lang / Wilkins

singing protects betrothed from yara (fairies), 474–484

—Russian / Ivanits, 246 (index)

—Vanishing / Mercer *

quest for wife abducted by giant bird, 42–49

—Witch Encyc / Guiley, 411 (index)

—Yep / Rainbow *

foolish boy: "Snake-spoke," 86–95

holy fool: The butterfly man, 60–68

Charmed life, or Princess and Liftman

—Nesbit / Fairy * 25–42

CHARMING (a character)

—Lang / Wilkins

Charming wins Goldilocks, 31–43

CHARYBDIS

—Gods / Schwab, 749 (index)

CHASE

see also ESCAPE . . .

—Allison / I'll Tell *

gingerbread boy, 22–23

CHASTITY (including tests)

—Clouston / Popular

virtuous wife, importunate suitors, II.289–316

of women, I.173–181

—Jewish / Sadeh

bride auctioned; bought by prince; chastity test, 332–333

—Trolls / Asbjornsen

goose-girl: "meant" to marry Prince of England, 60–63

Chaucer, Geoffrey (1345–1400) [by]

—Chaucer / Cohen *

franklin's tale, 67–84

nun's tale: Chauntecleer and Pertelote, 19–31

wife of Bath: must choose, 55–63

—Corrin / Six-Year *

Chanticleer and Pertelette, 195–198

CHAUCER, Geoffrey (1345–1400) [about]

—Animals / Rowland, 182 (index)

—Bird Symbol / Rowland, 202 (index)

—Clouston / Popular

Pardoner's tale: avarice and murder, II.379–412

—Fairies / Briggs

Wife of Bath's tale, 432–434

—Mercatante / Encyclopedia, 752 (index)

Chauntecleer and Pertelote
—Chaucer / Cohen * 19–31

CHEAT(-s; -ing)
—Bryan / Lion *
hide and seek: Jackal's favorite game, 40–59
—Caduto / Keepers *
coyote takes payment back, 57–59
Old Man Coyote and Grandfather Rock, 57–59
—Clouston / Popular
sharpers and the simpleton, II.27–42
tailor's dream; versions, II.79–85
three travellers and the loaf; et al., II.86–98
—Fahs / Old *
moon's origin: boy cheats at ball-game, 81–83
—Grimm / Complete *
musician promises to teach animals to play, 56–58
—Harris-Parks / Jump *
Brer Terrapin "wins" race with Brer Rabbit, 19–24
—High John / Sanfield *
Old Boss cheats ("de-ducks") John the sharecropper, 80–83
—Jaffrey / Seasons
king beaten with magic stick for taking magic bowl from old man, 103–109
—MacDonald / Sourcebook *
motif index, 279–280
—Starkey / Ghosts
"Dauntless girl," 72–79

CHEATER-CHEATED
—Clouston / Popular
lost purse; amount of money overstated, II.367–371
—Coyote / Bierhorst *

blind woman cured, but coyote steals all her possessions, [28]
—Jewish / Sadeh
two shopkeepers, eagle, mountain of gold, 271–273
—Turkish / Walker
jackel shows crow: destroy cheater by trick, 17–19
survive cold night; candle 100 meters away, 47–48

CHEESE
—Jonsen / Trolls *
stone cheese [troll tricked by youngest son], [24–32]

CHEETAH
—Greaves / Hippo * 33–34 @
how cheetah got his speed, 28–29
why cheetah's cheeks are tear-stained, 29–33

CHELM
—Jewish / Frankel, xvi (index)

Chermak, Sylvia
—Dramatized / Kamerman
Peter and the wolf, 375–380

CHERRY of Zennor
—Fairies / Briggs, 72–73

CHESS
—Jewish / Frankel
Solomon, 225–228
—Spring / Philip
dragon seen by unprotected men, 119–133
—Tall Tales / Downs: Bear
chess-machine in bar / E.B. White, 19–23
—Vietnam / Terada *
chess player dies; enters body of newly dead butcher, 75–77
—Yep / Rainbow *
after thousands of years: homecoming, 144–151

CHEST
—Lang / Wilkins

princess in the chest; faithful
guard, 369–384

CHESTNUT
—Bierhorst / Naked *
chestnut pudding: magic food
supply, 3–10

CHICKEN(-s)
see also HEN; ROOSTER
—Aesop / Alley *
daydreams: milkmaid and her
pail, 10–13
—Grimm / Complete *
crumbs on the table, 768
—MacDonald / Sourcebook *
motif index, 592–593
—Russian / Ivanits, 246 (index)

Chicken Licken
—Jones / Tales *
"sky is falling!" 16–20

Chicken Little
—Hall / Treasury * 80–83

CHILD(-ren)
see also BABY; DAUGHTER;
PARENT; etc.
—Am Child / Bronner, 1–281
—Baring-Gould / Curious
Piper of Hamelin: souls of children in the wind, 116–120 @
—Bomans / Wily *
each year witch takes two naughtiest children in Finland, 27–
36
return: rich man tries to restore
his childhood home, 76–78
—Bruchac / Iroquois *
monstrous, two-headed snake a
traitor, 97–102
—Cambodian / Carrison
lost, king tells child how to recognize a king, 86–89
—Celts / Hodges *
how Finn MacCool got his wisdom tooth, 34–52
—Chinese / Chin *

palace plot: cat put in place of
baby, 77–92
—Chorao / Child's *
Pied Piper (rat agreement broken), 51–55
—Clouston / Popular
precocious, II.12–14
—Dulac / Fairy *
Finn, and Queen of many-colored
bedchamber, 69–76
Snegorotchka: lives one winter,
melts in spring, 1–6
—Ghosts / Starkey
Whuppity Stoorie [promised un-
wittingly], 44–51
—Ghosts / Time-Life
utburd (child exposed to die), 38–
41
—Grimm / Complete *
Eve's various children: God bestows blessings unequally,
734–736
—Grimm / Legends (Ward), II:396 (index)
—Hopi Coyote / Malotki
coyote rescues children captured
by ogre, 179–193
—Igloo / Metayer
bear kills mother, raises her child,
118–121
child-killer escapes as shooting
star, 70–72
—Imaginary / Nigg
lost: king/queen and the hatthilinga, 109–111
—Jewish / Sadeh
dead child returns to earth to
atone for "Christian milk," 192–
194
learning wisdom from (three
ways), 363
—Legends / Cavendish
exposure and rescue, 400 (index)
fostering, training, 401 (index)

—Leonardo / Fables *
monkey and baby bird [child rearing], 98
—Lester / Leopard *
speaking harshly to; eyes filled with tears, 37–39
woman and the tree children, 37–39
—MacDonald / Sourcebook *
motif index, 593–594
—Russian / Ivanits, 246 (index)
—Scary / Young *
golem brought to life; answer children's questions (humor), 17–20
—Wilde / Happy *
selfish giant (children bring spring to garden), 59–69
—Wilde / Lynch *
selfish giant: always winter, 6–13
—Williams-Ellis / Tales *
magic bird unplows field, gives milk, lures children, 62–76
—Yolen / Faery Flag
faery flag (shawl); (fairy/mother returns), 3–11
foxwife (father's tears make "foxcubs" human), 12–20
CHILD(-ren), ABANDONED (- murdered)
see also Babes in the wood; Hansel and Gretel
—Animal Legends / Kerven *
mother bear adopts abandoned boy, [8–9]
—Arabian / Lewis
abandoned children (grown) restored, 166–173
—Arabian / Riordan
abandoned children, 78–87
—Bierhorst / Monkey *
giant takes, marries girl, tries to kill her brother, 92–93
—Bierhorst / Naked *

Porcupine's grandson [abandoned boy], 93–100
—Bruchac / Iroquois *
boy who lived with the bears (save human life), 24–30
—Carter / Sleeping *
Hop o' my Thumb, 69–80
—Crane / Beauty *
Princess Belle-Etoile, [21–33]
—Crane / McLean *
Princess Belle-Etoile; evil Queen, 16–27
—Lang / Wilkins
fate of king's son: marry a slave, 513–527
—Lewis / Proud
Le Fresne: twin "found" at sister's wedding, 20–28
—Lore of Love
Sir Eglamour and Lady Chrystobel, 128–139
—Old Wives / Carter
Nourie Hadig: ordered killed by jealous mother, 192–199
—Shah / Central Asia
prince who married a peri (fairy), 49–55
—Spanish-Am / Van Etten *
evil, elder sisters dispose of youngest's infants, 78–80
—Turkish (Art I) / Walker
Cengidilaver: abandoned children rescued by miller, 1–10
Child(-ren), Abducted, see ABDUCTION.
Child(-ren), Abused, see ABUSED CHILD.
CHILD(-ren): BIRTH
—Bell / Classical Dict, 48–50 @
—Bierhorst / Sacred
Indian women in labor; prayer/songs, 13, 137
—Davidson / Dictionary

amulet angels (seventy) invoked (list), 346–347
—Jewish / Frankel, 648 (index)
—Lore of Love
taboo: ill-starred mating of earth and sea, 87–95
—Lurker / Dict Gods, 395 (index)
—Mercatante / Encyclopedia, 753 (index)
CHILD(-ren): CHILDLESSNESS
—Jaffrey / Seasons
King Rudra, without heir, marries seven sisters, 110–114
—Jewish / Frankel, 648 (index)
punishment of man who breaks betrothal vow, 523–527
—Jewish / Sadeh
dead fiancee [apparition], 14–17
Jewish pope; bastard converts to Catholicism, 195–197
CHILD(-ren): LITERATURE FOR
—Wildlife / Gillespie, 244 (index)
CHILD(-ren): NURTURE and GROWTH
—Bryan / Lion *
Jumoke ("Foolish Boy") outwits Ananse, 60–86
—Cambodian / Carrison
guards propose punishment for treacherous prince, 73–76
—Childcraft 3 / Stories *
Anansi gives away his share of plantains, 108–113
Duny: boy who became a wizard (Le Guin), 176–186
—Egyptian / Harris
judgment by King of the Dead, 103–107
—Jaffrey / Seasons
how Ram, son of Dashrat, defeated demon king Ravan, 48–69
—Lang / Wilkins
Heart of ice (Caylus), 190–219

—Quayle / Shining *
mother's mirror warns Sachiko of stepmother in rat-form, 90–96
—Turkish / Walker
Hamal Hasan (porter) has trouble carrying babies, 123–126
CHILD(-ren): SUBSTITUTED
—Chinese / Chin *
palace plot: cat put in place of baby, 77–92
—Dramatized / Kamerman
peach tree kingdom; imposter, 288–305
—Grimm / Complete *
Elves: changeling, 200
—Lang / Wilkins
Grateful prince: girl helps hero escape old man, 394–414
—Turkish (Art I) / Walker
Cengidilaver: pups substituted for newborn twins, 1–10
Childe Rowland and Burd Ellen
—Hamilton / Dark * 65–72
—Williams-Ellis / Tales *
rescues Burd Ellen from Elfland, 24–36
CHIMERA [or] CHIMAERA
—Animals / Rowland, 54–58 @
—Creatures (illus) / Huber * 155 (index)
—South / Mythical
sources; bibliographical essay, 103–111, 381 (index)
CHIMNEY SWEEP
—Bomans / Wily *
chimney sweep's curse (personified) captured by curate, 93–96
CHINA
—Chinese / Christie
Han dynasty, 142 (index)
—Creatures (illus) / Huber * 82–93
—Dictionary / Leach, 1205 (index)
—Hamilton / In the Beginning *
Phan Ku: creation myth, 20–23

—Lynn / Fantasy * 747–748 (index)
—Man Myth & Magic, 3121 (index)
—Unicorn / Hathaway
  ancient; the unicorn, 41–51 @
CHINESE in AMERICA
—Yep / Rainbow *
  comfort for immigrants: Slippers,
  162–168
CHINESE MYTH / TALES
—Animal Legends / Kerven *
  mynah bird's revenge, [20–21]
—Chinese / Chin * 1–180
—Chinese / Christie, 1–144
  sources, 41–50
—Constellations / Gallant * 200 (in-
  dex)
—Corrin / Imagine *
  The living Kuan-Yin, 136–141
—Dramatized / Kamerman
  Lady Moon and the thief, 23–31
  Plum Blossom and the dragon,
  38–46
—Earth / Hadley *
  storm: Lin maiden (ghost) guides
  lost seamen to safety, [27–28]
—Fahs / Old *
  daughter saves father from pun-
  ishment by mutilation, 133–
  138
  magic pillow: dream projects future life, 121–124
—Frog Rider (Chinese)
  nine tales (Han, Tibetan, Uygur,
  etc), 1–140
—Hamilton / Dark *
  Ho Hsien Ku becomes immortal,
  73–75
—Journey Sun (Chinese)
  nine tales (Zhuang, Nong, Bai,
  Han, etc), 1–140
—Journeys / Norris *
  journey to hell/heaven and back,
  [26–28]
—Legends / Cavendish, 5 (index)

—Lore of Love
  deity keeps book; all are foreordained, 18–23
—Mercatante / Encyclopedia, 727 (index)
—Mercatante / Good/Evil, 127–135 @
—Old Wives / Carter
  Mrs. Number Three, 155–157
—Restless / Cohen *
  demon corpse: unburied body becomes monster-ghost, 52–59
—Spring / Philip
  ethnic (non-Chinese) groups, 7–
  9 @
  minority peoples in China, 1–144
—Water Buffalo (Chinese)
  twenty-two tales (Tibetan, Han,
  etc), 1–115
—Williams-Ellis / Tales *
  Sister Long-Hair steals stream
  from mountain god, 161–171
—Yep / Rainbow *
  Chinese America (four tales),
  116–151
  fools (four tales), 36–68
  love (four tales), 152–190
  tricksters (three tales), 1–35
  virtues and vices (five tales), 69–
  115
CHIPMUNK
—Bruchac / Iroquois *
  chipmunk ridicules bear, and
  pays, 37–39
—Hopi / Talashoma-Malotki
  Hopi boy and his two pet eagles,
  150–199
CHIRON
—Lore of Love
  groom for the sea-lord's daughter, 8–15
CHIVALRY
—Celts / Hodges *
  Gareth of Orkney wins his spurs,
  133–154

142

CHOICES
—Caduto / Keepers *
  small inconvenience, large gain:
  Gluscabi and Wind Eagle, 67–
  71
—Chaucer / Cohen *
  wife of Bath: must choose (good
  or beautiful), 55–63
—Douglas / Magic *
  choice: goodness or appearance; Beauty and the Beast,
  85–97
—Geras / Grandmother *
  woman chooses her own misery
  over that of others, 66–76
—Hoke / Giants
  choices; advice not heeded =
  ruin, 112–118
—Old Wives / Carter
  Maol a Chliobain repeatedly gets
  better of giant, 24–27
  she-ghoul: wife and children flee;
  man does not believe danger;
  is eaten, 216–220
—Russian Hero / Warner *
  Alesha (priest's son) battles Tu-
  garin, 72–76
—Unicorn / Coville *
  quest for unicorn horn: cure of
  winter sickness, 136–155
CHRETIEN de Troyes (fl.1160–90)
—Barber / Anthology
  Yvain, or the Knight with the Lion,
  53–71
—Lacy / Arth Ency, 104–110
CHRISTENING
—Nielsen / Old Tales *
  godmother keeps baby, [5–15]
CHRISTIAN CHURCHES
—Dictionary / Leach, 1205 (index)
CHRISTIAN LITERATURE
—Lycanthropy / Otten
  Housman: The were-wolf (alle-
  gory), 281–320

CHRISTIAN MYTHS
—Christian / Every, 1–144
—Legends / Cavendish, 422 (in-
  dex)
—Mercatante / Encyclopedia, 727–
  729 (index)
—Mercatante / Good/Evil, 49–60,
  234 (index)
CHRISTIANITY
—Man Myth & Magic, 3121 (index)
—Roman / Perowne
  Roman mythology and, 128–
  141 @
—Scandinavian / Davidson
  Scandinavian paganism, 124–
  140
—Unnatural / Cohen, 145 (index)
CHRISTIANITY and PAGANISM
—Baring-Gould / Curious
  Mountain of Venus, 78–82 @
CHRISTIANITY and POLITICS
—Bomans / Wily *
  satire: twelfth king (has hollow
  [brainless] head), 185–192
CHRISTMAS (including stories)
  see also MAGI
—American / Read Dgst
  miracle-gift: the Margil vine, 67–
  68
—Bomans / Wily *
  man with "Xmas spirit" turns
  away couple seeking shelter,
  174–175
  odyssey of the Christmas tree an-
  gel, 181–185
—Ghosts / Cohen, 269–273
—Grimm / Legends (Ward), II:397 (index)
—Jonsen / Trolls *
  trolls and the pussy cat [a white
  bear], 15–23
—Lynn / Fantasy * 748 (index)
—Scarry's Best *
  Bad twins, The, [39–42]

Best Christmas present ever, [25–28]
Big Hilda helps Santa, [21–24]
Christmas is coming! [5–8]
Dr. Bones is good all year round, [9–10]
Grouchy Mr. Gronkle, [11–14]
Mr. Frumble helps out, [29–33]
Postman Pig and Aunt Kitty, [15–16]
Trouble at Santa's workshop, [17–20]
Visit to grandma's house (game), [35–38]
What to give grandma for Christmas? [34]
words of Christmas, [43–44]
CHRISTMAS EVE
—Ghosts / Starkey
Black Annis (witch) defeated, 52–57
—Rockwell / Puss *
cat (white bear) on the dovrefell, 71–79
—Williams-Ellis / Tales *
trolls driven away by bear ("great white cat"), 17–23
CHRISTMAS GIFTS
—Nesbit / Fairy *
town in the library, 81–98
Christmas tree
—Bedtime / Padoan & Smith * 177–179
CHURCH(-es) (buildings)
—Crossley / British FT *
John Chapman, pedlar of Swaffham, 251–264
—Fairies / Briggs
foul-weather, 179–180
—Ghosts / Starkey
Broder Menine: expiation for crime, 16–23
—Grimm / Complete *

peasant boy thinks church is heaven, 828–829
—Grimm / Legends (Ward), II:397 (index)
—Scandinavian / Kvideland, xvii, 426 (index)
CHURCH SERVICE
—Quayle / Cornish *
borne by tidal wave, mermaid meets/mates carpenter-singer, 51–63
CHURCHMEN
—Jewish / Frankel
Rabbi's mirror allows king to see treachery in his bedroom, 405–409
CIBOLA
—Floyd / Gr Am Myst
the Seven Cities of Cibola, 33–38
—Speck / New World, 129–232
CICADA
—Hopi Coyote / Malotki
hawk eats all her children; coyote would learn her dirge, 105–111
CICERO, Marcus Tullius (106–43 b.c.)
—Roman / Perowne, 78–86 @
CID (= EL CID)
—Knights / Heller-Headon, 60–69
—Legends / Cavendish, 249–253
Cihansah and Semsi Bani
—Turkish (Art I) / Walker, 207–217
CIMIDYUE
—Legends / Cavendish, 354–356
Cinderella (Ashenputtel)
—Allison / I'll Tell * 50–52
—Bedtime / Padoan & Smith * 1–3
—Carter / Sleeping * 103–112
—Childcraft 1 / Once * 122–129
—Chorao / Childs FTB * 53–62
—Corrin / Favourite * 50–58
—Douglas / Magic * 109–117
—Grimm / Complete * 121–128
—Grimm / Sixty, 31, 188–196

—Hall / Treasury * 98–101

—Lang / Wilkins, 18–26

—Leete / Golden * 108–123

—Lynn / Fantasy *

adaptations, 748 (index)

—Scriven / Full Color * 69–73

—Strauss / Trail

reflections before Prince arrives

(poem), 18–19

—Zipes / Beauties * 25–30

Cinderella (*existential retelling*)

—Switzer / Existential, 38–45

CINDERELLA-TYPE TALES

—Brooke / Telling *

prince marries Cinderella albeit

slipper doesn't fit, 51–74

—Chinese / Chin *

golden carp (killed, bones do

magic for friend), 47–57

—Clarkson / World *

Indian Cinderella: Strong Wind

will marry truthful girl, 43–45

CIRCLE

—Russian / Ivanits, 246 (index)

CIRCUMCISION

—Jewish / Sadeh

accept demon's gift: fall into his

net, 169–172

Baal Shem Tov: Elijah comes to

every circumcision, 128–

129

—Schwartz / Gates, 799 (index)

CITY, EXTRAORDINARY

—Celts / Hodges *

Bells of Ys, 104–114

City mouse . . . *see* Aesop: Town

mouse . . .

CIVIL WAR (U.S.)

—American / Read Dgst, 287–303,

435 (index)

—Civil War Ghosts, 1–205

CLAIRVOYANCE

—High John / Sanfield *

eavesdrops on Master; pretends

foreknowledge of his plans,

24–33

—Occult & Parapsych / Shepard,

1590–91 (index)

**CLASSICAL MYTH(-ology): diction-
aries**

—Bell / Classical Dict, 1–390 @

—Grimal / Concise, 1–456

—Grimal / Dictionary, 1–603 @

—Preston / Dict Classical

in visual art, 1–311 @

—Room / Classical Dict, 1–343 @

CLERGY

—Bomans / Wily *

world-ending flood: clergy argue

about biblical text, 107–108

—Ghosts / Starkey

laying Black Lucott's ghost, 116–

123

CLEVER(-ness)

—Aesop / Reeves-Wilson *

fox tricks cock and vice versa,

115–117

thirsty Crow and pitcher, 99–100

—Allison / I'll Tell *

crow finds way to get to water in

pitcher, 109

—Bruchac / Iroquois *

Skunny-Wundy defeats the

Stone Giants, 161–167

—Cambodian / Carrison

rooster foils polecat's plan to eat

him, 49–51

—Carle / Treasury *

wolf falls for lamb's "last re-

quest": play music (Aesop),

108–9

—Childcraft 1 / Once *

turtle "killed" by being thrown into

water, 172–173

—Clarkson / World *

clever Manka (solves riddles;

problem-tasks), 93–95

—Clouston / Popular

clever thief tales: cobbler and
calf, etc, II.43–52
precocious children, II.12–14
—Corrin / Imagine *
Onsongo distracts Masai herds-
men; horn hidden, tied to
crane's leg, 80–96
—Coyote / Bierhorst *
pays to be clever when you're the
weaker one, [14]
—Douglas / Magic *
fisherman's promise to genie,
13–19
—Erdoes / Sound *
Iktome invited to dinner, 31–32
—Ghosts / Starkey
Tammy escapes from Lucky Min-
nie (troll), 110–115
—Hamilton / People *
Big John forces Little John, 81–
89
—Harris-Parks / Again
Brers Mink-Possum-Coon-Fox-
Bear guard butter, 14–21
Miss Wolf (Brer Wolf's niece) and
mosquitoes, 22–29
—Hoke / Giants
Quillo defeats tyrannical giant
Hundar, 41–64
—Jewish / Frankel
king and: contented simple man,
dissatisfied clever man, 538–
544
—Jewish / Sadeh
contest: champion of hot pepper,
296
man who agreed to be Moses,
298
master thief, 291–295
—Jones / Tales *
The three billy goats Gruff, 42–
44
—Lester / Brer Rabbit *
outwits Mr. Man, 137–141

—Lester / Leopard *
contest: how many spots does
leopard have? 53–57
—MacDonald / Sourcebook *
motif index, 219–234
—Paxton / Aesop *
poor old lion (eats animal-visitors), [14–15]
—Paxton / Belling *
crow and the pitcher (Aesop),
[22–23]
—Quayle / Shining *
white hare tricks crocodiles; revenge; kind prince heals hare,
24–32
—Shannon / More *
cock crow in kettle: clean hand
reveals thief, 31–34
devil will spare man as long as
candle "lasts," [not "burns"],
27–30
—Spring / Philip
king "never heard of this before,"
134–139
Tibetan envoy wins princess, 42–
49
—Turkish / Walker
bet lost; cook with candle one
meter from pot, 47–48
—Williams-Ellis / Tales *
Mr. Miacca would eat boy, 131–
133
—Witches / Iosa *
brothers envious of Pinkel's favor
with king, 23–31
CLEVER DETECTION OF TRUTH
—Geras / Grandmother *
tablecloth: rabbi determines
owner, 31–40
—Journey Sun (Chinese)
Fanjiangshan secures justice;
three episodes, 90–108
CLEVER DIVIDING
—Arabian / Lewis

glutton feigns message from
small fish, 210
—Arabian / McCaughrean, (as
above), 194–197
—Spanish-Am / Van Etten *
chicken dinner: guest divides,
keeps best part for self, 42–43
Clever Elsa
—Grimm / Complete * 171–174
—Grimm / Sixty * 177–181
Clever Grethel
—Grimm / Complete * 360–363
—Grimm / Sixty * 138–140
—Old Wives / Carter, 89–91
—Scriven / Full Color * 65
Clever Hans
—Grimm / Complete * 166–168
—Grimm / Sixty * 217–222
CLEVER JUDICIAL DECISIONS
—Arabian / Lewis
Scheherazod escapes execution
by storytelling, 6–9
—Arabian / McCaughrean (as
above), 1–9, 243–249
—Arabian / Riordan (as above)
merchant's life saved by story-
telling, 100–107
Scheherazod escapes (as
above), 8–11
—Clarkson / World *
judge: tiger cured of snakebite
threatens to eat man, 309–312
—Dramatized / Kamerman
baker would charge man for
smelling bakery, 471–480
—Spring / Philip
wise king exposes gold thief, 50–
57
—Turkish (Art I) / Walker
woodcutter's wife, once a mighty
warrior disguised as man, 200–
204
CLEVER LAW COURT
—Chinese / Chin *

palace plot: cat put in place of
baby, 77–92
—Corrin / Imagine *
goldsmith steals woodcarver-
friend's gold; woodcarver
"turns" goldsmith's children
into bears, 23–46
—Dramatized / Kamerman
Olive jar, 360–374
—Starkey / Ghosts
Tregeagle's ghost, 58–65
**Clever Manka [riddle re swift-
est . . .]**
—Childcraft 3 / Stories * 120–127
**CLEVER MEANS OF AVOIDING LE-
GAL PUNISHMENT**
—Egyptian / Harris
clever thief: treasure of
Rhumpsinitus, 114–116
—Shannon / More *
students outwit king's ruse for ex-
posing thief, 47–50
—Turkish (Art I) / Walker
poor man taken to court for three
disasters; complaints with-
drawn, 168–172
**CLEVER MEANS OF AVOIDING
PUNISHMENT**
—Bomans / Wily *
knight's three tasks: kill dragon,
defeat witch, be grateful, 197–
202
—Chinese / Chin *
clever daughter-in-law, 3–14
—Crossley / Animal (Grimm) *
fox helps old horse, 34–38
—Grimm / Complete *
master-thief given three tasks,
773–780
shepherd boy adopted by king,
651–652
three sons of fortune (trade for
gold), 342–344
—Shannon / More *

firefly defeats 100 club-wielding apes, 19–22

Clever peasant girl [riddles; values]
—Corrin / Imagine * 116–123

CLEVER PERSONS
see also BUNYAN, Paul; SOLO-MON
—Chinese / Chin *
clever daughter-in-law, 3–14
monkey: on road to fetch scriptures, 95–110
—Corrin / Eight-Year *
Little Claus and Big Claus, 13–26
—Earth / Hadley *
climbing to heaven on a pole, [8–9]
—Grimm / Complete *
cunning tailor: riddle, bear, princess, 525–528
little peasant, 311–316
—Grimm / Sixty *
little peasant, 142–148
—Rockwell / Puss *
nail soup [series of small lies], 12–18
—Spring / Philip
king "never heard of this before," 134–139
Tibetan envoy wins princess, 42–49
—Starkey / Ghosts
Tammy escapes from Lucky Minnie (troll), 110–115
—Turkish / Walker
fat sultan condemns doctors who can't cure him, 127–131
—Turkish (Art I) / Walker
man called "donkey"—doesn't smoke, drink, or sport with women, 176–177
—Williams-Ellis / Tales *
master thief, 77–95
—Yep / Rainbow *

gambler: "Professor of smells," 20–35

CLEVER PLEADING
—Dramatized / Kamerman
The price of eggs, 149–154
—Grimm / Complete *
peasant's wise daughter, 439–440

CLOAK, MAGIC
—Grimm / Complete *
spirit in the bottle, 458–462
—Manning / Cauldron *
amber witch: common man, loved by princess, sent to get amber, 18–31

CLOTHES (often magic)
see also Emperor's new clothes, The
—Crossley / British FT *
Mossycoat; marvelous transportation from coat made of moss, 86–99
—Hall / Treasury *
Little Black Sambo [trades with tigers], 68–76
—Igloo / Metayer
ghost hunter, 82–91
—Jewish / Frankel, 645 (index)
—Lang / Wilkins
little soldier (Deulin), 243–259
snake/woman regains human form (Deulin), 243–259
true story of Little Golden Hood, 132–136
—Old Wives / Carter
which is bigger fool: 1) wearing invisible clothes; 2) thinks he's dead, 102–3
—Reeves / Shadow
husband becomes werewolf; clothes effect change back, 99–110
—Wilde / Lynch *

young king dreams: the poor suffer to provide grandeur, 73–94

CLOUD(-s)
—Bomans / Wily *
prince plants tree so he can be above clouds, 131–134
—Caduto / Keepers *
Hero Twins and Swallower of Clouds, 79–81

CLUB, MAGIC
—O'Brien / Tales *
goatskin-clad Eamonn defeats giants; gets club, fife and ointment, 38–43

CLUMSINESS
—Yep / Rainbow *
Breaker's bridge, 118–123

CLURICAUNE (Irish elf)
—Clarkson / World *
field of Boliauns, 115–117

COAL
—Grimm / Complete *
personification: straw, coal, and bean, 102–103
—Grimm / Sixty * (as above), 29–30

COBOLD, The
—Grimm / Legends (Ward), II:397–399 (index)

Cock, see ROOSTER.

COFFIN
—Grimm / Complete *
glass coffin; bewitched maid, 672–678
—Scary / Young *
coffin follows boy; takes cough drops to "stop the coughin'," 33

COFITACHEQUI
—Southern [legends] / Floyd, 32–37

COIN
—Water Buffalo (Chinese)
woman's coin keeps rice-jar full, 55–61

COINCIDENCE
—Tibet / Timpanelli *
unwilling "seer": reputation made by luck/coincidence, 29–41
—Turkish / Walker
mosquito "hurts" water buffalo, 14

COLD
see also WINTER
—Earthmaker / Mayo *
Ice Man puts out big fire (Cherokee tale), 54–56
Snowmaker torments the people (Micmac tale), 48–52
—Turkish / Walker
survive cold night; candle 100 meters away, 47–48

COLLEGE STUDENTS
—Bronner / Piled
legends, beliefs, ghost stories, etc., 1–256

Collodi, Carlo (1826–1890)
—Childcraft 1 / Once *
Pinocchio, 212–226

COLORS
—Vietnam / Terada *
significance in lives of people, 34 @

Colson, J.G.
—Dramatized / Kamerman
Baron Barnaby's box, 549–558

Colt, see HORSE(-s)

Colum, Padraic (1881–1972)
—Grimm / Complete *
introduction to Grimms' tales, vii–xiv

COLUMBUS, Christopher (1451–1506)
—Speck / New World, 520 (index)

COMIC BOOKS
—Rovin / Superheroes
20th cent. folklore, 1–443

COMMON SENSE
see also FOOL
—Lester / Brer Rabbit *

Brer Fox and Brer Rabbit go hunting, 42–43

COMMUNICATION
see also ANIMAL-HUMAN COMMUNICATION
—Turkish / Walker
man asks wife, mother, daughter to shorten pants, 135–138

COMMUNITY
—Leonardo / Fables *
cedar and many other trees, 81

COMPANION(s)
—Turkey / Walker, 301 (index)

COMPASSION
—Fahs / Old *
loyalty to lowly dependent (dog), 33–36

COMPLAINING
—Geras / Grandmother *
peddler (angel) takes kvetch to Market of Misery, 66–76

COMPROMISE
—Fahs / Old *
grizzly vs. coyote on day/season lengths, 96–99

Compton, Margaret
—Hoke / Giants
The magic feather, 112–118

COMPULSORY BEHAVIOR
—Manning / Cauldron *
witch's flute: goatherd can't stop playing; goats and people can't stop dancing, 99–105

Conall Gulban
—Campbell / West Highlands, III.202–297

CONCEALED IDENTITY
—Egyptian / Harris
doomed prince: fate foretold, 71–76

CONCEIT
—Demi / Reflective *
peacocks: flattery not always true, [20]

—O'Brien / Tales *
Lord Mount Dhraggin: weaver "kills" three-score and ten; made Lord, 72–81

CONCEPTION AND BIRTH (often magic or miraculous)
see also CHILDBIRTH
—Arabian / Lewis
Moorish sorcerer vs. king, 60–64
—Arabian / McCaughrean
Moorish sorcerer vs. king, 133–141
—Celts / Hodges *
Merlin: life and magic powers, 117–132
—Chinese / Chin *
conscripted husband of Meng-Jiang Nyu, 128–139
—Douglas / Magic *
Merlin and Arthur, 141–149
—Egyptian / Harris
judgment by King of the Dead, 103–107
—Erdoes / Sound *
magic rock: Iyan Hokshi, the stone boy, 108–116
—Jaffrey / Seasons
how Ganesh got his elephant head, 121–123
King Rudra; Parvati forms baby from halva, 110–114
—Journey Sun (Chinese)
girl eats dragon pearl; child born, 81–89
—Lester / Leopard *
woman and the tree children, 37–39
—Lore of Love
ill-starred mating of earth and sea, 87–95
—Old Wives / Carter
Kakuarshuk: get children by digging from earth, 11–12
—Quayle / Shining *

Momotaro, the peach-warrior,
77–89
—Russian Hero / Warner *
Ivan son of Mare kills his treacherous brothers, 120–124
prodigy Volkh: Russian mother,
snake father, 92
—Turkish (Art I) / Walker
faithful son of lala [tutor]; quest
for arrogant princess, 123–136
—Vietnam / Terada *
worm and snail are born to two
sisters, 59–63
CONCUBINE
—Chinese / Chin *
palace plot: rival concubines, 77–
92
—Vietnam / Terada *
betrothed woman captured by
enemy kills self, 99–101
CONDITION NOT MET
see also PROMISE(-s)
—Greek / Osborne
Orpheus and Eurydice: quest in
underworld, 45–48
—Jewish / Sadeh
lost princess: king's curse, to Evil
One's kingdom, 386–389
—Trolls / Asbjornsen
spell: East of the sun . . . (poor
man's daughter given to white
bear), 26–35
CONDUCT OF LIFE
—Caduto / Keepers *
follow the "Good Red Road,"
187–188
—Jewish / Frankel
bird gives hunter three pieces of
wisdom, 378–379
slacken the reins (joy: lighten up),
496
—Jewish / Sadeh
father's advice on carousing, etc.
averts evil, 333–334

CONFESSION
—Egyptian / Mercatante
negative, before Osiris, 103–104
CONFIDENCE
see also SELF-CONFIDENCE
—Bomans / Wily *
three riddles; win princess; fear-
less woodcutter, 202–204
CONFLICT
—Legends / Cavendish
family, 403–404 (index)
CONFORMITY
—Coyote / Bierhorst *
coyote loses tail, tries to get oth-
ers to cut tails off, [12]
—Williams-Ellis / Tales *
monkeys steal forty-nine night-
caps, 173–174
CONFUCIAN ETHICS
—Vietnam / Terada * 34 @
CONFUCIUS (551?-497? b.c.)
—Chinese / Christie, 142 (index)
CONGO
—Dictionary / Leach, 1199 (index)
—Vanishing / Mercer *
pygmies help Lightning (personi-
fied) kill elephants, 71–73
CONGO BAMBUTI TALE
—Vanishing / Mercer *
pygmy befriended by monkeys,
steals fire, 68–70
CONJURER
—Hamilton / People *
defined, 103 @
CONQUERORS
—Legends / Cavendish, 394 (index)
CONQUISTADORS
—American / Read Dgst, 59–61
CONSCIENCE
—Allison / I'll Tell *
(lax) wolf needs excuse to eat
lamb, 111
CONSCRIPTION
—Chinese / Chin *

Great Wall; husband of Meng-
   Jiang Nyu, 128–139
Constellation, see STAR(-s)
CONTAINERS
—Jewish / Frankel, 645 (index)
CONTENTIOUSNESS
—Caduto / Keepers *
   punishment: Loo-Wit, the fire-
   keeper, 41–43
CONTENTMENT (dis-)
—Aesop / Reeves-Wilson *
   Town mouse and country mouse,
   40–42
—Allison / I'll Tell *
   be yourself: frog (tries to be big as
   ox) explodes, 108
—Jewish / Frankel
   mouse seeks a wife (fable), 463–
   465
—Leonardo / Fables *
   falcon dives into water after duck;
   regret, 83
   peach tree envies walnut tree, 26
—Lines / Magical *
   magic apple of contentment:
   highest value, 15–23
—Spanish-Am / Van Etten *
   Pedro and priest's mule trade
   places; bad for both, 90–94
—Water Buffalo (Chinese)
   stone-mason never satisfied, 89–
   92
—Yep / Rainbow *
   old woman: "old jar" never empties, 96–105
CONTEST(-s)
   see also ATHLETIC CONTEST
   . . . ; ENDURANCE . . . ;
   RACES (athletic)
—Afro-American / Abrahams, 219–
   262
—Bruchac / Iroquois *
   tall tales: four Iroquois hunters,
   156–159

—Coyote / Ramsey
   coyote vs. monster, 9–12
   turtle outswims buffalo, 22–23
—Greaves / Hippo *
   elephant versus rhino: produce
   most dung, 60–64
—Grimm / Complete *
   brothers: barber, blacksmith,
   fencing master (most skilled?),
   561–62
   willow-wren: contest to select
   king of birds, 705–708
—Hopi / Talashoma-Malotki
   how the Poqangwhoyas turned
   two girls to stone, 92–107
—Igloo / Metayer
   contest: swan vs. crane; dancing;
   neck-wrestling, 43–45
—Jewish / Frankel, 648 (index)
—Jewish / Sadeh
   debate won by misunderstanding: priest vs. town fool, 299–
   300
—Lester / Leopard *
   how many spots does leopard
   have? 53–57
—Old Coot / Christian *
   auguring match (talking contest),
   41–56
—Scary / Young *
   Indian boy (with turtle) vs. Stone
   Giant; rock-skipping, 14–16
—Shannon / More *
   little deer wins (counts to ten, by
   fives), 11–14
—Spanish-Am / Van Etten *
   doctor, rancher, sheepherder
   (winner) try to drive out skunk,
   101–105
CONTEST WON BY DECEPTION
   see also ATHLETIC CON-
   TESTS . . . ; STRENGTH:
   CONTESTS . . .
—Greaves / Hippo *

eating contest: elephant vs.
squirrel, 52–53
—Hoke / Giants
battle with King of the Giants,
119–129
—Lester / Leopard *
why monkeys live in trees; eat
pepper, 41–44
CONTRARINESS
—Yep / Rainbow *
old woman: "old jar" never empties, 96–105
Convent, see NUNS.
CONVERSATION
—Old Wives / Carter
tongue meat: sultan's wife
wastes away; poor man's wife
fat and happy, 215
CONVERSION (*moral or ethical*)
—Fahs / Old *
struggle: boy half-good, half-bad,
1–6
—Jewish / Sadeh
miser-innkeeper tells what happened after death, 172–176
—Scriven / Full Color *
proud princess reforms; King
Grizzly Beard, 89–92
CONVERSION (*religious*)
—Jewish / Frankel, 648 (index)
Baal Shem Tov: services in
house of leper; tailor, 477–482
Baal Shem Tov: storyteller returns
to tell forgotten story, 485–489
happy drunkard: Shimon must
convert or die, 498–503
Pope Elhanan: Jewish child,
raised Christian, returns to Judaism, 395–398
princess to God: restore my lover
or take my life, 360–365
—Jewish / Sadeh
better to hear of son's death than
of his conversion, 339

Conveyances, Magic, *see* MAGIC
TRANSPORT.
COOK, Captain James (1728–1779)
—Polynesians / Andersen, 477 (in-
dex)
COOK(-ing)
—Grimm / Complete *
Fundevogel, 241–244
Pink [carnation], The, 355–360
—Grimm / Sixty *
Fundevogel, 84–87
Pink [carnation], The, 171–176
—Lang / Wilkins
Dwarf Long Nose (boy under
spell), 534–556
—Pellowski / Story *
fire used for cooking; origin; sand
story, 70–74
—Scriven / Full Color *
cook eats meal prepared for
guests, 65–68
—Sioux / Standing Bear *
first fire brought to the Sioux, 77–
79
—Yep / Rainbow *
Virtue goes to town, 118–123
COON HUNTING
—Tall Tales / Downs: Bear
grinning the bark off a tree / D.
Crockett, 31–32
COOPERATION
—Aesop / Holder *
strong help weak: laden ass and
a horse, 10–13
—Allison / I'll Tell *
little red hen (industrious), 16–17
—Crossley / Animal (Grimm) *
Bremen Town musicians, 54–59
—Dramatized / Kamerman
Indian boy without a name, 526–
536
—Leonardo / Fables *
fish mobilize to destroy net, 63–
66

—Paxton / Belling *
    feet and stomach: who's helping
        whom (Aesop), [32–33]
—Spanish-Am / Van Etten *
    cat/rooster/sheep/ox escape
        from wolves/coyote, 97–100
—Williams-Ellis / Tales *
    mice repel invaders of kingdom of
        friendly humans, 45–54
—Yep / Rainbow *
    We are all one, 72–78

COPPER CANOEMAN
—Muddleheads / Harris
    weds human princess, 75–93

**Cormac Mac Art trades family for
apple branch**
—Lines / Magical * 141–149

CORN
    see also MAIZE
—Bierhorst / Monkey *
    origin of red and yellow corn, 52–
        55
    with Lightning's help, animals find
        fox's corn supply, 52–55
—Caduto / Keepers *
    drops of blood: corn's origin,
        137–138
—Fahs / Old *
    how Tewas came to live at Turtle
        Mountain, 7–14
    maize spirit: origin of corn, 148–
        151
—Grimm / Complete *
    ear of corn used to clean dress,
        791–792
—Hopi Coyote / Malotki
    Bird Girls, grinding corn, give
        feathers to Coyote Girl, 91–97
    corn and the Korowiste kachinas,
        195–227, 303, 307 @
—Tree / Kerven *
    origin: corn-maiden, love and re-
        spect the earth, [30–32]
—Yolen / Faery Flag

    minstrel killed: plant growing from
        grave, 41–46

CORNFIELD
—Bierhorst / Monkey *
    bird bride: toad helps youngest
        son re oft-ruined cornfield, 25–
        31
    youngest son, lazy Tup, gets ants
        to clear/plant/harvest cornfield,
        44–51

CORNISH (people)
—Humor / Midwest, 73–78

CORNISH TALES
—Quayle / Cornish *
    twelve tales, 1–108

CORNMEAL
—Hopi Coyote / Malotki, 291, 299 @

CORNSTALK-YOUNG-MAN
—Chorao / Child's FTB *
    ants push sky; rescue, from tree
        top, 43–50

CORNUCOPIA
—Bell / Classical Dict, 55 @
—Lurker / Dict Gods, 423 (index)

CORNWALL
—King Arthur / Senior, 319 (index)

**CORONADO, Francisco (1510–
1554)**
—Speck / New World, 520 (index)

CORPSE
    see also DEAD; EXHUMATION
—Bierhorst / Monkey *
    three would-be buyers of jar mur-
        dered; fool tricked: buries
        "one" thrice, 32–36
—Clouston / Popular
    parish-clerk: corpse "killed" three
        times, II.494–496
—Crossley / British FT *
    piper cuts off feet of frozen corpse,
        to steal shoes, 283–286
—Hamilton / People *
    give me back my "tailypo," 116–
        120

—Jewish / Sadeh
Shlomo Tamsut's hand, 254
—Restless / Cohen *
demon corpse: unburied body be-
comes monster-ghost, 52–59
Russian walking corpses; three
tales, 73–83
wife steals liver from corpse; hus-
band replaces with wife's 103–
109
—Turkey / Walker, 301 (index)
Corson, Hazel W.
—Dramatized / Kamerman
Dame Fortune and Don Money,
481–492
Fish in the forest, 388–399
Triumph for two, 47–60
CORTES, Hernando (1485–1547)
—Speck / New World, 520 (index)
COSTUME
—Man Myth & Magic, 3123 (index)
COUGH
—Scary / Young *
coffin follows boy; takes cough
drops to "stop the coughin',"
33
Counsel, see ADVICE.
COUNTING
—Beat / Bryan *
habit: husband counts spoonfuls;
loses wives, 30–40
—Shannon / More *
little deer wins contest (counts to
ten, by fives), 11–14
—Yolen / Baby Bear *
sheep can't count themselves (10
add up to "90"), [22–23]
Country mouse . . . see Aesop: Town
mouse . . .
Country mouse and city mouse (ex-
istential retelling)
—Switzer / Existential, 86–92
COURAGE
—Bruchac / Iroquois *

boy who lived with the bears, 24–
30
brave woman and the Flying
Head, 184–187
—Crossley / Animal (Grimm) *
kill Old Sultan, faithful dog, 11–
14
—Ghosts / Starkey
Dauntless girl; ghost reveals
treasure, 72–79
—Jewish / Frankel, 648 (index)
—Quayle / Shining *
Lord Bag-o'-Rice aids serpent
(Dragon King); kills giant centi-
pede, 33–43
—Turkish / Walker
Kazan kills forty flies, becomes
"hero," 67–74
Courlander, Harold
—Childcraft 3 / Stories *
The cow-tail switch, 32–37
Court, see CLEVER LAW COURTS.
COURTLY LOVE
—Knights / Heller-Headon, 136–137
COURTSHIP
see also INDIAN COURTSHIP
CUSTOMS; SUITORS
—Bierhorst / Monkey *
Lord Sun courts woman; suc-
ceeds over father's objections,
84–91
—Bierhorst / Naked *
Two Feathers: skills test, 11–18
—Bomans / Wily *
frog sends treacherous friend to
plead case, 109–111
—Brooke / Telling *
Sleeping Beauty: event after
awakening, 3–33
—Erdoes / Sound *
origin of use of flute, 3–9
—Grimm / Complete *
Fair Katrinelje and Pif-Paf-Poltrie,
593–594

spindle, shuttle, and needle help
girl marry prince, 764–767
—Harris-Parks / Again
Brer Rabbit wins Miss Molly Cot-
tontail, 30–39
—Hoke / Giants
Managing-Molly outwits ogre,
65–70
—Lang / Wilkins
enchantment: princess must stay
in tower . . . , 415–431
—Lester / Brer Rabbit *
King Deer's daughter, 131–134
—Russian Hero / Warner *
Dunai: archery contest ends in
death, 37–41
—Shah / Central Asia
Gushtasp and the Princess of
Roum, 78–81
warrior-hero leaves wife (Tah-
mina), 87–91
—Zipes / Beauties *
king sends to Beauty with the
golden hair (d'Aulnoy), 309–320

COVEN
—Witch Encyc / Guiley, 70–73

COVETING
—Igloo / Metayer
owl-suitor rejected by ptarmigan,
40–41
—Lore of Love
cursed embrace: Liba and Guntram, 32–35
—Shah / Central Asia
bead-seller and the jinn's sister,
62–68

Coville, Bruce
—Unicorn / Coville *
Homeward bound, 63–77
lore, 1–6 @
—Yolen / Werewolves
Passing of the pack, 151–171

COW(-s)
—American / Read Dgst

Foolish John gets dollar for each
hair in cow's hide, 52
—Animals / Rowland, 182 (index)
—Crossley / British FT *
cow that ate the piper, 283–286
—Fairies / Briggs
dun cow of Kirkham, 112–113
—Grimm / Complete *
peasant tricks the gullible/greedy
with wooden cow, 311–316
—Grimm / Sixty *
peasant tricks . . . [as above],
142–148
—Lester / Brer Rabbit *
[with] Fox, goes inside cow to cut
meat; the Man kills fox, 57–
60
steals Brer Wolf's fish; gives cow,
but ends up with the meat, 51–
53
tricks Sister Cow (horns stuck in
tree), 23–26
—MacDonald / Sourcebook *
motif index, 599–600
—O'Brien / Tales *
Paddy the Piper, to get boots,
cuts off leg of hanged man [did
cow eat?], 118–127
poor farmer trades cow for magic
"do your [whatever] duty" bottle, 46–52
—Old Wives / Carter
Beauty and Pock Face; dead
mother returns as yellow cow,
200–204
—Tall Tales / Downs: Bear
Harold Peavey's fast cow / G.
Cronyn, 229–248
—Water Buffalo (Chinese)
magic (cow hair) carrying-pole,
111–118
—Witches / Iosa *
Old witch (Jacobs); kind girl and
her selfish sister, 34–39

156

COWARDLY FOOLS
—Grimm / Complete *
  seven Swabians (numskulls),
  538–542
COWBOY(-s)
—American / Read Dgst, 306–310,
  436 (index)
—Folk Ballads / McNeil
  folk ballads, I.143–165
—Hopi Coyote / Malotki
  coyote foolishly tries to cut pocket
  in his skin; dies, 113–117
COWSLIPS
—Scriven / Full Color *
  children find cowslips: Keys of
  summer, 41–42
The cow-tail switch (Courlander)
—Childcraft 3 / Stories * 32–37
COYOTE
—Amer Ind / Erdoes
  twenty-four tales, 333–386
—Bierhorst / Monkey *
  rabbit gets caught; dupes coyote
  to take his place, 72–76
  rabbit marries coyote's daughter,
  81–83
—Caduto / Keepers *
  Old Man Coyote and Grandfather
  Rock, 57–59
  talebearer: how Coyote was the
  Moon, 111
—Coyote / Bierhorst *
  Aztec versions of Aesop, [1–46]
—Coyote / Ramsey
  coyote the eye-juggler, 245–247
  Crater Lake's origin, 210–211
  land of the dead: coyote and eagle, 81–84
  learning to hunt, 240–242
  makes mouth for mouthless man,
  49–51
  Oregon Indian legends, 1–295
  swallowing match: coyote/bear,
  118

—Curry / Beforetime *
  animals build mountains, to be rid
  of tale-bearer, 22–25
  bow length determines share in
  ruling; coyote gets shortest; tail
  between legs, 121–127
  coyote makes first man from clay;
  other animals give ideas, 107–
  115
  coyote rides sun (why his back
  and tail are dark), 100–106
  coyote tricks to get deer meat
  from badger; fails, 78–88
  helped by lookalike relatives, frog
  wins race with coyote, 57–59
  newly-made people given laughter, movement, language,
  food, 116–120
  pine-nut thieves: bluebirds put to
  sleep by coyote's chant, 90–99
  shape-changer: coyote steals
  sun and sets it on course, 10–
  21
  tries badger's hunting method;
  fails because ticklish, 74–77
  why coyote is thin: falls "ten
  snows," riding Evening Star,
  48–51
—Erdoes / Sound *
  Iktome's misadventures, 16–22
—Fahs / Old *
  grizzly vs. coyote on day/season
  lengths, 96–99
—Gullible Coyote / Malotki, 1–180, 1–
  23 @
  baby turtle left behind; coyote
  tricked to carry it home, 69–75
  Coyote Woman kills Antelope
  Woman; tries to get her children, 27–36
  dancing skeleton; eyes pop out,
  go sight-seeing, 77–82
  deceives beautiful maid: devil's-
  claw as rattlesnake, 119–129

eating watermelons; coyote swallows horned lizard alive, 149–154
joins ants in dance, 47–54
joins cats in dance challenge, 83–93
Maasaw (god of death) and coyote try to scare each other, 95–103
mate dies; Coyote Woman grinds his penis to enjoy sex, 55–67
maxim: rain when sun is shining means coyote is mating, 58
on prayer mission for rain, 105–117
swallows birds alive, goes crazy, predicts flood, 37–45
witch-coyote and skunk; skunk deceives rabbits, 131–148
—Haboo / Hilbert, 8–9, 45–56
dances with the sea shells, 153–154
eyes of coyote, 96–107
marries his own daughter, 87–95
son of coyote had two wives, 66–72
—Hamilton / In the Beginning *
Maidu Indian creation myth, 38
—Hopi Coyote / Malotki, 1–342, 293 @
abduction: coyote and Pavayoykyasi, 141–149
Bird Girls, grinding corn, give feathers to Coyote Girl, 91–97
birds play: pluck out/retrieve eyes, 63–67
Coyote-Boy marries Musangnuvi Girl, 229–283
Coyote Woman and Turkey Woman roast their children, 77–81
coyotes make coyote-chain to try to reach crow's nest, 151–159

duped by little bird, coyote kills his grandmother, 83–89
foolish imitation: crow standing on one leg, 69–75
foolishly tries to cut pocket in his skin; dies, 113–117
grasshopper dupes coyote (hold up roof with legs), 99–103
hawk eats all her children; coyote would learn her dirge, 105–111
imitates porcupine: meal from bark and nose-bleed; dies, 3–7
Korowiste kachinas, 195–227, 303, 307 @
learns sorcery; trans. to cottontail; eaten by his children, 166–177
lusts for girl resuscitated by badger, 23–41
rescues children captured by ogre, 179–193
salt expedition, 127–139
sheep-killer, duped into taking sweatbath; dies, 119–125
spider families entertain; lust for Spider Woman, 43–55
water serpent: coyote fashions long tail as ruse, 9–21
wren and coyote play hide and seek, 57–61
—MacDonald / Sourcebook *
motif index, 600–601
—Navajo Coyote / Haile, 1–146
beaver and coyote (bet their "clothes" [skins]), 12, 33–34
Changing Bear Maiden (widow) transformed to monster bear, 16, 82–84
coyote as predator-bungler, 13, 47–52
coyote died (after swallowing Horned Toad), 13, 47–52
coyote role: coyote as both hero and evil trickster, 14, 65–68

creator of the Ute people, 14,
59–62

gray lizard and coyote (called
"First Scolder"), 13, 40

how deer gets its spots, 10, 31–32

how people killed coyote, 15, 78–
81

imitate chickadee (pluck out
eyes) 12, 35

Old Man Owl raised Coyote's
son, 13, 53–54

porcupine tricks/kills elk; vies with
coyote for it, 13, 41–44

rabbit tricks, and escapes from,
coyote, 12, 38–39

range of status levels, 7–19 @

tingling maiden: coyote as suitor-
seducer, 15, 69–77

would imitate porcupine (turning
bark into meat), 12, 36–37

Youngest Brother; coyote resuscitated, 16, 22–24 @, 85–88

—Old Coot / Christian *
Coyote promises "gold" (i.e.,
tales) to Old Coot, 3–13

—Spanish-Am / Van Etten *
cat/rooster/sheep/ox escape
from wolves/coyote, 97–100
coyote disrupts farm's animals,
11–18
leaf monster: covered with (a)
honey, (b) leaves, 11–18

—Tall Tales / Downs: Bear
Senor Coyote and Senor Fox / D.
Storm, 106–108

—Wildlife / Gillespie, 240 (index)

CRAB

—Clarkson / World * 71–73

—Demi / Reflective *
crab thinks of self as beautiful,
[14]

—Old Wives / Carter
girl marries crab; it takes human
form from banyan tree, 19–21

—Pellowski / Story *
finger-play story, 97

CRAFTSMEN

—Cotterell / Encyclopedia, 252 (index)

Craik, Dinah M.M.

—Victorian / Hearn
Little lame prince and his travelling-cloak, 132–191

CRANE, T.F.

—Clouston / Popular, II.505 (index)

CRANE, Walter

—Crane / Beauty * [5–6]

Crane, see BIRD: CRANE.

CRATER, Joseph Force

—Floyd / Gr Am Myst
ride into the unknown, 128–131

CRATER LAKE: origin

—Coyote / Ramsey
coyote in love, 210–211

CRAYFISH

—Bruchac / Iroquois *
raccoon tricks the crayfish, 69–
72

—Dulac / Fairy *
fairy; hind of the wood: spell on
princess, 43–59

CREATION

see also EARTH: CREATION OF

—Schwartz / Gates, 799 (index)

CREATION MYTH(-s)

see also GODS and GOD-
DESSES; INDIAN CREATION
MYTHS

—Amer Ind / Erdoes
human (23 myths), 1–72
world (16 myths), 73–124

—Babylonia / Spence, 389 (index)

—Bierhorst / Monkey *
Blue Sun: beheads younger
brother every day; various origins, 107–112

—Bruchac / Iroquois *
creation of Earth, 15–17

two brothers: one brings good,
the other evil, 19–23
—Bullchild / Sun, 1–390
—Caduto / Keepers *
Earth on turtle's back, 25–26
Four Worlds: the Dine story, 31–
34
place, earth, trees (three tales),
21–37
—Childcraft 3 / Stories *
good and evil: Glooscap vs.
Malsum [and Lox], 143–
151
—Chinese / Christie, 51–68
—Christian / Every
myths, 20–31
—Cotterell / Encyclopedia
deities/myths, 252 (index)
—Coyote / Ramsey
four creations: Atfalati Kalapuya,
106–110
genesis: the Giver, 217–222
—Curry / Beforetime * 1–134
animals build mountains, to be rid
of coyote, 22–25
coyote makes first man from clay;
other animals give ideas, 107–
115
coyote steals sun and sets it on
course, 10–21
how Old-Man-Above created the
world, 1–4
waking of newly-made people:
laughter, language, etc., 116–
120
weather-bundles, in roadrunner's
pack, 5–9
—Earth / Hadley *
Baiame sends Yhi to bring earth
to life, [9–10]
—Egyptian / Harris, 18–20
—Egyptian / Ions
cosmogonies, 21–32 @
—Erdoes / Sound *

remaking of the (third) world,
126–129
—Fahs / Old *
Bakongo; stolen drum to dance
by, 86–90
Deucalion's flood; Zeus makes
new people from stones, 58–
63
Prometheus: prowess to animals;
fire to mankind, 145–147
—Greaves / Hippo *
African Bushman, 14 @
how cheetah got his speed, 28–
29
how tortoises' eggs are cared for,
134–136
—Haboo / Hilbert
fly: High World, Day, Night, people, 33–41
—Hamilton / Dark *
Joseph Golem: blood accusation
against Jews, 87–96
—Hamilton / In the Beginning * 1–161
[has full-page color illus. of each
"creator"]
Ananse vs. Wulbari (Krachi), 52–
57
Blackfoot Indians: Old Man, 24–27
Divine Woman: Huron myth, 58–
63
Earth Starter: Maidu Indians, 34–
41
Elohim: Genesis account, 148–
153
Imir: The frost giant, 68–71
Karora (Bandicoot ancestor), 46–
51
Lowa: sun, life, wind, and death,
104–109
Marduk, god of gods, 78–85
Mawu and Lisa (Fon myth), 42–45
Nyambi: Man copies god, 64–67
Old Man: traveling to form the
world, 24–27

Olorun: Owner of the sky, 72–77
Phan Ku: the cosmic egg, 20–23
Popul Vuh, 86–99
Quatgoro: finding night, 8–13
Ra: The sun-god and the dragon, 110–115
Raven (pea-pod man) and man; woman 2–7
Sa: death the creator, 14–19
Separation of earth and sky, 116–121
Ta-aroa: The angry gods, 100–103
Ulgen: first man becomes the devil, 28–33
—Indian Myth / Burland
Gluskap and Malsum (brothers), 57–59
Great Turtle and the swans, 66
Nesaru and Corn Maiden, 77–81
Wisagatcak, 57
—Indic / Ions, 29–36 @
—Jaffrey / Seasons
heavenly nectar of immortality: Vishnu, Moon, demon Rahu, 71–72
—Jewish / Frankel, vii, 648 (index)
—MacDonald / Sourcebook *
motif index, 27–41
—Man Myth & Magic, 3123 (index)
analytics, 3187 (index)
—Mercatante / Good/Evil, 235 (index)
—Mesoamerican / Leon-P, 99–147, 296 (index)
—Navajo / Klah, 1–237
—Navajo Coyote / Haile
prehuman flux, 12 @
—Persian / Hinnells, 59–62
—Polynesians / Andersen
Tane' and Rongo, 403–431
Tangaroa, 349–402
—Scandinavian / Davidson, 112–114
—Vanishing / Mercer *

Ainu people: earth and sea; insects, 95–98
Napi, the Old Man, (Blackfeet) as creator, 121–128
—Wolves / Lopez
Wolf Star left out at council to build Earth, 133
CREATION of HEAVENLY BODIES see also MOON; STAR; SUN; etc.
—Egyptian / Harris
murder of Isiris (Seth, Isis, Horus), 36–40
—Jewish / Frankel
God made sun/moon equal in brightness; moon wants more, 7–9
—Lester / Leopard *
why sun and moon [personified] are in sky, 1–4
Creation of mankind, see CREATION MYTH(-s); MANKIND: ORIGIN.
CREATOR(-s) (deities)
—Beat / Bryan *
Raluvhimba: how animals, birds, fish got tails, 53–70
—Bruchac / Iroquois *
how buzzard got his feathers, 61–63
—Caduto / Keepers *
Begochiddy; Four Worlds: the Dine story of creation, 31–34
Four Worlds (Dine); creation of animal life, 31–34
Loo-Wit, the fire-keeper, 41–43
Tabaldak (the Owner); Gluscabi, 21
—Childcraft 3 / Stories *
good and evil: Glooscap vs. Malsum [and Lox], 143–151
—Curry / Beforetime *
Old-Man-Above created the world, 1–4

—Grimm / Complete *
God creates animals; devil creates goats with long tails, 642–644
—Haboo / Hilbert
the Changer, 57–59
legend of the Three Sisters (mountains), 123–126
—Lurker / Dict Gods, 395–396 (index)
—Schwartz / Gates, 799 (index)
—Tree / Kerven *
Baiame: up Oobi-Oobi mountain to land of flowers, [22–25]
—Vanishing / Mercer *
Napi: the Old Man (Blackfeet) as creator, 121–128

CREDIBILITY
—Aesop / Reeves-Wilson *
"Wolf! Wolf!" 59–60
—Aesop / Zwerger *
Shepherd's boy and the wolf [cry "wolf"], 9
—Allison / I'll Tell *
boy who cried wolf, 105

CREDULITY
see also Emperor's new clothes, The; GULLIBILITY
—Childcraft 1 / Once *
foolish, timid rabbit: "earth breaking up," 166–168
—Folk-rhymes / Northall
England, 159–180

Cremation of Sam McGee
—Oral Trad / Cunningham, 105–107

CREOLE
—American / Read Dgst
'Tite Poulette [quadroon], 54

CREON, King of Thebes
—Greek / Switzer, 204 (index)

CRETE
—D'Aulaire / Greek * 190 (index)
—Man Myth & Magic, 3124 (index)

CRICKET
—Curry / Beforetime *

mountain lion "defeated" by mosquito (cricket's aide), 70–73

CRIME
see also MURDER; PIRATE(-s); THIEF; etc.
—Folk Ballads / McNeil
folk ballads, I.47–68
—Grimm / Complete *
apprentices' pact with devil; condemned for innkeeper's crime, 542–545
—Grimm / Sixty *
accidental discovery: Doctor Know-All, 281–283
—Old Wives / Carter
Mr. Fox: his betrothed dreams of him mutilating woman for ring, 8–10
—Turkish / Walker
accidental discovery: stargazer to the sultan, 98–107

CRIME PUNISHED
—Grimm / Complete *
bright sun brings it [murder] to light, 528–529
Snowdrop [=Snow White and the seven dwarfs], 249–258
—Grimm / Sixty *
Snowdrop [as above], 161–170
—Vietnam / Terada *
sea snake captures mandarin's wife, 88–94

CRIMINAL PSYCHOLOGY
—Strauss / Trail
Red Riding Hood; soliloquy of "waiting wolf" (poem), 14–16

CRIPPLES
—Bruchac / Iroquois *
origin: Okteondon defeats Workers of Evil, 109
—Crossley / British FT *
Billy: crippled tailor flees ghosts in graveyard, 244–246

CRISES
—Bomans / Wily *
    twelfth king (has hollow [brain-
        less] head), 185–192
CRITICISM
—Grimm / Complete *
    Master Pfriem [never rests; al-
        ways criticizes], 720–724
CROCKETT, Davy (1786–1836)
—American / Read Dgst, 122–125
—Crockett Almanacs
    facsimile ed., including fifty-three
        tales, 1–116
    the fictional, the historical, i-xlviii @
—Davy Crockett / Dewey *
    tall tales, 1–48
—Tall Tales / Downs: Bear
    Grinning the bark off a tree, 31–32
CROCODILE(-s)
    see also ALLIGATOR(-s)
—Animals / Rowland, 183 (index)
—Childcraft 1 / Once *
    Monkey and the crocodile, 169–
        171
—Corrin / Eight-Year *
    monkey to crocodile: my heart is
        hanging in tree, 102–109
—Coyote / Bierhorst *
    crocodile brags; coyote says:
        look at self, not ancestors, [40]
—Egyptian / Harris
    doomed prince: fate foretold by
        Seven Hatitors, 71–76
—Egyptian / Mercatante
    prince doomed to three fates:
        crocodile, serpent, dog, 36–38
—Greaves / Hippo *
    waterbuck runs into swamp; es-
        capes lion, 91–92
    why ostrich has a long neck, 128–
        130
—Leonardo / Fables *
    crocodile killed by ichneumon,
        108–109

—MacDonald / Sourcebook *
    motif index, 601
—Manning / Cats *
    would eat Soafara; she escapes
        with help of Roller Bird, 51–57
—Quayle / Shining *
    white hare tricks crocodiles; re-
        venge; kind prince heals hare,
        24–32
—Wildlife / Gillespie, 240 (index)
CROKER, T. Crofton
—Irish / Glassie, 11–16, 21–22 @
Crompton, Anne E.
—Yolen / Werewolves
    Met by moonlight, 224–237
CROPS
—Caduto / Keepers *
    corn's origin, 137–138
—Crossley / British FT *
    farmer and boggart (trick: crop
        above/below ground), 224–
        227
—Journey Sun (Chinese)
    qingke (barley) seed stolen from
        snake king by Achu, 24–46
CROSS (holy)
—Baring-Gould / Curious
    sacred sign, Christian and other,
        106–110 @
—Clarkson / World *
    witch made powerless by sign of,
        202–206
—Grimm / Legends (Ward), II:400 (in-
    dex)
—Hamilton / People *
    wicked man not wanted in
        heaven or hell, 126–132
—Man Myth & Magic, 3124 (index)
—Russian / Ivanits, 246 (index)
—Scary / Young *
    to steal baby, goblin's arms grow
        longer/longer; cross saves,
        43–46
Crow, see BIRD: CROW

Crow and the picture, *see under* Aesop.

CROW BUTTE
—Sioux / Standing Bear *
Crow Indians escape from the Sioux, 37–40

CRUCIFIXION
—Christian / Every, 46–60
—Man Myth & Magic, 3124 (index)

CRUELTY (including: of relatives; to animals; unnatural)
see also SACRIFICE, CRUEL; STEPMOTHER; Ugly duckling, The
—Arabian / McCaughrean
animals tell lion of man's cruelty, 51–57
—Bierhorst / Naked *
boy who learned the songs of the birds, 60–66
—Bruchac / Iroquois *
boy who lived with the bears, 24–30
—Cambodian / Carrison
Bodhisattva's old mother would kill him to marry pupil, 90–94
—Celts / Hodges *
How Finn MacCool got his wisdom tooth, 34–52
—Chinese / Chin *
golden carp (Cinderella-type), 47–57
—Chorao / Child's FTB *
girl given to the Ranee's pet fish Muchie Lal, 21–31
—Clouston / Popular
son cruel to father; his son plans same, II.372–378
—Coyote / Ramsey
chief, 100 wives, kills all his sons, 65–68
—Dulac / Fairy *
White Caroline, Black Caroline, 15–21

—Earthmaker / Mayo *
Snowmaker torments the people (Menominee tale), 48–52
—Grimm / Complete *
girl shares bread with three little men, 78–83
lambkin and the little fish, 625–627
spouse sharing joy and sorrow, 704–705
true bride; prince forgets betrothal, 752–760
—Hepburn / World *
Tattercoats: gooseherd plays flute; prince falls in love, 90–109
—Hoke / Giants
three giants tricked to death by boy's wits, 34–40
—Igloo / Metayer
Kautaluk: Great Spirit grants marvelous strength, 35–39
mother blinds her hunter-son, 92–98
—Jaffrey / Seasons
king unbearably arrogant when told he cannot be killed, 87–91
Shravan Kumar: wife feeds sour pudding to in-laws, 16–20
—Jewish / Frankel
stepmother sends Miriam to be killed in forest, 579–583
—Jewish / Sadeh
whom God loves, 149–152
—Lang / Wilkins
Blue Beard (murderous husband), 110–115
—Lines / Magical *
Joseph (in Egypt) and his brethren, 149–169
—MacDonald / Sourcebook *
motif index, 357–360
—Manning / Cats *

man marries bird-wife; his mother drives her out, 75–82

—Mex-Am / West
motif index, 301

—Old Wives / Carter
little red fish and clog of gold (Cinderella-type), 171–177

—Palestinian / Speak (Muhawi)
motif-index, 400

—Quayle / Shining *
tongue-cut sparrow: kind husband, cruel wife, 44–56

—Russian Hero / Warner *
bear bites off head of woman who cut off its leg, 117–120

—Scriven / Full Color *
Babes in the wood, 16–20

—Starkey / Ghosts
Joe Reardon and the three sister-ghosts, 102–109

—Turkish (Art I) / Walker
stepmother "kills" stepdaughter, takes her place as bride, 82–88

—Vietnam / Terada *
Prime Minister, in former life a tea server, 83–87
Tam kills stepsister Cam; takes her place as king's wife, 23–34

—Yep / Rainbow *
beggar woman: The child of calamity, 46–52
holy fool: The butterfly man, 60–68

Crumbs on the table
—Grimm / Complete * 768

CRUSADES
—Knights / Heller-Headon, 170–171
—Lore of Love
Aucassin and Saracen maid, 98–106

CRUSADES: Children's Crusade
—Yolen / Werewolves
Wolf's flock (finds redemption), 201–223

CRYSTAL GAZING
—Precious Stones / Kunz, 176–224 @

CUBA
—Speck / New World, 520 (index)

CUCHULAIN (Celtic hero) (also Cu Chulainn)
—Celtic / MacCana, 141 (index)
—Celts / Hodges *
The champion of Ireland, 17–31
—Dramatized / Kamerman
versus Finn McCool, disguised as baby, 218–226
—Ellis / Dict Irish Myth, 71–73
—Fairies / Briggs, 84
—Legends / Cavendish, 183–184

CUCUMBERS
—Arabian / McCaughrean
Price of cucumbers, 122–129

CUDGEL
—Grimm / Complete *
magic: wishing-table, gold-ass, cudgel in sack, 177–187

CULTS
—Egyptian / Ions, 7–20 @
—Southern [legends] / Floyd
handling poisonous snakes in churches, 133–140

CULTURE ACQUISITION by PRIMAL MAN
—Bierhorst / Naked *
chestnut pudding: unlimited food supply, 3–10
—Bruchac / Iroquois *
origin of legends (Hahskwahot), 12–13
—Caduto / Keepers *
Kokopilau, the hump-backed flute player, 151
—Curry / Beforetime *
measuring [inch]-worm's great climb (in search of fire), 26–32
—Earth / Hadley *
stone tells story of stories (to Seneca Indian), [29–31]

—Erdoes / Sound *
  flute, 3–9
—Fahs / Old *
  hoarded knowledge shared with
    all, 29–31
  how Tewas came to live at Turtle
    Mountain, 7–14
  maize spirit: origin of corn, 148–
    151
—Greaves / Hippo *
  ostrich tricked into losing fire,
    127–128
—Water Buffalo (Chinese)
  origin of horse-headed fiddle, 44–
    48

CUMULATIVE TALES
  see also CHAIN TALE(-s)
—Arabian / McCaughrean
  little beggar "killed" over and
    over, 97–103
—Arabian / Riordan
  little beggar . . . [as above], 122–
    124
  Zubaida's tale: the little hunch-
    back, 122–124
—Bierhorst / Naked *
  Turtle's war party vs. Seven Sis-
    ters, 31–36
—Bruchac / Iroquois *
  rabbit outwits fox (trying to eat
    him), 74–78
—Caduto / Keepers *
  Old Man Coyote and Grandfather
    Rock, 57–59
—Clarkson / World *
  cat eats enormous quantity: ani-
    mals, people, etc.; all escape,
    223–225
  mouse tries to regain bitten-off
    tail, 237–241
—Clouston / Popular, I.289–313
—Douglas / Magic *
  three billy goats Gruff, 119–121
—Egyptian / Harris

Hathor: Eye of the sun, 26–33
Wenamon: build sacred boat for
  Amon-Ra, 117–125
—Erdoes / Sound *
  Iktome's misadventures, 16–22
—Grimm / Complete *
  Clever Hans, 166–168
  death of the little hen, 365–367
  task: catch Golden Bird, apple
    thief, 272–279
—Grimm / Sixty *
  Clever Hans, 217–222
  task: catch Golden Bird, 1–9
—Hopi Coyote / Malotki
  coyotes make coyote-chain to
    try to reach crow's nest, 151–
    159
—Jewish / Sadeh
  bread cast upon the water [chain
    of being], 28–31
  infanticide: man who stole a rope,
    375–377
—Jones / Tales *
  Chicken Licken, 16–20
  The Gingerbread Boy, 35–41
  Munachar and Manachar, 27–
    34
  Titty Mouse and Tatty Mouse,
    21–26
—Lester / Brer Rabbit *
  noise in the woods: run! 113–115
—Norwegian / Hodne, 331–338
—Old Wives / Carter
  orphan twins visit mother: market
    of the dead, 166–169
—Rockwell / Puss *
  fisherman, his wife, and the floun-
    der, 42–52
—Turkish (Art I) / Walker
  community mourning for Brother
    Louse, 58–59
—Williams-Ellis / Tales *
  boy's series of trades: feather to
    village chief, 102–112

Johnny-Cake runs away from all
but fox, 96–101
CUNNING
—Aesop / Reeves-Wilson *
King Lion is ill, 105–107
—Allison / I'll Tell *
wolf and goat's kid, 130
Cunning little tailor
—Grimm / Complete * 525–528
CUPID
—Greek / Osborne
Cupid's arrows: Daphne and
Apollo, 23–26
CUPID and PSYCHE LEGEND
—Bulfinch / Sewell * 62–73
—Clouston / Popular, I.205–214
—Douglas / Magic *
Venus, Cupid and Psyche, 151–
165
—Greek / Osborne
Cupid and Psyche: the four tasks,
57–65
CURANDERO
—Ghost (S'west) / Young
death (personified) at foot/head
of bed, 111–112
CURE(-s) (magic; marvelous)
see also HEALING
—Arabian / McCaughrean
man with three wives, 185–193
—Bierhorst / Naked *
mother of ghosts; life-restored,
37–43
—Corrin / Imagine *
Pari hides in golden candelabra;
prince buys, falls in love, 151–
160
—Fahs / Old *
quest: healing waters for plague-
stricken wife, 52–56
—Grimm / Complete *
Godfather Death (head or foot of
bed), 209–212
godfather: water cures if death

stands at head of bed, 206–
208
surgeons; body parts removed;
cat eats; other parts substituted; effects, 535–538
—Jewish / Frankel
princess to God: restore my lover
or take my life, 360–365
—Jewish / Sadeh
lovesickness: leaves from Paradise, 365–367
—Lang / Wilkins
snake soup; queen poisons stepdaughter's suitor, 460–473
—Manning / Cats *
king loses sight; cure if washed in
Katchka's blood, 118–123
—O'Brien / Tales *
fairies take Gilly, abduct princess;
strike her dumb; Gilly learns of
curing herb, 106–117
—Old Wives / Carter
man marries snake-woman; falls
ill; cured when she is burnt up,
142–148
—Rockwell / Puss *
Kate Crackernuts breaks evil
spells, 19–26
—Scriven / Full Color *
Rapunzel, 9–12
—Spring / Philip
son test's father's advice; cures
king, 82–86
—Turkish (Art I) / Walker
Camesap eats part of Sahmeran,
learns language of plants,
218–224
—Unicorn / Coville *
quest for unicorn horn: cure of
winter sickness, 136–155
stealing water touched by unicorn
horn, to cure sick friend, 7–22
—Yep / Rainbow *
"We are all one," 72–78

CURIOSITY
—Dulac / Fairy *
   green serpent: one twin princess cursed, ugly, 124–138
—Hamilton / In the Beginning *
   Pandora's box, 138–142
—Spring / Philip
   dragon seen by unprotected men, 119–133
—Turkish (Art I) / Walker xxviii–xxix @

CURSE(-s)
   see also Sleeping Beauty (Briar Rose)
—Bomans / Wily *
   chimney sweep's curse (personified) captured by curate, 93–96
   lock of princess' hair; king's cruelty to "bird witch," 165–173
—Classic / Downer
   Jacksonboro, Georgia, 80–83
—Douglas / Magic *
   Sleeping Beauty, 55–61
—Dulac / Fairy *
   curse: not to see daylight; crayfish fairy, 43–59
   green serpent: one twin princess cursed, ugly, 124–138
—Ghosts / Time-Life
   Grettir the Strong defeats Glam, 132–139
   Hervor (Viking) and sword (Tyrfing), 109–111
—Grimm / Complete *
   seven ravens [transformed brothers], 137–139
—Grimm / Legends (Ward), II:400 (index)
—Grimm / Sixty *
   seven ravens [as above], 284–287
—Hamilton / Dark *
   phantom ship (Flying Dutchman) cursed by God, 38–42
—Hamilton / In the Beginning
   Ta-aroa: angry gods, 100–104
—Jewish / Frankel, 648 (index)
   angry king: daughter taken captive because of his curse, 531–536
—Lang / Wilkins
   Princess Mayblossom (good vs. evil fairies), 137–153
—Legends / Cavendish, 408 (index)
—Lewis / Proud
   Guigemar: find woman who will endure anguish and lift curse, 10–19
—Lore of Love
   curse causes husband to forget wife, 26–31
—Nesbit / Fairy *
   Belinda and Bellamant; ugly on certain days, 101–122
—Reeves / Shadow
   husband becomes werewolf "Garwal"; curse removed, 99–110
   white doe: curse put on Valdemar, 131–153
—Rockwell / Puss *
   Briar Rose; gifts of Wise Women, 53–59
—Scriven / Full Color *
   Sleeping Beauty, 48–51
—Turkish (Art I) / Walker
   faithful son of lala [tutor]; quest for arrogant princess, 123–136
—Witch Encyc / Guiley, 81–82, 411 (index)

CUSTOMS (including origins)
   see also MARRIAGE CUSTOMS
—Am Child / Bronner, 161–174
—Bruchac / Iroquois *
   husband; vampire skeleton, 129–133
—Caduto / Keepers *

Awi Usdi: deer and excessive hunting, 173–174

Kokopilau, the hump-backed flute player, 151

—Fahs / Old *
animals make sickness for man-enemy, 71–80

—Folk-rhymes / Northall England, 181–266

—Hoke / Giants
Hercules and the golden apples, 130–132

—Maori / Kanawa *
Mataora; husbands must not beat wives, 68–80

—Vietnam / Terada *
look-alike brothers love the same girl, 109–113

CYBELE
—Roman / Usher, 27–29 @

CYCLICAL TALE
—Bomans / Wily *
chimney sweep's curse (personi-fied) captured by curate, 93–96

CYCLOPS
—D'Aulaire / Greek * 190 (index)
—Greek / Switzer, 204 (index)
—Hamilton / In the Beginning *
illustration, 129
—McGowen / Encyclopedia * 17–18

CZAR
—Geras / Grandmother *
faces of Czar: clever repartee, 14–20
—Lines / Magical *
Little Fool Ivan and the little humpback horse, 70–85
—Russian Hero / Warner *
little simpleton: silver saucer and juicy apple, 106–108
Sister Alenushka and Brother Ivanushka, 108–109

CZECHOSLOVAKIAN TALE
—Dramatized / Kamerman
Triumph for two, 47–60

DAGDA (king)
—Celtic / MacCana, 141 (index)
—Ellis / Dict Irish Myth, 76–77

DAHOMEY
—Dictionary / Leach, 1199 (index)

DAHUT (evil princess)
—Celts / Hodges *
Bells of Ys, 104–114

DAKSHA (Sanskrit)
—Indic / Ions, 143 (index)
—Wolkstein / Love, 238 @

DAM
—Caduto / Keepers *
Koluscap turns Water Monster into bullfrog, 81–84

DANANN
—Celts / Hodges *
swan children restored by St. Patrick's coming, 5–14

DANCE(-ers; -ing)
see also INDIAN DANCE
—Aesop / Zwerger
monkey [dances] and camel [en-vies], 13
—Childcraft 3 / Stories *
imitator can't dance like man with bump on cheek, 58–65
—Clarkson / World *
taboo: dancing after midnight on Shrove Tuesday, 214–219
—Dramatized / Kamerman
Magic cloak; princesses wear out shoes, 435–446
—Dulac / Fairy *
magic pipe makes all dance, 114–123
—Fahs / Old *
stolen drum to dance by, 86–90

—Fairies / Briggs
Kate Crackernuts, 243–245
—Grimm / Complete *
magic fiddle makes everyone
dance, 503–508
—Grimm / Legends (Ward), II:401 (index)
—Grimm / Sixty *
magic fiddle (as above), 182–189
—Gullible Coyote / Malotki
buffalo dancers, 162–164 @
coyote joins ants in dance, 47–54
coyote joins cats in dance challenge, 83–93
—Hopi Coyote / Malotki
coyote and the Korowiste kachinas, 195–227, 303, 307 @
—Igloo / Metayer
contest: swan vs. crane; dancing; neck-wrestling, 43–45
—Lurker / Dict Gods, 424 (index)
—MacDonald / Sourcebook *
motif index, 603
—Man Myth & Magic, 3125 (index)
—Manning / Cauldron *
witch's flute: goatherd can't stop playing; goats and people can't stop dancing, 99–105
—Mex-Am / West, 180–184
—O'Brien / Tales *
goatskin-clad Eamonn: fife forces dancing (wolf and jealous rival Fiac) 38–43
—Oral Trad / Cunningham
Tree Deedle, The, 86–88
—Pellowski / Family *
Magic Mary, 54–57
—Polynesians / Andersen
hula, 432–451
—Yolen / Baby Bear *
Aldo the anteater teaches ants to waltz, [14–15]
Danced-out shoes, *see* Twelve dancing princesses.

DANES
—O'Brien / Tales *
goatskin-clad Eamonn: bring flail (keeps Danes away) from hell, 38–43
DANGER
—Aesop / Reeves-Wilson *
cooperation: Lion, goat, and vulture, 74–75
—Allison / I'll Tell *
mice in council: belling the cat, 121
—Jewish / Sadeh
foretold; prince who went off on his own, 101–105
—Paxton / Aesop *
bear whispers: choose friend who stands by in danger, [31–32]
—Paxton / Belling *
hare's "friends" exposed by danger (Aesop), [16–21]
—Turkish (Art I) / Walker
donkey and camel: irresistible urges, 44–45
—Water Buffalo (Chinese)
plop! spread of unquestioned danger, 30–32
DANGER: FOOLISH DISREGARD OF
—Childcraft 1 / Once *
Potter: Tale of Peter Rabbit, 192–196
—Water Buffalo (Chinese)
boastful tortoise, 9–12
DANIEL (O.T.)
—Babylonia / Spence, 390 (index)
DANISH TALES
—Clouston / Popular, II.505 (index)
DANTE Alighieri (1265–1321)
—Mercatante / Encyclopedia, 756 (index)
DAO PEOPLE
—Vietnam / Terada *

squash seeds: origin of Dao People, 54–58
DAPHNE
—Greek / Osborne
Cupid's arrows: Daphne and Apollo, 23–26
—Lore of Love
doomed trysts: Apollo; Pyramus, 77
DARK(-ness)
—Ghosts / Starkey
moon (personified) captured/rescued (bogles), 96–101
—Hall / Treasury *
Little Brown Bear afraid of the dark, 22–25
—Hamilton / In the Beginning *
Ananse creation myth, 52–57
DARK TOWER
—Hamilton / Dark *
elf king, Childe Rowland and Burd Ellen, 65–72
Dassie, see HYRAX.
DAUGHTER(-s)
see also FATHER and DAUGHTER
—Fahs / Old *
Capilano sisters bring peace and brotherhood, 104–107
—Russian Hero / Warner *
foolish man exchanges daughter for help, 57–60
—Women / Dyer, 235–241 @
Dauntless girl
—Crossley / British FT * 182–189
—Crossley / Dead * 57–62
DAVID, King (*Old Testament*)
—Christian / Every, 143 (index)
—Hoke / Giants
David and Goliath, 79–92
—Jewish / Frankel, x (index), 195–260
Pasha's lance recovered from David's tomb, 403–405
—Jewish / Sadeh

apparition; healing waters; Rabbi Reconnati, 41–43
baker's apprentice; pregnant princess thrown out/reconciled, 268–271
Joab and the Amalekites, 39–41
tomb of, 65–66
Davol, Marguerite W.
—Yolen / Werewolves
Flesh and blood, 172–188
DAY AND NIGHT (*origins*)
see also NIGHT
—Caduto / Keepers *
How Grandmother Spider stole the Sun, 49–50
—Earthmaker / Mayo *
daylight comes at last (Black Raven) (Lillooet tale), 12–16
origin, 11 @
Wahconda makes the earth shake (Oto tale), 54–56
—Fahs / Old *
grizzly vs. coyote on day/season lengths, 96–99
struggle: boy half-good, half-bad, 1–6
—Hamilton / In the Beginning *
Quat: "finding night," 8–13
Sa: Kono creation myth, 14–19
Sedi and Melo: too strong, 116–121
—Russian Hero / Warner *
traveler meets sun in her mother's house, 56–57
DAYDREAM(-s)
see also ABSURDITIES
—Jewish / Sadeh
egg seller strikes it rich; ends in misfortune, 303
DAYDREAMS: "counting chickens before they're hatched"
—Aesop / Alley *
milkmaid and her pail, 10–13
—Aesop / Reeves-Wilson * 97–98

—Aesop / Zwerger * 5
—Allison / I'll Tell *
  farmer's daughter, 107
—Clouston / Popular
  opulence, II.432–443
—Paxton / Belling * [34–37]
Daylight, see DAY AND NIGHT.
DEAD
  see also CORPSE; DEATH;
  GHOST(-s); IMMORTALITY;
  LIFE RESTORED; NECRO-
  MANCY; REVENANTS; ZOM-
  BIE
—Baring-Gould / Curious
  Fortunate Isles: Paradise for
  souls, 134–138 @
—Bierhorst / Naked *
  Last Remaining [after plague;
  bring back from lower world],
  87–92
—Celtic / MacCana
  Celtic myth, 128–131
—Coyote / Ramsey
  bringing back to life, 81–84
—Crossley / Dead *
  dead moon (boggles; marsh folk),
  1–9
  Suffolk miracle: ploughboy returns from dead; claims Rosamund, 11–19
—Erdoes / Sound *
  ghost: older Indian foils would-be
  robbers of dead man, 82–85
—Grimm / Complete *
  shroud wet; can't rest; child returns from the dead, 502–503
—Jewish / Frankel
  good man, bad man: temporal
  honor, eternal reward, 578–
  579
  grateful dead: youth buries Sultan's accused treasurer, 427–
  430
—Jewish / Sadeh

  dead man's trial: deposited
  money, 258–259
  ghost returns one month after
  death, as promised, 87–89
  Ja'akov repays dead rabbi's debt;
  rabbi returns to help him, 137–
  139
  revenant; mourner's prayer for
  the dead, 139–140
  self-knowledge, as dead, 367
—Lang / Wilkins
  Indian chief goes to lowerworld
  for his bride, 282–284
—MacDonald / Sourcebook *
  motif index, 122–130
—Mex-Am / West
  motif index, 299
—Old Wives / Carter
  orphan twins visit mother: market
  of the dead, 166–169
  which is bigger fool: 1) wearing
  invisible clothes; 2) thinks he's
  dead, 102–3
—Palestinian / Speak (Muhawi)
  motif-index, 390
—Scandinavian / Kvideland, 419 (index)
  binding the, x (index)
  revenge by the, ix (index)
—Scary / Young *
  Indian maid, married in Land of
  the Dead, returns with child,
  69–72
—Turkish (Art I) / Walker
  dead mother advises stepdaughter: nurse, teach, wed serpent-
  prince, 183–188
—Vietnam / Terada *
  beliefs re punishment, food offer-
  ings, etc., 82 @
DEAD, ABODE OF THE
  see also HADES; HELL; UNDER-
  WORLD
—Egyptian / Harris

Setna and the Book of Thoth,
92–102
—Scary / Young *
Indian maid reunited with lover in
Land of the Dead, 69–72
DEAD LOVER
—Crossley / Dead *
Suffolk miracle: ploughboy re-
turns from dead; claims Ro-
samund, 11–19
—Scary / Young *
ghost of murdered Oiwa haunts
samurai husband to death, 21–
25
Dead moon [*marshland*]
—Crossley / Dead * 1–9
DEAD: RETURN (*friendly*)
—Bruchac / Iroquois *
Hodadenon: last one left, 169–
182
—Corrin / Eight-Year *
painter (long dead) gives lessons
to servant, 51–61
—Dulac / Fairy *
suitor test: Ivan and the chestnut
horse, 60–68
—Egyptian / Harris
murder of Isiris (Seth, Isis, Horus), 36–40
—Geras / Grandmother *
ghost at peace after standing under wedding canopy, 86–96
—Grimm / Complete *
aged mother blames God for
death of sons, 826–827
brother transformed to fawn; sister faithful, 67–73
—Journey Sun (Chinese)
cruel stepmother, false wife,
ghost, 6–23
—Old Wives / Carter
Beauty and Pock Face; dead
mother returns as yellow cow,
200–204

—Starkey / Ghosts
"Dauntless girl," 72–79
ghost reveals deed to estate, 24–
29
—Turkish (Art I) / Walker
dead mother advises stepdaughter: nurse, teach, wed serpent-
prince, 183–188
—Yep / Rainbow *
dead relatives return: "Slippers,"
162–168
DEAD: RETURN TO PUNISH
—Hamilton / People *
give me back my "tailypo," 116–
120
—Journey Sun (Chinese)
cruel stepmother, false wife,
ghost, 6–23
—Lore of Love
stone avenger drags Don Juan to
hell, 61–63
—Old Wives / Carter
orphan twins visit mother: market
of the dead, 166–169
—Scary / Young *
Old Raw Head (butchered) borrows fangs, claws, tail, 11–
13
**DEAD: RETURN TO REPAY OBLI-
GATIONS**
—Bomans / Wily *
king's soul in statue 100 years;
unworthy of heaven; prayer
frees, 121–125
—Clarkson / World *
ghost returns to restore stolen
goods, 188–191
—Grimm / Complete *
stolen farthings: child returns
from dead, 654–655
—Jewish / Frankel
dim-witted boy buys box of bones
(chain tale), 414–418
man who breaks betrothal vow

punished by childlessness,
523–527
—Starkey / Ghosts
Tregeagle's ghost, 58–65
DEATH
see also AFTERLIFE; ANGEL
OF DEATH; BURIAL; DEAD;
IMMORTALITY;
JUDGMENT DAY; LIFE RE-
STORED; RESURRECTION;
RESUSCITATION
—Amer Ind / Erdoes
thirteen tales, 465–499
—Bell / Classical Dict, 61–62 @
—Bierhorst / Monkey *
Mole-Catcher marries daughter
of Death-Maker, 121–130
—Bierhorst / Naked *
Porcupine's grandson [real self
lives on], 93–100
—Bomans / Wily * 648 (index)
king, devoted to his mother, does
not want to die, 118–120
old man "invisible" so death (personified) can't find him, 104–
107
storyteller wants to see a gnome
before he dies, 141–142
wings: "madman" wants to go to
heaven without dying, 152–155
—Caduto / Keepers *
origin: woman has last word,
181–182
—Celts / Hodges *
Arthur's last battle, 157–169
—Clouston / Popular
old lady entices Death to climb
prune tree, I.389–390
—Cotterell / Encyclopedia, 252 (index)
—Coyote / Ramsey
origin of no-return from, 33–37
—Creatures (illus) / Huber * 155 (index)

—Crossley / Animal (Grimm) *
wolf and seven young goats;
death averted, 29–34
—Crossley / Dead *
green mist: girl lives only until
cowslip dies, 39–43
—Dulac / Fairy *
Snegorotchka: lives one winter,
melts in spring, 1–6
—Egyptian / Harris
divinities of, 103–113 @
journey of the soul, 48–50
—Erdoes / Sound *
doing a magic trick with eyeballs,
86–89
—Fahs / Old *
hunter in Walumbe's country of
Death, 181–184
Mawu's ways: apparent evil has
hidden good, 173–177
—Folk Ballads / McNeil
folk ballads, II.162–178
—Ghost (S'west) / Young
(personified) at foot/head of bed;
the curandero, 111–112
—Ghosts / Time-Life
appointment in Samarra (tale), 14
double, or Fetch, or co-walker,
13–14
ghostly heralds, 6–37
herald: Ankou, 16–19
herald: Dando, 19–23
omens, 10–13
—Grimm / Complete *
Death's messengers (symp-
toms), 718–720
Godfather Death (head or foot of
bed), 209–212
godfather: water cures if death
stands at head of bed, 206–208
rose given to child helping another gather wood, 819
—Grimm / Legends (Ward), II:401 (index)

—Gullible Coyote / Malotki
  coyote and Maasaw (god of
    death) try to scare each other,
    95–103
—Hamilton / Dark *
  banshee scream; death coming,
    1–4
  phantom ship (Flying Dutchman)
    cursed by God, 38–42
  Rolling Rio wrestles Death, and
    wins , 5–13
  Yama, god of Death, marries
    mortal (shrew; leaves), 137–
    142
  Yama: son dissuades his edict of
    death, 137–142
—Hamilton / In the Beginning *
  Blackfoot Indian myth (stone
    sinks), 26–27
  Lowa: creation myth, 104–109
  origin: Quat, creator myth, 11,
    13
  spirits go to far west (Huron
    myth), 63
—Irish / Glassie
  six tales, 121–126
—Jewish / Frankel
  death foretold: two socks on one
    foot, 482–483
  Moses resists his fate, 158–162
  three friends: what counts at time
    of death, 379
—Jewish / Sadeh
  Angel of Death's seven messen-
    gers, 180–181
  better to hear of son's death than
    of his conversion, 339
  charity saves peddler's wife from
    foreordained death, 335–336
  man in wagon: all are traveling
    toward death (Nachman), 378–
    379
  parrot's advice: escape by feign-
    ing death, 165–166

worms' complaint: men are too
    skinny, 167–168
—Journeys / Norris *
  road to death: old man takes form
    of bullock, [16–18]
—Legends / Cavendish
  mysterious deaths, 408 (index)
—Leonardo / Fables *
  swan: end in beauty, 29
—Lester / Leopard *
  town where sleeping was not al-
    lowed, 27–30
—Lurker / Dict Gods, 396–397 (index)
—Lycanthropy / Otten
  Housman: The were-wolf (alle-
    gory), 281–320
—MacDonald / Sourcebook *
  motif index, 604–605
—Man Myth & Magic, 3125 (index)
—Mercatante / Encyclopedia, 756 (in-
    dex)
—Mesoamerican / Leon-P
  death averted, 296 (index)
—Navajo / Klah
  creation myths, 68–72
—Pirate Ghosts / McSherry
  no ships pass; people cannot die,
    13–39
—Polynesians / Andersen, 477 (in-
    dex)
—Russian / Ivanits, 246 (index)
—Russian Hero / Warner *
  Koshchei the Deathless; "death"
    hidden in egg, 96–99
—Turkey / Walker, 301 (index)
DEATH: for BREAKING TABOO
—Jewish / Frankel
  demon princess/wife and the bro-
    ken oath, 432–437
—Quayle / Shining *
  Urashima opens forbidden box; is
    suddenly very old, 57–68
—Scary / Young *
  bride always wears ribbon around

neck; husband removes; her
head falls off, 61–63

DEATH: FEIGNED
—Bruchac / Iroquois *
hungry fox and boastful suitor,
80–83
rabbit outwits fox (trying to eat
him), 74–78
raccoon tricks the crayfish, 69–
72
—Clarkson / World *
Anansi plays dead (to steal
yams), 259–261
—Curry / Beforetime *
coyote tries badger's hunting
method; fails because ticklish,
74–77
—Gullible Coyote / Malotki
witch-coyote and skunk; skunk
deceives rabbits, 131–148
—Harris-Parks / Jump *
Brer Fox hunts, Brer Rabbit gets
the game, 11–16
—Igloo / Metayer
Coppermine River legend, 78–81
—Jewish / Frankel
starling and the princess (fable),
468–469
—Lester / Brer Rabbit *
Brer Fox feigns death; Brer Rab-
bit tricks him, 29–31
—Turkish / Walker
Deli feigns death, frightens
thieves, gets reward, 80–84
—Williams-Ellis / Tales *
Anansi and Mrs. Dove, 143–150

DEATH (a god)
—Hamilton / In the Beginning *
Sa: Kono creation myth, 14–19

Death of the little hen
—Grimm / Complete * 365–367

DEATH VALLEY
—Floyd / Gr Am Myst
moving stones, 43–45

Death's messengers
—Grimm / Complete * 718–720

DEBATE
—Jewish / Sadeh
won by misunderstanding: priest
vs. town fool, 299–300

DEBT
—Jewish / Sadeh
Ja'akov repays dead rabbi's debt,
137–139
pony's IOU: soul of departed one,
working off debt, 354

Decapitation, see BEHEAD(-ed)
(-ing).

Deceit, see DECEPTION.

**DECEIVER FALLS INTO OWN
TRAP**
—Carter / Sleeping *
Hop o' my Thumb, 69–80
—Childcraft 2 / Time *
borrows friend's coat, puts food in
pockets; friend finds food, 36–
39
—Clarkson / World *
Molly Whuppie: substitutions
cause giant to kill his children,
54–56
—Dramatized / Kamerman
lawyer/deceiver; backfire, 128–
148
—Egyptian / Harris
brothers (Lies and Truth personi-
fied), 84–85
—Jaffrey / Seasons
demon-wet-nurse Pootana tries
to poison Krishna, 22–25
—Lewis / Proud
King Equitan, seducer; dies in
boiling bathwater, 82–87
—Rockwell / Puss *
Boy who cried "Wolf," 40–41
—Williams-Ellis / Tales *
Anansi (death for saying "five"),
143–150

DECEPTION
see also ATHLETIC CONTEST
. . . ; BARGAIN, DECEPTIVE;
CLEVERNESS; CONTEST
WON BY DECEPTION;
DEATH: FEIGNED; DIS-
GUISE; ESCAPE . . . ; LIAR
—Allison / I'll Tell *
fox uses goat (escape from well),
120
—Arabian / McCaughrean
woman marries (a) robber (b)
pickpocket, 218–224
—Bierhorst / Monkey *
three would-be buyers of jar murdered; fool tricked: buries
"one" thrice, 32–36
—Bruchac / Iroquois *
turtle's race with bear, 51–53
—Caduto / Keepers *
marriage of Sedna: woman under
the sea, 95–97
—Cambodian / Carrison
father/son ride/carry donkey to
market, 102–106
woman tricked, endanger baby,
then robbed, 31–35
—Celts / Hodges *
Lad of Luck and monster of the
loch, 89–103
—Childcraft 1 / Once *
Monkey and the crocodile, 169–
171
—Chinese / Chin *
white snake (in woman form), 29–
44
—Clouston / Popular
Little Fairly, et al., versions,
II.229–288, 489–491
—Corrin / Eight-Year *
Little Claus and Big Claus, 13–26
—Coyote / Ramsey
cruel chief, 100 wives, kills all his
sons, 65–68

—Crossley / Animal (Grimm) *
kill Old Sultan, faithful dog, 11–14
—Curry / Beforetime *
lookalike relatives help frog win
race with coyote, 57–59
—Douglas / Magic *
ogre tricked: Jack the Giant Killer,
131–139
—Dramatized / Kamerman
covetous councilman (tricked; returns gold), 504–513
fierce creature bluffing, 3–6
gold found in the forest, 388–399
Merry Tyll and the three rogues,
162–176
stone soup, 381–387
tiger, brahman, and jackal, 212–
217
—Egyptian / Harris
capture of Joppa; cunning of
Djhuty, 69–70
clever thief: treasure of
Rhumpsinitus, 114–116
—Giant / Harrison *
boy tells secret to giant-capturers: measles, 7–17
—Greaves / Hippo *
eating contest: elephant vs.
squirrel, 52–53
—Grimm / Complete *
Brother Lustig and St. Peter,
367–377
grave-mound: devil and grave-
watchers, 792–796
Hans married: uncle deceives
bride's father, 387–388
little peasant (tricks the gullible/
greedy), 311–316
Old Sultan, 230–232
—Grimm / Sixty *
little peasant (as above), 142–
148
Old Sultan, 26–28
—Gullible Coyote / Malotki

coyote deceives beautiful maid: devil's-claw as rattlesnake, 119–129

—Hamilton / Dark *
free spirits: Bouki and Malice, 102–107

—Harris-Parks / Jump *
Brer Rabbit tricks Brer Wolf into trunk, 3–8

—High John / Sanfield *
eavesdrops on Master; pretends foreknowledge of plans, 24–33

—Igloo / Metayer
Coppermine River legend: feigned death, 78–81
Kajortoq: bears and wolf become fox's food, 19–23
Kajortoq (fox) outwitted by crow, 46–48
orphan and the bears [bear-men], 24–31
raven deceives/kills people, for food, 58–60

—Jaffrey / Seasons
King Rudra marries seven sisters; youngest becomes pregnant, 110–114
king's wife lies about eating barley; says it's pearls, 115–119

—Jewish / Frankel, 648 (index)

—Jewish / Sadeh
lamp that died, 305–306
parrot's advice: feign death, 165–166
two washerwomen on Passover eve, 131–132

—Lester / Brer Rabbit *
courting King Deer's daughter, 131–134
says molasses is "fox blood," 141–144

—Lester / Leopard *
tug-of-war: turtle cons elephant and hippo, 17–20

—MacDonald / Sourcebook *
motif index, 261–323

—Mex-Am / West
motif index, 300

—Muddleheads / Harris
haughty princess, arranged marriage, self-mutilation, 115–130

—O'Brien / Tales *
giants, McConigle vs. Finn (disguised as infant), 9–16

—Old Wives / Carter
wife gives rice to lover; tricks husband to accept chaff for grain, 72

—Palestinian / Speak (Muhawi)
motif-index, 395–397

—Paxton / Aesop *
boy who cried wolf, [33–35]

—Quayle / Shining *
hare tricks crocodiles to form bridge; he jeers; is punished, 24–32

—Rockwell / Puss *
Boy who cried "Wolf," 40–41
Nail Soup [series of small lies], 12–18
Puss in Boots, 80–88

—Russian Hero / Warner *
gypsy cons dragon: he's stronger, 71–72

—Scary / Young *
Indian boy (with turtle) vs. Stone Giant; rock-skipping, 14–16

—Scriven / Full Color *
cook eats meal prepared for guests, 65–68

—Spring / Philip
king "never heard of this before," 134–139
son tests father's advice; cures king, 82–86

—Trolls / Asbjornsen
Askelad and the silverducks, 11–16

—Turkish / Walker
  bear tricks (goat) kids; goat gets
  even, 4–7
  foolish parents give con man gifts
  for dead son, 85–87
  stargazer to the sultan, 98–107
—Turkish (Art I) / Walker
  Haci's daughter marries, is repeatedly assaulted, 24–33
—Vanishing / Mercer *
  hedgehog (cheating) wins race
  with ostrich, 102–105
—Water Buffalo (Chinese)
  arrogant fox pretends to be king,
  36–38
—Yep / Rainbow *
  bedtime snacks, 4–10
  claim to find lost things by smell,
  20–35

DECEPTION, FATAL
—Douglas / Magic *
  Puss in Boots; ogre becomes
  mouse, 99–107
—Dulac / Fairy *
  Bashtchelik (real steel), 91–
  113
—Erdoes / Sound *
  Iktome and the ducks, 91–92
—Geras / Grandmother *
  talking plants' contest: which is
  most beautiful? 57–65
—Lore of Love
  Aztec couple: reunion in flames,
  52–57
—Turkish (Art I) / Walker
  swindlers swindled: messenger
  rabbit; magic flute; underwater
  sheep, 147–153
—Williams-Ellis / Tales *
  Johnny-Cake runs away from all
  but fox, 96–101

**DECEPTION into FATAL SUBSTI-
TUTION**
—Bierhorst / Monkey *

rabbit gets caught; dupes coyote
  to take his place, 72–76
—Clarkson / World *
  Molly Whuppie: giant's wife takes
  girl's place; beaten to death,
  54–56

**DECEPTION into HUMILIATING
POSITION**
—Greaves / Hippo *
  jackal fools lion: hold up rock,
  50
—Grimm / Complete *
  Valiant tailor, 112–120
—Grimm / Sixty *
  Valiant tailor, 88–97
—Jaffrey / Seasons
  Doda and Dodi: daughter-in-law's
  cruel trick backfires, 38–46
—Journey Sun (Chinese)
  Fanjiangshan secures justice;
  three episodes, 90–108
—Lore of Love
  warlock tricked: hair from heifer,
  84
—Water Buffalo (Chinese)
  hare, crow, and greedy mer-
  chant, 18–20

DECEPTION into SELF-INJURY
—Animal Legends / Kerven *
  mynah commands judge: pluck
  beard; bows, [20–21]
—Bierhorst / Monkey *
  rabbit repeatedly dupes puma,
  77–80
—Bruchac / Iroquois *
  fox trickster: how bear lost his tail,
  32–34
—Childcraft 1 / Once *
  why bear has stumpy tail; frozen
  in ice, 96–97
—Clarkson / World *
  Buh Fox imitates Buh Rabbit, but
  is caught, 145–147
  pig-headed wife (does opposite

of what she is told; drowns),
381–384
—Grimm / Complete *
fox helps horse trick lion, 595–
596
little peasant, 311–316
—Grimm / Sixty *
fox helps horse trick lion, 241–243
little peasant, 142–148
—Hamilton / People *
Bruh Alligator meets trouble, 35–
41
—Hoke / Giants
deception through false doctor-
ing, 41–64
—Journey Sun (Chinese)
cruel stepmother, false wife,
ghost, 6–23
—Russian Hero / Warner *
captive tricks witch's daughter;
geese help escape, 82–85
—Scary / Young *
Ki'in spirits eat souls, take over
bodies; boy outwits Ki'in, 52–56
—Water Buffalo (Chinese)
origin of features (four animals),
82–84
rabbit get revenge on lion, 33–35
DECEPTION PUNISHED
—Caduto / Keepers *
Old Man Coyote and Grandfather
Rock, 57–59
—Dramatized / Kamerman
rich woman; poor woman, 191–
199
—Frog Rider (Chinese)
magic gourd; 120 monsters
burned up, 71–82
—Grimm / Complete *
Hans the hedgehog: princess
promised, 497–502
—Turkish (Art I) / Walker
donkey and camel: irresistible
urges, 44–45

good to the good, and damnation
to the evil: poor man and grand
vizier, 204–207
wicked aunt blinds girl; substitutes her own daughter as
bride, 159–168
DECEPTIVE BARGAIN(-s)
—Cambodian / Carrison
guards propose punishment for
treacherous prince, 73–76
—Clarkson / World *
fox's bag: a series of acts, 251–
253
—Crossley / Animal (Grimm) *
fox and geese: one last prayer,
26–28
—Dramatized / Kamerman
Stone soup, 381–387
—Geras / Grandmother *
Chelm couple's savings plan;
each leaves it to other, 49–56
—Grimm / Complete *
Old Sultan, 230–232
Wolf and the seven [goat] kids,
39–42
—Grimm / Sixty *
Old Sultan, 26–28
Wolf and the seven [goat] kids,
202–205
—Lore of Love
French soldier and Saracen
maid, 98–106
—Shah / Central Asia
wishes (three) granted by genie,
31–44
DECISIVENESS
—Rockwell / Puss *
Jack and the Beanstalk, 1–11
DEDUCTION(-s)
—High John / Sanfield *
Old Boss cheats ("de-ducks")
John the sharecropper, 80–
83
—Paxton / Aesop *

poor old lion (eats animal-visitors), [14–15]

—Turkey / Walker, 301 (index)

DEER (includes "hart")

—Aesop / Holder

stag and the hounds, 24–25

—Allison / I'll Tell *

value: stag's legs vs. antlers, 100

—Animals / Rowland, 185 ("hart")

—Bell / Classical Dict, 231 @

—Bierhorst / Monkey *

wife's head leaves body, eats hot coals, harasses husband, 113–117

—Caduto / Keepers *

Awi Usdi: tabu on excessive hunting, 173–174

—Douglas / Magic *

stag; Thumbelina, 43–53

—Fahs / Old *

animals make sickness for human enemy, 71–80

—Grimm / Complete *

brother transformed to fawn; sister faithful, 67–73

—Grimm / Legends (Ward), II:450 (index)

—Haboo / Hilbert

loon and deer hunt ducks with bow and arrow, 6–7

—Hamilton / People *

alliance: Bruh Alligator and Bruh Deer, 26–30

—High John / Sanfield *

John verifies: Master killed deer with "one shot," 63–68

—Lester / Brer Rabbit *

courting King Deer's daughter, 131–134

—Manning / Cats *

witch abducts king's two children; Katchen the cat helps escape, 9–15

—Navajo Coyote / Haile

coyote and deer: how deer gets its spots, 10, 31–32

—Shannon / More *

little deer wins contest (counts to ten, by fives), 11–14

—Sioux / Standing Bear *

Deer Dreamer: the Deer Run, 26–27

—Tall Tales / Downs: Bear

animal's spring; Mr. Deer escapes / W.H. Vann, 94–98

—Unicorn / Coville *

transfigured hart (Yolen), 79–89

—Yolen / Shape Shift

Indian girl unknowingly turns into deer (Johanna), 52–60

shapeshifting into, 69

DEFECATION

—Hopi Coyote / Malotki

coyotes make coyote-chain to try to reach crow's nest, 151–159

—Navajo Coyote / Haile

Youngest Brother, 16, 22–24 @, 85–88

DEFORMITY

—Bomans / Wily *

echo well: misshapen people not aware of defects, 97–100

—Jewish / Sadeh

girl who had a cow's mouth (healed), 275–276

king's horn: secrets can't be kept forever, 323–324

DEITY(-ies)

—Cotterell / Encyclopedia, 1–260 @

—Indic / Ions

mountains, rivers, pools, 109–116 @

—Russian / Ivanits, 246 (index)

DEKA-DEKA (island)

—Manning / Cauldron *

hero Tow-how: magic disk helps foil hideous old witch, 58–65

de la Mare, Walter (1873–1956)

—Clarkson / World *
  Hare and the hedgehog, 164–
    167
—Hoke / Giants
  David and Goliath, 79–92
de Lint, Charles
—Yolen / Werewolves
  One chance, 254–267
Deliverers of their country (Nesbit)
—Victorian / Hearn, 346–357
DELPHI
—Grimal / Dictionary, 573 (index)
DELPHIC ORACLE
—Greek / Switzer, 204 (index)
Deluge, see FLOOD.
DEMON(-s)
  see also DEVIL; DIV(-s); FEVER
    DEMON; IMP
—Childcraft 3 / Stories *
  man with bump on cheek dances
    for demons, 58–65
—Clouston / Popular, II.505 (index)
  devil on two sticks, I.395–397
—Corrin / Imagine *
  popplesnitch: huntsman's pact to
    produce unknown bird, 70–79
—Cotterell / Encyclopedia, 252 (in-
    dex)
—Creatures (illus) / Huber * 155 (in-
    dex)
—Crossley / Dead *
  black dog of Bungay, 73–76
  Tiddy Mun, marsh spirit, 65–70
—Demons / Gettings
  dictionary, 1–256
  spirits of Solomon (Lemegeton),
    229–231
—Earth / Hadley *
  Sararuma: fire destroys all but
    one couple, [21–22]
—Halloween ABC / Merriam * [9]
—Hamilton / Dark *
  One-Inch boy, the demon oni,
    and the princess, 23–26

—Hartland / English *
  seven tales, 153–182
—Hopi / Talashoma-Malotki
  goats rape/destroy demon-girl,
    136–149
—Jaffrey / Seasons
  heavenly nectar of immortality:
    Vishnu, Moon, demon Rahu,
    71–72
  how Ram, son of Dashrat, de-
    feated demon king Ravan, 48–
    69
  king Kans sends demon-wet-
    nurse to kill Krishna, 22–25
—Japanese / Tyler, 334 (index)
—Jewish / Frankel, 644 (index)
  demon princess/wife and the bro-
    ken oath, 432–437
—Jewish / Sadeh
  accept demon's gift: fall into his
    net, 169–172
  finger: she-demon claims bride-
    groom as her husband, 241–
    242
  form of gazelle; make princess
    talk, 111–112
  kiss: forced to marry she-demon,
    66–69
  piece of copper makes junk man
    rich, 183–186
  prince who went off on his own,
    101–105
  for sparing tree, demon makes
    owner rich, 186
  wandering merchant and
    trustworthy ghost, 87–89
  young man who had no luck,
    285–287
—Limburg / Weird , 120 (index)
—Lurker / Dict Gods, 1–451
—Lynn / Fantasy * 749 (index)
—Man Myth & Magic, 3126 (index)
—Occult & Parapsych / Shepard,
    1579–81 (index)

—Persian / Hinnells
  forces of evil, 52–59, 142 (index)
—Quayle / Shining *
  Momotaro's samurai: dog, pheasant, monkey, 77–89
—Russian Hero / Warner *
  spirits of forest, stream, home,
  24–25 @
—Scary / Young *
  Ki'in spirits eat souls, take over
  bodies; boy outwits Ki'in, 52–
  56
—Schwartz / Gates, 799 (index)
—Shah / Central Asia
  (seed and salt) seven divs for
  brothers, 13–18
—Starkey / Ghosts
  boggart of Castle Farn, 30–35
—Unnatural / Cohen, 71–90
  medieval conceptions; illus., 73
—Vietnam / Terada *
  worm and snail are born to two
  sisters, 59–63
—Witch Encyc / Guiley, 91–96
DEMONIC POSSESSION
—Fahs / Old *
  Jesus: evil spirit driven from boy,
  159–162
—Floyd / Gr Am Myst
  Mary Lurancy Vennum, 152–155
—Ghost (S'west) / Young
  by spirits, 143–154
—Japanese / Tyler, 340 (index)
—Jewish / Sadeh
  Baal Shem Tov and the dybbuk,
  345–346
  dybbuk: haunt of man who killed
  Zechariah, 159–160
—Witch Encyc / Guiley, 89–91, 412
  (index)
DEMONOLOGY
—Lycanthropy / Otten, 327 (index)
  scientific status (Clark), 168–
  194 @

—Occult & Parapsych / Shepard, 1–
  1617 @
—Plants / Dyer, 71–79
De Morgan, Mary
—Victorian / Hearn
  Necklace of Princess Fiori-
  monde, 210–227
DENMARK
—Jonsen / Trolls *
  trolls and the pussy cat [a white
  bear], 15–23
DENTIST
—Corrin / Six-Year *
  dragon; magic bag makes all who
  sniff it, laugh, 53–58
Derleth, August (1909-)
—Pirate Ghosts / McSherry
  The blue spectacles, 73–83
DERMOT O' DYNE
—Celts / Hodges *
  Dermot in the Land-under-Wave,
  57–73
DERVISH
—Arabian / Lewis
  princess elopes on wedding day,
  217–221
—Turkey / Walker, 301 (index)
—Turkish (Art I) / Walker
  golden pears: selfish farmer pun-
  ished, 53–57
  stonecutter: dervish-thieves in
  court of discernment, 72–80
DESERT
—Jewish / Frankel, 646 (index)
—Journeys / Norris *
  quest: city of ultimate beauty and
  happiness, [29–32]
DESERTION
—Jewish / Sadeh
  husband/father and girl who had
  a cow's mouth, 275–276
DESIRE
  see also COVET
—Bomans / Wily *

rich man: the truly happy lack
nothing; vs. the Three Wise
Men, 176–180
—Egyptian / Harris
brothers (Lies and Truth personified), false accusation, 84–85
—Jewish / Sadeh
horse that was an imp, 381–
382
—Leonardo / Fables *
river in fury to possess lily, 34
—Paxton / Aesop *
fox and the grapes, [10–13]
—Turkish (Art I) / Walker
donkey and camel: irresistible
urges, 44–45
De SOTO, Hernando (1496?-1542)
—Southern [legends] / Floyd
search for Cofitachequi, 32–37
DESPAIR
—Jewish / Sadeh
desperate man and prophet
Jonah, 154–158
DESTINY
—Clouston / Popular
miller's son: letter contains death-
warrant, II.458–466
—Lore of Love
Sir Eglamour and Lady Chrysto-
bel, 128–139
DESTITUTION
—Spring / Philip
wise king exposes gold thief, 50–
57
DEUCALION
—D'Aulaire / Greek * 76
—Fahs / Old *
flood; cruel greed punished by
Zeus, 58–63
Deulin, Charles
—Lang / Wilkins
The little soldier, 243–259
DEVIL (*including "pacts" with*)
see also DEMON; SATAN

—American / Read Dgst, 436 (index)
mansion in New Orleans, 55
—Animals / Rowland, 183 (index)
—Arabian / Lewis
Sinbad's first and last voyage,
94–105
—Arabian / McCaughrean [as above]
16–21
—Arabian / Riordan [as above] 38–55
—Baring-Gould / Curious
priest (sixth cent.) slandered, deposed, restored, 156–159 @
—Bomans / Wily *
stolen heart: man sells soul to
devil; becomes "heartless,"
158–165
—British / Briggs *
six tales, 129–139
—Clarkson / World *
Shrove Tuesday visitor, 214–219
—Classic / Downer
devil's tramping ground
(Pittsboro, NC), 74–79
how the Duyvil gave New Amster-
dam to the English, 210–212
—Clouston / Popular
demon in a bottle, I.381–388
—Creatures (illus) / Huber * 155 (index)
—Crossley / British FT *
priest's effective grace: "may
devils fear and fly," 153–154
—Davidson / Dictionary
worship: Yezidic archangels,
354
—Demons / Gettings
devil in literature, 84–95, 197
—Ghosts / Starkey
farmer's pact with farmhand
(devil), 8–15
—Grimm / Complete *
apprentices' pact with devil; condemned for innkeeper's crime,
542–545

bearskin: devil gives money-
providing cloak, 467–472

crafty peasant cheats devil, 767–
768

devil with the three golden hairs,
151–158

devil's grandmother solves riddle
for hero, 563–566

discharged soldier serves Devil
for seven years, 463–466

girl without hands; goodness
wins over devil, 160–166

God creates animals; devil creates
goats with long tails, 642–644

grave-mound: devil and grave-
watchers, 792–796

—Grimm / Legends (Ward), II:402–
403 (index)

—Hamilton / Dark *
servant opens forbidden book,
summons devil to work; can't
stop, 126–131

very large son: landowner tries to
exploit giant, 97–101

—Hamilton / In the Beginning *
Erlik vs. Ulgen: creation of
woman, 28–33

—Hamilton / People *
Devil's daughter helps John de
Conquer, 107–114

wicked man not wanted in
heaven or hell, 126–132

—High John / Sanfield *
devil tests John's memory (humor), 69–72

overhears the Lord and Devil "dividing up souls," 44–49

—Irish / Glassie
outwitting; two tales, 116–118

—Jewish / Frankel
Baal Shem Tov and the devil-
hearted werewolf, 473–475

king; contented simple man; dissatisfied clever man, 538–544

—Jewish / Sadeh
Baal Shem Tov and the Devil, 347

miser-innkeeper tells what happened after death, 172–176

rabbi and the devil worshippers,
217–220

tricked, 3–4

—Journey Sun (Chinese)
drink from Red Spring, under
power of Red Devil, 125–140

—Limburg / Weird , 43–47, 120

—Lurker / Dict Gods, 1–451

—Lycanthropy / Otten, 328 (index)

—MacDonald / Sourcebook *
motif index, 606

—Man Myth & Magic, 3126 (index)
analytics, 3184 (index)
Satanic pact, 3159 (index)

—Mercatante / Encyclopedia, 757 (index)

—Mercatante / Good/Evil, 235 (index)
argues with Jesus on doing good,
181–182

—Monsters / Cohen
devil's footprints, 103–106 @

—Pourrat / French
seven tales, 111–155

—Quayle / Cornish *
Duffy's pact: will do her spinning;
guess name for release, 75–87

Lord Pengerswick and the witch
of Fraddam, 103–108

—Russian / Afanasev, 658 (index)

—Russian / Ivanits, 245 (index)
pact with, 249 (index)

—Russian Hero / Warner *
turning old folk into young: smith
and devil, 19–20

—Scandinavian / Kvideland, xv, 419,
426 (index)

—Schwartz / Gates, 799 (index)

—Trolls / Asbjornsen
boy tricks devil into nut; smith
smashes it, 41

—Unnatural / Cohen, 71–90, 145 (index)
—Vanishing / Mercer *
    Gypsy girl gives parents/brothers to devil, 50–53
—Witch Encyc / Guiley, 96–102, 412 (index)
—Woman's Ency / Walker, 225–232 @
Devil and his grandmother, The
—Grimm / Complete * 563–566
DEVIL, CHEATED OF PROMISED SOUL
—Bomans / Wily *
    devil cheated of promised soul, 158–165
—Cambodian / Carrison
    greedy for silk robe, monk loses robe and money, 52–57
—Clarkson / World *
    Buh Fox's number nine shoes (used to lure bear), 145–147
    coyote pretends to ride home to get tools, 283–285
—Curry / Beforetime *
    coyote steals fire from yellowjacket (people), 33–41
    pine-nut thieves: bluebirds put to sleep by coyote's chant, 90–99
—Dramatized / Kamerman
    Queen of Hearts: stolen tarts, 98–105
—Grimm / Complete *
    bearskin: devil gives money-providing cloak, 467–472
    grave-mound: devil and grave-watchers, 792–796
    Strong Hans escapes from robber den, 688–695
—Hamilton / People *
    wicked man not wanted in heaven or hell, 126–132
—Lang / Wilkins
    Dragon of the North, 285–297
—Shannon / More *

devil will spare man as long as candle "lasts," [not "burns"], 27–30
—Starkey / Ghosts
    farmer's pact with farmhand (devil), 8–15
—Turkish (Art I) / Walker
    magic hen, and fate of two brothers, 61–69
—Vietnam / Terada *
    how tiger got its stripes, 7–9
Devil with the three golden hairs
—Grimm / Complete * 151–158
DEVIL'S CLAW (plant)
—Gullible Coyote / Malotki
    coyote deceives beautiful maid: rattlesnake, 119–129
DEVIL'S DAUGHTER
—Hamilton / People *
    helps John de Conquer escape, 107–114
Devil's sooty brother
—Grimm / Complete * 463–466
Devoted friend, The
—Wilde / Happy * 73–101
—Wilde / Lynch * 24–40
DEW BALLS
—O'Brien / Tales *
    giant Trencross abducts princess; white cat helps rescue, 92–105
DHARMA
—Fahs / Old *
    loyalty to lowly dependent (dog), 33–36
DIAMOND(-s)
—Arabian / Lewis
    king's quest: secure seventh diamond girl, 144–152
    Sinbad's first and last voyage, 94–105
—Arabian / McCaughrean
    Sinbad's first and last voyage, 16–21

—Arabian / Riordan [as above] 38–55

—Jewish / Sadeh Adam's diamond, 2

—Lang / Wilkins
 Toads and diamonds (kind girl and proud sister speak), 106–109

—Precious Stones / Kunz, 396 (index)

DIANA

—Roman / Usher, 131 (index)

—Witch Encyc / Guiley, 412 (index)

DIARMAID

—Campbell / West Highlands
 Diarmaid and Grainne, III.49–102

—Ellis / Dict Irish Myth, 84–87

Dick Whittington . . . see Puss in Boots

Dickens, Charles (1812–1870). The magic fishbone.

—Corrin / Eight-Year * 147–160

—Victorian / Hearn, 106–115

DICTIONARIES

—Astrology / Gettings, 365 @

—Bell / Classical Dict, 1–390 @

—Cotterell / Encyclopedia, 1–260 @

—Demons / Gettings, 1–256

—Dictionary / Leach, 1–1235

—Drury / Dictionary, 1–281 @

—Egyptian / Mercatante, 1–231

—Ellis / Dict Irish Myth, 1–240

—Fairies / Briggs, 1–481

—Grimal / Concise
 classical mythology, 1–456

—Grimal / Dictionary, 1–603 @

—Lacy / Arth Ency, 1–649

—Lurker / Dict Gods, 1–451

—Mercatante / Encyclopedia, 1–807 @

—Occult & Parapsych / Shepard, 1–1617 @

—Preston / Dict Classical
 classical subjects in visual art, 1–311 @

—Room / Classical Dict, 1–343 @

—Waters / Encyclopedia
 magic/magicians, 1–372

—Woman's Ency / Walker, 1–1124 @

DIDO

—Roman / Usher
 Dido and Aeneus, 40–45 @

DIET

—Turkish / Walker
 fat sultan condemns doctors who can't cure him, 127–131

DILEMMA TALES

—African / Abrahams, 109–110 @

DINADAN, Sir

—Pendragon / Ashley
 For to achieve your adventure (Roberts), 101–119

Dinesen, Isak (1883–1962)

—Yolen / Shape
 The sailor-boy's tale, 52–60

DINOSAURS

—Monsters / Hall, 84–99

DIONYSIUS

—D'Aulaire / Greek * 64

—Grimal / Dictionary, 574 (index)

—Man Myth & Magic, 3126 (index)

DIPLOMACY

—Fahs / Old *
 two kings dispute over land, 101–103

DIRGE

—Hopi Coyote / Malotki
 hawk eats all her children; coyote would learn her dirge, 105–111

DIRTY CLOTHES (a name)

—Bruchac / Iroquois *
 knowledge: gifts of the Little People, 41–44

DISABILITY

—Bomans / Wily *
 speech impediments treated with humor, 97–100

DISAPPEAR

—Southern [legends] / Floyd
 Paul Redfern's final flight, 83–87

DISASTER(-s)
—Arabian / Lewis
prohibitions disregarded; evils result, 10–16
—Corrin / Eight-Year *
Little Claus and Big Claus, 13–26
—Hamilton / In the Beginning *
Pandora's box, 138–147
DISASTER FUND
—Bomans / Wily *
evils wanted by four generations of wizards; people turn it to good, 71–75
DISCERNMENT
—Turkish (Art I) / Walker
stonecutter: dervish-thieves in court of discernment, 72–80
Discreet princess, The (L'Heritier)
—Zipes / Beauties * 77–94
DISCRETION
see also PRUDENCE
—Aesop / Reeves-Wilson *
Fox and goat: look before you leap, 14–15
Wolf and goat, 114
—Turkish / Walker
lion asks fox: how does my den smell? 16
DISEASE
—Lycanthropy / Otten, 328 (index)
DISENCHANTMENT
see also CURSE; MAGIC; SORCERY; SPELL
—Arabian / Lewis
abandoned children (grown) restored, 166–173
Anklet (magic pot; magic pins), 49–51
test for succession: prince marries tortoise, 43–51
—Arabian / McCaughrean
test for succession (as above), 142–149
—Arabian / Riordan
abandoned children (grown) restored, 78–87
—Bierhorst / Monkey *
bird bride: toad helps youngest son re oft-ruined cornfield, 25–31
—Celts / Hodges *
swan children restored by St. Patrick's coming, 5–14
—Clarkson / World *
wolf-child; semi-christian ritual removes curse, 202–206
—Corrin / Imagine *
Caliph and Vizier into storks; forget magic word; marriage to (enchanted) owl, 164–76
—Crossley / British FT *
small-tooth dog disenchanted when girl agrees he is sweet . . . , 112–117
—Douglas / Magic *
Beauty and the Beast, 85–97
behead the white cat (enchanted princess), 69–83
kiss: Sleeping Beauty, 55–61
six swans (enchanted princes saved by their sister), 35
—Dramatized / Kamerman
grants three wishes; capture bandit, 324–333
—Erdoes / Sound *
Iktome's misadventures, 16–22
—Giant / Harrison *
witch's spell: giant sees/fears butterflies, etc., 19–30
—Grimm / Complete *
bewitched: straw believed to be a beam, 645
frog; princess' promise; kissed, reverts to prince, 17–20
girl lost in wood; witch, ring, and dove/prince, 558–560
girl shares bread with three little men, 78–83

hero must hold crystal ball before enchantress to free princess, 798–801

Iron Hans, 612–620

iron stove: princess frees prince; breaks tabu, 571–577

Jorinda and Joringel, 339–342

King of the golden mountain, 425–430

lambkin and the little fish, 625–627

Raven, The, 431–436

Seven ravens [transformed brothers], 137–139

Three languages, The, 169–171

—Grimm / Sixty *

Iron Hans, 317–325

Jorinda and Joringel, 17–20

King of the golden mountain, 274–280

Raven, The, 250–256

Seven ravens [transformed brothers], 284–287

Three languages, The, 223–226

—Irish / Glassie

eight tales, 173–184

—Journey Sun (Chinese)

qingke seed stolen from snake king by Achu, 24–46

Wives in the mirror, 109–124

—Lang / Wilkins

Dwarf Long Nose (boy under spell), 534–556

Heart of ice (Caylus), 190–219

The little soldier (Deulin), 243–259

Snow White and Rose Red (befriend bear), 99–105

Water of life (brothers fail; sister succeeds), 362–368

Wounded lion (prince), 385–393

—Legends / Cavendish

enchantresses, 396 (index)

—Lines / Magical *

submission: true love; human form regained: Finist the Falcon, 31–45

—Lore of Love

warlock tricked: hair from heifer, 84

—Nesbit / Fairy *

Belinda and Bellamant; Carillon-Land, 101–122

magic apples: age with each wish, 125–138

princesses to golden apples, 141–158

—Old Wives / Carter

governor marries "Chinese princess" (snake-woman); becomes ill, 142–148

—Pourrat / French

twenty-three tales, 1–109

—Rockwell / Puss *

Kate Crackernuts (gets head of sheep), 19–26

—Russian Hero / Warner *

Sister Alenushka and [kid] Brother Ivanushka, 108–109

—Scriven / Full Color *

Frog prince, 57–59

Sleeping Beauty, 48–51

—Shah / Central Asia

bag: princess imprisoned in mountain of jade, 19–24

charcoal burner and enchanted bear (prince), 92–102

kiss: princess and the donkey, 82–86

ointment: serpent (enchanted princess), 109–117

princess imprisoned in mountain of jade, 19–24

—Turkey / Walker, 301 (index)

—Turkish / Walker

princess marries pig (prince under spell), 114–117

—Turkish (Art I) / Walker
   returned to human form; stepmother killed, 82–88
—Unicorn / Coville *
   princess, cat, and unicorn, 120–
   134
—Williams-Ellis / Tales *
   Childe Rowland rescues Burd Ellen from Elfland, 24–36
   frog-prince; Well of the World's
   End, 55–61
   The Laidly Worm of Spindlestone
   Heugh, 134–141
   youngest sister saves her two bewitched sisters, 125–130
—Yep / Rainbow *
   changeling: faithfulness effects
   disenchantment, 162–168
   enchanted dragons: rainbow people, 162–168
—Yolen / Faery Flag
   face in the cloth; princess and
   witches, 87–100
**DISENCHANTMENT: by faithful-
   ness**
—Bomans / Wily *
   disenchantment by faithfulness
   of others, 9–16
—Grimm / Complete *
   failing vs. non-failing in feeding
   animals, 698–704
   father vows to kill twelve brothers
   if daughter is born, 59–64
—Lang / Wilkins
   Fairer-than-a-Fairy, 274–281
**DISENCHANTMENT: by removing
   covering**
—Arabian / Lewis
   Hasan, the alchemist, and the
   Jinn princess, 138–143
—Clarkson / World *
   woman reverts to seal when hidden skin is found, 136–137
—Frog Rider (Chinese)
   Frog rider (man under spell); marriage, 1–23
—Grimm / Complete *
   Hans the hedgehog: princess
   promised, 497–502
   princess marries donkey; it removes animal skin at night,
   632–635
—Jewish / Frankel
   serpent (prince at night); wife
   burns skin; spell broken, 446–
   449
—Old Wives / Carter
   Nourie Hadig: magic sleep
   caused by ring sent by mother,
   192–199
—Shah / Central Asia
   wishes (three) granted by genie,
   31–44
—Spanish-Am / Van Etten *
   lizard: destroy skin; creature must
   remain old man, 19–24
—Turkish (Art I) / Walker
   Cihansah retains pigeon's skin; it
   remains a girl, 207–217
   dead mother advises stepdaughter: nurse, teach, wed serpent-
   prince, 183–188
   princess and the red-horse-
   husband, 12–19
   skin burned: princess and the
   red-horse-husband, 12–19
**DISENCHANTMENT: by rough
   treatment**
—Chorao / Child's FTB *
   girl given to the Ranee's pet fish
   Muchie Lal, 21–31
—Crossley / British FT *
   mule, beaten, transformed into
   fool's father, 295–303
—Douglas / Magic *
   white cat (enchanted princess),
   69–83
—Dulac / Fairy *

hind of the wood: crayfish fairy,
43–59
—Lang / Wilkins
Wounded lion, The, 385–393
DISGUISE
see also ESCAPE by DISGUISE
—Arabian / Lewis
princess elopes on wedding day
(to another), 217–221
—Bell / Classical Dict, 65–66 @
—Bruchac / Iroquois *
two daughters: wise obedience,
foolish disobedience, 116–121
—Chinese / Chin *
customs: marriage; scholarship
(Ju Yingtai), 61–73
—Clarkson / World *
Cluricaune shows hiding place of
treasure, 115–117
—Corrin / Imagine *
popplesnitch: huntsman's pact
with demon to produce un-
known bird, 70–79
—Erdoes / Sound *
ghost (older Indian foils would-be
robbers of dead man), 82–85
Indian in buffalo skin; captures
crow, 57–59
—Grimm / Complete *
lazy spinner: hides from woodcutter-husband; seeing tow, 577–
579
Maid Maleen, 801–807
—Gullible Coyote / Malotki
coyote and Maasaw (god of
death) try to scare each other,
95–103
—Igloo / Metayer
orphan and the bears [bear-men],
24–31
—Jewish / Frankel, 648 (index)
—Journey Sun (Chinese)
Fanjiangshan secures justice;
three episodes, 90–108

—Lang / Wilkins
Lute player: wife rescues husband from prison, 528–533
—Lore of Love
lovers forced apart; rendezvous
in dreams, 37–49
—O'Brien / Tales *
giants, McConigle vs. Finn (dis-
guised as infant), 9–16
—Old Wives / Carter
widowed king to marry his own
daughter; she flees in leather
suit, 39–46
—Quayle / Shining *
Rashomon: ogre loses/regains
arm, 103–111
—Shah / Central Asia
Feroz-Shah and the mechanical
flying horse, 131–145
—Turkish (Art I) / Walker
Haci's daughter marries, is re-
peatedly assaulted, 24–33
—Williams-Ellis / Tales *
Cap o' Rushes (loves father "like
salt"), 8–16
King O'Toole's goose made
young by St. Kevin, 37–43
—Yep / Rainbow *
Bedtime snacks, 4–10
Disillusion, *see* ILLUSION.
DISK, MAGIC
—Manning / Cauldron *
hero Tow-how: magic disk helps
foil hideous old witch, 58–65
DISLIKE
—Dramatized / Kamerman
The magic (!) grapes: make oth-
ers like boy, 258–264
—Nesbit / Fairy *
Billy and cousin: kite/bicycle, 45–
56
Disobedience, *see* OBEDIENCE.
Ditmars tale of wonders
—Grimm / Complete * 662

DIV(-s)
—Shah / Central Asia
    (chaos) princess and the donkey,
      82–86
    girl with seven divs for brothers,
      13–18
DIVIDING
    see also CLEVER DIVIDING
—Turkey / Walker, 301 (index)
DIVINATION
—Folk-rhymes / Northall
    England, 108–125
—Man Myth & Magic, 3127 (index)
—Witch Encyc / Guiley, 412 (index)
DIVINE . . .
—Jewish / Frankel, 648 (index)
DIVINE INTERVENTION
    see also MIRACLE; PROVI-
      DENCE
—Jewish / Sadeh
    rabbi Isaac Abrabanel and king's
      shoe, 222–223
DIVINE JUDGMENT
—Jewish / Sadeh
    pious rabbi punished for faulty
      vowel sounds, 211–213
    pious/wicked men die on same
      day, 213–214
    rabbi and the beardless rich man,
      214
DIVINE JUSTICE
—Jewish / Frankel
    death: good man, bad man: tem-
      poral honor, eternal reward,
      578–579
    God works in mysterious ways,
      594–596
    Maimonides and the limekiln: bad
      breath, 392–394
—Jewish / Sadeh
    rabbi scolds poor man offering
      bread to God, 238–239
DIVINE PRESENCE
—Schwartz / Gates, 799 (index)

Divine providence, *see* PROVI-
    DENCE, DIVINE
DIVINE PUNISHMENT
—Grimm / Complete *
    tailor throws footstool from
      heaven, 175–177
—Jewish / Sadeh
    atone for sin: reincarnated bride,
      243
    haunt: woman a nonbeliever in
      miracles, 245–246
DIVINE RESIDENCES
—Cotterell / Encyclopedia, 253 (in-
    dex)
DIVING BELL
—Nesbit / Fairy *
    Belinda and Bellamant; Carillon-
      Land, 101–122
DIVINING ROD
—Baring-Gould / Curious, 36–42 @
DIVORCE
—Clouston / Popular
    divorce averted by wife's devo-
      tion, II.327–331
—Jewish / Frankel
    tailor's sleeve: divorce, 521–523
—Jewish / Sadeh
    woman whose husband disap-
      peared, 81–83
DOCTOR(-s)
—Coyote / Bierhorst *
    doc always says "you're doing
      fine," [30]
    dead: the help comes too late,
      [32]
—Fairies / Briggs
    delivers baby of fairy princess,
      103–105
—Grimm / Sixty *
    peasant: Doctor Know-All, 281–
      283
—Jewish / Sadeh
    Elijah: the poor man who became
      a doctor, 133–134

—Scarry's Best *
Dr. Bones is good all year round,
[9–10]
—Turkish / Walker
fat sultan condemns doctors who
can't cure him, 127–131
DOCTORS: HUMOR
—Vietnam / Terada *
one ghost; doctor only had one
patient, 128–129
Doctor Knowall (Grimm)
—Grimm / Complete * 456–458
—Grimm / Sixty * 281–283
DOG(-s)
see also Bremen Town musi-
cians; Old Sultan
—Aesop / Alley *
Dog, carrying meat, and his re-
flection, 24–25
—Aesop / Holder
stag and the hounds, 24–25
—Aesop / Zwerger
ass [jealous of] lap dog, 25
dog and sow [argue: whose babies are better], 21
—Animal Legends / Kerven *
matchmaker: learns beloved's secret name, [18–19]
—Animals / Rowland, 183 (index)
—Baring-Gould / Curious
Gellert, Old Sultan et al., 56–61
—Bell / Classical Dict, 67–69 @
—Bierhorst / Monkey *
giant marries abandoned girl,
"kills" her brother; dog revives,
92–93
—Bruchac / Iroquois *
dogs who saved their master, 85–
91
—Carle / Treasury *
wolf and dog: rather be hungry
than a slave (Aesop), 104–
105
—Celts / Hodges *

Lad of Luck and monster of the
loch, 89–103
—Clarkson / World *
talk (by yam, dog, tree, stone,
etc.), 229–232
—Clouston / Popular
Llewellyn and his dog Gellert,
II.166–186
—Cotterell / Encyclopedia, 253 (index)
—Coyote / Ramsey
Chetco: monster tricked, swept
out to sea, 146–147
—Creatures (illus) / Huber * 155 (index)
—Crossley / British FT *
small-tooth dog disenchanted
when girl agrees he is sweet
. . . , 112–117
—Crossley / Dead *
black dog of Bungay, 73–76
—Curry / Beforetime *
why dog and man walk together,
128–131
—Egyptian / Harris
doomed prince: fate foretold by
Seven Hatitors, 71–76
—Egyptian / Mercatante
prince doomed to three fates:
crocodile, serpent, dog, 36–38
—Erdoes / Sound *
dogs electing a leader; satire,
23–24
origin: smelling other dogs' tail
ends, 23–24
woman works blanket 1,000
years; dog unravels, 124–125
—Fahs / Old *
loyalty to lowly dependent (dog),
33–36
—Fairies / Briggs
Bran (Finn MacCool), 37–38
guardian black dog, 207–208
Moddey Dhoo, 301

—Greaves / Hippo * 39 @
zebra and impala, special prey of
wild dog, 35–38
—Grimm / Complete *
carter runs over/kills dog; sparrow seeks revenge, 280–282
Three languages [dog, bird, frog],
169–171
—Grimm / Legends (Ward), II:404 (index)
—Grimm / Sixty *
carter runs over/kills dog; sparrow seeks revenge, 36–40
Three languages [dog, bird, frog],
223–226
—Hamilton / In the Beginning *
fur: Russian creation myth, 28–
33
—Hamilton / People *
give me back my "tailypo," 116–
120
—Hoke / Giants
Finlay, the giant killer, 142–149
—Igloo / Metayer
dog kills would-be girl takers,
122–127
—Jewish / Sadeh
father punished: reborn as dog,
361–362
Gehazi, for punishment, is reincarnated as dog, 134–136
—Lester / Brer Rabbit *
dog and fox become enemies,
4–6
—Lester / Leopard *
why dogs chase cats, 21–26
—Lurker / Dict Gods, 424–425 (index)
—MacDonald / Sourcebook *
motif index, 608–609
—McGowen / Encyclopedia *
Black Dog, 13–14
—Man Myth & Magic, 3127 (index)
—Manning / Cats *

Little Wonder; witch-stepmother
turns boy into dog, drives his
sister out, 65–74
—Manning / Cauldron *
can see witch, who makes self
invisible, steal farmer's eggs,
32–38
—Paxton / Aesop *
dog in the manger: keeping what
we can't use, [28–30]
—Quayle / Cornish *
good dog Devil; annual delivery
of maid to phantom cats, 37–
44
—Quayle / Shining *
old man makes dead trees
bloom; dog unearths treasure,
69–76
—Russian / Afanasev, 658 (index)
—Scary / Young *
dogs kill witch who would chop
down tree sheltering children,
47–51
Hobbyahs: master dismembers
barking dog (tragicomedy), 26–
30
—Sioux / Standing Bear *
first horse called "holy dog";
Sioux use of dogs, 71–74
wolves save woman caught in
blizzard, 3–9
—Spring / Philip
elder brother envies hardworking
brother, 114–118
—Tall Tales / Downs: Bear
Billingsley's bird dog / D. Anderson, 170–178
Blue Quail Dog / C. Arrowood,
151–153
A Boston Terrier / E.B. White,
16–18
dog that bit people / James
Thurber, 276–282
Rufus / H. A. Smith, 310–314

—Vanishing / Mercer *
  Nagas myth: originally dog had
    horns, goat none, 87–88
—Wildlife / Gillespie, 241 (index)
—Witches / Iosa *
  animals help kind children es-
    cape giant witch, 18–22
—Wolves / Lopez, 301 (index)
  which has better life: wolf or In-
    dian dog, 110–111
—Woman's Ency / Walker, 240–
    247 @
—Yep / Rainbow *
  cats and dogs as "Natural ene-
    mies," 12–18
  dog-spirit: stay in haunted house;
    boasting contest, 96–105
—Yolen / Shape Shift
  shape-shifter can't revert from,
    38–41
Dog and the bone see under Aesop
**Dog and the sow [argue: whose
    babies are better]**
—Aesop / Zwerger * 21
Dog and the sparrow
—Grimm / Complete * 280–282
—Grimm / Sixty * 36–40
DOG-DEER
—Hamilton / People *
  alliance: Bruh Alligator and Bruh
    Deer, 26–30
Dog in the manger
—Paxton / Aesop * [28–30]
Dog in the river
—Paxton / Belling *
  greed: foolish loss of meat
    (Aesop), [38–39]
DOGAI
—McGowen / Encyclopedia * 18
DOLL(-s)
—Bomans / Wily *
  children escape from witch with
    help of top, kite, doll, 88–93
—Grimm / Complete *

  maiden escapes marriage to
    hare, 332–334
—Hamilton / Dark *
  Baba Yaga, Vasilisa, and her
    doll, 14–22
—Pellowski / Family *
  nesting doll story: five clever girls,
    107–113
—Pellowski / Story *
  nesting dolls (matrioska), 78–83
  stories with dolls, 77–91
  trouble dolls, 84–86
—Russian Hero / Warner *
  magic doll helps Vasilisa escape
    Baba-Yaga, 86–92
DOLPHIN
—Bell / Classical Dict, 69–70 @
—Corrin / Imagine *
  Arion wins prize; is thrown over-
    board; saved by dolphin, 161–
    163
DOMOVOI
—McGowen / Encyclopedia * 18–19
—Russian / Ivanits, 246 (index)
DON JUAN
—Lore of Love
  stone avenger (statue) drags D.J.
    to hell, 61–63
DON JUAN TYPES
—Erdoes / Sound *
  flute entices girls to "ghostly
    lover," 95–97
DONKEY(-s) (includes "ass,"
    "burro")
  see also Aesop: Laden ass and
    a horse; Bremen Town musi-
    cians
—Aesop / Reeves-Wilson *
  miller, boy, and donkey, 51–53
  pretense: in lion's skin, 24–26
  quarrel over "rental" of shadow,
    64
  trickery backfires: Donkey carry-
    ing salt, 92–94

—Allison / I'll Tell *
farmer, son, and donkey: attempt to please everyone,
128–129
—Arabian / McCaughrean
donkey advises ox to feign illness, 104–107
—Birds / Carter & Cartwright *
prayer to go to heaven with (Jam-
mes/Wilbur), 50
—Cambodian / Carrison
father/son ride/carry donkey to
market, 102–106
—Grimm / Complete *
magic: wishing-table, gold-ass,
cudgel in sack, 177–187
princess marries donkey; it removes animal skin at night,
632–635
Salad; fed to witch, 551–558
—Grimm / Sixty *
Salad; fed to witch, 292–293
—Jewish / Frankel
rabbi's magic ring: mean-spirited
wife to donkey, 450–455
—Jewish / Sadeh
marriage: princess to donkey's
head, 4–8
singing donkey and dancing
camel, 167
—MacDonald / Sourcebook *
motif index, 609–610
—Manning / Cauldron *
donkey, gift of troll-child, helps
hunter rescue princess, 9–17
—Rockwell / Puss *
Miller (The), his son, and the donkey, 27–29
—Shah / Central Asia
(chaos; div) princess and the
donkey, 82–86
—Turkey / Walker, 302 (index)
—Turkish (Art I) / Walker
(drops gold coins), given to sim-
pleton, stolen by padishah, re-
covered, 195–198
donkey and camel: irresistible
urges, 44–45
Hoca joined by, selling pome-
granates, 71
—Water Buffalo (Chinese)
innkeeper steals magic donkey,
table cloth, stick, 103–110
Donkey, The
—Grimm / Complete * 632–635
Donkey cabbage
—Grimm / Complete * 551–558
—Grimm / Sixty * 60
—Lang / Wilkins, 266–273
Donkey-skin
—Carter / Sleeping * 81–92
—Zipes / Beauties * 67–74
Doodang, The
—Tall Tales / Downs: Bear
by Joel C. Harris, 109–111
DOPPELGAENGER
—Ghosts / Cohen, 215–218
DORANI
—Lang / Wilkins
Dorani: transport by magic stool,
432–440
Dove, see BIRD: DOVE.
Dove and the snake
—Aesop / Holder, 2–3
DOWRY
—Corrin / Imagine *
Onsongo, lazy artist, steals
Masai cattle for dowry, 80–
96
—Hoke / Giants
Managing-Molly outwits courting
ogre, 65–70
Doyle, Debra
—Yolen / Werewolves
Bad blood, 3–34
DRACULA
—Dracula / McNally, 1–233 @
beyond the grave, 183–190

fiction and film, 160–181 @

filmography, 216–223 @

German/Russian/Romanian stories, 192–208 @

history (15th cent.), 35–81, 125–
141 @

horror stories (15th cent.), 108–
124 @

DRAGON(-s)

—Animals / Rowland, 183 (index)

—Babylonia / Spence, 391 (index)

—Beasts / McHargue, 116 (index)
Oriental, 19–27 @

—Bell / Classical Dict, 71–73 @

—Bomans / Wily *
balloon message; with godmother's help, knight kills
dragon, 197–202

—British / Briggs *
five tales, 141–149

—Brooke / Telling *
Sleeping Beauty: event after
awakening, 3–33

—Childcraft 1 / Once *
Custard the Dragon (Nash), 272–
275

—Clouston / Popular, I.155–167

—Corrin / Six-Year *
laughing dragon; magic bag; all
who sniff it laugh, 53–58

—Cotterell / Encyclopedia, 253 (index)

—Creatures (illus) / Huber * 36–38,
155 (index)

—Demons / Gettings, 96–98

—Dragons / Baskin * [1–47]
Beowulf and Grendel's mother,
[14–15]
Colchis, [36–37]
Daniel and the dragon, [10–11]
eight-tailed, [42–43]
fire-breathing dragon, [32–33]
fold-up dragons, [24–25]
ghostly dragon, [38–39]
Krak's dragon, [30–31]

manuscript dragon, [44–45]
Perseus and the sea dragon,
[28–29]
Shen Lung, [12–13]

—Dragons / Hogarth
ancient and classical, 12–85 @
medieval, 88–161 @
modern, 190–206 @
renaissance, 164–187 @

—Dragons / Johnsgard, 1–163
ancient to modern, 46–61
child-stealing, 63–66
classification and types, 1–23,
138–147
fire-breathing, 33–35, 138
origins, 75–78

—Dramatized / Kamerman
king under spell, 79–87
Plum Blossom and the dragon,
38–46

—Fahs / Old *
people cooperate to "kill" pollution dragon, 169–171

—Fairies / Briggs, 106–108
Lambton Worm, 259–260

—Frog Rider (Chinese)
Shigar saves men; wife cuts
wings of flying horse, 60–70

—Gould / Mythical, 159–211, 377–
383, 392–407 @
Chinese, 212–247 @
classical and medieval, 192–
211 @
Japanese, 248–255 @

—Grimm / Complete *
youngest huntsman rescues
princesses from dragon, 420–
424

—Grimm / Legends (Ward), II:404 (index)

—Journey Sun (Chinese)
small yellow dragon defeats big
black dragon, 81–89

—Lang / Wilkins

Fairy of the Dawn; magic well
water, 571–601
—Legends / Cavendish
foam; Chinese, 53–54 @
—Lurker / Dict Gods, 425 (index)
—Lynn / Fantasy * 750–751 (index)
—MacDonald / Sourcebook *
motif index, 610
—McGowen / Encyclopedia * 19–
20
—Man Myth & Magic, 3128 (index)
—Maori / Kanawa *
talking dragon (Taniwah) of Ro-
torua trapped/killed, 52–60
taniwah (Hotu-puku) killed by
brave warriors, 88–89
—Monsters / Cohen, 228–235 @
—Monsters / Hall, 6–23
Chinese, 10–11, 18–19
—Nesbit / Fairy *
last dragon; pet of princess, 161–
171
last dragon; tamed; becomes first
airplane, 161–171
two-headed, killed by Billy the
King, 1–22
—O'Brien / Tales *
Lord Mount Dhraggin: weaver
"kills" three-score and ten;
made Lord, 72–81
—Quayle / Shining *
Lord Bag-o'-Rice aids serpent
(Dragon King); kills giant centipede, 33–43
—Russian / Afanasev, 658 (index)
—Russian / Ivanits, 246 (index)
—Russian Hero / Warner *
Dobrynya spares abductor/
dragon, 69–70
gypsy cons dragon: he's
stronger, 71–72
Russian folk tales, 62–63 @
tsar's son flees smithy, to escape,
18–19

Vasilisa (Golden Braid) and Ivan
the Pea, 63–68
—Saint George / Fox, 23–38, 184 (in-
dex)
—South / Mythical
sources; bibliographical essay,
27–58 (J. Evans), 381 (index)
—Spring / Philip
loses power when seen by unpro-
tected men, 119–133
—Trolls / Asbjornsen
boy who became lion, falcon, ant,
64–70
—Unicorn / Hathaway
Knight of the Lion / Lady of the
Unicorn, 88–99 @
—Victorian / Hearn
Reluctant dragon, The (Gra-
hame), 326–344
—Vietnam / Terada *
sea snake captures mandarin's
wife, 88–94
—Water Buffalo (Chinese)
trifles may cause disasters, 13–17
—Williams-Ellis / Tales *
The Laidly Worm of Spindlestone
Heugh, 134–141
—Yep / Rainbow *
freed from spell: rainbow people,
162–168
—Yolen / Faery Flag
making: head, trunk, tale, options
(poem), 82–84
DRAGON KING
—Journey Sun (Chinese)
Dragon King of Langqiong; five
tales, 61–80
—Spring / Philip
girl sheepherder finds water and
salt, 98–102
Dragon of the North
—Lang / Wilkins, 285–297
Dragon's boy, The / Jane Yolen
—Pendragon / Ashley, 32–48

DRAWING
—Pellowski / Family *
  picture-drawing stories, 47–76
  in sand, snow, or mud, 119–125
—Yolen / Faery Flag
  dumb child draws unicorns; is
  healed, 48–57

DREAM(-s)
—Arabian / Lewis
  Princess Dunja: all men are faith-
  less, 52–59
—Bruchac / Iroquois *
  Okteondon defeats Workers of
  Evil, 104–114
—Cambodian / Carrison
  Siva believes eagle's dreams;
  owl asks equal treatment, 67–
  72
—Chaucer / Cohen *
  Chauntecleer: ignoring prophetic
  dreams, 19–31
—Clouston / Popular
  falling in love through dreams,
  II.228, 488
—Crossley / British FT *
  butterfly soul flutters, goes into
  horse skull, 365–367
  John Chapman, pedlar of Swaff-
  ham, 251–264
—Crossley / Dead *
  Pedlar of Swaffham: dream dis-
  closes treasure, 27–37
—Douglas / Magic *
  prophetic: Europa and Zeus,
  181–184
—Fahs / Old *
  magic pillow: dream projects fu-
  ture life, 121–124
—Grimm / Complete *
  Jorinda and Joringel; flower
  breaks spell, 339–342
—Grimm / Sixty *
  Jorinda . . . (as above), 17–20
—Jewish / Frankel, 649 (index)

—Jewish / Sadeh
  fly and spider; incense: knowledge
  and understanding, 389–392
  king and forty crows; demon-child
  interprets, 31–34
  king saved by rabbi's wife, 232–
  233
  king's bad dream; prediction, 329
  lovesickness: leaves from Paradise, 365–367
  rich man prepared for rainy day,
  178–179
  two tailors and wonderful photograph, 204–208
—Man Myth & Magic, 3128 (index)
—Old Wives / Carter
  Mr. Fox: his betrothed dreams of
  him mutilating woman for ring,
  8–10
—Pirate Ghosts / McSherry
  before I wake: Pedro goes to sea,
  182–200
—Plants / Dyer
  dream-plants, 103–113
—Restless / Cohen *
  snow-ghost wife: reveal dream =
  death, 16–23
—Schwartz / Gates, 799 (index)
—Shah / Central Asia
  magic dream of Habeeb, 56–61
—Tree / Kerven *
  bamboo-princess freed from
  spell, [28–29]
—Turkey / Walker, 302 (index)

DRESS
—Jewish / Sadeh
  charm causes lewdness, 20–21

DRINK, MAGIC
—Jaffrey / Seasons
  heavenly nectar of immortality:
  Vishnu, Moon, demon Rahu,
  71–72

DRINKING
—Paxton / Belling *

crow and the pitcher (Aesop),
[22–23]

DRINKING TABOO
—Caduto / Keepers *
Manabozho and the maple trees,
145
—Grimm / Complete *
Raven, The, 431–436
—Grimm / Sixty *
Raven, The, 250–256
—Jaffrey / Seasons
Karvachauth: husband dies when
wife breaks taboo; Nine Earth
Mothers, 75–79

DROLL(-s)
—Hartland / English *
eight tales, 249–282

DROUGHT
—Caduto / Keepers *
Hero Twins and Swallower of
Clouds, 79–81
Koluscap turns Water Monster
into bullfrog, 81–84
—Chinese / Christie
Sea Girl finds key to unlock lake,
137–138
—Chorao / Child's FTB *
ants push sky; rescue Indian from
tree top, 43–50
—Earth / Hadley *
ends when snake makes frog
laugh, [23–24]
—Fahs / Old *
lizard keeps others from well, 91–
95
—Gullible Coyote / Malotki
coyote on prayer mission for rain,
105–117
—Imaginary / Nigg
fire spirits and the dew-eagle oshadegea, 133–135
—Journey Sun (Chinese)
Yangang saves village incinerated by shooting star, 47–60

—Spring / Philip
Akui frees water; turns to stone,
87–93
girl sheepherder finds water and
salt, 98–102
—Williams-Ellis / Tales *
Sister Long-Hair steals stream
from mountain god, 161–171

DROWN
—Russian / Ivanits, 246 (index)

DRUID(-s)
—Campbell / West Highlands, IV.432
(index)
—Celtic / MacCana, 141 (index)
—Ellis / Dict Irish Myth, 90–92
—Lines / Magical *
Oisin's mother captured by Dark
Druid, 169–174
—Man Myth & Magic, 3128 (index)
—Witch Encyc / Guiley, 107–109,
412 (index)

DRUM(-s) (*sometimes magic*)
—Fahs / Old *
stolen drum to dance by, 86–
90
—Igloo / Metayer
woman a walking skeleton: magic
drum, 13–18
—Spanish-Am / Van Etten *
must guess what drum is made of
(flea hide), 65–72
—Water Buffalo (Chinese)
enormous candy-man; magic
drum; long nose, 70–77
—Yep / Rainbow *
Wong I, II and III: boasting contest, 96–105

Drummer, The
—Grimm / Complete * 781–791

DRUNK
—Crossley / British FT *
Slam impersonates ghost; frightened to death by real ghost,
140–141

DUALISM
—Mercatante / Good/Evil, 235 (index)
DUCK(-s)
see also Ugly duckling, The
—Birds / Carter & Cartwright *
Duck and the kangaroo (Lear), 44
—Dramatized / Kamerman
Peter and the wolf, 375–380
—Grimm / Complete *
Fundevogel, 241–244
Queen bee, The, 317–319
—Grimm / Sixty *
Fundevogel, 84–87
Queen bee, The, 206–208
—High John / Sanfield *
Old Boss cheats ("de-ducks")
John the sharecropper, 80–83
—Manning / Cats *
Istvan climbs pea-plant into heav-
ens; finds seven-eyed goat;
falls into swamp, 107–110
DUMB
—O'Brien / Tales *
fairies take Gilly, abduct princess;
strike her dumb; Gilly learns of
curing herb, 106–117
DUMUZI
—Wolkstein / Love
Inanna and Dumuzi, 37–71,
239 @
DUNCE
—Grimm / Complete *
cat (princess) gives horse to
miller's apprentice, 482–485
—Tall Tales / Downs: Bear
duck that flew backwards / D.
Tracy, 345–351
—Vanishing / Mercer *
abduction: little duck and big water-rat, 54–57
DUNG
—Greaves / Hippo *
elephant/rhino contest: produce
most dung, 60–64

rhino loses porcupine's quill, 64–
65
why hippo scatters dung on riverbank, 67
—Navajo Coyote / Haile
chart; the seventeen tales, 11 @
**Duny: boy who became a wizard
(Le Guin)**
—Childcraft 3 / Stories * 176–186
DUPE(-s)
see also FOOL; GULLIBILITY;
TRICKERY
—Bierhorst / Monkey *
rabbit gets caught; dupes coyote
to take his place, 72–76
rabbit repeatedly dupes puma,
77–80
—Childcraft 1 / Once *
the three little pigs [tricked to self-
destruct], 102–106
—Hopi Coyote / Malotki
coyote sheep-killer, duped into
taking sweatbath; dies, 119–
125
grasshopper dupes coyote (hold
up roof with legs), 99–103
—Navajo Coyote / Haile
rabbit tricks, and escapes from,
coyote, 12, 38–39
Duration of life, The
—Grimm / Complete * 716–718
DUST
—Jewish / Frankel, 646 (index)
DUTCH TALES
—Restless / Cohen *
death and tragedy follow haunted
hooded-chair, 94–102
—Scriven / Full Color *
children find cowslips: Keys of
summer, 41–42
DWARF(-s)
see also Snow-White . . .
—Arabian / McCaughrean
Sinbad's second voyage, 22–28

—Arabian / Riordan
Sinbad's second voyage, 38–55

—Bomans / Wily *
echo well: misshapen people not/aware of defects, 97–100

—Crane / Beauty *
Yellow Dwarf and proud princess, [34–47]

—Grimm / Complete *
girl shares bread with three little men, 78–83

—Grimm / Legends (Ward), II:405–406 (index)

—Lang / Wilkins
Snow White and Rose Red (befriend bear), 99–105

—MacDonald / Sourcebook *
motif index, 612

—McGowen / Encyclopedia * 20

—Norse / Crossley, 266 (index)

—Strauss / Trail
Snow White . . . ; soliloquy (poem), 5–7

—Zipes / Beauties *
Yellow dwarf (d'Aulnoy), 459–476

Dwarf Long Nose (boy under spell)
—Lang / Wilkins, 534–556

DYBBUK (a haunt)
—Jewish / Sadeh
Baal Shem Tov and the dybbuk, 345–346

DYER
—Arabian / Lewis treachery: good barber and evil dyer, 123–130

Dying for others, see SELF-SACRIFICE.

EA (god)
—Babylonia / Spence, 391 (index)
Eagle, see BIRD: EAGLE.

Ear of corn, The
—Grimm / Complete * 791–792
EAR SCOOP
—Yep / Rainbow *
treasure unearthed by pet mouse, 80–85
EARHART, Amelia (1898–1937)
—Floyd / Gr Am Myst
last flight, 132–135
EARTH (including creation; origin of present order)
see also WORLD
—Bierhorst / Naked *
Turtle's glory: support earth on its back, 31–36
—Bruchac / Iroquois *
creation of Earth; turtle supports, 15–17
—Bullchild / Sun
beginnings, 1–126
—Caduto / Keepers *
beginnings of life: Grandfather Rock, 57
earth's origin; primal water; turtle's back, 25–26
how Thunder and Earthquake made Ocean, 93–95
Woman from the Sky, 25–26
—Chinese / Christie, 69–85
—Constellations / Gallant * 200 (index)
—Cotterell / Encyclopedia, 253 (index)
—Coyote / Ramsey, 258–259
—Curry / Beforetime *
how Old-Man-Above created the world, 1–4
—Earth / Hadley *
Baiame sends Yhi to bring earth to life, [9–10]
—Earthmaker / Mayo *
Earth is on Big Turtle's back (Wyandot tale), 2–4
—Erdoes / Sound *

remaking of the (third) world,
126–129
—Hamilton / In the Beginning *
Enuma elish, 84
Hesiod's Theogony, 126–131
Olorun: Owner of the sky, 72–77
Sedi and Melo (gods), 116–121
turtle back: Huron creation myth,
58–63
—MacDonald / Sourcebook *
motif index, 18–24
—Man Myth & Magic, 3129 (index)
—Schwartz / Gates, 800 (index)
—Southern [legends] / Floyd
Teed's theory: Earth a concave
sphere, 21–23
—Tree / Kerven *
corn-maiden: love and respect
the earth, [30–32]
—Vanishing / Mercer *
Ainu myth: tides, quakes, hills,
etc., 95–98

EARTH GOD
—Jaffrey / Seasons
birth of Krishna: wicked king Kans
tries to kill him, 22–25

EARTH MOTHERS
—Jaffrey / Seasons
Karvachauth: husband dies when
wife breaks taboo, 75–79

EARTHQUAKE
—Bierhorst / Monkey *
underground: witch escapes from
great-horned-snake, 118–120
—Caduto / Keepers *
how Thunder and Earthquake
made Ocean, 93–95
—Earthmaker / Mayo *
origins, 1 @
Wahconda makes the earth
shake (Oto tale), 54–56

EARTH STARTER
—Hamilton / In the Beginning *
Maidu creation myth, 34–41

**East of the sun and west of the
moon . . .**
—Corrin / Favourite * 1–15
—Old Wives / Carter, 122–132
—Trolls / Asbjornsen, 26–35

EASTER EGG
—Russian Hero / Warner, 96 @

EASY PROBLEM MADE HARD
—Bomans / Wily *
obvious solutions ignored, 147–
151
—Dramatized / Kamerman
Peach tree kingdom; imposter;
bride test, 288–305

EATING
—Greaves / Hippo *
contest: elephant vs. squirrel,
52–53
—Grimm / Complete *
shepherd chooses bride who
eats properly, 655–656
—High John / Sanfield *
bet on eating forty-pound watermelon (eats one for practice),
41–43
—Jewish / Sadeh
contest: champion of hot pepper,
296
—Trolls / Asbjornsen
(prodigious) Rumble-Mumble
Goose-Egg, 71–82

EATING TABOO
—Grimm / Complete *
Raven, The, 431–436
youngest huntsman rescues prin-
cesses from dragon, 420–424
—Grimm / Sixty *
Raven, The, 250–256
—Old Wives / Carter
to be safe, girl must share food
with cat, 160–165

ECHO (god/nymph)
—Bulfinch / Sewell *
Echo and Narcissus, 74–77

—D'Aulaire / Greek * 92
—Greek / Osborne
    punished: can only repeat last
      words heard, 29–32
—Lore of Love
    vanity's reflection: Echo and Nar-
      cissus, 74

ECOLOGY
—Caduto / Keepers *
    White Buffalo Calf Woman and
      sacred pipe, 187–188

ECSTASY
—Man Myth & Magic, 3129 (index)

ECTOR de Maris, Sir
—Douglas / Magic *
    Merlin and Arthur: the sword,
      141–149
—King Arthur / Senior, 319 (index)

EDUCATION
—Clarkson / World *
    folktales in the college class-
      room, 399–412 @
    folktales in the elementary class-
      room, 385–398 @

Eel, *see* FISH: EEL.

Effect, *see* CAUSE and EFFECT.

EFREET
—Arabian / Lewis
    prince detests women; princess
      disgusted by men, 66–80
—Arabian / Riordan
    prince detests . . . [as above],
      66–77

EGG(-s)
—Dramatized / Kamerman
    The price of eggs, 149–154
—High John / Sanfield *
    devil tests John's memory, 69–72
—Jewish / Sadeh
    egg seller strikes it rich; ends in
      misfortune, 303
—MacDonald / Sourcebook *
    motif index, 613
—Man Myth & Magic, 3129 (index)

—Russian / Ivanits, 247 (index)
—Russian Hero / Warner *
    extended soul in, 96 @

Ego, *see* SELF . . .

EGOTISM
—Manning / Cats *
    baby wrens lie; father wren
      "scares off" King Tiger, 124–
      125

EGYPT
—Cotterell / Encyclopedia, 10–13 @
—Dictionary / Leach, 1206 (index)
—Egyptian / Harris
    fifth dynasty: King Khufu and the
      magicians, 53–62
—Hamilton / In the Beginning *
    Ra: The sun-god and the dragon,
      110–115
—Jewish / Frankel, 654 (index)
—Man Myth & Magic, 3129 (index)
—Medicine-Plants / Read Dgst
    ancient lore, 13
—Schwartz / Gates, 800 (index)
—Wolkstein / Love Two Lands, 255 @

EGYPTIAN . . .
—Constellations / Gallant * 200 (in-
    dex)
—Egyptian / Ions, 1–144 @
    sacred animals, 120–125 @
—Egyptian / Mercatante, 1–231
—Legends / Cavendish, 5 (index)
—Mercatante / Encyclopedia, 729 (in-
    dex)
—Mercatante / Good/Evil, 13–19 @
—Old Wives / Carter
    widowed king to marry his own
      daughter; she flees in leather
      suit, 39–46
—Restless / Cohen *
    the mummy's ghost, 3–15
—Roman / Perowne
    influence on Roman, 88–97 @
—Wolkstein / Love
    Isis and Osiris, 1–36, 261 @

Elders, *see* AGED.
EL DORADO
—Speck / New World, 521 (index)
ELECTION
—Erdoes / Sound *
    dogs electing a leader; satire,
    23–24
ELEMENTALS
—Demons / Gettings, 100
—Man Myth & Magic, 3130 (index)
—Occult & Parapsych / Shepard,
    405–407 @
—Witch Encyc / Guiley, 412 (index)
ELEPHANT(-s)
—Animals / Rowland, 183 (index)
—Beat / Bryan *
    stronger? why bush cow and ele-
    phant always fight, 14–29
—Cambodian / Carrison
    Siva believes eagle's dreams;
    owl asks equal treatment, 67–
    72
—Corrin / Imagine *
    Arap Sang: bigger head = bigger
    headache, 47–53
—Creatures (illus) / Huber * 155 (in-
    dex)
—Greaves / Hippo * 58–59 @
    contest with rhino: produce most
    dung, 60–64
    eating contest: vs. squirrel, 52–
    53
    elephant vs. Rain Spirit: who is
    greater? 53–58
    rhino borrows porcupine's quill to
    treat wound, 64–65
—Jaffrey / Seasons
    how Ganesh got his elephant
    head, 121–123
    wrestling, Krishna defeats ele-
    phant and two giants; kills
    Kans, 32–36
—Leonardo / Fables *
    characteristics; behavior, 46–47

—Lester / Brer Rabbit *
    with Brer Elephant's help, causes
    Brer Tiger to leave area, 62–
    65
—Lester / Leopard *
    Tug-of-war: turtle cons elephant
    and hippo, 17–20
—MacDonald / Sourcebook *
    motif index, 614
—Vanishing / Mercer *
    pygmies help Lightning (personi-
    fied) kill elephants, 71–73
—Yolen / Baby Bear *
    Morris the elephant packs "trunk"
    for trip, [7]
ELEVATOR OPERATOR
—Nesbit / Fairy *
    Charmed life, or Princess and
    Lift-man, 25–42
ELF (elves)
—Dramatized / Kamerman
    happy adults: children at wishing
    well, 15–22
—Fairies / Briggs
    ellyllon, 121–122
—Hall / Treasury *
    a home for Tandy, 54–61
—Lynn / Fantasy * 752 (index)
—McGowen / Encyclopedia * 21
ELFLAND
—Williams-Ellis / Tales *
    Childe Rowland rescues Burd El-
    len from Elfland, 24–36
    Tamlane (knight) rescued from
    elfland, 151–159
ELIJAH (*the prophet*)
—Jewish / Frankel, xvii, 654 (index)
    Elijah appears as slave; sold to
    help poor man, 584–585
    Elijah in heaven: recording angel,
    577–578
    Elijah's cup to be sold to provide
    needs for seder, 605–606
    father dreams: son to hang on

thirteenth birthday; saved by
Elijah, 597–600
fifteen tales, 575–607
soft like reed, not hard like cedar;
race, 583–584
stepmother sends Miriam to be
killed in forest, 579–583
student marries ugly girl; leaves
her; Elijah makes her beautiful,
588–594
tramp (Elijah), stranger to be
treated kindly, 604–605
—Jewish / Sadeh
Baal Shem Tov: comes to every
circumcision, 128–129
bookseller, 130
poor man who became a doctor,
133–134
prophet's magic box, 126
Rabbi Nissim and the poor Talmud scholar, 122–124
sold as slave to help poor man,
124–126
—Schwartz / Gates, 800 (index)
ELK
—Coyote / Ramsey
elk, hunter, greedy father, 64–65
twig to boy to elk; transformation,
153–156
—Earthmaker / Mayo *
Black Elk digs up the mountains
(Apache tale), 18–22
—Erdoes / Sound *
courtship: origin of use of flute,
3–9
—Haboo / Hilbert
wolf brothers kill elk and beaver,
10–13
—Navajo Coyote / Haile
porcupine tricks/kills elk; vies with
coyote for it, 13, 41–44
ELOHIM
—Hamilton / In the Beginning *
creation (Genesis), 148–153

ELOPE(-ment)
—Arabian / Lewis
princess elopes on wedding day
(to another), 217–221
—Clouston / Popular, II.212–228
ELOQUENCE
—Egyptian / Harris
peasant: Khunanup vs. Nem-
tynakht, 60–62
Elves, see ELF (elves).
Elves (second story)
—Grimm / Complete * 199
Elves (third story)
—Grimm / Complete * 200
**Elves and the shoemaker, The
(Grimm)**
—Allison / I'll Tell * 57
—Corrin / Six-Year * 49–52
—Grimm / Complete * 197–198
—Grimm / Sixty * 209–210
Elwes, Alfred
—Pendragon / Ashley
Jaufrey (knight) and fair Brunis-
sende, 260–321
EMBALMMENT
—Egyptian / Ions, 143 (index)
EMERALD
—Precious Stones / Kunz, 397 (index)
Emerson, Ru
—Yolen / Werewolves
The werewolf's gift, 35–44
EMPEROR
—Chinese / Chin *
palace plot: rival concubines, 77–
92
—Grimm / Legends (Ward), II:407 (in-
dex)
—Lang / Wilkins
Nightingale (sings for emperor),
317–326
—Manning / Cats *
able to call twelve sailors at will,
Vasily saves Leeshy Cat, 37–
50

Emperor's new clothes, The
—Allison / I'll Tell * 24–25
—Childcraft 3 / Stories * 100–106
—Corrin / Favourite * 219–225
—Hepburn / World * 30–47
—Leete / Golden * 8–15
EMPLOYEES
—Aesop / Reeves-Wilson *
  clever! cock and the maids, 62–
  63
EMPLOYMENT AGENCY
—Nesbit / Fairy *
  Billy the King [hired to be eaten
  by dragon], 1–22
Enchantment, see DISENCHANT-
  MENT; SPELL(-s).
Encyclopedias, see DICTIONAR-
  IES.
END OF DAYS
—Schwartz / Gates, 800 (index)
END OF THE WORLD
—Bomans / Wily *
  flood: clergy argue about biblical
  text interpretation, 107–108
—Earthmaker / Mayo *
  beaver brings, 81 @
—Erdoes / Sound *
  old Sioux woman works blanket
  1,000 years, 124–125
—Indian Myth / Burland
  Pawnee mythology, 88–89
—Jewish / Frankel
  end of days, 649 (index)
ENDLESS TALES
—Clarkson / World *
  rats jump from ship . . . , 247–248
—Old Coot / Christian *
  wager: gambler won't say
  "enough" to stories, 29–38
ENDURANCE CONTEST
—Greaves / Hippo *
  elephant vs. Rain Spirit: who is
  greater, 53–58
—Turkish (Art I) / Walker

  seven-year siege lifted by
  woman's cleverness, 144–
  146
ENEMY
—Coyote / Bierhorst *
  enemies in sinking boat; re-
  venge-minded forget all else,
  [20]
—Fahs / Old *
  Capilano sisters bring peace and
  brotherhood, 104–107
ENGINE
—Hall / Treasury *
  Little Engine that could, 1–9
ENGLAND
  see also BRITISH . . .
—British / Briggs *
  historical traditions; seventeen
  tales, 205–229
  local legends; seventeen tales,
  231–249
—Celts / Hodges *
  Merlin: life and magic powers,
  117–132
—Dictionary / Leach, 1207 (index)
—Folk-rhymes / Northall, 1–565
—Ghosts / Time-Life
  Tower of London, 81–84
—Hope / Holy Wells
  antiquities; saints, 1–222
—Lynn / Fantasy * 752 (index)
—Saint George / Fox
  St. George; history, 59–97
ENGLISH LANGUAGE
—Bosma / Classroom
  folk literature, 1–116
ENIGMAS
—Grimm / Complete *
  Four clever brothers, 580–584
—Grimm / Sixty *
  Four clever brothers, 220–234
—Turkish / Walker
  son "loves father like salt," 108–
  113

ENKI (Sumerian)
—Wolkstein / Love, 239 @
ENLIGHTENMENT
—Indic / Ions
  Buddhist, 132 @
ENLIL (god)
—Babylonia / Spence, 392 (index)
ENNEAD
—Egyptian / Harris, 131 (index)
  throne of Egypt: Horus vs. Seth,
  41–47
ENSLAVEMENT
  see also SLAVE
—Douglas / Magic *
  roc, its egg eaten, gets venge-
  ance on Sinbad, 21–25
ENTERTAINMENT
—Lester / Leopard *
  town where snoring was not al-
  lowed, 27–30
ENTRAPMENT
—Cambodian / Carrison
  Princess Amaradevi: husband ac-
  cused of treachery, 23–30
ENUMA ELISH
—Hamilton / In the Beginning *
  Marduk, god of gods, 78–85
ENVIRONMENT
—Spanish-Am / Van Etten *
  proper/improper use of river:
  good/bad life, 37–41
ENVY
  see also JEALOUSY
—Aesop / Reeves-Wilson *
  freedom better than comfort:
  Wolf and house-dog, 110–
  111
—Bomans / Wily *
  Anita: little maybug desires hap-
  piness, 83–86
—Clouston / Popular
  king's favorite envied and plotted
  against, II.444–457
—Geras / Grandmother *

rabbi determines owner of tablecloth, 31–40
—Jewish / Frankel, 649 (index)
  dog, cheese, and water (fable),
  459
  lion and two apes: request
  granted, double, 465–466
—Jewish / Sadeh
  Pearlneck: coveted by foe's
  daughter, 143–146
—Leonardo / Fables *
  peach tree envies walnut tree, 26
—Paxton / Belling *
  bird who lost his song (Aesop),
  [28–31]
—Scandinavian / Kvideland, viii (index)
—Spring / Philip
  elder brother envies hardworking
  brother, 114–118
—Witches / Iosa *
  brothers envious of Pinkel's favor
  with king, 23–31
EPITAPH
—Bomans / Wily *
  return: rich man learns: "happiness is within," 76–78
EQUALITY
—Bomans / Wily *
  king in undershirt, sans regalia, a
  common man, 155–157
—Cambodian / Carrison
  poor cook's helper says he's rich
  as king, 77–78
—Coyote / Bierhorst *
  coyote, puma and donkey divide
  catch unequally, [36]
EQUIVOCATION
  see also DECEPTION
—Grimm / Complete *
  Hans married: uncle deceives
  bride's father, 387–388
ERIDU
—Babylonia / Spence, 392 (index)

ERIS (goddess of discord)
—Gods / Schwab, 752 (index)
EROS (god)
—Lore of Love
  doomed trysts: Apollo; Pyramus,
  77
—Wolkstein / Love
  Psyche and Eros, 111–146, 241,
  265 @
ERROR
—My Mama / Viorst *
  mother in error re monsters, [1–
  45]
ESCAPE(-s) and PURSUIT(-s)
  see also CAPTIVE(-s); FLIGHT
  see also particular tales, e.g.,
  Hansel and Gretel
—Allison / I'll Tell *
  wolf and [goat's] kid, 130
—Arabian / Lewis
  Ghanim, the slave of love, 35–41
—Arabian / Riordan
  Sinbad makes wine in pumpkin,
  51–55
—Bierhorst / Monkey *
  with help of giant's daughter,
  young man does four impossible tasks, 56–65
—Bomans / Wily *
  toys help escape, 83–86
—Bruchac / Iroquois *
  brave woman and the Flying
  Head, 184–187
  chipmunk ridicules bear, and
  pays, 37–39
  hungry fox and boastful suitor,
  80–83
  rabbit outwits fox (trying to eat
  him), 74–78
—Carter / Sleeping *
  Hop o' my Thumb; seven-league
  boots, 69–80
—Celts / Hodges *
  Lad of Luck and monster, 89–103

—Childcraft 3 / Stories *
  Baba Yaga's geese abduct girl's
  brother, 114–118
—Corrin / Six-Year *
  captured field mouse escapes
  with acorn, 113–115
—Coyote / Bierhorst *
  escape from well; coyote tricks
  goat, [24]
—Coyote / Ramsey
  magic power: boy and sister escape from At'at'a'hlia, 75–76
—Crossley / British FT *
  giant's daughter helps prince escape death, 313–330
—Curry / Beforetime *
  mink and bluejay retrieve Little
  Weasel, stolen by lizard, 60–67
—Douglas / Magic *
  Androcles and the lion, 167–175
  Rapunzel: her daughter promised
  to witch, 27–33
  roc's vengeance; make captor
  drunk, 21–25
  three billy goats Gruff, 119–121
  Thumbelina, 43–53
—Dulac / Fairy *
  Finn, and Queen of many-colored
  bedchamber, 69–76
—Frog Rider (Chinese)
  magic brush: things painted become real, 47–59
—Ghosts / Starkey
  Tammy escapes from Lucky Min-
  nie (troll), 110–115
—Grimm / Complete *
  Maid Maleen, in menial disguise,
  at lover's court, 801–807
  nixie (mill-pond) captures young
  man; wife rescues, 736–742
  stupid giant conned by boastful
  tailor's "power," 745–747
  Sweetheart Roland, 268–271
  Tom Thumb, 187–193

true bride; prince forgets be-
trothal, 752–760
—Grimm / Sixty *
Sweetheart Roland, 156–160
Tom Thumb, 125–132
—Gullible Coyote / Malotki
Coyote Woman kills Antelope
Woman; tries to get her chil-
dren, 27–36
—Hamilton / People *
Devil's daughter helps John de
Conquer, 107–114
Little Daughter sings, and es-
capes from wolf, 60–63
—Hopi / Talashoma-Malotki
Kokosori and his witch wife, 23–
41
—Igloo / Metayer
Coppermine [magic] River leg-
end: feigned death, 78–81
forced marriage: The huntress,
99–107
—Imaginary / Nigg
Sindbad and the roc, 57–59
—Jewish / Sadeh
parrot's advice: feign death, 165–
166
prince who went off on his own,
101–105
—Journeys / Norris *
Dermot and Grania: escape from
Finn, [22–25]
—Lang / Wilkins
Grateful prince: girl helps hero
escape old man, 394–414
—Lore of Love
Aucassin and Saracen maid, 98–
106
—MacDonald / Sourcebook *
motif index, 280–290
—Manning / Cats *
crocodile would eat Soafara; she
escapes with help of Roller
Bird, 51–57

—Muddleheads / Harris
Mink Being wants to marry human princess, 5–25
—Nesbit / Fairy *
Billy and cousin: kite/bicycle, 45–
56
—O'Brien / Tales *
swan bride: king's son's quest for
Scolog's daughter, 82–95
—Old Wives / Carter
ghoul follows trail of girl's blood,
160–165
prince and giant's daughter escape using her magic, 76–85
—Russian Hero / Warner *
captive tricks witch's daughter;
geese help escape, 82–85
Dunai: archery contest ends in
death, 37–41
witch (blood sister) and sun's sister, 60–61
—Shah / Central Asia
seven divs for brothers, 13–18
—Shannon / More *
trapped in bucket of cream, frog
churns it to butter and escapes,
23–26
—Sioux / Standing Bear *
Crow Butte: escape from the
Sioux, 37–40
Hawk Dreamer invokes hawk,
leaps to safety, 28–31
—Spanish-Am / Van Etten *
cat/rooster/sheep/ox escape
from wolves/coyote, 97–100
—Spring / Philip
lovers reincarnated as butterflies,
35–41
princess's veil; father demands
many tests, 75–81
—Starkey / Ghosts
Tammy escapes from Lucky Minnie (troll), 110–115
—Tree / Kerven *

imprisoned boys in tree, use nose
bone, [6–7]

—Trolls / Asbjornsen
stepsisters: one kind, one cruel;
escape service of witch, 42–50

—Turkish / Walker
Teeny-Tiny and Witch-Woman,
49–51

—Turkish (Art I) / Walker
Cihansah pursues/finds pigeon-
girl, 207–217

—Water Buffalo (Chinese)
wolf pretends to be grandmother,
62–69

—Williams-Ellis / Tales *
Baba Yaga; Marusia's kindness
helps escape, 113–124
magic bird unplows field, gives
milk, lures children, 62–76
Mr. Miacca would eat boy, 131–
133

—Witches / Iosa *
animals help kind children escape giant witch, 18–22

—Yolen / Shape Shift
Dinesen, I. / The sailor-boy's
tale, 52

—Yolen / Werewolves
gypsy werewolf, Nazi soldiers,
Jewish children, 238–253

ESCAPE by DECEPTION

—Corrin / Eight-Year *
monkey to crocodile: my heart is
hanging in tree, 102–109

—Douglas / Magic *
escape from death: three billy
goats Gruff, 119–121

—Dulac / Fairy *
Bashtchelik (real steel), 91–113

—Grimm / Complete *
Old Sultan, 230–232
Snowdrop [=Snow White and the
seven dwarfs], 249–258
Three languages, The, 169–171

—Grimm / Sixty *
Old Sultan, 26–28
Snowdrop [as above], 161–170
Three languages, The, 223–
226

—Jewish / Frankel
fox escapes from Angel of Death,
and Leviathan's fish, 11–14

—Lang / Wilkins
gnome king Rubezahl captures
princess, 497–512

—Lester / Leopard *
town where snoring was not allowed, 27–30

**ESCAPE by DISGUISE; SHAM;
SUBSTITUTION**

—Cambodian / Carrison
Bodhisattva's old mother would
kill him to marry pupil, 90–94

—Clarkson / World *
fox's bag: dog substituted for boy,
251–253

—Grimm / Complete *
wizard captures three sisters;
Fitcher's bird, 216–220

—Dramatized / Kamerman
Finn McCool, 218–226

—Old Wives / Carter
Maol a Chliobain repeatedly gets
better of giant, 24–27

—Russian Hero / Warner *
captive Mashen'ka tricks bear,
116–117

ESCAPE by FALSE PLEA

—Chaucer / Cohen *
fox talks; Chauntecleer escapes,
19–31

—Grimm / Complete *
blue light summons tiny servant,
530–534

—Grimm / Sixty *
blue light summons tiny servant,
244–249

—Lang / Wilkins

Blue Beard (murderous husband), 110–115
ESCHATOLOGY
—Persian / Hinnells, 63–70
ESKIMO(-s) (tales by and about)
—Animal Legends / Kerven *
  Sedna marries seabird; unhappy; father kills bird, [30–32]
—Caduto / Keepers *
  Sedna, woman under the sea, 95–97
—Dictionary / Leach, 1207,1222 (index)
—Fahs / Old *
  Niyak, Umak, and the eagle, 71–80
—Hamilton / In the Beginning *
  creation myth: The pea pod man, 2–7
—Igloo / Metayer
  legends of Inuit people (Copper Eskimos), 1–127
—Indian Myth / Burland
  fishermen of the Northwest coast, 16–25
—Man Myth & Magic, 3130 (index)
—Northern / Norman, 1–343
—Old Wives / Carter
  blubber boy: chunk of blubber animated by being rubbed against genitals, 31–32
  grandmother to "male" hunter; impregnates granddaughter, 181–182
  Kakuarshuk: all reversed in other world, 11–12
  Sermerssuaq: remarkably strong woman, 1
  two women who found freedom, 225–226
  woman married her son's wife, 170
—Speck / New World, 521 (index)
—Vanishing / Mercer *
  blind boy and the loon, 36–39
  otter living on both land and water; origin, 40–41
  quest for wife abducted by giant bird, 42–49
ESSAY (*homework*)
—Clarkson / World *
  writing a comparative "tale" paper (4th grade), 390 @
—Nesbit / Fairy *
  Billy and cousin: kite/bicycle, 45–56
ESTATE
—Ghosts / Starkey
  ghost reveals deed to estate, 24–29
ETAIN
—Fairies / Briggs, 123–125
ETHIOPIA (-ian)
—Legends / Cavendish, 6 (index)
—Man Myth & Magic, 3131 (index)
ETHNIC INDEX
—MacDonald / Sourcebook * 739–778
ETHNOZOOLOGY
—Wildlife / Gillespie, 1–251 @
ETRUSCANS
—Roman / Usher, 131 (index)
EULENSPIEGEL, Till (or Tyll)
—Dramatized / Kamerman
  Merry Tyll and the three rogues, 162–176
EURIPIDES
—Greek / Switzer, 204 (index)
EUROPE
—Wolves / Lopez, 301 (index)
EURYDICE
—Greek / Osborne
  Orpheus and Eurydice: quest in underworld, 45–48
Eve, *see* ADAM and EVE.
Eve's various children
—Grimm / Complete * 734–736
Evil, *see* GOOD AND EVIL.

EVIL BEING(-s): (*deceived into releasing prisoner*)
—Douglas / Magic *
   fisherman's promise to genie, 13–19
—Giant / Harrison *
   boy tells secret to giant-capturers: measles, 7–17
—Grimm / Complete *
   wizard captures three sisters; Fitcher's bird, 216–220
—Williams-Ellis / Tales *
   boy uses sofa leg to escape Mr. Miacca, 131–133
EVIL BEING: (*deceived into self-injury*)
—Hoke / Giants
   three giants tricked to death by boy's wits, 34–40
—Old Wives / Carter
   ogre tricked into drinking river; bursts, 24–27
—Scary / Young *
   Sally-Bally: grandma jumps into giant's ear; he kills self trying to eject, 89–92
EVIL BEING: (*defeated*)
—Bierhorst / Naked *
   Animal-Foot hitter kills sorcerer, 24–30
—Bruchac / Iroquois *
   monstrous, two-headed snake a traitor, 97–102
—Celts / Hodges *
   how Finn MacCool got his wisdom tooth, 34–52
—Corrin / Six-Year *
   dragon; magic bag makes all who sniff it, laugh, 53–58
—Grimm / Complete *
   drummer rescues princess from glass mountain, 781–791
   girl without hands; goodness wins over devil, 160–166

   stupid giant conned by boastful tailor's "power," 745–747
—Hoke / Giants, 150–155
   ogre defeated, 41–64, 65–70
—Lang / Wilkins
   Dragon of the North, 285–297
—Shah / Central Asia
   wishes (three) granted by genie, 31–44
—Starkey / Ghosts, 80–87
   McGregor and the kelpy, 66–71
—Turkish / Walker
   Karacor and the giants, 52–61
—Turkish (Art I) / Walker
   youngest son becomes milk-child of nine-headed female giant, 230–239
EVIL BEING: (*killed/maimed/captured*)
—Caduto / Keepers *
   Hero Twins and Swallower of Clouds, 79–81
—Crossley / Dead *
   Tom Hickathrift [remarkable strength; giant killed], 11–19
—Douglas / Magic *
   Jack the Giant Killer, 131–139
   ogre defeated: three billy goats Gruff, 119–121
—Dulac / Fairy *
   Bashtchelik (real steel), 91–113
—Grimm / Complete *
   skillful huntsman, 508–514
—Hoke / Giants
   Finlay, the giant killer, 142–149
   Hercules and the golden apples, 130–132
—Journey Sun (Chinese)
   wives in the mirror, 109–124
—Lester / Leopard *
   monster swallows three villages, 13–15
—Lines / Magical *

Beowulf and Grendel [battle], tears off arm, 105–116
—Old Wives / Carter
ghoul trapped, killed by girl's seven brothers, 160–165
—Russian Hero / Warner *
Alesha (priest's son) battles Tugarin, 72–76
—Scriven / Full Color *
Hansel and Gretel, 43–47
Jack and the beanstalk, 53–56
—Turkish (Art I) / Walker
youngest son kills seven- and eight-headed giants, 230–239
—Williams-Ellis / Tales *
great greedy beast eats everything, 177–184
EVIL BEING: (*relative of, aids hero*)
—Bruchac / Iroquois *
Stone Coat Woman aids hunters, 135–144
—Chorao / Child's *
Jack and the Beanstalk; giant's wife, 9–20
—Grimm / Complete *
devil with the three golden hairs, 151–158
devil's grandmother solves riddle for hero, 563–566
kings' daughters aid hero in tasks: win girl or die, 515–524
—Hamilton / People *
Devil's daughter helps John de Conquer, 107–114
—Lang / Wilkins
Fairer-than-a-Fairy, 274–281
grateful prince: girl helps hero escape old man, 394–414
—Old Wives / Carter
giant's daughter aids hero in tasks required to win her, 76–85
EVIL BEING: (*witch, ogre, devil, person, etc. in power*)
—Carter / Sleeping *
Hop o' my Thumb; shelter with ogre, 69–80
—Chorao / Child's *
Hansel and Gretel, 29–40
—Journey Sun (Chinese)
drink from Red Spring, under power of Red Devil, 125–140
—Lang / Wilkins
Dragon of the North, 285–297
—Scriven / Full Color *
Hansel and Gretel, 43–47
—Williams-Ellis / Tales *
Mr. Miacca would eat boy, 131–133
EVIL EYE
—Russian / Ivanits, 247 (index)
—Scandinavian / Kvideland, vii (index)
—Witch Encyc / Guiley, 413 (index)
EVIL HABIT PUNISHED
—Arabian / Lewis
slave girl (Sweet-Friend) and Ali Nur, 25–34
—Greaves / Hippo *
how buffalo became a grass eater, 73–77
how jackal got its markings, 47
—Grimm / Complete *
hospitality: poor man rewarded; rich man punished, 394–398
—Maori / Kanawa *
Rona screams at moon, is snatched up to moon's surface, 102–104
—Spring / Philip elder brother envies hardworking brother, 114–118
Evil king (Andersen)
—Carle / Treasury * 147–152
EVOLUTION
—Yolen / Shape Shift
shapeshifting, 181–182
Ewing, Juliana Horatia
—Hoke / Giants
The ogre courting, 65–70

EXAGGERATION (humor)
see also BUNYAN, Paul; FINN
Mac COOL [etc.]; TALL
TALES
—Arabian / McCaughrean
wonderful bag: impossible list of
contents, 130–132
—Childcraft 1 / Once *
lie or "story": sheep with wooden
collar, 147–157
—Corrin / Eight-Year *
attempts to prevent princess
wanting the moon, 91–101
—Grimm / Complete *
Ditmars tale of wonders, 662
Knoist and his three sons,
622
Schlauraffen land, 660
—Old Coot / Christian *
auguring match (talking contest),
41–56
—Old Wives / Carter
furburger: animal demolishes ob-
jects named (husband: "my
ass,"), 92–93
—Vietnam / Terada *
tombstone grateful: soldier (practice shooting) never hit,
130
—Williams-Ellis / Tales *
white-faced simini (forced to use
foolish words), 142–144
—Yep / Rainbow *
The boasting contest, 96–105
—Yolen / Baby Bear *
sheep can't count themselves: 10
add up to "90," [22–23]
EXAMINATIONS
—Vietnam / Terada *
mandarin exams, 49 @
EXCALIBUR
—King Arthur / Senior, 319 (index)
EXCESS
—Allison / I'll Tell *

too much heat (if sun marries and
has children), 113
—Greek / Osborne
self-confidence: chariot of the
sun god, 1–6
—Grimm / Complete *
magic pot produces porridge;
can't stop, 475–476
—Paxton / Aesop *
patience: fox eats lunch found in
hollow tree, [6–9]
EXCHANGES
—Williams-Ellis / Tales *
boy's series of trades: feather to
village chief, 102–112
Excrement, *see* DUNG.
EXCUSE
—Allison / I'll Tell *
wolf needs excuse to eat lamb,
111
EXECUTION(-s) *(often avoided)*
—Arabian / Lewis
treachery: good barber and evil
dyer, 123–130
—Clouston / Popular
miller's son: letter contains death-
warrant, II.458–466
—Dramatized / Kamerman
King who was bored; endless
tale, 334–345
—Grimm / Legends (Ward), II:407 (index)
—Hopi / Talashoma-Malotki
hide and seek with life at stake,
50–69
—Jewish / Sadeh
casual; master thief, 291–295
—Lester / Leopard *
body parts argue: which is most
important, 45–51
—Manning / Cats *
Little Wonder; witch-stepmother
turns boy into dog, drives his
sister out, 65–74

—Nesbit / Fairy *
    Charmed life, or Princess and
      Lift-man, 25–42
—Southern [legends] / Floyd
    Will Purvis: man who wouldn't
      die, 96–98
—Turkish / Walker
    son "loves father like salt," 108–
      113

EXHUMATION
    see also CORPSE; DEAD
—Hopi / Talashoma-Malotki
    old wizard plots to seduce beauti-
      ful girl, 70–91

EXISTENTIAL TALES
—Switzer / Existential
    Cinderella (mediocrity), 38–45
    country mouse and city mouse
      (dietary purity), 86–92
    fisherman and his wife (discon-
      tent), 63–70
    gallant tailor (overachievement),
      102–111
    Goldilocks and the three bears
      (nothingness), 17–23
    goose girl (paranoid hysteria), 1–8
    Hansel and Gretel (guilt), 142–
      149
    hen who baked the bread (posi-
      tivism), 9–16
    Henney Penney (nuclear dread),
      79–85
    Jack and the beanstalk (amoral-
      ity), 112–118
    Little Red Riding Hood (dread),
      32–37
    Peter Rabbit (technitis: computer
      programming), 134–141
    Rapunzel (fundamentalism), 71–
      78
    Rumpelstiltskin at gambling table
      (identity crisis), 17–23
    shoemaker and the elves (schizo-
      phrenia), 54–62

    Sleeping Beauty (bored; wants
      brains, not beauty), 38–45
    Snow White (anguish), 119–125
    three little pigs (political ideal-
      ism), 93–101
    Tom Thumb (academic excel-
      lence), 126–133
    ugly duckling (first woman in ma-
      jor league baseball), 150–157

EXORCISM
—Chinese / Chin *
    monkey: on road to fetch scrip-
      tures, 95–110
—Demons / Gettings, 107–108
—Ghosts / Starkey
    laying of the Pakenham ghost
      [three times], 37–43
—Ghosts / Time-Life
    Dorothy Dinglet, 125
—Witch Encyc / Guiley, 87–88, 412
    (index)

EXPECTATION(-s)
    see also DISILLUSIONMENT
—Aesop / Reeves-Wilson *
    Widow Martin and her hen, 54
—Clouston / Popular
    counting chickens before hatched
      [opulence], II.432–443
—Leonardo / Fables *
    flea leaves dog; looks for better
      life on sheep, 71

EXPEDIENCE
—Allison / I'll Tell *
    lion, fox, ass: dividing spoils
      "equally," 116

EXPEDITION
—Egyptian / Harris
    shipwrecked sailor and the huge
      serpent, 64–65

EXPLOITATION
—Bierhorst / Monkey *
    bad compadre oft exploits Juan;
      animals perform his impossible
      tasks, 94–106

—Coyote / Bierhorst *
blackbird caught; powerful hurt
the weak, [26]
—Hamilton / Dark *
very large son: landowner tries to
exploit giant, 97–101
EXPLORING
—Jones / Tales *
Goldilocks and the three bears,
8–15
EXPOSER
—Caduto / Keepers *
How Coyote was the Moon, 111
External soul, *see* SOUL, EXTER-
NAL.
EXTINCTION
—Gould / Mythical
fabulous animal species, 42–
77 @
EXTORTION
—Jewish / Frankel
pound of flesh: Shylock and Pope
Sixtus IV, 400–403
EXTRAORDINARY EVENTS
—Crossley / British FT *
hazel twig defeats men trying to
put Jemmy in coffin, 77–85
—Quayle / Shining *
wooden bowl (worn to hide girl-
bride's beauty), 97–102
EXTRAORDINARY PEOPLE
see also HERO; GIANT; THUMB-
SIZED
—Bierhorst / Naked *
Whirlwinds vs. Stone Coats, 19–
23
—Corrin / Eight-Year *
Sir Gawaine and the Green
Knight, 161–172
—Crossley / Dead *
green children (from a land where
everything is green), 87–96
—Dulac / Fairy *
Snegorotchka, 1–6

—Grimm / Complete *
goose-girl at well; princess weeps
pearls, 725–734
—Lynn / Fantasy *
miniature people, 762–763 (index)
—Water Buffalo (Chinese)
seven remarkably endowed sons
"reason" with tyrant, 49–54
EYE(-s)
—Arabian / Lewis
tale of the one-eyed beggar, 10–
16
—Bierhorst / Naked *
Quilt of men's eyes, 101–109
—Erdoes / Sound *
doing a trick with eyeballs, 86–89
—Gullible Coyote / Malotki
dancing skeleton; eyes pop out,
go sight-seeing, 77–82
—Hopi Coyote / Malotki
coyote and bird play: pluck out/
retrieve eyes, 63–67
—Jewish / Sadeh
brothers' widow-mother marries
lion, 92–95
—Lurker / Dict Gods, 426 (index)
three-eyed, 443 (index)
—Navajo Coyote / Haile
chickadee and coyote (pluck out
eyes) 12, 35
—Spanish-Am / Van Etten *
old woman's eyes (removed at
night) eaten by cat, 88–89
—Turkish (Art I) / Walker
"A bouquet of roses for an eye,"
159–168
—Women / Dyer
blue, 249 (index)
world, 48–62 @
EYE OF RA
—Egyptian / Ions, 143 (index)
EYEGLASSES
—Pirate Ghosts / McSherry

blue spectacles: user not wholly
  good, 73–83
Eyesight, see BLIND . . .
EZECHIEL
—Jewish / Sadeh
  tomb: besieged guardians rescued, 153

FABLE(-s)
—Allison / I'll Tell * 97–98 @, 99–
  131
—Bosma / Classroom
  critical reading, 25–26 @
—Campbell / West Highlands, I.275–
  288
—Clouston / Popular
  of Bidpai, II.506 (index)
  origin, I.274–276 @
—Coyote / Bierhorst *
  Aztec versions of Aesop, [1–46]
—Demi / Reflective *, [1–27]
—Jewish / Frankel
  Benedictus le Puncteur: thirteen
  "fox" fables, 458–469
—Leonardo / Fables * 1–118
—Mercatante / Encyclopedia
  definition, xviii @
**FABULOUS ANIMAL(-s) or CREA-
  TURE(-s)**
—Gould / Mythical, 1–407 @
  extinction of species, 42–77 @
  remarkable animal forms, 31–
  41 @
—Jewish / Frankel, 646 (index)
—South / Mythical
  glossary, xxxi-xxxv
  illustrations; bibliographical es-
  say, xvii-xlix
  taxonomy; bibliography; index,
  372–377, 382
Face on the barroom floor, The
—Oral Trad / Cunningham, 119–121

FAFNIR
—Dragons / Baskin * [26–27]
—McGowen / Encyclopedia * 22
FAILURE
  see also SUCCESS
—Aesop / Reeves-Wilson *
  Fox and [sour] grapes, 57–58
—Curry / Beforetime *
  coyote tries badger's hunting
  method; fails because ticklish,
  74–77
—Egyptian / Harris
  shipwrecked sailor and the huge
  serpent, 64–65
—Jewish / Sadeh
  young man who had no luck,
  285–287
Fair Katrinelje and Pif-Paf-Poltrie
—Grimm / Complete * 593–594
Fairer-than-a-Fairy
—Lang / Wilkins, 274–281
Fairies [toads and diamonds]
—Zipes / Beauties * 61–63
FAIRY(-ies)
  see also: GIFTS FROM FAIRIES;
    LEPRECHAUN; MERMAID;
    SPRIGGAN, etc.
  see also particular stories, e.g.,
    Cinderella
—British / Briggs *
  fourteen tales, 151–167
—Bruchac / Iroquois *
  knowledge: gifts of the Little Peo-
  ple, 41–44
—Campbell / West Highlands, II.57–
  84; IV.432 (index)
—Carle / Treasury *
  Magic boots (Andersen), 31–35
—Celts / Hodges *
  swan children of Lir, 5–14
—Chinese / Chin *
  cowherd's marriage to fairy weav-
  ing maid, 113–125
—Clarkson / World *

appearance: Te Kanawa and the
fairies, 140–141
Selena Moor: taboo; souls of the
dead, 109–111
—Clouston / Popular
hunchback and fairies; versions,
I.352–372
subaqueous halls, I.192–198
—Corrin / Eight-Year *
princess: save magic fishbone
(fairy gift) until needed, 147–160
—Corrin / Six-Year *
fairy punishes selfish boy for mis-
treating cow, duck, pig, 191–
194
ungrateful old woman lives in vinegar-bottle, 13–18
—Crane / Beauty *
Yellow Dwarf, Fairy of the Desert,
and proud princess, [34–47]
—Crossley / British FT *
baker's daughter turned into owl;
refuses bread to fairy/old
woman, 331–333
Dathera Dad: fairy child steps out
of pudding, 45–46
fairies cure good-tempered
hunchback, 145–152
midwife uses ointment; fairy husband blinds eye, 287–292
Tam Lin (poem), 270–282
three blows: man catches fairy
with half-baked bread, 353–
364
—Douglas / Magic *
white cat (enchanted princess),
69–83
—Dramatized / Kamerman
Plum Blossom and the dragon,
38–46
—Fairies / Briggs
Allies's list, 4–5
bathing, 17–19
borrowing, 235–237

captured, 66–68
crafts, 137–139
departure of, 94–96
diminutive, 98–102
drama: Wisdome of Dr. Dodypol,
438–440
dress and appearance, 108–111
encyclopedia, 1–481
faults condemned by, 167–168
golden hair, 194–195
grateful, 197–199
infringement of privacy, 233
lake maidens, 211–212
market or fair, 151–153
medieval chronicles, 282–284
morality, 153–156
origin, 318–320, 393–394
power over, 334–335
protection against, 335–336
Robert Burton's account, 52–54
seeing fairies, 350–353
size, 368–369
small people, the, 374–375
solitary, 375–376
spells to obtain power over, 376–
378
sports, 378–380
Strangers, The, 383–385
theft: Laird of Balmachie's wife,
257–258
thefts from, 158, 391–393
traffic with, 409–412
trooping, 412
—Hartland / English *
twenty-three tales, 89–152
—Irish / Glassie
four encounters, 148–157
traits and treasure; eleven tales,
157–173
—Lang / Wilkins
captured children; Little King Loc,
441–459
Little good mouse (fairy helps imprisoned queen), 116–127

magic ring: happiness and power if . . . , 220–227

mistreated Tontlawald girl lives with fairies, 557–570

Princess Mayblossom (good vs. evil fairies), 137–153

princess sent to check on gifts asked of fairies, 186–189

Sylvain and Jocosa (befriended by fairy), 178–185

—Lynn / Fantasy * 754–755 (index)

—MacDonald / Sourcebook * motif index, 132–138

—McGowen / Encyclopedia * 1–64

—Man Myth & Magic, 3132 (index)

—Manning / Cats *
advice: when heads are cut off, mouse-queen spell broken, 83–91

—Manning / Cauldron *
Moti-katika to be eaten by Water Witch; fairy provides magic, saving bones, 118–127

—Maori / Kanawa *
Patupaiarehe come to visit chief Te Kanawa, 62–66

—Monsters / Cohen, 235–238 @

—Nesbit / Fairy *
Melisande [curse on hair-growth], 59–78

—O'Brien / Tales *
fairies take Gilly for ride to France; abduct princess; strike her dumb, 106–117

—Occult & Parapsych / Shepard, 1512 (index)

—Palestinian / Speak (Muhawi) motif-index, 391

—Plants / Dyer, 80–91

—Polynesians / Andersen, 478 (index)
Tura, Te Kanawa, Taniwha, 115–156

—Rockwell / Puss *

Kate Crackernuts breaks evil spells, 19–26

—Scandinavian / Kvideland, 426 (index)
lover, xiii (index)

—Scriven / Full Color *
how to catch a leprechaun, 85–87

—Shah / Central Asia
fairy queen; prince who married a peri (fairy), 49–55

gifts: wisdom (nobleman and slave), 103–108

transformed to mortal, 49–55

wishes (three) granted by genie, 31–44

—South / Mythical
bibliographical essay, 325–348 (J. Carter); 383 (index)

sources; 1–393 passim

—Tree / Kerven *
fairies' revenge for cutting down hawthorn bush, [26–27]

—Turkey / Walker, 302 (index)

—Turkish (Art I) / Walker
grateful fairy-padishah teaches farmer (with termagant wife) to cure the sick, 188–190

—Unnatural / Cohen, 107–118

—Vanishing / Mercer *
fishing nets: Maoris custom origin, 28–31

—Victorian / Hearn
The fairies [poem by Allingham], 128–130

Melilot (H. Morley), 117–127

—Williams-Ellis / Tales *
Tamlane rescued from elfland, 151–159

—Witch Encyc / Guiley, 117–121, 413 (index)

—Woman's Ency / Walker, 298–301 @

—Yolen / Faery Flag

faery flag (shawl; wife/mother for one year), 3–11
—Zipes / Beauties *
little mouse (story by d'Aulnoy), 350–361
FAIRY: *appearance*
—Arabian / McCaughrean
man with three wives, 185–193
—Bomans / Wily *
secret behavior of gnomes, 138–140
Sunday child, gigantic, goes to sun to live, 169–173
—Clarkson / World *
fairies take shape/form of gifts, 140–141
—Lang / Wilkins
mistreated Tontlawald girl lives with fairies, 557–570
—Maori / Kanawa *
fairies come to visit chief Te Kanawa, 62–66
FAIRY BRIDE
—Fairies / Briggs
Sir Launfal, 366–367
Wild Edric, 432–434
FAIRY: *defeated*
—Clarkson / World *
brownie of Blednock (fairy leaves when given clothes), 115–117
—Lang / Wilkins
charm protects betrothed from yara (fairies), 474–484
gnome king Rubezahl captures princess, 497–512
—Muddleheads / Harris
Mink Being wants to marry human princess, 5–25
—Rockwell / Puss *
Kate Crackernuts (gets head of sheep), 19–26
FAIRY GODMOTHER
see also Cinderella; GIFT(-s) from FAIRIES

—Dulac / Fairy *
blue bird (prince transformed), 77–90
FAIRY: *malevolent*
—Crossley / Dead *
Yallery Brown (malevolent being), 79–85
—Dulac / Fairy *
green serpent: one twin princess cursed, ugly, 124–138
hind of the wood: crayfish fairy, 43–59
—Lang / Wilkins
Heart of ice (Caylus), 190–219
FAIRY: *marriage/liaison with mortals*
—Baring-Gould / Curious
Melusina: mortal wed to water-sprite, 129–133 @
—Bruchac / Iroquois *
wife of Thunderer, 146–154
—Celts / Hodges *
Dermot in the Land-under-Wave, 57–73
—Chinese / Chin *
cowherd's marriage to fairy weaving maid, 113–125
—Crossley / British FT *
three blows: man catches fairy with half-baked bread, 353–364
—Maori / Kanawa *
Mataora meets underworld Turehu; marries, 68–80
—Quayle / Shining *
Urashima: fisherman marries under-sea-king's daughter, 57–68
—Russian Hero / Warner *
rusalka (water-spirit) and the seal-hunter, 28–29
—Shah / Central Asia
prince who married a peri (fairy), 49–55
—Yolen / Faery Flag
faery flag (shawl), 3–11

Fairy of the Dawn
—Lang / Wilkins, 571–601
FAIRY TALES (*about the genre*)
—Allison / I'll Tell * 3–5 @
—Bosma / Classroom
     critical reading, 24–25 @
—Lynn / Fantasy *
     annotated bibliography, 3–60
—Schwartz / Gates, 801 (index)
—Victorian / Hearn
     history in England, to the Victori-
     ans, xv-xxvii @
FAIRYLAND
—Celts / Hodges *
     Dermot in the Land-under-Wave,
     57–73
     Tam Lin freed from evil spell by
     love, 76–83
—Crossley / British FT *
     shepherd visits fairyland; breaks
     taboo (drinks from well), 248–
     250
—Fairies / Briggs
     dwelling on Selena Moor, 141–
     143
     Elidor and the golden ball, 118–
     120
     fairy widower, 161–165
     time in, 398–400
     visitors to, 422–425
—Lang / Wilkins
     Fairer-than-a-Fairy, 274–281
FAIRYLAND: *mortals transported to*
—Celts / Hodges *
     Dermot in the Land-under-Wave,
     57–73
—Clarkson / World *
     Cherry of Zennor: nursemaid to
     fairy/human child, 129–134
     Selena Moor: former sweetheart
     now a servant of fairy, 109–111
—Dulac / Fairy *
     childless queen: crayfish fairy,
     43–59

—Lang / Wilkins
     Fairer-than-a-Fairy, 274–281
     Little King Loc, 441–459
—Turkish (Art I) / Walker
     Cihansah enters palace of pa-
     dishah of birds, 207–217
—Williams-Ellis / Tales *
     Tamlane rescued from elfland,
     151–159
FAITH
—Fahs / Old *
     evil Jesus: spirit driven from boy,
     159–162
—Jewish / Frankel, xii, 649 (index)
—Jewish / Sadeh
     rich man will pay to say: I don't
     believe in God, 324–326
Faithful John
—Grimm / Complete * 43–51
Faithlessness in marriage,
     see FIDELITY.
FALCONRY
—Knights / Heller-Headon, 106–107
Fall, *see* AUTUMN.
FALL OF MAN (evil comes)
—Bruchac / Iroquois *
     two brothers: one brings good,
     the other evil, 19–23
—Fahs / Old *
     animals make sickness for man-
     enemy, 71–80
—Schwartz / Gates, 801 (index)
Falling in love, *see* LOVE, FALLING
     IN.
False accusation, *see* ACCUSA-
     TION(-s).
False bride, *see* MARITAL IMPOS-
     TORS.
FALSE FACE SOCIETY
—American / Read Dgst
     disease; Stone Giant; Iroquois;
     51
FALSE LOGIC
—Lester / Brer Rabbit *

noise in the woods: run! 113–115

False pretense, see PRETENSE.

FALSEHOOD
see also DECEPTION; LIAR
—Leonardo / Fables *
mole killed by exposure, 89

FAMILIAR(-s) (spirit, imp, witch)
—Clarkson / World *
cats and witches, 211–212 @
—Limburg / Weird , 77–78
—Man Myth & Magic, 3133 (index)
—Pirate Ghosts / McSherry
witch's toad: Pedro goes to sea, 182–200
—Witch Encyc / Guiley, 121–122, 413 (index)

FAMILY
—Bierhorst / Naked *
Moose wife; broken promise brings bad luck, 52–59
—Coyote / Ramsey
quarrels: brothers become sun and moon, 78–81
—Jewish / Frankel
figures, 643 (index)
—Jewish / Sadeh
reunited; desperate man and prophet Jonah, 154–158
—Lore of Love
reunion; King Nala and Princess Damayanti, 110–119
—Yep / Rainbow *
mouse: superior pet, 80–85

FAMINE
—Baring-Gould / Curious
Bishop Hatto: famine and rats, 122–126 @
—Hoke / Giants
giant steals all [Blackfeet] buffaloes, 150–155
—Igloo / Metayer
Taligvak: ostracized shaman saves village, 61–69

—Lester / Leopard *
magic bird makes milk for famine-stricken people, 5–11

FANTASY
—Lynn / Fantasy *
overview, xix-xxxv @

FARM(-s; -ers; -ing)
—Allison / I'll Tell *
bequest: working hard is a treasure, 99
farmer, son, and donkey: attempt to please everyone, 128–129
—Arabian / McCaughrean
donkey advises ox to feign illness, 104–107
Price of cucumbers, 122–129
—Bierhorst / Monkey *
lazy farmer trades places with buzzard; dies foolishly, 37–43
—Coyote / Ramsey
cruel chief, 100 wives, kills all his sons, 65–68
quarrels: sons become sun and moon, 78–81
—Crossley / Animal (Grimm) *
fox helps old horse, 34–38
—Crossley / Dead *
Suffolk miracle: ploughboy returns from dead; claims Rosamund, 11–19
—Dramatized / Kamerman
wise woman helps man be good overseer, 265–277
—Ghosts / Starkey
boggart of Castle Farm, 30–35
farmer's pact with farmhand (devil), 8–15
—Hamilton / People *
fast-growing: Papa John's tall tale, 76–80
—Humor / Midwest, 175–189
—Jonsen / Trolls *

trolls and the pussy cat [a white
  bear], 15–23
—Pellowski / Story *
  string-story: farmer and yams, 9–
  15
—Scandinavian / Kvideland, xiv, 427
  (index)
—Williams-Ellis / Tales *
  magic bird unplows field, gives
  milk, lures children, 62–76
—Yolen / Faery Flag
  kill minstrel; his song continues;
  corn grows, 41–46
—Yolen / Shape Shift
  wer-cat: Moon change / A.W.
  Turner, 38–41
**Farmer and boggart [trick: crop
  above/below ground]**
—Crossley / British FT * 224–227
Farmer in the dell
—Allison / I'll Tell * 180
Farrington, Beatrice
—Unicorn / Coville *
  Ragged John (poem), 61–62
FASHION
—Witch Hndbk / Bird * 62–69
FASTING
—Jaffrey / Seasons
  Karvachauth: husband dies when
  wife breaks taboo; Nine Earth
  Mothers, 75–79
—Jewish / Frankel
  sin of pride, 516–517
FATE
  see also CHANCE; DESTINY
—Arabian / Lewis
  changing luck: destiny or capital,
  17–24
—Arabian / McCaughrean
  keys of destiny; Iram, 65–82
—Bell / Classical Dict, 83 @
—Crossley / Dead *
  Yallery Brown (offended, sends
  harm and bad luck), 79–85

—Egyptian / Harris
  doomed prince: fate foretold by
  Seven Hatitors, 71–76
—Egyptian / Mercatante
  prince doomed to three fates:
  crocodile, serpent, dog, 36–38
—Grimm / Complete *
  dog and sparrow: "it will cause
  death yet," 280–282
—Grimm / Sixty *
  dog and sparrow (as above), 36–
  40
—Jaffrey / Seasons
  by pretending madness, faithful
  sister changes brother's fate,
  96–101
—Jewish / Frankel
  father dreams: son to hang on
  13th birthday; saved by Elijah,
  597–600
  student marries ugly girl; leaves
  her; Elijah makes her beautiful,
  588–594
—Jewish / Sadeh
  charity saves peddler's wife from
  foreordained death, 335–336
  Solomon and the stars, 63
  Solomon's wager with fate, 64–
  65
—Lang / Wilkins
  fate of king's son: marry a slave,
  513–527
  prince saved from fates: crocodile, serpent, dog, 485–496
—Lore of Love
  deity keeps book; all are foreordained, 18–23
—Lurker / Dict Gods, 399 (index)
—Palestinian / Speak (Muhawi)
  motif-index, 398
—Turkish (Art I) / Walker
  magic hen, and fate of two brothers, 61–69
—Yep / Rainbow *

foolish boy: "Snake-spoke," 86–95

FATES (*goddesses*)
—D'Aulaire / Greek * 191 (index)
—Roman / Usher, 131 (index)

FATHER(-s)
—Bomans / Wily *
    stolen heart: man sells soul to devil; becomes "heartless," 158–165
—Jewish / Sadeh
    advice on carousing, etc. averts evil, 333–334
—Reeves / Shadow
    white doe: curse put on Valdemar, 131–153
—Strauss / Trail
    Hansel and Gretel; soliloquy (poem), 3–5

FATHER and DAUGHTER
—Grimm / Complete *
    goose-girl at well; princess weeps pearls, 725–734
—Turkish / Walker
    ruler gives daughter to poor man as punishment, 139–147
—Williams-Ellis / Tales *
    Cap o' Rushes (loves father "like salt"), 8–16

FATHER and SON
—Clouston / Popular
    son cruel to father; his son plans same, II.372–378
—Dulac / Fairy *
    suitor test: Ivan and the chestnut horse, 60–68
—Jewish / Sadeh
    fish with golden tail and pearls for eyes, 95–97
—Lewis / Proud
    Milun/lover wait 20 years to be wed, 65–75
—Shannon / More *
    devil will spare man as long as candle "lasts," [not "burns"], 27–30
—Turkish / Walker
    son "loves father like salt," 108–113

FAULTS
—Geras / Grandmother *
    peddler (angel) takes kvetch to Market of Misery, 66–76

FAUN (deity)
—Animals / Rowland, 184 (index)

FAWN
—Lines / Magical *
    Oisin's mother transformed, 169–174

FAY
—McGowen / Encyclopedia * 24

FEAR (*including learning; tests*)
    see also DEATH; PANIC
—Aesop / Zwerger
    hares and [even more timid] frogs, 11
—Allison / I'll Tell *
    city mouse and country mouse, 124–125
—Animal Legends / Kerven *
    (foolish) breadfruit falls: hare heralds earthquake, [26–27]
—Ghosts / Starkey
    test: Joe Reardon and the three sister-ghosts, 102–109
—Giant / Harrison *
    witch's spell: giant sees/fears butterflies, etc., 19–30
—Greaves / Hippo *
    lion steals ostrich chicks, 130–132
—Grimm / Complete *
    fear of owl, people burn down barn to kill it, 711–713
    the youth who could not shudder, 29–39
—Grimm / Sixty *
    the youth who could not shudder, 300–311

—Gullible Coyote / Malotki
coyote and Maasaw (god of
death) try to scare each other,
95–103
—Hall / Treasury *
Little Brown Bear afraid of the
dark, 22–25
—Jewish / Frankel
city mouse and country mouse
(fable), 460–461
—Lang / Wilkins
Princess in the chest; faithful
guard, 369–384
—McGowen / Encyclopedia * 24
—Scary / Young *
who's following me? [flapping
sole of shoe], 57
—Starkey / Ghosts
buggane, Broder Menine, the tailor, 16–23
Joe Reardon and the three sister-
ghosts, 102–109
laying Black Lucott's ghost, 116–
123
—Yolen / Baby Bear *
Milly the mole fears noises at
night, [10–11]
FEARLESSNESS (*rewarded*)
see also COURAGE
—Bomans / Wily *
three riddles; win princess; fear-
less woodcutter, 202–204
—Quayle / Shining *
Lord Bag-o'-Rice aids serpent
(Dragon King); kills giant centi-
pede, 33–43
—Spanish-Am / Van Etten *
skeleton gives treasure to brave
boy, 109–114
FEASTING
—Knights / Heller-Headon, 104–105
FEASTS (religious)
—Folk-rhymes / Northall
England, 181–266

Feather, Jean
—Dramatized / Kamerman
One wish too many, 191–199
Quick-witted Jack, 400–412
FEATHER
—Grimm / Complete *
three feathers: youngest prince
marries toad, 319–322
—Hamilton / People *
wolf insults birds; borrowed feath-
ers taken back, 43–48
—Hopi Coyote / Malotki
Bird Girls, grinding corn, give
feathers to Coyote Girl, 91–97
—Lines / Magical *
girl requests red flower; must
marry Finist the Falcon, 31–
45
FEET
—Paxton / Belling *
feet and stomach: who's helping
whom (Aesop), [32–33]
FEET-WATER
—Hamilton / Dark *
horned women: twelve witches
vs. Spirit of the Well, 32–37
—Old Wives / Carter
wash water, not thrown out, lets
wool spinners in, 211–212
FELIMID
—Pendragon / Ashley
Buried silver (Taylor), 227–259
FENCING MASTER
—Grimm / Complete *
brothers: barber, blacksmith:
most skilled? 561–62
Fenelon, F. (1651–1715?)
—Lang / Wilkins
The Enchanted Ring, 220–227
FENIAN TALES
—Irish / Glassie
three tales, 237–256
FENODEREE
—Fairies / Briggs, 170–172

FENRIS
—Hamilton / Dark *
   wolf-child of Loki, 82–86
FERAL CHILDREN
—Yolen / Faery Flag
   wolf/child: she-wolf and the colo-
   nel, 61–78
**Ferdinand Faithful and Ferdinand
Unfaithful**
—Grimm / Complete * 566–571
Ferguson, David
—Dramatized / Kamerman
   A most special dragon, 79–87
FERRYMAN
—Jewish / Sadeh
   man who went to the "dickens,"
   146–149
FERTILITY
—Cotterell / Encyclopedia, 253 (in-
   dex)
—Egyptian / Ions, 143 (index)
—Man Myth & Magic, 3133 (index)
   analytics, 3187 (index)
—Mercatante / Encyclopedia, 762 (in-
   dex)
—Russian / Ivanits, 247 (index)
—Scandinavian / Davidson, 142 (in-
   dex)
FERTILITY RITE
—Hamilton / Dark *
   Wanjiru: girl swallowed by the
   earth, 108–112
FESTIVAL
—Mercatante / Encyclopedia, 762 (in-
   dex)
FEVER DEMON
—Egyptian / Harris
   princess, healing by Kohns the
   Determiner, 88–91
FIANNA
—Celts / Hodges *
   Dermot in the Land-under-Wave,
   57–73
—Fairies / Briggs, 174–175

FICKLE
—Wilde / Lynch *
   nightingale gives life for student-
   in-love, 14–23
FIDDLE
—Grimm / Complete *
   magic fiddle makes everyone
   dance, 503–508
—Grimm / Sixty *
   magic fiddle . . . , 182–189
—Water Buffalo (Chinese)
   origin of horse-headed fiddle, 44–
   48
FIDELITY (*especially in love;
   marriage*)
   see also LOYALTY
—Bierhorst / Naked *
   moose wife; broken promise
   brings bad luck, 52–59
—Chinese / Chin *
   conscripted husband of Meng-
   Jiang Nyu, 128–139
—Clouston / Popular
   parrot tales; wife's fidelity, II.196–
   211
   unwittingly eating lover's heart,
   II.187–195
—Coyote / Ramsey
   Wasco woman, 54–56
—Douglas / Magic *
   Beauty and the Beast, 85–97
—Egyptian / Harris
   Anpu and Bata; betrayed, 77–83
—Fahs / Old *
   girl chooses death over unfaith-
   fulness, 44–51
   loyalty to lowly dependent (dog),
   33–36
—Grimm / Complete *
   Marriage of Mrs. Reynard [Fox],
   193–196
—Grimm / Sixty *
   Marriage . . . [as above], 288–291
—Jewish / Sadeh

dying father to son: beware of hypocrite (wife), 260–261

father's advice on carousing, etc. averts evil, 333–334

lute player: cuckolding wife, 288–289

woman who was almost stoned to death, 18–20

—Lang / Wilkins

captured children; Little King Loc, 441–459

—Lore of Love

cursed embrace: Liba and Guntram, 32–35

King Nala and Princess Damayanti, 110–119

—Old Wives / Carter

hare seduces woman; she tricks, cooks, feeds him to husband, 47

wife gives rice to lover; tricks husband to accept chaff for grain, 72

—Spring / Philip

woman's love: wife rejects series of suitors, 58–74

—Turkish (Art I) / Walker

Haci's daughter marries, is repeatedly assaulted, 24–33

shah spares lustful pilgrim; favor later returned, 93–98

unfaithful wife detected by blind hoca, 89–91

—Vietnam / Terada *

look-alike brothers love the same girl, 109–113

ugly man changes self to test wife's fidelity, 64–68

Field, Eugene (1850–1895)

—Childcraft 1 / Once *

Wynken, Blynken, and Nod, 298–299

—Lycanthropy / Otten

The werewolf, 262–268

FIELD

—Coyote / Bierhorst *

field (estate); gold assumed; real legacy is hard work, [46]

FIGHT(-ing)

—Beat / Bryan *

bush cow vs. elephant: who is stronger? 14–29

—Bruchac / Iroquois *

Skunny-Wundy defeats the Stone Giants, 161–167

—Coyote / Bierhorst *

wolf and puma fight; coyote steals the kill, [22]

—Ghosts / Starkey

Joe Reardon and the three sister-ghosts, 102–109

—Shannon / More *

firefly defeats 100 club-wielding apes, 19–22

FIGS

—Tree / Kerven *

one banyon tree covers moon, [4–5]

FIJI TALES

—Hoke / Giants

The giant and his swing, 130–132

FILIAL PIETY

—Bomans / Wily *

king, devoted to his mother, does not want to die, 118–120

—Clouston / Popular

son cruel to father; his son plans same, II.372–378

—Jewish / Sadeh

sons neglect father; three tales, 282–284

Finette Cendron (d'Aulnoy)

—Zipes / Beauties * 400–416

FINGAL, KING

—Campbell / West Highlands, IV.433 (index)

FINGER-PLAY STORIES

—Pellowski / Story * 92–98

Finist the Falcon
—Lines / Magical *, 31–45
FINLAND
—Bomans / Wily *
 each year witch takes two naugh-
 tiest children in Finland, 27–36
—Dictionary / Leach, 1208 (index)
FINLAY (Scottish hero)
—Hoke / Giants
 giant killer, 142–149
Finn and the young hero's children
—Lines / Magical * 122–127
FINN Mac COOL
—Celtic / MacCana
 Fionn mac Cumhaill, 142 (index)
—Celts / Hodges *
 How Finn Mac Cool got his wis-
 dom tooth, 34–52
 The poem of Finn, 53–56
—Crossley / British FT *
 Gruagach, Finn, and the Lady of
 the Green Gown, 228–243
—Dramatized / Kamerman
 disguised as baby, he frightens
 Cuchullin, 218–226
—Dulac / Fairy *
 Queen of many-colored bed-
 chamber, 69–76
—Ellis / Dict Irish Myth, 124–126
—Journeys / Norris *
 Dermot and Grania: escape from
 Finn, [22–25]
—Lines / Magical *
 Oisin's mother, 169–174
—O'Brien / Tales *
 giants, McConigle vs. Finn
 (whose wife has him disguised
 as infant), 9–16
FINNEGAS (poet)
—Celts / Hodges *
 How Finn Mac Cool got his wis-
 dom tooth, 34–52
FINNISH . . .
—Earth / Hadley *

 spark: Vainamoinen recaptures
 stolen fire, [19–20]
—Humor / Midwest, 113–129
—Manning / Cauldron *
 Whirlwind abducts queen and
 son, 106–117
—Mercatante / Encyclopedia, 729 (in-
 dex)
—Scandinavian / Kvideland, 420 (in-
 dex)
Fionn . . . see FINN . . .
Fir tree, see Little fir tree.
FIRE(-s)
 see also FLAME
—Bell / Classical Dict, 86–89 @
—Bruchac / Iroquois *
 brave woman; Flying Head; misunderstanding by monster,
 184–187
—Caduto / Keepers *
 Loo-Wit, the fire-keeper, 41–43
—Cotterell / Encyclopedia, 253 (index)
—Coyote / Ramsey
 Cayuse Indians get fire, 15–17
 Coos people discover fire, 144–
 146
 theft: coyote and turtle, 216–217
—Curry / Beforetime *
 coyote steals fire from yellowjacket (people), 33–41
 learning to make, from willow
 sticks, 33–41
 measuring [inch]-worm's great
 climb (in search of fire), 26–32
—Dulac / Fairy *
 fire bird: princess, heart of prince,
 153–164
 origin, 153–164
—Earth / Hadley *
 Sararuma: fire destroys all but
 one couple, [21–22]
 spark: Vainamoinen recaptures
 stolen fire, [19–20]

—Earthmaker / Mayo *
    Ice Man puts out big fire (Chero-
    kee tale), 54–56
—Fahs / Old *
    Prometheus brings fire to man-
    kind, 145–147
—Greaves / Hippo *
    fight with baboon: how zebra got
    stripes, 99–102
    ostrich tricked into losing fire,
    127–128
—Grimm / Complete *
    personification: straw, coal, and
    bean, 102–103
—Grimm / Legends (Ward), II:409 (in-
    dex)
—Grimm / Sixty *
    personification (as above), 29–
    30
—Indian Myth / Burland
    origin: Rabbit, and the Hitchiti,
    111
—Jewish / Frankel, 646 (index)
—Lang / Wilkins
    Fairer-than-a-Fairy, 274–281
—Lester / Brer Rabbit *
    test: Brer Rabbit eats the butter;
    accuses Brer Possum, 46–50
—Lore of Love
    King Nala and Princess Damay-
    anti, 110–119
—MacDonald / Sourcebook *
    motif index, 619
—Man Myth & Magic, 3133 (index)
—Mercatante / Encyclopedia, 762 (in-
    dex)
—Pellowski / Story *
    fire used for cooking; origin; sand
    story, 70–74
—Persian / Hinnells, 142 (index)
—Polynesians / Andersen, 478 (in-
    dex)
—Russian / Ivanits, 247 (index)
—Sioux / Standing Bear *

    first fire brought to the Sioux, 77–
    79
—Southern [legends] / Floyd
    rains of snakes, etc., 74–77
—Tree / Kerven *
    coal given to willows and birches;
    rub them, make fire, [8–9]
    pines have fire; beaver steals a
    coal, [8–9]
—Turkey / Walker, 302 (index)
—Vanishing / Mercer *
    how men first got fire; Bushman
    tale, 76–79
    pygmy befriended by monkeys,
    steals fire, 68–70
—Williams-Ellis / Tales *
    white-faced simini (forced to use
    foolish words), 142–144
FIRE (*world catastrophe*)
—Corrin / Six-Year *
    fairy punishes selfish boy for mis-
    treating cow, duck, pig, 191–
    194
—Earth / Hadley *
    Sararuma: fire destroys all but
    one couple, [21–22]
—Lang / Wilkins
    Heart of ice (Caylus), 190–219
—Maori / Kanawa *
    Kahukura and fairies (fishing with
    net), 46–50
Firebird, *see* BIRD: MYTHICAL.
FIREFLY
—Shannon / More *
    defeats 100 club-wielding apes,
    19–22
Firestarters/Firewalkers
—Floyd / Gr Am Myst, 52–56
FIREWOOD
—Jonsen / Trolls *
    stone cheese [troll tricked by
    youngest son], 24–32
**FIREWORKS (personified; royal
    wedding)**

—Wilde / Happy *
  remarkable rocket, 105–133
—Wilde / Lynch *
  (same as above), 55–72
FIRST-AID
—Trolls / Asbjornsen
  cock would aid hen with nut stuck
  in throat, 22–24
First man, *see* MANKIND.
FISH(-es)
—Arabian / Lewis
  glutton feigns message from
  small fish, 210
—Arabian / McCaughrean
  glutton feigns . . . , 194–197
—Clouston / Popular
  men swallowed by monster fish,
  I.403–411
  ring and fish legends, I.398–403
—Creatures (illus) / Huber * 155 (in-
  dex)
—Douglas / Magic *
  Thumbelina, 43–53
—Earth / Hadley *
  Beebyeebyee marries water god
  (fish-man), [25–26]
—Greaves / Hippo *
  Creator forbids hippo to eat fish,
  67
—Hamilton / Dark *
  Manabozo: manitou hare swal-
  lowed by king of fishes, 27–31
—Jewish / Frankel
  fox escapes from Angel of Death,
  and Leviathan's fish, 11–14
—Jewish / Sadeh
  bread cast upon the water, 28–31
  fish with golden tail and pearls for
  eyes, 95–97
  Maimonides: king's ring found in
  fish, 215–217
—Leonardo / Fables *
  mobilize to destroy net, 63–66
—Lester / Brer Rabbit *

steals Brer Wolf's fish; gives cow,
  but ends up with the meat, 51–
  53
—MacDonald / Sourcebook *
  motif index, 619–621
—Manning / Cats *
  king loses sight; cure if washed in
  Katchka's blood, 118–123
—Old Wives / Carter
  little red fish and clog of gold
  (Cinderella-type), 171–177
—Spring / Philip
  golden fish rewards kindness,
  103–113
—Vanishing / Mercer *
  Ainu myth: origin of tides,
  quakes, hills, etc., 95–98
FISHBONE, MAGIC
—Corrin / Eight-Year *
  princess: save fishbone until
  needed, 147–160
FISH: CARP
—Chinese / Chin *
  golden carp (killed, its bones do
  magic for friend), 47–57
FISH: CATFISH
—High John / Sanfield *
  slaves forbidden to catch catfish,
  34–39
FISH (dinner)
—Manning / Cats *
  rhyming water-nick fries fish; bear
  and monkeys feast, 97–100
FISH: EEL
—Spring / Philip
  wise king exposes gold thief, 50–
  57
—Yep / Rainbow *
  husband (fool) and Eel's disguise, 38–44
FISH: FLOUNDER
—Rockwell / Puss *
  fisherman, his wife, and the flounder, 42–52

FISH: GOLDFISH
—Grimm / Complete *
  goldfish gives magic castle to
  fisherman, 388–393
Fish: Hagfish, *see* HAGFISH.
FISH-HOOK
—Maori / Kanawa *
  Maui uses New Zealand as hook
  (!) to catch South Island, 17–22
Fish-horse, *see* WALRUS.
Fish-men, *see* MERMAN (-men).
FISH: SALMON
—Celts / Hodges *
  How Finn MacCool got his wis-
  dom tooth, 34–52
—Curry / Beforetime *
  Ixkareya: witches steal all
  salmon; coyote destroys secret
  dam, 42–47
—Haboo / Hilbert
  legend of the humpy salmon,
  118–121
  sockeye salmon in Baker River,
  137–144
  steelhead, 127–129
—Hoke / Giants
  giant, no heart in his body, 93–
  102
FISH-SELLER
—Water Buffalo (Chinese)
  fish-seller and the one-eyed yak,
  5–8
FISH: SOLE
—Grimm / Complete *
  punished: mouth on side, 709
FISHER, Gabriel
—Ghosts / Time-Life, 62–69
FISHER (*animal*)
—Caduto / Keepers *
  skyland: origin of Big Dipper,
  117–120
Fisherman and his wife (Grimm)
—Allison / I'll Tell * 26–27
—Carle / Treasury * 21–30

—Grimm / Complete * 103–112
—Grimm / Sixty * 47–56
—Rockwell / Puss * 42–52
  Fisherman and his wife (*existential retelling*)
—Switzer / Existential, 63–70
FISHING / FISHERMAN
—Arabian / Lewis
  merman trades jewels for fruit,
  131–137
  well's magic objects do "impossible" tasks, 117–122
—Arabian / McCaughrean
  jinni tricked back into bottle, 29–
  35
  merman trades jewels for fruit,
  83–96
—Arabian / Riordan
  jinni tricked back into bottle, 26–
  37
—Corrin / Imagine *
  Pari hides in golden candelabra;
  prince buys, falls in love, 151–
  160
—Douglas / Magic *
  promise to the genie, 13–19
—Dramatized / Kamerman
  Quick-witted Jack; suitor tests,
  400–412
—Grimm / Complete *
  goldfish gives magic castle to
  fisherman, 388–393
—Hamilton / Dark *
  Rolling Rio, gray man, and Death,
  5–13
—Harris-Parks / Jump *
  moon in millpond: Brers Rabbit
  and Tortoise play trick, 35–38
—Jewish / Sadeh
  fish with golden tail and pearls for
  eyes, 95–97
—Journeys / Norris *
  great chase: Mirragen the Catman vs. Gurangatch, [10–12]

—Lester / Brer Rabbit *
moon in the pond: fishing party,
96–99
—Russian Hero / Warner *
wolf tricked: tail frozen in ice, 111
—Tall Tales / Downs: Bear
perfect bait / S. Corbett, 24–28
—Vietnam / Terada *
lady of stone: man unknowingly
marries his sister, 115–118
FISHING NET
—Vanishing / Mercer *
Maori custom, origin, 28–31
origin: Australian Abo tale, 54–57
FISHING: ORIGIN OF CUSTOMS
—Coyote / Ramsey
coyote invents rituals, 135–138
coyote kills giantess; herds
salmon, 138–140
Fitcher's bird
—Grimm / Complete * 216–220
Flail from heaven
—Grimm / Complete * 514–515
FLAME
—Leonardo / Fables *
flames and the cauldron, 84
pleasure: butterfly and the flame,
68
FLATTERY
—Aesop / Reeves-Wilson *
fool listens; Fox and crow, 66–67
—Aesop / Zwerger
fox [flatterer] and [gullible] crow,
19
—Allison / I'll Tell *
falling for fox flattery, crow loses
cheese, 127
—Demi / Reflective *
peacocks: flattery not always
true, [20]
—Spanish-Am / Van Etten *
animals (except mouse) flatter
mountain lion, 106–108
—Turkish / Walker

lion asks monkey: how does my
den smell? 16
—Zipes / Beauties *
Ram [a King Lear type, by
d'Aulnoy], 389–399
FLEA
—Grimm / Complete *
louse and the flea, 158–160
—Leonardo / Fables *
flea leaves dog; looks for better
life on sheep, 71
—Spanish-Am / Van Etten *
magic: finding suitor's secret
sleeping place, 29–31
task: make flea grow to size of
cow, 65–72
FLEMISH TALES
—Dulac / Fairy *
White Caroline, Black Caroline,
15–21
FLEXIBILITY
—Aesop / Reeves-Wilson *
oak and reed (weaker survives),
27
FLIGHT(-s) (*often magic*)
see also ESCAPE . . .
—Bierhorst / Naked *
Last Remaining [after plague],
87–92
—Celts / Hodges *
how Finn MacCool got his wisdom tooth, 34–52
—Coyote / Bierhorst *
coyote eats all his animals; people discreetly leave, [8]
—Crossley / British FT *
Mossycoat goes to ball; leaves
slipper behind, 86–99
—Grimm / Complete *
Fundevogel, 241–244
kings' daughters aid hero in
tasks: win girl or die, 515–524
queen dies; king would marry
their daughter, 326–331

Sweetheart Roland, 268–271
Water-nixie, The, 364–365
—Grimm / Sixty *
   Fundevogel, 84–87
   Sweetheart Roland, 156–160
—Hamilton / People *
   People could fly [to freedom],
     166–172
—Maori / Kanawa *
   Hinemoa and Tutanekai; guided
     by flute, 36–44
—Old Wives / Carter
   Juleidah: princess disguised as
     lowly kitchen-worker, 39–46
—Scriven / Full Color *
   Cinderella, 69–73
—Switzer / Existential
   Cinderella (*existential retelling*),
     38–45
—Williams-Ellis / Tales *
   Cap o' Rushes (loves father "like
     salt"), 8–16
FLOOD(-s)
—Bierhorst / Monkey *
   boy-servant of Chac (rain-god);
     repeated disobedience, 66–
     69
—Bierhorst / So Am
   Indian religion and mythology,
     266 (index)
—Bomans / Wily *
   deluge: clerics argue while water
     rises, 107–108
—Cotterell / Encyclopedia, 253 (in-
   dex)
—Earth / Hadley *
   bit of earth: Weesack-Kachak's
     world destroyed by flood, [6–7]
—Earthmaker / Mayo * 5 @
   thirsty lizard ends the big flood
     (Ute tale), 6–10
—Erdoes / Sound *
   how Sioux Nation came into be-
     ing, 72–73

   remaking of the (third) world,
     126–129
—Fahs / Old *
   Deucalion saved; cruel greed of
     human race punished, 58–63
—Gullible Coyote / Malotki, 165 @
   coyote swallows birds alive, goes
     crazy, predicts flood, 37–45
—Indian Myth / Burland
   Creek Indian myth, 115–116
—Vanishing / Mercer *
   Brazil: why Pamaris huts are on
     stilts, 20–21
—Vietnam / Terada *
   squash seeds: origin of Dao Peo-
     ple, 54–58
—Yep / Rainbow *
   origin: Trouble-snake, 118–123
FLOOD (O.T., Genesis)
—Babylonia / Spence, 390 (index)
—Gould / Mythical
   not a myth, 101–136, 375–376, @
FLORIDA
—Southern [legends] / Floyd
   monsters of the deep (Florida
     coast), 141–147
—Speck / New World, 521 (index)
Flounder, *see* FISH: FLOUNDER.
FLOWER(-s)
—Crossley / Dead *
   green mist: girl lives only until
     cowslip dies, 39–43
—Dramatized / Kamerman
   Plum Blossom and the dragon,
     38–46
—Geras / Grandmother *
   talking plants' contest: which is
     most beautiful? 57–65
—Grimm / Complete *
   Our Lady's Little Glass, 825–826
   Pink [carnation], The, 355–360
—Grimm / Sixty *
   Pink [carnation], The, 171–176
—Scary / Young *

ghost sucks blood from Indian mother/child; origin of Indian paintbrush, 87–88
—Tree / Kerven *
    creator Baiame gives seeds; flower life cycle, [22–25] mystery man of the peonies, [10–13]
Flowerbell (Grimm)
—Corrin / Six-Year * 82–86
Flute, see MUSIC: FLUTE.
FLY (flies) (insect)
—Beat / Bryan *
    how animals, birds, fish got tails, 53–70
—Childcraft 2 / Time *
    I know old lady who swallowed . . . (folksong) 206–211
—Hopi / Talashoma-Malotki
    hide and seek with life at stake, 50–69
—Turkish (Art I) / Walker
    foolish servant checks on fly in water glass, 91–92
FLYING
—Bomans / Wily *
    wings: "madman" wants to go to heaven without dying, 152–155
—Greaves / Hippo *
    ostrich tricked into losing fire, 127–128
—Hamilton / People *
    the people could fly [to freedom], 166–172
—Hopi Coyote / Malotki
    Bird Girls, grinding corn, give feathers to Coyote Girl, 91–97
—Sioux / Standing Bear *
    Hawk Dreamer invokes hawk, leaps to safety, 28–31
—Tall Tales / Downs: Bear
    the doodang / J.C. Harris, 109–111

—Witch Encyc / Guiley, 413 (index)
Flying carpet, see MAGIC TRANS-PORT.
FLYING DUTCHMAN
—Hamilton / Dark *
    phantom ship cursed by God, 38–42
FLYING HEAD
—Bruchac / Iroquois *
    brave woman and the Flying Head, 184–187
FOG
—Childcraft 3 / Stories *
    Duny: boy who became a wizard (Le Guin), 176–186
—Earthmaker / Mayo *
    Evil-Doer: when fog comes drifting, 76–80
    origins, 75 @
FOLK BELIEF
—Wildlife / Gillespie, 241 (index)
FOLK EVENTS
—American / Read Dgst
    USA guide (by state), 404–423
FOLK LITERATURE
—Bosma / Classroom
    form, theme, content, 39–54
    reading aloud, 10–13
    recommended books (142 titles annotated), 81–107
    story mapping, 13–16
    themes, 36–38
—MacDonald / Sourcebook *
    themes; motives, 1–818
FOLKLORE
—Bosma / Classroom
    classifications and definitions, 3–4
—Folk-rhymes / Northall
    England, 1–565
—MacDonald / Sourcebook *
    classification, 1–818
—Man Myth & Magic
    analytics, 3197–98 (index)

—Schwartz / Gates, 801 (index)
FOLK-MEDICINE
—Plants / Dyer, 281–299
FOLK MUSIC
—Folk Ballads / McNeil, 1–219; 1–223 (2 vols.)
    cowboys, I.143–165
    crime ballads, I.47–68
    death and dying ballads, II.168–178
    humorous ballads, II.32–65
    lovers, I.69–141
    murder ballads, II.67–89
    supernatural ballads, II.115–159
    tragedy; disasters, II.91–113
    war ballads, I.33–46
FOLK NARRATIVES
—Brown / Amer Folklore
    categories, 10 @
FOLKSONGS
—Mex-Am / West, 117–136
FOLKTALES (*about*)
—Bosma / Classroom
    criteria for evaluating (MacDonald), 80
—Grimm / Complete *
    types, history, meaning (by J. Campbell), 840–864
—Mercatante / Encyclopedia
    definition, xviii @
FOLKTALES: one-act plays
—Dramatized / Kamerman, 1–575
FOLKWAYS
—American / Read Dgst, 437 (index)
FON PEOPLE
—Hamilton / In the Beginning *
    Mawu and Lisa (creation myth), 42–45
FOOD (*often magic*)
    see also CORN; EATING; INDIAN FOOD; MEAL; etc.
—Bierhorst / Monkey *
    Mole-Catcher marries daughter of Death-Maker, 121–130
—Bierhorst / Naked *
    Chestnut pudding: magic food supply, 3–10
—Grimm / Complete *
    kings' daughters aid hero in tasks: win girl or die, 515–524
—Hopi Coyote / Malotki
    spider entertains coyote; food grows in size, 43–55
—Jewish / Frankel, 646 (index)
—Jewish / Sadeh
    old bachelor lost a bean, 22–25
—Muddleheads / Harris
    seal of Mouse Children recovered from Big Raven, 60–74
—Polynesians / Andersen, 479 (index)
—Tibet / Timpanelli *
    pancakes; unwilling "seer"; coincidence, 29–41
—Vietnam / Terada *
    unusual food: rice cakes for New Year, 105–108
—Williams-Ellis / Tales *
    magic bird unplows field, gives milk, lures children, 62–76
—Witch Hndbk / Bird *
    witch's kitchen, 14–25, 88
FOOD RELIEF
—Hopi Coyote / Malotki
    coyote and the Korowiste kachinas, 195–227, 303, 307 @
FOOD: SEAFOOD
—Caduto / Keepers *
    how Raven made the tides, 103
FOOD SUPPLY
—Bruchac / Iroquois *
    Hodadenon: last one left; chestnut tree, 169–182
—Caduto / Keepers *
    Kokopilau, the hump-backed flute player, 151
—Igloo / Metayer

Kajortoq: bears and wolf become fox's food, 19–23

—Spanish-Am / Van Etten *
ant and (begging) grasshopper visit spider's home, 95–96

FOOL(-s) (foolish acts)
see also BUNGLING FOOL(-s); COWARDLY FOOL; EXCESS; GULLIBILITY; NUMSKULL TALES; SIMPLETON
see also particular tales, e.g., Emperor's new clothes, The

—Aesop / Reeves-Wilson *
counting chickens before they're hatched, 97–98
pride ends in ruin: Donkey, cock, and lion, 120

—Aesop / Zwerger
ass [jealous of] lap dog, makes "ass" of self, 25
comparisons: dog and sow [argue: whose babies are better], 21

—Allison / I'll Tell *
farmer, son, and donkey: attempt to please everyone, 128–129

—Arabian / McCaughrean
thief pretends to be ass under spell, 150–152

—Bierhorst / Monkey *
buzzard-man: lazy farmer trades places with buzzard; dies, 37–43
three would-be buyers of jar murdered; fool tricked: buries "one" thrice, 32–36

—Bomans / Wily *
extremes: Princess Steppie: absurdities, 20–27
king's even more foolish sons are misunderstood as "wise," 143–146

—Bruchac / Iroquois *
girl not satisfied with simple things, 123–127

hungry fox and boastful suitor, 80–83

—Cambodian / Carrison
father/son ride/carry donkey to market, 102–106
rider holds rice on head to lessen load for buffalo, 97–99

—Chinese / Chin *
unwise acts: magic brush of artist Ma Liang, 143–153

—Clarkson / World *
carries complaints to God, who gives him gift of luck, 319–323
foolish grief: Bastianelo, 362–364
wives wager: whose husband is biggest fool, 377–380

—Greaves / Hippo *
ostrich tricked into losing fire, 127–128
why ostrich has a long neck, 128–130

—Greek / Osborne
golden touch: Bacchus grants King Midas' wish, 9–11

—Grimm / Complete *
going a traveling, 630–631
good bargain: peasant thinks frog and dog are speaking, 51–55
seven Swabians (numskulls), 538–542

—Hamilton / Dark *
free spirits: Bouki and Malice, 102–107
servant opens forbidden book, summons devil to work; can't stop, 126–131

—Hamilton / People *
Big John forces Little John; results, 81–89

—Hopi Coyote / Malotki
coyote foolishly tries to cut pocket in his skin; dies, 113–117
excess: coyote and bird play: pluck out/retrieve eyes, 63–67

fear of reflection in water, 105–111

—Irish / Glassie
seven tales, 83–90

—Jewish / Frankel, xiv, 649 (index)
box of bones (and three other tales), 414–424
foolish imaginings: "what if" disasters as real, 571–573

—Jewish / Sadeh
bread cast upon the water, 28–31
daughter wiser than her father, 289–291
debate between priest and town fool, 299–300
horse that was an imp, 381–382
wise men of Chelm, 313–314

—Jonsen / Trolls *
[troll's greed] The three billy goats Gruff, [4–14]

—MacDonald / Sourcebook *
motif index, 234–261

—Muddleheads / Harris
Mink Being wants to marry human princess, 5–25

—Navajo Coyote / Haile
chart: the seventeen tales, 11 @
how people killed coyote, 15, 78–81

—O'Brien / Tales *
poor farmer trades cow for magic "do your [whatever] duty" bottle, 46–52

—Old Wives / Carter
three sillies: crying over imagined harm to unborn child, 104–107
which is bigger fool: 1) wearing invisible clothes; 2) thinks he's dead, 102–103

—Oral Trad / Cunningham
Big Klaus and Little Klaus, 72–76

—Palestinian / Speak (Muhawi)
motif-index, 394–395

—Paxton / Aesop *

goose that laid golden eggs, [16–18]

—Paxton / Belling *
dog in river: greed: foolish loss of meat, (Aesop), [38–39]

—Rockwell / Puss *
Mr. Vinegar (makes series of bad trades), 60–65

—Russian Hero / Warner *
foolish man exchanges daughter for help, 57–60

—Turkish (Art I) / Walker
brothers quarrel, don't speak; one sends blank letter, 69–70

—Water Buffalo (Chinese)
plop! spread of unquestioned danger, 30–32

—Yep / Rainbow *
husband (fool): Eel's disguise, 38–44

FOOLISH BARGAIN(-s)

—Celts / Hodges *
Lad of Luck and monster, 89–103

—Clarkson / World *
Gudbrand on Hill-side, 75–78

—Grimm / Complete *
Fred and Kate [repeated foolish acts], 283–289
Hans in luck; series of foolish tradings, 381–386
nixie (mill-pond) captures young man; wife rescues, 736–742

—Grimm / Sixty *
Fred and Kate . . . , 144–155
Hans in luck . . . , 10–16

—Jaffrey / Seasons
how Ram, son of Dashrat, defeated demon king Ravan, 48–69

Foolish wishes [pudding on wife's nose]

—Carter / Sleeping * 41–44
—Zipes / Beauties * 64–66

FORBIDDEN . . .
 see also OBEDIENCE; TABOO
—Fahs / Old *
 how Tewas came to live at Turtle
 Mountain, 7–14
—Jewish / Frankel
 Adam/Eve tempt phoenix; does
 not eat forbidden fruit; immor-
 tal, 15–17
—Nesbit / Fairy *
 drawers; town in the library, 81–98
Ford, Ford Madox (1873–1939)
—Victorian / Hearn
 Brown owl, The, 260–316
FOREIGN LANGUAGES
—Pellowski / Family *
 finger stories, when traveling,
 102–106
FOREIGN POPULATION (U.S.)
—American / Read Dgst, 333–351
FOREKNOWLEDGE
—High John / Sanfield *
 eavesdrops on Master; pretends
 foreknowledge of his plans,
 24–33
FORESIGHT
—Aesop / Reeves-Wilson *
 Ant and grasshopper, 44–45
 mouse frees lion from net, 16–18
—Coyote / Bierhorst *
 escape from well; coyote tricks
 goat, [24]
FOREST
 see also LOGGING
—Demi / Reflective *
 boar declares war on forest, [10]
—Jewish / Frankel, 646 (index)
FOREST SPIRIT
—Tree / Kerven *
 ugarri imprisons boys in tree,
 [6–7]
FORETELLING THE FUTURE
 see also CLAIRVOYANCE; FU-
 TURE; PROPHECY

—Man Myth & Magic
 analytics, 3184–85 (index)
FORETHOUGHT
—Caduto / Keepers *
 Awi Usdi: deer and excessive
 hunting, 173–174
—Cambodian / Carrison
 rooster foils polecat's plan to eat
 him, 49–51
—Corrin / Six-Year *
 little jackal tricks alligator into revealing self, 93–97
—Crossley / British FT *
 Pict keeps secret of brewing ale
 from Scots, 142–144
—Curry / Beforetime *
 pine-nut thieves: bluebirds put
 to sleep by coyote's chant, 90–
 99
—Grimm / Complete *
 peasant's wise daughter, 439–
 440
—Old Wives / Carter
 girl rid of unwanted suitors by
 immobilizing them, 76–85
 rich farmer covets young girl; she
 substitutes mare for wedding,
 61–63
—Russian Hero / Warner *
 sun, frost, wind: honor most powerful, 32
—Scary / Young *
 tiger's eyes: sister recognizes imposter; throws pepper in eyes,
 73–77
—Turkish / Walker
 Hoca: tax collector keeps records
 on pastries, 45–46
—Water Buffalo (Chinese)
 fish-seller and the one-eyed yak,
 5–8
FORGET(-ing)
—Bierhorst / Monkey *
 with help of giant's daughter,

young man does four impossible tasks, 56–65

—Jewish / Frankel
Baal Shem Tov: storyteller returns to tell forgotten story, 485–489

—Jewish / Sadeh
servant of Baal Shem Tov forgets all stories save one, 357–361

—O'Brien / Tales *
giant Trencross abducts princess; white cat helps rescue, 92–105

—Yep / Rainbow *
magic forgetfulness: The homecoming, 144–151

FORGIVE(-ness)

—Caduto / Keepers *
gods and Loo-Wit, the fire-keeper, 41–43

—Lines / Magical *
Joseph (in Egypt) and his brethren, 149–169

—Vietnam / Terada *
ugly man changes self to test wife's fidelity, 64–68

FORMULA TALES (*framework of tales*)

—Ashliman / Guide
titles arranged in Aarne-Thompson system, 300–318 @

—Clarkson / World *
gold in chimney; witch: "have you seen a maid o mine?" 26–29
eight tales, 221–255

—Grimm / Complete *
juniper tree: murder exposed by singing bird, 220–229
my household, 624
Snowdrop [=Snow White and the seven dwarfs], 249–258

—Grimm / Sixty *
Snowdrop . . . , 161–170

—Hall / Treasury *
Teeny-tiny, 13–16

—Old Coot / Christian *
wager: gambler won't say "enough" to Coot's stories, 29–38

—Starkey / Ghosts
brothers encounter ogre, 80–87

—Turkish / Walker
just say Hic! 76–79

FORTUNATE ISLES

—Baring-Gould / Curious
Paradise for souls of the dead, 134–138 @

Fortune reversed, *see* REVERSAL OF FORTUNE.

FORTUNE-TELLING

—Witch Hndbk / Bird * 36–41

FOSTER-MOTHER

—Imaginary / Nigg
foster-mother: the alan, 113–115

Found objects, *see* LOST AND FOUND.

FOUNDER

—Cotterell / Encyclopedia, 253 (index)

FOUNDLING

—Manning / Cats *
kind witch raises foundling to be knight; bewitched Cat-Johann his aide, 111–117

—Reeves / Shadow
twin girls parted at birth; reunited at wedding of one, 113–128

FOUNTAIN OF YOUTH

—Speck / New World
early exploration, 21–31

FOUR (*number*)

—Gullible Coyote / Malotki, 169 @

—Hopi Coyote / Malotki, 311 @

—Navajo Coyote / Haile
request repeated four times, best to grant, 68 @

Four clever brothers
—Grimm / Complete * 580–584
—Grimm / Sixty * 220–234
FOURTH WORLD: PLANTS
—Caduto / Keepers *
    Kokopilau, the hump-backed
    flute player, 151
FOX
    see also Aesop: Fox . . .
—Aesop / Reeves-Wilson *
    cunning: King Lion is ill, 105–107
    flattery; fox and crow, 66–67
    guest's food in plate/bottle: fox
    and stork, 95–96
—Allison / I'll Tell *
    falling for fox flattery, crow loses
    cheese, 127
    fox and grapes: contempt for
    what one can't obtain, 131
    fox and stork; dinner invitations;
    victim of joke, 110
    fox uses goat (escape from well),
    120
    gingerbread boy, 22–23
    lion, fox, ass: dividing spoils
    "equally," 116
—Animals / Rowland, 184 (index)
—Arabian / McCaughrean
    old fox wants crow as hunting
    partner, 198–202
—Bierhorst / Monkey *
    with Lightning's help, animals find
    fox's corn supply, 52–55
—Bruchac / Iroquois *
    hungry fox and boastful suitor,
    80–83
    rabbit outwits fox (trying to eat
    him), 74–78
    trickster: how bear lost his tail,
    32–34
—Carle / Treasury *
    monkey chosen king; foolishly
    falls into trap (Aesop), 40–41
—Childcraft 1 / Once *
    why bear has stumpy tail; tricked;
    frozen in ice, 96–97
—Childcraft 2 / Time *
    went out on chilly night (folk
    song), 118–123
—Clarkson / World *
    hares safe in burrow; in unsuit-
    able houses, eaten by fox,
    159–161
    Mighty Mikko, 33–41
    travels: a swapping story, 251–
    253
—Crossley / Animal (Grimm) *
    fox and cat; arrogance and mod-
    esty, 8–10
    fox and geese: one last prayer,
    26–28
    fox helps old horse, 34–38
    wolf (master) outsmarted by fox,
    45–48
—Glooskap / Norman *
    panther-witch and her scissorbill
    birds, 39–49
—Grimm / Complete *
    catch Golden Bird; advice by fox
    ignored, 272–279
    Fox helps horse trick lion, 595–
    596
    gossip wolf and the fox, 353–354
    Old Sultan, 230–232
    sea-hare: suitor must conceal
    self from princess, 769–772
    test: Marriage of Mrs. Reynard
    [Fox], 193–196
    Wolf and the man [fox's warning],
    350–351
—Grimm / Sixty *
    catch Golden Bird; advice by fox
    ignored, 1–9
    Fox helps horse trick lion, 241–
    243
    Old Sultan, 26–28
    test: Marriage of Mrs. Reynard
    [Fox], 288–291

Wolf and the man [fox's warning], 211–212
—Hamilton / People *
Bruh Fox makes Tar Baby; rabbit gets stuck, 13–19
—Harris-Parks / Again
Brer Rabbit "fishing" in a well, 2–5
Tar-Baby story, 6–13
—Harris-Parks / Jump *
Brer Fox hunts, Brer Rabbit gets the game, 11–16
Brer Rabbit uses Brer Fox as riding horse, 27–32
—Igloo / Metayer
Kajortoq: bears and wolf become fox's food, 19–23
Kajortoq (fox) outwitted by crow, 46–48
—Japanese / Tyler, 334 (index)
—Jewish / Frankel fables, xiv (index)
fox escapes from Angel of Death, and Leviathan's fish, 11–14
—Lester / Brer Rabbit *
[note: even if not mentioned, Brer Rabbit is the principal character in each of these tales]
Brer Fox and Brer Rabbit go hunting, 42–43
Brer Fox feigns death; Brer Rabbit tricks him, 29–31
Brer Fox tricked; gets beaten by Mr. Man, 75–78
Brer Fox would eat Brer Rabbit's children; bird gives advice on tasks, 54–56
Brer Rabbit and the Tar Baby, 10–16
Brer Rabbit in the well, tricks Brer Fox, 44–46
Brer Rabbit says that molasses is "fox blood," 141–144
Brer Rabbit steals Brer Fox's peanuts; puts blame on Brer Bear, 71–74
Brer Rabbit warns Sister Goose re Brer Fox, 4–6
Brer Turtle as traveler, 26–29
Brer Turtle put in sack; replaced with hornet's nest, 110–112
courting King Deer's daughter, 131–134
"Hold'im [horse] down" [tricked by Brer Rabbit] 6–8
invitation to dinner: Brer Fox seeks revenge, 8–10
killed; Brer Rabbit has The Man cut off his head; Mrs. Fox, 57–60
riddle: bee hive in gum tree, 91–95
tattletale: Mr. Jack Sparrow meets his end, 35–37
trapped in Mr. Man's garden; cons Brer Fox to take his place, 81–86
tricks Brer Fox into being his saddle-horse, 16–23
with Brer Rabbit, goes inside cow to cut meat; the Man kills fox, 57–60
—Lines / Magical *
Ian Direach to bring the blue falcon; multiple transformations, 45–55
—MacDonald / Sourcebook *
motif index, 623–625
—Manning / Cats *
chain-tale: boy, hare, fox, wolf, bear vs. Baba Yaga, 58–64
—Paxton / Aesop *
patience: fox eats lunch found in hollow tree, [6–9]
poor old lion (eats animal-visitors), [14–15]
—Russian / Afanasev, 658 (index)
—Tall Tales / Downs: Bear

Senor Coyote and Senor Fox / D. Storm, 106–108
—Vanishing / Mercer *
  hedgehog tricks, makes fox his "saddle-horse," 99–101
—Water Buffalo (Chinese)
  arrogant fox pretends to be king, 36–38
  monkey trick: tie tails, eat horse's rump, 82–84
  origin of features (four animals), 82–84
—Wildlife / Gillespie, 242 (index)
—Williams-Ellis / Tales *
  Johnny-Cake runs away from all but fox, 96–101
—Yolen / Shape Shift
  wer-fox: The stranger / S. Oppenheim, 52–60
Fox and the cat
—Crossley / Animal (Grimm) * 8–10
—Grimm / Sixty * 227–228
Fox and the crane [invitations to dinner]
—Carle / Treasury * 106–107
Fox and the geese
—Crossley / Animal (Grimm) * 26–28
Fox and the horse
—Crossley / Animal (Grimm) * 35
—Grimm / Complete * 595–596
—Grimm / Sixty * 241–243
Fox [flatterer] and the [gullible] crow
—Aesop / Zwerger, 19
Fox-woman
—Strauss / Trail
  woman reflects on her fox-life (poem), 22–23
France, Anatole (1844–1924)
—Lang / Wilkins
  Little King Loc, 441–459
FRANCE
—Dictionary / Leach, 1208 (index)
—Lynn / Fantasy * 755 (index)

Francis of Assisi, *see* SAINT FRANCIS . . .
FRANK, Jacob
—Jewish / Sadeh
  visions; wonders, 248–250
FRANKLIN, Benjamin (1706–1790)
—American / Read Dgst, 98–100
Frau Holle
—German-American / Barrick, 110
Frau Trude
—Grimm / Complete * 208–209
FRECKLES
—Bomans / Wily *
  spoiled prince, perfectionist, is reformed by witch, 126–131
Fred and Kate [repeated foolish acts]
—Grimm / Complete * 283–289
—Grimm / Sixty * 144–155
FREEDOM
see also LIBERTY
—Aesop / Reeves-Wilson *
  freedom better than comfort: Wolf and house-dog, 110–111
—Unicorn / Coville *
  king would own unicorns; princess: they must be free, 24–37
  stealing water touched by unicorn horn, to cure sick friend, 7–22
FRENCH (*people***)**
—Humor / Midwest, 67–71
FRENCH TALES
—Dramatized / Kamerman
  The price of eggs, 149–154
—Dulac / Fairy *
  blue bird (prince transformed), 77–90
  green serpent: one twin princess cursed, ugly, 124–138
  hind of the wood: crayfish fairy, 43–59
—Legends / Cavendish, 424 (index)
—Manning / Cauldron *
  gives Jack ring (can change self

to any size); rescues princess from giant, 78–89
—Mercatante / Encyclopedia, 730 (index)
—Pourrat / French, 1–484
—Provencal / De Larrabeiti, 1–222
FREYR and FREYJA
—Norse / Crossley, 267 (index)
—Scandinavian / Davidson
deities of the earth, 72–79, 142 (index)
FRIAR
—Dulac / Fairy *
magic pipe makes all dance, 114–123
—Fahs / Old *
blood of defrauded poor, 125–126
FRIDAY
—Grimm / Legends (Ward), II:411 (index)
FRIEND(-s; -ship)
—Allison / I'll Tell *
bear and travelers: misfortune as test, 117
—Animal Legends / Kerven *
friends ask too much: guinea's crest feathers; lizard's skin, [24–25]
—Bell / Classical Dict, 94–95 @
—Bryan / Lion *
son of Mother Wind [name a secret], 24–39
true friendship: Jackal's favorite game, 40–59
—Demi / Reflective *
wild bird killed by kindness, [16]
—Dulac / Fairy *
White Caroline, Black Caroline, 15–21
—Jewish / Frankel
king's loaves: giving one's life, 353–355
—Legends / Cavendish
fast friends, 403 (index)

—Nesbit / Fairy *
Billy and cousin: kite/bicycle, 45–56
—Paxton / Aesop *
bear whispers: choose friend who stands by in danger, [31–32]
—Paxton / Belling *
hare's "friends" exposed by danger (Aesop), [16–21]
—Wilde / Happy *
devoted [false] friend: miller exploits gardener, 73–101
—Wilde / Lynch *
devoted friend: Little Hans and the miller, 24–40
—Yep / Rainbow *
Trouble-snake (unlikely friend), 118–123
Friesner, Esther M.
—Yolen / Werewolves
A winter's night, 238–253
FRIGHT
see also FEAR
—Hopi / Talashoma-Malotki
Maasaw and Oraibi People once got scared to death, 108–117
FROG(-s)
see also TOAD
—Aesop / Zwerger
hares and [even more timid] frogs, 11
—Beat / Bryan *
call cat: frog threatens hen; hawk gets frog, 3–13
frog/snake children play until told: snakes eat frogs, 41–52
—Bomans / Wily *
Joshua: frog/poet has an unreasoning deep sorrow, 116–118
marriage proposal: shy frog, 109–111
—Caduto / Keepers *
origin: Koluscap turns Water Monster into bullfrog, 81–84

—Cambodian / Carrison
frog boasts to bee: to Himalayas
in one day, 100–101

—Carle / Treasury *
frog wishes to be big as ox
(Aesop), 70–71

—Corrin / Six-Year *
enormous apple pie (frogs provide marvelous picnic), 132–
141

—Coyote / Ramsey
coyote and two frog-women;
physical characteristics, 152–
153

—Curry / Beforetime *
with help of lookalike relatives,
frog wins race with coyote, 57–
59

—Douglas / Magic *
Thumbelina, 43–53

—Earth / Hadley *
drought ends when snake makes
frog laugh, [23–24]

—Frog Rider (Chinese)
Frog Rider (man under spell);
wife fails task; frog dies, 1–
23

—Grimm / Complete *
Three languages [dog, bird, frog],
169–171

—Grimm / Sixty *
Three languages (as above),
223–226

—Hamilton / Dark *
marriage to boar/man; secret not
kept; woman turned into frog,
113–118

—Jewish / Sadeh
Baal Shem Tov and the transmuted Torah scholar, 344–
345

—MacDonald / Sourcebook *
motif index, 625–626

—Shannon / More *

frog wins bet; facing west he still
sees dawn-rays first, 51–52
trapped in bucket of cream, churns
it to butter and escapes, 23–26

—Victorian / Hearn
Melilot (H. Morley), 117–127

—Wilde / Lynch *
remarkable rocket: fireworks at
prince's wedding, 55–72

—Williams-Ellis / Tales *
Well of the World's End [frog-
prince], 55–61

Frog and the ox
—Carle / Treasury * 70–71

Frog-king, or Iron Henry
—Grimm / Complete * 17–20

**Frog prince, The (princess makes
rash promise)**
—Allison / I'll Tell * 14–15
—Corrin / Favourite * 141–147
—Corrin / Six-Year * 38–41
—Crane / McLean * 4–15
—Crossley / British FT * 24–27
—Grimm / Sixty * 60–63
—Hall / Treasury * 102–103
—Rockwell / Puss, 66–74 *
—Scriven / Full Color * 57–59

Frog princess (a parody; poem)
—Strauss / Trail
revolted by frog before turning to
prince, 24–26

FROG WOMAN
—Muddleheads / Harris
Asdilda desecrates Cormorant
Hat, 94–114

Froggie went a courtin'
—Allison / I'll Tell * 144–145

FRONTIER
see also CROCKETT, Davy
—American / Read Dgst
sodbusters: Feboldson, et al.,
207–210

FROST
—Hamilton / Dark *

evil stepmother: reward/punish-
ment by Father Frost, 49–53
—Russian Hero / Warner *
Morozko the frost demon, and his
bride, 33–37
sun, frost, wind: honor most pow-
erful, 32
FRUGALITY
—Turkish (Art I) / Walker
prince disguised as gooseherd to
win proud wife's love, 138–144
FRUIT
—Greaves / Hippo *
why lion does not eat fruit, 18–20
FRUSTRATION
—Demi / Reflective *
boar declares war on forest, [10]
Fundevogel
—Grimm / Complete * 241–244
—Grimm / Sixty * 84–87
FUNERAL(-s)
—Arabian / Lewis
joyful funeral of merpeople, 131–
137
—Arabian / McCaughrean
(same as above), 83–96
—Campbell / West Highlands
poor brother, rich brother, I.237–
243
—Egyptian / Ions
funerary rites, 143 (index)
—Egyptian / Mercatante
customs, 47–48 @
—Fairies / Briggs, 145–147
FUR
—Grimm / Complete *
queen dies; king would marry
their daughter, 326–331
FURIES
—Gods / Schwab, 753 (index)
FUTURE
—Bomans / Wily *
three riddles; wizard can read fu-
ture in magic book, 202–204

—Palestinian / Speak (Muhawi)
ordaining the future; motif-index,
397
Future life, *see* AFTERLIFE; ETER-
NITY; JUDGMENT DAY.

GAELIC TALES
see also IRISH . . .
—Clouston / Popular, II.507 (index)
Gag, Wanda
—Childcraft 1 / Once *
Millions of cats, 258–263
GALAHAD, Sir
—King Arthur / Senior, 319 (index)
—Knights / Heller-Headon, 156–
169
Gallant tailor (*existential retelling*)
—Switzer / Existential, 102–111
GAMBLER(-ing)
—Aleichem / Holiday *
Benny's luck: boy cheats friends,
playing with dreydl, 17–44
—Hopi / Talashoma-Malotki
life lost: Hopi boy and his two pet
eagles, 150–199
—Lore of Love
King Nala and Princess Damay-
anti, 110–119
—Old Coot / Christian *
wager: saying "enough" to Old
Coot's stories, 29–38
—Yep / Rainbow *
claim to find lost things by smell,
20–35
Gambling Hansel
—Grimm / Complete * 378–380
GAME(-s)
—Am Child / Bronner, 175–197
—Bell / Classical Dict, 96–98 @
—Coyote / Ramsey
Numuzo'ho plays ball, 248–250
—Fahs / Old *

moon's origin: boy cheats at ball-
game, 81–83
—Folk-rhymes / Northall
England, 352–429
—Hopi / Talashoma-Malotki
[shinny] how the Poqangwhoyas
turned two girls to stone, 92–
107
—Igloo / Metayer
The ball players [losers die], 32–
34
—Mex-Am / West, 187–195
GANESH
—Jaffrey / Seasons
how Ganesh got his elephant
head, 121–123
GARBAGE
—Jewish / Sadeh
unearthing of the Wailing Wall,
250–251
**GARDEN(-ing) (plants, fruit, vegeta-
bles)**
—Arabian / Lewis
abandoned children (grown) restored, 166–173
—Arabian / Riordan
abandoned children (grown) restored, 78–87
—Jewish / Frankel, 646 (index)
—Lester / Brer Rabbit *
tries to trick Brer Buzzard out of
his share of garden, 69–71
—Nesbit / Fairy *
magic apples: age with each
wish, 125–138
—Rockwell / Puss *
Jack and the Beanstalk, 1–11
—Spanish-Am / Van Etten *
wise woman asks three sisters:
why do you clear your field?
52–53
—Turkish / Walker
magic pumpkin (provides food)
stolen and recovered, 62–66

ruler gives daughter to poor man
as punishment, 139–147
—Turkish (Art I) / Walker
golden pears: dervish punishes
selfish farmer, 53–57
—Wilde / Happy *
selfish giant keeps children from
garden, 59–69
—Witch Hndbk / Bird * 26–35
GARETH, SIR
—Celts / Hodges *
Gareth of Orkney wins his spurs,
133–154
—King Arthur / Senior, 319 (index)
—Knights / Gross *
kitchen knight: "Big Hands," 77–
99
—Knights / Heller-Headon, 108–
119
Gareth and Linette
—Lines / Magical * 127–139
GARGOYLES
—Creatures (illus) / Huber * 30–35,
155 (index)
Garis, Howard R.
—Hall / Treasury *
Uncle Wiggily and the red spots,
26–31
GARTER(-s)
—O'Brien / Tales *
fairy-cobbler can lead to gold;
Bridget tricked with red garters,
17–20
GARWAL
—Reeves / Shadow
husband becomes werewolf
three days each week, 99–
110
GATILOKE
—Cambodian / Carrison, 11–18 @
GAWAIN, Sir
—Celts / Hodges *
Arthur's last battle, 157–169
—King Arthur / Senior, 319 (index)

—Knights / Gross *
  Sir Gawain and the Lady Ragnell,
  59–76
—Knights / Heller-Headon, 92–103
**GAWAIN: Sir Gawain and the Green
  Knight**
—Barber / Anthology, 112–134
—Corrin / Eight-Year * 161–172
—Lacy / Arth Ency, 506–511
GAZELLE
—Jewish / Frankel
  pursuit of white gazelle; "sixty
  days" [one hour] learning com-
  mon life, 410–414
GEB
—Egyptian / Ions, 143 (index)
GECKO (lizard)
—Vietnam / Terada *
  hunter given one wish; origin of
  the gecko, 69–71
Geese, see GOOSE / GEESE.
GEM
  see also JEWEL(-s)
—Precious Stones / Kunz
  talisman, 115–142 @
GENEROSITY (usually rewarded)
—Arabian / Lewis
  Attaf's hospitality; Jafar's misfor-
  tunes, 199–209
  commoner (more generous)
  made king, 81–90
—Arabian / McCaughrean
  price of cucumbers, 122–129
—Childcraft 3 / Stories *
  Anansi gives away his share of
  plantains, 108–113
  Chin has three questions for the
  Living Kuan-yin, 93–99
—Dramatized / Kamerman
  Dame Fortune and Don Money,
  481–492
  Hans Brinker: skates for poor
  children, 200–211
—Frog Rider (Chinese)

  advice from God of the West,
  92–99
—Scriven / Full Color *
  Golden goose, 61–63
—Turkish (Art I) / Walker
  shah spares lustful pilgrim; favor
  later returned, 93–98
—Wilde / Lynch *
  devoted friend: Little Hans and
  the miller, 24–40
GENETICS
—Yolen / Werewolves
  green messiah (genetic engineer-
  ing), 189–200
Genie, see JINN.
GENTILES
—Jewish / Frankel, 649 (index)
**GEOFFREY of Monmouth
  (ca.1100–ca.1155)**
—Barber / Anthology
  history of the kings of Britain, 12–
  28
—King Arthur / Ashe, 190 (index)
—Lacy / Arth Ency, 209–214
GEOGRAPHIC INDEX
—MacDonald / Sourcebook * 739–778
GEOGRAPHICAL MYTHS
—Speck / New World
  early discovery and exploration,
  1–531
George, Saint, see SAINT GEORGE.
GEORGIA
—Southern [legends] / Floyd
  mysterious sounds, Rabun
  County, GA, 91–95
  Rock Oven (Georgia), 68–71
GERMAN-AMERICANA
—German-American / Barrick, 1–
  264
GERMAN TALE(-s)
—Clouston / Popular, II.507 (index)
—Dramatized / Kamerman
  Merry Tyll and the three rogues,
  162–176

—Hoke / Giants
  Strong Gottlieb, 103–111
—Legends / Cavendish, 6 (index)
—Manning / Cauldron *
  prince and retinue turned into
  trees; girl breaks spell, 39–
  45
—Old Wives / Carter
  Juniper tree, The, 183–191
—Restless / Cohen *
  Amherst mystery: Tweed house,
  31–39
GERMANS (people)
—Humor / Midwest, 79–86
GERMANY
—Dictionary / Leach, 1208 (index)
—Lynn / Fantasy * 756 (index)
—Yolen / Werewolves
  Cologne; Jew shelters werewolf,
  70–83
Gesta Romanorum
—Clouston / Popular, II.507 (index)
GHOST(-s)
  see also ANIMAL GHOSTS;
  APPARITION(-s);
  DEAD: RETURN . . . ;
  HAUNT . . . ; REVENANT(-s)
—Am Child / Bronner, 144–147
—Amer Ind / Erdoes
  twelve tales, 427–463
—American / Read Dgst, 438 (index)
  ghost-ships, 236–237
  ghost-wrestler weakens when
  close to fire, 205
  Jack-o-Lantern; Plat-eye, 266–
  267
—Bierhorst / Naked *
  Mother of ghosts; life-restored,
  37–43
—Bomans / Wily *
  soldier's wager with King; traps
  ghost; becomes king, 37–43
—British / Briggs *
  sixteen tales, 169–196

—Bronner / Piled
  college legends, 252 (index)
—Bruchac / Iroquois *
  husband; vampire skeleton, 129–
  133
—Civil War Ghosts, 1–205
—Clarkson / World *
  fear test: tinker must spend night
  in castle, 188–191
  laid; aspen stake driven through
  heart of corpse, 197–198
  laid, when money is distributed to
  beggars, 188–191
—Classic / Downer
  Beckwith, George (Maryland,
  ca.1675), 39–42
  Big Liz (Greenbriar Swamp, Md.),
  134–135
  Bailes, John Perry, 14–16
  blond hitchhiker on Skyway
  Bridge (Florida), 100–103
  Bryarley, John; Peddler's Run,
  Md., 17–19
  Burr, Theodosia, 163–164
  coffin hollow, Confederate
  graves, 183–184
  Colorado spirits (by B. Kelly),
  104–106
  cry on Blackbird Hill (Nebraska),
  181–182
  Drawbridge Ghost, Md., 138–139
  fifty-one U.S. nonfiction accounts
  (200-year span), 1–214
  floating coffin (Hooper Island,
  Md.), 142–143
  ghost ship: the Sarah, 196–198
  ghostly theater usher (Minneapolis), 94–99
  haunted house (Lake Pleasant,
  NY), 112–116
  headless Frenchman: Etienne
  Brule (ca.1614), 107–110
  Heavy Collar (Blackfeet) and the
  ghost woman, 170–176

Idaho lore, 159–162

image comes to life (Alaska), 71–72

Indian maid, Waconda (Kansas), 47–53

lady in white (New Castle, Del.), 190–195

lady of the heath (Kentucky), 189

Lobo Girl, Devil's River (Texas), 56–62

Moodus Noises (CT, ca.1765), 68–70

mourning bride of Glendale (CO) Station, 34–38

Mt. Moosilauke, NH, 120–126

O'Donnell Heights (E. Baltimore, Md.), 136–137

Old Joe (Jewell County, Kansas), 205–209

opera house (Berks Co., Pa.), 127–132

phantom bugler (Forest Grove, OR), 199–200

San Antonio physician's emergency night call, 21–25

Savannah: Florence Martus (1869–1943), 43–46

Savannah: Willie and Nellie Gordon, 28–33

Seattle horrors, 152–158

Stanford Hall, Md., 150–151

strange tale (Montpelier, VT ca.1887), 165–168

Tacaluma, the phantom Indian, 186–188

treasure on Neahkahnie Mt. (Oregon), 117–119

USS Constitution, 146–147

White Marsh Church, Md., 140–141

—Coyote / Ramsey

spirit of dead wife, 33–37

—Crossley / British FT *

Billy: crippled tailor flees ghosts in graveyard, 244–246

burnt to ashes, Samuel must walk until he finds all his parts, 73–76

disappears when man embraces her, 58

Slam impersonates ghost; is frightened to death by real ghost, 140–141

—Earth / Hadley *

storm: Lin maiden (ghost) guides lost seamen to safety, [27–28]

—Egyptian / Harris

Anpu and Bata; ghost reborn as baby, 77–83

—Erdoes / Sound *

flute entices girls to "ghostly lover," 95–97

very angry ghost (older Indian in disguise), 82–85

—Fairies / Briggs

great giant of Henllys, 199–200

roaring bull of Bagburg, 341

—Floyd / Gr Am Myst

a case of retrocognition: Colleen Baterbaugh, 74–78

graveyards and ghostly lights, 148–151

Irving, Washington, in the Astor Library, 160–162

Vennum, Mary Lurancy, 152–155

—Geras / Grandmother *

ghost at peace after standing under wedding canopy, 86–96

—Ghost (South) / McNeil, 1–170

banshees, ghostly lights, etc., 107–126

grave humor, 127–133

haunts (other than houses), 49–68

headless and screaming, 69–77

hidden treasure, 79–87

malevolent, 99–106

traveling, 89–98

—Ghost (S'west) / Young

ghostly lights, 41–52

haunted places, other than houses, 87–107

jokes, 27–32

roadway ghosts, 53–65

Sally Baker, 120–123

southwestern U.S., 1–192

urban legends, 33–40

—Ghosts / Cohen, 1–307

moving-coffins of Barbados, 219–224

phenomena, 199–263

Radiant Boy stories, 296–301

revenge, warnings, crisis apparitions, 171–198

—Ghosts / Starkey

British Isles: sixteen stories, 1–123

Dauntless girl; ghost reveals treasure, 72–79

ghost reveals deed to estate, 24–29

Joe Reardon and the three sister-ghosts, 102–109

laying Black Lucott's ghost, 116–123

The laying of the Pakenham ghost [three times], 37–43

—Ghosts / Time-Life, 1–143

Baubie Skithawa, 120–122

cold lad of Gilsland Castle, 76

Dame Elizabeth Hoby, 93–94

harp: strings from hair of murdered sister, 32–37

heralds of death, 6–37

hooded congregation, 100–107

Jim Tregeagle case; ghost of dead man testifies, 126–131

malevolence: Invasions by the angry dead, 39–61

marsh gases, 42–43

necromancy: Lucan and Pompey, 113–117

O'lwa (Japanese) murdered ghost-wife's revenge, 51–55

phantom battle (Killiecrankie, 1689), 70–74

phantom tenants of Castle Glamis, 85–91

raising the dead, 112–113

screaming skulls, 56–60

Tower of London, 81–84

utburd (child exposed to die), 38–41

walkers [ghosts] after death (Iceland; Glam), 132–139

woman with severed head (G. Fisher), 62–69

—Grimm / Complete *

unafraid: Youth who could not shudder, 29–39

—Grimm / Legends (Ward), II:411–412 (index)

—Grimm / Sixty *

unafraid: Youth . . . [as above], 300–311

—Hamilton / People *

give me back my "tailypo," 116–120

—Hartland / English *

eleven tales, 206–246

—Indian Myth / Burland

the rolling heads (Natchez), 116–118

—Irish / Glassie

six tales, 127–141

—Jaffrey / Seasons

days of the banyan tree, 9 @

—Jewish / Sadeh

charity saves peddler's wife from foreordained death, 335–336

Ja'akov repays dead rabbi's debt; rabbi returns to help Ja'akov, 137–139

Jew executed: failure to say "Amen," 210–211

merchant buys dead partner's sin and guilt, 83–86

wandering merchant and
  trustworthy ghost, 87–89
woman a nonbeliever in miracles,
  245–246
—Journey Sun (Chinese)
  cruel stepmother, false wife,
    ghost, 6–23
—Limburg / Weird , 52–55, 121
—Lore of Love
  cursed embrace: Etelinda and
    Guntram, 32–35
  head of murdered lover buried in
    pot of basil, 64–65
—Lynn / Fantasy *
  annotated bibliography, 135–
    154
—MacDonald / Sourcebook *
  motif index, 628
—Man Myth & Magic
  analytics, 3136, 3200 (index)
—Mex-Am / West
  amorous, 79–80
—Pirate Ghosts / McSherry, 1–206
  Anty Bligh: hanged pirate's ghost
    gets buried, 40–44
  gallows guests, Gibbet Island:
    Vanderscamp and Old Pluto,
    145–157
  red swimmer: father and daugh-
    ter murdered by Luke Treach,
    45–68
  treasure: digging at Pistol Key,
    166–181
—Quayle / Cornish *
  old woman dies, leaves shawl to
    little girl; rests, 88–90
—Restless / Cohen *
  Australia: fate of George
    Woodfall, 84–93
  China: demon corpse: unburied
    body, 52–59
  Egypt: the mummy's ghost, 3–15
  eleven tales from eleven coun-
    tries, 1–109

Japan: the woman in white, 16–
  23
Malta: dust: naval officers invited
  to Suarez home, 40–51
Russian walking corpses; three
  tales, 73–83
Turkey: horse-back ride: girl ten-
  years-dead, 24–30
wife steals liver from corpse; husband replaces with wife's 103–
  109
—Scandinavian / Kvideland, x, 427
  (index)
—Scary / Young *
  Bloody Mary (a tale in rhyme),
    58–60
  ghost of murdered Oiwa haunts
    samurai husband to death, 21–
    25
  ghost sucks blood from Indian
    mother and child, 87–88
  Indian maid, married in Land of
    the Dead, returns with child,
    69–72
  Rap! Shylock Bones finds
    "ghost" to be "wrapping" pa-
    per, 31–32
  white wolf—eventually thought to
    be boy's ghost, 40–42
—Schwartz / Gold
  haunted treasure, 105–110, 124
—Shah / Central Asia
  nobleman and slave; gift of wis-
    dom, 103–108
—Southern [legends] / Floyd
  Rock Oven (Georgia), 68–71
  Surrency (GA) haunting, 109–
    114
—Spanish-Am / Van Etten *
  skeleton gives treasure to brave
    boy, 109–114
—Starkey / Ghosts
  Joe Reardon vs. three sister-
    ghosts, 102–109

Whuppity Stoorie [exorcism], 44–
51
—Talk / Goss
fourteen tales, and commentary,
299–359
—Tree / Kerven *
bamboo-princess freed from
spell, [28–29]
—Vietnam / Terada *
betrothed woman captured by
enemy kills self, 99–101
one ghost; doctor only had one
patient (humor), 128–129
spirits ask man to die and be their
leader, 78–80
student enamored of two women
(spirits), 95–98
—Yep / Rainbow *
changeling: husband kidnapped
by ghosts, 162–168
dead relatives return: Slippers,
162–168
holy fool: butterfly man, 60–68
marriage: ghost's bride, 54–59
GHOST-FACE WOMAN
—Yolen / Werewolves
White Wolf: boy's initiation to
manhood, 45–69
GHOST: UNQUIET GRAVE
—Egyptian / Harris
Setna and the Book of Thoth,
92–102
—Erdoes / Sound *
flute entices girls to "ghostly
lover," 95–97
—Grimm / Complete *
shroud: the unquiet grave, 502–
503
Willful child, The, 534–535
—Lore of Love
cursed embrace: Liba and Guntram, 32–35
illicit love; head buried in pot of
basil, 64–65

—Vietnam / Terada *
Da Trang crab: grateful snake
gives magic pearl, 37–41
student enamored of two women
(spirits), 95–98
GHOUL
—McGowen / Encyclopedia * 25–26
—Old Wives / Carter
ghoul gives ember for strip of
girl's skin, 160–165
she-ghoul fattens poor woodcutter, wife, children (to eat them),
216–220
GIANT(-s)
see also FINN Mac COOL;
STONE GIANT(-s)
—Bierhorst / Monkey *
helped by giant's daughter,
young man does four impossi-
ble tasks, 56–65
takes abandoned children, marries girl, tries to kill brother,
92–93
—Bierhorst / Naked *
Lodge Boy and Thrown Away
[chipmunk-sized boy], 79–86
Whirlwinds vs. Stone Coats, 19–
23
—British / Briggs *
six tales, 197–203
—Caduto / Keepers *
Hero Twins and Swallower of
Clouds, 79–81
—Campbell / West Highlands, IV.433
(index)
—Celts / Hodges *
Lad of Luck and monster of the
loch, 89–103
—Chorao / Child's *
Jack and the Beanstalk, 9–20
—Clarkson / World *
Molly Whuppie: substitutions
cause giant to kill his children,
54–56

—Clouston / Popular, I.133–154

—Corrin / Imagine *

  Black Thief tells story of faithless
  apprentice, 106–108

—Cotterell / Encyclopedia, 253 (index)

—Coyote / Ramsey

  Cry-Because-He-Have-No-Wife,
  29–30

  Tillamook man lives with Thunderer, 140–144

—Crossley / British FT *

  giant's daughter helps prince escape death, 313–330

—Douglas / Magic *

  Jack the Giant Killer, 131–139

  roc, its egg eaten, gets vengeance on Sinbad, 21–25

—Dramatized / Kamerman

  Frost Giant: Builder of the wall,
  422–434

—Earthmaker / Mayo *

  hunter and Rainbow Woman;
  husband lost (Hoh tale), 38–40

—Erdoes / Sound *

  stone-boy, his mother, his ten lost
  uncles, 108–116

  thunderbirds: when the earth was
  young, 33–36

  tree for arrow; Iktome's misadventures, 16–22

—Fairies / Briggs, 186–190

  young king of Esaidh Ruadh,
  356–359

—Giant / Harrison *

  boy tells secret to giant-capturers: measles, 7–17

  giant named Groans (limerick),
  32

  witch's spell: giant sees/fears
  butterflies, etc., 19–30

—Glooskap / Norman *

  human beings created by
  Glooskap, 1–10

—Grimm / Complete *

captain makes false claim for killing, 508–514

king's son who feared nothing,
  545–550

princess under spell, broken by
  persistence, 431–436

stupid giant conned by boastful
  tailor's "power," 745–747

thumbling nursed by giant acquires fabulous strength, 412–
  420

valiant tailor (seven at one blow),
  112–120

—Grimm / Legends (Ward), II:412–
  413 (index)

—Grimm / Sixty *

princess under spell, broken by
  persistence, 250–256

valiant tailor . . . , 88–97

—Hamilton / Dark *

  elf king, Childe Rowland and
  Burd Ellen, 65–72

  Rolling Rio, gray man, and Death,
  5–13

  tiny thing: Anishinaba and Boshk-
  wadosh, 54–59

—Hamilton / In the Beginning *

  Imir: frost giant, 68–71

—Hartland / English * 85–88

—Hoke / Giants

  Antaeus wrestles with Hercules,
  130–132

  battle with King of the Giants,
  119–129

  Bulai: short-sighted acts, 130–
  132

  defeat of tyrannical giant Hundar,
  41–64

  Finlay, the giant killer, 142–149

  giant, no heart in his body, 93–
  102

  giant ogre, 41–64

  Hercules and the golden apples,
  130–132

hummingbird directs slaying of Sinulu, 71–78

Indian boy kills giants; then falls, 112–118

physical characteristics of giant ogres, 71–78

poem: In the orchard (Stephens), 156

steals all [Blackfeet] buffaloes, 150–155

Strong Gottlieb, 103–111

three giants tricked to death by boy's wits, 34–40

—Jewish / Frankel

angry king: daughter taken captive because of his curse, 531–536

—Jewish / Sadeh

lost princess: king's curse, to Evil One's kingdom, 386–389

—Journey Sun (Chinese)

Yangang saves village incinerated by shooting star, 47–60

—Lang / Wilkins

Fairy of the Dawn; magic well water, 571–601

wounded lion (prince), 385–393

—Lester / Leopard *

healing leaves for blind king, 59–68

—Lurker / Dict Gods, 428 (index)

—Lynn / Fantasy * 756–757 (index)

—MacDonald / Sourcebook *

motif index, 628–629

—Man Myth & Magic, 3136 (index)

—Manning / Cauldron *

gives Jack ring (can change self to any size); rescues princess from giant, 78–89

—Maori / Kanawa *

Kupe battles giant octopus, 28–34

—Mercatante / Encyclopedia, 764 (index)

—Monsters / Cohen, 245–251 @

—Navajo / Klah

creation myths, 85–87

—Norse / Crossley, 268 (index)

—O'Brien / Tales *

Amada defeats (they daily return to life) a series of monsters, 21–30

giant Trencross abducts princess; white cat helps rescue, 92–105

goatskin-clad Eamonn defeats giants; gets magic club, fife and ointment, 38–43

Hookedy Crookedy frees [enchanted] mare and bear from giant, 53–71

swan bride: king's son's quest for Scolog's daughter, 82–95

—Old Wives / Carter

battle of the birds, 76–85

—Quayle / Cornish *

St. Michael's Mount: cruel Cormoran killed by Jack, 13–20

—Quayle / Shining *

Lord Bag-o'-Rice aids serpent (Dragon King); kills giant centipede, 33–43

—Rockwell / Puss *

Jack and the Beanstalk, 1–11

—Russian Hero / Warner *

last of the giants: Svyatogor, 125–128

—Scandinavian / Davidson, 142 (index)

—Scandinavian / Kvideland, xvi (index)

—Scary / Young *

Sally-Bally: grandma jumps into giant's ear; he kills self trying to eject, 89–92

—Scriven / Full Color *

Jack and the beanstalk, 53–56

—South / Mythical
sources; bibliographical essay,
293–324 (J. Pallister), 384 (index)
—Turkey / Walker, 303 (index)
—Turkish / Walker
Karacor and the giants, 52–61
—Turkish (Art I) / Walker
princess and the red-horse-husband, 12–19
sons seek Hazaran nightingale for padishah's mosque, 230–239
—Unnatural / Cohen, 91–106
illus. from Arabian Nights, 95
—Vanishing / Mercer *
quest for wife abducted by giant bird, 42–49
—Wilde / Happy *
selfish giant keeps children from garden, 59–69
—Wilde / Lynch *
selfish giant: always winter, children not allowed in garden, 6–13
Giant and the tailor, The
—Grimm / Complete * 745–747
GIANTESS
—Quayle / Cornish *
shrinks when husband, Cormoran, is killed by Jack, 13–20
Gift, *see* GIVING AND RECEIVING.
GIFT FROM FAIRIES
—Carter / Sleeping *
Ricky with the Tuft; ugly man and princess, 93–102
Sweetheart (given ring by fairy), 113–124
—Clarkson / World *
Cluricaune shows hiding place of treasure, 115–117
—Corrin / Six-Year *
ungrateful old woman lives in vinegar-bottle, 13–18

—Crossley / British FT *
Hughbo works for farmer, until wife makes clothes for him, 265–269
piper and pooka; given wits and memory for music, 17–23
—Douglas / Magic *
Cinderella; gift from fairy, 109–117
—Dulac / Fairy *
uninvited: the crayfish fairy, 43–59
White Caroline, Black Caroline, 15–21
—Grimm / Complete *
elves and the shoemaker, 197–198
tailor and goldsmith see little folk dancing, 742–745
—Grimm / Sixty *
elves and the shoemaker, 209–210
—Hoke / Giants, 34–40
—Lang / Wilkins
happiness? princess sent to check on fairy gifts, 186–189
Sylvain and Jocosa (befriended by fairy), 178–185
—Quayle / Shining *
tongue-cut sparrow-princess: gold to kind man; demons to cruel wife, 44–56
—Russian Hero / Warner *
Sadko of Novgorod: musician becomes rich merchant, 44
—Scriven / Full Color *
Cinderella, 69–73
how to catch a leprechaun, 85–87
—Shah / Central Asia
nobleman and slave; gift of wisdom, 103–108
—Switzer / Existential
shoemaker and the elves (schizophrenia), 54–62

—Turkish (Art I) / Walker
grateful fairy-padishah teaches
farmer (with termagant wife) to
cure the sick, 188–190
jinn and witches give magic gifts
to newborn girl, 159–168
—Vietnam / Terada *
Tam kills stepsister Cam; takes
her place as king's wife, 23–34
—Zipes / Beauties *
Ricky with the Tuft, 52–57, 95–100
Gifted, see TALENT.
GILDED MAN
—Speck / New World
eight legends, 63–127
GILGAMESH
—Babylonia / Spence, 393 (index)
—Gray / Near East, 143 (index)
—Legends / Cavendish, 91–94
—Wolkstein / Love, 242 @
Gingerbread boy
—Childcraft 1 / Once * 89–91
—Corrin / Six-Year * 28–32
—Clarkson / World * 242–243
GINGERBREAD BOY
—Jones / Tales *
vanity, gullibility = ruin, 35–41
Gipsy, see GYPSY.
GIRAFFE
—Greaves / Hippo *
giraffe watches over sun; re-
warded by Creator, 89
why giraffe and oxpecker are
friends, 84–86
why giraffe has a long neck, 86–
88
GIRL(-s)
—Hopi / Talashoma-Malotki
how the Poqangwhoyas turned
two girls to stone, 92–107
—Igloo / Metayer
dog kills would-be girl takers,
122–127
—Yolen / Faery Flag

words of power: Late Blossoming
Flower, 21–39
—Yolen / Shape Shift
Indian unknowingly turns into
deer (Johanna), 52–60
Girl without hands
—Grimm / Complete * 160–166
GIVING AND RECEIVING
—Caduto / Keepers *
corn's origin, 137–138
—Jewish / Frankel
Elijah, three sons, three wishes,
587–588
—Jewish / Sadeh
little shoemakers; backfire, 314–
315
—Nesbit / Fairy *
magic apples: younger with each
gift, 125–138
GLAM (ghost)
—Ghosts / Time-Life, 132–139
GLASS
—Grimm / Complete *
kings' daughters aid hero in
tasks: win girl or die, 515–524
Glass coffin
—Grimm / Complete * 672–678
GLASS MOUNTAIN
—Grimm / Complete *
Drummer rescues princess from
glass mountain, 781–791
Glass slipper, The, see Cinderella.
GLASTONBURY
—King Arthur / Ashe
Abbey, 189 (index)
Tor, 191 (index)
—Lacy / Arth Ency, 237–243
GLOOSKAP [spellings vary]
—Caduto / Keepers *
folly: trap all animals in magic
bag, 165–167
Glooskap made himself from left-
over dust, 21
Gluscabi and Wind Eagle, 67–71

—Childcraft 3 / Stories *
good and evil: Glooscap vs. Malsum [and Lox], 143–151
—Fahs / Old *
Glooskap ignored by baby, 153–155
—Glooskap / Norman *
baby's tantrums more powerful than, 29–37
giant bird, Wuchowsen, strength of sea winds, 21–28
human beings created by, 1–10
Ice Giants outwitted by, 11–19
panther-witch and her scissorbill birds, 39–49
secluded home found by wolves, 51–60
sorcerers plot to kill him, 29–37
—Indian Myth / Burland
Algonquin creation tale, 57–59
Gluscabi [or] Gluskap. *see* GLOOSKAP.

GLUTTON(-y)
—Arabian / Lewis
glutton feigns message from small fish, 210
—Arabian / McCaughrean
glutton . . . [as above], 194–197
—Crossley / Animal (Grimm) *
wolf (master) outsmarted by fox, 45–48
—Jewish / Sadeh
eating much, can bear much torture, 338

GNOME
—Bomans / Wily *
cobbler's three wishes; learns money's limitations, 53–61
secret: three gnomes living under chestnut tree, 138–140
storyteller wants to see a gnome before he dies, 141–142
—Grimm / Complete *
youngest huntsman rescues princesses from dragon, 420–424
—Lang / Wilkins
captured children; Little King Loc, 441–459
king Rubezahl captures princess, 497–512
—Lynn / Fantasy * 757 (index)
—McGowen / Encyclopedia * 27

Gnome, The
—Grimm / Complete * 420–424

GOAT(-s)
see also Three billy goats Gruff
—Aesop / Reeves-Wilson *
trust: Wolf and goat, 114
—Allison / I'll Tell *
fox uses goat (escape from well), 120
wolf and [goat's] kid, 130
—Animals / Rowland, 184 (index)
—Crossley / Animal (Grimm) *
wolf and seven kids [saved], 29–34
—Grimm / Complete *
God creates animals; devil creates goats with long tails, 642–644
One-eye, Two-eyes, and Three-eyes, 585–592
Wolf and the seven [goat] kids, 39–42
—Grimm / Sixty *
Wolf and the seven [goat] kids, 202–205
—Hopi / Talashoma-Malotki
goats rape/destroy demon-girl, 136–149
—Jewish / Frankel
goat's horns and the snuffbox, 549
two she-goats from Shebreshin, 564–566
—MacDonald / Sourcebook *
motif index, 630
—Man Myth & Magic, 3136 (index)

—Manning / Cats *
    Istvan climbs pea-plant into heav-
    ens; finds seven-eyed goat;
    falls into swamp, 107–110
—Manning / Cauldron *
    Elsa, abducted by witch to tend
    her baby, escapes aided by
    goat, 90–98
    witch's flute: goatherd can't stop
    playing; goats and people can't
    stop dancing, 99–105
—Old Wives / Carter
    escaping slowly: goat and kids in
    Lion's house, 221
—Trolls / Asbjornsen
    the three Billikin Whiskers vs. troll
    under bridge, 17–18
—Turkish / Walker
    bear tricks (goat) kids; goat gets
    even, 4–7
—Vanishing / Mercer *
    Nagas myth: originally dog had
    horns, goat none, 87–88
GOAT-MAN
—Southern [legends] / Floyd
    Charles McCartney: goat man of
    Dixie, 150–153
GOBLIN
—Lang / Wilkins
    Fairy of the Dawn; magic well
    water, 571–601
—McGowen / Encyclopedia * 27
—Monsters / Cohen
    Hopkinsville, 200–203 @
—Scary / Young *
    to steal baby, goblin's arms grow
    longer/longer; cross saves,
    43–46
—Water Buffalo (Chinese)
    enormous candy-man; magic
    drum; long nose, 70–77
**Goblin market [poem by C. Ros-
setti]**
—Victorian / Hearn, 192–208

GOD (*monotheistic*)
    see also CREATOR; YAHWEH
—Fahs / Old *
    being: can't see or feel; still real,
    20–23
—Gray / Near East, 143 (index)
—Grimm / Complete *
    Eve's various children: God be-
    stows blessings unequally,
    734–736
    hospitality: poor man rewarded;
    rich man punished, 394–398
—Grimm / Legends (Ward), II:414 (in-
    dex)
—Hamilton / Dark *
    phantom ship (Flying Dutchman)
    cursed by God, 38–42
—Jewish / Frankel
    bird's nest: human ladder to
    God's love, 495
    praise: paying God's wages,
    497
—Jewish / Sadeh
    existence: whom God loves,
    149–152
    Rabbi Joseph de la Reina; fight
    against Samael, 233–237
    sees all: reaper and his daughter,
    152
—Lycanthropy / Otten, 329 (index)
—Mesoamerican / Leon-P
    dual, 289 and 296 (index)
—Russian / Ivanits, 247 (index)
—Schwartz / Gates
    feminine presence of, 801 (index)
    names of, 808 (index)
—Unnatural / Cohen, 146 (index)
—Water Buffalo (Chinese)
    five wishes: crow-messenger dis-
    obeys God, 23–29
Goddesses, *see* GODS and GOD-
DESSES.
Godfather, The
—Grimm / Complete * 206–208

Godfather Death
—Grimm / Complete * 209–212
GODFREY of Bouillon
—Baring-Gould / Curious
   Helias: Knight of the Swan, 146–
   150
—Jewish / Sadeh
   rabbi; prediction: defeat at
   Jerusalem, 227–228
GODMOTHER(-s)
—Bomans / Wily *
   balloon message; with god-
   mother's help, knight kills
   dragon, 197–202
—Nielsen / Old Tales *
   takes mother's first three chil-
   dren, [5–15]
GODS and GODDESSES
   see also IMMORTALS; SKY
      GODS; SUPERNATURALS;
   see also names of individual gods
      and goddesses
—Babylonia / Spence, 394 (index)
—Bell / Classical Dict, 1–390 @
—Celtic / MacCana, 72–81
   Gaulish, and Irish equivalents,
   20–53
   goddesses: insular Celts, 82–95
—Celts / Hodges *
   Camelot, 155–156
—Childcraft 3 / Stories *
   Chin has three questions for the
   Living Kuan-yin, 93–99
—Chinese / Christie, 107–122
—Dramatized / Kamerman
   Frost Giant: Builder of the wall
   (Norse), 422–434
—Earth / Hadley *
   hideous Kanya, god of fire, tries
   in vain to get a wife, [17–18]
—Egyptian / Harris, 1–132, 7–20 @
   deeds of Hathor: Eye of the sun,
   26–33
   divinities of death, 113–115 @

divinities of the first time, 34–87 @
fertility and birth, 103–113 @
princess, healing by Kohns the
   Determiner, 88–91
protective divinities of the phar-
   aohs, 34–87 @
voyage of Wenamon: build sacred boat for Amon-Ra, 117–
   125
—Egyptian / Mercatante
   dictionary, 1–231
—Ellis / Dict Irish Myth, 1–240
—Fahs / Old *
   Zoroaster: Mazda vs. Manyu,
   140–147
—Ghost (S'west) / Young
   killer-of the alien-gods, 139–140
—Gods / Schwab
   Greek; dictionary/index, 745–764
—Gray / Near East
   Canaan gods, 68–76
   Mesopotamian, 14–25
—Greek / Osborne
   list, 71–74
—Grimal / Dictionary
   genealogical tables, 525–559 @
—Hamilton / Dark *
   pretender sacrificed to Tezcut-
   lipoca after year of high living,
   60–64
—Hamilton / In the Beginning *
   coming of all things, 126–131
   Kamonu (first man) at odds with
   creator, 64–67
—Hoke / Giants, 119
—Imaginary / Nigg, 1–160 passim
—Indian Myth / Burland
   chief gods and spirits, 140–142
—Indic / Ions
   early deities, 12–15 @
   goddesses: Hindu triad, 92–100 @
   polytheism, 36–39 @
   Vedic deities, 16–27 @
—Japanese / Tyler, 335 (index)

260

—Lore of Love
traits of gods, 112
—Lurker / Dict Gods, 1–451
supreme, 412–413 (index)
—MacDonald / Sourcebook *
motif index, 7–9
—Mesoamerican / Leon-P
dual, 289 and 296 (index)
—Occult & Parapsych / Shepard,
1585–88 (index)
—Persian / Hinnells, 24–33, 142 (index)
—Roman / Usher
city and state, 19–24 @
countryside, 14–16 @
family, 17–18 @
—Room / Classical Dict, 1–343 @
—Russian Hero / Warner * 15–17 @
—Scandinavian / Davidson
coming of the gods, 16–29
deities of the earth, 72–79
—Scary / Young *
Pele, Spirit of Fire, vs. Na-Maka;
Kilauea, 84–86
—Unnatural / Cohen, 146 (index)
—Vietnam / Terada *
mountain/water gods rivals for
princess, 50–53
scholar (Do Be) offends temple
god, 42–49
—Witch Encyc / Guiley, 413 (index)
—Woman's Ency / Walker, 1–1124 @

God's food
—Grimm / Complete * 822

GODS: MUTUAL RELATIONS
—Douglas / Magic *
Europa and Zeus, 181–184
gods: Cupid and Psyche, 151–165
—Egyptian / Harris
Hathor: Eye of the sun, 26–33
murder of Isiris (Seth, Isis, Horus), 36–40
throne of Egypt: Horus vs. Seth,
41–47

—Vietnam / Terada *
mountain/water gods rivals for
princess, 50–53

GODS: RELATIONS WITH MORTALS
—Caduto / Keepers *
Four Worlds (Dine); gods / mortals, 31–34
—Chinese / Chin *
conscripted husband of MengJiang Nyu, 128–139
—Douglas / Magic *
gods and mortals: Cupid and
Psyche, 151–165
—Earth / Hadley *
Beebyeebyee marries water god
(fish-man), [25–26]
—Egyptian / Harris
murder of Isiris (Seth, Isis, Horus), 36–40
princess, healing by Kohns the
Determiner, 88–91
Ra's anger over rebellious mankind, 34–35
Wenamon: build sacred boat for
Amon-Ra, 117–125
—Erdoes / Sound *
White Buffalo Woman (Lakota),
117–123
—Fahs / Old *
stolen drum to dance by, 86–
90
—Grimm / Complete *
tailor throws footstool from
heaven, 175–177
—Jewish / Frankel
thornbush: Moses and the burning bush, 107–109
—Lore of Love
curse causes husband to forget
wife, 26–31
vanity's reflection: Echo and Narcissus, 74
—Russian Hero / Warner *

Dobrynya spares abductor/
dragon, 69–70
—Vietnam / Terada *
sea snake captures mandarin's
wife, 88–94
Going a traveling
—Grimm / Complete * 630–631
GOLD
—American / Read Dgst
Mezcla men; gold hidden in giant-
figure's stomach, 70–71
—Coyote / Bierhorst *
field (estate); gold assumed; real
legacy is hard work, [46]
hidden, hoarded gold might as
well be stone, [10]
—Crossley / Dead *
Callow Pit coffer [protected by
black hand], 45–54
—Dramatized / Kamerman
Covetous councilman (tricked; returns gold), 504–513
gold found in the forest, 388–399
—Fahs / Old *
wish of Midas: all touched turns to
gold, 115–117
—Greek / Osborne
golden touch: Bacchus grants
King Midas' wish, 9–11
—Grimm / Complete *
King of the golden mountain,
425–430
three sons of fortune (trade for
gold), 342–344
—Grimm / Legends (Ward), II:414 (index)
—Grimm / Sixty *
King of the golden mountain,
274–280
—Jewish / Frankel, 646 (index)
—Jewish / Sadeh
fish with golden tail and pearls for
eyes, 95–97
old bachelor lost a bean, 22–25

two shopkeepers, eagle, mountain of gold, 271–273
—Lang / Wilkins
Sylvain and Jocosa (heart of yellow bird), 178–185
—MacDonald / Sourcebook *
motif index, 631
—Norse / Crossley, 268 (index)
—O'Brien / Tales *
adventures of Marteen: grateful
beggar gives magic gold-
producing ring, 31–37
leprechaun: catch, keep fairy-
cobbler; can lead to gold;
tricked with red garter, 17–20
—Old Coot / Christian *
Coyote promises "gold" (i.e.,
tales) to Old Coot, 3–13
—Quayle / Cornish *
miser would steal gold from fairy
Gump; foiled, 64–71
—Schwartz / Gold, 113 @
—Southern [legends] / Floyd
search for Cofitachequi, 32–37
—Spring / Philip
brothers: one honest, one
greedy, 94–97
wise king exposes gold thief, 50–
57
—Turkish (Art I) / Walker
apprentice shoe merchant dis-
missed for request to Allah,
116–122
—Witch Encyc / Guiley, 413 (index)
GOLD BUCKET
—Tibet / Timpanelli *
evil helper takes real daughter's
place, 15–27
Gold-children, The
—Grimm / Complete * 388–393
GOLD RUSH (1849)
—American / Read Dgst, 213–229
Joaquin Murrieta, 220–222
Roaring Camp, 216–219

Golden arm
—Clarkson / World * 194–195
Golden bird, The
—Grimm / Complete * 272–279
—Grimm / Sixty * 1–9
GOLDEN BOUGH
—Roman / Usher
    Aeneas in the Underworld, 51–
    57 @
Golden branch, The (d'Aulnoy)
—Zipes / Beauties * 362–386
Golden Fleece, The
—Bulfinch / Sewell * 96–99
GOLDEN FLEECE
—D'Aulaire / Greek * 162–175
Golden goose, The (Grimm)
—Allison / I'll Tell * 28–29
—Grimm / Complete * 322–326
—Grimm / Sixty * 257–263
—Leete / Golden * 124–143
—Rockwell / Puss * 30–39
—Scriven / Full Color * 61–63
Golden key, The
—Grimm / Complete * 812
Golden key, The (G. Macdonald)
—Victorian / Hearn, 228–251
Golden mermaid [=Golden bird]
—Lang / Wilkins, 228–237
Golden shoes (worn on hands to
    keep them clean)
—Geras / Grandmother * 21–29
Goldfish, see FISH: GOLDFISH.
Goldilocks and the three bears
—Allison / I'll Tell * 6–7
—Childcraft 1 / Once * 92–95
—Corrin / Favourite * 178–183
—Crossley / British FT * 135–
    139
—Hall / Treasury * 10–11
—Jones / Tales * [8–115]
—Lang / Wilkins, 31–43
—Leete / Golden * 74–78
—Scriven / Full Color * 27–28
—Switzer / Existential, 17–23

GOLDSMITH
—Grimm / Complete *
    tailor and goldsmith see little folk
    dancing, 742–745
GOLEM
—Hamilton / Dark *
    Joseph Golem: blood accusation
    against Jews, 87–96
—Jewish / Frankel
    rabbi fashions golem to thwart
    evil priest of Prague, 455–
    458
—Jewish / Sadeh
    golem of Prague, 228–230
—Scary / Young *
    brought to life; told to answer chil-
    dren's questions; reverts to
    stone, 17–20
—Schwartz / Gates, 802 (index)
GOLIATH
—Hoke / Giants
    David and Goliath, 79–92
—Jewish / Frankel, 197–199
GOO-TEEKHL
—McGowen / Encyclopedia * 28
GOOD AND EVIL
—Aesop / Holder
    good may be drawn out of evil:
    dove and the snake, 2–3
—Bomans / Wily *
    evils wanted by four generations
    of wizards; people turn it to
    good, 71–75
—Bruchac / Iroquois *
    two brothers: one brings good,
    the other evil, 19–23
—Chinese / Chin *
    magic brush of artist Ma Liang,
    143–153
—Clouston / Popular
    male companions; reversal of for-
    tune, I.249–261
—Corrin / Imagine *
    Pari hides in golden candelabra;

prince buys, falls in love, 151–
160
—Crossley / British FT *
wishes: three heads of the well,
28–35
—Erdoes / Sound *
Rabbit Boy (good) vs. Iktome
(evil), 98–102
—Fahs / Old *
Deucalion's flood; Zeus finds only
one good couple, 58–63
Mawu's ways: apparent evil has
hidden good, 173–177
struggle: boy half-good, half-bad,
1–6
war: Krishna helps good king win
over evil, 108–113
Zoroaster: Mazda vs. Manyu,
140–147
—Frog Rider (Chinese)
Big Lang and Little Lang divide
property, 100–110
—Grimm / Complete *
girl shares bread with three little
men, 78–83
—Hamilton / In the Beginning *
Hina vs. Ta-aroa; creation myth,
100–103
Huron creation myth, 58–63
—Hoke / Giants
David and Goliath, 79–92
—Jaffrey / Seasons
Dussehra: defeat of Ravan; celebration in Sri Lanka, 47 @
—Jewish / Sadeh
good suffer along with the evil, 3
—Lang / Wilkins
magic ring: happiness and power
if . . . , 220–227
Princess Mayblossom (good vs.
evil fairies), 137–153
—Lycanthropy / Otten
Housman (Clemence): The were-
wolf (allegory), 281–320

—Mercatante / Good/Evil, 1–242 @
—Quayle / Shining *
tongue-cut sparrow: kind husband, cruel wife, 44–56
—Spanish-Am / Van Etten *
proper/improper use of river:
good/bad life, 37–41
—Spring / Philip
elder brother envies hardworking
brother, 114–118
wise king exposes gold thief, 50–
57
—Tibet / Timpanelli *
evil helper takes real daughter's
place; exposed, 15–27
—Turkish (Art I) / Walker
—Vanishing / Mercer *
origin of good/bad people; Brazil-
ian Tupis, 16–19
—Victorian / Hearn
Melilot (H. Morley), 117–127
—Water Buffalo (Chinese)
enormous candy-man; magic
drum; long nose, 70–77
GOOD AND EVIL: *evil emphasized*
see also EVIL BEING(-s)
—Bruchac / Iroquois *
Okteondon defeats Workers of
Evil, 104–114
—Celts / Hodges *
Bells of Ys, 104–114
—Cotterell / Encyclopedia, 253 (index)
—Coyote / Ramsey
Little Raccoon and Grandmother,
58–60
—Earthmaker / Mayo *
Evil-Doer: When fog comes drift-
ing, 76–80
—Egyptian / Harris
Anpu and Bata, 77–83
bread cast upon the water, 28–31
—Egyptian / Mercatante
Set, god of evil and darkness,
143–145

—Hamilton / In the Beginning *
   Pandora's box, 138–147
—Indic / Ions
   rakshasas: enemies of human
      race, 116 @
—Jewish / Sadeh
   think of God as hard as you can,
      348–350
—Journeys / Norris *
   hell: prayers of good person
      make evils disappear, [26–28]
—Man Myth & Magic, 3131 (index)
—Persian / Hinnells, 142 (index)
Good bargain, The
—Grimm / Complete * 51–55
GOOD DEEDS / WORKS
—Jewish / Frankel
   death: good man, bad man: tem-
      poral honor, eternal reward,
      578–579
—Vietnam / Terada *
   Prime Minister, in former life a tea
      server, 83–87
Good girl and ornery girl
—Old Wives / Carter, 133–134
Good little mouse (fairy)
—Zipes / Beauties * 350–361
Good luck, *see* LUCK, GOOD.
Good Purim, Good Purim!
—Jewish / Frankel, 528–530
Good woman, The (LaForce)
—Zipes / Beauties * 103–118
GOODNESS (*usually rewarded*)
—Arabian / Lewis
   slave girl (Sweet-Friend) and Ali
      Nur, 25–34
—Bomans / Wily *
   each year witch takes two naugh-
      tiest children in Finland, 27–36
   evil wizards (four generations):
      "we all have our weaknesses,"
      71–75
   stolen heart: power over devil,
      158–165

—Childcraft 1 / Once *
   the little red hen, 98–99
—Crossley / Animal (Grimm) *
   fox and cat; arrogance and mod-
      esty, 8–10
—Dramatized / Kamerman
   Bridge to Killybog Fair, 227–
      238
—Fahs / Old *
   loyalty to lowly dependent (dog),
      33–36
   Zoroaster: Mazda vs. Manyu,
      140–147
—Geras / Grandmother *
   faces of Czar: clever man re-
      warded, 14–20
—Grimm / Complete *
   two travellers: tailor and shoe-
      maker, 386–496
—Jewish / Frankel
   out of evil: God works in mysteri-
      ous ways, 594–596
   scorpion in goblet: virtuous rabbi
      rewarded, 437–446
—Journeys / Norris *
   hell: prayers of good person
      make evils disappear, [26–28]
—Lang / Wilkins
   Little King Loc, 441–459
—Lore of Love
   King Nala and Princess Damay-
      anti, 110–119
—Spanish-Am / Van Etten *
   coyote disrupts farm's animals,
      11–18
   honesty rewarded: to lie to a
      witch means death, 48–49
—Turkish (Art I) / Walker
   defendant rewarded for not re-
      vealing judge's philandering,
      168–172
—Vietnam / Terada *
   hunter given one wish; origin of
      the gecko, 69–71

scholar (Do Be) offends temple god, 42–49

Tam kills stepsister Cam; takes her place as king's wife, 23–34

—Williams-Ellis / Tales *

Cap o' Rushes (loves father "like salt"), 8–16

—Yep / Rainbow *

The boasting contest, 96–105

The "old jar" never empties, 96–105

GOODOO, the CODFISH

—Pellowski / Story *

fire used for cooking; origin; sand story, 70–74

GOOSE / GEESE

see also Golden goose, The

—Allison / I'll Tell *

greed: goose that laid golden egg; ends in nothing, 118

—Bird Symbol / Rowland, 204 (index)

—Childcraft 3 / Stories *

Baba Yaga's geese abduct girl's brother, 114–118

—Crossley / Animal (Grimm) *

fox and geese: one last prayer, 26–28

—Lester / Brer Rabbit *

Brer Rabbit warns Sister Goose re Brer Fox, 4–6

—Paxton / Aesop *

goose that laid golden eggs, [16–18]

—Russian Hero / Warner *

captive tricks witch's daughter; geese help escape, 82–85

—Trolls / Asbjornsen

Goose-Girl "meant" to marry Prince of England, 60–63

Goose girl (Grimm)

—Corrin / Eight-Year * 110–119

—Corrin / Favourite * 40–49

—Hall / Treasury * 77–79

—Grimm / Complete * 404–411

—Grimm / Sixty * 67–73

Goose girl (existential retelling)

—Switzer / Existential, 1–8

Goose girl at the well

—Grimm / Complete * 725–734

Goose that laid golden eggs

—Paxton / Aesop * [16–18]

GOOSEHERD

—Hepburn / World *

Tattercoats: gooseherd plays flute; prince falls in love, 90–109

GOPHER

—Bierhorst / Monkey *

Blue Sun: beheads younger brother every day; various origins, 107–112

—Curry / Beforetime *

gopher kills hagfish, causer of parents' death, 52–56

—Earthmaker / Mayo *

Black Elk digs up the mountains (Apache tale), 18–22

—Erdoes / Sound *

man outruns bullet, 71

GORGON(-s)

—Hamilton / Dark *

Perseus' task: behead Medusa, 43–48

—McGowen / Encyclopedia * 28–29

—South / Mythical

Medusa: sources; bibliographical essay, 163–178 (J. Suther), 384 (index)

GORLAGON

—Lycanthropy / Otten

King Arthur and, 234–255

GOSSIP

—Curry / Beforetime *

animals build mountains to be rid of coyote, 22–25

Gossip wolf and the fox

—Grimm / Complete * 353–354

Gottfried von Strassburg
—Barber / Anthology
  Tristan, 72–92
—Lacy / Arth Ency, 249–256
GOTTLIEB
—Hoke / Giants
  greedy landowner bested, 103–111
GOURD
—Frog Rider (Chinese)
  magic gourd; 120 monsters
  burned up, 71–82
GRACE (at meals)
—Lester / Brer Rabbit *
  tricks Brer Wolf into saying grace,
  37–40
GRACES (goddesses)
—Gods / Schwab, 753 (index)
GRAEAE (sisters of the Gorgons)
—Hamilton / Dark *
  Perseus' task: behead Medusa,
  43–48
Grahame, Kenneth (1859–1932)
—Childcraft 3 / Stories *
  Toad's escape, 6–21
—Victorian / Hearn
  Reluctant dragon, The, 326–344
GRAIL
—Baring-Gould / Curious
  The Sangreal, 152–155 @
—King Arthur / Senior
  see under "Sangrail," 321 (index)
—Knights / Heller-Headon, 154–155
—Lacy / Arth Ency, 257–260
—Legends / Cavendish, 425 (index)
—Man Myth & Magic, 3137 (index)
GRAIN
—Greek / Osborne
  kidnapping: Ceres and Proserpina, 35–39
—Quayle / Cornish *
  piskie threshers; leave after gift of
  suits of clothes, 45–50
—Water Buffalo (Chinese)
  five staples: grain only at the top,
  23–29
GRAND CANYON
—Gullible Coyote / Malotki
  coyote on prayer mission for rain,
  105–117
GRANDFATHER
—Grimm / Complete *
  child teaches parents to respect
  grandfather, 363–364
—Grimm / Sixty *
  child teaches . . . (as above), 141
GRANDMOTHER(-s)
—Bomans / Wily *
  spell begets "Sunday child"; gigantic, leaves earth for sun,
  169–173
—Corrin / Eight-Year *
  Little Claus and Big Claus, 13–26
—Hopi / Talashoma-Malotki
  Hopi boy and his two pet eagles,
  150–199
  how Palongawhoya killed his
  grandmother, 42–49
—Hopi Coyote / Malotki
  duped by little bird, coyote kills
  his grandmother, 83–89
—Lang / Wilkins
  prince's mother would eat princess and children, 14–17
—Old Wives / Carter
  Eskimo male hunter impregnates
  granddaughter, 181–182
—Scarry's Best *
  Visit to grandma's house (game),
  [35–38]
—Scary / Young *
  Sally-Bally: grandma jumps into
  giant's ear; he kills self trying to
  eject, 89–92
—Scriven / Full Color *
  Little Red Riding Hood, 37–39
—Sioux / Standing Bear *
  grandmother and the bear, 58–60

—Water Buffalo (Chinese)
  wolf pretends to be grandmother, 62–69
GRAPES
  see also Aesop: Fox and the grapes
—Allison / I'll Tell *
  contempt for what one can't obtain, 131
GRASS
—Russian / Ivanits, 247 (index)
GRASSHOPPER
  see also Aesop: Grasshopper and the ants
—Carle / Treasury *
  improvident grasshopper plays music for ants (Aesop), 110–111
—Hopi Coyote / Malotki
  coyote duped (lie on back; hold up roof with legs), 99–103
—Spanish-Am / Van Etten *
  ant and (begging) grasshopper visit spider's home, 95–96
Grateful animals, *see* ANIMAL(-s), GRATEFUL.
GRATITUDE (and INGRATITUDE)
—Aesop / Reeves-Wilson *
  Wolf and crane [bone stuck in throat], 48–49
—Allison / I'll Tell *
  Androcles and lion (with thorn in paw), 119
—Arabian / Lewis
  treachery: good barber and evil dyer, 123–130
—Bomans / Wily *
  hardest task; with godmother's help, knight kills dragon, 197–202
—Bruchac / Iroquois *
  (arrow) monstrous, two-headed snake a traitor, 97–102
—Clarkson / World *

tiger cured of snakebite threatens to eat man, 309–312
—Clouston / Popular
  ungrateful animals, I.262–265
—Corrin / Six-Year *
  ungrateful old woman lives in vinegar-bottle, 13–18
—Jewish / Frankel
  favor returned: lion, mouse, and snare (fable), 462
—Lang / Wilkins
  Snow White and Rose Red (befriend bear), 99–105
—Turkish / Walker
  ingratitude: duck as judge: rabbit removed stone from wolf's back, 15
—Wilde / Happy *
  ungrateful for nightingale's sacrifice, 41–56
GRAVE
  see also CEMETERY; GHOST: UNQUIET GRAVE
—Classic / Downer
  scared to death (skirt caught), 84
—Grimm / Legends (Ward), II:415 (index)
—Scary / Young *
  white wolf eventually thought to be boy's ghost, 40–42
Grave-Mound, The
—Grimm / Complete * 792–796
Great Bear, *see under* STARS.
Great Britain, *see* BRITISH . . . ; ENGLAND.
GREAT SPIRIT
—Fahs / Old *
  Capilano sisters bring peace and brotherhood, 104–107
  unseen Spirit speaks through nature, 24–28
—Igloo / Metayer
  Kautaluk: Great Spirit grants marvelous strength, 35–39

GREAT WALL OF CHINA
—Chinese / Chin *
    conscripted husband of Meng-
    Jiang Nyu, 128–139
—Frog Rider (Chinese)
    seeks husband, working on con-
    struction, 83–91
Greaves, Margaret
—Unicorn / Coville *
    A net to catch the wind, 24–37
GREECE, ANCIENT
    see also GREEK . . .
—Cotterell / Encyclopedia, 20–23 @
—Creatures (illus) / Huber * 5–8
—Dictionary / Leach, 1209 (index)
—Hoke / Giants
    Hercules and the golden apples,
    130–132
—Legends / Cavendish, 154–164
—Man Myth & Magic, 3137 (index)
GREED
—Aesop / Alley *
    dog, carrying meat, and his re-
    flection, 24–25
—Aesop / Reeves-Wilson *
    dog and dog's reflection, 36–37
    Tom and the pitcher, 119
    Widow Martin and her hen, 54
—Allison / I'll Tell *
    goose that laid golden egg; ends
    in nothing, 118
—Cambodian / Carrison
    greedy for silk robe, monk loses
    robe and money, 52–57
—Chinese / Chin *
    golden carp (killed, its bones do
    magic for friend), 47–57
    magic brush of artist Ma Liang,
    143–153
    Wali and the magic saddle-bag,
    69–77
—Corrin / Six-Year *
    ungrateful old woman lives in vin-
    egar-bottle, 13–18

—Coyote / Ramsey
    elk, hunter, greedy father, 64–65
—Fahs / Old *
    Deucalion's flood; human race
    punished, 58–63
—Greaves / Hippo *
    how buffalo became a grass
    eater, 73–77
    hyena tries to catch impala and
    its baby, 40–41
—Greek / Osborne
    golden touch: Bacchus grants
    King Midas' wish, 9–11
—Grimm / Complete *
    little peasant tricks the gullible/
    greedy, 311–316
    tailor and goldsmith see little folk
    dancing, 742–745
—Grimm / Sixty *
    little peasant (as above), 142–148
—Hoke / Giants
    Strong Gottlieb, 103–111
—Jewish / Frankel, 649 (index)
    rich beggar and the wonderful
    purse, 375
    three sons in the orchard, 371–
    373
    two brothers (rich/poor) granted
    wish ("enough"), 602–604
—Jewish / Sadeh
    bread cast upon the water, 28–31
    horse that was an imp, 381–382
    merchant buys dead partner's sin
    and guilt, 83–86
    peasant and the snake, 190–191
    poor brother and three beasts,
    140–143
    rabbi and the devil worshippers,
    217–220
    wish granted: anything touched
    turns to gold, 181–182
—Jonsen / Trolls *
    three billy goats Gruff, [4–14]
—Manning / Cats *

old couple: repeated tries to cut down tree; bird, instead, supplies needs, 101–106

Pussy Cat Twinkle sells fur (life) to wizard; saved by female cat, 19–28

—Muddleheads / Harris
seal of Mouse Children recovered from Big Raven, 60–74

—Oral Trad / Cunningham
Big Klaus and Little Klaus, 72–76

—Paxton / Aesop *
goose that laid golden eggs, [16–18]

—Paxton / Belling *
dog in river: greed: foolish loss of meat (Aesop), [38–39]

—Quayle / Shining *
tongue-cut sparrow: kind husband, cruel wife, 44–56

—Rockwell / Puss *
Fisherman, his wife, and the flounder, 42–52

—Russian Hero / Warner *
Morozko the frost demon, and his bride, 33–37

—Shannon / More *
banker denies having received money Brahman entrusted to him, 39–42

—Spring / Philip brothers: one honest, one greedy, 94–97

—Switzer / Existential
fisherman and his wife (discontent), 63–70

—Trolls / Asbjornsen
the three Billikin Whiskers vs. troll under bridge, 17–18

—Vietnam / Terada *
elder brother inherits all but starfruit tree, 3–6

GREEK MYTH(-s)/TALES
—Bulfinch / Sewell * 1–126
—Childcraft 3 / Stories *

flight of Icarus, 208–211
Theseus and the minotaur, 202–207

—Colum / Golden * 1–316
—Constellations / Gallant * 201 (index)
—Corrin / Imagine *
Arion and the dolphin, 161–163

—D'Aulaire / Greek * 1–192
—Douglas / Magic *
Cupid and Psyche, 151–165

—Gods / Schwab, 1–764
—Greek / Osborne, 1–81
—Greek / Switzer, 1–208
—Lore of Love
groom for the sea-lord's daughter, 8–15

—Medicine-Plants / Read Dgst
ancient lore, 14–16

—Mercatante / Encyclopedia, 730–732 (index)

—Mercatante / Good/Evil, 75–82 @
—Old Wives / Carter
woman seeks Golden Sun for information on thief, 4–7

—Preston / Dict Classical
classical subjects in visual art, 1–311 @

—Wolkstein / Love
Psyche and Eros, 111–146, 265 @

Green, Roger Lancelyn (1918–1987)
—Hoke / Giants
The giant and the pygmies, 133–141

—Pendragon / Ashley
Sir Percivale of Wales, 89–100

Green children (land where everything is green)
—Crossley / British FT * 100–111
—Crossley / Dead * 87–96

Green serpent, The (d'Aulnoy)
—Zipes / Beauties * 477–500

GREENLAND
—Speck / New World, 522 (index)

GRENDEL
—Lines / Magical *
　　Beowulf and Grendel [battle],
　　105–116
GRETTIR the Strong
—Ghosts / Time-Life
　　defeats Glam, is cursed, 132–139
GRIEF
—Bell / Classical Dict, 106 @
—Greek / Osborne
　　lost at sea: Ceyx and Alcyone,
　　13–16
GRIFFIN
—Beasts / McHargue, 77–87 @, 117
　　(index)
—Bird Symbol / Rowland, 205 (index)
—Creatures (illus) / Huber * 155 (in-
　　dex)
—Crossley / British FT *
　　Gruagach transforms self into
　　mare; fights griffin, 228–243
—Lynn / Fantasy * 758 (index)
—McGowen / Encyclopedia * 29
—South / Mythical
　　sources; bibliographical essay,
　　85–101, 385 (index)
—Yolen / Faery Flag
　　Sir John Mandeville's report
　　(poem), 58–60
Griffin, The
—Grimm / Complete * 681–688
Grimm Brothers
*for locations of individual stories, see
　　these title entries:*
　　Ashenputtel [= Cinderella]
　　Blue light, The
　　Bremen Town musicians
　　Cat and mouse in partnership
　　Chanticleer and Partlet
　　Clever Elsa
　　Clever Grethel
　　Clever Hans
　　Cunning little tailor
　　Elves and the shoemaker

Four clever brothers
Fox and the cat
Fox and the geese
Fox and the horse
Frau Trude
Fred and Kate [repeated foolish
　　acts]
Frog Prince
Fundevogel
Golden bird, The
Goosegirl
Gossip wolf and the fox
Hans in luck
Hansel and Gretel
The hare and the hedgehog
Hedge-King
How six men got on in the world
Iron stove, The
Jorinda and Joringel
King of the golden mountain
Lady and the lion
Little peasant
Little Red Riding Hood
Man among the thorns
Mother Hulda
Mouse, bird, sausage [trade du-
　　ties = disaster]
Old man and his grandson
Old Sultan
Pink [carnation], The
Queen bee, The
Rapunzel
Red Riding Hood
Robber bridegroom
Rumpelstiltskin
Singing, soaring lark, The
Sleeping Beauty (Briar Rose)
Snow White and Rose Red (be-
　　friend bear)
Snowdrop [=Snow White and the
　　seven dwarfs]
Straw, coal, and bean
Sweetheart Roland
Three languages [dog, bird, frog]

Tom Thumb
Tom Thumb (Thumbling's travels [variant])
Turnip, The
Twelve huntsmen, The
Two brothers
Two kings' children
Valiant tailor
Water nixie
Water of life, The
White snake, The
Wolf and the man [fox's warning]
Wolf and the seven [goat] kids

GRIMM BROTHERS (writings about)
—Allison / I'll Tell * 10–11 @
—Ashliman / Guide
   list: 210 titles, with type numbers, 319–327 @
—Campbell / West Highlands, IV.434 (index)
—Grimm / Complete *
   commentary by Joseph Campbell, 833–864
   introduction by Padraic Colum, vii-xiv
—Grimm / Legends (Ward)
   life, work, role, sources, etc., v.2, p.341–384
GRIMOIRE(-s)
—Demons / Gettings, 123–127
—Witch Encyc / Guiley, 144–145, 414 (index)
Grizzly, see under BEAR.
GROTESQUE
—Hamilton / People *
   Big John forces Little John; results, 81–89
GROUCH
—Scarry's Best *
   Grouchy Mr. Gronkle, [11–14]
GROWTH (marvelous or magic)
—Caduto / Keepers *
   Koluscap turns Water Monster into bullfrog, 81–84

—Lang / Wilkins
   plums cause horns to grow on humans (Deulin), 243–259
—Nesbit / Fairy *
   Melisande [fairy curse on hair], 59–78
—Russian Hero / Warner *
   prodigy Volkh Vseslav'evich, 92
—Williams-Ellis / Tales *
   great greedy beast eats everything, 177–184
GRUAGACH
—Crossley / British FT *
   Gruagach, Finn, and the Lady of the Green Gown, 228–243
—Fairies / Briggs
   young king of Esaidh Ruadh, 356–359
Gruff, see Three billy goats Gruff.
GUARDIAN SPIRITS
—Coyote / Ramsey
   elk, hunter, greedy father, 64–65
—Man Myth & Magic, 3138 (index)
GUATEMALA
—Hamilton / In the Beginning *
   Popul Vuh, 86–99
—Turkish / Walker
   stargazer to the sultan, 98–107
GUESSING GAME
—Hopi / Talashoma-Malotki
   sosotukwpi, 207 @
GUILT
—Strauss / Trail
   Red Riding Hood; soliloquy of "waiting wolf" (poem), 14–16
—Switzer / Existential
   Hansel and Gretel (existential retelling), 142–149
GUINEA
—Animal Legends / Kerven *
   friends ask too much: guinea's crest feathers; lizard's skin, [24–25]

GUINEVERE, Queen [spelling varies]
see also ARTHURIAN ROMANCES
—King Arthur / Ashe, 190 (index)
—King Arthur / Senior, 319 (index)
—Lacy / Arth Ency
[five other spellings], 262–263
—Lewis / Proud
Lanval: knight boasts, nearly loses his lady, 26–47
—Reeves / Shadow
accuses Launfal: secret love for Rosamund, 49–83
GULLAH DIALECT
—Hamilton / People * 42 @
GULLIBILITY (usually foolish)
—Aesop / Zwerger
fox [flatterer] and [gullible] crow, 19
—Allison / I'll Tell *
falling for fox flattery, crow loses cheese, 127
—Arabian / Lewis
test for succession: prince marries tortoise, 43–51
—Arabian / McCaughrean
test . . . (as above), 142–149
thief pretends to be ass under spell, 150–152
—Cambodian / Carrison
four rogues pretend to be Buddhist monks, 36–48
—Clarkson / World *
gulled: naked man believes he is clothed, 377–380
—Corrin / Eight-Year *
Little Claus and Big Claus, 13–26
—Coyote / Bierhorst *
escape from well; coyote tricks goat, [24]
—Douglas / Magic *
Bremen Town musicians, 123–129

—Erdoes / Sound *
Iktome and the ducks, 91–92
—Greaves / Hippo *
jackal fools lion: hold up rock, 50
—Grimm / Complete *
Little peasant (tricks the gullible/greedy), 311–316
stupid giant conned by boastful tailor's "power," 745–747
will not beat wife if he finds someone more stupid, 476–480
—Grimm / Sixty *
Little peasant . . . [as above], 142–148
—Gullible Coyote / Malotki
twelve bilingual stories, 1–180
—Hamilton / People *
Big John forces Little John; results, 81–89
—Hoke / Giants
Quillo defeats tyrannical giant Hundar, 41–64
—Hopi Coyote / Malotki
coyote learns sorcery; transformed to cottontail; eaten by children, 166–177
—Jewish / Sadeh
swindler, bachelor, and chicken; woman, 309–311
—Jones / Tales *
The Gingerbread Boy, 35–41
—Muddleheads / Harris
rejection of arranged marriages: evil result, 115–130
—Old Wives / Carter
old woman courts young man; wraps up in wet sheet; freezes, 101
which is bigger fool: 1) wearing invisible clothes; 2) thinks he's dead, 102–103
—Russian Hero / Warner *
wolf tricked: tail frozen in ice, 111

—Turkish / Walker
  foolish parents give con man gifts
  for dead son, 85–87
GUMBEROOS (mythical beast)
—Hoke / Giants
  Paul Bunyan and Babe, 11–29
GUM-MAN
—Clarkson / World *
  Anansi captured by gum-man (tar
  baby), 259–261
GURRANGATCH
—McGowen / Encyclopedia * 30
GWINTER
—Beasts / McHargue, 58–59 @
GYPSY TALES
—Dictionary / Leach, 1209 (index)
—Legends / Cavendish, 7 (index),
  298–304
—Russian Hero / Warner *
  gypsy cons dragon: he's
  stronger, 71–72
—Turkish (Art I) / Walker
  patience stone: gypsy girl usurps
  lady's position, 111–116
—Vanishing / Mercer *
  devil's violin; girl gives parents/
  brothers to devil, 50–53
—Witch Encyc / Guiley, 414 (index)
—Woman's Ency / Walker, 360–
  363 @
—Yolen / Werewolves
  gypsy werewolf, Nazi soldiers,
  Jewish children, 238–253

HABETROT
—Fairies / Briggs, 213–216
HABIT, POWER OF
—Beat / Bryan *
  husband counts spoonfuls; loses
  wives, 30–40
HADES
  see also UNDERWORLD

—Cotterell / Encyclopedia, 254 (in-
  dex)
—D'Aulaire / Greek * 191 (index)
—Greek / Switzer, 205 (index)
—Grimal / Dictionary, 578 (index)
—Man Myth & Magic, 3138 (index)
HAG
—Fairies / Briggs
  Cailleach Bheur, 58–60
—Witch Encyc / Guiley, 414 (index)
HAGFISH
—Curry / Beforetime *
  gopher kills hagfish, causer of
  parents' death, 52–56
HAIR
—Bell / Classical Dict, 107–108 @
—Bomans / Wily *
  curse: lock of princess' hair;
  king's cruelty to "bird witch,"
  165–173
—Grimm / Legends (Ward), II:415 (in-
  dex)
—Lang / Wilkins
  wounded lion (prince), 385–393
—Lore of Love
  warlock tricked: hair from heifer,
  84
—MacDonald / Sourcebook *
  motif index, 635
—Nesbit / Fairy *
  Melisande [fairy curse on
  growth], 59–78
—Russian / Ivanits, 247 (index)
—Scriven / Full Color *
  Rapunzel, 9–12
HAIRPIN
—Vietnam / Terada *
  sea snake captures mandarin's
  wife, 88–94
HAITIAN TALE(-s)
—Dictionary / Leach, 1210 (index)
—Fahs / Old *
  drought: lizard keeps others from
  well, 91–95

—Hamilton / Dark *
  free spirits: Bouki and Malice,
    102–107
—Restless / Cohen *
  deadly dinner: Matthieu Toussel,
    60–72

HALFWITS
—Dramatized / Kamerman
  avoid tax: appear half-witted
    (Gotham), 88–97

Hall, Margaret C.
—Dramatized / Kamerman
  King Horn, 447–457

HALLOWEEN
—Celts / Hodges *
  Tam Lin freed from evil spell by
    love, 76–83
—Halloween ABC / Merriam * [1–30]
—Limburg / Weird , 1–122 @
—MacDonald / Sourcebook *
  motif index, 635
—Witch Hndbk / Bird * 80–83
—Witches / Iosa *
  Halloween song (poem, by Bar-
    rows), 1

HAMELIN
—Baring-Gould / Curious
  Piper of Hamelin, 116–120 @
—Victorian / Hearn
  Pied Piper (Browning), 24–34

HAMMER (religious symbol)
—Scandinavian / Davidson, 142 (in-
    dex)

HAND
—Clarkson / World *
  toad-witch recognized by missing
    (cut off) hand, 185–187
—Grimm / Complete *
  girl without hands; goodness
    wins over devil, 160–166

HANDKERCHIEF STORIES
—Pellowski / Family * 62–73

HANGING
—Bell / Classical Dict, 109 @

—Jewish / Frankel
  father dreams: son to hang on
    thirteenth birthday; saved by
    Elijah, 597–600
—Pirate Ghosts / McSherry
  hangman's rope: Saul Macart-
    ney and Capt. Fawcett, 84–
    144

Hans in luck (Grimm)
—Carle / Treasury * 85–98
—Grimm / Complete * 381–386
—Grimm / Sixty * 10–16

Hans married
—Grimm / Complete * 387–388

Hans the hedgehog
—Grimm / Complete * 497–502

Hansel and Gretel (Grimm)
—Allison / I'll Tell * 40–42
—Bedtime / Padoan and Smith *
    161–163
—Chorao / Child's * 29–40
—Corrin / Favourite * 30–39
—Grimm / Complete * 86–94
—Grimm / Sixty * 98–107
—Lang / Wilkins, 91–98
—Leete / Golden * 32–47
—Scriven / Full Color * 43–47
—Strauss / Trail
  father's soliloquy, 3–5

Hansel and Gretel (*existential retell-
    ing*)
—Switzer / Existential, 142–149

HAPPINESS
—Arabian / McCaughrean
  Keys of destiny; Iram, 65–82
—Bomans / Wily *
  Anita: little maybug desires hap-
    piness, 83–86
  cobbler's three wishes from
    gnome; learns money's limita-
    tions, 53–61
  Happy Hughie: how laughwort
    began; can't kill happiness,
    62–70

return: rich man learns: happiness is within, 76–78

rich man: the truly happy lack nothing; vs. the Three Wise Men, 176–180

wind-man controls four winds: happiness to one is sorrow to another, 76–78

—Dramatized / Kamerman

Dame Fortune and Don Money, 481–492

happy adults: children at wishing well, 15–22

—Fahs / Old *

weeping of the birch tree, 15–18

—Imaginary / Nigg

bird of happiness, 81–83

—Jewish / Sadeh

no possessions: "shirt of a happy man," 183

—Journeys / Norris *

quest: city of ultimate beauty and happiness, [29–32]

—Lang / Wilkins

princess sent to check on gifts asked of fairy, 186–189

HAPPY HUNTING GROUNDS

—Erdoes / Sound *

souls of the dead walk Milky Way, 93–94

Happy prince, The

—Wilde / Happy * 15–38

—Wilde / Lynch * 41–54

HARASSMENT

see also SEXUAL HARASSMENT

—Jewish / Frankel

Shah, in disguise, tests cobbler's faith (wooden sword), 344–346

HARDHEARTEDNESS

—Bomans / Wily *

man with "Xmas spirit" turns away couple seeking shelter, 174–175

—Grimm / Complete *

rogue and old beggar-woman; clothes catch fire, 646

HARDING, Ben

—Crockett Almanacs, xlvii (index)

HARE (see also RABBIT)

see also Aesop: Hare . . .

—Allison / I'll Tell *

hare and tortoise: slow/steady wins race, 102

—Animal Legends / Kerven *

breadfruit falls: hare heralds earthquake, [26–27]

—Animals / Rowland, 185 (index)

—Bryan / Lion *

hide and seek: Jackal's favorite game, 40–59

—Chorao / Child's *

hare repeatedly tricks lion, 43–49

—Clouston / Popular

race: hare and tortoise, I.266–273

—Crossley / Animal (Grimm) *

hare and hedgehog race, 39–44

—Dramatized / Kamerman

steals sun and foils pursuers, 7–9

—Greaves / Hippo * 121 @

baboon tricks/escapes leopard, 79–80

hare kills leopard's cubs; blames men, 22–26

how hippo lost his hair, 68–71

tortoise tricks hare in race, 114–118

tug-of-war: vs. hippo and rhino, 118–120

why lion roars, 15–18

zebra and impala, special prey of wild dogs, 35–38

—Grimm / Complete *

maiden escapes marriage to hare, 332–334

—Hamilton / Dark *

Manabozo: manitou hare swallowed by king of fishes, 27–31

—MacDonald / Sourcebook *
  motif index, 636–638
—Man Myth & Magic, 3138 (index)
—Manning / Cats *
  chain-tale: boy, hare, fox, wolf,
  bear vs. Baba Yaga, 58–64
—Old Wives / Carter
  hare seduces woman; she tricks,
  cooks, feeds him to husband,
  47
—Paxton / Aesop *
  race: tortoise and the hare, [22–
  27]
—Paxton / Belling *
  hare's "many friends" exposed
  by danger (Aesop), [16–21]
—Quayle / Shining *
  white hare tricks crocodiles; kind
  prince heals hare, 24–32
—Water Buffalo (Chinese)
  origin of features (four animals),
  82–84

Hare and the hedgehog (Grimm)
—Clarkson / World * 164–167
—Grimm / Complete * 760–764
Hare and the tortoise see under
  Aesop.
Hares and [even more timid] frogs
—Aesop / Zwerger, 11
Hare's bride
—Grimm / Complete * 332–334
Harp(-s), see under MUSIC.
HARPIES
—South / Mythical
  sources; bibliographical essay,
  155–161 (B. Rowland), 385 (in-
  dex)
HARRIS, George Washington
—Brown / Amer Folklore, 166 (index)
Harris, Joel Chandler (1848–1908)
—Harris-Parks / Jump *
  six Brer Rabbit tales, 1–40
—Lester / Brer Rabbit * xiii-xxi @
Hart, see DEER.

HARVEST
—Folk-rhymes / Northall
  England, 257–266
—Man Myth & Magic, 3138 (index)
—Quayle / Cornish *
  piskie threshers; leave after gift of
  suits of clothes, 45–50
—Russian / Ivanits, 247 (index)
HASIDIC TALES
—Schwartz / Gates, 1–815
HASIDIM / HASIDISM
—Schwartz / Gates, 802 (index)
HASTE
—Grimm / Complete *
  merchant, in a hurry, does not
  replace horseshoe nail, 748
HAT
—Muddleheads / Harris
  Asdilda desecrates Cormorant
  Hat, 94–114
HATHOR (*goddess*)
—Egyptian / Harris, 131 (index)
  Hathor: Eye of the sun, 26–33
—Egyptian / Ions, 143 (index)
—Egyptian / Mercatante, 53–54
—Wolkstein / Love, 242 @
HATTO, Bishop
—Baring-Gould / Curious
  Bishop Hatto: famine and rats,
  122–126 @
Hauff, Wilhelm
—Corrin / Imagine *
  Caliph Stork, 164–176
HAUGHTINESS
—Grimm / Complete *
  King Thrushbeard; haughty prin-
  cess, 244–248
—Grimm / Sixty *
  King Thrushbeard, 312–316
HAUNTED / HAUNTING
—Ghosts / Cohen, 79–136
—Ghost (South) / McNeil, 27–47
—Ghost (S'west) / Young, 67–85
—Hamilton / People *

better "wait till Martin [ghost]
comes," 133–137
—Occult & Parapsych / Shepard,
1594 (index)
**Haunted house (poem, by Prelut-
sky)**
—Witches / Iosa * 33
HAWAIIAN TALES
—Polynesians / Andersen, 480 (index)
—Scary / Young *
Pele, Spirit of Fire, vs. Na-Maka;
Kilauea, 84–86
Hawk, see BIRD: HAWK.
Hazel-branch, The
—Grimm / Complete * 830
Head, Faye E.
—Dramatized / Kamerman
Spouse for Susie Mouse, 317–323
HEAD
—Bell / Classical Dict, 111 @
—Bierhorst / Monkey *
wife's head leaves body, eats hot
coals, harasses husband, 113–
117
—Bomans / Wily *
Happy Hughie: beheaded, contin-
ues to laugh and tell jokes, 62–
70
—Ghost (S'west) / Young
flying (human) head, 114–116
—Jewish / Sadeh
Solomon and the man with two
heads, 56–58
—Lurker / Dict Gods
four-headed, 428 (index)
—Scary / Young *
bride always wears ribbon around
neck; husband removes; her
head falls off, 61–63
Old Raw Head: hillbilly steals/
butchers witch's hog, 11–13
HEALING (often magic)
see also CURE(-s); WOUND
—American / Read Dgst

disease; Stone Giant; Iroquois
False Face Society, 51
—Arabian / Lewis
Moorish sorcerer vs. king, 60–64
sea rose cures king's blindness,
212–216
—Arabian / McCaughrean
Moorish sorcerer vs. king, 133–
141
—Bell / Classical Dict, 112 @
—Egyptian / Harris
murder of Isiris (Seth, Isis, Horus), 36–40
princess, healing by Kohns the
Determiner, 88–91
—Fahs / Old *
quest: waters for plague-stricken
wife, 52–56
—Hamilton / Dark *
Yama, god of Death, gives power
to his son, 137–142
—Igloo / Metayer
woman a walking skeleton: flesh
and youth restored, 13–18
—Imaginary / Nigg
caladrius cures king, 25–27
—Indian Myth / Burland
beauty chant (Navajo), 102–104
—Japanese / Tyler, 336 (index)
—Jewish / Sadeh
leaves; whom God loves, 149–152
marriage: princess to donkey's
head, 4–8
one trouble drives another away,
326
poor brother and three beasts,
140–143
—Lester / Leopard *
healing leaves for blind king, 59–
68
—Lurker / Dict Gods, 401 (index)
—Man Myth & Magic, 3139 (index)
—Mercatante / Encyclopedia, 767 (index)

—Scandinavian / Kvideland, xi, 420
(index)
—Southern [legends] / Floyd
South Carolina's healing springs,
88–90
—Turkish / Walker
Keloglan overhears jinns' secrets, 23–28
—Turkish (Art I) / Walker
Camesap eats part of Sahmeran,
learns language of plants,
218–224
grateful fairy-padishah teaches
farmer (with termagant wife) to
cure the sick, 188–190
—Unicorn / Hathaway
Magical horn [poison; river impu-
rities], 113–123 @
—Witch Encyc / Guiley, 153–155,
414 (index)
—Yolen / Faery Flag
dumb child draws unicorns, 48–
57

HEALTH
—Tree / Kerven *
good sister: brother shares soul
with mango tree, [20–21]

HEARING
—Clarkson / World *
marvelous talent of honey-gatherer's son, 301–304

HEART
see also SOUL
—Baring-Gould / Curious
Swan maidens: hearts of seven
Samoyeds, 140–144
—Bomans / Wily *
stolen heart: man sells soul to
devil; becomes "heartless,"
158–165
—Bruchac / Iroquois *
Hodadenon: external soul, 169–
182
—Childcraft 1 / Once *

external heart: monkey and the
crocodile, 169–171
—Corrin / Eight-Year *
monkey to crocodile: my heart is
hanging in tree, 102–109
—Dulac / Fairy *
fire bird: princess, heart of prince,
153–164
—Egyptian / Harris
external; Anpu and Bata, 77–83
—Strauss / Trail
Beast's thoughts, waiting for
Beauty to return (poem), 30–32
Heart of ice (Caylus)
—Lang / Wilkins, 190–219
HEATHEN
—Grimm / Legends (Ward), II:416 (in-
dex)
HEATHER
—Crossley / British FT *
Pict keeps secret of brewing ale
from Scots, 142–144
HEAVEN
see also PARADISE
—Birds / Carter & Cartwright *
prayer to go to, with donkeys,
(Jammes/Wilbur), 50
—Bomans / Wily *
wings: "madman" wants to go to
heaven without dying, 152–155
—Fahs / Old *
loyalty to lowly dependent (dog),
33–36
—Grimm / Complete *
Hansel gambles in heaven and in
hell, 378–380
herb (rape-seed): flail from
heaven, 514–515
Master Pfriem [never rests; always criticizes], 720–724
poverty and humility lead to
heaven, 820–821
rich and poor men enter heaven,
695–696

tailor throws footstool from
heaven, 175–177
—Hamilton / People *
wicked man not wanted in
heaven or hell, 126–132
—Jewish / Frankel
Elijah in heaven: recording angel,
577–578
heavenly voice, 649 (index)
Heavenly wedding
—Grimm / Complete * 828–829
HEAVENS (cosmos)
see also SKY; STAR(-s); UPPER
WORLD
—Earth / Hadley *
lifting the sky (Ru; blue stone),
[13–14]
—Egyptian / Harris
creation of, 36
—Hamilton / In the Beginning *
Wulbari: raises self higher and
higher, 52–53
—MacDonald / Sourcebook *
motif index, 10–18
HEBREW MYTH / TALES
see also JEWISH . . .
—Dictionary / Leach, 1210 (index)
—Mercatante / Good/Evil, 39–48 @
—Wolkstein / Love
Song of Songs, The, 91–109,
265 @
HEBREWS
—Schwartz / Gates, 803 (index)
HECTOR
—Gods / Schwab, 754 (index)
HEDGEHOG
see also Hare and the hedgehog
—Crossley / Animal (Grimm) *
hare and hedgehog race, 39–
44
—Grimm / Complete *
Hans the hedgehog: princess
promised, 497–502
—Vanishing / Mercer *

by cheating, wins race with os-
trich, 102–105
tricks fox; makes him his "saddle-
horse," 99–101
HEDGE-KING (bird)
—Crossley / Animal (Grimm) *
Hedge-king [choosing king of
birds], 15–20
Hedge-king defeats bear, 49–
53
HEEDLESSNESS
—Turkish (Art I) / Walker
donkey and camel: irresistible
urges, 44–45
HEIMDALL (god)
—Norse / Crossley, 269 (index)
HEIR
—Chinese / Chin *
palace plot: rival concubines, 77–
92
HELEN of Troy
—Gods / Schwab, 754 (index)
—Greek / Switzer, 205 (index)
—Grimal / Dictionary, 579 (index)
HELIOPOLIS
—Egyptian / Ions, 143 (index)
HELIOS
—D'Aulaire / Greek * 82
—Greek / Osborne
chariot of the sun god, 1–6
HELL
see also DEVIL; HADES; PUN-
ISHMENT; HELL; UNDER-
WORLD
—Christian / Every
The harrowing of hell, 61–73
—Demons / Gettings, 130–134
—Grimm / Complete * 378–380
Hansel gambles in heaven and in
hell
—Hamilton / People *
wicked man not wanted in
heaven or hell, 126–132
—Jewish / Sadeh

Baal Shem Tov's dream; sentence commuted 346

miser given one hour to repent; fails, 177

miser-innkeeper tells what happened after death, 172–176

man who visited hell (dream), 256–257

—Journeys / Norris *

prayers of good person make evils disappear, [26–28]

—Man Myth & Magic, 3139 (index)

—Mercatante / Good/Evil, 237 (index)

—O'Brien / Tales *

goatskin-clad Eamonn: bring flail (keeps Danes away) from hell, 38–43

—Schwartz / Gates, 803 (index)

HELP(-ing; -ers)

—Arabian / Lewis

sea rose of Princess Brow of Lilies, 212–216

—Chinese / Chin *

joy: doing good with magic brush, 143–153

—Coyote / Bierhorst *

dead: the help comes too late, [32]

—Crossley / Animal (Grimm) *

disinterested helpers: fox helps old horse, 34–38

—Dulac / Fairy *

boy gathers six helpers: the seven conquerors, 22–28

—Jewish / Frankel

dim-witted boy buys box of bones (chain tale), 414–418

—Turkish / Walker

helpfulness: the heroic mouse-child, 8–10

Helpful . . . see ANIMALS, HELPFUL; BIRDS, HELPFUL; TASKS, HELP with.

HEN(-s)

—Allison / I'll Tell *

little red hen (industrious), 16–17

—Beat / Bryan *

call cat: frog threatens hen; hawk gets frog, 3–13

—Bomans / Wily *

Frederica: hen learns life cycles: love, birth, etc., 86–87

—Grimm / Complete *

cock and hen, in cart pulled by duck, trick innkeeper, 65–66

death of the little hen, 365–367

—Trolls / Asbjornsen

cock would aid hen with nut stuck in throat, 22–24

—Turkish (Art I) / Walker

magic hen, and fate of two brothers, 61–69

Hen who baked the bread (existential retelling)

—Switzer / Existential, 9–16

Henny-Penny

—Corrin / Six-Year * 104–107

—Switzer / Existential

"Henney Penney" (existential retelling), 79–85

HENSLEY, George Went

—Southern [legends] / Floyd

handling poisonous snakes in churches, 133–140

HERA

—D'Aulaire / Greek * 191 (index)

—Gods / Schwab, 754 (index)

—Greek / Switzer, 205 (index)

—Man Myth & Magic, 3140 (index)

Heracles, see HERCULES.

HERACLIDAE

—Gods / Schwab, 277–295

HERALDRY

—Knights / Heller-Headon, 152–153

HERB(-s) (magic)

—Greaves / Hippo *

why giraffe has a long neck, 86–88

—Medicine-Plants / Read Dgst
ancient lore, 1–464 *passim*
—O'Brien / Tales *
fairies take Gilly, abduct princess;
strike her dumb; Gilly learns of
curing herb, 106–117
—Witch Hndbk / Bird *
witch's garden, 28

HERCULES (or) HERACLES
[*Latin or Greek form for the
same god*]
—Bulfinch / Sewell * 102–107
—Constellations / Gallant * 201 (index)
—Cotterell / Encyclopedia, 254 (index)
—D'Aulaire / Greek * 191 (index)
—Douglas / Magic *
golden apples of immortality,
177–179
—Gods / Schwab, 156–201
—Grimal / Dictionary, 580 (index)
—Hoke / Giants
Antaeus (giant) and the pygmies,
130–132
—Man Myth & Magic, 3140 (index)
—Mercatante / Encyclopedia, 767 (index)
—Rovin / Superheroes
mass media, 139

HERMES
—D'Aulaire / Greek * 191 (index)
—Greek / Switzer, 205 (index)
—Hamilton / Dark *
Perseus' task: behead Medusa,
43–48

HERMIT(-s)
—Celts / Hodges *
swan children restored by St. Patrick's coming, 5–14
—Grimm / Complete *
three green twigs: hermit must do
penance, 823–825
—Manning / Cauldron *
amber witch: common man, loved

by princess, sent to get amber,
18–31
—Vietnam / Terada *
Prime Minister, in former life a tea
server, 83–87
—Yolen / Werewolves
wolf's flock (finds redemption in
Children's Crusade), 201–223

HERO(-es) (*including demigods and
culture heroes*)
see also YOUNGEST SON; *also
individuals by name,
e.g.,* FINN Mac COOL
—Amer Ind / Erdoes, 177–242
—American / Read Dgst, 439 (index)
Blood-Clot boy (Blackfoot) rids
world of monsters, 188–189
—Brooke / Telling *
John Henry wins tunnel-digging
race, 77–110
—Bruchac / Iroquois *
Okteondon defeats Workers of
Evil, 104–114
—Caduto / Keepers *
Hero Twins and Swallower of
Clouds, 79–81
Kokopilau, the hump-backed
flute player, 151
Koluscap turns Water Monster
into bullfrog, 81–84
Sedna, woman under the sea,
95–97
—Celts / Hodges *
Arthur's last battle, 157–169
Cuchulain: "The champion of Ireland," 17–31
Gareth of Orkney wins his spurs,
133–154
Lad of Luck and monster of the
loch, 89–103
—Chorao / Child's FTB *
ants push sky; rescue Indian from
tree top, 43–50
—Clarkson / World *

Strong-Man-Jack kills boar, unicorn, etc., for king, 264–271
—Corrin / Eight-Year *
Sir Gawaine and the Green Knight, 161–172
—Cotterell / Encyclopedia, 254 (index)
—Crossley / British FT *
devil (changeling) thrown into fire; child's return demanded, 212–214
—Douglas / Magic *
Merlin and Arthur: the sword, 141–149
—Dramatized / Kamerman
Big Paul Bunyan; Babe, the blue ox, 514–525
test for William Tell, 493–503
—Dulac / Fairy *
Bashtchelik (real steel), 91–113
—Earth / Hadley *
spark: Vainamoinen recaptures stolen fire, [19–20]
—Frog Rider (Chinese)
Shigar saves birds from python; men from dragon, 60–70
—Grimm / Complete *
Brother Lustig and St. Peter, 367–377
Ferdinand the Faithful and Ferdinand the Unfaithful, 566–571
king's son who feared nothing (Grimm), 545–550
kings' daughters aid hero in tasks: win girl or die, 515–524
Strong Hans escapes from robber den, 688–695
—Grimm / Legends (Ward), II:417 (index)
—Indian Myth / Burland
lazy boy with supernatural strength, 49–50
Stoneribs, son of Volcano Woman, 45–49
—Jaffrey / Seasons

Lakshmi, goddess of good fortune, can find only washerwoman, 81–84
—Journey Sun (Chinese)
Yangang saves village incinerated by shooting star, 47–60
—Lang / Wilkins
Fairy of the Dawn; magic well water, 571–601
—Legends / Cavendish, 395 and 398 (index)
animal parentage, 399 (index)
miraculous conception, 399 (index)
parentage, 399 (index)
—Lines / Magical *
Beowulf and Grendel [battle], tears off arm, 105–116
—Man Myth & Magic, 3140 (index)
analytics, 3188–89 (index)
—Maori / Kanawa *
birth; found on shore by sea god, Tama, 12–16
Kahukura and fairies (fishing with net), 46–50
—Mercatante / Encyclopedia, 767 (index)
—Navajo Coyote / Haile
chart: the seventeen tales, 11 @
—Quayle / Cornish *
good dog Devil; annual delivery of maid to phantom cats, 37–44
—Rovin / Superheroes
mass media: 20th cent. folklore, 1–443
—Russian Hero / Warner *
Il'ya saves city; captures Nightingale (monster), 76–80
Ivan son of Mare kills his treacherous brothers, 120–124
prodigy Volkh leads invasion of India, 92–94
Sukhman kills 40,000 Tartars, 41–42

—Shah / Central Asia
  Rustam and Tahmina; woman to animal, 87–91
—Sioux / Standing Bear *
  bow broken, hunter repels enemy by throwing arrows, 14–19
—Spring / Philip
  Akui frees water; turns to stone, 87–93
  girl sheepherder finds water and salt, 98–102
—Starkey / Ghosts
  Draiglin' Hogney defeated by youngest brother, 80–87
—Turkey / Walker, 303 (index)
—Turkish (Art I) / Walker
  Cihansah shipwrecked, carried to mountain top by bird, 207–217
—Williams-Ellis / Tales *
  great greedy beast eats everything, 177–184
  Sister Long-Hair steals stream from mountain god, 161–171

HEROES, UNLIKELY/UNPROMISING
  see also SUCCESS
—Allison / I'll Tell *
  mercy repaid: mouse rescues lion, 115
—Bierhorst / Naked *
  Lodge Boy and Thrown Away [chipmunk-sized boy], 79–86
—Bomans / Wily *
  stupid brothers find success as king's jesters, 143–146
—Corrin / Imagine *
  Onsongo, lazy artist, steals Masai cattle for dowry, 80–96
—Dramatized / Kamerman
  Simple Olaf becomes king's advisor, 413–421
—Ghosts / Starkey
  Joe Reardon and the three sister-ghosts, 102–109

—Lines / Magical *
  Little Fool Ivan and the little humpback horse, 70–85
—Nielsen / Old Tales *
  widow's son (in disguise), [16–36]
—Oral Trad / Cunningham
  small boy (Willy) traps wild hog, kills bull and three giants, 65–68
—Russian Hero / Warner *
  Mikula (peasant) and Vol'ga (prince), 21–22
—Turkish / Walker
  Kazan kills 40 flies; becomes "hero," 67–74
  Muslim preacher sells wisdom to king, 37–42
—Williams-Ellis / Tales *
  mice repel invaders of kingdom of friendly humans, 45–54

HEROINE
—Bierhorst / Monkey *
  with help of giant's daughter, young man does four impossible tasks, 56–65
—Bomans / Wily *
  Lady of the lake: spoiled prince loved/saved by young girl, 9–16
—Bruchac / Iroquois *
  Stone Coat Woman aids hunters, 135–144
  wife of Thunderer, 146–154
—Childcraft 3 / Stories *
  Baba Yaga's geese abduct girl's brother, 114–118
—Chinese / Chin *
  clever daughter-in-law, 3–14
—Chinese / Christie
  Sea Girl finds key to unlock lake, 137–138
—Corrin / Imagine *
  prince unwittingly marries Sorfarina four times, 11–22

—Crane / McLean *
Princess Belle-Etoile; evil Queen, 16–27
—Crossley / British FT *
giant's daughter helps prince escape death, 313–330
—Ellis / Dict Irish Myth
female champions, 115–116
—Erdoes / Sound *
Buffalo Calf Woman saves brother; battle of the Rosebud, 10–15
—Fahs / Old *
daughter saves father from punishment by mutilation, 133–138
girl chooses death over unfaithfulness, 44–51
—Grimm / Complete *
father vows to kill 12 brothers if daughter is born, 59–64
Seven ravens [transformed brothers], 137–139
Six swans: sister faithful to transformed brothers, 232–237
—Grimm / Sixty *
Seven ravens, 284–287
—Hamilton / People *
helps hero with tasks/escapes, 114 @
—Hepburn / World *
Tattercoats: gooseherd plays flute; prince falls in love, 90–109
—Hoke / Giants
Managing-Molly outwits courting ogre, 65–70
—Jewish / Sadeh
helps suitor; prince who went off on his own, 101–105
Pearlneck rescued by princess, 143–146
—Lang / Wilkins
grateful prince: girl helps hero escape old man, 394–414

prince saved from fates: crocodile, serpent, dog, 485–496
water of life (brothers fail; sister succeeds), 362–368
—Legends / Cavendish
religious, 405 (index)
—Manning / Cats *
Pussy Cat Twinkle sells fur (life) to wizard; saved by female cat, 19–28
—Manning / Cauldron *
amber witch: common man, loved by princess, sent to get amber, 18–31
—O'Brien / Tales *
swan bride: king's son's quest for Scolog's daughter, 82–95
—Old Wives / Carter
battle of the birds, 76–85
Maol a Chliobain repeatedly gets better of giant, 24–27
—Scriven / Full Color *
Snow Queen [Gerda rescues seduced boy], 35–36
—Sioux / Standing Bear *
grandmother and the bear, 58–60
woman kills hooting owl (really an enemy Crow), 55–57
—Spring / Philip
girl sheepherder finds water and salt, 98–102
—Turkish (Art I) / Walker
seven-year siege lifted by woman's cleverness, 144–146
using disguise and bracelet, girl seeks bride for her widowerfather, 224–230
woodcutter's wife, once a mighty warrior disguised as man, 200–204
—Williams-Ellis / Tales *
Janet: Tamlane rescued from elfland, 151–159

Sister Long-Hair steals stream from mountain god, 161–171

youngest sister saves her two bewitched sisters, 125–130

HERON-FEATHER
—Bruchac / Iroquois *
hungry fox and boastful suitor, 80–83

Herr Korbes
—Grimm / Complete * 205–206

HIAWATHA
—Indian Myth / Burland, 63

HIDDEN SAINTS
—Jewish / Sadeh
Jewish maid weds old Torah scholar, to escape Graf's son, 368–369

HIDE AND SEEK
—Hopi / Talashoma-Malotki
with life at stake, 50–69
—Hopi Coyote / Malotki
coyote and wren play, 57–61

HIEROGLYPHICS
—Egyptian / Harris, 128–129

HIGH JOHN the Conqueror
—High John / Sanfield *
sixteen trickster tales, 1–113

HIGH-PRIEST
—Precious Stones / Kunz
Jewish high-priest's breastplate, 275–306 @

HINA (*goddess*)
—Polynesians / Andersen
Hina, sister of Maui, 236–266, 481 (index)
—Tree / Kerven *
one banyon tree covers moon, [4–5]

Hind of the wood: crayfish fairy
—Dulac / Fairy * 43–59

HINDU . . .
—Dictionary / Leach, 1211 (index)
—Fahs / Old *

being: can't see or feel; still real, 20–23

war: Krishna helps good king win over evil, 108–113
—Indic / Ions, 40–127 @
demigods and rishis, 120–121 @
Vedic gods, 69–78 @
—Legends / Cavendish, 5 (index), 16–27
—Man Myth & Magic, 3141 (index)
—Mercatante / Encyclopedia, 732 (index)
—Mercatante / Good/Evil, 107–116 @
—Wolkstein / Love
Shiva and Sati, 73–89, 264 @

Hinemoa and Tutanekai
—Maori / Kanawa * 36–44

HIPPOCAMPUS
—Beasts / McHargue, 49 @

HIPPOGRIF
—Beasts / McHargue, 83–84 @

HIPPOMENES
—Greek / Osborne
Atalanta: golden apples, 51–54

HIPPOPOTAMUS
—Animals / Rowland, 185 (index)
—Greaves / Hippo * 72 @
Creator permits hippo to live in water, 67
how hippo lost his hair, 68–71
tug-of-war: hare vs. hippo and rhino, 118–120
why hippo scatters dung on riverbank, 67
—Lester / Leopard *
tug-of-war: turtle cons elephant and hippo, 17–20

Hirsch, Audrey and Harvey
—Hall / Treasury *
a home for Tandy, 54–61

HISTORY
—Persian / Hinnells
myth and, 110–119

HITCHHIKER
—Ghosts / Cohen
   phantom hitchhiker, 291–293
HO HSIEN KU
—Hamilton / Dark *
   Ho Hsien Ku becomes immortal,
   73–75
HOARDING
—Coyote / Bierhorst *
   hidden, hoarded gold might as
   well be stone, [10]
—Paxton / Aesop *
   dog in the manger: keeping what
   we can't use, [28–30]
HOAX
—Beasts / McHargue
   sea serpents, 95–101 @
—Floyd / Gr Am Myst
   Cardiff Giant, 102–104
HOB
—Fairies / Briggs, 222
Hobbyahs
—Scary / Young
   scared away by barking dog *
   26–30
HOBGOBLIN(-s)
   see also BOGGART(-s)
—Fairies / Briggs
   Robin Goodfellow, 341–343
HOBO
—Southern [legends] / Floyd
   Charles McCartney: goat man of
   Dixie, 150–153
HOCA (or HODJA) TALES
—Clarkson / World * 290–292 @
—MacDonald / Sourcebook *
   motif index, 640–641
—Turkish (Art I) / Walker, xii-xiii @
   Haci's daughter marries, is re-
   peatedly assaulted, 24–33
   three "reformed" brigands granted
   wishes; two fail test, 155–159
HOG
   see also BOAR; PIG; WILD HOG

—Scary / Young *
   Old Raw Head: hillbilly steals/
   butchers witch's hog, 11–13
—Tall Tales / Downs: Bear
   indestructible razorback, C.F. Ar-
   rowood, 126–142
HOLDA (*goddess*) (or THORGERDA)
—Baring-Gould / Curious
   Mountain of Venus, 78–82 @
Holi, spring festival in India
—Jaffrey / Seasons, 85–86 @
HOLIDAY
—Jewish / Frankel, 641 (index)
Holland, see NETHERLANDS.
HOLY FOOL
—Yep / Rainbow *
   The butterfly man, 60–68
Holy Grail, see GRAIL.
HOLY ONE (God)
—Schwartz / Gates, 803 (index)
HOLY THURSDAY
—Russian / Ivanits, 247 (index)
HOLY WELLS
—Hope / Holy Wells
   England; antiquities, 1–222
HOME
—Bomans / Wily *
   return: rich man tries to restore
   his childhood home, 76–
   78
HOMELESS
—Bomans / Wily *
   man with "Xmas spirit" turns
   away couple seeking shelter,
   174–175
HOMER
—Greek / Switzer, 205 (index)
—Mercatante / Encyclopedia, 769 (in-
   dex)
HOMOSEXUALITY
—Bell / Classical Dict, 118–120 @
HONESTY
   see also TRUTHFULNESS
—Dramatized / Kamerman

Baron Barnaby's box; reward, 549–558
—Jewish / Frankel
Moshele's gift: poor water-carrier prays for 1,000 rubles, 554–556
—Jewish / Sadeh
pious thief saves king's life, 262–263
poor man and thieving ministers, 264–266
selling old donkey, 179–180
—Paxton / Belling *
honesty is the best policy (Aesop's "lost ax"), [24–27]
—Williams-Ellis / Tales *
Cap o' Rushes (loves father "like salt"), 8–16
—Yep / Rainbow *
beggar woman: child of calamity, 46–52

HONEY
—Bierhorst / Monkey *
Blue Sun: beheads younger brother every day; various origins, 107–112
—Lester / Brer Rabbit *
covered with honey and leaves; seen as monster, 127–131
end of Brer Bear; the honey tree, 74–75
—MacDonald / Sourcebook *
motif index, 642

Honey-gatherer's three sons: Hear, Follow, Piece
—Clarkson / World * 301–304

HONOR
—Old Wives / Carter
for her fidelity, king-robber-ogre absolve woman of promise(s), 13–15

HOODIE
—Campbell / West Highlands, IV.434–435 (index)

Hookedy Crookedy
—O'Brien / Tales, 53–71

HOOPOE
—Bird Symbol / Rowland, 206 (index)
—Grimm / Complete *
bittern and the hoopoe, 710–711

Hop o' my Thumb
—Carter / Sleeping *, 69–80

HOPE
—Hamilton / In the Beginning *
Pandora's box, 138–147
—Jewish / Frankel
only the dead lose hope, 350–352

HOPELESS SITUATION
—Allison / I'll Tell *
wolf and [goat's] kid, 130

HOPI (*the word*)
—Hopi / Talashoma-Malotki
"good in every way," 203 @

Hopi Indians, *see* INDIANS: HOPI.

HOPI LANGUAGE
—Gullible Coyote / Malotki
alphabet, pronunciation, glossary, 157–180 @
—Hopi / Talashoma-Malotki
glossary, 201–209 @
—Hopi Coyote / Malotki
alphabet; sounds, 340–343 @

HORAE (goddesses of order)
—Gods / Schwab, 755 (index)

HORAPOLLO
—Animals / Rowland, 185 (index)

HORN(-s)
—Grimm / Complete *
singing bone: murder revealed, 148–150
—Jewish / Sadeh
king's horn: secrets can't be kept forever, 323–324
—Man Myth & Magic, 3142 (index)
—O'Brien / Tales *
magic apples: red produce horns on eater; golden apples remove, 31–37

—Vanishing / Mercer * Nagas myth: originally dog had horns, goat none, 87–88

HORNED GOD
—Witch Encyc / Guiley, 414 (index)

HORNED LIZARD
—Gullible Coyote / Malotki, 165 @ coyote and horned lizard eat watermelons; coyote swallows horned lizard alive, 149–154

HORNED TOAD
—Navajo Coyote / Haile coyote died (after swallowing Horned Toad), 13, 47–52

HORNET'S NEST
—Lester / Brer Rabbit * Brer Turtle, in sack, replaced with hornet's nest, 110–112

HORROR STORIES
—Am Child / Bronner, 147–159

HORSE(-s) (often magic)
see also MARE
—Aesop / Holder laden ass and a horse, 10–13
—Animals / Rowland, 185 (index)
—Arabian / Lewis king trades daughter for flying ebony horse, 106–116
—Arabian / McCaughrean king trades . . . [same as above], 225–242
—Arabian / Riordan king trades . . . [same as above], 56–65
—Bell / Classical Dict, 121–126 @
—Clouston / Popular enchanted (Arabian nights; Pegasus, etc), I.373–380
—Corrin / Eight-Year * Atri: ring bell if wrongly dealt with, 75–78
—Cotterell / Encyclopedia, 254 (index)
—Creatures (illus) / Huber * 155 (index)

—Crossley / Animal (Grimm) * fox helps old horse, 34–38
—Dulac / Fairy * suitor test: Ivan and the chestnut horse, 60–68
—Earthmaker / Mayo * making of whirlwind [horse: Red Wind; Kiowa tale], 24–26
—Fairies / Briggs speaking horse; king of Esaidh Ruadh, 356–359
—Grimm / Complete * cat (princess) gives horse to miller's apprentice, 482–485 Ferdinand the Faithful and Ferdinand the Unfaithful, 566–571 fox helps horse trick lion, 595–596 goosegirl: servant's imposture of princess revealed, 404–411
—Grimm / Legends (Ward), II:419 (index)
—Grimm / Sixty * fox helps horse trick lion, 241–243 goosegirl . . . [as above], 67–73
—Hamilton / People * tall tale: horse arrives before it leaves, 76–80
—Jewish / Sadeh horse that was an imp, 381–382 pony's IOU: soul of departed one, working off debt, 354
—Journey Sun (Chinese) drink from Red Spring, under power of Red Devil, 125–140
—Knights / Heller-Headon knight's horse in armor, 88–89
—Lang / Wilkins Fairy of the Dawn; magic well water, 571–601
—Legends / Cavendish hero's horse, 402 (index)
—Lester / Brer Rabbit * tricks Brer Fox: "Hold 'im [horse] down," 6–8

—Lines / Magical *
    Little Fool Ivan and the little
      humpback horse, 70–85
—Lurker / Dict Gods, 430 (index)
—MacDonald / Sourcebook *
    motif index, 642–643
—Man Myth & Magic, 3142 (index)
—Manning / Cats *
    small-small cat seeks advice on
      growing large, 126–127
—Mercatante / Encyclopedia, 769 (in-
    dex)
—Nesbit / Fairy *
    magic apples: age with each
      wish, 125–138
—Nielsen / Old Tales *
    wonder horse (enchanted
      prince) helps widow's son,
      [16–36]
—Paxton / Aesop *
    dog in the manger: keeping what
      we can't use, [28–30]
—Paxton / Belling *
    neighing: bird who lost his song
      (Aesop), [28–31]
—Russian / Afanasev, 659 (index)
—Russian / Ivanits, 247 (index)
—Russian Hero / Warner *
    Dobrynya spares abductor/
      dragon, 69–70
    wolf helps quest; warnings ig-
      nored, 112–116
—Scandinavian / Davidson, 143 (in-
    dex)
—Shah / Central Asia
    enchanted horse (man) under-
      stands, obeys, 31–44
    Feroz-Shah and the mechanical
      flying horse, 131–145
—Sioux / Standing Bear *
    faithful horse: victory dance after
      war excursion, 61–64
    first horse called "holy dog";
      Sioux use of dogs, 71–74

    Horse Dreamer and Singing Colt,
      51–54
    how medicine-man found lost
      horses, 10–13
    Standing Bear's horse; facing
      starvation, 32–36
    Thunder Horse leaves hoofprint
      in rock, 75–76
—Spanish-Am / Van Etten *
    start/stop monastery mare;
      farmer starts, at edge of cliff,
      44–47
—Spring / Philip
    Akui frees water; turns to stone,
      87–93
—Tall Tales / Downs: Bear
    horse in the apartment / F. Eisen-
      berg, 315–332
    horse that played third base for
      Brooklyn / W. Schramm, 285–
      297
    memoirs of the stable / H.L.
      Mencken, 59–65
    A very friendly horse / J. Bailey,
      5–7
    wonder horse / G. Byram, 207–
      219
—Tibet / Timpanelli *
    speaks: kill me; skin becomes
      palace, 1–13
—Turkey / Walker, 303 (index)
—Turkish (Art I) / Walker
    tyrant Bolu Bey blinds man; son
      gets revenge, 99–109
—Water Buffalo (Chinese)
    origin of features (four animals),
      82–84
    Suhe's pony: origin of horse-
      headed fiddle, 44–48
—Yolen / Shape Shift
    shapeshifting into, 61
HORSEHIDE, MAGIC
—Oral Trad / Cunningham
    Big Klaus and Little Klaus, 72–76

HORSEMANSHIP
—Lore of Love
 King Nala and Princess Damay-
 anti, 110–119
HORSEMEN
—Hamilton / Dark *
 Baba Yaga and Vasilisa: Dawn,
 Day, and Night, 14–22
HORSESHOE
—Clarkson / World *
 protection against witches, 202–
 209
—Grimm / Complete *
 merchant, in a hurry, does not
 replace horseshoe nail, 748
HORUS
—Egyptian / Harris, 131 (index)
 throne of Egypt: Horus vs. Seth,
 41–47
—Egyptian / Ions, 143 (index)
—Egyptian / Mercatante
 Horus and Set contend for king-
 ship, 57–68
—Wolkstein / Love
 Isis and Osiris, 1–36, 242 @
HOSPITALITY (*lack punished*)
—Arabian / Lewis
 Attaf's hospitality; Jafar's misfor-
 tunes, 199–209
—Bell / Classical Dict, 126–127 @
—Bruchac / Iroquois *
 Stone Coat Woman aids hunters,
 135–144
—Greek / Osborne
 mysterious visitors: Baucis and
 Philemon, 67–70
—Grimm / Complete *
 poor man rewarded; rich man
 punished, 394–398
—Jewish / Frankel, 649 (index)
—Jewish / Sadeh
 Abraham and the solitary tsaddik,
 38
—Spanish-Am / Van Etten *

 beggar-woman turned away:
 curse for not sharing, 50–51
—Turkish (Art I) / Walker, xxix @
 host's supreme authority (not to
 be contradicted), 41–44
—Wilde / Happy *
 selfish giant [spring doesn't
 come], 59–69
HOSTAGE
—Jewish / Sadeh
 giving life for one's friend, 121–
 122
**Hotu-puku (dragon) killed by brave
warriors**
—Maori / Kanawa * 88–89
HOUDINI, Harry (1874–1926)
—Floyd / Gr Am Myst, 64–67
HOUSE
—Clarkson / World *
 hares safe in burrow; in unsuitable houses, eaten by fox,
 159–161
—Geras / Grandmother *
 overcrowded house (move animals in/out; seems larger), 77–
 85
—Hall / Treasury *
 a home for [elf] Tandy, 54–61
—MacDonald / Sourcebook *
 motif index, 644
—Rockwell / Puss *
 fisherman, his wife, and the flounder, 42–52
—Scriven / Full Color *
 Hansel and Gretel: gingerbread
 house, 43–47
HOUSE-SPIRITS
—Clarkson / World *
 brownie of Blednock (does
 household tasks), 115–117
—Ghosts / Starkey
 boggart of Castle Farm, 30–35
—Russian Hero / Warner *
 domovoi, living in stove, 29–30

House that Jack built, The
—Allison / I'll Tell * 78–79
—Clouston / Popular, I.284–291
HOUSEWORK
—Hoke / Giants
   Managing-Molly outwits courting
      ogre, 65–70
—Imaginary / Nigg
   the kikimora, 33–35
—Trolls / Asbjornsen
   man and wife exchange jobs for a
      day, 19–20
—Water Buffalo (Chinese)
   inanimate objects take over; per-
      ish, 21–22
Housman, Clemence (1865–1959)
—Lycanthropy / Otten
   The Were-wolf, 281–320
Housman, Laurence (1865–1959)
—Victorian / Hearn
   Rocking-horse land, 318–324
How six men got on in the world
—Grimm / Complete * 344–49
HUDSON BAY
—Speck / New World, 523 (index)
HUGHES, Thomas
—Southern [legends] / Floyd
   Rugby colony, 50–54
HUICHOL
—Dictionary / Leach, 1217 (index)
HUITZILOPOCHTLI
—Mesoamerican / Leon-P, 290, 297
   (index)
Hula dance
—Polynesians / Andersen, 432–
   451
HUMAN-ANIMAL COMPOSITES
   see also BEAST-MEN; MER-
      MAID; MERMAN
—South / Mythical
   sources; bibliographical essay,
      123–239, 371 (index)
HUMAN CONDITION
—Coyote / Bierhorst *

loss can sometimes make us see
   our good fortune, [44]
—Gods / Schwab
   ages of man (Hesiod), 36–38
—Hamilton / In the Beginning *
   Pandora's box, 138–147
—Jewish / Sadeh
   worms' complaint: men are too
      skinny, 167–168
—Mesoamerican / Leon-P, 297 (index)
HUMAN RELATIONS
—Caduto / Keepers *
   death: woman has last word,
      181–182
—Paxton / Aesop *
   boy who cried wolf, [33–35]
HUMAN SACRIFICE
   see also SACRIFICE
—Bell / Classical Dict, 127–130 @
—Cotterell / Encyclopedia, 254 (index)
—Hamilton / Dark *
   pretender: sacrificed to Tezcut-
      lipoca after year of high living,
      60–64
—Jewish / Sadeh
   mother sells son for human sacri-
      fice, 330–331
   rabbi and the devil worshippers,
      217–220
—Lurker / Dict Gods, 431 (index)
—Man Myth & Magic, 3142 (index)
—Nesbit / Fairy *
   Billy the King [hired to be eaten
      by dragon], 1–22
—Quayle / Cornish *
   good dog Devil; annual delivery of
      maid to phantom cats, 37–44
HUMANOIDS
—Monsters / Cohen, 3–37 @
HUMILITY
   see also PRIDE
—Aesop / Reeves-Wilson *
   stag: proud of antlers; ashamed
      of legs, 29

—Erdoes / Sound *
  Iktome: hawk gets even for being ridiculed, 60–61
—Leonardo / Fables *
  snowflake becomes avalanche, 20

HUMMINGBIRD
—Hoke / Giants
  slaying of giant Sinulu, 71–78

HUMOR
  see also ANAL HUMOR; EXAGGERATION; INDIAN HUMOR; JOKE(-s); TALL TALE(-s)
—Bomans / Wily *
  king's even more foolish sons are misunderstood as "wise," 143–146
—British / Briggs *
  sixteen tales, 51–65
—Hamilton / People *
  better "wait till Martin [ghost] comes," 133–137
—High John / Sanfield *
  bet on eating 40-pound watermelon (eats one for practice), 41–43
  Christmas turkey: "what you do to it, we'll do to you," (John kisses its butt), 99–102
  John in court ("owned wagon since it was wheelbarrow"), 85–88
—Humor / Midwest, 1–268
—Lore of Love
  warlock tricked: hair from heifer, 84
—Lynn / Fantasy *
  annotated bibliography, 235–272
—MacDonald / Sourcebook *
  motif index, 374–380
—Old Wives / Carter
  rich farmer covets young girl; she substitutes mare for wedding, 61–63

—Palestinian / Speak (Muhawi)
  motif-index, 402
—Scary / Young *
  coffin follows boy; takes cough drops to "stop the coughin'," 33
  Rap! Shylock Bones finds "ghost" to be "wrapping" paper, 31–32
—Talk / Goss, 361–434
—Turkish / Walker
  Hamal Hasan (porter) has trouble carrying babies, 123–126
  man asks wife, mother, daughter to shorten pants, 135–138
—Turkish (Art I) / Walker
  foolish servant checks on fly in water glass, 91–92
  Hoca, selling pomegranates, joined by donkey, 71
  man called "donkey": doesn't smoke, drink, or sport with women, 176–177

HUNCHBACK
—Arabian / Riordan
  Zubaida's tale: the little hunchback, 122–124
—Clouston / Popular, II.508 (index)
  hunchback and fairies; versions, I.352–372
—Crossley / British FT *
  fairies cure good-tempered hunchback, 145–152

HUNDAR (giant)
—Hoke / Giants
  Quillo defeats tyrannical giant, 41–64

HUNGER
—Geras / Grandmother *
  Bavsi's feast: rich man experiences hunger, 6–13

HUNT, Robert (1807–1887)
—Quayle / Cornish * 11–12

HUNT(-er; -ing)

see also COON HUNTING; IN-
DIAN HUNTING
—Animal Legends / Kerven *
    Iroquois tale: never kill a small
    bear, [6–7]
—Animals / Rowland, 186 (index)
—Bierhorst / Naked *
    Moose wife; broken promise
    brings bad luck, 52–59
    Mother of ghosts; life-restored,
    37–43
—Bierhorst / Sacred
    Indian prayer/songs, 123–139
—Bomans / Wily *
    hunter spares deer, swan, raven;
    saves man accused of theft,
    16–19
—Bruchac / Iroquois *
    boy who lived with the bears, 24–
    30
    dogs who saved their master, 85–
    91
    hunting of the Great Bear (Big
    Dipper), 189–195
    Okteondon defeats Workers of
    Evil, 104–114
    Stone Coat Woman aids hunters,
    135–144
—Caduto / Keepers *
    ask permission before killing; ask
    pardon, 173–174
    folly: trap all animals in magic
    bag, 165–167
    myth: man ordained to be hunter,
    181–182
—Corrin / Imagine *
    popplesnitch: huntsman's pact
    with demon to produce un-
    known bird, 70–79
—Coyote / Ramsey
    arrow-point maker and tobacco-
    hunter, 76–78
    coyote and wolf, 242–245
—Curry / Beforetime *
    coyote: many tricks trying to get
    deer meat from badger; fails,
    78–88
    coyote tries feigning death; fails
    because ticklish, 74–77
—Dramatized / Kamerman
    Peter and the wolf, 375–380
—Erdoes / Sound *
    courtship: origin of use of flute,
    3–9
—Fahs / Old *
    animals make sickness for hu-
    man enemy, 71–80
—Greaves / Hippo *
    why cheetah's cheeks are tear-
    stained, 29–33
—Grimm / Complete *
    Four clever brothers, 580–584
    Salad; fed to witch, 551–558
    Twelve huntsmen; prince forgets
    his betrothed, 334–336
—Grimm / Legends (Ward), II:420 (in-
    dex)
—Grimm / Sixty *
    Four clever brothers, 220–234
    Salad; fed to witch, 292–293
    Twelve huntsmen (as above),
    271–273
—Haboo / Hilbert
    seal-hunting brothers, 73–86
—High John / Sanfield *
    John verifies: Master killed deer
    with "one shot," 63–68
—Hopi / Talashoma-Malotki
    Hopi boy and his two pet eagles,
    150–199
—Hopi Coyote / Malotki
    Coyote Boy marries Musangnuvi
    Girl, 229–283
—Humor / Midwest, 213–222
—Igloo / Metayer
    marriage to seductress-ghost,
    82–91

orphan and the bears [bear-men],
24–31

seal hunters on ice floe: Lost at
sea, 49–54

—Jonsen / Trolls *
trolls and the pussy cat [a white
bear], 15–23

—Lester / Brer Rabbit *
Brer Fox and Brer Rabbit go hunting, 42–43

—Manning / Cauldron *
donkey, gift of troll-child, helps
hunter rescue princess, 9–
17

—Muddleheads / Harris
sea hunters swallowed by whirlpool, 26–43

—Northern / Norman
ten tales, 245–276

—Russian Hero / Warner *
Ivan son of Mare kills his treacherous brothers, 120–124

—Tibet / Timpanelli *
hunter's son can't kill animals;
father buries him, 1–13

—Unicorn / Hathaway
hunt of the unicorn, 77–87 @

—Vanishing / Mercer *
how Bushmen came to be hunters and gatherers, 74–75

—Wildlife / Gillespie, 243 (index)

—Wolves / Lopez, 302 (index)

HUNTER RIGHTS

—Navajo Coyote / Haile
porcupine tricks/kills elk; vies with
coyote for it, 13, 41–44

HUNTRESS

—Igloo / Metayer
wife-killer, forced marriage: huntress, 99–107

Hurds, The

—Grimm / Complete * 656

HURLING

—Fairies / Briggs, 228–229

HURRICANE

—Lester / Brer Rabbit *
tricks Brer Lion: "hurricane coming," 60–62

—Vanishing / Mercer *
why hurricane lives apart; personified; Australian Abo tale,
61–64

HUSBAND

—Earthmaker / Mayo *
hunter and Rainbow Woman; lost
(Quileute tale), 38–40

—Jewish / Frankel
missing ruble: man sent for jewels brings deserting husband,
509–514

—Lore of Love
foretell: who will be my future
husband? 24–25

—Reeves / Shadow
becomes werewolf "Garwal,"
three days each week, 99–
110

HUSBAND and WIFE

see also Blue Beard

—Arabian / McCaughrean
man with three wives, 185–193

—Bierhorst / Monkey *
wife's head leaves body, eats hot
coals, harasses husband, 113–
117

—Bierhorst / Naked *
mother of ghosts; life-restored,
37–43

—Clarkson / World *
cow on roof: man does wife's
work for a day; disaster, 54–56
pig-headed (obstinate) wife,
381–384
wives wager: whose husband is
biggest fool, 377–380

—Clouston / Popular
wager: who will speak first, II.15–
26

wicked wife causes husband to
be beaten, II.497
—Dramatized / Kamerman
gold found in the forest, 388–
399
—Egyptian / Harris
doomed prince: fate foretold by
Seven Hatitors, 71–76
—Fahs / Old *
Navajo First Man/Woman quarrel, 128–132
—Geras / Grandmother *
savings plan; each leaves it to
other; wheels on chest, 49–56
—Grimm / Complete *
dog and sparrow: "it will cause
death yet," 280–282
lazy spinner: hides from woodcutter-husband; seeing tow, 577–
579
nixie (mill-pond) captures young
man; wife rescues, 736–742
—Grimm / Sixty *
dog and sparrow: "it will cause
death yet," 36–40
—Jewish / Sadeh
father's advice on carousing, etc.
averts evil, 333–334
Solomon, the tin sword; ruthless
woman, 52–54
—Journey Sun (Chinese)
drink from Red Spring, under
power of Red Devil, 125–140
—Lewis / Proud
Bisclavret: wife keeps husband in
wolf-form, 29–35
—Old Wives / Carter
tongue meat: sultan's wife
wastes away; poor man's wife
fat and happy, 215
which is bigger fool: 1) wearing
invisible clothes; 2) thinks he's
dead, 102–3
—Quayle / Shining *

tongue-cut sparrow: kind husband, cruel wife, 44–56
—Reeves / Shadow
nightingale: cruel husband; young
wife loves neighbor, 87–95
—Restless / Cohen *
wife steals liver from corpse; husband replaces with wife's 103–
109
—Scary / Young *
ghost of murdered Oiwa haunts
samurai husband to death, 21–
25
—Shah / Central Asia
Ahmad and the nagging wife,
126–130
—Trolls / Asbjornsen
man and wife exchange jobs for a
day, 19–20
—Vietnam / Terada *
ugly man changes self to test
wife's fidelity, 64–68
—Yep / Rainbow *
changeling: husband kidnapped
by ghosts, 162–168
gambler: Professor of smells, 20–
35
**Husband who was to mind the
house**
—Old Wives / Carter, 118–119
Hussey, Leigh Ann
—Yolen / Werewolves
White Wolf, 45–69
Hut in the forest
—Grimm / Complete * 696–698
HYDRA
—Beasts / McHargue, 93 @
—Dragons / Baskin * [16–17]
—McGowen / Encyclopedia * 31
HYENA
—Animals / Rowland, 186 (index)
—Greaves / Hippo * 44 @
greedy hyena tries to catch im-
pala and its baby, 40–41

why leopard hides his food in
tree, 26
HYPOCRITE(-s)
—Grimm / Complete *
gossip wolf and the fox, 353–354
wolf and the seven [goat] kids,
39–42
—Grimm / Sixty *
wolf and the seven [goat] kids,
202–205
—Jewish / Sadeh
dying father to son: beware of
hypocrites, 260–261
—Lang / Wilkins
true story of Little Golden Hood,
132–136
—Scriven / Full Color *
Little Red Riding Hood, 37–39
—Water Buffalo (Chinese)
wolf pretends to be grandmother,
62–69
—Wilde / Happy *
devoted [false] friend: miller exploits gardener, 73–101
HYRAX
—Greaves / Hippo * 124–126 @
why dassie has no tail, 122–124

Ian Direach brings the blue falcon
—Lines / Magical * 45–55
ICE
—Earthmaker / Mayo *
origins, 61 @
—Glooskap / Norman *
Ice Giants outwitted by Glooskap,
11–19
—Haboo / Hilbert
grizzly and rabbit play on ice-
covered lake, 155–157
—Igloo / Metayer
seal hunters on ice floe: Lost at
sea, 49–54

ICELANDIC . . .
—Clouston / Popular, II.508 (index)
—Dictionary / Leach, 1211 (index)
—Ghosts / Time-Life
Glam's tale, 132–139
—Hamilton / In the Beginning *
Imir: The frost giant, 68–71
—Norse / Crossley, 270 (index)
—Old Wives / Carter
which is bigger fool: 1) wearing
invisible clothes; 2) thinks he's
dead, 102–3
ICON
—Russian / Ivanits, 247 (index)
IDEAS
—Allison / I'll Tell *
mice in council: belling the cat,
121
IDENTIFICATION by TOKENS
—Crossley / British FT *
three blows: recognition by
unique sandals, 353–364
—Grimm / Complete *
Maid Maleen, in menial disguise,
at lover's court, 801–807
Seven ravens [transformed broth-
ers], 137–139
—Grimm / Sixty *
Seven ravens . . . , 284–287
—Old Wives / Carter
Juleidah: princess disguised
as lowly kitchen-worker, 39–
46
little red fish and clog of gold
(Cinderella-type), 171–177
—Turkish (Art I) / Walker
using disguise and bracelet, girl
seeks bride for her widower-
father, 224–230
IDOL(-s)
—Jewish / Frankel, 649 (index)
jewel dropped in sea, to avoid
adorning idol, 596–597
—Jewish / Sadeh

piece of copper makes junk man rich, 183–186

IFRIT
—Douglas / Magic *
  fisherman's promise to genie, 13–19

IKTOME (spider-man)
—Erdoes / Sound *
  coming of the white man (wasicum), 74–81
  hawk gets even for being ridiculed, 60–61
  Iktome's misadventures, 16–22
  invited to dinner; frightened by hostess, 31–32
  mudhen stays away from ducks, 91–92
  Rabbit Boy (good) vs. Iktome (evil), 98–102

ILELE
—Legends / Cavendish, 314–315
Iliad
—Mercatante / Encyclopedia, 770 (index)

ILLEGITIMACY
—Crossley / British FT *
  fine field of flax: girl cared for by her mother, 218–223
—Lore of Love
  Sir Eglamour and Lady Chrystobel, 128–139
Illness, see SICK(-ness).
[dis-]ILLUSION
—Caduto / Keepers *
  Kokopilau, the hump-backed flute player, 151
—Demi / Reflective *
  life a butterfly's dream, [22]
—Grimm / Complete *
  lazy spinner hides from woodcutter-husband; seeing tow, 577–79
—Leonardo / Fables *

disillusion: willow, magpie, and pumpkin, 92–95
—Lycanthropy / Otten, 330 (index)
—Old Wives / Carter
  governor marries "Chinese princess" (snake-woman); unmasking by Guru, 142–148
  nuns (i.e., witches) prepare to eat Parsley-Girl, 86–88
—Quayle / Shining *
  wooden bowl (worn to hide girl's beauty), 97–102

ILLUSTRATIONS
  see also INDIAN ILLUSTRATIONS
—Bosma / Classroom appreciation, 33–35 @
—Creatures (illus) / Huber * 1–155
—Edens / Glorious ABC *
  ABCs, with illus. by best artists from the past, 1–32

ILLUSTRATOR(-s) [order: artist first, location second]
Alley, R.W.
—Aesop / Alley *
Ambrus, Victor G.
—Arabian / Riordan
—McGowen / Encyclopedia *
Anderson, Scoular
—Manning / Cauldron *
Anderson, Walter
—Douglas / Magic *
Barrett, Angela
—Lewis / Proud
Bennett, Jill
—Corrin / Imagine *
Bozzo, Frank
—Beasts / McHargue
Browne, Anthony
—Strauss / Trail
Bryan, Ashley
—Beat / Bryan *
—Bryan / Lion *
Burgevin, Daniel

—Bruchac / Iroquois
Carle, Eric
—Carle / Treasury *
Cartwright, Reg
—Birds / Carter & Cartwright *
Chorao, Kay
—My Mama / Viorst *
Christelow, Eileen
—Old Coot / Christian *
Christiana, David
—Schwartz / Gold
Clement, Rod
—Greaves / Hippo *
Crane, Walter
—Crane / Beauty *
Dalton, Anne
—Reeves / Shadow
Darke, Alison Claire
—Hepburn / World *
Davis, Lambert
—Hamilton / Dark *
di Grazia, Thomas
—Aleichem / Holiday *
Dillon, Leo and Diane
—Hamilton / People *
Dulac, Edmund
—Dulac / Fairy *
Durer, Albrecht
—Baring-Gould / Curious
Dyer, Jane
—Yolen / Baby Bear *
Egielski, Richard
—Brooke / Telling *
Evora, Tony
—Vanishing / Mercer *
Fadden, John Kahionhes
—Caduto / Keepers *
Felts, Shirley
—Crossley / Dead *
Firmin, Hannah
—Crossley / British Isles *
Fix, Philippe
—Giant / Harrison *
Ford, H.J.

—Lang / Wilkins
Foreman, Michael
—Carter / Sleeping *
—Jaffrey / Seasons
—Maori / Kanawa *
—O'Brien / Tales *
—Quayle / Cornish *
—Quayle / Shining *
Frampton, David
—Imaginary / Nigg
Frasconi, Antonio
—Owl Poems / Livingston
Fraser, Eric
—Legends / Cavendish
Frolich, Lorenz
—Andersen / Eighty *
Georges, Bernard
—Animal Legends / Kerven *
Goble, Paul
—Erdoes / Sound *
Green, Norman
—Knights / Gross *
Hall, Wendell E.
—Jameson / Burland
—Scary / Young *
Hauman, George and Doris
—Hall / Treasury *
Hay, Michael
—Kimmel / [Bibliog.] *
Heller, Julek
—Knights / Heller-Headon
Heller, Linda
—Elijah / Schwartz
Hildebrandt, Tim
—Unicorn / Coville *
Holder, Heidi
—Aesop / Holder *
Hood, G.P. Jacomb
—Lang / Wilkins
Hoogendijk, Wouter
—Bomans / Wily *
Howell, Troy
—Greek / Osborne
Hughes, Shirley

—Corrin / Eight-Year *
Humphreys, Ginny
—Hepburn / World *
Hyman, Trina Schart
—Chaucer / Cohen *
Iosa, Ann
—Witches / Iosa *
Jacques, Robin
—Manning / Cats *
Jones, Harold
—Jones / Tales *
Jordan, Jael
—Geras / Grandmother *
Keith, Eros
—Celts / Hodges *
Kellogg, Steven
—Pecos Bill / Kellogg *
Kemp, Moira
—Williams-Ellis / Tales *
Koshkin, Alexander
—Russian Hero / Warner *
Larsen, Janet
—Vietnam / Terada *
Lavis, Stephen
—Arabian / McCaughrean
—Hoke / Giants
Lee, Brian
—Hepburn / World *
Lewin, Betsy
—Gobble / Graham-Barber *
—Limburg / Weird *
Lockwood, Elizabeth Kelly
—Tibet / Timpanelli *
Lynch, P.J.
—Wilde / Lynch *
Malotki, Anne-Marie
—Gullible Coyote / Malotki
—Hopi / Talashoma-Malotki
Manson, Beverlie
—Leete / Golden *
McCurdy, Michael
—Glooskap / Norman *
Marlowe, Christopher
—Hepburn / World *

Mazza, Adriana Saviozzi
—Leonardo / Fables *
Moser, Barry
—Hamilton / In the Beginning *
—Harris-Parks / Again
—Harris-Parks / Jump *
Nanogak, Agnes
—Igloo / Metayer
Nielsen, Kay
—Nielsen / Old Tales *
O'Brien, John
—Jonsen / Trolls *
O'Connor, David
—Egyptian / Harris
Parker, Robert Andrew
—Bierhorst / Monkey *
Pedersen, Vilhelm
—Andersen / Eighty *
Pieck, Anton
—Arabian / Lewis
Pienkowski, Jan
—Ghosts / Starkey
Pinkney, Jerry
—Lester / Brer Rabbit *
Pogany, Willy
—Colum / Golden *
Rackham, Arthur
—Grimm / Sixty *
Raverat, Gwen
—Andersen / Raverat *
Rayevsky, Robert
—Paxton / Aesop *
—Paxton / Belling *
Robb, Brian
—Nesbit / Fairy *
Robinson, Charles
—Wilde / Happy *
Rockwell, Anne
—Rockwell / Puss *
Sargood, Corinna
—Old Wives / Carter
Scharl, Josef
—Grimm / Complete *
Schiller, Sophie

—Russian / Ivanits
Schlesinger, John
—Bell / Classical Dict
Sewell, Helen
—Bulfinch / Sewell *
Shannon, David
—Lester / Leopard *
Shorensen, Hans Gerhard
—Trolls / Asbjornsen
Sibbick, John
—Roman / Usher
Siegl, Helen
—Turkish (Art I) / Walker
Sis, Peter
—Shannon / More *
Skilleter, Andrew
—Scriven / Full Color *
Smith, Lane
—Halloween ABC / Merriam *
Smith, Sandra
—Bedtime / Padoan & Smith *
Speed, Lancelot
—Lang / Wilkins
Stoops, Herbert Morton
—Sioux / Standing Bear *
Sweat, Lynn
—Pellowski / Family *
—Pellowski / Story
Tait, Douglas
—Muddleheads / Harris
Tudor, Tasha
—Hall / Treasury *
Varley, Susan
— Crossley / Animal (Grimm) *
Waldman, Bryna
—Earth / Hadley *
—Journeys / Norris *
—Tree / Kerven *
Wallwork, Richard
—Polynesians / Andersen
Wang, Lu
—Chinese / Chin *
Ward, John
—High John / Sanfield *

Watson, Wendy
—Coyote / Bierhorst *
Watts, James
—Curry / Beforetime *
Wiesner, David
—Yep / Rainbow *
Wijngaard, Juan
—Corrin / Favourite *
Wilson, Maurice
—Aesop / Reeves-Wilson *
Wood, Carol
—Caduto / Keepers *
Zimmer, Dirk
—Bierhorst / Naked *
Zwerger, Lisbeth
—Aesop / Zwerger *
IMAGINATION (foolish)
—Old Wives / Carter
   three sillies: crying over imagined
      harm to unborn child, 104–107
IMIR (evil god)
—Hamilton / In the Beginning *
   Ask and Embla: Prose Edda, 68–
      71
IMITATION (*often foolish*)
—Arabian / Lewis
   Ali Baba and the forty thieves,
      188–198
—Arabian / McCaughrean
   Ali Baba (as above), 108–121
—Arabian / Riordan
   Ali Baba (as above), 88–99
—Bomans / Wily *
   rich man seeks childhood happi-
      ness, 76–78
—Childcraft 1 / Once *
   Lazy Jack (follows suggestions
      foolishly), 110–114
—Childcraft 3 / Stories *
   imitator can't dance like man with
      bump on cheek, 58–65
—Clarkson / World *
   cow on roof: man does wife's
      work for a day; disaster, 54–56

do-all ax chops wood, plows, etc.,
on command, 49–51
—Corrin / Eight-Year *
Little Claus and Big Claus, 13–
26
—Crossley / British FT *
Welsh boy tries to take gold; King
Arthur's sleeping army, 38–44
—Curry / Beforetime *
coyote tries badger's hunting
method; fails because ticklish,
74–77
—Grimm / Complete *
old man made young again, 640–
642
Simeli Mountain: treasure secret
overheard, 627–630
Turnip, The, 637–640
—Grimm / Sixty *
Turnip, The, 213–216
—Hamilton / People *
Big John forces Little John; results, 81–89
—Hopi Coyote / Malotki
coyote and porcupine: meal from
bark and nosebleed, 3–7
Coyote Woman and Turkey
Woman roast their children,
77–81
crow stands on one leg; coyote
cuts off his own leg, 69–75
duped by little bird, coyote kills
his grandmother, 83–89
ruse: badger pretends to cut out
his own intestines, 23–41
—Navajo Coyote / Haile
chart: the seventeen tales, 11 @
imitator-fool: gray lizard and
coyote ("First Scolder"), 13,
40
—Old Coot / Christian *
Old Coot and rustler: crow envies
hawk, 17–26
—Old Wives / Carter

evil attempt to make daughter
beautiful fails (Cinderella-
type), 171–177
—Paxton / Belling *
neighing: bird who lost his song
(Aesop), [28–31]
—Russian Hero / Warner *
foolish man exchanges daughter
for help, 57–60
—Williams-Ellis / Tales *
monkeys steal forty-nine nightcaps, 173–174
IMMIGRANTS
—American / Read Dgst, 333–351
IMMOBILITY
—Grimm / Complete *
soldier can reduce others to im-
mobility, 808–811
IMMORTALITY
—Bell / Classical Dict, 133–134 @
—Douglas / Magic *
golden apples of immortality,
177–179
—Jaffrey / Seasons
heavenly nectar of immortality:
Vishnu, Moon, demon Rahu,
71–72
—Jewish / Frankel
phoenix does not eat forbidden
fruit; Luz, 15–17
—Legends / Cavendish
quest for, 402 (index)
—Mercatante / Encyclopedia, 771 (in-
dex)
gambler: professor of smells, 20–
35
IMMORTALS
—Hamilton / Dark *
Ho Hsien Ku becomes immortal,
73–75
—Japanese / Tyler, 336 (index)
—Journey Sun (Chinese)
Green Peony: wives in the mirror,
109–124

—Persian / Hinnells
   forces of good, 44–52
—Yep / Rainbow *
   after thousands of years: home-
      coming, 144–151
   crooked old man: Breaker's
      Bridge, 118–123

IMP(-s)
—Jewish / Sadeh
   Baal Shem Tov and the imps
      [lust], 352–353
   old bachelor lost a bean, 22–
      25
—Manning / Cats *
   becomes gigantic when threat-
      ened; shifts shape to cat, 16–
      18

IMPALA
—Greaves / Hippo *
   special prey of wild dogs, 35–38

Impatience, see PATIENCE.

IMPERSONATION
   see also DISGUISE
—Southern [legends] / Floyd
   Peter Stuart Ney: Napoleon's
      General? 162–165

IMPIETY PUNISHED
—Earth / Hadley *
   Beebyeebyee marries water god
      (fish-man), [25–26]
—Egyptian / Harris
   Ra's anger over rebellious man-
      kind, 34–35
—Turkish (Art I) / Walker
   Hoca punished for not saying "If
      Allah wills," 51–52
—Williams-Ellis / Tales *
   Sister Long-Hair steals stream
      from mountain god, 161–171

IMPORTANCE
—Lester / Leopard *
   body parts argue: which is most
      important, 45–51

"Impossible" tasks, see TASKS.

IMPOSTOR (*imposture*)
   see also MARITAL IMPOSTORS
—Animal Legends / Kerven *
   mynah commands judge in voice
      of emperor, [20–21]
—Bierhorst / Naked *
   Mother Swan's daughters, 72–78
   Two Feathers: skills test, 11–18
—Bomans / Wily *
   tries to hide from death; hires
      servant who "is" death, 104–
      107
—Clouston / Popular
   lucky: pretence to knowledge of
      secrets, II.413–431
—Dramatized / Kamerman
   Peach tree kingdom; bride test,
      288–305
—Frog Rider (Chinese)
   wooden horse, 24–46
—Grimm / Complete *
   brothers: one rescues princess; is
      rescued by other, 290–311
   girl shares bread with three little
      men, 78–83
   Goosegirl: servant's imposture of
      princess revealed, 404–411
   white bride and black bride, 608–
      612
—Grimm / Sixty *
   Goosegirl . . . (as above), 67–73
—Jewish / Frankel
   imposter rebbe: healing the ha-
      sid, 519–520
   king's counselor pretends shep-
      herd's wisdom is his own, 422–
      424
—Jewish / Sadeh
   Ashmodai rules in Solomon's
      place, 58–61
—Lang / Wilkins
   magic ring: happiness and power
      if . . . , 220–227
—Lore of Love

lovers forced apart; rendezvous in dreams, 37–49

—Old Wives / Carter
Pock Face drowns Beauty; tells husband she has small pox, 200–204
servant forces girl and maid to change places, 160–165

—Scary / Young *
tiger's eyes: it eats man, puts on his clothes, eats wife, 73–77

—Scriven / Full Color *
Little Red Riding Hood, 37–39

—Switzer / Existential
Little Red Riding Hood (existential retelling), 32–37

—Turkey / Walker, 303 (index)

—Turkish / Walker
bear tricks (goat) kids; goat gets even, 4–7
pretense: three tricksters "steal" pot of butter, 88–90

—Turkish (Art I) / Walker
patience stone: gypsy girl usurps lady's position, 111–116

Imprisonment, see PRISON.

IMPROVIDENCE

—Carle / Treasury *
grasshopper plays music for ants (Aesop), 110–111

INA (wife of the moon)

—Polynesians / Andersen, 483 (index)

INANIMATE OBJECTS (as if living)

—Bomans / Wily *
Christmas tree angel describes celebrations, 181–185

—Childcraft 1 / Once *
Pinocchio: puppet becomes alive, 212–226

—Childcraft 3 / Stories *
Baba Yaga's geese abduct girl's brother, 114–118

—Clarkson / World *

talk (by yam, dog, tree, stone, etc.), 229–232

—Dulac / Fairy *
Snegorotchka, 1–6

—Frog Rider (Chinese)
Wooden horse, 24–46

—Grimm / Complete *
cock, hen, et al, attack Herr Korbes, 205–206

—Hall / Treasury *
Little Engine that could, 1–9

—Jones / Tales *
Titty Mouse and Tatty Mouse, 21–26

—Water Buffalo (Chinese)
minding the house, 21–22
woman's coin keeps rice-jar full, 55–61

—Wilde / Happy *
fireworks discuss their showing at king's wedding, 105–133
happy prince (statue sends swallow with jewels for poor), 15–38

Inanna and Dumuzi

—Wolkstein / Love, 37–71, 243, 264 @

INCANTATION

—Arabian / Lewis
king's quest: secure seventh diamond girl, 144–152

—Scary / Young *
witch would chop down tree sheltering children, 47–51

INCENSE

—Jewish / Sadeh
fly and spider; incense: knowledge and understanding, 389–392

—Russian / Ivanits, 248 (index)

INCEST

—Bell / Classical Dict, 135–136 @

—Egyptian / Harris
Anpu and Bata; betrayed, 77–83

—Grimm / Complete *

queen dies; king would marry
their daughter, 326–331
—Old Wives / Carter
widowed king to marry his own
daughter; she flees in leather
suit, 39–46

INCH-WORM
—Curry / Beforetime *
measuring [inch]-worm's great
climb (in search of fire), 26–32

INCONSISTENCY
—Aesop / Zwerger *
man [blows on hands; on hot por-
ridge] and satyr, 7

INCONVENIENCE: gaining from
—Caduto / Keepers *
Gluscabi and Wind Eagle, 67–71

Incredibility, see CREDIBILITY.

INDEXES
—Ashliman / Guide, 1–368
—MacDonald / Sourcebook * 1–818

INDIA: INDIC TALES
—Cotterell / Encyclopedia, 30–33 @
—Creatures (illus) / Huber * 79–81
—Dictionary / Leach, 1211 (index)
—Dramatized / Kamerman
tiger, brahman, and jackal, 212–
217
—Hamilton / Dark *
Yama, god of Death, marries
mortal (shrew; leaves), 137–
142
—Hamilton / In the Beginning
Minyony tribe: creation myth *
116–121
—Indic / Ions, 1–144 @
—Jaffrey / Seasons, 1–128
Karvachauth, 73–74 @
—Legends / Cavendish, 426 (index)
—Lore of Love
curse causes husband to forget
wife, 26–31
—Man Myth & Magic, 3143 (index)
—Russian Hero / Warner *

prodigy Volkh leads invasion of
India, 92–94
—Vanishing / Mercer *
Nagas people; four myths, 84–
94

INDIAN(-s) (Native Americans)
*[Subheads are arranged in two
alphabets:
1. Indians considered generally, with subheads from
"Bibliography" to "Women."
2. Particular tribes/nations or
geographical areas, with
subheads "Abenaki" to
"Zuni"]*
—Amer Ind / Erdoes
myths and legends, 1–527
—American / Read Dgst, 439–440
(index)
—Bierhorst / Sacred
birth and infancy, 11–27
dying and the dead, 141–154
growing up, 29–43
hunters, 123–139
love songs, love magic, 45–61
planting and gathering, 109–121
poetry, 1–191
prayer sticks, 7–8
prayers, 1–191
sickness and evil, 77–91
travelers, 63–75
weather, 93–107
—Bierhorst / So Am
male domination, 267 (index)
—Caduto / Keepers *
essay on education, values, the
natural world, 193–196
Great Stone (a standing rock)
tales, 3–4
Native Americans and environmental activities, 1–209
—Clouston / Popular, II.508 (index)
—Constellations / Gallant *
legends, 201 (index)

—Curtis-Bierhorst / Girl
girl who married a ghost, and other tales from the North American Indian, 1–115
—Dictionary / Leach, 1220–1225 (index)
—Dramatized / Kamerman
Indian boy without a name, 526–536
—Earthmaker / Mayo *
map (U.S. and Canada), iv @
weather phenomena; origins, 1–89
—Erdoes / Sound *
courtship: origin of use of flute, 3–9
Fox Warrior Society, 25–30
Spotted Eagle and Black Crow both love Red Bird; treachery, 25–30
—Gobble / Graham-Barber *
Thanksgiving Day words; etymology, 121 (index)
—Humor / Midwest, 49–65
—Imaginary / Nigg
oshadegea vs. the fire spirits, 133–135
—Indian Myth / Burland, 1–144
farmers of the eastern woodlands, 60–71
hunters of the northern forests, 52–59
main tribal areas (map), 7
—Lang / Wilkins
chief goes to lowerworld for dead bride, 282–284
—Legends / Cavendish, 321–328
—Lynn / Fantasy * 764 (index)
—Man Myth & Magic
North American, 3157 (index)
—Mercatante / Encyclopedia
North American, 737 (index)
—Mercatante / Good/Evil, 153–160 @
—Native American / Lankford, 1–265

—Northern / Norman, 1–343
—Old Wives / Carter
girl marries crab; it takes human form from banyan tree, 19–21
wife gives rice to lover; tricks husband to accept chaff for grain, 72
—Scary / Young *
Indian maid, married in Land of the Dead, returns with child, 69–72
—Sioux / Standing Bear *
weather: Thunder Horse leaves hoofprint in rock, 75–76
—Southern [legends] / Floyd
Melungeons, 14–16
prehistory: Prince Madoc, 38–43
—Thompson / NA Indians
Tales of the North American Indians, 1–386
—Wildlife / Gillespie, 245 (index)
—Wolves / Lopez, 304 (index)
—Yolen / Faery Flag
words of power: Late Blossoming Flower, 21–39

INDIAN BIBLIOGRAPHY
—Native American / Rock
in American literature, 1–211
INDIAN CHIEF
—Glooskap / Norman *
panther-witch and her scissorbill birds, 39–49
INDIAN COURTING CUSTOMS
—Bierhorst / Naked *
Animal-Foot hitter kills sorcerer, 24–30
Two Feathers: skills test, 11–18
—Bruchac / Iroquois *
marriage bread, 116–121
—Hopi Coyote / Malotki
abduction: coyote and Pavayoykyasi, 141–149
INDIAN CREATION MYTHS
—Coyote / Ramsey, 232–236

—Hamilton / In the Beginning *
   Blackfoot: Old Man, 24–27
   Huron myth, 58–63
   Maidu Indians: Earth Starter, 34–41
INDIAN DANCE
—Erdoes / Sound *
   Sitting Bull, his dancing horse, his death, 103–107
INDIAN FOOD
—Coyote / Ramsey
   wren kills elk, 60–63
INDIAN HUMOR
—Clarkson / World *
   coyote tricks the white man, 283–285
INDIAN HUNTING
—Coyote / Ramsey
   elk, hunter, greedy father, 64–65
   wren kills elk, 60–63
—Sioux / Standing Bear *
   bow broken, hunter repels enemy by throwing arrows, 14–19
   Deer Dreamer: the Deer Run, 26–27
   Hawk Dreamer invokes hawk, leaps to safety, 28–31
   hunter on ledge, saved by young eagles, 20–25
INDIAN ILLUSTRATIONS
—Creatures (illus) / Huber * 145–151
INDIAN LANGUAGES
—Erdoes / Sound *
   how Sioux Nation came into being, 72–73
—Hopi Coyote / Malotki
   alphabet; sounds, 340–343 @
INDIAN LEGENDS
—Erdoes / Sound *
   twenty-nine tales, 1–134
INDIAN MARRIAGE CUSTOMS
—Amer Ind / Erdoes
   twenty-one myths, 271–331
—American / Read Dgst

   friend-turned-snake and monster serpent woman, 49–50
—Bierhorst / Naked *
   Mother Swan's daughters, 72–78
—Earthmaker / Mayo * 53 @
   Wahconda takes Sun-Flower (Oto tale), 54–56
—Hopi Coyote / Malotki
   Coyote Boy marries Musangnuvi Girl, 229–283
—Muddleheads / Harris
   princess rejects arranged marriage, 115–130
—Sioux / Standing Bear *
   snow-woman: news-carrier in winter, 48–50
Indian medicine man, *see* MEDICINE MAN.
INDIAN PRAYERS
—Coyote / Ramsey
   Modoc prayers, 186–187
INDIAN RELATIONS with WHITES
—Coyote / Ramsey
   white men are snakes, 258
—Erdoes / Sound *
   coming of the white man (wasicum), 74–81
   dogs electing a leader; satire, 23–24
   girl saves brother; battle of the Rosebud, 10–15
   Sitting Bull, his dancing horse, his death, 103–107
   white man = "steal-all" or "fat taken," 81
INDIAN RELIGION
—Indian Myth / Burland, 140–142
   medicine-bundles, 80ff
—Sioux / Standing Bear *
   facing starvation; God: the Great Mystery, 32–36
   first horse, "holy dog"; the Great Mystery, 71–74

INDIAN SONGS
—Hopi Coyote / Malotki, 327 @
INDIAN WARS
—Amer Ind / Erdoes
  counting coup; warrior code (ten
  myths), 243–270
—Earthmaker / Mayo *
  Smoking Waters; hot springs (Ute
  tale), 42–46
—Erdoes / Sound *
  Chimney Rock, Neb., 45–46
  girl saves brother; battle of the
  Rosebud, 10–15
  treachery: two warriors love same
  girl, 25–30
—Sioux / Standing Bear *
  faithful horse: victory dance after
  war excursion, 61–64
Indian wedding, see INDIAN MAR-
  RIAGE.
INDIAN WOMEN
—Erdoes / Sound *
  Brave Woman (Sioux), 51–56
INDIANS (particular nations or tribes)
—Amer Ind / Erdoes
  basic information on seventy-one
  tribes, 500–521 @
—Erdoes / Sound *
  Sioux, Pahani, Cheyenne, Crow,
  45–56
—Vanishing / Mercer *
  Brazil: Tupis, Pamaris, Juruna
  tales, 13–27
INDIANS: ABENAKI
—Caduto / Keepers *
  Gluscabi made himself from lefto-
  ver dust, 21
INDIANS: ALGONQUIN
—Fahs / Old *
  Glooskap ignored by baby, 153–
  155
—Journeys / Norris *
  visit to spirits of Mt. Katahdin,
  [19–21]

—Scary / Young *
  Skunnee Wundee [Indian boy]
  and the stone giant, 14–16
INDIANS: APACHE
—Dictionary / Leach, 1221 (index)
Indians: Aztec, see AZTECS.
INDIANS: BILOXI
—Southern [legends] / Floyd
  sea-maiden of the Biloxi, 116–
  121
INDIANS: BLACKFEET
—American / Read Dgst
  Blood-Clot boy rids world of mon-
  sters, 188–189
—Bullchild / Sun, 1–390
—Hoke / Giants
  giant steals all buffaloes, 150–
  155
—Vanishing / Mercer *
  Akaiyan and the beavers, 106–
  111
  Medicine Bundle, 106–111
  Napi as creator; tribal customs,
  121–128
INDIANS: CALIFORNIA
—Curry / Beforetime *
  creation myths, 1–134
INDIANS: CANADIAN
—Hoke / Giants
  three giants tricked to death by
  boy's wits, 34–40
INDIANS: CENTRAL AMERICA
—Bierhorst / Mexico
  religion and mythology, 1–239
—Mesoamerican / Leon-P, 1–300
INDIANS: CHEROKEE
—Dictionary / Leach, 1221 (index)
—Fahs / Old *
  animals make sickness for hu-
  man enemy, 71–80
  moon's origin: boy cheats at ball-
  game, 81–83
INDIANS: CHEYENNE
—Erdoes / Sound *

Cheyenne Chief Roman Nose, 45–46
—Vanishing / Mercer *
bears' tower: rock grows, to protect girls, 118–120
INDIANS: CHINOOK
—Scary / Young *
Indian maid, married in Land of the Dead, returns with child, 69–72
INDIANS: CHIPPEWAS
—Fahs / Old *
maize spirit: origin of corn, 148–151
INDIANS: CREE
—Earth / Hadley *
bit of earth: Weesack-Kachak; flood, [6–7]
INDIANS: CROW
—Sioux / Standing Bear *
Crow Butte: escape from the Sioux, 37–40
INDIANS: DAKOTA
—Hoke / Giants
magic feather, 112–118
INDIANS: HAIDA
—Muddleheads / Harris
Asdilda desecrates Cormorant Hat, 94–114
INDIANS: HOPI
—Dict / Leach, 1222 (index)
—Gullible Coyote / Malotki
twelve bilingual stories, 1–180
—Hopi / Talashoma-Malotki, 1–213
—Hopi Coyote / Malotki, 1–342
Coyote Boy marries Musangnuvi Girl, 229–283
chiefs of the four directions, 289 @
INDIANS: INCA
—Dictionary / Leach, 1231 (index)
—Legends / Cavendish, 346–351
INDIANS: IROQUOIS
—American / Read Dgst

Deganawidah, the real Hiawatha, 50–51
disease; Stone Giant; False Face Society, 51
underground: the Great Little People, 48
—Animal Legends / Kerven *
mother bear adopts abandoned boy, [8–9]
—Bierhorst / Naked *
tale sources, xvii-xx @
—Dictionary / Leach, 1222 (index)
—Earth / Hadley *
Ga-oh (creator) has animals help control the four winds, [11–12]
—Fahs / Old *
quest: healing waters for plague-stricken wife, 52–56
—Indian Myth / Burland, 143 (index)
—Old Wives / Carter
clog of gold (Cinderella-type), 171–177
INDIANS: JURUNA
—Vanishing / Mercer *
sun: origin of present order; personification, 22–27
INDIANS: LAKOTA
—Erdoes / Sound *
White Buffalo Woman, 117–123
INDIANS: LUMBEES
—Southern [legends] / Floyd, 10–13
INDIANS: LUSHOOTSEED
—Haboo / Hilbert, 1–204
INDIANS: MAKAN
—Floyd / Gr Am Myst
return of a lost village, 46–49
INDIANS: MAORIS
—Vanishing / Mercer *
fishing net; landmark rock; tree (three myths), 28–35
INDIANS: MARITIME
—Glooskap / Norman * 1–60
Indian: Maya, *see* MAYA(-s).

INDIANS: MEXICO
—Bierhorst / Mexico
  religion and mythology, 1–239
—Mesoamerican / Leon-P, 1–300
INDIANS: NAVAHO
—Animal Legends / Kerven *
  rewarded for saving eagle chicks, [22–23]
—Caduto / Keepers *
  Four Worlds: the Dine story of creation, 31–34
—Dictionary / Leach, 1223 (index)
INDIANS: NEZ PERCE
—Tree / Kerven *
  beaver steals fire from pine trees, [8–9]
INDIANS: OMAHA
—Vanishing / Mercer *
  how Rabbit caught the sun, 115–117
INDIANS: OREGON: Legends
—Coyote / Ramsey, 1–295
INDIANS: PAI
—Journeys / Norris *
  scatter throughout the land; tribal origins, [13–15]
INDIANS: PASSAMAQUODDY
—Fairies / Briggs
  the little people, 268–270
INDIANS, PERUVIAN
—Dictionary / Leach, 1231 (index)
INDIANS: PLAINS
—Dictionary / Leach, 1224 (index)
—Fahs / Old *
  Navajo First Man/Woman quarrel, 128–132
—Indian Myth / Burland, 143 (index)
  emergence myth, 92–96
  twins: Nagenatzoni and Thobadestchin, 97–100
—Navajo / Klah
  ceremonial songs, 127–162

creation myths, 1–237
glossary, 210–237
—Navajo Coyote / Haile, 1–146
INDIANS: PUEBLO
—American / Read Dgst
  miracle of San Felipe, 69
  White Corn introduces Snake Order to Pueblos, 62–65
—Chorao / Child's FTB *
  ants push sky; rescue Indian from tree top, 43–50
—Dictionary / Leach, 1224 (index)
—Indian Myth / Burland, 120–133, 143
—Scary / Young *
  ghost sucks blood from Indian mother and child, 87–88
INDIANS: SENECA
—Earth / Hadley *
  stone tells story of stories, [29–31]
INDIANS: SHAWNEE
—American / Read Dgst
  star lore, 132–133
—Dictionary / Leach, 1224 (index)
INDIANS: SIOUX
—Erdoes / Sound *
  how Sioux Nation came into being, 72–73
  old woman works blanket 1,000 years, 124–125
—Sioux / Standing Bear *
  twenty tales, 1–79
INDIANS: SOUTH AMERICA
—Bierhorst / So Am
  religion and mythology, 1–269
—Dictionary / Leach, 1230–31 (index)
—Earth / Hadley *
  Sararuma: fire destroys all but one couple, [21–22]
—Mercatante / Good/Evil, 161–172 @
INDIANS: TAOS
—Dictionary / Leach, 1225 (index)

INDIANS: TEWA
—Fahs / Old *
　　how Tewas came to live at Turtle
　　　Mountain, 7–14
INDIANS: TOLTECS
—Mesoamerican / Leon-P, 294 and
　　299 (index)
INDIANS: UTE
—Navajo Coyote / Haile
　　coyote: creator of the Ute people,
　　　14, 59–62
INDIANS: ZUNI
—Caduto / Keepers *
　　Hero Twins and Swallower of
　　　Clouds, 79–81
—Dictionary / Leach, 1225 (index)
—Indian Myth / Burland, 144 (index)
—Speck / New World, 531 (index)
Indic . . . , see INDIA.
INDISCRETION
—Leonardo / Fables *
　　oyster in love with the moon, 30
—Shah / Central Asia
　　Wali (talk) and the magic saddle-
　　　bag, 69–77
INDOCHINA
—Dictionary / Leach, 1212 (index)
INDONESIA
—Creatures (illus) / Huber * 109–115
INDRA
—Indic / Ions, 143 (index)
INDUSTRIOUS
—Bierhorst / Monkey *
　　lazy farmer trades places with
　　　buzzard; dies foolishly, 37–43
—Grimm / Complete *
　　hurds (discarded flax) 656
INEXHAUSTIBLE . . .
—Clouston / Popular
　　purse, I.461–462
INFANTICIDE
—Jewish / Sadeh
　　man who stole a rope, 375–377
Infidelity, see FIDELITY.

INFLUENCE
—Clouston / Popular
　　advantages of speaking to a king,
　　　II.360–366
Ingratitude, see GRATITUDE.
INITIATION
—Man Myth & Magic, 3143 (index)
—Witch Encyc / Guiley, 168–170,
　　415 (index)
INJURING
—Russian Hero / Warner *
　　bear bites off head of woman who
　　　cut off its leg, 117–120
Injustice, see under JUSTICE.
IN-LAWS
　　see also CRUELTY; MOTHER-
　　　IN-LAW
—Jaffrey / Seasons
　　Shravan Kumar: wife feeds sour
　　　pudding to in-laws, 16–20
INNKEEPER
—Bomans / Wily *
　　famine: roasts his own leg to sat-
　　　isfy guests, 111–115
—Grimm / Complete *
　　apprentices' pact with devil; con-
　　　demned for innkeeper's crime,
　　　542–545
—Jewish / Sadeh
　　desperate man and prophet
　　　Jonah, 154–158
　　miser-innkeeper tells what hap-
　　　pened after death, 172–
　　　176
INSANITY
—Bell / Classical Dict, 137–139 @
INSATIABILITY
—Rockwell / Puss *
　　fisherman, his wife, and the floun-
　　　der, 42–52
INSCRIPTIONS
—Am Child / Bronner
　　autographs; "remember me,"
　　　etc., 83–94

INSECT(-s)
—Bomans / Wily *
    Anna: mayfly born, weds, begets,
    grows old (all in one day), 43–
    46
—Caduto / Keepers *
    Four Worlds (Dine); creation of
    insects, 31–34
    helpful spider: Hero Twins and
    Swallower of Clouds, 79–81
—Jewish / Frankel, 646 (index)
—Scary / Young *
    ghost sucks blood from Indian
    mother/child; origin of mosqui-
    tos, 87–88
—Vanishing / Mercer *
    Ainu myth: origin of gnats, mos-
    quitoes, etc., 97–98
INSULT: *avenged*
—Crossley / Animal (Grimm) *
    hedge-king (bird) defeats bear,
    49–53
INTELLIGENCE: *personified*
—Dramatized / Kamerman
    Triumph for two, 47–60
INTESTINES
—Hopi Coyote / Malotki
    ruse: badger pretends to cut out
    own intestines, 23–41
INTIMIDATION
—Bryan / Lion *
    lion steals ostrich chicks, 3–23
INTRUDERS
    see also Goldilocks . . . ; Snow-
    drop . . . ; Snow White . . .
—Switzer / Existential
    Goldilocks and the three bears
    (*existential retelling*), 17–23
—Turkish (Art I) / Walker
    outcast stepdaughter keeps
    house for forty thieves, 82–88
INUIT PEOPLE
    see also ESKIMO
—Indian Myth / Burland, 143 (index)

INVASION
—Williams-Ellis / Tales *
    mice repel; kingdom of friendly
    humans, 45–54
INVISIBILITY
—Clarkson / World *
    truthful girl admits she can't see
    Strong Wing, 43–45
—Clouston / Popular
    caps, cloaks, etc., I.72–122
—Dramatized / Kamerman
    magic cloak; princesses wear out
    shoes, 435–446
—Imaginary / Nigg
    cloak; the tengu, 101–103
—Jewish / Sadeh
    Blackface: merchant's son in love
    with princess, 117–121
—Lang / Wilkins
    Dorani: transport by magic stool,
    432–440
—Manning / Cauldron *
    her cat advises witch (who makes
    self invisible) to steal farmer's
    eggs, 32–38
—Quayle / Cornish *
    magic ointment put on eye makes
    one invisible, 13–20
—Shah / Central Asia
    power of horse's hair, 19–24
    Rustam and the iron fortress, 25–
    30
INVULNERABILITY
—Grimm / Complete *
    Pink [carnation], The, 355–360
—Grimm / Sixty *
    Pink [carnation], The, 171–176
—Hall / Treasury *
    Little Black Sambo, 68–76
—Old Wives / Carter
    Nourie Hadig ordered killed by
    jealous mother, 192–199
IRANIAN MYTHOLOGY
—Dictionary / Leach, 1213 (index)

—Persian / Hinnells, 1–143
IRELAND / the IRISH / IRISH TALES
—Campbell / West Highlands
Conall Cra Bhuidhe, I.105–127
—Celtic / MacCana
early history: battles and invasions, 54–71
—Celts / Hodges *
Cuchulain: champion of Ireland, 17–31
how Finn MacCool got his wisdom tooth, 34–52
—Corrin / Imagine *
Black Thief (O'Faolain), 97–111
—Dictionary / Leach, 1213 (index)
—Dramatized / Kamerman
Bridge to Killybog Fair, 227–238
Leprechaun shoemakers, 239–249
—Dulac / Fairy *
Finn, and Queen of many-colored bedchamber, 69–76
—Ellis / Dict Irish Myth, 1–240
—Ghosts / Starkey
buggane, Broder Menine, the tailor, 16–23
—Hamilton / Dark *
priest becomes proud, denies afterworld, until visited by angel of death, 119–125
—Humor / Midwest, 87–92
—Irish / Glassie, 1–353
history; fourteen tales, 207–233
—Lynn / Fantasy * 758–759 (index)
—O'Brien / Tales * 1–127
—Tree / Kerven *
fairies' revenge for cutting down hawthorn bush, [26–27]
—Williams-Ellis / Tales *
King O'Toole's goose made young by St. Kevin, 37–43

IRON
—Jewish / Sadeh
mice that ate the iron, 317–318
Iron Hans
—Grimm / Complete * 612–620
—Grimm / Sixty * 317–325
Iron stove, The
—Grimm / Complete * 571–577
IRONIC TALES
—Bierhorst / Monkey *
buzzard-man: lazy farmer trades places with buzzard; dies foolishly, 37–43
—Bomans / Wily *
donkeys and camels: brothers help others, foolishly can't help selves, 147–151
man with "Xmas spirit" turns away couple seeking shelter, 174–175
misunderstanding: old man "invisible" so death can't find him, 104–107
—Crossley / Animal (Grimm) *
verbal irony: cat/mouse partnership, 21–25
—Schwartz / Gold
partners celebrate; murder; poisoned wine, 103–104
—Spanish-Am / Van Etten *
start/stop monastery mare; farmer starts, at edge of cliff, 44–47
Iroquois, see INDIANS: IROQUOIS.
Irving, Washington (1783–1859)
—Floyd / Gr Am Myst
ghost in the Astor Library, 160–162
—Pirate Ghosts / McSherry
Guests from Gibbet Island, 145–157
ISAAC
—Jewish / Frankel, 655 (index)
—Schwartz / Gates, 803 (index)

ISEULT
—Wolkstein / Love
  Tristan and Iseult, 181–233,
  266 @
ISHTAR / INANNA
—Babylonia / Spence, 396 (index)
—Gray / Near East, 143 (index)
ISIS (goddess)
  see also HORUS [her son]
—Egyptian / Harris, 131 (index)
  murder of Isiris ("mistress of
  magic"), 36–40
  throne of Egypt: Horus vs. Seth,
  41–47
—Egyptian / Ions, 143 (index)
—Egyptian / Mercatante, 72–76,
  113–114
—Wolkstein / Love
  Isis and Osiris, 1–36, 243 @
Isis and Osiris
—Wolkstein / Love, 1–36, 261 @
ISKANDAR
—Shah / Central Asia
  Iskandar and the emerald ring
  (jinn), 118–125
ISLAM/ISLAMIC . . .
—Creatures (illus) / Huber * 76–78
—Dictionary / Leach, 1218 (index)
—Legends / Cavendish, 5 (index)
—Man Myth & Magic, 3144 (index)
—Mercatante / Encyclopedia, 734 (in-
  dex)
—Mercatante / Good/Evil, 67–73 @
→Turkish (Art I) / Walker 1–250
Island of happiness, The (d'Aulnoy)
—Zipes / Beauties * 299–308
ISLANDS
—Arabian / McCaughrean
  Voyage of Sinbad, 10–15
—Baring-Gould / Curious
  Fortunate Isles: Paradise for
  souls of the dead, 134–138 @
ISO ISHVARA
—Cambodian / Carrison
  Siva believes pet eagle's dreams;
  justice, 67–72
ISRAEL, ANCIENT
—Hoke / Giants
  David and Goliath, 79–92
—Schwartz / Gates, 803 (index)
Israelites, see JEWS.
ITALIAN TALE(-s)
—Calvino / Italian
  200 tales, 1–763
—Clouston / Popular, II.508 (index)
—Dictionary / Leach, 1213 (index)
—Dramatized / Kamerman
  The magic box, 265–277
  The magic grapes, 258–264
—Dulac / Fairy *
  serpent-prince: marries, regains
  human form, 29–42
—Earth / Hadley *
  North Wind (lady) wishes to marry
  Zephyr, [15–16]
—Restless / Cohen *
  wife steals liver from corpse; hus-
  band replaces with wife's, 103–
  109
**Ivan [trades wages for master's ad-
  vice]**
—Clarkson / World * 314–317

Jabberwocky (Lewis Carroll)
—Childcraft 3 / Stories * 187
JACINTH (hyacinth)
—Precious Stones / Kunz, 399 (index)
Jack and the Beanstalk
—Allison / I'll Tell * 36–37
—Bedtime / Padoan & Smith * 113–
  115
—Brooke / Telling *
  uncle and boy work on retelling,
  113–132
—Childcraft 1 / Once * 137–147
—Chorao / Child's * 9–20

—Corrin / Favourite * 170–177
—Corrin / Six-Year * 182–190
—Crossley / British FT * 118–131
—Douglas / Magic, 131
—Hepburn / World * 66–89
—Lang / Wilkins, 154–166
—Leete / Golden * 144–157
—Rockwell / Puss * 1–11
—Scriven / Full Color * 53–56
Jack and the beanstalk (*existential retelling*)
—Switzer / Existential, 112–118
JACK-O'-LANTERN
—Halloween ABC / Merriam * [14]
JACK TALES
—Clarkson / World *
  Strong-Man-Jack kills boar, unicorn, etc., for king, 264–271
Jack the Giant Killer
—Douglas / Magic * 131–139
—Hartland / English * 3–17
—Quayle / Cornish *
  St. Michael's Mount: cruel giant Cormoran killed, 13–20
JACKAL(-s)
—Bryan / Lion *
  hide and seek: Jackal's favorite game, 40–59
—Corrin / Six-Year *
  little jackal tricks alligator into revealing self, 93–97
—Dramatized / Kamerman
  deception: tiger, brahman, and jackal, 212–217
—Greaves / Hippo * 51 @
  how jackal got its markings, 47
  jackal boast: can outrun dogs, 40–41
  jackal fools lion: hold up rock, 50
  why leopard hides his food in tree, 26
  why lion does not eat fruit, 18–20
—MacDonald / Sourcebook *
  motif index, 648

—Turkish / Walker
  jackal shows crow: destroy cheater by trick, 17–19
JACKSON, Andrew (1767–1845)
—American / Read Dgst, 130–131
JACOB
—Jewish / Frankel, 655 (index)
—Schwartz / Gates, 804 (index)
Jacobi, Carl
—Pirate Ghosts / McSherry
  The digging at Pistol Key, 166–181
Jacobs, Elizabeth [by]
—Coyote / Ramsey
  Exploits of South Wind, 130–133
Jacobs, Joseph
—Chorao / Child's *
  Pied Piper, 51–55
—Witches / Iosa * 34–39
  Old witch, The
JADE
—Chinese / Christie, 143 (index)
—Precious Stones / Kunz, 399 (index)
JADE EMPEROR
—Chinese / Chin *
  monkey: on road to fetch scriptures, 95–110
JAGUAR
—Bierhorst / So Am
  Indian religion and mythology, 266 (index)
JAMAICAN TALES
—Animal Legends / Kerven *
  Anansi: how tiger and monkey both escaped, [28–29]
—Dictionary / Leach, 1219 (index)
—Williams-Ellis / Tales *
  dialect tale: Anansi and Mrs. Dove, 143–150
JAPANESE TALES
—Creatures (illus) / Huber * 91–99
—Dictionary / Leach, 1213 (index)
—Dramatized / Kamerman

Great samurai sword, 306–316
Ogre who built a bridge, 278–287
Peach tree kingdom, 288–305
—Dulac / Fairy *
Urashima Taro; Dragon Sea-
King's palace, 140–152
—Earth / Hadley *
climbing to heaven, [8–9]
—Ghosts / Time-Life
O'Iwa murdered ghost-wife's re-
venge, 51–55
—Japanese / Tyler
220 tales, 1–340
—Legends / Cavendish, 5 (index),
61–67
—Lore of Love
Howori: ill-starred mating of earth
and sea, 87–95
—Mercatante / Encyclopedia, 734 (in-
dex)
—Mercatante / Good/Evil, 137–143 @
—Quayle / Shining *
ten tales, 1–111
—Restless / Cohen *
snow-ghost wife bears ten chil-
dren, 16–23
—Scary / Young *
ghost of murdered Oiwa haunts
samurai husband to death, 21–
25
—Tree / Kerven *
mystery man of the peonies, [10–
13]
JAR(-s)
—Bierhorst / Monkey *
three would-be buyers of jar murdered; fool tricked: buries
"one" thrice, 32–36
—Yep / Rainbow *
old woman: old jar never empties,
96–105
JASON (*and the golden fleece*)
—Corrin / Eight-Year * 79–88
—Gods / Schwab, 756 (index)

JASPER
—Precious Stones / Kunz, 399 (in-
dex)
JATAKA TALES
—Childcraft 1 / Once *
foolish, timid rabbit: "earth break-
ing up," 166–168
turtle "killed" by being thrown into
water, 172–173
JAUFREY
—Pendragon / Ashley
Jaufrey (knight) and fair Brunis-
sende, 260–321
JEALOUSY
see also ENVY
—Arabian / Lewis
Ghanim, the slave of love, 35–41
—Douglas / Magic *
Venus, Cupid and Psyche, 151–
165
—Erdoes / Sound *
treachery: two warriors love same
girl, 25–30
—Ghosts / Time-Life
harp: strings from hair of murdered sister, 32–37
—Greek / Osborne
Cupid and Psyche: the four tasks,
57–65
—Hamilton / Dark *
John (brother) kills Little Tom,
takes credit for his feat, 132–
136
—Igloo / Metayer
owl-suitor rejected by ptarmigan,
40–41
—Jewish / Sadeh
nightingale and shroud wearers;
queen's evil sisters, 25–28
—Lewis / Proud
Yonec: lover killed by jealous
husband's trap, 53–60
—O'Brien / Tales *
goatskin-clad Eamonn: fife forces

dancing (wolf and jealous rival Fiac), 38–43

—Palestinian / Speak (Muhawi)
motif-index, 402

—Shah / Central Asia
nobleman and slave (later king), 103–108

—Trolls / Asbjornsen
Askelad and the silverducks, 11–16

—Vietnam / Terada *
husband accuses faithful wife of infidelity, 10–13

JEFFERIES, Anne
—Fairies / Briggs, 239–242, 318–320

JENNY HANIVERS
—Monsters / Cohen, 255–258 @

JERICHO, BATTLE OF
—Jewish / Frankel, 174–176

JERUSALEM
—Jewish / Frankel, 656 (index)
—Jewish / Sadeh
unearthing of the Wailing Wall, 250–251

—Schwartz / Gates, 804 (index)

JESTER
—Corrin / Eight-Year *
attempts to prevent princess wanting the moon, 91–101

JESUS CHRIST
—Animals / Rowland, 182 (index)
—Baring-Gould / Curious
crucifixion; the Wandering Jew, 18–25 @

—Bierhorst / Monkey *
birth: how animals warmed the Christ-Child, 131–132
Christ chased; betrayed by mag-pie-jay, 133–135
Christ chased; birds help/hinder his flight, 133–135

—Christian / Every, 143 (index)
—Fahs / Old *

evil spirit driven from boy, 159–162
miracle of loaves and fishes, 156–158
rich young man: sell all, give to poor, 118–120

—Jewish / Sadeh
Sanhedrin's verdict, 230–231

—Legends / Cavendish, 426 (index)
—Man Myth & Magic, 3145 (index)
—Mercatante / Encyclopedia, 772 (index)
—Mercatante / Good/Evil, 238 (index)
—Russian / Ivanits, 246 (index)
—Wilde / Happy *
selfish giant led to Paradise by Christchild, 59–69

—Wilde / Lynch *
"coronation" of beggar-king, 73–94

Jew among thorns (Grimm)
—Grimm / Complete * 503–508

JEWEL(-s)
—Aesop / Holder
cock and the jewel, 20–21

—Arabian / Lewis
merman trades jewels for fruit, 131–137

—Arabian / McCaughrean
merman trades . . . , 83–96

—Clouston / Popular
luminous jewels, I.412

—Dramatized / Kamerman
Plum Blossom and the dragon, 38–46

—Jewish / Frankel, 646 (index)
dropped in sea, to avoid its adorning idol, 596–597

—Tibet / Timpanelli *
magic turquoise: only real owner can safely wear, 43–51

JEWISH TALES
—Aleichem / Holiday *

feasts and fasts; seven stories, 1–145
—Dictionary / Leach, 1214 (index)
—Dramatized / Kamerman
    bee rewards King Solomon's kindness, 250–257
—Elijah / Schwartz, 1–302
—Hamilton / Dark *
    Joseph Golem: blood accusation against Jews, 87–96
—Jewish / Frankel
    glossary, 631–639
    history, viii-ix (index)
    Yahweh: ten plagues punish Egyptians, 109–113
—Jewish / Sadeh, 1–443
    dead fiancee [apparition], 14–17
    king makes impossible demands; taught lesson by Ari, 239–241
    Rome; two tailors and wonderful photograph, 204–208
    tailor and Haman: "years" really only fifteen minutes, 201–204
—Legends / Cavendish, 5 (index)
—Mercatante / Encyclopedia, 734 (index)
—Schwartz / Gates, 1–815
—Yiddish / Weinreich
    Eastern Europe, 1–413

JEWS
    see also RABBI
—Baring-Gould / Curious
    Wandering Jew, 18–25 @
—Grimm / Complete *
    bright sun brings murder to light, 528–529
—Jewish / Sadeh
    pogrom: king saved by rabbi's wife, 232–233
—Precious Stones / Kunz
    Jewish high-priest's breastplate, 275–306 @
—Yolen / Werewolves

gypsy werewolf, Nazi soldiers, Jewish children, 238–253
shelters werewolf in Cologne, 70–83

JEWS and CHRISTIANS
—Jewish / Frankel
    Pope Elhanan: Jewish child, raised Christian, returns to Judaism, 395–398
    Rabbi's mirror allows king to see treachery in his bedroom, 405–409
—Jewish / Sadeh
    better to hear of son's death than of his conversion, 339
    Bishop of Salzburg converted, 225–226
    child returns to earth to atone for "Christian milk," 192–194
    eagle takes rabbi's son to Christian palace, 273–275
    Elchanan the pope, 197–199
    Jewish pope; bastard converts to Catholicism, 195–197
    man who visited heaven, 257–258
    two shopkeepers, eagle, mountain of gold, 271–273

JINNI [JINN; GENIE; GENII]
—Arabian / Lewis
    Ala al-Din finds, loses, regains magic lamp, 153–165
    giant helps prince; sea rose of Princess Brow of Lilies, 212–216
    Hasan, the alchemist, and the Jinn princess, 138–143
    princess loved by cousins (three brothers), 174–183
—Arabian / McCaughrean
    Ala al-Din finds . . . [as above], 153–184
    man with three wives; well, 185–193

tricked back into bottle by fisherman, 29–35
—Arabian / Riordan
Ala al-Din finds . . . [as above],
12–25
merchant's life saved by storytelling, 100–107
summoned to lift curses from all,
122–124
tricked back . . . [as above], 26–
37
—Douglas / Magic *
fisherman's promise to genie,
13–19
—Lore of Love
lovers forced apart; rendezvous
in dreams, 37–49
—McGowen / Encyclopedia * 31–32
—Shah / Central Asia
bead-seller and the jinn's sister,
62–68
Iskandar and the emerald ring,
118–125
princess imprisoned in mountain
of jade, 19–24
wishes (three) granted by genie,
31–44
—Turkey / Walker, 303 (index)
—Turkish / Walker
Keloglan overhears jinns' secrets, 23–28
—Turkish (Art I) / Walker
huge man-eating jinn enticed
back into bottle, 60

JOHN HENRY
—Brooke / Telling *
wins tunnel-digging race, 77–110
—Hamilton / Dark *
Rolling Rio, gray man, and Death,
5–13
JOHN of Calais
—Mex-Am / West, 99–101
John the Conqueror, see HIGH
JOHN the Conqueror.

Johnny Appleseed, see
APPLESEED, Johnny.
JOHNNY-CAKE
—Williams-Ellis / Tales *
runs away from all but fox, 96–101
JOKE(-s)
—Allison / I'll Tell *
fox and stork; dinner invitations;
victim of joke, 110
—Am Child / Bronner, 113–142
—Bomans / Wily *
Happy Hughie: beheaded, contin-
ues to laugh and tell jokes, 62–
70
—Ghost (S'west) / Young, 27–32
—Humor / Midwest
bibliographic essay, 11–29 @
—Kessler / Turtle Knock * 1–48
—Kessler / Turtle Riddle * 1–48
—Mex-Am / West, 105–111
motif index, 303–304
—Wildlife / Gillespie, 243 (index)
JONAH
—Jewish / Sadeh
desperate man and prophet
Jonah, 154–158
Jones, Gwyn
—Hoke / Giants
giant who had no heart in his
body, 93–102
JOPPA
—Egyptian / Mercatante
taking of, 173–175
Jorinda and Joringel
—Grimm / Complete * 339–342
—Grimm / Sixty * 17–20
Joseph de la Reina
—Jewish / Frankel, 424–427
JOSEPH of Arimathea
—King Arthur / Ashe, 190 (index)
—Lacy / Arth Ency, 305–308
**Joseph (sold into Egypt) and his
brethren**
—Lines / Magical * 149–169

JOURNEY(-s)
—Haboo / Hilbert
    journey to sky and back down to
        earth, 3–5
—Jewish / Frankel, 649 (index)
—Jones / Tales *
    Chicken Licken, 16–20
—Journeys / Norris *
    scatter throughout the land; tribal
        origins, [13–15]
    stories from eight cultures, [1–32]
JOYOUS GARD (castle)
—King Arthur / Senior, 320 (index)
JUAN del Oso
—Mex-Am / West, 101–104
JUDAISM
—Aleichem / Holiday *
    glossary for festivals, 142–145 @
—Man Myth & Magic, 3145 (index)
—Unnatural / Cohen, 146 (index)
JUDGE(-s)
—Chinese / Chin *
    palace plot: rival concubines, 77–
        92
—Dramatized / Kamerman
    baker would charge man for
        smelling bakery, 471–480
    tiger does work of ox he killed,
        32–37
—Fahs / Old *
    stolen drum to dance by, 86–90
—MacDonald / Sourcebook *
    motif index, 649–650
—Turkish (Art I) / Walker
    defendant rewarded for not re-
        vealing judge's philandering,
        168–172
—Vietnam / Terada *
    chess player dies; enters corpse
        of butcher (whose wife?), 75–
        77
JUDGMENT
    see also DIVINE JUDGMENT
—Jewish / Frankel, 649 (index)

    Solomon: the egg and the boiled
        beans, 208–210
JUDGMENT DAY (*judgment of the
    dead*)
—Bomans / Wily *
    storyteller wants to see a gnome
        before he dies, 141–142
—Egyptian / Harris
    judgment by King of the Dead
        (Osiris), 103–107
—High John / Sanfield *
    overhears the Lord and Devil "di-
        viding up souls," 44–49
—Jewish / Sadeh
    merchant buys dead partner's sin
        and guilt, 83–86
    miser-innkeeper tells what hap-
        pened after death, 172–176
—Persian / Hinnells
    Zoroastrian universal judgment,
        68–70
JUMPING TO CONCLUSIONS
—Lester / Brer Rabbit *
    noise in the woods: run! 113–115
Juniper tree, The
—Grimm / Complete * 220–229
—Old Wives / Carter, 183–191
JUNO
—Douglas / Magic *
    Cupid and Psyche, 151–165
—Greek / Osborne
    Callisto and Arcus: Great Bear
        and Little Bear, 41–43
—Roman / Usher, 131 (index)
JUPITER
—Greek / Osborne
    chariot of the sun god, 1–6
    Callisto and Arcus: Great Bear
        and Little Bear, 41–43
    mysterious visitors: Baucis and
        Philemon, 67–70
—Roman / Usher, 131 (index)
—Room / Classical Dict
    by-names (list), 330–335 @

JUST MEN
—Schwartz / Gates, 804 (index)
JUSTICE / (IN-) (*administration of justice*)
see also DIVINE JUSTICE
—Arabian / Lewis
injustice: Ghanim, the slave of love, 35–41
—Bierhorst / Monkey *
bad compadre oft exploits Juan; animals perform his impossible tasks, 94–106
—Cambodian / Carrison
Siva believes eagle's dreams; owl asks equal treatment, 67–72
—Chinese / Chin *
palace plot: cat put in place of baby, 77–92
—Chinese / Christie
Qilin: justice by ordeal, 130–136
—Corrin / Eight-Year *
Atri: ring bell if wrongly dealt with, 75–78
—Dramatized / Kamerman
Olive jar; thief caught, 360–374
Robin Hood outwits the sheriff, 61–78
—Egyptian / Harris
brothers (Lies and Truth personified), false accusation, 84–85
eloquent peasant: Khunanup vs. Nemtynakht, 60–62
—Egyptian / Mercatante
peasant robbed, pleads eloquently for redress, 117–120
—Ghosts / Starkey
ghost reveals deed to estate, 24–29
—Hoke / Giants
injustice: Strong Gottlieb, 103–111
—Jewish / Frankel
rabbi's mirror allows king to see treachery in his bedroom, 405–409
—Jewish / Sadeh
peddler and the woman who lied, 327–328
—Journey Sun (Chinese)
Fanjiangshan secures justice; three episodes, 90–108
—Lurker / Dict Gods, 402 (index)
—Manning / Cats *
Little Wonder; witch-stepmother turns boy into dog, drives his sister out, 65–74
—Turkish (Art I) / Walker
stonecutter: dervish-thieves revealed in court of discernment, 72–80

KABUKI
—Dramatized / Kamerman
Great samurai sword, 306–316
KACHINAS
—American / Read Dgst
supernaturals, 63
—Hopi / Talashoma-Malotki, 203 ff @
Hopi boy and his two pet eagles, 150–199
jealousy: two girls in love with same boy, 118–135
old wizard plots to seduce beautiful girl, 70–91
—Hopi Coyote / Malotki
coyote and the Korowiste kachinas, 195–227, 303, 307 @
KAFKA, Franz (1883–1924)
—Schwartz / Gates, 804 (index)
Kahukura and fairies (fishing with net)
—Maori / Kanawa * 46–50
KALI MA
—Woman's Ency / Walker, 488–494 @

KALMUK TALES
—Clouston / Popular, II.509 (index)
KAMA (Sanskrit)
—Wolkstein / Love, 244 @
Kanawa (chief) visited by Patupaia-rehe (fairies)
—Maori / Kanawa * 62–66
KANGAROO
—Animal Legends / Kerven *
  first human encounter: comes in windstorm, [12–14]
—Birds / Carter & Cartwright *
  Duck and the kangaroo (Lear), 44
—Childcraft 3 / Stories *
  why kangaroo hops on two legs, 83–86
KANNON
—Japanese / Tyler, 336 (index)
KAPPA
—McGowen / Encyclopedia * 32
KARACOR
—Turkish / Walker
  Karacor and the giants, 52–61
KARAKIA (Maori charm)
—Polynesians / Andersen, 486 (index)
KARKADANN
—Unicorn / Hathaway, 52–62 @
KARORA (Bandicoot ancestor)
—Hamilton / In the Beginning *
  creation (imperfect) myth, 46–51
Karr, Phyllis Ann
—Pendragon / Ashley
  The Lady of Belec, 344–353
KARVACHAUTH
—Jaffrey / Seasons
  husband dies when wife breaks taboo, 75–79
KASHMIRI TALES
—Clouston / Popular, II.509 (index)
Katchen the cat
—Manning / Cats * 9–15
KATCHKA
—Manning / Cats *

king loses sight; cure if washed in Katchka's blood, 118–123
Kate Crackernuts
—Fairies / Briggs, 243–245
—Old Wives / Carter, 16–18
—Rockwell / Puss, 19–26 *
KATHA SARIT SAGARA
—Clouston / Popular, II.509 (index)
Kauffman, Reginald Wright
—Hall / Treasury *
  Puss in Boots (in verse), 94–97
KAY, Sir
—Douglas / Magic *
  Merlin and Arthur: the sword, 141–149
Kelea and Kalamakua
—Polynesians / Andersen, 71–92
KELOGLAN
—Turkey / Walker, 304 (index)
—Turkish / Walker
  lazy, bald Keloglan wins sultan's daughter, 20–22
  the twelve dancing princesses, 29–34
—Turkish (Art I) / Walker
  Haci's daughter marries, is repeatedly assaulted, 24–33
KELPIE
—Beasts / McHargue, 54 @
—Ghosts / Starkey
  McGregor and the kelpy, 66–71
Kendall, Carol
—Childcraft 3 / Stories *
  the Living Kuan-yin, 93–99
KENYAN TALE
—Hamilton / Dark *
  Wanjiru: girl swallowed by the earth, 108–112
KETTLE
—Hamilton / Dark *
  Bumbuku, the tanuki magic tea-kettle, 76–81
—Shannon / More *

cock crow in kettle: clean hand
reveals thief, 31–34
KEY(-s)
—Arabian / McCaughrean
Keys of destiny; Iram, 65–82
KHAEMWESE
—Egyptian / Harris, 131 (index)
KHEPRI (Egyptian)
—Wolkstein / Love, 245 @
KHOJA
—Turkey / Walker, 304 (index)
KIDD, Captain (pirate) (1645?-1701)
—Schwartz / Gold, 87–96, 120 @
KIDNAPPED
see also ABDUCTION
—Curry / Beforetime *
mink and bluejay retrieve Little
Weasel, stolen by lizard, 60–67
—Igloo / Metayer
child kidnapped by wolf-men, 73–
77
KI'IN
—Scary / Young *
Ki'in spirits eat souls, take over
bodies, 52–56
KILLING
—Arabian / McCaughrean
little beggar "killed" over and
over, 97–103
—Arabian / Riordan
little beggar . . . [as above], 122–
124
—Bruchac / Iroquois *
snakes make war of revenge, 93–
95
—Hamilton / People *
Big John forces Little John; re-
sults, 81–89
[father of] Beautiful girl of the
moon tower, 53–59
—Wolves / Lopez, 302 (index)
Kimbriel, Katharine Eliska
—Yolen / Werewolves
Night calls, 95–118

KINDNESS (usually rewarded)
see also Golden goose, The
—Aesop / Alley *
lion and the mouse, 16–19
—Aesop / Reeves-Wilson *
mouse frees lion from net, 16–18
—Allison / I'll Tell *
dove saves ant; ant warns dove
of trap, 106
—Animal Legends / Kerven *
rewarded for saving eagle chicks,
[22–23]
—Bomans / Wily *
curse: lock of princess' hair;
king's cruelty to "bird witch,"
165–173
hunter spares deer, swan, raven;
saves man accused of theft,
16–19
—Bruchac / Iroquois *
dogs who saved their master, 85–
91
gifts of the Little People, 41–44
—Celts / Hodges *
Dermot in Land-under-Wave, 57–
73
—Clarkson / World *
gold in chimney; animals help girl
escape witch, 26–29
—Demi / Reflective *
wild bird killed by kindness, [16]
—Douglas / Magic *
Androcles and the lion, 167–175
to bird; Thumbelina, 43–53
—Dramatized / Kamerman
bee rewards King Solomon's
kindness, 250–257
price of eggs, 149–154
rich woman; poor woman, 191–
199
—Dulac / Fairy *
magic pipe makes all dance,
114–123
—Greaves / Hippo *

waterbuck runs into swamp; escapes lion, 91–92
why giraffe and oxpecker are friends, 84–86
—Grimm / Complete *
failing vs. non-failing in feeding animals, 698–704
hospitality: poor man rewarded; rich man punished, 394–398
Queen bee, The, 317–319
white bride and black bride, 608–612
—Grimm / Sixty *
Queen bee, The, 206–208
—Hoke / Giants
giant, no heart in his body, 93–102
—Hopi Coyote / Malotki
coyote and the Korowiste kachinas, 195–227, 303, 307 @
—Igloo / Metayer
forced marriage: huntress, 99–107
—Jewish / Frankel
dim-witted boy buys box of bones (etc., chain tale), 414–418
scorpion in goblet: virtuous rabbi rewarded, 437–446
tramp (Elijah), stranger to be treated kindly, 604–605
—Jewish / Sadeh
fish with golden tail and pearls for eyes, 95–97
—Lang / Wilkins
Charming wins Goldilocks, 31–43
—Lines / Magical *
Raja's son feeds ants; removes thorn from tiger's foot, 56–66
—Old Wives / Carter
little red fish and clog of gold (Cinderella-type), 171–177
—Quayle / Shining *
kind prince heals hare; is chosen by princess, 24–32

—Rockwell / Puss *
cat (white bear) on the dovrefell, 71–79
unkindness punished: Dummling: The Golden Goose, 30–39
—Russian Hero / Warner *
little simpleton: silver saucer and juicy apple, 106–108
Morozko the frost demon, and his bride, 33–37
—Shah / Central Asia
charcoal burner and enchanted bear, 92–102
—Spring / Philip
golden fish rewards kindness, 103–113
—Trolls / Asbjornsen
stepsisters: one kind, one cruel; brush, cow, ram, appletree, 42–50
—Turkish (Art I) / Walker
kind girl rewarded with chest of jewels, 46–51
shoemaker saves snake; later, executioner-snake returns favor, 178
—Unicorn / Coville *
Unicorn in the maze (Lindholm), 7–22
—Vanishing / Mercer *
quest for wife abducted by giant bird, 42–49
—Water Buffalo (Chinese)
innkeeper steals magic donkey, table cloth, stick, 103–110
—Wilde / Lynch *
selfish giant: always winter, children not allowed in garden, 6–13
—Williams-Ellis / Tales *
Baba Yaga; Marusia's escape, 113–124
—Witches / Iosa *

animals help kind children escape giant witch, 18–22
Old witch (Jacobs); kind girl and her selfish sister, 34–39
—Yep / Rainbow *
butterfly man, 60–68
pet white mouse, 80–85
we are all one, 72–78
—Yolen / Shape, 78–96
KING(-s)
—Arabian / Lewis
commoner (more generous) made king, 81–90
holy man sent to make king aware of his gifts, 184–87
king trades daughter for flying ebony horse, 106–116
king's quest: secure seventh diamond girl, 144–152
merman trades jewels for fruit, 131–137
Moorish sorcerer claims prince, 60–64
test for succession: prince marries tortoise, 43–51
treachery: good barber and evil dyer, 123–130
well's magic objects do "impossible" tasks, 117–122
—Arabian / McCaughrean
holy man . . . [as above], 208–217
king trades . . . [as above], 225–242
merman . . . [as above], 83–96
Moorish . . . [as above], 133–141
test for succession . . . [as above], 142–149
—Arabian / Riordan
king trades . . . [as above], 56–65
porter's tale: king's son and lover buried alive, 112–116
—Babylonia / Spence, 397 (index)
—Bomans / Wily *
balloon message; with god-mother's help, knight kills dragon, 197–202
cobbler's three wishes from gnome; learns money's limitations, 53–61
curse: lock of princess' hair; cruelty to "bird witch," 165–173
echo well: misshapen people not aware of defects, 97–100
king, devoted to his mother, does not want to die, 118–120
king totally bored; has all, = nothing; learns work, 101–103
naked soul of King Pim, 121–125
Princess Steppie and King Boruba's rigid "principles," 20–27
satire: twelfth king (has hollow [brainless] head), 185–192
soldier's wager with king; traps ghost; becomes king, 37–43
in undershirt, sans regalia, a common man, 155–157
—Cambodian / Carrison
King Bimbisara: punishment for treacherous prince, 73–76
lost, king tells child how to recognize a king, 86–89
—Campbell / West Highlands
King of Lochlin's three daughters, I.244–258
—Carle / Treasury *
evil king (Andersen), 147–152
—Celts / Hodges *
Merlin: life and magic powers, 117–132
—Clouston / Popular
advantages of speaking to a king, II.360–366
king's favorite envied and plotted against, II.444–457
king's life saved by maxim, II.317–321, 491–493
—Corrin / Imagine *

Black Thief: quest for King
Conal's horses, 97–111
—Crane / Beauty *
Yellow Dwarf, Fairy of the Desert,
and proud princess, [34–47]
—Crossley / Animal (Grimm) *
Hedge-king [choosing king of
birds], 15–20
—Douglas / Magic *
Thumbelina; king of little people,
43–53
white cat (enchanted princess),
69–83
—Dramatized / Kamerman
avoid tax: appear half-witted
(Gotham), 88–97
happy adults: children at wishing
well, 15–22
intelligence and luck; make prin-
cess speak, 47–60
a most special dragon, 79–87
Simple Olaf becomes advisor,
413–421
—Fahs / Old *
two kings dispute over land, 101–
103
—Fairies / Briggs
King Herla, 247–249
King Orfeo, 249–251
young king of Esaidh Ruadh,
356–359
—Frog Rider (Chinese)
magic brush: things painted become real, 47–59
—Ghosts / Cohen, 22–29
—Gods / Schwab
King Oedipus, 230–250
—Gray / Near East
Canaan, 92–105
Mesopotamian myths, 53–63
—Greek / Osborne
birds: King Ceyx and Alcyone,
13–16
—Grimm / Complete *

blue light summons tiny servant,
530–534
devil with the three golden hairs,
151–158
girl without hands; goodness
wins over devil, 160–166
peasant's wise daughter, 439–
440
queen dies; king would marry
their daughter, 326–331
success through magic knapsack, hat, horn, 258–264
willow-wren: contest to select
king of birds, 705–708
—Grimm / Legends (Ward), II:422 (index)
—Grimm / Sixty *
blue light summons tiny servant,
244–249
—Hamilton / People *
Manuel's riddle; fills sack with
lies; fortune, 65–75
—Hathaway / Unicorn
King Charles VI, of France, 101–
107
—Imaginary / Nigg
golden peacock befriends captor,
97–99
—Jaffrey / Seasons
birth of Krishna: wicked king Kans
tries to kill him, 22–25
how Ram, son of Dashrat, defeated demon king Ravan, 48–
69
king beaten with magic stick for
taking magic bowl from old
man, 103–109
king Kans sends demon-nurse to
kill Krishna, 22–25
king's wife lies about eating barley; says it's pearls, 115–119
Krishna defeats elephant and two
giants; kills Kans, 32–36
—Jewish / Frankel

angry king: daughter taken captive because of his curse, 531–536

pursuit of gazelle; "sixty days" [really one hour] learning common life, 410–414

—Jewish / Sadeh

Abraham ben Ezra and the bishop, 220–221

daughter wiser than her father, 289–291

fish with golden tail and pearls for eyes, 95–97

fly and spider; incense: knowledge and understanding, 389–392

king and forty crows; dream, 31–34

king who couldn't sleep, 208–210

king's horn: secrets can't be kept forever, 323–324

makes impossible demands on Jews; taught lesson, 239–241

master thief, 291–295

pious thief saves king's life, 262–263

poor man and thieving ministers, 264–266

princess who refused to talk, 106–111

riddle; mother sells son for human sacrifice, 330–331

tailor and Haman: "years" really only fifteen minutes, 201–204

—King Arthur / Senior

King Mark of Cornwall, 320 (index)

King Pelles, 320 (index)

—Lang / Wilkins

King Loc's children captured by fairies, 441–459

Little good mouse (fairy helps imprisoned queen), 116–127

Rubezahl: gnome captures princess; she escapes, 497–512

Sylvain and Jocosa (has yellow bird cooked), 178–185

—Legends / Cavendish

dragon kings (Iran), 130–132

ideal king, 394 (index)

King Duttabaung, 68–70

pious king, 395 (index)

wise king, 394 (index)

—Lewis / Proud

King Equitan, seducer; dies in boiling bathwater, 82–87

—Lines / Magical *

magic apple of contentment: only true owner can pick, 15–23

—Lore of Love

curse causes husband to forget wife, 26–31

King Nala and Princess Damayanti, 110–119

—Man Myth & Magic, 3147 (index)

—Manning / Cats *

kind witch raises foundling to be knight; bewitched Cat-Johann his aide, 111–117

king loses sight; cure if washed in Katchka's blood, 118–123

witch abducts king's two children; Katchen the cat helps escape, 9–15

—Nesbit / Fairy *

Billy the King [hired to be eaten by dragon], 1–22

Charmed life, or Princess and Lift-man, 25–42

—Nielsen / Old Tales *

blue belt (Arabia; boy succeeds in winning princess), [37–62]

widow's son (made ugly) joins staff, [16–36]

—O'Brien / Tales *

Hookedy Crookedy: to serve king, transformed as knight,

marries king's daughter, 53–71

Lord Mount Dhraggin: weaver "kills" three-score and ten; made Lord, 72–81

swan bride: king's son's quest for Scolog's daughter, 82–95

—Persian / Hinnells
Persian, 98–109, 143 (index)

—Reeves / Shadow
husband becomes werewolf "Garwal"; king tames, 99–110

—Roman / Usher
King Numa, 93–95 @

—Scriven / Full Color *
Brian Boru: how to catch a leprechaun, 85–87

—Shah / Central Asia
bead-seller and the jinn's sister, 62–68

—Shannon / More *
never seen, never heard: king vs. Aesop, 35–38

—Spring / Philip
king "never heard of this before," 134–139

—Tibet / Timpanelli *
takes jewel of "girl who was already queen," 43–51

—Tree / Kerven *
abducts beautiful bride (thorn tree) of poor man, [16–19]

—Trolls / Asbjornsen
Askelad and the silverducks, 11–16

Rumble-Mumble Goose-Egg, 71–82

—Turkish / Walker
Muslim preacher sells wisdom to king, 37–42

—Unicorn / Coville *
king would own unicorns; princess: they must be free, 24–37

—Vietnam / Terada *

Tam kills stepsister Cam; takes her place as king's wife, 23–34

—Water Buffalo (Chinese)
arrogant fox pretends to be king, 36–38

—Wilde / Lynch *
young king dreams: the poor suffer to provide grandeur, 73–94

—Williams-Ellis / Tales *
King O'Toole's goose made young by St. Kevin, 37–43

mice repel invaders of kingdom, 45–54

Tom-Tit-Tot spins skeins for girl, 185–195

—Witches / Iosa *
brothers envious of Pinkel's favor with king, 23–31

—Yolen / Faery Flag
confined; questions "tower bird" re kingdom, 82–84

—Zipes / Beauties *
king sends to Beauty with the golden hair (d'Aulnoy) * 309–320

Ram [a King Lear type, by d'Aulnoy], 389–399

KING(-s) and QUEEN(-s)
see also QUEEN(-s)

—Crane / McLean *
Princess Belle-Etoile; evil Queen, 16–27

—Dramatized / Kamerman
King Horn; chamberlain deceives queen, 447–457

Quick-witted Jack; suitor test, 400–412

—Jewish / Sadeh
demons: prince who went off on his own, 101–105

nightingale and shroud wearers; queen gives birth to animals, 25–28

—Lang / Wilkins

Charming wins Goldilocks, 31–43

Lute player: wife rescues husband from prison, 528–533

—Yolen / Faery Flag

face in the cloth; princess and witches, 87–100

—Zipes / Beauties *

little mouse (fairy; story by d'Aulnoy) * 350–361

King Arthur, see ARTHUR, King.

King Grisly-beard (Grimm)

—Corrin / Six-Year * 146–150

—Scriven / Full Color * 89–92

KING, Katie

—Ghosts / Cohen, 22–29

King of the golden mountain

—Grimm / Complete * 425–430

—Grimm / Sixty * 274–280

King of the Golden River (Ruskin)

—Victorian / Hearn, 3–23

King Thrushbeard

—Grimm / Complete * 244–248

—Grimm / Sixty * 312–316

KINGDOM(s)

—Russian / Afanasev, 659 (index)

King's man: Merlin and Niniane (Miller)

—Pendragon / Ashley, 78–88

King's son who feared nothing (Grimm)

—Grimm / Complete * 545–550

KINGSHIP

—Carle / Treasury *

chosen king; foolishly falls into trap (Aesop), 40–41

—MacCana / Celtic

sacral kingship, 114–121

—Philip / Spring

woman chosen to be "king" "marries" her husband, 58–74

KINSMEN

—Scary / Young *

Ki'in spirits eat souls, take over bodies; boy outwits Ki'in, 52–56

Kipling, Rudyard (1865–1936)

—Childcraft 1 / Once *

how camel got hump, 268–271

—Corrin / Eight-Year *

Rikki-Tikki-Tavi, 173–191

—Lynn / Fantasy *

bibliography (about the author), 519–521

KISMET

—Turkey / Walker, 304 (index)

KISS

—Corrin / Eight-Year *

Sir Gawaine and the Green Knight, 161–172

—Douglas / Magic *

disenchantment: Sleeping Beauty, 55–61

—Riordan / Arabian

Safia's tale: merchant bites her; husband beats her, 119–122

—Turkey / Walker, 304 (index)

KITE

—Bomans / Wily *

children escape from witch with help of top, kite, doll, 88–93

—Nesbit / Fairy *

Billy and cousin: kite/bicycle, 45–56

KIVA

—Gullible Coyote / Malotki, 166 @

—Hopi / Talashoma-Malotki, 204 @

—Hopi Coyote / Malotki, 305 @

Knapsack, hat, and horn

—Grimm / Complete * 258–264

KNIFE (magic)

—Igloo / Metayer

forced marriage: The huntress, 99–107

KNIGHT(-s)

see also ARTHURIAN ROMANCES

—Bomans / Wily *

balloon message; with godmother's help, knight kills
dragon, 197–202
—Campbell / West Highlands
Knight of the Red Shield, II.451–
493
—Corrin / Eight-Year *
Sir Gawaine and the Green
Knight, 161–172
—Grimm / Legends (Ward), II:423 (index)
—Hathaway / Unicorn
Knight of the Lion / Lady of the
Unicorn, 88–99 @
—Knights / Heller-Headon, 1–190
armor, 86–87
characterization, 90–91
courtly love, 136–137
dubbings, 58–59
feasting, 104–105
helmets, 84–85
horse in armor, 88–89
initiation of squires, 54–55
pages and, 38–39
tournaments, 120–121
weapons, 122–123
—Lang / Wilkins
queen poisons stepdaughter's
suitor (Kristensen), 460–473
—Lewis / Proud
Eliduc: knight unfaithful; wife enters convent, 88–100
Lanval boasts; Queen Guinivere
accuses, 26–47
Le Fresne: abandoned twin
"found" at sister's wedding,
20–28
lovers' nightingale (Laustic) killed
by cruel husband, 61–64
Milun/lover wait 20 years to be
wed, 65–75
Yonec: lover killed by jealous
husband's trap, 53–60
—Lore of Love

cursed embrace: Liba and Guntram, 32–35
Sir Eglamour and Lady Chrystobel, 128–139
—Manning / Cats *
kind witch raises foundling to be
knight; bewitched Cat-Johann
his aide, 111–117
—O'Brien / Tales *
Hookedy Crookedy: to serve
king, transformed as knight,
marries king's daughter, 53–71
—Pendragon / Ashley
midnight, moonlight, and secret
of the sea (Schweitzer), 385–
401
—Reeves / Shadow
nightingale: cruel husband;
young wife loves bachelor/
neighbor, 87–95
—Russian Hero / Warner *
Alesha (priest's son) battles Tu-
garin, 72–76
Il'ya saves city; captures Nightin-
gale (monster), 76–80
—Williams-Ellis / Tales *
Tamlane (enchanted) rescued
from elfland, 151–159
**Knight with the two swords, The
(Steinbeck)**
—Pendragon / Ashley, 49–69
KNIGHTS TEMPLAR
—Knights / Heller-Headon, 172–173
KNOCKERS
—Fairies / Briggs, 254–256
KNOCK-KNOCK JOKES
—Kessler / Turtle Knock * 1–48
Knoist and his three sons
—Grimm / Complete * 622
KNOTS
—Witch Encyc / Guiley, 415 (index)
KNOWLEDGE
—Bruchac / Iroquois *
gifts of the Little People, 41–44

—Clouston / Popular
   lucky imposter: pretends to know
   secrets, II.413–431
—Demi / Reflective *
   non-knowledge results in error,
   [2]
   river god/ocean god: exhalted image deflated, [26]
—Fahs / Old *
   hoarded by tortoise, shared with
   all, 29–31
—Grimm / Sixty *
   accidental; Doctor Know-All,
   281–283
—High John / Sanfield *
   eavesdrops on Master; pretends
   foreknowledge of his plans,
   24–33
—Jewish / Sadeh
   king and forty crows; dream, 31–
   34
—Philip / Spring
   dragon seen by unprotected
   men, 119–133
KNOWLEDGE, MAGIC
—Arabian / McCaughrean
   Keys of destiny; Iram, 65–82
—Jewish / Frankel
   Rabbi's mirror allows king to see
   treachery in his bedroom, 405–
   409
—Lang / Wilkins
   Dragon of the North, 285–297
—Lines / Magical *
   Cormac Mac Art: magic cup
   breaks when lie is told, 141–
   149
—Scriven / Full Color *
   Ali Baba and the forty thieves,
   20–25
—Turkish (Art I) / Walker
   death, if shepherd does not keep
   secret his knowing language of
   animals, 190–194

—Vietnam / Terada *
   Da Trang crab: grateful snake
   gives magic pearl, 37–41
KNUCKLEBONE
—Manning / Cats *
   Altin's golden knucklebone, water
   cat, and stallion, 29–36
KOALAS
—Animal Legends / Kerven *
   magic song: koalas created by
   boy's transformation, [6–7]
KOLUSCAP
—Caduto / Keepers *
   turns Water Monster into bullfrog,
   81–84
KONO PEOPLE
—Hamilton / In the Beginning
   Death (Sa) the Creator, 14–19
Koon, Helene
—Kamerman / Dramatized
   Pierre Patelin, 128–148
KOREAN TALE(-s)
—Fahs / Old *
   girl chooses death over unfaith-
   fulness, 44–51
—Kamerman / Dramatized
   Spouse for Susie Mouse, 317–323
Koropanga and Rukutia
—Polynesians / Andersen, 45–70
**Koshalki-Opalki (how simpleton
   became king)**
—Clarkson / World * 19–22
KRAKEN
—Beasts / McHargue, 91–92 @
—McGowen / Encyclopedia * 33
—Monsters / Cohen, 163–169 @
KRISHNA
—Fahs / Old *
   Krishna helps good king win over
   evil, 108–113
—Indic / Ions, 143 (index)
—Jaffrey / Seasons
   birth of Krishna: wicked king Kans
   tries to kill him, 22–25

Krishna defeats evil five-headed serpent-king, 30–31

wrestling, Krishna defeats elephant and two giants; kills King Kans, 32–36

Kristensen, Evald Tang
—Lang / Wilkins
The Green Knight, 460–473

KRONOS (Greek god)
—Cotterell / Encyclopedia, 255 (index)
—Hamilton / In the Beginning, 128–131, 137

KUMARA
—Polynesians / Andersen, 488 (index)

Kunz and his shepherd
—Clarkson / World * 81–83

KUPE
—Maori / Kanawa *
discovery of Aotearoa, 28–34

Kuttner, Henry
—Pirate Ghosts / McSherry
Before I wake . . . , 182–200

KUT-TOE-YIS
—Bullchild / Sun
Bloodclot tales, 229–266

LABICHE, Emmeline
—American / Read Dgst, 52–53

LABOR(-ers)
see also WAGES; WORK
—Yep / Rainbow *
Virtue goes to town, 118–123

Laden ass and a horse
—Aesop / Holder, 10–13

Lady and the lion
—Grimm / Complete * 398–404
—Grimm / Sixty * 235–240

Lady in Blue
—Ghost (S'west) / Young
Maria de Agreda, 116–117

Lady of Belec, The (Karr)
—Pendragon / Ashley, 344–353

LADY OF THE LAKE
—Bomans / Wily *
spoiled prince loved/saved by young girl, 9–16
—Fairies / Briggs, 257, 349

LAFITTE, Jean (1780?-1826?)
—Pirate Ghosts / McSherry
blue spectacles: user not wholly good, 73–83

LaForce, Charlotte-Rose Caumont de
—Zipes / Beauties *
The good woman, 103–118

LAIDERONNETTE
—Dulac / Fairy *
green serpent: one twin princess cursed, ugly, 124–138

LAIDLY WORM
—Dragons / Baskin * [22–23]

LAKE
—Grimm / Legends (Ward), II:424 (index)

LAKE TE ANAU
—Maori / Kanawa *
taboo; woman looks into spring; drowns village, 85–86

LAKSHMI
—Jaffrey / Seasons
goddess of good fortune, can find only washerwoman, 81–84
—Wolkstein / Love, 245 @

LAMAISM
—Dictionary / Leach, 1215 (index)

LAMB
—Animals / Rowland, 186 (index)
—Grimm / Complete *
lambkin and the little fish, 625–627
—Hamilton / Dark *
free spirits: Bouki and Malice, 102–107

Lambkin and the little fish
—Grimm / Complete * 625–627

LAMBTON WORM
—Crossley / British FT * 339–346
—McGowen / Encyclopedia * 34
LAMIA
—Fairies / Briggs, 260–262
Lamp, see Aladdin . . .
LANCELOT, Sir (Lancelot du Lake)
    see also ARTHURIAN RO-
    MANCES
—Celts / Hodges *
    Arthur's last battle, 157–169
—King Arthur / Senior, 320 (index)
—Knights / Gross *
    Lancelot and the Round Table,
    26–40
—Knights / Heller-Headon, 138–151
—Lacy / Arth Ency, 323–329
LAND
—Grimm / Legends (Ward), II:424 (in-
    dex)
LAND OF JOY
—Zipes / Beauties *
    little mouse (fairy; story by
    d'Aulnoy), 350–361
LAND OF NO RETURN
—Lester / Leopard *
    healing leaves for blind king, 59–
    68
LAND OF SOULS
—Lang / Wilkins
    Indian goes to lowerworld for
    dead bride, 282–284
Land of the dead, see UNDER-
    WORLD.
LANDLORD
—Yep / Rainbow *
    wizard: The rainbow people,
    162–168
LANDMARK
—Vanishing / Mercer *
    origin of Rangitoto channel rock,
    32–33
LANGUAGE(-s)
    see also INDIAN LANGUAGES

—Babylonia / Spence, 398 (index)
—Curry / Beforetime *
    newly-made people given laugh-
    ter, movement, language,
    food, 116–120
—Mesoamerican / Leon-P, 290 (in-
    dex)
LANKA
—Jaffrey / Seasons
    how Ram, son of Dashrat, de-
    feated demon king Ravan, 48–
    69
LAOTIAN TALE
—Scary / Young *
    tiger's eyes: it eats man, puts on
    his clothes, eats wife, 73–77
LAPIS-LAZULI
—Precious Stones / Kunz, 400 (in-
    dex)
LAPLAND
—Dictionary / Leach, 1215 (index)
LAPPS
—Yolen / Shape Shift
    The sailor-boy's tale / I. Dinesen,
    52–60
Large person, see SIZE.
LAST WISHES (father's)
—Dulac / Fairy *
    suitor test: Ivan and the chestnut
    horse, 60–68
LATIN MYTH
—Preston / Dict Classical
    classical subjects in visual art,
    1–311 @
LAUGH(-ing; -ter)
—Bomans / Wily *
    Happy Hughie: how laughwort
    began; can't kill happiness,
    62–70
—Corrin / Imagine *
    taboo: Caliph and Vizier into
    storks; forget magic word; mar-
    riage to (enchanted) owl, 164–
    76

—Corrin / Six-Year *
dragon; magic bag makes all who
sniff it, laugh, 53–58
—Curry / Beforetime *
newly-made people given laugh-
ter, movement, language,
food, 116–120
—High John / Sanfield *
freedom, on bet he can make
mean Master laugh, 73–78
LAUGHWORT
—Bomans / Wily *
Happy Hughie: how laughwort
began; can't kill happiness,
62–70
LAUNDRY
—Lester / Brer Rabbit *
"battling clothes," 4–6
Launfal: secret love for Rosamund
—Reeves / Shadow, 49–83
LAVAINE, Sir
—King Arthur / Senior, 320 (index)
LAW
see also CLEVER DETECTION
. . . ; CLEVER LAW . . . ;
CLEVER JUDICIAL . . . ;
CLEVER MEANS . . .
—Schwartz / Gates, 805 (index)
LAW COURTS
—Dramatized / Kamerman
tiger does work of ox he killed,
32–37
LAWYER
—Dramatized / Kamerman
client told to say "baa" to all; (his
fee!), 128–148
—Jewish / Sadeh
young man and princess/lawyer,
277–279
LAY(-s)
—Campbell / West Highlands, IV.436
(index)
Layla and Majnun
—Wolkstein / Love, 147–180, 266 @

LAZY(-iness)
see also Mother Hulda
—Aesop / Reeves-Wilson *
wolf in sheep's clothing, 20–21
—Bierhorst / Monkey *
youngest son, Tup, gets ants to
clear/plant/harvest cornfield,
44–51
—Bruchac / Iroquois *
hunting of the Great Bear (Big
Dipper), 189–195
—Childcraft 1 / Once *
punished; the little red hen, 98–
99
—Corrin / Imagine *
Onsongo, lazy artist, steals
Masai cattle for dowry, 80–96
—Fahs / Old *
Niyak, Umak, and the eagle, 71–
80
—Ghosts / Starkey
Jack Mackintosh: Treasure ghost
of Fife, 88–95
—Grimm / Complete *
lazy Harry weds fat Trina, 678–
681
Mother Hulda; lazy sister, 133–
136
three sluggards, 647
twelve idle servants, 648–650
—Grimm / Sixty *
Mother Hulda; lazy sister, 111–
115
—Igloo / Metayer
The lazy son-in-law, 112–117
—Indian Myth / Burland
boy with supernatural strength,
49–50
—Jewish / Frankel
cicada and the ant (fable), 463
—Leonardo / Fables *
razor: escapes, loafs, rusts, 54
—MacDonald / Sourcebook *
motif index, 655

—Old Wives / Carter
  with their own hands, dig hole in
  which they fall, 220
—Turkish / Walker
  lazy, bald Keloglan wins sultan's
  daughter, 20–22
Lazy Harry
—Grimm / Complete * 678–681
Lazy Jack
—Clarkson / World * 351–352
Lazy spinner, The
—Grimm / Complete * 577–579
LEADER(-s)
—Aesop / Reeves-Wilson *
  mice and weasels fight for leader-
  ship, 30–31
Lean Lisa
—Grimm / Complete * 696–698
Lear, Edward (1812–1888)
  see also Owl and the pussycat,
  The
—Birds / Carter & Cartwright *
  Duck and the kangaroo, The, 44
  Pelican chorus, The, 10–11
LEARN (by experience, etc.)
  see also WISDOM
—Allison / I'll Tell *
  lion, fox, ass: dividing spoils
  "equally," 116
—Coyote / Bierhorst *
  ocean advises coyote to become
  merchant; ship's cargo lost; in-
  jury, [38]
—Curry / Beforetime *
  coyote rides sun (why his back
  and tail are dark), 100–106
—Demi / Reflective *
  lifetime venture: the phoenix, [12]
—Hamilton / People *
  Bruh Alligator meets trouble, 35–
  41
—Jewish / Frankel
  Elijah, three sons, three wishes,
  587–588

LEAVES
—Grimm / Complete *
  snake-leaves revive treacherous
  wife, 94–96
—Jewish / Sadeh
  lovesickness: leaves from Para-
  dise, 365–367
—Lester / Leopard *
  healing leaves for blind king, 59–
  68
LEGEND(-s)
  see also INDIAN LEGENDS
—Bosma / Classroom
  study and teaching (elementary),
  1–116
—Bruchac / Iroquois *
  origin: voice from standing rock
  (Hahskwahot), 12–13
—Cotterell / Encyclopedia, 1–260 @
—Ghosts / Cohen, 265–304
—Mercatante / Encyclopedia, 1–
  807 @
  definition, xvii @
—Schwartz / Gates, 805 (index)
LeGuin, Ursula K.
—Childcraft 3 / Stories *
  Duny: boy who became a wizard,
  176–186
LEMURIANS
—Floyd / Gr Am Myst
  mystic village, 39–42
L'Engle, Madeleine
—Unicorn / Coville *
  Valley of the unicorns [excerpt],
  41–60
LEONARDO da Vinci (1452–1519)
—Leonardo / Fables * 8–14 @
LEOPARD(-s)
—Animals / Rowland, 186 (index)
—Greaves / Hippo * 27 @
  baboon tricks/escapes leopard,
  79–80
  hare kills leopard's cubs; blames
  men, 22–26

why leopard hides his food in tree, 26
—Lester / Leopard *
contest: how many spots does leopard have? 53–57
why monkeys live in trees; eat pepper, 41–44

LEPRECHAUN(-s)
—Dramatized / Kamerman
bridge to Killybog Fair, 227–238
leprechaun shoemakers, 239–249
—Fairies / Briggs
poem by William Allingham, 264–266
—Lynn / Fantasy * 761 (index)
—McGowen / Encyclopedia * 35
—O'Brien / Tales *
catch, keep fairy-cobbler; can lead to gold; tricked with red garter, 17–20
—Scriven / Full Color *
how to catch a leprechaun, 85–87

Le Prince de Beaumont, Marie (1711–1780)
—Carter / Sleeping *
Madame Sweetheart, 113–124
—Zipes / Beauties *
Beauty and the beast, 233–245
Prince Desir and Princess Mignone, 233–245

LESHII (*or Leshy; spirit of forest*)
—McGowen / Encyclopedia * 36
—Russian / Ivanits, 248 (index)
—Russian Hero / Warner * 24–25 @

LETTUCE
—Lester / Brer Rabbit *
lettuce patch; Mr. Man's daughter, 78–81

Leuser, Eleanor D. (author)
—Dramatized / Kamerman
The magic grapes, 258–264
Secret of the wishing well, 15–22

The wise people of Gotham, 88–97

LEVIATHAN
—Beasts / McHargue, 117 (index)
—Dragons / Baskin * [6–7]
—Jewish / Frankel
cast your bread upon the waters, 385–387
fox escapes from Angel of Death, and Leviathan's fish, 11–14

LEVITATION
—Fairies / Briggs, 148–150

LEWIS, C.S. (1898–1963)
—Lynn / Fantasy *
bibliography (about the author), 535–543
—Unicorn / Coville *
What news the eagle brought [excerpt], 105–117

L'Heritier, Marie-Jeanne
—Zipes / Beauties *
The discreet princess, 77–94

LIABILITY
—Geras / Grandmother *
fault (scratch on diamond) made into asset, 41–48

LIAR(-s; lie; lying)
see also ACCUSATION; DECEPTION; TALL TALES
—Aesop / Alley *
Shepherd boy and the wolf, 4–9
—Aesop / Reeves-Wilson *
"Wolf! Wolf!" [loss of credibility] 59–60
—Aesop / Zwerger
Shepherd's boy and the wolf [cry "wolf"], 9
—Allison / I'll Tell *
boy who cried wolf, 105
—Coyote / Bierhorst *
doc always says "you're doing fine," [30]
—Crossley / Animal (Grimm) *
cat/mouse partnership, 21–25

—Egyptian / Harris
  brothers (Lies and Truth person-
    ified), false accusation, 84–
    85
—Ghosts / Starkey
  Dauntless girl; ghost reveals
    treasure, 72–79
—Hamilton / People *
  Manuel's riddle; fills sack with
    lies; fortune, 65–75
—Igloo / Metayer
  the lazy son-in-law, 112–117
—Jaffrey / Seasons
  Parvati provides palace to cover
    Queen's well-intentioned lie,
    115–119
—Leonardo / Fables *
  the tongue and the teeth, 40
—Lines / Magical *
  Cormac Mac Art: magic cup
    breaks when lie is told, 141–
    149
—Mex-Am / West
  jokes; motif index, 304
—Paxton / Aesop *
  boy who cried wolf, [33–35]
—Spanish-Am / Van Etten *
  owl wishes: to lie to a witch
    means death, 48–49
—Tibet / Timpanelli *
  evil helper takes real daughter's
    place, 15–27
—Trolls / Asbjornsen
  Askelad and the silverducks, 11–
    16
—Turkey / Walker, 305 (index)
LIBAN
—Fairies / Briggs, 266–267
Liber de Donis
—Clouston / Popular, II.509 (index)
LIBERATION
—Chinese / Chin *
  finding wife for cruel River God,
    17–26

LIBERTY
  see also FREEDOM
—Carle / Treasury *
  wolf and dog: rather be hungry
    than a slave (Aesop), 104–105
—Leonardo / Fables *
  goldfinch: rather death than loss
    of liberty, 24–25
  thrushes and the owl, 110–111
LIBRARY
—Egyptian / Mercatante
  goddess: Sefkhet-Aabut, 140
—Nesbit / Fairy *
  town in the library, 81–98
Lie, see LIAR . . .
LIFE (life events; living)
  see also CONDUCT OF LIFE;
    SOUL; WATER of LIFE
—Bomans / Wily *
  Anita: little maybug desires hap-
    piness, 83–86
  Anna: mayfly born, weds, begets,
    grows old—all in one day, 43–
    46
  Frederica: hen learns life cycles:
    love, birth, 86–87
—Clouston / Popular
  depending on extraneous object,
    I.347–351 @
  king's life saved by maxim,
    II.317–321, 491–493
  tokens, I.170
—Crossley / Dead *
  green mist: girl lives only until
    cowslip dies, 39–43
—Grimm / Complete *
  formula for human duration: add
    dog, ass, monkey expectan-
    cies, 716–718
—Hamilton / In the Beginning *
  Lowa: creation myth, 104–109
—Hamilton / Dark
  life sign * 136 @
—Hamilton / People *

suitor must find/kill; in egg, inside
hog, 53–59
—Jewish / Frankel
Elijah: gift of seven years of prosperity, 585–586
lion, man, pit, and snake (fable),
466–467
—Jewish / Sadeh
king for a year (then banished to
desert isle), 379–381
—Leete / Golden *
shortness/quality: the Little fir
tree, 80–93
—Old Wives / Carter
blubber boy: chunk of blubber animated by being rubbed
against genitals, 31–32
—Turkey / Walker
dependent on external object,
305 (index)
token, 305 (index)
LIFE-RESTORED
—Baring-Gould / Curious
swan maidens: hearts of seven
Samoyeds, 140–144
—Bierhorst / Monkey *
giant marries abandoned girl,
"kills" her brother, 92–93
—Bierhorst / Naked *
Animal-Foot kills sorcerer, 24–
30
mother of ghosts, 37–43
quilt of men's eyes, 101–109
—Erdoes / Sound *
Rabbit Boy (good) vs. Iktome
(evil), 98–102
stone-boy, his mother, his ten lost
uncles, 108–116
—Grimm / Complete *
Brother Lustig and St. Peter,
367–377
snake-leaves revive treacherous
wife, 94–96
—Hopi / Talashoma-Malotki

grandmother frozen, thaws, lives
again, 42–49
grandmother shot through heart
(accident), 42–49
hide and seek with life at stake,
50–69
old wizard plots to seduce beautiful girl, 70–91
—Jewish / Frankel
scorpion in goblet: virtuous rabbi
rewarded, 437–446
vengeful widow: bride brought
back to life, 484–485
—Jewish / Sadeh
errant soul, 384–385
woman whose husband disap-
peared, 81–83
—Journeys / Norris *
hell: prayers of good person
make evils disappear, [26–
28]
—Lang / Wilkins
Water of life (brothers fail; sister
succeeds), 362–368
—O'Brien / Tales *
Amada defeats giants (who daily
return to life), and series of
monsters, 21–30
—Russian Hero / Warner *
little simpleton: silver saucer and
juicy apple, 106–108
wolf helps quest; warnings ignored, 112–116
—Williams-Ellis / Tales *
Childe Rowland rescues Burd Ellen from Elfland, 24–36
LIFE, SHORTNESS OF
—Jewish / Frankel
Solomon visits deserted palace;
learns "vanities," 251–254
LIGHT
—Schwartz / Gates, 805 (index)
LIGHT (fire)
—Russian Hero / Warner *

magic doll helps Vasilisa escape
   Baba-Yaga, 86–92
LIGHTNING
—Bell / Classical Dict, 149–151 @
—Bierhorst / Monkey *
   with Lightning's help, animals find
      fox's corn supply, 52–55
—Bruchac / Iroquois *
   wife of Thunderer, 146–154
—Davy Crockett / Dewey * 38–39
—Earthmaker / Mayo *
   how thunder and lightning came
      (Puget Sound tale), 34–36
   origins, 33 @
—Indian Myth / Burland
   earth and sky spirits, 69–71
—Plants / Dyer, 41–54
—Russian / Ivanits, 248 (index)
—Sioux / Standing Bear *
   Thunder Horse leaves hoofprint
      in rock, 75–76
—Vanishing / Mercer *
   pygmies help Lightning (personi-
      fied) kill marauding elephants,
      71–73
LILITH
—Davidson / Dictionary, 174, 351
—Schwartz / Gates, 805 (index)
LIMERICKS
—Giant / Harrison * 6, 18, 32, 44
**Lin maiden (ghost) guides lost sea-
   men to safety**
—Earth / Hadley * [27–28]
LINCOLN, Abraham (1809–1865)
—American / Read Dgst, 282–286,
   441 (index)
—Ghosts / Cohen, 7–11
Lindholm, Gegan
—Unicorn / Coville *
   Unicorn in the maze, 7–22
LION(-s)
—Aesop / Alley *
   Lion and the mouse, 16–19
—Aesop / Reeves-Wilson *

cunning: King Lion is ill, 105–
   107
—Allison / I'll Tell *
   Androcles and lion (with thorn in
      paw), 119
   lion, fox, ass: dividing spoils
      "equally," 116
   mercy repaid: mouse rescues
      lion, 115
—Animals / Rowland, 187 (index)
—Arabian / McCaughrean
   animals tell lion of man's cruelty,
      51–57
—Bell / Classical Dict, 151–152 @
—Bryan / Lion *
   lion steals ostrich chicks, 3–23
—Chorao / Child's *
   hare repeatedly tricks lion, 43–49
—Creatures (illus) / Huber * 155 (index)
—Douglas / Magic *
   Androcles and the lion, 167–175
—Egyptian / Harris
   lion and mouse; extended story,
      32–33
—Greaves / Hippo * 20–21 @
   how buffalo became a grass
      eater, 73–77
   jackal fools lion: hold up rock, 50
   lion steals ostrich chicks, 130–
      132
   waterbuck runs into swamp; es-
      capes lion, 91–92
   why dassie has no tail, 122–124
   why lion does not eat fruit, 18–20
   why lion roars, 15–18
   why wart hog goes on his knees,
      108
   why wart hog is so ugly, 109–112
—Grimm / Complete *
   fox helps horse trick lion, 595–
      596
   king's son who feared nothing
      (Grimm), 545–550

lady and lion [man by night], 398–
404
—Grimm / Sixty *
fox helps horse trick lion, 241–
243
lady and lion [man by night], 235–
240
—Hamilton / People *
Anton's shapechange: beautiful
girl of the moon tower, 53–59
—Jewish / Sadeh
brothers' widow-mother marries
lion (three heads), 92–95
Rabbi Alfasi and the lion, 252–
253
—Lang / Wilkins
Wounded lion (prince), 385–393
—Lester / Brer Rabbit *
Brer Lion meets the creature (Ole
Boy), 65–68
tricks Brer Lion: "hurricane coming," 60–62
—Lurker / Dict Gods, 432–433 (index)
—MacDonald / Sourcebook *
motif index, 657–658
—Man Myth & Magic, 3148 (index)
—Manning / Cauldron *
Martin kills witch; lions freed of
enchantment, 66–77
—Nielsen / Old Tales *
blue belt (mother conspires with
troll to kill son), [37–62]
—Old Wives / Carter
escaping slowly: goat and kids in
Lion's house, 221
—Paxton / Aesop *
gratitude: lion spares mouse;
mouse frees lion from net, [19–
21]
poor old lion (eats animal-visitors), [14–15]
—Trolls / Asbjornsen
boy who became lion, falcon, ant,
64–70

—Turkey / Walker, 305 (index)
—Turkish / Walker
lion asks: how does my den
smell? 16
—Unicorn / Hathaway
Knight of the Lion / Lady of the
Unicorn, 88–99 @
—Water Buffalo (Chinese)
rabbit gets revenge on lion, 33–35
Lion and the mouse see under
Aesop.
LIONESS
—Jewish / Sadeh
brothers' widow-mother marries
lion, 92–95
LIR
—Celts / Hodges *
swan children restored by St. Pat-
rick's coming, 5–14
LISABETTA
—Lore of Love
head of murdered lover buried in
pot of basil, 64–65
LITHUANIAN TALES
—Corrin / Imagine *
The Popplesnitch, 70–79
—Dictionary / Leach, 1215 (index)
Little Briar Rose, see Sleeping
Beauty.
Little engine that could, The
—Hall / Treasury * 1–9
Little Fairly
—Clouston / Popular
versions, II.229–288, 489–491
Little fir tree
—Hall / Treasury * 42–53
—Leete / Golden * 80–93
Little folks' presents, The
—Grimm / Complete * 742–745
**Little Fool Ivan and the little hump-
back horse**
—Lines / Magical * 70–85
Little good mouse
—Lang / Wilkins, 116–127

Little Ida's flowers
—Andersen / Raverat * 57–76
Little King Loc
—Lang / Wilkins, 441–459
Little Klaus and Big Klaus
—Andersen / Raverat * 22–49
—Carle / Treasury * 72–84
Little lame prince and his travelling-cloak (Craik)
—Victorian / Hearn, 132–191
Little peasant, The
—Grimm / Complete * 311–316
—Grimm / Sixty * 142–148
LITTLE PEOPLE
see also ELF; LEPRECHAUN; PISKIES; PYGMIES
—Quayle / Cornish *
Cherry Winbroome in service of shape-changer, 91–102
piskie threshers; leave after gift of suits of clothes, 45–50
Little Red Engine: talks with animals; ill (needs oil)
—Corrin / Six-Year * 24–27
Little Red Riding Hood (Grimm)
—Allison / I'll Tell * 30–31
—Bedtime / Padoan & Smith * 129–131
—Carter / Sleeping * 21–25
—Corrin / Favourite * 102–106
—Corrin / Six-Year * 142–145
—Grimm / Complete * 139–143
—Grimm / Sixty * 116–119
—Hall / Treasury * 35–39
—Lang / Wilkins
True story of Little Golden Hood, 132–136
—Old Wives / Carter
[in this version, gobbled up by wolf], 208–210
—Scriven / Full Color * 37–39
—Strauss / Trail
soliloquy of "waiting wolf" (poem), 14–16

—Wolves / Lopez, 302 (index)
—Yolen / Faery Flag
retelling in "old wolves' home," 103–119
—Zipes / Beauties * 58–60
Little Red Riding Hood (existential retelling)
—Switzer / Existential, 32–37
Little Thumbling
—Zipes / Beauties * 36–43
Little tin soldier
—Bedtime / Padoan & Smith * 33–35
Little turtle that could not stop talking
—Hall / Treasury * 84–87
LITTLE WEASEL
—Williams-Ellis / Tales *
boy's series of trades: feather to village chief, 102–112
Little Wonder
—Manning / Cats * 65–74
LIVER
—Restless / Cohen *
wife steals liver from corpse; husband replaces with wife's, 103–109
LIVERY BOY
—Jewish / Sadeh
lovesickness: leaves from Paradise, 365–367
Living Kuan-Yin
—Corrin / Imagine * 136–141
Livingston, Myra Cohn
—Unicorn / Coville *
Riddle (poem), 40
LIZARD(-s)
—Animal Legends / Kerven *
friends ask too much: guinea's crest feathers; lizard's skin, [24–25]
—Curry / Beforetime *
mink and bluejay retrieve Little Weasel, stolen by lizard, 60–67
—Earthmaker / Mayo *

thirsty lizard ends the big flood
(Ute tale), 6–10
—Fahs / Old *
drought: lizard keeps others from
well, 91–95
—Hamilton / People *
Bruh Rabbit: how stop stolen
magic hoe? 31–34
—MacDonald / Sourcebook *
motif index, 658
—Pellowski / Story *
string-story, 22–30
—Polynesians / Andersen, 489 (in-
dex)
—Spanish-Am / Van Etten *
captive bride in lizard's den, 19–
24
LOAD
—Cambodian / Carrison
rider holds rice on head to lessen
load for buffalo, 97–99
Lobel, Arnold
—Childcraft 2 / Time *
Frog and toad, 44–53
LOCH NESS MONSTER
—Beasts / McHargue, 103–113 @,
117 (index)
—Monsters / Cohen, 125–134 @
—Monsters / Hall, 62–83
—Werewolves / Aylesworth, 104–110
LOCOMOTIVE
—Hall / Treasury *
Little Engine that could, 1–9
LOGGERS (people)
—Humor / Midwest, 141–161
LOGGING
—Hoke / Giants
how we logged Katahdin Stream
(verse), 30–33
Paul Bunyan and Babe, 11–29
LOHENGRIN
—Baring-Gould / Curious
Helias: Knight of the Swan, 146–
150
—Knights / Heller-Headon, 176–185
LOKI
—Dramatized / Kamerman
builder of the wall, 422–434
—Hamilton / Dark *
Fenris, wolf-child of Loki, 82–86
—Norse / Crossley, 270 (index)
—Scandinavian / Davidson
trickster, 104, 143 (index)
LONELINESS
see Ugly duckling, The.
LONGEVITY
—Grimm / Complete *
formula for human: add dog, ass,
monkey expectancies, 716–
718
**LONGSTREET, Augustus Baldwin
(1790–1870)**
—Brown / Amer Folklore, 167 (index)
LONO (deity)
—Polynesians / Andersen, 489 (index)
Looking for a bride
—Grimm / Complete * 655–656
LOOKING TABOO
—Clarkson / World *
gold in chimney; witch's servant
forbidden to look, 26–29
—Corrin / Favourite *
while asleep: East of the sun . . . ,
1–15
—Maori / Kanawa *
woman looks into spring; drowns
village, 85–86
—Muddleheads / Harris
Copper Canoeman weds human
princess, 75–93
—Nesbit / Fairy *
town in the library, 81–98
—Quayle / Shining *
Urashima opens forbidden box; is
suddenly very old, 57–68
Loon, see BIRD: LOON.
LORD, The
—Schwartz / Gates, 805 (index)

Lord's animals and the devil's
—Grimm / Complete * 642–644
LORD'S PRAYER
—Ghosts / Starkey
    moon (personified) captured/
    rescued (bogles), 96–101
LOSS
—Coyote / Bierhorst *
    loss can sometimes make us see
    our good fortune, [44]
    wolf and puma fight; coyote
    steals the kill, [22]
—Grimm / Complete *
    gifts lost: Clever Hans, 166–
    168
—Grimm / Sixty *
    gifts lost: Clever Hans, 217–222
LOST and FOUND
—Dramatized / Kamerman
    Baron Barnaby's box, 549–558
—Fahs / Old *
    (child) Niyak, Umak, and the ea-
    gle, 71–80
—Ghosts / Starkey
    ghost reveals deed to estate, 24–
    29
—Grimm / Complete *
    lost girl: failing vs. non-failing in
    feeding animals, 698–704
—Jewish / Frankel
    Moshele's gift: poor water-carrier
    prays for 1,000 rubles, 554–
    556
—Sioux / Standing Bear *
    how medicine-man found lost
    horses, 10–13
—Tibet / Timpanelli *
    unwilling "seer": reputation made
    by luck/coincidence, 29–41
—Yep / Rainbow *
    Professor of smells, 20–35
LOTUS
—Egyptian / Ions, 143 (index)
—Lurker / Dict Gods, 433 (index)

LOTUS SUTRA
—Japanese / Tyler, 337 (index)
LOUISIANA
—Southern [legends] / Floyd
    Last Island's last day, 56–60
LOUSE
—Turkish (Art I) / Walker
    community mourning for Brother
    Louse, 58–59
Louse and the flea
—Grimm / Complete * 158–160
LOVE
    see also CHARITY; COURTLY
    LOVE
—Amer Ind / Erdoes
    marriage: twenty-one myths,
    271–331
—Arabian / Lewis
    Ghanim, the slave of love, 35–
    41
    prince detests women; princess
    disgusted by men, 66–80
—Arabian / Riordan
    prince . . . [same as above], 66–
    77
—Bierhorst / Sacred
    Indian songs, 45–61
—Bomans / Wily *
    Lady of the lake: spoiled prince
    loved/saved by young girl, 9–
    16
—Brooke / Telling *
    marries Cinderella albeit slipper
    doesn't fit, 51–74
—Carter / Sleeping *
    Ricky with Tuft; man not ugly to
    princess who loves him, 93–
    102
—Celts / Hodges *
    Gareth of Orkney wins his spurs,
    133–154
    Tam Lin freed from evil spell by
    love, 76–83
—Chaucer / Cohen *

the franklin's tale: will love when
stones are gone, 67–84
—Childcraft 1 / Once *
Velveteen Rabbit (becomes real
when loved), 175–181
—Clouston / Popular
falling in love through dreams,
II.228, 488
—Corrin / Imagine *
Chura ("Simba"); his love returns
from underworld; can marry
only Simba, 142–150
Pari hides in golden candelabra;
prince buys, falls in love, 151–
160
—Cotterell / Encyclopedia, 255 (in-
dex)
—Douglas / Magic *
Beauty and the Beast, 85–97
Rapunzel: daughter promised to
witch, 27–33
—Dulac / Fairy *
green serpent: one twin princess
cursed, ugly, 124–138
—Fahs / Old *
girl chooses death over unfaithfulness, 44–51
—Greek / Osborne
Cupid's arrows: Daphne and
Apollo, 23–26
mysterious visitors: Baucis and
Philemon, 67–70
—Hodges / Celts *
freed from evil spell by love, 76–
83
—Hopi / Talashoma-Malotki
jealousy: two girls (friends) in love
with same boy, 118–135
—Jewish / Frankel, xiii (index)
Rashi's companion-to-be in Paradise, 388–392
ruby/serpent: Solomon's daughter shut in tower; power of love,
254–257

—Legends / Cavendish
romantic, 406 (index)
—Leonardo / Fables *
mother pelican's blood restores
babies to life, 56
—Lewis / Proud
Eliduc: her knight unfaithful; she
enters convent, 88–100
Guigemar: find woman who will
endure anguish and lift curse,
10–19
—Lore of Love
enchanted world series (Time-
Life), 1–143
love potions, 58–59
obstacles: French soldier and
Saracen maid, 98–106
vanity's reflection: Echo and Narcissus, 74
—Lurker / Dict Gods, 403–404 (index)
—Lycanthropy / Otten
Housman: The were-wolf (allegory), 281–320
—Manning / Cauldron *
amber witch: common man, loved
by princess, sent to get amber,
18–31
—Muddleheads / Harris
asked to prove by slashing
cheeks, 115–130
—Plants / Dyer
love-charms, 92–102
—Russian Hero / Warner *
rusalka (water-spirit) and the
seal-hunter, 28–29
—Scandinavian / Kvideland
changing someone's mind, vii (index)
—Spanish-Am / Van Etten *
Santa Fe soldier buys love [unre-
quited] potion, 33–36
witch asks: you love wife more
than child? 48–49
—Strauss / Trail

Bluebeard: reflection on women destroyed (poem), 20–21

—Tree / Kerven *
bamboo-princess freed from spell, [28–29]

—Turkish (Art I) / Walker
overhears secrets: how to win princess, escape spell, 123–136

—Wilde / Lynch *
nightingale gives life to produce red rose for student-in-love, 14–23
selfish giant: always winter, children not allowed in garden, 6–13

—Williams-Ellis / Tales *
Cap o' Rushes (loves father "like salt"), 8–16

—Women / Dyer
love tests, 92–98, 101–107 @

—Zipes / Beauties *
Ricky with Tuft; man not ugly to princess who loves him, 52–57, 95–100

LOVE, FALLING IN
—Arabian / Lewis
Ghanim, the slave of love, 35–41
prince detests women; princess disgusted by men, 66–80
Princess Dunja: all men are faithless, 52–59
princess elopes on wedding day (to another), 217–221

—Arabian / McCaughrean
Pearl-Harvest, 36–50

—Arabian / Riordan
prince detests women (as above), 66–77

—Brooke / Telling *
prince marries Cinderella; slipper doesn't fit, 51–74

—Carter / Sleeping *

Ricky with the Tuft; ugly man and princess, 93–102

—Jaffrey / Seasons
Savitri and Satyavan: love for woodcutter, 10–15

—Lewis / Proud
Guigemar: find woman who will lift curse, 10–19

—Lore of Love
illicit love; head buried in pot of basil, 64–65

—Maori / Kanawa *
Hinemoa and Tutanekai; her father opposes, 36–44

—Quayle / Shining *
wooden bowl (worn to hide girl-bride's beauty), 97–102

—Yolen / Shape, 52–60

—Zipes / Beauties *
Ricky with the Tuft; ugly man and princess, 52–57, 95–100

LOVE: MAGIC AS CAUSE
—Caduto / Keepers *
span of human life, 181–182

—Grimm / Complete *
duration of life: dog, ass, monkey, man, 716–718

—Scriven / Full Color *
Snow Queen [seduces boy; girl rescues], 35–36

LOVE STORIES
—Old Wives / Carter
battle of the birds, 76–85

—Wolkstein / Love, 1–270

LOVE, TRAGIC (*unrequited*)
—Chinese / Chin *
customs: marriage; scholarship (Ju Yingtai), 61–73

—Clouston / Popular
women whose love is slighted, II.499–502

—Hodges / Celts *
Dermot in the Land-under-Wave, 57–73

—Lang / Wilkins
  Princess Mayblossom, 137–153
—Lewis / Proud
  Chaitivel: Four Sorrows; the Sor-
    rowful One, 74–78
  Nightingale (Laustic) killed by
    cruel husband, 61–64
  Yonec: lover killed by jealous
    husband's trap, 53–60
—Lines / Magical *
  Oisin's mother captured by Dark
    Druid, 169–174
—Lore of Love
  curse causes husband to forget
    wife, 26–31
  doomed trysts: Apollo; Pyramus,
    77
  illicit love; head buried in pot of
    basil, 64–65
  interwoven branches: tragic love,
    122–127
  sculptor carves palace (solid
    rock) for princess, 79–83
  Sir Eglamour and Lady Chrysto-
    bel, 128–139
  trees with interwoven branches:
    tragic love, 122–127
—Turkish (Art I) / Walker
  fairy-monster kills Cihansah's pi-
    geon-girl, 207–217
—Vietnam / Terada *
  betrothed woman captured by
    enemy kills self, 99–101
  lady of stone: man unknowingly
    marries his sister, 115–118
  magic crossbow used to kill king,
    120–125
**Lovecraft, Howard Phillips (1890–
1937)**
—Pirate Ghosts / McSherry
  Terrible Old Man, 69–72
LOVER(-s)
  see also COURTSHIP; DEAD
    LOVER; FIDELITY

—Arabian / Lewis
  generous commoner made king;
    reunited with lost love, 81–90
  Ghanim, the slave of love, 35–41
  princess elopes on wedding day
    (to another), 217–221
  sea rose of Princess Brow of Lil-
    ies, 212–216
  slave girl (Sweet-Friend) and Ali
    Nur, 25–34
—Arabian / Riordan
  porter's tale: king's son and lover
    buried alive, 112–116
—Bomans / Wily *
  secret: three gnomes living under
    chestnut tree, 138–140
—Fahs / Old *
  girl chooses death over unfaith-
    fulness, 44–51
—Folk Ballads / McNeil
  disguises and tricks, I.77–83
  faithful/unfaithful, I.85–141
  family opposition, I.69–76
—German-American / Barrick
  Jorinde and Goringel, 109
—Grimm / Complete *
  Jorinda and Joringel, 339–342
  Twelve huntsmen; prince forgets
    his betrothed, 334–336
—Grimm / Legends (Ward), II:424 (in-
    dex)
—Grimm / Sixty *
  Jorinda and Joringel, 17–20
  Twelve huntsmen (as above),
    271–273
—Jewish / Frankel
  princess to God: restore my lover
    or take my life, 360–365
—Jewish / Sadeh
  Blackface: merchant's son in love
    with princess, 117–121
—Lang / Wilkins
  enchantment: princess must stay
    in tower . . . , 415–431

—Lewis / Proud
  Chevrefoil (hazel and honey-
  suckle); Tristram, 79–81
  Eliduc: her knight/husband un-
  faithful; she enters convent,
  88–100
  Milun (swan-messenger) waits
  twenty years to wed lover, 65–
  75
  Nightingale (Laustic) killed by
  cruel husband, 61–64
—Lore of Love
  Prince Camaralzaman and Princess Badoura, 37–49
—Maori / Kanawa *
  Hinemoa and Tutanekai; her father opposes, 36–44
—Nesbit / Fairy *
  Charmed life, or Princess and
  Lift-man, 25–42
—Quayle / Cornish *
  borne by tidal wave, mermaid
  meets/mates carpenter-singer,
  51–63
—Reeves / Shadow
  Launfal: secret love for Rosamund, 49–83
  nightingale: cruel husband;
  young wife loves bachelor/
  neighbor, 87–95
  white doe: knotted garment;
  pledge, 131–153
  young bride locked in tower;
  shape-change knight as lover,
  1–48
—Scary / Young *
  Indian maid, married in Land of the
  Dead, returns with child, 69–72
—Spring / Philip
  lovers reincarnated as butterflies,
  35–41
—Vietnam / Terada *
  betrothed woman captured by
  enemy kills self, 99–101

—Wilde / Happy *
  nightingale seeks rose for stu-
  dent's love, 41–56
LOVER SCORNED
—Arabian / Lewis
  Princess Dunja: all men are faith-
  less, 52–59
—Grimm / Complete *
  Twelve huntsmen, The, 334–336
—Grimm / Sixty *
  Twelve huntsmen, The, 271–273
—Lore of Love
  sculptor carves palace for prin-
  cess, 79–83
LOVESICK(-ness)
—Jewish / Sadeh
  eagle takes rabbi's son to Chris-
  tian palace, 273–275
  leaves from Paradise, 365–367
LOWA (god)
—Hamilton / In the Beginning *
  sun, life, wind, and death, 104–
  109
LOWE, Rabbi Judah
—Hamilton / Dark *
  Joseph Golem: blood accusation
  against Jews, 87–96
LOWER WORLD, JOURNEY TO
see also UNDERWORLD
—Arabian / Lewis
  merman trades jewels for fruit,
  131–137
—Arabian / McCaughrean
  merman trades jewels for fruit,
  83–96
—Fahs / Old *
  hunter in Walumbe's country of
  Death, 181–184
—Lang / Wilkins
  Indian chief goes to Land of Souls
  for dead bride, 282–284
—Lore of Love
  loved one in the lower world, 108
—Maori / Kanawa *

Mataora meets underworld
Turehu; marries, 68–80
—Vietnam / Terada *
sea snake captures mandarin's
wife, 88–94
LOYALTY
—Crossley / Animal (Grimm) *
kill Old Sultan, faithful dog, 11–14
—Legends / Cavendish, 403 (index)
—Yep / Rainbow *
old woman: old jar never empties,
96–105
Lubert, Mlle de
—Zipes / Beauties *
Princess Camion, 261–293
LUCIFER
—Demons / Gettings, 150–153
LUCK
—Arabian / Lewis
changing luck: destiny or capital,
17–24
test for succession: prince marries tortoise, 43–51
—Arabian / McCaughrean
test . . . (as above), 142–149
—Clarkson / World *
fool carries complaints to God,
who gives him gift of luck, 319–
323
—Clouston / Popular
imposter: pretence to knowledge
of secrets, II.413–431
luckily, they are not peaches,
II.467–472
—Dramatized / Kamerman
Triumph for two [personified], 47–
60
—Jewish / Frankel
man never takes oath; result: first
misfortune then good, 383–
385
—Jewish / Sadeh
poor brother and three beasts,
140–143

—Lester / Brer Rabbit *
Brer Wolf steals Brer Rabbit's
lucky rabbit foot, 145–151
—Lore of Love
lovers forced apart; rendezvous
in dreams, 37–49
—MacDonald / Sourcebook *
motif index, 660
—O'Brien / Tales *
poor farmer trades cow for magic
"do your [whatever] duty" bottle, 46–52
—Tibet / Timpanelli *
unwilling "seer": reputation made
by luck/coincidence, 29–41
—Turkish / Walker
stargazer to the sultan, 98–107
—Yep / Rainbow *
beggar woman: child of calamity,
46–52
gambler: Professor of smells, 20–
35
LUCK, BAD
—Arabian / McCaughrean
keys of destiny; Iram, 65–82
—Frog Rider (Chinese)
Big Lang and Little Lang divide
property, 100–110
—Grimm / Complete *
juniper tree: murder exposed by
singing bird, 220–229
robber bridegroom, 200–204
—Grimm / Sixty *
robber bridegroom, 120–124
—Jewish / Frankel
fate: can't change wheel of fortune, 394–395
—Jewish / Sadeh
coachman; poor man (two anecdotes), 302
desperate man and prophet
Jonah, 154–158
young man who had no luck,
285–287

—Quayle / Shining *
greedy neighbor kills treasure-
finding dog; burns magic pot,
69–76

LUCK, GOOD
—Crossley / Dead *
Yallery Brown (does other's
work), 79–85
—Egyptian / Harris
shipwrecked sailor and the huge
serpent, 64–65
—Jaffrey / Seasons
Lakshmi, goddess of good fortune, can find only washerwoman, 81–84
—Turkish (Art I) / Walker
laborer purchases four pieces of
advice, to his good fortune,
179–183
—Yep / Rainbow *
child of calamity, 46–52

LUCKY ACCIDENTS
see also TREASURE
—Arabian / Lewis
Ghanim, the slave of love, 35–41
—Lang / Wilkins
Princess Mayblossom (good vs.
evil fairies), 137–153
—Turkish / Walker
Kazan kills forty flies, becomes
"hero," 67–74

LUGH (god)
—Celtic / MacCana, 142 (index)

LUSHOOTSEED TALES
—Haboo / Hilbert, 1–204

LUST
—Ghosts / Time-Life
O'Iwa (Japanese) murdered
ghost-wife's revenge, 51–55
—Gullible Coyote / Malotki
coyote deceives beautiful maid:
devil's-claw as rattlesnake,
119–129
—Hopi / Talashoma-Malotki

old wizard plots to seduce beautiful girl, 70–91
—Hopi Coyote / Malotki
coyote and spider families entertain; lust for Spider Woman,
43–55
coyote lusts for girl resuscitated
by badger, 23–41
—Jewish / Sadeh
Baal Shem Tov and the imps,
352–353
dress: charm causes lewdness,
20–21
—Lore of Love
enchanter's snare, 121

LUTE PLAYER
—Arabian / McCaughrean
Pearl-Harvest, 36–50
—Lang / Wilkins
wife (queen) rescues husband
from prison, 528–533

LUXURY
—Aesop / Holder *
country mouse and city mouse,
4–7
—Allison / I'll Tell *
(costly) city mouse and country
mouse, 124–125

LUZ
—Jewish / Frankel
Milham's walled city, barred to
Angel of Death, 15–17

LYCANTHROPY
—Lycanthropy / Otten, 1–337, 331
(index)
—Witch Encyc / Guiley, 208–210

Lying, see LIAR(s).

Lynch, May
—Dramatized / Kamerman
Finn McCool, 218–226

LYNETTE
—Pendragon / Ashley
King's damosel: Lynette
(Chapman), 120–203

Lady of the Fountain [Luned]
(Mabinogion), 204–226
LYNX
—Animals / Rowland, 187 (index)

MAASAW (god of death)
—Gullible Coyote / Malotki, 167 @
coyote and Maasaw try to scare
each other, 95–103
—Hopi / Talashoma-Malotki, 205 @
Maasaw and Oraibi People once
got scared to death, 108–117
**Mabie, Hamilton Wright (1846–
1916)**
—Hoke / Giants
Thor's wonderful journey, 119–
129
MABINOGION
—Barber / Anthology
Culhweh and Olwen, 33–43
—Celtic / MacCana, 142 (index)
—Lacy / Arth Ency, 346–349
—Lines / Magical *
birth of Pryderi, 116–122
—Pendragon / Ashley
Lady of the Fountain [Luned =
Lynette], 204–226
MACABRE STORIES
see also HORROR STORIES;
MURDER; MUTILATION
—Bomans / Wily *
famine: innkeeper roasts his own
leg to satisfy guests, 111–115
—Yolen / Shape Shift
girl unknowingly turns into deer
(Johanna), 52–60
McCARTNEY, Charles
—Southern [legends] / Floyd
goat man of Dixie, 150–153
MacDONALD, George (1824–1905)
—Lynn / Fantasy *
bibliography (about the author),
549–552

—Victorian / Hearn
Golden key, The, 228–251
Macdonald, J. D. (James D., 1954-)
—Yolen / Werewolves
Bad blood, 3–34
McDowell, Ian
—Pendragon / Ashley
Son of the morning [Mordred],
322–343
McFarlan, Ethel
—Dramatized / Kamerman
Olive jar, 360–374
MACHINERY
—Brooke / Telling *
John Henry wins tunnel-digging
race, 77–110
Macmillan, Cyrus
—Hoke / Giants
The boy who overcame the gi-
ants, 34–40
The giant with grey feathers,
150–155
McNeill, James
—Hoke / Giants
Finlay, the giant killer, 142–149
McPHERSON, Aimee Semple
—Floyd / Gr Am Myst, 123–126
MADNESS
—Jaffrey / Seasons
by pretending madness, faithful
sister changes brother's fate,
96–101
MADOC, Prince
—Southern [legends] / Floyd, 38–43
**MAGELLAN, Ferdinand (1480?-
1521)**
—Speck / New World, 525 (index)
MAGI
—Bomans / Wily *
rich man: the truly happy lack
nothing; vs. the Three Wise
Men, 176–180
MAGIC
see also DISENCHANTMENT;

INCANTATIONS; SOR-
CERER; SPELLS; WITCH;
WIZARD
—Ashliman / Guide
titles arranged in Aarne-Thompson system, 51–149 @
—Babylonia / Spence, 399 (index)
—Bierhorst / Monkey *
with help of giant's daughter,
young man does four impossible tasks, 56–65
—Bomans / Wily *
cobbler's three wishes from
gnome; learns money's limitations, 53–61
—Clouston / Popular, II.510 (index)
—Cotterell / Encyclopedia, 255 (index)
—Crossley / British FT *
Gruagach, Finn, and the Lady of
the Green Gown, 228–243
hazel twig defeats men trying to
put Jemmy in coffin, 77–85
—Curry / Beforetime *
mink and bluejay retrieve Little
Weasel, stolen by lizard, 60–
67
pine-nut thieves: trapped by
magic ice-wall, 90–99
—Egyptian / Harris
Setna and the Book of Thoth,
92–102
—Egyptian / Mercatante
Setna and the magic book, 145–
153
—Hamilton / Dark *
Baba Yaga, Vasilisa, and her
doll, 14–22
People could fly [to freedom],
166–172
servant opens forbidden book,
summons devil to work; can't
stop, 126–131
—Hamilton / People *

Devil's daughter helps John de
Conquer, 107–114
—Hoke / Giants
defeat: Thor loses to giants, 119–
129
Indian boy kills giants; then falls,
112–118
—Hopi / Talashoma-Malotki
hide and seek with life at stake,
50–69
old wizard plots to seduce beautiful girl, 70–91
—Igloo / Metayer
child kidnapped by wolf-men, 73–
77
Coppermine River legend:
feigned death, 78–81
loon; the ball players [losers die],
32–34
—Japanese / Tyler, 337 (index)
—Jewish / Frankel, 649 (index)
—Jewish / Sadeh
scholar who fell into the water,
89–90
Talmud student who wished to
study magic, 90–92
—Journeys / Norris *
great chase: Mirragen the Catman vs. Gurangatch, [10–12]
—Legends / Cavendish, 427 (index)
powers and equipment, 396 (index)
—Lycanthropy / Otten, 331 (index)
—Lynn / Fantasy *
adventures; annotated bibliography, 273–310
—MacDonald / Sourcebook *
motif index, 93–121
—Man Myth & Magic, 3150 (index)
—Manning / Cats *
old couple: repeated tries to cut
down tree; bird, instead, supplies needs, 101–106
—Manning / Cauldron *

crusader beaten, robbed by comrades; witches reveal secrets,
= reversal, 46–57
—Medicine-Plants / Read Dgst
ancient lore, 21–23
—Mex-Am / West
motif index, 298, 302
—Norwegian / Hodne, 57–162
—Occult & Parapsych / Shepard, 1–
1617 @
—Palestinian / Speak (Muhawi)
motif-index, 388–390
—Quayle / Cornish *
magic ointment makes one eye
invisible, 13–20
—Russian / Ivanits, 248 (index)
—Russian Hero / Warner *
foolish man exchanges daughter
for help, 57–60
—Scandinavian / Kvideland, 421 (index)
—Scriven / Full Color *
Rumpelstiltskin, 13–15
—Shah / Central Asia
(div) princess and the donkey,
82–86
—Switzer / Existential
Rumpelstiltskin at gambling table
(*existential retelling*), 17–23
—Turkish (Art I) / Walker
witches' gifts: tears to pearls,
laugh to roses, water to gold,
159–168
—Unnatural / Cohen, 146 (index)
—Vanishing / Mercer *
sea frozen; giant bird caught, 42–
49
—Water Buffalo (Chinese)
rescued by lad, gives him magic
gifts, 103–110
—Waters / Encyclopedia, 1–372
—Williams-Ellis / Tales *
Tom-Tit-Tot spins skeins for girl,
185–195

—Witch Encyc / Guiley, 213–220,
416 (index)
—Woman's Ency / Walker, 566–
570 @
—Yep / Rainbow *
old woman: "The old jar" never
empties, 96–105
Magic carpet, *see* MAGIC TRANS-
PORT.
MAGIC CONTROL OF ELEMENTS
—Chaucer / Cohen *
the franklin's tale: will love when
stones are gone, 67–84
—Russian Hero / Warner *
Il'ya saves city; captures Nightin-
gale (monster), 76–80
Magic fish-bone, The (Dickens)
—Victorian / Hearn, 106–115
Magic lamp, *see* ALADDIN . . .
Magic Mary
—Pellowski / Family * 54–57
**MAGIC OBJECT(-s) (- acts; -
events, etc.)**
see also ARROW; BONES;
BOOK; BOTTLE; BOW and
ARROW; BOWL; BROOM;
CAP; CHANGE; CLOAK;
CLOTHES; CLUB; CURE;
DISK; DREAM; DRINK;
DRUM; FISHBONE; FLIGHT;
FLOWER; FOG; FOOD SUP-
PLY; GROWTH; HEALING;
HERBS; HORSE; HORSE-
HIDE; KETTLE; KNIFE;
KNOWLEDGE; LOVE; MEDI-
CINE; MILL; MIRROR;
RHYME; RING; SHIP; SHOE;
SONG; STICK; STONE;
SWORD; TABLE; TALK;
TREE; UTENSILS; WAND;
WATER; WEAPONS; WORDS
—Arabian / Lewis
carpet; telescope; apple (test to
win princess), 174–183

—Bomans / Wily *
balloon message; with godmother's help, knight kills
dragon, 197–202
Lady of the lake: spoiled prince
loved/saved by young girl, 9–
16
protection: toys help children escape witch, 83–86
—Bruchac / Iroquois *
finger-pointer: Stone Coat
Woman aids hunters, 135–144
flute: Okteondon defeats Workers of Evil, 104–114
—Chinese / Chin *
cow's hide, 113–125
drink: white snake (in woman
form), 29–44
—Chorao / Child's *
Jack and the Beanstalk; hen;
harp, 9–20
—Clarkson / World *
Boots outperforms brothers;
magic ax, shovel, walnut, 277–
281
Koshalki-Opalki (how simpleton
became king), 19–22
magic beer: Cluricaune shows
hiding place of treasure, 115–
117
—Corrin / Six-Year *
dragon; magic bag makes all who
sniff it, laugh, 53–58
—Douglas / Magic *
works physical change: Rapunzel, 27–33
—Dramatized / Kamerman *
farm prospers; magic sand, 265–
277
—Fahs / Old *
magic pillow: dream projects future life, 121–124
—Frog Rider (Chinese)
wooden horse, 24–46

—Grimm / Complete *
brothers: one rescues princess; is
rescued by other, 290–311
cure: spirit in the bottle, 458–
462
princess under spell, broken with
help of, 431–436
Salad; fed to witch, 551–558
—Grimm / Sixty *
princess under spell, broken with
help, 250–256
Salad; fed to witch, 292–293
Water of life, The, 264–270
—Hamilton / People *
magic cowhide dipper: how turtle
got marks on back, 20–25
—Jewish / Sadeh
baker's apprentice and gold-
spewing cup, 268–271
magic staff; silver/gold; princess
who refused to talk, 106–111
—Journeys / Norris *
magic dagger; quest: city of ultimate beauty and happiness,
[29–32]
—Lang / Wilkins
charm protects betrothed from
yara (fairies), 474–484
enchantment, wishes, horns
(Deulin), 243–259
grateful prince: girl helps hero escape old man, 394–414
—Man Myth & Magic
analytics, 3182 (index)
—Old Wives / Carter
Aunt Kate's goomer-dust causes
mighty breaking of wind, 73–75
—Quayle / Shining *
mother's mirror speaks/warns Sachiko of stepmother in rat-form,
90–96
—Russian Hero / Warner *
magic doll helps Vasilisa escape
Baba-Yaga, 86–92

magic whip: Dobrynya spares abductor/dragon, 69–70
three kingdoms: copper, silver, gold; magic guides, 53–56
—Shah / Central Asia
bag; princess imprisoned in mountain of jade, 19–24
Iskandar and the emerald ring, 118–125
—Trolls / Asbjornsen
(axe, pick, walnut) task: cut oak; provide year-around water well, 36–40
—Turkey / Walker, 305 (index)
—Turkish / Walker
Teeny-Tiny and Witch-Woman, 49–51
—Williams-Ellis / Tales *
Baba Yaga; comb and towel help escape, 113–124
—Witches / Iosa *
animals help kind children escape giant witch, 18–22
—Yolen / Faery Flag
cure: dumb child draws unicorns, 48–57

MAGIC OBJECT DRAWS PERSON TO IT
—Chorao / Child's *
Pied Piper, 51–55
—Grimm / Complete *
blue light summons tiny servant, 530–534
—Grimm / Sixty *
blue light (as above), 244–249

MAGIC OBJECT, GIFT OF
—Dulac / Fairy *
magic pipe makes all dance, 114–123
—Grimm / Complete *
kings' daughters aid hero in tasks: win girl or die, 515–524
—Jaffrey / Seasons
goddess Parvati gives magic bowl to old man, 103–109
—Lines / Magical *
North Wind gives boy meal-producing cloth; gold-producing ram, 66–70
—Quayle / Shining *
Lord Bag-o'-Rice aids Dragon King; kills giant centipede, 33–43
—Turkish (Art I) / Walker
shrewd one cheats his simpleton brother, who ends up rich, 195–198
—Vietnam / Terada *
Da Trang crab: grateful snake gives magic pearl, 37–41

MAGIC OBJECT LOST
—Grimm / Complete *
success through magic knapsack, hat, horn, 258–264
wishing-table, gold-ass, cudgel in sack, 177–187
—Lore of Love
lovers forced apart; rendezvous in dreams, 37–49
—Yep / Rainbow *
cats and dogs as "natural enemies," 12–18

MAGIC OBJECT OBTAINED BY TRICKERY
—Grimm / Complete *
hero must hold crystal ball before enchantress to free princess, 798–801
King of the golden mountain, 425–430
One-eye, Two-eyes, and Three-eyes, 585–592
—Grimm / Sixty *
King of the golden mountain, 274–280
—Lines / Magical *

suitor test: Raja's son gets magic objects from fakirs, 56–66

MAGIC OBJECT OTHERWISE OBTAINED

—Chinese / Chin *
magic brush of artist Ma Liang, 143–153

—Douglas / Magic *
seeing; transport; healing, 3–11

—Hodges / Celts *
Merlin: life and magic powers, 117–132

—Lines / Magical *
apple of contentment: magic seed exchanged for cap, 15–23
Cormac Mac Art trades family for apple branch, 141–149

—Water Buffalo (Chinese)
enormous candy-man, 70–77

—Yep / Rainbow *
boasting contest, 96–105
pellets grow to be piers, 118–123

MAGIC OBJECT as PROVIDER

—Arabian / Lewis
Ala al-Din finds, loses, regains magic lamp, 153–165

—Arabian / McCaughrean
Ala al-Din finds . . . (as above), 153–184

—Arabian / Riordan
Ala al-Din finds . . . (as above), 12–25

—Bomans / Wily *
magic provider: golden slippers, 53–61

—Bruchac / Iroquois *
Hodadenon: chestnut, provider of food, 169–182

—Chinese / Chin *
golden carp (Cinderella-type), 47–57

—Frog Rider (Chinese)
magic gourd; 120 monsters burned up, 71–82

—Grimm / Complete *
Brother Lustig and St. Peter, 367–377
magic pot produces porridge, 475–476
One-eye, Two-eyes, and Three-eyes, 585–592
spirit in the bottle, 458–462
success through magic knapsack, hat, horn, 258–264

—Hamilton / People *
Tappin: how turtle got marks on back, 20–25

—Igloo / Metayer
magic plate; Taligvak: shaman saves village from famine, 61–69

—Jaffrey / Seasons
Doda and Dodi: poor woman's father in heaven provides needs, 38–46

—Jewish / Frankel
pursuit of gazelle; "60 days" [one hour] learning common life, 410–414

—Journeys / Norris *
ox-horn magically supplies needs, [6–9]

—Lines / Magical *
Cormac Mac Art: given magic table cloth, 141–149
North Wind gives boy meal-producing cloth; gold-producing ram, 66–70

—Old Wives / Carter
battle of birds: prince given magic bag, 76–85

—Scriven / Full Color *
Aladdin and the wonderful lamp, 79–83

—Shah / Central Asia

Wali and the magic saddle-bag, 69–77
—Turkish / Walker
magic pumpkin (provides food) stolen and recovered, 62–66
Magic object provides transport, *see* MAGIC TRANSPORT.
MAGIC OBJECT RECOVERED
—Caduto / Keepers *
Gluscabi hunting; bag never fills, 165–167
—Russian Hero / Warner *
cock and the corn mill, 52–53
MAGIC OBJECT RENDERS PERSON HELPLESS
—Grimm / Complete *
man among the thorns, 503–508
success through magic knapsack, hat, horn, 258–264
—Grimm / Sixty *
man among the thorns, 182–189
—Muddleheads / Harris
seal of Mouse Children recovered from Big Raven, 60–74
MAGIC OBJECT SERVES OWNER
—Caduto / Keepers *
folly: Gluscabi hunting; bag never fills, 165–167
—Dulac / Fairy *
blue bird (prince transformed), 77–90
magic pipe makes all dance, 114–123
—Shah / Central Asia
(seed and salt) seven divs for brothers, 13–18
Magic passage of time, *see* TIME.
MAGIC POWERS
—Arabian / Lewis
Moorish sorcerer vs. king, 60–64
—Arabian / McCaughrean
Moorish sorcerer vs. king, 133–141

—Childcraft 3 / Stories *
Duny: boy who became a wizard, 176–186
—Crossley / British FT *
midwife uses ointment meant for child on own eye, 287–292
—Grimm / Complete *
Pink [carnation], The, 355–360
soldier can reduce others to immobility, 808–811
three spinners help attain bride's mother's boast, 83–86
—Grimm / Sixty *
Pink, The, 171–176
—Hamilton / People *
Wiley triumphs over Hairy Man, 90–103
—Hodges / Celts *
Merlin: life and magic powers, 117–132
—Yep / Rainbow *
Dream Flier, 144–151
MAGIC POWERS: ACQUISITION or LOSS
—Egyptian / Harris
Setna and the Book of Thoth, 92–102
—Grimm / Complete *
White snake, The, 98–101
—Grimm / Sixty *
White snake, The, 197–201
—Hamilton / People *
beautiful girl of the moon tower, 53–59
—Turkish / Walker
lazy, bald Keloglan wins sultan's daughter, 20–22
—Water Buffalo (Chinese)
magic (cow hair) carrying-pole, 111–118
—Yolen / Werewolves
White Wolf, 45–69
MAGIC TRANSPORT
—Arabian / Lewis

king trades daughter for flying,
ebony horse, 106–116

—Arabian / McCaughrean [as above],
225–242

—Arabian / Riordan [as above], 56–
65

—Carle / Treasury *
Magic boots (Andersen), 31–35

—Corrin / Six-Year *
by mistake, crossing-sweeper
takes magic broom, 87–92

—Crossley / British FT *
Mossycoat; marvelous transportation from coat made of moss,
86–99

—Jewish / Frankel
princess to God: restore my lover
or take my life, 360–365
Solomon uses flying cloak to visit
palace, 251–254

—Jewish / Sadeh
Rabbi Adam Baal Shem: palace,
340–341

—Lang / Wilkins
Dorani: transport by magic stool,
432–440

—Manning / Cauldron *
Whirlwind abducts queen and
(evil) son; magic shoes take
him away, 106–117

—Shah / Central Asia
cobbler's son and serpent
(enchanted princess), 109–
117
dream of Habeeb, 56–61

—Water Buffalo (Chinese)
magic (cow hair) carrying-pole,
111–118

—Yep / Rainbow *
Dream Flier, 144–151

MAGICIAN(-s)
see also CONJURER; SOR-
CERY; TRANSFORMATIONS;
WIZARD(-s)

—Egyptian / Mercatante
tales of the, 175–182

—Jewish / Frankel, 643 (index)

—Jewish / Sadeh
adventures of David El-Ro'i, 246–
247
Rabbi Yehiel and King of France,
223–224

—Lang / Wilkins
King Solomon's ring; Dragon of
the North, 285–297

—Legends / Cavendish, 396 (index)

—Nesbit / Fairy *
princesses transformed to golden
apples, 141–158

—Shah / Central Asia
Feroz-Shah and the mechanical
flying horse, 131–145

MAGNETIC MOUNTAIN
—Arabian / Lewis
prohibitions disregarded; evils result, 10–16

MAGOTINE
—Dulac / Fairy *
green serpent: one twin princess
cursed, ugly, 124–138

Mahabharata
—Indic / Ions, 121–127 @, 143 (index)

—Mercatante / Encyclopedia, 778 (index)

Maid Maleen
—Grimm / Complete * 801–807

Maid of Brakel
—Grimm / Complete * 623

MAIDEN
—Grimm / Legends (Ward), II:427 (index)

Mailly, Jean de
—Zipes / Beauties *
Queen of the island of flowers,
121–127

MAIMONIDES (1125–1204)
—Jewish / Sadeh
king's ring found in fish, 215–217

MAIZE: origin
—Indian Myth / Burland, 112–115
MALAY TALE
—Tree / Kerven *
 bamboo-princess freed from
  spell, [28–29]
MALAYA
—Dictionary / Leach, 1212, 1215 (index)
MALICE (spirit)
—Hamilton / Dark *
 free spirits: Bouki and Malice,
  102–107
Malleus Maleficarum
—Lycanthropy / Otten, 106–114 @
MALORY, Sir Thomas (c.1408–1471)
—Barber / Anthology
 the Morte Arthur Saunz Guerdon,
  135–150
—King Arthur / Ashe, 190 (index)
—King Arthur / Senior
 Malory-Caxton, 9–24 @
—Lacy / Arth Ency, 352–357
MALSUM
—Childcraft 3 / Stories *
 good and evil: Glooscap vs. Mal-
  sum, 143–151
MALTESE TALE
—Restless / Cohen *
 dust: naval officers invited to
  Suarez home, 40–51
Man [human], see MANKIND.
Man among the thorns
—Grimm / Complete * 503–508
—Grimm / Sixty * 182–189
Man and the satyr
—Aesop / Zwerger * 7
Manabozo, a manitou hare
—Hamilton / Dark * 27–31
MANDARIN EXAMINATIONS
—Vietnam / Terada * 49 @
MANDRAKE
—Grimm / Legends (Ward), II:427 (index)

—Medicine-Plants / Read Dgst
 ancient lore, 12
—Plants / Dyer, 325 (index)
MANGAIA
—Polynesians / Andersen, 491 (index)
MANITOU
—Fahs / Old *
 quest: healing waters for plague-
  stricken wife, 52–56
—Hamilton / Dark *
 Manabozo: manitou hare swallowed by king of fishes, 27–31
MANKIND (origin; first human pair)
 see also CREATION MYTH;
  CULTURE; FALL OF MAN
—Babylonia / Spence, 399 (index)
—Caduto / Keepers *
 death: woman has last word,
  181–182
 Gluscabi made himself from lefto-
  ver dust, 21
—Cotterell / Encyclopedia, 255 (index)
—Curry / Beforetime *
 coyote makes first man from clay;
  other animals give ideas, 107–
  115
 length of bows determine man/
  animal share in ruling, 121–
  127
 newly-made people given laughter, movement, language,
  food, 116–120
—Egyptian / Harris
 Anpu and Bata; betrayed, 77–83
—Erdoes / Sound *
 man (species) created from blood
  clot, 98–102
 woman/eagle mate: origin of
  Sioux nation, 72–73
—Fahs / Old *
 how Tewas came to live at Turtle
  Mountain, 7–14

—Glooskap / Norman *
Glooskap as creator, 1–10
—Grimm / Complete *
King of the golden mountain,
425–430
—Grimm / Sixty *
King of the golden mountain,
274–280
—Hamilton / In the Beginning *
Ask and Embla: Prose Edda, 68–
71
four creations to make man, 96
God wants praisegiver/food-
bringer, 89–90
Kamonu at odds with creator, 64–
67
Karora: imperfect creation, 46–51
knowing too much, 97
man evil, woman good (Hina),
100–103
Marduk, god of gods, 84–85
Popul Vuh: four creations, 86–99
Raven, the creator: The pea pod
man, 2–7
Quat: creation myth, 8–13
Sa: Kono creation myth, 14–19
tears of God-Ra, 114
Ulgen vs. Erlik, 28–33
—Hamilton / People *
fear: He lion, Bruh bear, Bruh
rabbit, 5–12
—Jewish / Sadeh
fall of angels and, 1
—Mercatante / Encyclopedia
primal ancestors, 789 (index)
—Mesoamerican / Leon-P, 290 and
297 (index)
MANNERS
—Turkish (Art I) / Walker
host's supreme authority (not to
be contradicted), 41–44
MANTICORA (or Manticore)
—McGowen / Encyclopedia * 38
—South / Mythical

sources; bibliographical essay,
125–131, 386 (index)
Manus
—Campbell / West Highlands,
III.367–395
Man-wolf, see WEREWOLF.
MAORI TALES
—Clarkson / World *
Te Kanawa and the fairies, 140–
141
—Maori / Kanawa *
New Zealand, 1–118
—Polynesians / Andersen, 1–513
MAPLE SYRUP
—Caduto / Keepers *
Manabozho and the maple trees,
145
Mapp, Frances
—Dramatized / Kamerman
Ogre who built a bridge, 278–
287
MARDI GRAS
—Pirate Ghosts / McSherry
blue spectacles: user not wholly
good, 73–83
MARDUK (god)
—Hamilton / In the Beginning *
Apsu and Tiamat, 78–85
MARE(-s)
—Animals / Rowland, 187 (index)
—Crossley / British FT *
Gruagach transforms self into
mare; fights griffin, 228–243
—O'Brien / Tales *
Hookedy Crookedy frees [en-
chanted] mare and bear, 53–
71
—Old Wives / Carter
rich farmer covets young girl; she
substitutes mare for wedding,
61–63
—Russian Hero / Warner *
Ivan son of Mare kills his treach-
erous brothers, 120–124

Marelles, Ch.
—Lang / Wilkins
   True story of Little Golden Hood,
   132–136
Marie de France (12th century)
—Barber / Anthology
   lay of Sir Launfal, 44–52
—Lewis / Proud
   the author; the "lays," 7–9 @
—Lycanthropy / Otten
   lay of the were-wolf, 256–261
MARITAL IMPOSTORS
—Bierhorst / Naked *
   Mother Swan's daughters, 72–78
—Corrin / Imagine *
   Sorfarina escapes dungeon; marries prince three times, 11–22
—Dramatized / Kamerman
   servant tells stories, in exchange
   for clothes, 10–14
—Dulac / Fairy *
   blue bird (prince transformed),
   77–90
   hind of the wood: crayfish fairy,
   43–59
—Grimm / Complete *
   brother transformed to fawn; sister faithful, 67–73
   girl shares bread with three little
   men, 78–83
   Goosegirl: servant's imposture of
   princess revealed, 404–411
   white bride and black bride, 608–
   612
—Grimm / Sixty *
   Goosegirl . . . , 67–73
—Journey Sun (Chinese)
   cruel stepmother, false wife,
   ghost, 6–23
—Old Wives / Carter
   Pock Face drowns Beauty; tells
   husband she has small pox,
   200–204
—Turkish (Art I) / Walker

prince disguised as gooseherd
   to win proud wife's love, 138–
   144
wicked aunt blinds girl; substitutes her own daughter as
   bride, 159–168
MARKET
—Yep / Rainbow *
   husband (fool) and Eel's disguise, 38–44
MARKSMAN
—Vietnam / Terada *
   tombstone grateful: soldier (practice shooting) never hit, 130
MAROONED
—Igloo / Metayer
   seal hunters on ice floe, 49–54
MARRIAGE
   see also BIGAMY; BRIDE;
   COURTSHIP; FAIRY: mar-
   riage; FIDELITY; MARITAL
   . . . ; MATE SELECTION;
   REMARRIAGE; WEDDING
—Aesop / Holder *
   marriage of the sun, 16–19
—Arabian / Lewis
   Hasan, the alchemist, and the
   Jinn princess, 138–143
   king under spell must marry ugly
   old crone, 184–87
—Arabian / McCaughrean
   king under spell must marry ugly
   old crone, 208–217
—Baring-Gould / Curious
—Bell / Classical Dict, 157–158 @
—Bierhorst / Monkey *
   Mole-Catcher marries daughter
   of Death-Maker, 121–130
   rabbit marries coyote's daughter,
   81–83
—Bierhorst / Naked *
   Turtle, his sister, and Great Wind,
   110–115
—Bomans / Wily *

360

Anita: little maybug desires happiness, 83–86

—Bruchac / Iroquois *
avoiding forced marriage: wife of Thunderer, 146–154
two daughters: wise obedience, foolish disobedience, 116–121

—Caduto / Keepers *
deception of Sedna, woman under the sea, 95–97

—Cambodian / Carrison
Bodhisattva's old mother would kill him to marry pupil, 90–94

—Chaucer / Cohen *
wife of Bath: must choose whether good or beautiful, 55–63

—Chinese / Chin *
conscripted husband; fidelity of Meng-Jiang Nyu, 128–139
cowherd's marriage to fairy weaving maid, 113–125
white snake (in woman form), 29–44

—Corrin / Imagine *
prince unwittingly marries Sorfarina four times, 11–22

—Coyote / Ramsey
South Wind marries ocean's daughter, 129–130

—Crane / Beauty *
Yellow Dwarf, Fairy of the Desert, and proud princess, [34–47]

—Crossley / Animal (Grimm) *
wife as partner: hare and hedgehog race, 39–44

—Douglas / Magic *
mortal and god: Cupid and Psyche, 151–165
six swans: king forced to marry witch's daughter, 35–41

—Earth / Hadley *
North Wind (lady) wishes to marry Zephyr, [15–16]

—Fahs / Old *
girl's promise to boy half-good, half-bad, 1–6

—Frog Rider (Chinese)
Frog rider (man under spell); wife fails task; frog dies, 1–23

—Grimm / Complete *
lazy Harry weds fat Trina, 678–681

—Hamilton / Dark *
marriage to boar/man; secret must be kept, 113–118

—Igloo / Metayer
ghost hunter, 82–91
woman a walking skeleton: magic drum, 13–18

—Jewish / Frankel, 650 (index)
demon princess/wife and the broken oath, 432–437
dim-witted boy buys box of bones (chain tale), 414–418
student marries ugly girl; leaves her; Elijah makes her beautiful, 588–594

—Jewish / Sadeh
bride and the angel of death, 11–13
Jewish maid weds old Torah scholar, to escape Graf's son, 368–369
marriage of man and snake-woman, 79–80
oath broken; merchant's son and Ashmodai's daughter, 69–76
princess to donkey's head, 4–8

—Lang / Wilkins
fate of king's son: marry a slave, 513–527

—Leonardo / Fables *
willow and the grape vine, 99

—Lewis / Proud
Le Fresne: abandoned twin "found" at sister's wedding, 20–28

—Lore of Love
deity keeps book; all are foreordained, 18–23
demon-bride's (snake) marriage to mortal, 68–73
groom for the sea-lord's daughter, 8–15
—Man Myth & Magic, 3151 (index)
—Manning / Cats *
man marries bird-wife; his mother drives her out, 75–82
—Muddleheads / Harris
chief mistreats Robin Woman and Sawbill Duck Woman, 44–59
Copper Canoeman weds human princess, 75–93
—Northern / Norman
twelve tales, 277–326
—Norwegian / Hodne, 244–254
—Oral Trad / Cunningham
Socrates Snooks, 122–124
—Pourrat / French
twenty-one tales, 387–473
—Russian / Ivanits, 248 (index)
—Russian Hero / Warner *
Dunai: archery contest ends in death, 37–41
—Shah / Central Asia
Ahmad and the nagging wife, 126–130
prince who married a peri (fairy), 49–55
—Turkish (Art I) / Walker
princess and the red-horse-husband, 12–19
—Vietnam / Terada *
customs: betel leaf, areca nut, limestone, 109–113
lady of stone: man unknowingly marries his sister, 115–118
student enamored of two women (spirits), 95–98
—Yolen / Faery Flag
foxwife, 12–20

MARRIAGE: ANIMAL AND HUMAN
—Animal Legends / Kerven *
Sedna marries seabird; unhappy; father kills bird, [30–32]
—Bierhorst / Naked *
Moose wife; broken promise, bad luck, 52–59
—Chinese / Christie
dog who married a princess, 124–125
—Grimm / Complete *
maiden escapes marriage to hare, 332–334
—Yolen / Faery Flag
foxwife (driven away; father finds fox-cubs), 12–20
MARRIAGE to ANIMAL in HUMAN FORM
—Caduto / Keepers *
Sedna, woman under the sea, 95–97
—Chinese / Chin *
marriage to white snake (in woman form), 29–44
—Clarkson / World *
seal's skin: marriage to seal in human form, 136–137
—Journey Sun (Chinese)
gingko seed stolen from snake king by Achu, 24–46
—Old Wives / Carter
girl marries hyena in human form, 64–65
governor marries "Chinese princess" (snake-woman), 142–148
—Turkish (Art I) / Walker
Cihansah marries pigeon-girl; she finds skin; leaves, 207–217
father forces youngest son to take "frog wife," 172–176
—Vietnam / Terada *
snake princess, 14–17

MARRIAGE CUSTOMS
see also INDIAN MARRIAGE
CUSTOMS
—Geras / Grandmother *
phantom at the wedding, 86–96
—Lore of Love
deity keeps book; all are foreordained, 18–23
—Muddleheads / Harris
rejection of arranged marriages:
evil result, 115–130
**MARRIAGE to HUMAN in ANIMAL
FORM**
—Arabian / Lewis
test for succession: prince marries tortoise, 43–51
—Arabian / McCaughrean
test . . . (as above), 142–149
—Chorao / Child's FTB *
girl given to the Ranee's pet fish
Muchie Lal, 21–31
—Corrin / Favourite *
youngest daughter weds white
bear: East of the sun . . . , 1–15
—Crossley / British FT *
small-tooth dog saves father;
claims daughter, 112–117
—Dulac / Fairy *
serpent-prince: marries, regains
human form, 29–42
—Frog Rider (Chinese)
Frog rider (man under spell); marriage, 1–23
—Grimm / Complete *
Hans the hedgehog: princess
promised, 497–502
princess marries donkey; it removes animal skin at night,
632–635
three feathers: youngest prince
marries toad, 319–322
—Lines / Magical *
girl requests red flower; must
marry Finist the Falcon, 31–45

—Old Wives / Carter
girl marries crab; it takes human
form from banyan tree, 19–21
—Turkish / Walker
princess marries pig (prince un-
der spell), 114–117
—Turkish (Art I) / Walker
princess and the red-horse-
husband, 12–19
stepdaughter nurses, teaches,
weds serpent-prince, 183–188
—Williams-Ellis / Tales *
Well of the World's End, 55–61
Marriage of Mrs. Reynard [Fox]
—Grimm / Complete * 193–196
—Grimm / Sixty * 288–291
Marriage of the sun
—Aesop / Holder, 16–19
MARRIAGE TESTS
—Grimm / Complete *
Marriage of Mrs. Reynard [Fox],
193–196
—Grimm / Sixty *
Marriage of Mrs. Reynard [Fox],
288–291
—Turkish (Art I) / Walker
to win beautiful mute, prince must
make her speak, 34–41
MARRIAGE, UNUSUAL
—Arabian / Lewis
Hasan, the alchemist, and the
Jinn princess, 138–143
—Arabian / McCaughrean
woman marries (a) robber (b)
pickpocket, 218–224
—Chinese / Chin *
marriage to white snake (in
woman form), 29–44
—Dramatized / Kamerman
spouse (most powerful?) for
Susie Mouse, 317–323
—Lewis / Proud
Eliduc: her knight unfaithful; she
enters convent, 88–100

—Lore of Love
   groom for the sea-lord's daughter, 8–15
   ill-starred mating of earth and sea, 87–95
Married life, see MARRIAGE.
MARS
—Roman / Usher, 131 (index)
MARSH
—Crossley / Dead *
   dead moon [boggles; marsh folk], 1–9
Marsh king's daughter (Andersen)
—Carle / Treasury * 112–130
MARSHALL ISLANDS
—Hamilton / In the Beginning *
   Lowa: creation myth, 104–109
MARSHMEN
—Crossley / Dead *
   Tiddy Mun, marsh spirit, 65–70
MARTYR(-s)
—Baring-Gould / Curious
   persecution of Decius: Seven Sleepers of Ephesus, 44–49
—Christian / Every, 93–97, 144 (index)
—Jewish / Frankel
   Polish king and the tavern-keeper, 561–562
—Mercatante / Encyclopedia, 779 (index)
MARUSIA
—Williams-Ellis / Tales *
   Baba Yaga; kindness helps escape, 113–124
MARVELS
   see also GROWTH; MAGIC; PLANTS; STRENGTH; TALL TALES; TASK(-s); TIME; etc.
—Arabian / Lewis
   abandoned children (grown) restored, 166–173

test for succession: prince marries tortoise, 43–51
   well's magic objects do "impossible" tasks, 117–122
—Arabian / McCaughrean
   test . . . [as above], 142–149
—Arabian / Riordan
   abandoned children (grown) restored, 78–87
—Bierhorst / Naked *
   Last Remaining [arrows; plague], 87–92
—Chinese / Chin *
   magic brush of artist Ma Liang, 143–153
—Grimm / Complete *
   glass coffin; bewitched maid, 672–678
   godfather: water cures if death stands at head of bed, 206–208
   Raven, The, 431–436
—Grimm / Sixty *
   Raven, The, 250–256
—Lore of Love
   enchanter's snare, 121
   love potents, 58–59
—MacDonald / Sourcebook *
   motif index, 131–156
—Mex-Am / West
   motif index, 299
—Nesbit / Fairy *
   Billy and cousin: kite/bicycle, 45–56
—Old Wives / Carter
   old Indian woman ties crab to belly, "gives birth," 19–21
—Palestinian / Speak (Muhawi)
   motif-index, 391
—Scriven / Full Color *
   Rapunzel, 9–12
—Yep / Rainbow *
   boasting contest, 96–105
   "Dream Flier," 144–151
   old jar never empties, 96–105

**MARVELOUS OBJECT OR ANI-
MAL, QUEST FOR**
—Bruchac / Iroquois *
  Hodadenon: last one left, 169–
  182
—Crossley / Dead *
  Callow Pit coffer [protected by
  black hand], 45–54
—Dulac / Fairy *
  fire bird: princess, heart of prince,
  153–164
—Grimm / Sixty *
  Water of life, The, 264–270
—Lang / Wilkins
  Dragon of the North, 285–297
  Water of life (brothers fail; sister
  succeeds), 362–368
—Lester / Leopard *
  healing leaves for blind king, 59–
  68
—Lines / Magical *
  girl wears out iron shoes seeking
  Finist the Falcon, 31–45
  Ian Direach to bring the blue falcon, 45–55
  Little Fool Ivan sent for gold-
  bristled sow, 70–85
—Spring / Philip
  princess's veil; father demands
  many tests, 75–81
  wonderful brocade picture, 23–34
—Turkish (Art I) / Walker
  sons seek Hazaran nightingale
  for padishah's mosque, 230–
  239
—Unicorn / Coville *
  quest for unicorn horn: cure of
  winter sickness, 136–155
—Wilde / Happy *
  nightingale seeks rose for student's love, 41–56
MARY, Blessed Virgin
—Christian / Every, 144 (index)
  lives of, 74–88

—Floyd / Gr Am Myst
  weeping Madonna (Hempstead,
  NY), 79–82
—Grimm / Complete *
  hazel-branch protects against
  snakes, etc., 830
  Our Lady's Little Glass, 825–826
  Virgin Mary, the woodcutter; for-
  bidden room, 23–29
—Grimm / Legends (Ward), II:457 (in-
  dex)
—Legends / Cavendish
  Our Lady of Guadalupe, 341–
  343
—Man Myth & Magic, 3151 (index)
—Nielsen / Old Tales *
  godmother; returns prince's chil-
  dren, [5–15]
—Southern [legends] / Floyd
  alleged apparitions in Lubbock
  (1988), 100–103
Mary had a little lamb
—Allison / I'll Tell * 152
Masefield, John
—Pirate Ghosts / McSherry
  Anty Bligh: hanged pirate's ghost
  gets buried, 40–44
MASK
—Man Myth & Magic, 3151 (index)
MASS MEDIA
—Rovin / Superheroes
  20th cent. folklore, 1–443
Master cat, see Puss in Boots.
**Master of all masters [gives odd
  names to things]**
—Corrin / Eight-Year * 89–90
MASTER OF LIFE
—Lang / Wilkins
  Indian goes to lowerworld for
  dead bride, 282–284
Master Pfriem
—Grimm / Complete * 720–724
Master-thief, The
—Grimm / Complete * 773–780

MATCHMAKER
—Animal Legends / Kerven *
  boy's dog learns beloved's secret
  name, [18–19]
—Geras / Grandmother *
  use of messy wool to test brides,
  41–48
MATE SELECTION
—Bomans / Wily *
  spoiled prince, perfectionist, is reformed by witch, 126–131
—Bruchac / Iroquois *
  girl not satisfied; snake to man,
  123–127
—Jewish / Sadeh
  daughter wiser than her father,
  289–291
—Manning / Cats *
  juniper bush: when heads are cut
  off, mouse-queen spell broken,
  83–91
—Old Wives / Carter
  girl marries crab; it takes human
  form from banyan tree, 19–21
MATRIOSKA
—Pellowski / Story *
  nesting dolls, 78–83
MAUI
—Fahs / Old *
  takes bird-shape, to Underworld
  seeking parents, 37–43
—Maori / Kanawa *
  birth; found on shore by sea god,
  Tama, 12–16
  Maui tames the sun, 24–26
  Maui uses North Island as hook
  (!) to catch South Island, 17–22
—Polynesians / Andersen, 192–235,
  492 (index)
MAWU and LISA
—Fahs / Old *
  Mawu's ways: apparent evil has
  hidden good, 173–177
—Hamilton / In the Beginning *

Fon creation myth: sky gods, 42–
  45
MAXIMS
—Clouston / Popular
  king's life saved by maxim,
  II.317–321, 491–493
—Folk-rhymes / Northall
  England, 1–565
—Turkish / Walker
  Muslim preacher sells wisdom to
  king, 37–42
  stargazer to the sultan, 98–107
MAYA(-s; -n)
—Bierhorst / Monkey
  the Maya people * 3–23 @
  Maya tales * 1–152
—Creatures (illus) / Huber * 126–134
—Dictionary / Leach, 1217 (index)
—Mercatante / Encyclopedia, 735 (in-
  dex)
—Mesoamerican / Leon-P, 291 (in-
  dex)
MAYBUG / MAYFLY
—Bomans / Wily *
  Anita: little maybug desires hap-
  piness, 83–86
  Anna: mayfly born, weds, begets,
  grows old (all in one day), 43–
  46
MAYFLOWER (ship)
—Gobble / Graham-Barber *
  Thanksgiving Day words; etymol-
  ogy, 121 (index)
Mayhar, Ardath
—Unicorn / Coville *
  The snow white pony, 92–104
MAZE
—Unicorn / Coville *
  stealing water touched by unicorn
  horn, to cure sick friend, 7–22
Mc . . . [names are interfiled with
  "Mac" names]
ME, The (Sumerian)
—Wolkstein / Love, 246 @

MEAL(-s; dinner, etc.)
—Aesop / Zwerger *
   simple (in safety) better than
   feast (in fear): Town mouse
   and country mouse, 3
—Allison / I'll Tell *
   fox and stork; dinner invitations;
   victim of joke, 110
—Erdoes / Sound *
   Iktome invited to dinner; frightened away, 31–32
—Lester / Brer Rabbit *
   invitation to dinner: Brer Fox
   seeks revenge, 8–10
—Turkish / Walker
   bet lost; cook with candle one
   meter from pot, 47–48
MEASLES
—Giant / Harrison *
   boy tells secret to giant-captur-
   ers, 7–17
—Hall / Treasury *
   Uncle Wiggily and the red spots,
   26–31
MEAT
—Navajo Coyote / Haile
   coyote would imitate porcupine
   (bark into meat), 12, 36–37
—Wolves / Lopez
   sacred; "medicine," 92 @
MECCA
—Dictionary / Leach, 1216 (index)
MEDDLING PUNISHED
—Caduto / Keepers *
   How Coyote was the Moon,
   111
MEDEA
—Gods / Schwab, 757 (index)
MEDICINAL PLANTS
—Medicine-Plants / Read Dgst
   ancient lore, 1–464 *passim*
MEDICINE (*including magic*)
   see also FOLK-MEDICINE
—Fahs / Old *

   animals make sickness for man-
   enemy; plants heal, 71–80
—Hopi / Talashoma-Malotki
   fire controlled; So'yoko monsters
   killed by Poqangwhoyas, 1–21
—Lycanthropy / Otten, 331 (index)
MEDICINE-MAN
—Curry / Beforetime *
   [crane] coyote steals sun and
   sets it on course, 10–21
—Erdoes / Sound *
   vision quest [spirits can't be
   forced], 63–67
—Sioux / Standing Bear *
   how medicine-man found lost
   horses, 10–13
   Thunder Dreamer, the medicine
   man, 41–43
   year of the buffalo; the Buffalo
   Dreamer, 68–70
MEDICINE SACK
—Hamilton / Dark *
   tiny thing: Anishinaba and Boshk-
   wadosh, 54–59
Medium, *see* PSYCHIC MEDIUM.
MEDUSA
—Hamilton / Dark *
   Perseus' task: behead Medusa,
   43–48
—McGowen / Encyclopedia * 38
Meehan, John
—Hoke / Giants
   The wicked giant of stone, 71–78
MELAMPUS
—D'Aulaire / Greek * 130
MELANCHOLY
—Lycanthropy / Otten, 332 (index)
MELANESIA
—Dictionary / Leach, 1216 (index)
—Hamilton / In the Beginning *
   creation myth: Finding night, 8–13
—Man Myth & Magic, 3152 (index)
Melilot (H. Morley)
—Victorian / Hearn, 117–127

Melisande, or long and short division
—Corrin / Eight-Year * 34–50
MELUNGEONS
—Southern [legends] / Floyd, 14–16
MELUSINE
—Baring-Gould / Curious
mortal wed to water-sprite, 129–133 @
—Fairies / Briggs, 285–287
MEMORATE
—Russian / Ivanits, 249 (index)
—Scandinavian / Kvideland, 429 (index)
MEMORY
—High John / Sanfield *
devil tests John's memory (humor), 69–72
MEMPHIS (Egypt)
—Egyptian / Harris, 131 (index)
—Egyptian / Ions, 144 (index)
MEN (males)
see also OLD MEN
—Arabian / Lewis
Princess Dunja: all men are faithless, 52–59
—Grimm / Complete *
Wolf and the man [fox's warning], 350–351
—Grimm / Sixty *
Wolf and the man . . . , 211–212
—Jewish / Sadeh
whatever a man does, he does for himself, 281–282
MENELAUS
—Gods / Schwab, 757 (index)
—Greek / Switzer, 206 (index)
MERCHANT(-s)
—Jewish / Sadeh
Blackface: merchant's son in love with princess, 117–121
merchant buys dead partner's sin and guilt, 83–86

wandering merchant and trustworthy ghost, 87–89
—Shah / Central Asia
dream of Habeeb, 56–61
—Turkish / Walker
Muslim preacher sells wisdom to king, 37–42
MERCURY (god)
—Celtic / MacCana, 142 (index)
—Greek / Osborne
mysterious visitors: Baucis and Philemon, 67–70
—Wolkstein / Love, 247 @
MERCY
—Allison / I'll Tell *
mercy repaid: mouse rescues lion, 115
—Jewish / Frankel, 650 (index)
have mercy on animals, not men, 376–378
MERFOLK
—American / Read Dgst, 244–247
—Lynn / Fantasy * 762 (index)
MERLIN
see also ARTHURIAN ROMANCES
—Celts / Hodges *
life and magic powers, 117–132
—Hamilton / Dark *
Childe Rowland and Burd Ellen, 65–72
—King Arthur / Ashe, 88–109 @ ; 190 (index)
—Knights / Gross *
sword in the stone, 7–25
—Lacy / Arth Ency, 382–386
—Pendragon / Ashley
Morte d'Alain / Maxey Brooke, 70–77
—Williams-Ellis / Tales *
Childe Rowland rescues Burd Ellen from Elfland, 24–36
—Witch Encyc / Guiley, 229

MERMAID(-s)
—Animals / Rowland, 187 (index)
—Celts / Hodges *
   Lad of Luck and monster of the
      loch, 89–103
—Fairies / Briggs, 287–289
   Ben-Varrey, 22–23
   Lutey, 274–275
—Grimm / Legends (Ward), II:428 (index)
—McGowen / Encyclopedia * 38–40
—Monsters / Cohen, 260–264 @
—Monsters / Hall, 24–36
—Quayle / Cornish *
   borne by tidal wave, meets/mates
      carpenter-singer, 51–63
—Scandinavian / Kvideland, 426 (index)
—South / Mythical
   sources; bibliographical essay,
      133–145 (R. Berman), 387 (index)
—Southern [legends] / Floyd
   sea-maiden of the Biloxi, 116–121

MERMAN (-men) ("fish-men")
—Arabian / Lewis
   trades (fisherman) jewels for fruit,
      131–137
—Arabian / McCaughrean
   trades . . . [as above], 83–96
—Coyote / Ramsey
   woman married to merman, 150–152
—Crossley / British FT *
   wildman: merman captured, es-
      capes, 334–337
—Grimm / Legends (Ward), II:428 (index)
—Hodges / Celts *
   Lad of Luck, and monster, 89–103
—Lang / Wilkins

   enchantment: princess must stay
      in tower . . . , 415–431
MERODACH
—Babylonia / Spence, 400 (index)
MERROWS
—Fairies / Briggs, 290–294
MERRY-GO-ROUND
—Yolen / Faery Flag
   dumb child draws unicorns, 48–57
MESOAMERICA
—Mesoamerican / Leon-P, 13–34 @
      291 (index)
MESOPOTAMIA
—Dictionary / Leach, 1216 (index)
—Gray / Near East, 26–52, 144 (index)
—Man Myth & Magic, 3152 (index)
MESSAGE
—Erdoes / Sound *
   Owl Woman (Hinhan Win) is mes-
      senger; pay attention, 93–94
—Jewish / Frankel, 646 (index)
MESSIAH
—Gray / Near East, 134–141
—Jewish / Frankel
   birthday hidden until world is
      ready, 338–340
—Jewish / Sadeh
   Sambation river and Sabbatai
      Zevi, 247–248
—Schwartz / Gates, 806 (index)
METAMORPHOSIS
—Lycanthropy / Otten
   philosophical/theological ap-
      proaches, 99–133 @
—Mercatante / Encyclopedia, 780 (index)
—Witch Encyc / Guiley, 416 (index)
METEOR-s)
—Igloo / Metayer
   child-killer escapes as shooting
      star, 70–72

MEXICAN-AMERICANS
—Mex-Am / West, 1–314
   ballads and folksongs, 117–136
   beliefs and superstitions, 137–
   146, 279
   customs and festivals, 147–172,
   281–286
   folk drama and dance, 173–185
   names; speech, 33–38
   religious/supernatural legends,
   67–79
MEXICAN TALES
—Dramatized / Kamerman
   King who was bored, 334–345
   Pepe and the cornfield bandit,
   324–333
   Sleeping mountains, 346–359
MEXICO
—Dictionary / Leach, 1216,1218 (in-
   dex)
—Mesoamerican / Leon-P, 291 (in-
   dex)
—Speck / New World, 525 (index)
MIACCA, MR.
—Williams-Ellis / Tales *
   would eat bad boy, but . . . ,
   131–133
Mice, see MOUSE.
MICRONESIA
—Dictionary / Leach, 1218 (index)
MIDAS (King)
—Corrin / Favourite *
   Midas and the golden touch,
   204–211
—D'Aulaire / Greek * 124
—Dramatized / Kamerman
   anything touched, turns to gold,
   177–190
—Fahs / Old *
   all touched turns to gold, 115–
   117
—Greek / Osborne
   golden touch: Bacchus grants
   King Midas' wish, 9–11

MIDDLE AGES
   see also ARTHURIAN RO-
   MANCES; KNIGHT(-s)
—Baring-Gould / Curious, 1–159
Middle West, see MIDWEST.
MIDNIGHT
—Russian / Ivanits, 249 (index)
**Midnight, moonlight, and secret of
   the sea (Schweitzer)**
—Pendragon / Ashley, 385–401
MIDRASH
—Schwartz / Gates, 807 (index)
MIDWEST
—Humor / Midwest, 1–268
MIDWIFE
—Crossley / British FT *
   midwife uses ointment meant for
   child on own eye, 287–292
—Fairies / Briggs, 296–298
—Grimm / Legends (Ward), II:429 (in-
   dex)
Mighty Mikko
—Clarkson / World * 33–41
MILITARY AFFAIRS
—Chinese / Chin *
   secret of the moon cake [upris-
   ing], 171–180
MILK
—Grimm / Legends (Ward), II:429 (in-
   dex)
—Lester / Leopard *
   magic bird makes milk for famine-
   stricken people, 5–11
—Scandinavian / Kvideland
   stealing, xii (index)
—Tree / Kerven *
   Elder Tree Witch steals milk;
   burnt by Granny, [14–15]
—Turkish / Walker
   magpie spills milk; loses/regains
   tail, 11–13
—Williams-Ellis / Tales *
   magic bird unplows field, gives
   milk, lures children, 62–76

Milkmaid and her pail, *see under*
Aesop.
MILKY WAY
—Erdoes / Sound *
souls wake, to reach happy hunt-
ing grounds, 93–94
MILL, MAGIC
—Clarkson / World *
why sea is salt, 336–339
Miller, Sasha
—Pendragon / Ashley
King's man: Merlin and Niniane,
78–88
MILLER(-s)
—Clouston / Popular
miller's son: letter contains death-
warrant, II.458–466
—Grimm / Legends (Ward), II:429 (in-
dex)
—Rockwell / Puss *
Miller (The), his son, and the don-
key, 27–29
—Wilde / Lynch *
devoted friend: Little Hans and
the miller, 24–40
Millions of cats (Gag)
—Childcraft 1 / Once * 258–263
Milne, A.A. (1882–1956)
—Childcraft 1 / Once *
Pooh goes visiting, 201–207
MILTON, John (1608–1674)
—Demons / Gettings, 164–169
MINERS
—Humor / Midwest, 163–173
—Journey Sun (Chinese)
Dragon King of Langqiong; five
tales, 61–80
MINERVA
—Bulfinch / Sewell * 78–80
—Greek / Osborne
weaving contest: Arachne and
Minerva, 19–21
—Room / Classical Dict
by-names (list), 327–329 @

Miniature people, *see* EXTRAORDI-
NARY . . . ; THUMB-SIZED . . .
MINK
—Curry / Beforetime *
mink and bluejay retrieve Little
Weasel, stolen by lizard, 60–
67
MINOTAUR
—McGowen / Encyclopedia * 40–41
—South / Mythical
sources; bibliographical essay,
193–205, 387 (index)
MINSTREL
—Yolen / Faery Flag
reincarnation: plant growing from
grave, 41–46
MIRACLES
see also SHAM MIRACLES
—Grimm / Complete *
Brother Lustig and St. Peter,
367–377
Hans the hedgehog: princess
promised, 497–502
princess marries donkey; it re-
moves animal skin at night,
632–635
—Hoke / Giants
miracle manifested to unbeliev-
ers, 79–92
—Jewish / Frankel, 650 (index)
—Jewish / Sadeh
drowning man (far away), 351–
352
promise: man who agreed to be
Moses, 298
—Legends / Cavendish, 396 (index)
MIRAGE
—Journeys / Norris *
quest: city of ultimate beauty and
happiness, [29–32]
MIRAGE ISLAND
—Pirate Ghosts / McSherry
no ships pass; people cannot die,
13–39

MIRROR (sometimes magic)
—Arabian / Lewis
king's quest: secure seventh diamond girl, 144–152
—Clarkson / World *
humor: not recognizing selves in mirror, 367–369
—Demi / Reflective *
reflections on a Chinese mirror, [28]
seeing properly, [2]
—Jewish / Frankel
Rabbi's mirror allows king to see treachery in his bedroom, 405–409
—Journey Sun (Chinese)
wives in the mirror, 109–124
—Manning / Cats *
able to call twelve sailors at will, Vasily saves Leeshy Cat, 37–50
—Quayle / Shining *
mother's mirror warns Sachiko of stepmother in rat-form, 90–96
—Scary / Young *
Bloody Mary (a tale in rhyme), 58–60

Mirror, carpet, and lemon
—Turkish / Walker, 132–134

MISADVENTURE
—Bierhorst / Monkey *
boy-servant of Chac (rain-god); repeated disobedience, 66–69

MISER(-s)
—Arabian / McCaughrean
miser's everlasting shoes, 58–64
—Fairies / Briggs
fairy group, 299–300
—Jewish / Frankel
kamzan: two keys to each coffer, 369–371
mirror and the glass, 552–553
Yossele the holy miser gives secretly, as God gives, 557–560

—Jewish / Sadeh
accept demon's gift: fall into his net, 169–172
charity: eternally dirty pastry, 169
given one hour to repent; fails, 177
miser-innkeeper tells what happened after death, 172–176
—Quayle / Cornish *
would steal gold from fairy Gump; foiled, 64–71

MISFORTUNE
—Aesop / Holder *
lasting remembrance: bat, bramblebush, and cormorant, 8–9
—Allison / I'll Tell *
bear and travelers: test of friendship, 117
—Arabian / Lewis
Attaf's hospitality; Jafar's misfortunes, 199–209
—Arabian / Riordan
porter's tale: king's son and lover buried alive, 112–116
Safia's tale: merchant bites her; husband beats her, 119–122
Zubaida's tale: the little hunchback, 122–124
—Clarkson / World *
foolish man (fails to take advantage of opportunities), 319–323
—Geras / Grandmother *
complainer (kvetch) chooses her own misery, 66–76
—Jewish / Sadeh
egg seller strikes it rich; ends in misfortune, 303
—Vietnam / Terada *
Prime Minister, in former life a tea server, 83–87

MISOGYNY (*prince detests women; princess disgusted by men*):
—Arabian / Lewis, 66–80

—Arabian / Riordan, 66–77

MISSION
—Allison / I'll Tell *
  mice in council: belling the cat,
  121

MISSIONARIES, CHRISTIAN
—Mesoamerican / Leon-P, 288 (index)

MISSISSIPPI
—Southern [legends] / Floyd
  Will Purvis: man who wouldn't
  die, 96–98

MISSISSIPPI RIVER
—American / Read Dgst, 442 (index)
—Speck / New World, 525 (index)

MISTAKES
—Coyote / Bierhorst *
  coyote mistakes statue for (brain-
  less) live person, [42]
  divide catch unequally; profit from
  others mistakes, [36]
—O'Brien / Tales *
  Paddy the Piper, to get boots,
  cuts off leg of hanged man,
  118–127

MISTLETOE
—Plants / Dyer, 325 (index)

MISTRESS
—Lewis / Proud
  King Equitan, seducer; dies in
  boiling bathwater, 82–87

MISUNDERSTANDING
  see also ABSURDITIES: misunderstandings
—Arabian / McCaughrean
  little beggar "killed" over and
  over, 97–103
—Arabian / Riordan
  little beggar . . . , 122–124
—Bomans / Wily *
  king's even more foolish sons are
  misunderstood as "wise," 143–
  146
—Grimm / Sixty *

peasant: Doctor Know-All, 281–
  283
—Jones / Tales *
  Chicken Licken [physical phenomena misunderstood], 16–
  20
—Williams-Ellis / Tales *
  Cap o' Rushes (loves father "like
  salt"), 8–16

**MISUNDERSTANDING CAUSING
INAPPROPRIATE ACTION**
—Corrin / Six-Year *
  Silly Simon (follows suggestions
  foolishly), 120–124
—Grimm / Complete *
  going a traveling, 630–631
—Scary / Young *
  Hobbyahs: master dismembers
  barking dog (tragicomedy), 26–
  30
—Spanish-Am / Van Etten *
  thieves flee, leaving gold, 25–
  28
—Turkish / Walker
  boys steal hoca (teacher) saddle-
  bags, 36
  man asks wife, mother, daughter
  to shorten pants, 135–138

MITHRAS / MITHRAISM
—Persian / Hinnells, 74–90, 143 (in-
  dex)
—Roman / Perowne, 105–109 @
—Roman / Usher, 29–30 @

MJOLLNIR
—Norse / Crossley, 271 (index)

MODESTY
—Crossley / Animal (Grimm) *
  fox and cat; arrogance and mod-
  esty, 8–10
—Jewish / Sadeh
  Jewish shepherd, 328

MOHAMMEDANISM
  see also ISLAM
—Dictionary / Leach, 1218 (index)

MOKELE-MBEMBE
—McGowen / Encyclopedia * 42
MOLASSES
—Lester / Brer Rabbit *
  says that molasses is "fox blood,"
    141–144
MOLE
—Animals / Rowland, 188 (index)
—Bierhorst / Monkey *
  Mole-Catcher marries daughter
    of Death-Maker, 121–130
—Bomans / Wily *
  thrush-girl: learns to understand
    birds, bees, mole, 135–137
—Curry / Beforetime *
  eyes squint, paws bent (from ef-
    fort to replace sun in sky), 89
—Douglas / Magic *
  Thumbelina, 43–53
—Fahs / Old *
  how Tewas came to live at Turtle
    Mountain, 7–14
—Haboo / Hilbert
  moose, wolf, and mole, 145–149
—Hopi / Talashoma-Malotki
  Hopi boy and his two pet eagles,
    150–199
—Yolen / Baby Bear *
  Milly the mole fears noises at
    night, [10–11]
Molloy, Lida Lisle
—Dramatized / Kamerman
  The stolen tarts, 98–105
Molly Whuppie
—Clarkson / World * 54–56
MOLOCH
—Babylonia / Spence, 400 (index)
Momotaro, the peach-warrior
—Quayle / Shining * 77–89
MONASTERY
—Spanish-Am / Van Etten *
  start/stop monastery mare;
    farmer starts, at edge of cliff,
    44–47

MONEY
  see also WEALTH
—Jewish / Frankel, 647 (index)
—Jewish / Sadeh
  dead man's trial: deposited
    money, 258–259
—Lester / Brer Rabbit *
  Mr. Man with wagon load of
    money, 104–106
—MacDonald / Sourcebook *
  motif index, 666
MONGOLS (tales, etc.)
—Chinese / Chin *
  secret of the moon cake [upris-
    ing], 171–180
—Clouston / Popular, II.510 (index)
—Legends / Cavendish, 45–51 (in-
  dex)
MONGOOSE
—Bryan / Lion *
  lion steals ostrich chicks, 3–23
—Corrin / Eight-Year *
  Rikki-Tikki-Tavi (mongoose) kills
    cobras, 173–191
—Greaves / Hippo *
  lion steals ostrich chicks, 130–
    132
MONK(-s)
  see also BUDDHIST MONKS
—Chinese / Chin *
  white snake (in woman form), 29–
    44
—Ghosts / Cohen
  ghostly monks of Glastonbury,
    97–100
—Grimm / Legends (Ward), II:430 (in-
  dex)
—Lore of Love
  demon-bride's marriage to mor-
    tal, 68–73
MONKEY(-s)
—Aesop / Zwerger *
  monkey [dances] and camel [en-
    vies], 13

—Animal Legends / Kerven *
Anansi: how tiger and monkey
both escaped, [28–29]
—Beat / Bryan *
messenger to chief: why bush-
cow and elephant always fight,
14–29
—Bierhorst / Monkey *
monkey's haircut; steals razor,
gives to butcher; takes guitar,
138–143
—Carle / Treasury *
chosen king; foolishly falls into
trap (Aesop), 40–41
—Chinese / Chin *
on road to fetch scriptures, 95–
110
—Chinese / Christie
Chinese pantheon, 126–130
—Corrin / Eight-Year *
monkey to crocodile: my heart is
hanging in tree, 102–109
—Hamilton / Dark *
free spirits: Bouki and Malice,
102–107
—Hamilton / In the Beginning *
origin, 94
—Jewish / Sadeh
Pinchas and the dead monkey,
189–190
—Lester / Leopard *
why monkeys live in trees; eat
pepper, 41–44
—MacDonald / Sourcebook *
motif index, 666–667
—Manning / Cats *
rhyming water-nick fries fish; bear
and monkeys feast, 97–100
—Scriven / Full Color *
organ grinder's monkey; spider;
forced dance, 29–33
—Spring / Philip
elder brother envies hardworking
brother, 114–118

—Vanishing / Mercer *
Nagas myth: originate from hu-
man children, 84–86
pygmy befriended by monkeys,
steals fire, 68–70
—Water Buffalo (Chinese)
origin of features (four animals),
82–84
—Williams-Ellis / Tales *
monkeys steal forty-nine night-
caps, 173–174
Monkey and the camel
—Aesop / Zwerger * 13
Monkey and the crocodile
—Childcraft 1 / Once * 169–171
Monkey [as king] and the fox
—Carle / Treasury * 40–41
**Monkey [dances] and the camel
[envies]**
—Aesop / Zwerger * 13
MONSOON
—Vietnam / Terada *
mountain/water gods rivals for
princess, 50–53
MONSTER(-s)
see also SEA MONSTERS
—Amer Ind / Erdoes, 177–242
—Babylonia / Spence, 400 (index)
—Bruchac / Iroquois *
brave woman and the Flying
Head, 184–187
dogs who saved their master, 85–
91
two-headed snake a traitor, 97–
102
—Caduto / Keepers *
Koluscap turns Water Monster
into bullfrog, 81–84
—Celts / Hodges *
Allyn: how Finn MacCool got his
wisdom tooth, 34–52
Lad of Luck and monster of the
loch, 89–103
—Coyote / Ramsey

Amhuluk at Wapato Lake, 111–112

boy and sister escape from At'at'a'hlia, 75–76

Chetco: monster swept out to sea, 146–147

coyote swallowed-alive, 9–12

skookum and Clackamas boy, 94–95

—Douglas / Magic *

Beauty and the Beast, 85–97

—Earthmaker / Mayo *

Brave Girl and the storm monster (Seneca tale), 28–32

—Floyd / Gr Am Myst

behemoth (bones, mounds, etc.) in New World, 98–101

Minnesota Iceman, 105–108

—Frog Rider (Chinese)

magic gourd; 120 monsters burned up, 71–82

—Gould / Mythical, 1–407 @

—Hamilton / In the Beginning *

Babylonian creation myth, 81

—Hopi / Talashoma-Malotki

So'yoko monsters killed by Poqangwhoyas, 1–21

—Imaginary / Nigg

Scipio vs. Hannibal: the perytons, 69–71

—Indian Myth / Burland

whirlpool; lady Hanging Hair, 40–41

—Journeys / Norris *

great chase of monster fish: Mirragen the Catman vs. Gurangatch, [10–12]

—Legends / Cavendish

battles with, 401 (index)

—Lester / Brer Rabbit *

covered with honey and leaves; seen as monster, 127–131

—Lester / Leopard *

magic bird makes milk for famine-stricken people, 5–11

monster swallows three villages, 13–15

—Limburg / Weird , 58–63

—Lynn / Fantasy * 763 (index)

—McGowen / Encyclopedia * 1–64

—Man Myth & Magic

analytics, 3190 (index)

—Monsters / Cohen

encyclopedia, 1–287 @

river and lake, 117–146 @

—Monsters / Hall, 1–144

fiction and movies, 130–143

North American, 116–129

—My Mama / Viorst *

mother in error re monsters, [1–45]

—Navajo / Klah

creation myths, 85–99

—O'Brien / Tales *

Amada defeats giants (who daily return to life), and a series of monsters, 21–30

—Quayle / Cornish *

good dog Devil; annual delivery of maid to phantom cats, 37–44

—Russian Hero / Warner *

Alesha (priest's son) battles Tugarin, 72–76

Nightingale (half-man, half-bird) captured, 76–80

—South / Mythical

sources; bibliographical essay, 1–393 passim

—Southern [legends] / Floyd

Scape Ore Swamp (SC): the "Lizard-Man," 127–132

—Tall Tales / Downs: Bear

Ozark legends, 126–142

—Tree / Kerven *

one banyon tree covers moon; natural wonders, [4–5]

—Unnatural / Cohen
man-made, 130–141

—Williams-Ellis / Tales *
great greedy beast eats everything, 177–184

—Yep / Rainbow *
cautious brother, and Dagger
Claws, 4–10

MOON

—Aesop / Zwerger *
moon [always changing] and her
[dressmaker] mother, 23

—Amer Ind / Erdoes, 125–175

—Babylonia / Spence, 400 (index)

—Baring-Gould / Curious
Jack and Jill (rhyme), 77 @
Man in the Moon, 74–77 @

—Bierhorst / Mexico
religion and mythology, 236 (index)

—Bierhorst / Monkey *
Blue Sun: beheads younger
brother every day; various origins, 107–112
Lord Sun courts woman; she becomes moon; origin of wasps,
flies, etc., 84–91

—Caduto / Keepers *
meddling punished: how Coyote
was the Moon, 111

—Celts / Hodges *
traditional Scottish folk prayer, 86

—Constellations / Gallant * 202 (index)

—Corrin / Eight-Year *
attempts to prevent princess
wanting the moon, 91–101

—Cotterell / Encyclopedia, 256 (index)

—Coyote / Ramsey
land of the dead: coyote and eagle, 81–84
origin: brothers become sun and
moon, 78–81

—Creatures (illus) / Huber * 155 (index)

—Crossley / Dead *
dead moon [taken; brought to
earth], 1–9

—Curry / Beforetime *
newly-made people given laughter, movement, language,
food, 116–120

—Davidson / Dictionary
angels (28) in twenty-eight man-
sions of moon, 348

—Dramatized / Kamerman
Lady Moon and the thief, 23–31

—Dulac / Fairy *
buried moon (captured by evil
bog creatures), 7–14

—Fahs / Old *
moon's origin: boy cheats at ball-
game, 81–83

—Ghosts / Starkey
moon (personified) captured/
rescued (bogles), 96–101

—Glooskap / Norman *
panther-witch (banishment) and
her scissorbill birds, 39–49

—Grimm / Complete *
origin of position: moon stolen by
four men; St. Peter, 713–715

—Hamilton / In the Beginning *
Ananse creation myth, 52–57
Mawu and Lisa (Fon myth), 42–
45

—Harris-Parks / Jump *
moon in millpond: Brers Rabbit
and Terrapin play trick, 35–38

—Indian Myth / Burland, 39–40, 143
(index)

—Jaffrey / Seasons
eclipse as punishment by demon
Rahu, 71–72

—Jewish / Frankel
"captured," reflection locked in
barrel of borscht, 570

God made sun/moon equal in
brightness; moon wants more,
7–9
—Lester / Brer Rabbit *
animals like to look at Sister
Moon, 1–3
moon in the pond: fishing party,
96–99
origin of marks on, 3
—Lester / Leopard *
why sun and moon [personified]
are in sky, 1–4
—MacDonald / Sourcebook *
motif index, 668
—Man Myth & Magic, 3154 (index)
—Maori / Kanawa *
Rona screams at moon, is
snatched up to moon's surface,
102–104
—Oral Trad / Cunningham
Tree Deedle: man in the moon,
86–88
—Plants / Dyer, 325 (index)
—Polynesians / Andersen
Ina, wife of the moon, 483 (index)
personified (Marama), 491 (in-
dex)
—Quayle / Shining *
Shining Princess (from Moon
People) and deceptive suitors,
13–23
—Russian Hero / Warner *
foolish man exchanges daughter
for help, 57–60
—Witch Encyc / Guiley, 416 (index)
—Woman's Ency / Walker, 669–
673 @
—Yolen / Shape Shift
wer-cat: Moon change / A.W.
Turner, 38–41
Moon, The
—Grimm / Complete * 713–715
MOON CAKE
—Chinese / Chin *

secret of the moon cake [upris-
ing], 171–180
MOON GODS / DEITIES
—Crossley / Dead *
dead moon [marshland], 1–9
—Lurker / Dict Gods, 404–405, 434
(index)
—Mercatante / Encyclopedia, 781 (in-
dex)
MOONSHINERS
—American / Read Dgst, 363
MOOSE
—Haboo / Hilbert
moose, wolf, and mole, 145–
149
—Igloo / Metayer
Kajortoq (fox) outwitted by crow,
46–48
MORAL TALES
—African / Abrahams, 109–110 @
MORALITY TALES
—Clarkson / World *
six tales, 299–326
MORDRED, Sir
—Celts / Hodges *
Arthur's last battle, 157–169
—King Arthur / Senior, 320 (index)
—Pendragon / Ashley
Son of the morning [McDowell],
322–343
MORGAN Le Fey
—King Arthur / Senior, 50–59, 320
(index)
—Knights / Gross *
beautiful witch, 41–58
Morley, Henry (1822–1884)
—Victorian / Hearn
Melilot, 117–127
Morley, Olive J.
—Dramatized / Kamerman
King Arthur and his knights, 106–
127
MORMONS
—American / Read Dgst, 200–203

MOROCCAN TALE
—Old Wives / Carter
    girl who banished seven broth-
    ers, 160–165
Morris, William (1834–1896)
—Barber / Anthology
    Defence of Guenevere, 190–194
Morte d'Alain / Maxey Brooke
—Pendragon / Ashley, 70–77
MOSES
—Jewish / Frankel, 657 (index)
    death of (Ethiopian tale), 167–
    169
    golden calf, 133–137
    thornbush: Moses and the burn-
    ing bush, 107–109
—Schwartz / Gates, 807 (index)
MOSQUE
—Turkey / Walker, 306 (index)
MOSQUITO(-es)
—Childcraft 1 / Once *
    why mosquitoes buzz in people's
    ears, 130–136
—Curry / Beforetime *
    mountain lion "defeated" by mos-
    quito (cricket's aide), 70–73
—Harris-Parks / Again
    Miss Wolf (Brer Wolf's niece) and
    mosquitoes, 22–29
—Lester / Brer Rabbit *
    mosquitoes, and Brer Wolf's
    daughter, 124–127
—McGowen / Encyclopedia *
    origin, 28
—Pellowski / Story *
    string-story, 5–8
—Scary / Young *
    ghost sucks blood from Indian
    mother/child; origin of mosqui-
    tos, 87–88
—Turkish / Walker
    mosquito "hurts" water buffalo,
    14
Mossycoat [a Cinderella type]

—Crossley / British FT * 86–99
Mossycoat (in dialect)
—Old Wives / Carter, 48–56
MOTHER(-s)
    see also FOSTER MOTHER;
    PARENT; STEPMOTHER; UN-
    MARRIED MOTHER
—Grimm / Legends (Ward), II:431 (in-
    dex)
—Igloo / Metayer
    bear kills mother, raises her child,
    118–121
    cruel mother blinds her hunter-
    son, 92–98
—Jewish / Sadeh
    desperate man and prophet
    Jonah, 154–158
    mother sells son for human sacri-
    fice, 330–331
    widow-mother marries lion; lion
    seeks to kill her sons, 92–95
—My Mama / Viorst *
    in error re monsters, [1–45]
—Nielsen / Old Tales *
    blue belt (conspires with troll to
    kill son), [37–62]
—Old Wives / Carter
    escaping slowly: goat and kids in
    Lion's house, 221
—Strauss / Trail
    Rumplestiltskin: reflections of
    mother on child (poem), 28–
    29
MOTHER AND CHILD
—Manning / Cauldron *
    she takes water from Water
    Witch's lake; son to die, 118–
    127
—Old Wives / Carter
    daughter who stayed in fork of
    tree, 33–38
—Yep / Rainbow *
    daughter: ghost's bride, 54–59
    Trouble-snake, 118–123

MOTHER GODDESS
see also EARTH MOTHERS
—Man Myth & Magic, 3154 (index)
—Mercatante / Encyclopedia, 782 (index)
MOTHER HOLLA
—Grimm / Legends (Ward), II:431 (index)
Mother Hulda
—Grimm / Complete * 133–136
—Grimm / Sixty * 111–115
MOTHER-IN-LAW
—Bruchac / Iroquois *
    Okteondon defeats Workers of
    Evil, 104–114
MOTHER OF GOD
—Russian / Ivanits, 249 (index)
MOTHMAN
—Monsters / Cohen, 211–215 @
MOTIF INDEX (Stith Thompson)
—MacDonald / Sourcebook * 3–390
—Mex-Am / West, 298–304 (index)
MOUND FOLK
—Scandinavian / Kvideland, 426 (index)
MOUNDS
—Southern [legends] / Floyd, 17–20
MOUNT HOOD
—Caduto / Keepers *
    transformation: Loo-Wit, the fire-
    keeper, 41–43
MOUNT KATAHDIN
—Journeys / Norris *
    visit to spirits of Mt. Katahdin,
    [19–21]
MOUNT MERU
—Indic / Ions, 143 (index)
MOUNT OOBI-OOBI
—Tree / Kerven *
    creator Baiame to land of flowers,
    [22–25]
MOUNT SAINT HELENS
—Caduto / Keepers *
    Loo-Wit, the fire-keeper, 41–43

—Earthmaker / Mayo *
    monster overeats and erupts,
    65 @
MOUNT SHASTA
—Curry / Beforetime *
    Old-Man-Above lives in ice
    "teepee": smoke-hole, 1–4
—Floyd / Gr Am Myst
    mystic village, 39–42
MOUNT SINAI
—Schwartz / Gates, 807 (index)
MOUNTAIN(-s)
see also MAGNETIC MOUNTAIN
—Babylonia / Spence, 401 (index)
—Cotterell / Encyclopedia, 256 (index)
—Curry / Beforetime *
    animals build Sierras, to be rid of
    coyote, 22–25
—Earthmaker / Mayo *
    Black Elk digs up the mountains
    (Apache tale), 18–22
    origins, 17 @
—Grimm / Complete *
    glass; princess under spell, bro-
    ken by persistence, 431–436
    glass; seven ravens [transformed
    brothers], 137–139
—Grimm / Legends (Ward), II:431 (index)
—Grimm / Sixty *
    glass; seven ravens . . . , 284–
    287
    glass; princess under spell, bro-
    ken by persistence, 250–256
—Haboo / Hilbert
    legend of the Three Sisters, 123–
    126
—Jewish / Sadeh
    fly and spider; incense: knowl-
    edge and understanding, 389–
    392
—Legends / Cavendish, 428 (index)
—Lewis / Proud

Two Lovers Mountain: carry princess to top, 48–52

—Man Myth & Magic, 3154 (index)

MOUNTAIN: CREATION/ORIGIN

—Caduto / Keepers *

Four Worlds (Dine); creation of mountains, 31–34

—Curry / Beforetime *

animals build Sierras, to be rid of coyote, 22–25

—Journey Sun (Chinese)

Yangang saves village incinerated by shooting star, 47–60

MOUNTAIN GOD

—Spring / Philip

Akui frees water; turns to stone, 87–93

—Williams-Ellis / Tales *

Sister Long-Hair steals stream from mountain god, 161–171

MOUNTAIN LION

—Childcraft 3 / Stories *

Tony Beaver: how it snowed fur and rained fry cakes, 199–201

—Curry / Beforetime *

mountain lion "defeated" by mosquito (cricket's aide), 70–73

—Spanish-Am / Van Etten *

animals (except mouse) flatter mountain lion, 106–108

MOUNTAIN MEN

—American / Read Dgst, 174–189

MOURNING

—Fahs / Old *

Krishna helps good king win over evil, 111

—Hopi Coyote / Malotki

hawk eats all her children; coyote would learn her dirge, 105–111

—Jewish / Sadeh

children live again: rabbi will not mourn on Sabbath, 336–337

MOUSE / MICE

see also Aesop: Belling the cat

Aesop: Lion and the mouse

Aesop: Town mouse . . .

—Animals / Rowland, 188 (index)

—Clarkson / World *

mouse tries to regain bitten-off tail, 237–241

—Corrin / Six-Year *

captured field mouse escapes with acorn, 113–115

farm couple adopt boy-mouse; he seeks a wife, 125–131

—Crossley / Animal (Grimm) *

cat/mouse partnership, 21–25

—Douglas / Magic *

Thumbelina, 43–53

—Dramatized / Kamerman

Spouse (sun? cloud? wind?) for Susie Mouse, 317–323

—Egyptian / Harris

lion and mouse; extended story, 32–33

—Erdoes / Sound *

gives one eye to trickster Veeho, 86–89

mice powwow in elk skull, 68–70

—Grimm / Complete *

mouse, bird, sausage [trade duties = disaster], 131–133

—Grimm / Sixty *

mouse, bird . . . , (as above), 108–110

—Jewish / Frankel

mouse seeks a wife (fable), 463–465

mouse wants not to share food with cat; God punishes, 41–42

—Jewish / Sadeh

mice that ate the iron, 317–318

—Jones / Tales *

Titty Mouse and Tatty Mouse, 21–26

—Lang / Wilkins

Little good mouse (fairy helps imprisoned queen), 116–127

—MacDonald / Sourcebook *
   motif index, 670
—Manning / Cats *
   juniper bush: when heads are cut
      off, mouse-queen spell broken,
      83–91
—Nesbit / Fairy *
   clockwork; town in the library, 81–
      98
—Paxton / Belling *
   belling the cat (Aesop; a verse
      version), [6–9]
—Pellowski / Family *
   handkerchief story, 69–72
—Pellowski / Story *
   finger-play story, 96
—Rowland / Animal, 188 (index)
—Spanish-Am / Van Etten *
   animals (except mouse) flatter
      mountain lion, 106–108
   ant, etc. tell suitor what drum is
      made of (flea hide), 65–72
—Tall Tales / Downs: Bear
   the young man and the mouse /
      W. Saroyan, 333–335
—Turkish / Walker
   boasting mouse misunder-
      stands natural phenomena,
      1–3
—Vanishing / Mercer *
   Nagas myth: rice as food for men
      and mice; origin, 89–90
—Williams-Ellis / Tales *
   mice repel invaders of kingdom of
      friendly humans, 45–54
—Witches / Iosa *
   animals help kind children es-
      cape giant witch, 18–22
**Mouse, bird, sausage [trade duties
   = disaster]**
—Grimm / Complete * 131–133
—Grimm / Sixty * 108–110
MOUSE-CHILD
—Turkish / Walker

Hasan, the heroic mouse-child,
   8–10
—Zipes / Beauties *
   little mouse (fairy; story by
      d'Aulnoy), 350–361
MOUSE WOMAN
—Muddleheads / Harris
   Asdilda desecrates Cormorant
      Hat, 94–114
   Copper Canoeman weds human
      princess, 75–93
   Mink Being wants to marry hu-
      man princess, 5–25
   princess rejects arranged mar-
      riage, 115–130
   seal of Mouse Children recovered
      from Big Raven, 60–74
   wives: Robin Woman and Sawbill
      Duck Woman, 44–59
MOUTH(-s)
—Lang / Wilkins
   Toads and diamonds (kind girl
      and proud sister speak), 106–
      109
—Ramsey / Coyote
   coyote and mouthless man, 49–
      51
Mr. Vinegar
—Rockwell / Puss, 6–65 *
MUCHIE LAL
—Chorao / Child's FTB *
   girl given to the Ranee's pet fish,
      21–31
MUDDLEHEADEDNESS
—Muddleheads / Harris
   Mouse Woman stories, 1–131
MULE
—Crossley / British FT *
   fool and mule follow bird; mule's
      marvelous acts, 295–303
—Spanish-Am / Van Etten *
   Pedro and priest's mule trade
      places; bad for both, 90–
      94

MULLAH
—MacDonald / Sourcebook *
   motif index, 671
MUMMY
—Egyptian / Mercatante, 97–98
—Restless / Cohen *
   the mummy's ghost, 3–15
—Unnatural / Cohen, 119–129
MUNACHAR and MANACHAR
—Jones / Tales *, 27–34
MUONG PEOPLE
—Vietnam / Terada * 63 @
Murat, Henriette Julie de
—Zipes / Beauties *
   Palace of revenge, The, 131–141
MURDER(-s; -ed; -ers)
   see also Blue Beard
—Arabian / Lewis
   Ali Baba and the forty thieves,
     188–198
—Arabian / McCaughrean
   Ali Baba (as above), 108–121
   little beggar "killed" over and
     over, 97–103
—Arabian / Riordan
   Ali Baba (as above), 88–99
   little beggar (as above), 122–124
—Bell / Classical Dict
   by class (brother, father, etc.),
     165–169 @
—Bierhorst / Monkey *
   three would-be buyers of jar mur-
     dered; fool tricked: buries
     "one" thrice, 32–36
—Clouston / Popular
   Chaucer's Pardoner's tale: ava-
     rice and murder, II.379–412
   disposal of bodies, II.332–359
—Egyptian / Harris
   murder of Isiris (Seth, Isis, Ho-
     rus), 36–40
—Folk Ballads / McNeil
   folk ballads, II.67–89
—Ghosts / Time-Life

harp: strings from hair of murdered sister, 32–37
O'Iwa (Japanese) murdered
   ghost-wife's revenge, 51–55
—Grimm / Complete *
   bright sun brings murderer to
     light, 528–529
   juniper tree: murder exposed by
     singing bird, 220–229
   man tied in sack; Turnip, The,
     637–640
   singing bone: murder revealed,
     148–150
   wizard captures three sisters;
     Fitcher's bird, 216–220
—Grimm / Legends (Ward), II:432 (in-
   dex)
—Grimm / Sixty *
   man tied in sack; Turnip, The,
     213–216
—Hamilton / Dark *
   John (brother) kills Little Tom;
     talking bone reveals truth,
     132–136
—Jewish / Sadeh
   intended; Bishop of Salzburg
     converted, 225–226
—Lore of Love
   illicit love; head buried in pot of
     basil, 64–65
   stone avenger drags Don Juan to
     hell, 61–63
—Lycanthropy / Otten, 332 (index)
—Maori / Kanawa *
   Kupe leaves, to drown so as to
     marry, 28–34
—Old Wives / Carter
   Pock Face drowns Beauty; tells
     husband she has small pox,
     200–204
—Pirate Ghosts / McSherry
   red swimmer: father and daugh-
     ter murdered by Luke Treach,
     45–68

treasure: digging at Pistol Key, 166–181
—Ramsey / Coyote
red willow, maiden's blood, 31
—Scandinavian / Kvideland
murdered children, x (index)
—Scary / Young *
beheads boy; makes his sister think she killed him; cooks boy, 78–83
boy reincarnated as bird; sings tale of murder; revenge, 78–83
—Turkish / Walker
strategy: Karacor and the giants, 52–61
—Vietnam / Terada *
Tam kills stepsister Cam; takes her place as king's wife, 23–34
—Yolen / Shape Shift
Dinesen, I. / The sailor-boy's tale, 52–60
MURPHY, Bridey
—Floyd / Gr Am Myst, 136–141
MUSES (goddesses)
—D'Aulaire / Greek * 191 (index)
MUSHROOM
—Corrin / Six-Year *
Tim Rabbit uses mushroom as umbrella, 161–165
MUSIC
see also FOLK MUSIC; SONG(-s)
—Japanese / Tyler, 338 (index)
—Lurker / Dict Gods, 406, 435 (index)
—Man Myth & Magic, 3155 (index)
MUSIC: FIFE
—O'Brien / Tales *
goatskin-clad Eamonn: fife forces dancing (wolf and jealous rival Fiac) 38–43
MUSIC: FLUTE
—Erdoes / Sound *

flute entices girls to ghostly lover, 95–97
origins, 3–9
—Jewish / Frankel
Yom Kippur flute carries synagogue prayers to heaven, 475–477
—Manning / Cauldron *
witch's flute: goatherd can't stop playing; goats and people can't stop dancing, 99–105
—Maori / Kanawa *
Hinemoa and Tutanekai; guided by flute, 36–44
—Yep / Rainbow *
enchanted dragons: the rainbow people, 162–168
MUSIC: GUITAR
—Bierhorst / Monkey *
monkey's haircut; steals razor, gives to butcher; takes guitar, 138–143
MUSIC: HARP(-s)
—Fahs / Old *
weeping of the birch tree, 15–18
—Ghosts / Time-Life
strings from hair of murdered sister, 32–37
MUSIC: HORN
—Corrin / Imagine *
Onsongo distracts Masai herdsmen; horn hidden, tied to crane's leg, 80–96
MUSIC: PIANO
—Pellowski / Story *
lion on the path: thumb-piano story, 103–106
rabbit and hyena play sanza; thumb-piano story, 107–110
MUSICAL INSTRUMENTS (sometimes magic)
see also REINCARNATION as MUSICAL INSTRUMENT
—Hepburn / World *

Tattercoats: gooseherd plays flute; prince falls in love, 90–109
—Pellowski / Story * 102–112

MUSICIANS
see also Bremen Town musicians
—Dramatized / Kamerman
Musicians of Bremen Town, 155–161
—Grimm / Complete *
promises to teach animals to play, 56–58
—Vietnam / Terada *
woman cries when musician plays (husband couldn't play either), 132

Musil, Rosemary G.
—Kamerman / Dramatized
Peach tree kingdom, 288–305

MUSKRAT
—Caduto / Keepers *
earth's origin; primal water; turtle's back, 25–26
—Earth / Hadley *
bit of earth: Weesack-Kachak's world destroyed by flood, [6–7]

MUTILATION(-s)
—Arabian / Lewis
Moorish sorcerer vs. king, 60–64
—Arabian / McCaughrean
Moorish sorcerer vs. king, 133–141
Sinbad's second voyage, 22–28
—Arabian / Riordan
porter's tale: blinded by vizier, 112–116
—Caduto / Keepers *
Sedna, woman under the sea, 95–97
—Corrin / Eight-Year *
Sir Gawaine and the Green Knight, 161–172
—Egyptian / Harris

brothers (Lies and Truth personified), 84–85
murder of Isiris (Seth, Isis, Horus), 36–40
—Fahs / Old *
daughter saves father from punishment, 133–138
—Grimm / Complete *
girl without hands; goodness wins over devil, 160–166
two travellers: tailor and shoemaker, 386–496
—Hopi / Talashoma-Malotki
how the Poqangwhoyas turned two girls to stone, 92–107
—Jewish / Frankel
stepmother sends Miriam to be killed in forest, 579–583
—Old Wives / Carter
Mr. Fox: his betrothed dreams of him mutilating woman for ring, 8–10
—Ramsey / Coyote
coyote and two frog-women, 152–153
—Turkish (Art I) / Walker
tyrant Bolu Bey blinds man; son gets revenge, 99–109
wicked aunt blinds girl; substitutes her own daughter as bride, 159–168

MUTTON
—High John / Sanfield *
caught killing sheep, pretends self-defense, 19–22

My household
—Grimm / Complete * 624

MYSTERY
—Mesoamerican / Leon-P, 297 (index)

Mystery Hill, NH
—Floyd / Gr Am Myst, 28–32

MYSTICISM / MYSTICS
—Drury / Dictionary, 1–281 @

—Man Myth & Magic
analytics, 3200–01 (index)
—Schwartz / Gates, 807 (index)
MYTH(-s; -ology)
see also particular national or
ethnic entries:
BRITISH . . . ; CHINESE . . . ;
GREEK . . . ; etc.
—Bosma / Classroom
study and teaching (elementary),
1–116
—Campbell / West Highlands
theory; origin, IV.274–315 @
—Clarkson / World *
pourquoi tales compared with,
345 @
—Cotterell / Encyclopedia, 1–260 @
—Every / Christian, 144 (index)
necessity of, 123–129
—Gould / Mythical
transference from Old to New
World, 137–157 @
—Hamilton / In the Beginning
introduction; description, [ix]-xi
types, in this collection, 155–157
—Hinnells / Persian
history and, 110–119
nature of, 20–21
—Lurker / Dict Gods, 1–451
—Lynn / Fantasy *
annotated bibliography, 185–210
—Mercatante / Encyclopedia, 1–807 @
definition, xiv @
—Schwartz / Gates, 807 (index)
—Walker / Woman's Ency, 1–1124 @
Mythical animals, see ANIMAL(-s),
MYTHICAL.

NABU
—Babylonia / Spence, 401 (index)
NABUCHADNEZZAR
—Babylonia / Spence, 402 (index)

NACHMAN of Bratslav, Rabbi
—Schwartz / Gates, 807 (index)
NAGAS
—Indic / Ions, 143 (index)
—McGowen / Encyclopedia * 42
NAHMAN, Reb
—Jewish / Frankel, xvi (index)
NAHUAS
—Mesoamerican / Leon-P, 292 (in-
dex)
Nail, The
—Grimm / Complete * 748
Nail Soup
—Rockwell / Puss, 12–18 *
NAKATI (playmate)
—Bryan / Lion *
son of Mother Wind, 24–39
NAME(-s)
—Bryan / Lion *
son of Mother Wind [name a se-
cret], 24–39
—MacDonald / Sourcebook *
motif index, 672
NAME-GUESSING
see also Rumpelstiltskin
—Animal Legends / Kerven *
matchmaker: boy's dog learns be-
loved's secret name, [18–19]
—Corrin / Imagine *
popplesnitch: huntsman's pact
with demon to produce un-
known bird, 70–79
—Dramatized / Kamerman
ogre; guess name; carpenter's
ear, 278–287
—Ghosts / Starkey
"Whuppity Stoorie," 44–51
—Quayle / Cornish *
Duffy's pact: devil will do spinning; guess name for release,
75–87
—Williams-Ellis / Tales *
Tom-Tit-Tot spins skeins for girl,
185–195

NAME TABOO
—Dramatized / Kamerman
    ogre; guess name; carpenter's
    ear, 278–287
—Turkish (Art I) / Walker
    must not explain actions; quest
    for arrogant princess, 123–136
—Yep / Rainbow *
    "Snake-spoke," 86–95
NAPI TALES
—Bullchild / Sun, 127–228
**NAPOLEON Bonaparte (1729–
    1821)**
—Restless / Cohen *
    death and tragedy follow haunted
    hooded-chair, 94–102
—Southern [legends] / Floyd
    Peter Stuart Ney: Napoleon's
    General? 162–165
NARCISSUS
—Greek / Osborne
    face in the pool: Echo and Narcis-
    sus, 29–32
NARNAUK
—Muddleheads / Harris
    Mouse Woman stories, 1–131
Nash, Ogden (1902–1971)
—Childcraft 1 / Once *
    Custard the Dragon, 272–275
NASREDDIN HOCA
—Turkish / Walker
    Emperor Tamerlane; two tales,
    37–47
Nasr-ed-din Hodja in the pulpit
—Clarkson / World * 289–290
Native American, see INDIAN(-s).
NATURAL LAWS
—Old Wives / Carter
    nature helps man understand
    God's laws, 222–224
NATURAL ORDER
—Bruchac / Iroquois *
    first man/woman, 15–17
—Chinese / Chin *

    year of the rat [etc., Chinese cal-
    endar], 157–167
—Childcraft 3 / Stories *
    creation: Glooscap vs. Malsum,
    143–151
—Curry / Beforetime *
    length of bows determine man/
    animal share in ruling, 121–
    127
—Erdoes / Sound *
    remaking of the (3rd) world, 126–
    129
NATURAL PHENOMENA
—Cotterell / Encyclopedia, 256 (in-
    dex)
NATURE
    see also ABSURDITIES: disre-
    gard of proper nature
—Aesop / Reeves-Wilson *
    cat to woman; nature can't
    change, 61
—Bomans / Wily *
    simple blackberry-picker has
    riches in beauties of nature,
    47–53
—Fahs / Old *
    unseen Spirit speaks through na-
    ture, 24–28
—Hamilton / Dark *
    cycles: Wanjiru girl swallowed by
    the earth, 108–112
—Man Myth & Magic
    analytics, 3187 (index)
—Victorian / Hearn
    King of the Golden River
    (Ruskin), 3–23
**NATURE: EXTRAORDINARY PHE-
    NOMENA**
—Erdoes / Sound *
    boulder rolls back up hill; vision
    quest, 63–67
—Maori / Kanawa *
    Maui tames [catches in net] the
    sun, 24–26

—Turkish / Walker
Teeny-Tiny and Witch-Woman, 49–51
NATURE WILL SHOW ITSELF
—Beat / Bryan *
why frog and snake never play together, 41–52
—Lang / Wilkins
queen poisons stepdaughter's suitor, 460–473
—Spanish-Am / Van Etten *
father kills meadowlark, dies; need "spirit of song" to live, 54–56
Navaho Indians, see INDIANS: NAVAHO.
NAZIS
—Yolen / Werewolves
gypsy werewolf, Nazi soldiers, Jewish children, 238–253
NEAR EASTERN
—Mercatante / Encyclopedia, 736 (index)
NEBO
—Babylonia / Spence, 401 (index)
Necessities, see NEED(-s).
NECKLACE
—Jaffrey / Seasons
crow drops queen's necklace on washerwoman's doorstep, 81–84
Necklace of Princess Fiorimonde (M. de Morgan)
—Victorian / Hearn, 210–227
NECROMANCY
See also DEAD
—Ghosts / Cohen
prophetic corpses, 232–235
—Ghosts / Time-Life
Lucan and Pompey, 113–117
summoning the dead, 114–117
—Witch Encyc / Guiley, 417 (index)
NECROPOLIS
—Egyptian / Harris, 131 (index)

NEED(-s)
—Coyote / Bierhorst
sickness: promises come easy in time of need, [18]
—Manning / Cats *
old couple: repeated tries to cut down tree; bird supplies needs, 101–106
—Shah / Central Asia
Wali and the magic saddle-bag, 69–77
NEEDLE
—Grimm / Complete *
spindle, shuttle, and needle help girl marry prince, 764–767
NEGRO(-es)
see also AFRICANS; AFRO-AMERICANS; SLAVE(-s)
—American / Read Dgst
got religion? 264–265
King Cotton: the 19th century South, 256–278
why hard work is blacks' lot, 263
—Dictionary / Leach, 1219 (index)
—Pirate Ghosts / McSherry
gallows guests, Gibbet Island: Vanderscamp and Old Pluto, 145–157
West Indies: Saul Macartney and Capt. Fawcett, 84–144
NEITH (Egyptian)
—Wolkstein / Love, 248 @
NELSON, Mary
—Fairies / Briggs, 305–308
NEMESIS (goddess of revenge)
—Lore of Love
vanity's reflection: Echo and Narcissus, 74
NENNIUS
—King Arthur / Ashe, 191 (index)
NEPHTHYS
—Egyptian / Ions, 144 (index)
NEPTUNE
—Roman / Usher, 132 (index)

388

NEREUS
—Lore of Love
A Groom for the sea-lord's
daughter, 8–15
**NESBIT, Edith (1858–1924) [author
and subject]**
—Corrin / Eight-Year *
Melisande, or long and short divi-
sion, 34–50
—Corrin / Imagine *
Belinda and Bellamant, 54–69
—Lynn / Fantasy *
bibliography (about the author),
566–568
—Nesbit / Fairy *
by Naomi Lewis, vii-xvii
—Victorian / Hearn
Deliverers of their country, 346–
357
NESTOR
—Gods / Schwab, 758 (index)
NETHERLANDS
—Scriven / Full Color *
children find cowslips: Keys of
summer, 41–42
NEW ENGLAND
—Dictionary / Leach, 1220 (index)
NEW GUINEA
see also PAPUA NEW GUINEA
TALES
—Dictionary / Leach, 1216 (index)
NEW MEXICO
—Jameson / Buried
legendary lost mines, gold, etc.,
95–130
NEW ORLEANS
—American / Read Dgst, 442 (in-
dex)
NEW YEAR
—Gray / Near East, 144 (index)
—Man Myth & Magic, 3156 (index)
—Vietnam / Terada *
unusual food: rice cakes for New
Year, 105–108

NEW YORK CITY
—American / Read Dgst, 442 (index)
NEW ZEALAND
—Maori / Kanawa *
Maori tales, 1–118
Maui uses North Island as hook
(!) to catch South Island, 17–22
—Vanishing / Mercer *
fishing nets: origin of Maori cus-
tom, 28–31
Newman, Deborah
—Dramatized / Kamerman
Plum Blossom and the dragon,
38–46
NEWS
—Jewish / Sadeh
better to hear of son's death than
of his conversion, 339
NEY, Peter Stuart
—Southern [legends] / Floyd
Napoleon's General? 162–165
NIAGARA FALLS
—Bruchac / Iroquois *
wife of Thunderer, 146–154
—Davy Crockett / Dewey * 40–41
Nicholson, Mary Ann
—Dramatized / Kamerman
The price of eggs, 149–154
Nicht Nought Nothing
—Fairies / Briggs, 308–310
Nicolette, see AUCASSIN.
NIGERIAN TALES
—Beat / Bryan * 1–70
—Dictionary / Leach, 1220 (index)
NIGHT
see also DAY AND NIGHT
—Coyote / Ramsey
coyote shoots the night, 253–
254
—Curry / Beforetime *
origin: bundles, in roadrunner's
pack, 5–9
NIGHTCAPS
—Williams-Ellis / Tales *

monkeys steal forty-nine night-
caps, 173–174
Nightingale, The [sings for emperor]
—Corrin / Eight-Year * 134–146
—Hepburn / World * 48–65
—Lang / Wilkins, 317–326
Nightingale and the rose, The
—Wilde / Happy * 41–56
—Wilde / Lynch * 14–23
NIGHTMARE
—Grimm / Legends (Ward), II:432 (in-
dex)
NILE RIVER
—Egyptian / Harris
seven-year famine, 51–52, 131
(index)
—Egyptian / Ions, 144 (index)
NIMROD
—Babylonia / Spence, 402
NINIB
—Babylonia / Spence, 402
NIPPOR
—Babylonia / Spence, 403
NISSE
—McGowen / Encyclopedia * 42
NIXIE
—Grimm / Legends (Ward), II:432 (in-
dex)
—Manning / Cats *
rhyming water-nick fries fish; bear
and monkeys feast, 97–100
—McGowen / Encyclopedia * 42–43
Nixie of the mill-pond
—Grimm / Complete * 736–742
NIYAK
—Fahs / Old *
Umak and the eagle, 71–80
NOAH
—Jewish / Frankel
mouse wants not to share food
with cat; God punishes, 41–42
NOAH'S ARK
—Unicorn / Hathaway
unicorn, 38–39 @

NOBLES
—Mesoamerican / Leon-P, 298 (in-
dex)
NONSENSE
—Williams-Ellis / Tales *
white-faced simini (forced to use
foolish words), 142–144
NOODLES (sillies)
—Clarkson / World *
stories of bumbling sons, 353–
354 @
NORDIC/FINNISH MYTH
—Mercatante / Good/Evil, 83–91 @
NORSE (-nation; -myths; -tales)
—Campbell / West Highlands, IV.438
(index)
—Clouston / Popular, II.511 (index)
—Dramatized / Kamerman
Frost Giant: Builder of the wall,
422–434
—Hamilton / Dark * 86 @
—Mercatante / Encyclopedia, 736 (in-
dex)
—Norse / Crossley, 1–276
glossary, 237–253
Norsemen, 272 (index)
—Scandinavian / Davidson, 1–143
NORTH CAROLINA
—Floyd / Gr Am Myst
Barisal Guns, 114–116
—Southern [legends] / Floyd
Edward Teach: Blackbeard the
Pirate, 154–161
Peter Stuart Ney: Napoleon's
General? 162–165
Norton, Andre
—Pendragon / Ashley
Artos, son of Marius, 344–371
NORWEGIAN TALES
—Manning / Cauldron *
amber witch: common man, loved
by princess, sent to get amber,
18–31
—Norwegian / Asbjornsen, 1–188

—Norwegian / Hodne 1–400
—Old Wives / Carter
rich farmer covets young girl; she
substitutes mare for wedding,
61–63
—Trolls / Asbjornsen, 1–82
—Williams-Ellis / Tales *
trolls driven away by bear, 17–
23
NOSE
—Lewis / Proud
Bisclavret: girl children born with-
out noses, 29–35
—Water Buffalo (Chinese)
enormous candy-man; magic
drum; long nose, 70–77
Nose, The (Grimm)
—Corrin / Six-Year * 74–81
NOSE BONE
—Tree / Kerven *
escape of imprisoned boys in
tree, [6–7]
NOSTALGIA
—Carle / Treasury *
magic boots (Andersen) ("good
old days"), 31–35
NOTHINGNESS
—Switzer / Existential
Goldilocks and the three bears,
17–23
Nourie Hadig
—Old Wives / Carter, 192–199
NOVELLE (form)
—British / Briggs *
eight tales, 67–97
NUADHA (king)
—Celtic / MacCana, 143 (index)
NUBIA
—Egyptian / Harris, 131 (index)
challenge: read letter without
breaking seal, 108–113
NUCKELAVEE
—Beasts / McHargue, 55–56 @
—Fairies / Briggs, 311–313

NUCLEAR HOLOCAUST
—Yolen / Werewolves
Night calls, 95–118
NUDITY
—Bomans / Wily *
naked soul of King Pim, 121–
125
Number four, *see* FOUR (number).
NUMBER SONGS
—Beat / Bryan *
husband counts spoonfuls; loses
wives, 30–40
Number story
—Pellowski / Story *
picture-drawing story, 58–59
NUMSKULL TALES
see also SIMPLETON
—Bomans / Wily *
donkeys and camels: brothers
help others, foolishly can't help
selves, 147–151
—Clarkson / World *
seven tales, 349–384
—Grimm / Complete *
seven Swabians (terrified by
hare; etc.), 538–542
—Norwegian / Hodne, 229–243
—Turkey / Walker, 306 (index)
NUN(-s)
—Egyptian / Ions, 144 (index)
—Grimm / Legends (Ward), II:434 (in-
dex)
—Lewis / Proud
Eliduc: her knight unfaithful;
she enters convent, 88–
100
—Old Wives / Carter
Parsley-Girl: woman steals from
nuns' (i.e., witches') garden,
86–88
Nunda, eater of people
—Lang / Wilkins, 602–614
NURSE
—Bell / Classical Dict, 173–175 @

NURSERY TALES
—British / Briggs *
   eight tales, 101–114
NUT
—Trolls / Asbjornsen
   boy tricks devil into nut; smith
      smashes it, 41
NUT (god)
—Egyptian / Ions, 144 (index)
NYAMBI (god)
—Hamilton / In the Beginning *
   Lozi creation myth, 64–67
NYMPH(-s)
   see also WOOD NYMPHS
—Grimal / Dictionary, 590 (index)
—McGowen / Encyclopedia * 43–44
—Mercatante / Encyclopedia, 784 (index)

OAHU
—Polynesians / Andersen, 496 (index)
OATH
—Bell / Classical Dict, 175–176 @
—Jewish / Frankel
   man never takes oath; result, first
      misfortune then good, 383–
      385
—Jewish / Sadeh
   marriage: merchant's son and
      Ashmodai's daughter, 69–76
   promise never to make oath; results, 154–158
OBEAH (charm)
—Pirate Ghosts / McSherry
   treasure: digging at Pistol Key,
      166–181
OBEDIENCE / DISOBEDIENCE
—Arabian / Lewis
   abandoned children (grown) restored, 166–173
—Arabian / Riordan
   abandoned . . . [as above], 78–
      87
—Bierhorst / Monkey *
   boy-servant of Chac (rain-god);
      repeated disobedience, 66–69
—Bierhorst / Naked *
   Mother Swan's daughters, 72–78
—Bomans / Wily *
   each year witch takes two naughtiest children in Finland, 27–36
—Bruchac / Iroquois *
   two daughters: wise obedience,
      foolish disobedience, 116–121
—Bryan / Lion *
   son of Mother Wind [name a secret], 24–39
—Douglas / Magic *
   Cinderella; midnight deadline,
      109–117
   Cupid and Psyche, 151–165
—Erdoes / Sound *
   doing a trick with eyeballs, 86–89
   three brothers transformed to rattlers; remain friendly, 37–42
—Fahs / Old *
   Niyak, Umak, and the eagle, 71–
      80
—Ghosts / Starkey
   Tammy escapes from Lucky Minnie (troll), 110–115
—Greaves / Hippo *
   zebra/impala, special prey of wild
      dogs, 35–38
—Greek / Osborne
   Cupid and Psyche: four tasks,
      57–65
—Grimm / Complete *
   disobedient child visits Frau
      Trude, 208–209
—Hamilton / Dark *
   servant opens forbidden book,
      summons devil to work; can't
      stop, 126–131
—Hamilton / People *

Little Daughter sings, and escapes from wolf, 60–63

—Hoke / Giants
Indian boy kills giants; then falls,
112–118

—Jewish / Sadeh
absolute, enjoined on younger
brother, 149–152
marriage: princess to donkey's
head, 4–8

—Lore of Love
Howori: ill-starred mating of earth
and sea, 87–95

—O'Brien / Tales *
giant Trencross abducts princess; white cat helps rescue,
92–105

—Russian Hero / Warner *
Dobrynya spares abductor/
dragon, 69–70
milk cows and the leshii, 24–25
Sister Alenushka and Brother
Ivanushka, 108–109
wolf helps quest for firebird; warnings ignored, 112–116

—Scary / Young *
bunny disobeys mother; is nearly
eaten by snake, 34–36

—Turkish / Walker literal obedience:
just say Hic! 76–79

—Water Buffalo (Chinese)
five wishes: crow-messenger disobeys God, 23–29

—Williams-Ellis / Tales *
Childe Rowland rescues Burd Ellen from Elfland, 24–36
magic bird unplows field, gives
milk, lures children, 62–76

—Yep / Rainbow *
after thousands of years: homecoming, 144–151
foolish boy: "Snake-spoke," 86–
95
ghost's bride, 54–59

protector of sailors: "Dream
Flier," 144–151
trouble-snake, 118–123

OBJECTIVITY
—Demi / Reflective *
crab thinks of self as beautiful,
[14]

OBSERVANCE
—Cambodian / Carrison
lost, king tells child how to recognize a king, 86–89

OCCULT(-ism; -ists)
—Drury / Dictionary, 1–281 @
—Man Myth & Magic
analytics, 3202 (index)
—Occult & Parapsych / Shepard, 1–
1617 @

OCEAN
—Caduto / Keepers *
how Thunder and Earthquake
made Ocean, 93–95
—Coyote / Bierhorst
ocean advises coyote to become
merchant; ship's date cargo
lost, [38]
—Coyote / Ramsey
origins: South Wind marries
ocean's daughter, 129–130
—Demi / Reflective *
river god/ocean god: exhalted image deflated, [26]

OCEANIA
—Creatures (illus) / Huber * 116–119

OCTOPUS
—Maori / Kanawa *
Kupe battles giant octopus, 28–
34
—Monsters / Cohen
giant, 153–160 @

ODIN
—Hamilton / Dark *
Fenris, wolf-child of Loki, 82–86
—Imaginary / Nigg
Hugin and Munin, 37–39

—Man Myth & Magic, 3157 (index)
—Norse / Crossley, 272 (index)
—Scandinavian / Davidson
  cult of, 31–49, 143 (index)
ODYSSEUS
—Gods / Schwab, 609–743, 759 (index)
—Greek / Switzer, 206 (index)
—Grimal / Dictionary, 590 (index)
Odyssey
—Mercatante / Encyclopedia, 784 (index)
OEDIPUS, King
—Gods / Schwab, 230–250
OFFERING(-s)
—Jewish / Sadeh
  rabbi scolds poor man offering
  bread to God, 238–239
OGOPOGO
—Monsters / Cohen, 136–141 @
OGRE(-s)
  see also DIVS; GIANT(-s); JINNI;
  TROLL(-s)
—Bierhorst / Naked *
  Naked Bear, xv @
—Carter / Sleeping *
  Hop o' my Thumb, 69–80
—Clarkson / World *
  devil (well-dressed man) tempts
  girl to dance, 214–219
—Clouston / Popular, I.466–468
—Crossley / British FT *
  giant's daughter helps prince es-
  cape death, 313–330
—Douglas / Magic *
  Puss in Boots; ogre becomes
  mouse by trickery, 99–107
—Dramatized / Kamerman
  ogre; guess name; carpenter's
  ear, 278–287
—Ghosts / Starkey
  Draiglin' Hogney defeated by
  youngest brother, 80–87
—Giant / Harrison *

giant who threw tantrums, 33–
  42
witch's spell: giant sees/fears
  butterflies, etc., as larger than
  himself, 19–30
—Grimm / Complete *
  grateful Iron Hans, 612–620
—Grimm / Sixty *
  Iron Hans, 317–325
—Hamilton / People *
  Wiley triumphs over Hairy Man,
  90–103
—Hoke / Giants
  Managing-Molly outwits courting
  ogre, 65–70
—Hopi Coyote / Malotki
  coyote rescues children captured
  by So'yoko ogre, 179–193
—Igloo / Metayer
  forced marriage: "The huntress,"
  99–107
—Imaginary / Nigg
  golden apples, prince, and fire-
  bird, 89–91
—Indian Myth / Burland
  twins: Nagenatzoni and
  Thobadestchin, 97–100
—Lang / Wilkins
  grateful prince: girl helps hero es-
  cape old man, 394–414
—MacDonald / Sourcebook *
  motif index, 156–171
—McGowen / Encyclopedia * 44–46
—Mex-Am / West
  motif index, 299
—Norwegian / Hodne
  stupid, 207–226
—Palestinian / Speak (Muhawi)
  motif-index, 391–393
—Rockwell / Puss *
  Puss in Boots, 80–88
—Williams-Ellis / Tales *
  Mr. Miacca would eat boy, 131–
  133

OGRESS
—Coyote / Ramsey
 coyote kills giantess; herds
  salmon, 138–140
—Haboo / Hilbert, 17–22, 42–44,
 108–110, 150
OINTMENT, MAGIC
—Crossley / British FT *
 midwife uses ointment, meant for
  child, on own eye, 287–292
—O'Brien / Tales *
 Amada defeats giants (who daily
  return to life), and series of
  monsters, 21–30
 goatskin-clad Eamonn defeats giants, 38–43
—Quayle / Cornish *
 Cherry Winbroome in service of
  little people, 91–102
—Witch Encyc / Guiley, 417 (index)
Oisin's mother
—Lines / Magical * 169–174
OKLAHOMA
—Jameson / Buried
 legendary lost mines, gold, etc.,
  131–156
OLD AGE
 see also Bremen Town Musicians; Old Sultan; etc.
—Arabian / McCaughrean
 old fox wants crow as hunting
  partner, 198–202
—Crossley / Animal (Grimm) *
 fox helps old horse, 34–38
 kill Old Sultan, faithful dog, 11–14
—Grimm / Complete *
 Fox helps horse trick lion, 595–
  596
—Grimm / Sixty *
 Fox helps horse trick lion, 241–
  243
—Jewish / Sadeh
 Angel of Death's seven messengers, 180–181

 Solomon asks: most unusual
  thing you ever saw? 49–
  50
—Williams-Ellis / Tales *
 King O'Toole's goose made
  young by St. Kevin, 37–43
—Yep / Rainbow *
 old woman: old jar never empties,
  96–105
Old beggar-woman
—Grimm / Complete * 646
OLD COOT
—Old Coot / Christian *
 Coyote promises "gold" (i.e.,
  tales) to Old Coot, 3–13
OLD COUPLE
—Dulac / Fairy *
 Snegorotchka: snow-child melts
  in spring, 1–6
—Manning / Cats *
 repeated tries to cut down tree;
  bird, instead, supplies needs,
  101–106
—Quayle / Shining *
 Shining Princess (from Moon
  People) and deceptive suitors,
  13–23
Old Echo (poem)
—Crossley / British FT * 304–306
Old Hildebrand
—Grimm / Complete * 440–444
Old MacDonald had a farm
—Allison / I'll Tell * 150
OLD MAN
—Bomans / Wily *
 misunderstanding: old man "in-
  visible" so death can't find him,
  104–107
—Grimm / Complete *
 child teaches parents to respect
  grandfather, 363–364
—Grimm / Sixty *
 child teaches parents . . . , 141
—Journeys / Norris *

road to death: old man takes form
of bullock, [16–18]
—Manning / Cats *
caught cranes carry cart into sky;
bear pulls cart, 91–96
—Pirate Ghosts / McSherry
Terrible Old Man and three
would-be robbers, 69–72
Old man and his grandson (Grimm)
—Clarkson / World * 324–325
—Grimm / Complete * 363–364
—Grimm / Sixty * 141
Old man made young again
—Grimm / Complete * 640–642
Old man with the bump (Uchida),
—Childcraft 3 / Stories * 58–65
Old Mother Hubbard
—Allison / I'll Tell * 83
Old Rinkrank
—Grimm / Complete * 798–801
Old Sultan [bravery rewarded]
—Crossley / Animal (Grimm) *
11–14
—Grimm / Complete * 230–232
—Grimm / Sixty * 26–28
OLD WIVES' TALES
—Witch Hndbk / Bird * 50–55
OLD WOMAN
—Bomans / Wily *
balloon message; with god-
mother's help, knight kills
dragon, 197–202
—Cambodian / Carrison
Bodhisattva's old mother would
kill him to marry pupil, 90–94
—Childcraft 2 / Time *
I know . . . who swallowed a fly
(folksong) 206–211
—Corrin / Six-Year *
ungrateful old woman lives in vin-
egar-bottle, 13–18
—Grimm / Complete *
goose-girl at well; princess weeps
pearls, 725–734

nixie (mill-pond) captures young
man; wife rescues, 736–742
—Old Wives / Carter
courts young man; stays on roof,
wrapped in wet sheet; freezes,
101
—Quayle / Cornish *
to buy a house, she seizes sprig-
gans' plunder, 72–74
—Water Buffalo (Chinese)
woman's coin keeps rice-jar full;
tiger would steal, 55–61
Old woman and the tramp
—Clarkson / World * 370–374
Old woman in the wood
—Grimm / Complete * 558–560
**Old woman who lived in vinegar
bottle**
—Old Wives / Carter, 109–111
OLORUN (god)
—Hamilton / In the Beginning *
"Owner of the sky," 72–77
OLYMPUS
—D'Aulaire / Greek * 192 (index)
—Hamilton / Dark * 23–26
OMEN
—Scandinavian / Kvideland, 421 (in-
dex)
OMEN (princess)
—Muddleheads / Harris
Eagle Clan princess sends chil-
dren home, 94–114
ONE-ACT PLAYS
—Dramatized / Kamerman
fifty folk tales, 1–575
**One-eye, Two-eyes, and Three-
eyes**
—Grimm / Complete * 585–592
ONE GOOD TURN . . .
—Allison / I'll Tell *
dove saves ant; ant warns dove
of trap, 106
ONI (*demon*)
—Hamilton / Dark *

One-Inch boy, the oni, and the
princess, 23–26
—McGowen / Encyclopedia * 45
OPAL
—Precious Stones / Kunz, 402 (index)
OPOSSUM
—High John / Sanfield *
John eats George's possum
while George sleeps, 58–61
stolen piglet, "just possum," 14–
18
—Lester / Brer Rabbit *
Brer Rabbit eats the butter; accuses Brer Possum, 46–50
tricked: Brer Possum hears the
singing, 87–91
—Tall Tales / Downs: Bear
how Mr. Rabbit fooled Mr.
Possum / W.H. Vann, 99–
102
OPPORTUNISM
—Coyote / Bierhorst
wolf and puma fight; coyote
steals the kill, [22]
OPPRESSION
—Jewish / Sadeh
peasant Gabriel and Count Samael, 374–375
OPTIMISM
—Bomans / Wily *
Happy Hughie: how laughwort
began; can't kill happiness,
62–70
ORACLES
—Cotterell / Encyclopedia, 256 (index)
—Greek / Switzer
Delphic Oracle, 204 (index)
ORAL . . .
—Hearne / [Bibliog.]
For reading out loud! 1–266
—Oral Trad / Cunningham
traditional recitations, 1–264

—Turkish (Art I) / Walker
tales, ix-xxxvii @
—Wildlife / Gillespie
narrative, 246 (index)
ORDEAL BY BATTLE, FIRE, ETC.
—Grimm / Legends (Ward), II:435 (index)
OREGON TRAIL
—American / Read Dgst, 196–197
ORGAN GRINDER
—Scriven / Full Color *
grinder's monkey; spider; forced
dance, 29–33
ORIGAMI
—Pellowski / Family * 74–84
ORIGIN(-s)
see also particular entities by
name: ANIMAL; EARTH;
PLANTS; WEATHER; etc.
—Earthmaker / Mayo *
weather phenomena; Indian legends, 1–89
—Northern / Norman
sixteen tales, 61–98
ORNAMENTS, MAGIC
—Corrin / Imagine *
poor mother parts with magic
buckle; pilgrim grants wishes,
124–135
—Jewish / Frankel
rabbi's magic ring: rabbi to
werewolf; wife to donkey, 450–
455
ruby/serpent: Solomon's daughter shut in tower; power of love,
254–257
—Lang / Wilkins
magic ring: happiness and power
if . . . , 220–227
—Shah / Central Asia
Iskandar and the emerald ring,
118–125
ORPHAN(-s)
—Cambodian / Carrison

Phnong family murdered; one
child is saved, 78–85
—Igloo / Metayer
Kautaluk: Great Spirit grants marvelous strength, 35–39
—Old Wives / Carter
co-wives must care for real
mother's children (Dahomey
tale), 166–169
ORPHEUS
—D'Aulaire / Greek * 102
—Gods / Schwab, 759 (index)
—Greek / Osborne
Orpheus and Eurydice: quest in
underworld, 45–48
OSEBERG (ship-burial)
—Scandinavian / Davidson, 143 (in-
dex)
OSIRIS
—Cotterell / Encyclopedia, 257 (in-
dex)
—Egyptian / Harris, 131 (index)
challenge: read letter without
breaking seal, 108–113
judgment by King of the Dead,
103–107
murder of Isiris (Seth, Isis, Ho-
rus), 36–40
throne of Egypt: Horus vs. Seth,
41–47
—Egyptian / Ions, 144 (index)
afterlife; cult, 126–139 @
—Egyptian / Mercatante
Horus and Set contend for king-
ship, 57–68
—Man Myth & Magic, 3158 (index)
—Wolkstein / Love
Isis and Osiris, 1–36, 250 @
OSSIAN
—Campbell / West Highlands, IV.5–
147, 438–439 (index)
OSTRICH
—Bird Symbol / Rowland, 208 (index)

—Bryan / Lion *
lion steals ostrich chicks, 3–23
—Greaves / Hippo *
lion steals ostrich chicks, 130–
132
ostrich tricked into losing fire,
127–128
why ostrich has a long neck, 128–
130
—Vanishing / Mercer *
hedgehog, by cheating, wins
race, 102–105
OTHERWORLD
see also AFTERLIFE; HADES;
HEAVEN; HELL; UNDER-
WORLD
—Celtic / MacCana
Celtic myth, 122–131, 143 (index)
—Celts / Hodges *
apple tree, 75
Dermot in the Land-under-Wave,
57–73
—Hamilton / In the Beginning *
fate of bad/good people, 108–
109
—Legends / Cavendish
journey to, 398 (index)
—Lynn / Fantasy *
annotated bibliography, 155–185
travel to, 210–234
—Russian Hero / Warner *
wonder tales, 51–52 @
—Yolen / Werewolves
unhappy children find key to otherworld, 254–267
**OTHER WORLDS (TERRESTRIAL),
JOURNEY TO**
—Corrin / Eight-Year *
painter (long dead) gives lessons
to servant, 51–61
—Crossley / Dead *
green children (from a land where
everything is green), 87–96

—Dulac / Fairy *
Urashima Taro; Dragon Sea-
King's palace, 140–152
—Grimm / Complete *
Mother Hulda, 133–136
—Grimm / Sixty *
Mother Hulda, 111–115
—Muddleheads / Harris
sea hunters swallowed by whirl-
pool, 26–43
—Nesbit / Fairy *
town in the library, 81–98
—Old Wives / Carter
Kakuarshuk: woman digs to other
side of world, 11–12
—Scriven / Full Color *
Snow Queen [seduces boy; girl
rescues], 35–36
—Yolen / Faery Flag
faery flag (shawl), 3–11
—Yolen / Werewolves
unhappy children find key to oth-
erworld, 254–267
**OTHER WORLDS (TERRESTRIAL),
NATURE OF**
—Corrin / Six-Year *
enormous apple pie (frogs pro-
vide marvelous picnic), 132–
141
—Egyptian / Harris
judgment by King of the Dead,
103–107
—Hodges / Celts *
freed from evil spell by love, 76–
83
—Old Wives / Carter
Kakuarshuk: all reversed in other
world, 11–12
OTTER(-s)
—Animals / Rowland, 188 (index)
—Celts / Hodges *
Lad of Luck and monster of the
loch, 89–103
—Erdoes / Sound *

remaking of the (third) world,
126–129
—Vanishing / Mercer *
living on both land and water;
origin, 40–41
Our Lady's child
—Grimm / Complete * 23–29
Our Lady's little glass
—Grimm / Complete * 825–826
OUTCASTS
—Jewish / Frankel, 643 (index)
OUTLAWS
—Legends / Cavendish, 398 (index)
OUT-OF-BODY EXPERIENCE
—Occult & Parapsych / Shepard,
1600 (index)
OUTSIDERS
—Legends / Cavendish, 401 (index)
OVEN
—Witches / Iosa *
Old witch (Jacobs); kind girl and
her selfish sister, 34–39
OVERLAND TRAIL (to the Pacific)
—American / Read Dgst, 190–211
OVER-PROTECTED
—Jewish / Sadeh
prince who went off on his own,
101–105
Overweening, *see* ARROGANCE;
PRIDE.
OVERWEIGHT
—Paxton / Aesop *
patience: fox eats lunch found in
hollow tree, [6–9]
—Turkish / Walker
fat sultan condemns doctors who
can't cure him, 127–131
Ovid
—Lycanthropy / Otten
Lycaon and Jupiter, 227–230
OVID (43 B.C.?–17 A.D.)
—Greek / Switzer, 206 (index)
—Mercatante / Encyclopedia, 785 (in-
dex)

Owl, *see* BIRD: OWL.
Owl, The
—Grimm / Complete * 711–713
Owl and the pussy-cat / Edward Lear
—Childcraft 1 / Once * 264–265
—Hall / Treasury * 40–41
—Owl Poems / Livingston, 49–50
Ownership, *see* PROPERTY.
OX(-en)
—Animals / Rowland, 188 (index)
—Arabian / McCaughrean
  donkey advises ox to feign illness, 104–107
—Bell / Classical Dict, 178–181 @
—Carle / Treasury *
  frog wishes to be big as ox (Aesop), 70–71
—Chinese / Chin *
  year of the rat [etc., Chinese calendar], 157–167
—Chinese / Christie
  helper of farmers, 97–99
  twisted horns (origin), 123–124
—Egyptian / Harris
  brothers (Lies and Truth personified), false accusation, 84–85
—Turkey / Walker, 306 (index)
OX HORN
—Journeys / Norris *
  ox-horn magically supplies needs, [6–9]
OZARK TALES
—Scary / Young *
  beheads boy; makes his sister think she killed him; cooks boy, 78–83
  Old Raw Head: hillbilly steals/ butchers witch's hog, 11–13
  Sally-Bally: grandma jumps into giant's ear; he kills self trying to eject, 89–92

PACE (running)
—Allison / I'll Tell *
  hare and tortoise: slow/steady wins race, 102
Pack of ragamuffins
—Grimm / Complete * 65–66
PADISHAH
—Turkey / Walker, 306 (index)
PAGANISM
—Russian / Ivanits, 249 (index)
PAINT(-er; ing)
—Chinese / Chin *
  magic paintbrush: artist Ma Liang, 143–153
—Corrin / Eight-Year *
  painter (long dead) gives lessons to servant, 51–61
—Frog Rider (Chinese)
  magic brush: things painted become real, 47–59
—Jewish / Sadeh
  Kerikoz; Maimonides: king's ring found in fish, 215–217
—Pirate Ghosts / McSherry
  hangman's rope: Saul Macartney and Capt. Fawcett, 84–144
PALACE
—Babylonia / Spence, 403 (index)
—Jewish / Frankel
  Solomon visits deserted palace; learns "vanities," 251–254
—Jewish / Sadeh
  Rabbi Adam Baal Shem: magical transport, 340–341
—Lore of Love
  sculptor carves palace (solid rock) for princess, 79–83
Palace of revenge, The (Murat),
—Zipes / Beauties * 131–141
PALESTINE
—Dictionary / Leach, 1226 (index)
PALESTINIAN-ARAB TALES
—Palestinian / Speak (Muhawi), 1–420

PAN
—D'Aulaire / Greek * 90
PANDORA
—D'Aulaire / Greek * 74
—Hamilton / In the Beginning *
  created by Zeus, for revenge,
  136–137
  evils released on human race,
  138–147
PANIC
—Water Buffalo (Chinese)
  plop! spread of unquestioned
  danger, 30–32
PANTHEON
—Babylonia / Spence, 403 (index)
PANTHER
—Animals / Rowland, 188 (index)
—Creatures (illus) / Huber * 155 (index)
—Glooskap / Norman *
  panther-witch and her scissorbill
  birds, 39–49
PAPA GOD
—Fahs / Old *
  drought: lizard keeps others from
  well, 91–95
PAPAGO
—Dictionary / Leach, 1217 (index)
PAPUA NEW GUINEA TALES
—Animal Legends / Kerven *
  how turtle got her shell, [15–17]
—Manning / Cauldron *
  hero Tow-how: magic disk helps
  foil hideous old witch, 58–65
PARADISE
  see also HEAVEN
—Baring-Gould / Curious
  Fortunate Isles: Paradise for
  souls of the dead, 134–138 @
  Terrestrial Paradise, 89–91 @
—Japanese / Tyler, 338 (index)
—Jewish / Frankel, 650, 657 (index)
  two she-goats from Shebreshin,
  564–566

—Jewish / Sadeh
  little window that delivereth from
  death, 319
  location: in the saints, 378
—Man Myth & Magic, 3159 (index)
—Schwartz / Gates, 801 (Eden), 809
  (index)
PARADOX
—Bomans / Wily *
  wind-man controls four winds:
  happiness to one is sorrow to
  another, 76–78
PARANORMAL
—Man Myth & Magic
  analytics, 3199 (index)
PARAPSYCHOLOGY
—Occult & Parapsych / Shepard, 1–
  1617 @
PARENT(-s) and CHILD(-ren)
  see also CHILD; FATHER; FIL-
  IAL PIETY; MOTHER; etc.
—Chinese / Chin *
  clever daughter-in-law, 3–14
—Crossley / Animal (Grimm) *
  wolf and seven young goats, 29–
  34
—Fahs / Old *
  Maui in bird-shape, to Underworld, 37–43
—Grimm / Complete *
  child teaches parents to respect grandfather, 363–
  364
—Grimm / Sixty *
  child teaches parents to respect
  grandfather, 141
—Jaffrey / Seasons
  Shravan Kumar: wife feeds sour
  pudding to parent in-laws, 16–
  20
—Jewish / Frankel, 650 (index)
  ape and leopard: love equally (fable), 468
—Old Wives / Carter

mother foils attempt to abduct
daughter, 33–38
—Yep / Rainbow *
comfort for immigrants: "Slip-
pers," 162–168
—Yolen / Faery Flag
words of power: Late Blossoming
Flower, 21–39
PARIS
—Greek / Switzer, 206 (index)
Parks, Van Dyke
—Harris-Parks / Jump *
six Brer Rabbit tales, 1–40
PARODIES
—Am Child / Bronner
song parodies, 95–111
Parrot, see BIRD: PARROT.
PARSIFAL
—Knights / Heller-Headon, 42–53
PARSIS
—Persian / Hinnells, 143 (index)
PARSONS (clergy)
—Grimm / Complete *
Old Hildebrand: husband vs.
adultress, 440–444
—Norwegian / Hodne, 298–314
PARTNERSHIP
—High John / Sanfield *
tops or bottoms; sharecropper
outwits owner, 89–96
PARTY
—Lester / Brer Rabbit *
breaks up party, 134–137
PARVATI (Sanskrit)
—Indic / Ions, 144 (index)
—Jaffrey / Seasons
goddess gives magic bowl to old
man, 103–109
how Ganesh got his elephant
head, 121–123
King Rudra marries seven sis-
ters; youngest becomes preg-
nant, 110–114
provides palace to cover Queen's

well-intentioned lie, 115–
119
—Wolkstein / Love, 250 @
PASSOVER
—Aleichem / Holiday *
exiles: men chased room to
room while women clean, 109–
121
first commune: three families join
to celebrate; it doesn't work,
122–141
ruined Passover: new clothes
don't fit, 45–68
—Jewish / Sadeh
two washerwomen on Passover
eve, 131–132
PASTORES, Los
—Mex-Am / West, 174–177
PATIENCE / IMPATIENCE
—Caduto / Keepers *
impatience: how Turtle flew south
for winter, 157–158
—Jewish / Frankel
Gentile's impatience at seder
meal, 562–563
—Leonardo / Fables *
the caterpillar, 114
—Old Wives / Carter
Nourie Hadig tells her tragic story
to Stone of Patience, 192–199
—Paxton / Aesop *
patience: fox eats lunch found in
hollow tree, [6–9]
race: tortoise and the hare, [22–
27]
—Williams-Ellis / Tales *
Anansi (death for saying "five"),
143–150
—Yep / Rainbow *
foolish boy: "Snake-spoke," 86–
95
**Patience stone: gypsy girl usurps
lady's position**
—Turkish (Art I) / Walker, 111–116

PATRIOTISM
—Bell / Classical Dict, 182–183 @
PEA(-s)
—Manning / Cats *
    old man: caught cranes carry cart
    into sky; bear pulls cart, 91–96
PEA-PLANT
—Manning / Cats *
    Istvan climbs, into heavens; finds
    seven-eyed goat; falls into
    swamp, 107–110
PEA SOUP
—Bomans / Wily *
    Princess Steppie: King Boruba
    and his rigid "principles," 20–
    27
PEACE
—Fahs / Old *
    Capilano sisters bring peace and
    brotherhood, 104–107
—Leonardo / Fables *
    stone leaves solitude for the
    road; regret, 80
PEACEMAKER
—Dramatized / Kamerman
    Indian boy without a name, 526–
    536
PEACE OF MIND
—Lang / Wilkins
    a quiet spirit valued over beauty,
    etc., 186–189
—Paxton / Belling *
    town mouse and country mouse
    (Aesop), [12–15]
PEACH
—Clouston / Popular
    Luckily, they are not peaches,
    II.467–472
PEACOCK
- -Bird Symbol / Rowland, 209 (index)
PEAR
—Turkish (Art I) / Walker
    golden pears: dervish punishes
    selfish farmer, 53–57

PEARL(-s)
—Frog Rider (Chinese)
    wishing-pearl; God of the West,
    92–99
—Grimm / Complete *
    goose-girl at well; princess weeps
    pearls, 725–734
—Journey Sun (Chinese)
    Yangang saves village inciner-
    ated by shooting star, 47–60
—Precious Stones / Kunz, 402 (in-
    dex)
—Vietnam / Terada *
    Da Trang crab: grateful snake
    gives magic pearl, 37–41
PEASANT(-s)
—Egyptian / Harris
    eloquent peasant: Khunanup vs.
    Nemtynakht, 60–62
—Egyptian / Mercatante
    robbed, pleads eloquently for re-
    dress, 117–120
—Grimm / Complete *
    Little peasant (tricks the gullible/
    greedy), 311–316
—Grimm / Sixty *
    Little peasant (as above), 142–
    148
—Jewish / Sadeh
    peasant Gabriel and Count Sa-
    mael, 374–375
—Pellowski / Family *
    handkerchief story, 64–66
—Turkey / Walker, 306 (index)
Peasant and the devil
—Grimm / Complete * 767–768
Peasant in heaven
—Grimm / Complete * 695–696
Peasant's wise daughter, The
—Grimm / Complete * 439–440
PECOS BILL
—American / Read Dgst, 310
—Pecos Bill / Dewey * 1–56
—Pecos Bill / Kellogg * 1–40

—Tall Tales / Downs: Bear
and the mountain lion / M.
Boatright, 149–150
Pedlar of Swaffham
—Crossley / British FT * 251–264
—Crossley / Dead * 27–37
PEDRO de Urdemalas
—American / Read Dgst, 68
—Clarkson / World *
sells buried pigs' tails, 293–295,
296–297 @
—Ghost (S'west) / Young, 112–114
—Mex-Am / West, 107–111
PEGASUS (*winged horse*)
—Beasts / McHargue, 84–86 @
—Corrin / Eight-Year * 27–33
—Gods / Schwab, 759 (index)
PEHE-IPE
—Hamilton / In the Beginning *
Maidu creation myth, 34–41
PELE (*the fire goddess*)
—Polynesians / Andersen, 267–287,
498 (index)
—Scary / Young *
Pele, Spirit of Fire, vs. Na-Maka;
Kilauea, 84–86
PELEUS
—Lore of Love
A Groom for the sea-lord's
daughter, 8–15
Pelican chorus, The
—Birds / Carter & Cartwright * 10–
11
PENANCE
—Grimm / Legends (Ward), II:436 (in-
dex)
—Mesoamerican / Leon-P, 298 (in-
dex)
—Turkish (Art I) / Walker
three "reformed" brigands
granted wishes; two fail test,
155–159
PENGERSWICK CASTLE
—Quayle / Cornish *

Lord Pengerswick and the witch
of Fraddam, 103–108
PENITENCE
—Jewish / Sadeh
Baal Shem Tov and the frog
(transmuted Torah scholar),
344–345
lead and the honey, 200–201
PEONIES
—Tree / Kerven *
mystery man of the peonies, [10–
13]
PEOPLE
—Baring-Gould / Curious
Tailed men, 62–66 @
PEPPER
—Lester / Leopard *
why monkeys live in trees; eat
pepper, 41–44
PERCEPTIONS
—Yep / Rainbow *
things not what they seem: "The
butterfly man," 60–68
PERCIVAL de Gales, Sir
—King Arthur / Senior, 320 (index)
PERFECTIONISM
—Bomans / Wily *
spoiled prince, perfectionist, is re-
formed by witch, 126–131
—Grimm / Complete *
Master Pfriem [never rests; al-
ways criticizes], 720–724
Peri, *see* FAIRY.
PERRAULT, Charles (1628–1703)
see title entries for the following:
Blue Beard
Cinderella
Donkey-skin
Fairies [toads and diamonds]
Foolish wishes
Hop o' my Thumb
Little Red Riding Hood
Little Thumbling
Puss in Boots

Ricky with the tuft [Riquet ???]
Sleeping Beauty in the woods
Toads and diamonds
—Allison / I'll Tell * 49 @
PERSECUTION
—Jewish / Sadeh
tailor and Haman: "years" really
only 15 minutes, 201–204
PERSEPHONE
—D'Aulaire / Greek * 58
—Scriven / Full Color *
winter and summer, 75–78
PERSEUS
—Bulfinch / Sewell * 88–93
—Constellations / Gallant * 202 (index)
—Hamilton / Dark *
task: behead Medusa, 43–48
PERSEVERANCE (*usually rewarded*)
see also Aesop: Hare and the
tortoise
—Crossley / British FT *
John Chapman, pedlar of Swaffham, 251–264
—Fahs / Old *
girl chooses death over unfaithfulness, 44–51
—Hall / Treasury *
Little Engine that could, 1–9
—Jones / Tales *
Munachar and Manachar, 27–34
—Lewis / Proud
Milun/lover wait 20 years to be
wed, 65–75
—Lines / Magical *
Little Fool Ivan and the little
humpback horse, 70–85
—Paxton / Aesop *
race: tortoise and the hare, [22–27]
—Shannon / More *
trapped in bucket of cream, frog
churns butter and escapes,
23–26

—Yep / Rainbow *
building "Breaker's bridge," 118–123
PERSIA (-ian; -myth; -tales)
—Clouston / Popular, II.512 (index)
—Corrin / Imagine *
The golden candelabra, 151–160
—Dictionary / Leach, 1226 (index)
—Dramatized / Kamerman
Olive jar, 360–374
—Fahs / Old *
Zoroaster: Mazda vs. Manyu,
140–147
—Legends / Cavendish, 5 (index)
—Mercatante / Encyclopedia, 737 (index)
—Mercatante / Good/Evil, 31–37 @
—Persian / Hinnells, 143 (index)
—Shah / Central Asia
Feroz-Shah and the mechanical
flying horse, 131–145
Rustam and the iron fortress, 25–30
—Wolkstein / Love
Layla and Majnun, 147–180,
266 @
PERSISTENCE
—Aesop / Reeves-Wilson *
race: Hare and Tortoise, 68–73
—Leonardo / Fables *
flint stone and the steel, 73
PERSONAL CHARACTERISTICS
—Coyote / Ramsey
mouthless man, 49–51
PERSONIFICATION
[*note: in tales, it is common for
animals and even inanimate
things to be presented as
"human"; the titles that follow
are a selection.*]
—Bomans / Wily *
overcoming curse (personified),
93–96
winds personified, 79–82

—Bryan / Lion *
  son of Mother Wind [name a se-
    cret], 24–39
—Caduto / Keepers *
  how Thunder and Earthquake
    made Ocean, 93–95
  Winter as old man; Spring as
    young, 129–131
—Corrin / Six-Year *
  Little Red Engine: talks with
    animals; ill (needs oil), 24–
    27
  pig (Harold Trotter) with human
    feelings, 62–69
—Crossley / British FT *
  Sir John Barleycorn (poem; liquor
    personified), 132–134
—Crossley / Dead *
  dead moon [visits earth], 1–9
—Curry / Beforetime *
  because it's easier, sun rolls on
    ground; with help, mole re-
    places, 89
—Dramatized / Kamerman
  Dame Fortune and Don Money,
    481–492
  intelligence and luck; make prin-
    cess speak, 47–60
—Dulac / Fairy *
  buried moon (captured by evil
    bog creatures), 7–14
—Earth / Hadley *
  North Wind (lady) wishes to marry
    Zephyr, [15–16]
—Egyptian / Harris
  brothers (Lies and Truth), false
    accusation, 84–85
—Grimm / Complete *
  Death's messengers (symp-
    toms), 718–720
—Grimm / Sixty *
  straw, coal, and bean, 29–30
—Jewish / Frankel
  God made sun/moon equal in

  brightness; moon wants more,
    7–9
—Lester / Leopard *
  body parts argue: which is most
    important, 45–51
  why sun and moon [personified]
    are in sky, 1–4
—Russian Hero / Warner *
  Black Stream (personified); dam
    removed, 43
  sun, frost, wind: honor most pow-
    erful, 32
PERU
—Speck / New World, 527 (index)
PESTS
—Bierhorst / Monkey *
  Lord Sun courts woman; she be-
    comes moon; origin of wasps,
    flies, etc., 84–91
PET(-s)
—Witch Hndbk / Bird * 34–35
Peter and the Wolf
—Bedtime / Padoan & Smith * 49–
    51
—Yolen / Faery Flag
  retelling in "old wolves' home,"
    103–119
Peter Pan
—Childcraft 1 / Once *
  Come away! (J.M. Barrie), 276–
    295
**Peter Pan in Kensington Gardens
[excerpt]**
—Victorian / Hearn, 358–379
Peter Rabbit (*existential retelling*)
—Switzer / Existential, 134–141
Peterson, Mary Nygaard
—Dramatized / Kamerman
  The magic box, 265–277
  Pedro and the burro, 458–470
  Simple Olaf, 413–421
Petronius Arbiter
—Lycanthropy / Otten
  Satyricon, 231–233

PHAETON
—Bulfinch / Sewell * 32–39
—Greek / Osborne
  Chariot of the sun god, 1–6
PHAN KU
—Hamilton / In the Beginning *
  The cosmic egg, creation myth,
  20–23
PHANTOM
—Monsters / Cohen, 97–115 @
PHANTOM SHIP
—Hamilton / Dark *
  Flying Dutchman cursed by God,
  38–42
PHARAOH
—Egyptian / Harris
  Anpu and Bata, 77–83
—Egyptian / Ions, 144 (index)
  protective divinities of, 34–87 @
PHILANTHROPY
—Jewish / Sadeh
  baker's apprentice gets king's at-
  tention, 268–271
PHILIPPINE ISLANDS
—Dictionary / Leach, 1212,1227 (in-
  dex)
PHILISTINES
—Hoke / Giants
  David and Goliath, 79–92
Phoenix, see under BIRDS: MYTHI-
  CAL.
PHOUKA
—Fairies / Briggs, 326–327
Piano, see MUSIC: PIANO.
PIASA
—Beasts / McHargue, 48–49 @
PICKPOCKET
—Arabian / McCaughrean
  woman marries (a) robber (b)
  pickpocket, 218–224
PICNIC
—Corrin / Six-Year *
  enormous apple pie (frogs provide
  marvelous picnic), 132–141

PICT
—Crossley / British FT *
  Pict keeps secret of brewing ale
  from Scots, 142–144
PICTURE
—Spring / Philip
  wonderful brocade picture, 23–34
PICTURE-DRAWING STORIES
—Pellowski / Story * 47–76
PIE
—Gobble / Graham-Barber *
  Thanksgiving Day words; etymol-
  ogy, 121 (index)
—Russian Hero / Warner *
  captive Mashen'ka tricks bear,
  116–117
Pied piper of Hamelin (R. Browning)
—Victorian / Hearn, 24–34
PIETY [rewarded]
—Dulac / Fairy *
  suitor test: Ivan and the chestnut
  horse, 60–68
—Jewish / Frankel, 650 (index)
—Russian Hero / Warner *
  old woman honors the wind, 31
PIG(-s)
  see also HOG(-s); SOW
—Childcraft 1 / Once *
  the three little pigs, 102–106
—Clarkson / World *
  stolen pig disguised as baby in
  crib, 286–288
—Corrin / Six-Year *
  discontented pig: some unpleas-
  antness in all work, 116–119
  pig (Harold Trotter) with human
  feelings, 62–69
—German-American / Barrick
  why pigs have curly tails, 106–107
—Hamilton / In the Beginning *
  Quat: creation myth, 11–12
—Lurker / Dict Gods, 436 (index)
—MacDonald / Sourcebook *
  motif index, 680

—Pellowski / Story *
  hungry Piggy Wig and Piggy
  Wee; finger-play, 94–95
—Tall Tales / Downs: Bear
  Pigs is pigs / E.P. Butler, 336–
  344
—Turkish / Walker
  princess marries pig (prince un-
  der spell), 114–117
PIIKI (Hopi dish)
—Hopi / Talashoma-Malotki, 206 @
—Hopi Coyote / Malotki, 317 @
PILGRIM
—Gobble / Graham-Barber *
  Thanksgiving Day words; etymol-
  ogy, 121 (index)
PINE NUTS
—Curry / Beforetime *
  pine-nut thieves: bluebirds put to
  sleep by coyote's chant, 90–99
Pink [carnation], The
—Grimm / Complete * 355–360
—Grimm / Sixty * 171–176
PINKEL
—Witches / Iosa *
  brothers envious of Pinkel's favor
  with king, 23–31
PIONEERS
—American / Read Dgst
  Overland Trail, 190–211
PIPE (*musical*)
—Dulac / Fairy *
  magic pipe makes all dance,
  114–123
PIPE (*sacred*)
—Erdoes / Sound *
  White Buffalo Woman (Lakota),
  117–123
PIPE (*smoking*)
—Bierhorst / Naked *
  Two Feathers: skills test, 11–18
—Caduto / Keepers *
  symbol of unity of creation, 187–
  188

PIPER
—Baring-Gould / Curious
  Piper of Hamelin: souls of chil-
  dren in the wind, 116–120 @
—Crossley / British FT *
  piper and pooka; carried to moun-
  tain top to play for weeping
  woman, 17–23
  piper cuts off feet of frozen
  corpse, to steal shoes, 283–
  286
—O'Brien / Tales *
  Paddy the Piper, to get boots,
  cuts off leg of hanged man,
  118–127
PIRATE(-s)
—American / Read Dgst
  Edward Teach, Blackbeard, 76–
  78
  Jean Lafitte, 80–81
  Mary Read and Anne Bonny, 82–
  83
  Satanic sea robbers, 84–87
—Arabian / McCaughrean
  Sinbad's second voyage, 22–28
—Arabian / Riordan
  Sinbad's second voyage, 38–55
—Bell / Classical Dict, 185 @
—Ghosts / Starkey
  laying Black Lucott's ghost, 116–
  123
—Pirate Ghosts / McSherry, 1–206
  gallows guests, Gibbet Island:
  Vanderscamp and Old Pluto,
  145–157
  hangman's rope: Saul Macartney
  and Capt. Fawcett, 84–144
—Southern [legends] / Floyd
  Edward Teach: Blackbeard the
  Pirate, 154–161
Pisces, *see* STARS.
PISKIES / PIXIES
—Fairies / Briggs, 328–331
  Old Farmer Mole, 329

—McGowen / Encyclopedia * 45
—Quayle / Cornish *
  Piggin: care and conditions of
    changelings, 29–36
  piskie threshers; leave after gift of
    suits of clothes, 45–50
PLACES
—Legends / Cavendish
  foundation legends, 409 (index)
**PLACES, EXTRAORDINARY/MAR-
  VELOUS**
  see also HEAVENS; UNDER-
    GROUND
—Douglas / Magic *
  roc, its egg eaten, gets venge-
    ance on Sinbad, 21–25
—Dulac / Fairy *
  Urashima Taro; Dragon Sea-
    King's palace, 140–152
—Grimm / Complete *
  Seven ravens [transformed broth-
    ers], 137–139
—Grimm / Sixty *
  Seven ravens [as above], 284–
    287
**PLACES, GEOGRAPHICAL, ORI-
  GIN**
—Caduto / Keepers *
  Loo-Wit, the fire-keeper, 41–43
—Dramatized / Kamerman
  Sleeping mountains: Ixtlaccihuatl
    and Popocatepetl, 346–359
—Erdoes / Sound *
  thunderbirds: Black Hills; Bad
    Lands, 33–36
—Lore of Love
  Aztec couple: reunion in flames,
    52–57
  sculptor carves palace for prin-
    cess, 79–83
—Maori / Kanawa *
  Kupe battles giant octopus; for-
    mation of Aotearoa features,
    28–34

Maui uses North Island as hook
  (!) to catch South Island, 17–
  22
—Scary / Young *
  Pele, Spirit of Fire, vs. Na-Maka;
    Kilauea, 84–86
PLAGUE(-s)
—Bell / Classical Dict, 186–187 @
—Fahs / Old *
  quest: healing waters for wife,
    52–56
—Grimm / Legends (Ward), II:437 (in-
  dex)
—Indian Myth / Burland
  twins: Nagenatzoni and
    Thobadestchin, 97–100
—Jewish / Frankel
  Yahweh: ten plagues punish
    Egyptians, 109–113
—Jewish / Sadeh
  clay barrel: plague averted, 244
PLANET(-s)
—Man Myth & Magic, 3161 (index)
PLANNING: feasibility
—Aesop / Reeves-Wilson *
  plan to bell the cat, 80–84
**PLANT(-s) (botany) (including ori-
  gins)**
  see also REINCARNATION as
    PLANT
—Bierhorst / Sacred
  planting; Indian prayers/songs,
    109–121
—Bruchac / Iroquois *
  hunting of the Great Bear (Big
    Dipper), 189–195
  two brothers: one brings good,
    the other evil, 19–23
—Caduto / Keepers * 3–4
  corn's origin, 137–138
  earth's origin; primal water; tur-
    tle's back, 25–26
  Four Worlds (Dine); origin of
    plants, 31–34

punishment: Manabozho and the
maple trees, 145
—Clarkson / World *
sisters changed into wind-trem-
bling aspen trees, 43–45
—Coyote / Ramsey
origin: red willow, maiden's
blood, 31
—Fahs / Old *
animals make sickness for human enemy; medicine, 71–80
—Journey Sun (Chinese)
qingke seed stolen from snake
king by Achu, 24–46
—Man Myth & Magic
analytics, 3185–87 (index)
—Medicine-Plants / Read Dgst
useful plants: ancient lore, 1–464
passim
—Mercatante / Encyclopedia, 738 (index)
—Occult & Parapsych / Shepard,
1611 (index)
—Plants / Dyer, 1–328
[*text includes tales and summaries of
tales*]
calendar, 216–232
ceremonial use, 145–162
children's rhymes and games,
233–242
demonology, 71–79
doctrine of signatures, 201–215
fabulous, 188–200
fairy-lore, 80–91
folk-medicine, 281–299
language; symbolism, 176–187
legendary history, 300–311
lightning, 41–54
love-charms, 92–102
mystic, 312–219
names, 163–175
primitive beliefs, 18–29
proverbs, 128–144
sacred, 243–261

saints, 326–327 (index)
superstitions, 262–280
weather, 114–127
witchcraft, 55–70
worship, 28–40
—Scary / Young *
ghost sucks blood from Indian
mother/child; origin of Indian
paintbrush, 87–88
—Tree / Kerven *
eleven tales, [1–32]
—Turkish (Art I) / Walker
Camesap eats part of Sahmeran,
learns language of plants,
218–224
—Yolen / Faery Flag
reincarnation: plant growing from
grave, 41–46
PLANT(-s), MARVELOUS
—Bomans / Wily *
cloud tree brings happiness to
three generations, 131–134
—Fahs / Old *
weeping of the birch tree, 15–18
—Grimm / Complete *
flail from heaven, 514–515
—Old Wives / Carter
wicked stepmother: fruit tree low-
ers branches when boy sings,
178–180
—Turkish / Walker
princess marries pig (prince under spell), 114–117
—Unicorn / Coville *
hunting season: children try to
save unicorn, 79–89
PLANTER RIGHTS
—Navajo Coyote / Haile
coyote died (after swallowing
Horned Toad), 13, 47–52
PLATYPUS
—Vanishing / Mercer *
origin: little duck and big water-
rat, 54–57

PLAY
—Am Child / Bronner
    rhymes of play, 51–82
—Paxton / Aesop *
    grasshopper and the ants, [36–39]
PLAYMATES
—Beat / Bryan *
    frog/snake children play until told: snakes eat frogs, 41–52
PLEASING EVERYONE
—Aesop / Reeves-Wilson *
    miller, boy, and donkey, 51–53
—Cambodian / Carrison
    father/son ride/carry donkey to market, 102–106
—Rockwell / Puss *
    Miller (The), his son, and the donkey, 27–29
PLEASURE
—Hoke / Giants
    excess has a bad end (Fiji; Bulai), 130–132
—Leonardo / Fables *
    butterfly and the flame, 68
PLEDGE
—Jewish / Frankel
    unpaid pledge: man wants wife to die, 520–521
Pleides, see STARS.
PLINY
—Animals / Rowland, 189 (index)
Plop!
—Clarkson / World * 233–234
PLOW (-ing; -man)
—Arabian / McCaughrean
    donkey advises ox to feign illness, 104–107
—Russian Hero / Warner * 18 @
    Mikula (peasant) and Vol'ga (prince), 21–22
    No Bigger than a Finger, 128–129

PLUTO
—Greek / Osborne
    Kidnapping: Ceres and Proserpina, 35–39
    Orpheus and Eurydice: quest in underworld, 45–48
PLYMOUTH ROCK
—Gobble / Graham-Barber *
    Thanksgiving Day words; etymology, 122 (index)
POEMS (*poetic verses; poetry*)
    see also Owl and the pussy-cat; RHYMES
—Halloween ABC / Merriam * [1–30]
—Oral Trad / Cunningham
    recitations, 1–264
—Paxton / Aesop *
    ten fables, retold in verse, [1–40]
—Rockwell / Puss *
    Fisherman, his wife, and the flounder, 42–52
—Strauss / Trail, 1–35
—Williams-Ellis / Tales *
    Tamlane (knight) rescued from elfland, 151–159
—Yolen / Faery Flag
    making dragons: head, trunk, tale, options, 82–84
POET(-s)
—Bomans / Wily *
    Joshua: frog/poet has an unreasoning deep sorrow, 116–118
POETIC JUSTICE
—Legends / Cavendish, 407 (index)
POETRY (*American Indian*)
—Mesoamerican / Leon-P, 292 (index)
POISON(-ed; -ing)
—Egyptian / Harris
    murder of Isiris (Seth, Isis, Horus), 36–40
—Hamilton / People *
    Manuel's riddle; fills sack with lies; fortune, 65–75

—Jewish / Sadeh
whatever a man does, he does
for himself, 281–282

—Lester / Brer Rabbit *
with Brer Wolf kills a cow; pretends to be poisoned, 115–117

—Turkish (Art I) / Walker
to cure ruler, Camesap eats part
of Sahmeran, learns language
of plants, 218–224

—Unicorn / Hathaway
Magical horn [healing; river impu-
rities], 113–123 @

—Witch Encyc / Guiley, 270–272,
418 (index)

POLAND
—Dictionary / Leach, 1227 (index)

POLE
—Water Buffalo (Chinese)
magic (cow hair) carrying-pole,
111–118

POLECAT
—Cambodian / Carrison
rooster foils polecat's plan to eat
him, 49–51

POLES (*people*)
—Humor / Midwest, 131–135

POLITICAL SATIRE
—Bomans / Wily *
twelfth king (has hollow [brain-
less] head), 185–192

—Erdoes / Sound *
dogs electing a leader, 23–24

POLITICIANS
—Tall Tales / Downs: Bear
grinning the bark off a tree / D.
Crockett, 31–32

POLLUTION
—Fahs / Old *
people cooperate to "kill" pollution dragon, 169–171

POLTERGEIST(-s)
—Ghosts / Cohen, 151–169
—Ghosts / Time-Life, 45–50

—Restless / Cohen *
Amherst mystery: Tweed house,
31–39

POLYNESIA(-n) (-ian tales)
—Dictionary / Leach, 1227 (index)

—Earth / Hadley *
lifting the sky (Ru; blue stone),
[13–14]

—Legends / Cavendish, 370–378

—Lore of Love
loved one in the lower world, 108

—Man Myth & Magic, 3162 (index)

—Polynesians / Andersen, 1–513
Polynesia and its people, 13–44 @

POMEGRANATE (*magic*)
—Greek / Osborne
kidnapping: Ceres and Proserpina, 35–39

—Turkish / Walker
ruler gives daughter to poor man
as punishment, 139–147

POND
—Grimm / Complete *
nixie (mill-pond) captures young
man; wife rescues, 736–742

—Spring / Philip
lovers reincarnated as butterflies,
35–41

POOKA
—Crossley / British FT *
piper and pooka; carried to mountain top to play for weeping
woman, 17–23

—McGowen / Encyclopedia * 46

POOL
—Grimm / Complete *
Iron Hans, 612–620

—Grimm / Sixty *
Iron Hans, 317–325

POOR
see also RICH
—Bomans / Wily *
echo well: misshapen people not
aware of defects, 97–100

—Fahs / Old *
  blood of defrauded poor, 125–
  126
  rich young man: sell all, give to
  poor, 118–120
—Frog Rider (Chinese)
  wishing pearl; all wealthy men
  die, 92–99
—Jewish / Frankel
  Good Purim, Good Purim! 528–
  530
  Moshele's gift: poor water-carrier
  prays for 1,000 rubles, 554–
  556
—Jewish / Sadeh
  poor brother and three beasts,
  140–143
  Rabbi Nissim and the poor Talmud scholar, 122–124
  rabbi scolds poor man offering
  bread to God, 238–239
  rich man prepared for rainy day,
  178–179
  rich man will pay to say: I don't
  believe in God, 324–326
—Spanish-Am / Van Etten *
  father kills meadowlark, dies; need
  "spirit of song" to live, 54–56
—Turkish / Walker
  Deli feigns death, frightens
  thieves, gets reward, 80–84
—Wilde / Lynch *
  happy prince: statue persuades
  swallow to help the poor, 41–
  54
Poor boy in the grave, The
—Grimm / Complete * 749–752
Poor man and the rich man, The
—Grimm / Complete * 394–398
Poor miller's boy and the cat
—Grimm / Complete * 482–485
POPE(-s)
—Grimm / Legends (Ward), II:437 (in-
  dex)

—Jewish / Frankel
  Pope Elhanan: Jewish child,
  raised Christian, returns to Ju-
  daism, 395–398
—Jewish / Sadeh
  Elchanan the pope, 197–199
  Jewish pope; bastard converts to
  Catholicism, 195–197
  secretly a Jew; "Christian milk,"
  192–194
  two tailors and wonderful photo-
  graph, 204–208
POPE JOAN (legendary)
—Baring-Gould / Curious
  Antichrist and Pope Joan, 68–
  73 @
POPE SIXTUS IV
—Jewish / Frankel
  pound of flesh: Shylock and the
  Pope, 400–403
Popplesnitch, The
—Corrin / Imagine * 70–79
POPUL VUH
—Bierhorst / Monkey * 18–19 @
—Hamilton / In the Beginning *
  "Four creations to make man,"
  86–99
—Mesoamerican / Leon-P, 101–134
POPULARITY: foolish desire
—Aesop / Zwerger *
  monkey [dances] and camel [en-
  vies], 13
PORCUPINE
—Bierhorst / Naked *
  Porcupine's grandson [aban-
  doned boy], 93–100
  Turtle's war party vs. Seven Sis-
  ters, 31–36
—Greaves / Hippo *
  rhino borrows porcupine's quill to
  treat wound, 64–65
  why wart hog is so ugly, 109–
  112
—Hopi Coyote / Malotki

coyote imitates: meal from bark
and nose-bleed; dies, 3–7
—Navajo Coyote / Haile
coyote would imitate porcupine
(turning bark into meat), 12,
36–37
porcupine tricks/kills elk; vies with
coyote for it, 13, 41–44

PORRIDGE
—Grimm / Complete *
magic pot produces porridge,
475–476

PORTENT
—Grimm / Legends (Ward), II:438 (index)

PORTUGAL
—Dictionary / Leach, 1227 (index)
—Speck / New World, 527 (index)

POSEIDON
—D'Aulaire / Greek * 192 (index)
—Greek / Switzer, 207 (index)
—Lore of Love
A Groom for the sea-lord's
daughter, 8–15

Possession, see DEMONIC POS-
SESSION.

POSSESSIONS (ownership)
—Aesop / Holder*
excess: marriage of the sun, 16–
19
—Bomans / Wily *
rich man: the truly happy lack
nothing; vs. the Three Wise
Men, 176–180
—Grimm / Complete *
Hans in luck; a light heart: free of
possessions, 381–386
—Grimm / Sixty *
Hans in luck (as above), 10–16
—Jewish / Sadeh
shirt of a happy man, 183

Possum, see OPOSSUM.

POSTMAN
—Spanish-Am / Van Etten *

cons robber to shoot holes in uniform (until gun is empty), 83–
87

POT, MAGIC
—Arabian / Lewis
Anklet [magic pot; magic pins]
49–51
—Grimm / Complete *
magic pot produces porridge,
475–476
—Jewish / Sadeh
old bachelor lost a bean, 22–25
—Quayle / Shining *
greedy neighbor kills treasure-
finding dog; burns magic pot,
69–76

POTION
—Lewis / Proud
Two Lovers Mountain: carry prin-
cess to top (endurance), 48–52
—Russian / Ivanits, 250 (index)

Potter, Beatrix (1866–1943)
—Childcraft 1 / Once *
Tale of Peter Rabbit, 192–196
—Lynn / Fantasy *
bibliography (about the author),
581–584

POURQUOI TALES
see also ANIMAL CHARACTER-
ISTICS
—Afro-American / Abrahams, 37–79
—Hamilton / Dark *
Manabozo: manitou hare swal-
lowed by king of fishes, 27–31

POURRAT, Henri
—Pourrat / French, xi-xxvi @

POVERTY
see also POOR
—Chinese / Chin *
finding wife for cruel River God,
17–26
—Grimm / Complete *
poverty and humility lead to
heaven, 820–821

—Jewish / Frankel, 650 (index)
—Victorian / Hearn
Magic fish-bone, The (Dickens), 106–115
Poverty and humility lead to heaven
—Grimm / Complete * 820–821
POWER (*often marvelous*)
—Allison / I'll Tell *
lion, fox, ass: dividing spoils "equally," 116
—Bierhorst / Naked *
Cannibal Island; rescue; commanding nature, 44–51
—Clarkson / World *
three sons, marvelous talents: hearing, following, assembly, 301–304
—Coyote / Bierhorst
blackbird caught; powerful hurt the weak, [26]
—Coyote / Ramsey
cruel chief, 100 wives, kills all his sons, 65–68
—Dramatized / Kamerman
Spouse (most powerful?) for Susie Mouse, 317–323
—Egyptian / Harris
challenge: read letter without breaking seal, 108–113
—Erdoes / Sound *
remaking of the (third) world, 126–129
—Fahs / Old *
Glooskap ignored by baby, 153–155
magic pillow: dream projects vanity, 121–124
—Grimm / Complete *
six servants help prince win daughter of sorceress, 600–607
—Hamilton / People *

People could fly [to freedom], 166–172
—Lang / Wilkins
how six men travelled the wide world, 299–304
magic ring: happiness and power if . . . , 220–227
—Russian Hero / Warner *
Mikula (peasant) and Vol'ga (prince), 21–22
—Water Buffalo (Chinese)
seven remarkably endowed sons "reason" with tyrant, 49–54
PRACTICAL WISDOM
see also PRUDENCE
—Coyote / Bierhorst
coyote, puma and donkey divide catch unequally, [36]
PRAGUE
—Hamilton / Dark *
Joseph Golem: blood accusation against Jews, 87–96
PRAISE
—Leonardo / Fables *
lion: awaken sleeping virtue, 55
Prankster, *see* TRICKSTER.
PRAYER(-s)
see also INDIAN PRAYERS
—Bomans / Wily *
for the dead: soul of King Pim released from statue, 121–125
prayer heard: wind-man controls four winds: happiness to one is sorrow to another, 76–78
—Caduto / Keepers *
Koluscap turns Water Monster into bullfrog, 81–84
pipe/breath/wind carry prayers to Creator, 187–188
—Crossley / Animal (Grimm) *
fox and geese: one last prayer, 26–28
—Ghosts / Starkey

evil man saved from hell; remains
on earth, 58–65
—Grimm / Complete *
maid of Brakel, 623
Twelve Apostles (sleep 300
years, awaiting Redeemer),
818–819
—Gullible Coyote / Malotki
prayer feather, 172 @
—Jewish / Frankel, 650 (index)
alphabet recited; God to put it into
words, 547–548
jar of tears, 373–374
—Jewish / Sadeh
say ABC's (humor), 395
shepherd's pipe, 396; commentary, 413–421 @
—Journeys / Norris *
hell: prayers of good person
make evils disappear, [26–28]
—Russian Hero / Warner *
Alesha (priest's son) battles Tugarin, 72–76
—Witch Encyc / Guiley, 418 (index)
PRAYER BOOK(-s)
—Jewish / Frankel
a mother's prayerbook: son re-
turns to the faith, 560–561
—Jewish / Sadeh
orphan boy's gift to God, 395
PRAYER STICK(-s)
—Caduto / Keepers *
origin; Kokopilau, the hump-
backed flute player, 151
—Hopi Coyote / Malotki, 321 @
Preaching, see SERMON(-s)
PRECAUTION
—Jewish / Sadeh
king for a year (then banished to
desert isle), 379–381
PRECIOUS STONE(-s)
—Precious Stones / Kunz, 1–406 @
Jewish high-priest's breastplate,
275–306 @

ominous/luminous, 143–175 @
planetary/astral influences, 338–
366 @
religious uses, 225–274 @
superstition, 1–18 @
talisman and amulet, 19–114 @
therapeutic use, 367–391 @
PRECOGNITION
—Occult & Parapsych / Shepard,
1601 (index)
PREDICTION
—Jewish / Sadeh
rabbi; prediction: defeat at
Jerusalem, 227–228
PREGNANCY
—Jewish / Sadeh
baker's apprentice, princess
and gold-spewing cup, 268–
271
PREHISTORIC ANIMALS
—Tall Tales / Downs: Bear
mid-west (James Thurber), 258–
263
PREJUDICE
see also RACE PREJUDICE
—Cambodian / Carrison
Phnong family murdered; one
child is saved, 78–85
Prelutsky, Jack
—Witches / Iosa *
The haunted house (poem), 33
PREMONITIONS
—Floyd / Gr Am Myst
sinking of the Titanic, 164–168
PREPAREDNESS
—Paxton / Belling *
night singer: bat and caged bird
(Aesop), [10–11]
**PRESTER JOHN (legendary; 12th
century)**
—Baring-Gould / Curious, 26–34 @
PRETENSE
see also DECEPTION; IMPOS-
TOR

—Aesop / Alley *
Fox and the grapes, 14–15
—Aesop / Holder *
despising what one can't obtain:
fox and the grapes, 14–15
—Aesop / Reeves-Wilson *
Donkey in lion's skin, 24–26
—Dramatized / Kamerman
avoid tax: appear half-witted
(Gotham), 88–97
—Grimm / Complete *
Three languages [dog, bird, frog],
169–171
Valiant tailor (seven at one blow),
112–120
—Grimm / Sixty *
Three languages, 223–226
Valiant tailor, 88–97
—Hopi Coyote / Malotki
ruse: badger pretends to cut out
own intestines, 23–41
—Jaffrey / Seasons
by pretending madness, faith-
ful sister changes fate, 96–
101
—Lester / Brer Rabbit *
with Brer Wolf kills a cow; pre-
tends to be poisoned, 115–
117
—O'Brien / Tales *
Lord Mount Dhraggin: weaver
"kills" three-score and ten;
made Lord, 72–81
—Rockwell / Puss *
Puss in Boots, 80–88
—Scriven / Full Color *
Little Red Riding Hood, 37–39
PREY
—Coyote / Bierhorst
pays to be clever when you're the
weaker one, [14]
—Wolves / Lopez, 305 (index)
PRIAM
—Gods / Schwab, 761 (index)

PRICE(-s)
—Arabian / McCaughrean
price of cucumbers, 122–129
PRIDE / VANITY
see also BOAST; Emperor's new
clothes, The
—Aesop / Holder *
utility (legs) vs. ornament (antlers), 24–25
—Aesop / Reeves-Wilson *
disappointed: Mercury, the god,
32–33
Eagle and jackdaw, 22–23
Leopard and fox: good looks
aren't everything, 34–35
Oak and reed [weaker survives],
27
—Bierhorst / Monkey *
bird bride: toad helps youngest
son re oft-ruined cornfield, 25–
31
—Carle / Treasury *
vain blackbird wears peacock
feathers; ridiculed (Aesop),
64–65
—Douglas / Magic *
humbled; Cinderella, 109–117
—Earth / Hadley *
hideous Kanya, god of fire, tries
in vain to get a wife, [17–18]
—Erdoes / Sound *
vision quest [spirits can't be
forced], 63–67
—Greaves / Hippo *
how hippo lost his hair, 68–71
—Hamilton / Dark *
priest becomes proud, denies afterworld, until visited by angel
of death, 119–125
—Jewish / Frankel, 650 (index)
crow and fox: pride surpasses
greed, 461
Elijah: soft like reed, not hard like
cedar; race prejudice, 583–584

stag and the dogs (fable), 467
vanity, 651 (index)
—Lang / Wilkins
Toads and diamonds (kind girl
and proud sister speak), 106–
109
—Leonardo / Fables *
the walnut tree, 109
—Muddleheads / Harris
princess rejects arranged marriage, 115–130
—Scriven / Full Color *
princess and King Grizzly Beard,
89–92
—Spanish-Am / Van Etten *
animals (except mouse) flatter
mountain lion, 106–108
—Turkish (Art I) / Walker
Hoca punished for not saying "If
Allah wills," 51–52
prince disguised as gooseherd to
win proud wife's love, 138–144
seven-year siege lifted by
woman's cleverness, 144–146
—Wilde / Lynch *
remarkable rocket: vain illusions
unto the end, 55–72
—Yep / Rainbow *
foolish boy: Snake-spoke, 86–95
**PRIDE-BROUGHT-LOW (the proud
humbled)**
—Bomans / Wily *
king without crown: ordinary man,
155–157
—Chorao / Child's *
hare repeatedly tricks lion, 43–49
—Crossley / Animal (Grimm) *
fox and cat; arrogance and modesty, 8–10
hare and hedgehog race, 39–44
—Fahs / Old *
Glooskap ignored by baby, 153–
155
—Geras / Grandmother *

Bavsi's feast: rich man experiences hunger, 6–13
—Greaves / Hippo *
how hippo lost his hair, 68–71
jackal boast: can outrun dogs,
45–47
—Grimm / Complete *
King Thrushbeard; haughty princess, 244–248
—Grimm / Sixty *
Fox [100 tricks] and the cat, 227–
228
King Thrushbeard . . . , 312–316
—Jones / Tales *
The Gingerbread Boy, 35–41
—Leonardo / Fables *
fig tree berates elm because it
has no fruit, 95
—Maori / Kanawa *
totara tree boasts, fails, hides in
forest, 83
—Spanish-Am / Van Etten *
animals (except mouse) flatter
mountain lion, 106–108
—Turkish / Walker
ruler gives daughter to poor man
as punishment, 139–147
—Turkish (Art I) / Walker
tyrant Bolu Bey blinds man; son
gets revenge, 99–109
—Water Buffalo (Chinese)
arrogant fox pretends to be king,
36–38
rabbit get revenge on lion, 33–
35
—Wilde / Happy *
fireworks [personified]: proud
rocket gets thrown out, 105–
133
PRIDE, FALSE
—Cambodian / Carrison
frog boasts to bee: to Himalayas
in one day, 100–101
—Clarkson / World *

marvelous talents of honey-
gatherer's sons, 301–304
—Grimm / Complete *
Master Pfriem [never rests; always criticizes], 720–724
PRIEST(-s)
—Babylonia / Spence, 404 (index)
—Bomans / Wily *
chimney sweep's curse (personified) captured by curate, 93–96
return: rich man tries to restore
his childhood home, 76–78
—Clarkson / World *
Shrove Tuesday visitor: priest
routs devil, 214–219
—Clouston / Popular
parish-clerk: corpse "killed" three
times, II.494–496
—Egyptian / Ions, 144 (index)
—Hamilton / Dark *
becomes proud, denies after-
world, until visited by angel of
death, 119–125
—Irish / Glassie
twelve tales, 66–79
—Jewish / Frankel
rabbi fashions golem to thwart
evil priest of Prague, 455–458
Rabbi's mirror allows king to see
treachery in his bedroom, 405–
409
—Man Myth & Magic, 3162 (index)
—Mesoamerican / Leon-P, 292 and
298 (index)
—Persian / Hinnells, 143 (index)
—Russian / Ivanits, 250 (index)
—Spanish-Am / Van Etten *
Pedro and priest's mule trade
places; bad for both, 90–94
Primal ancestors, see MANKIND.
PRIMEVAL DEITIES
—Lurker / Dict Gods, 407 (index)
PRIMITIVE MAN
—Curry / Beforetime *

learning to make fire, from willow
sticks, 33–41
—Man Myth & Magic
beliefs; analytics, 3197–98 (index)
—Vanishing / Mercer *
how South Africans came to be
hunters and gatherers, 74–
75
PRINCE(-s)
see also PRINCE(-s) and
PRINCESS(-es) [below]
—Bomans / Wily *
king's even more foolish sons are
misunderstood as "wise," 143–
146
Lady of the lake: spoiled prince
loved/saved by young girl, 9–
16
—Brooke / Telling *
marries Cinderella albeit slipper
doesn't fit, 51–74
—Cambodian / Carrison
guards propose punishment for
treacherous prince, 73–76
—Corrin / Imagine *
Pari hides in golden candelabra;
prince buys, falls in love, 151–
160
prince abducted; Volkh uses his
six, prince's three wishes to
rescue, 124–135
prince unwittingly marries Sorfarina four times, 11–22
—Crossley / British FT *
prince bets head in card game
with giant, 313–330
—Douglas / Magic *
Cinderella, 109–117
Rapunzel: her daughter promised
to witch, 27–33
six swans (enchanted princes
saved by their sister), 35–41
—Egyptian / Harris

doomed prince: fate foretold by
Seven Hatitors, 71–76
—Grimm / Complete *
abduction; Pink [carnation], The,
355–360
girl lost in wood; witch, ring, and
dove/prince, 558–560
spindle, shuttle, and needle help
girl marry prince, 764–767
three feathers: youngest prince
marries toad, 319–322
true bride; prince forgets betrothal, 752–760
twelve huntsmen; prince forgets
his betrothed, 334–336
—Grimm / Sixty *
abduction; Pink [carnation], The,
171–176
twelve huntsmen . . . , 271–273
—Imaginary / Nigg
golden apples, prince, and firebird, 89–91
—Jewish / Frankel
serpent (prince at night); wife
burns skin; spell broken, 446–
449
—Jewish / Sadeh
bride auctioned; bought by
prince; chastity test, 332–333
child returns to earth to atone for
"Christian milk," 192–194
prince who went off on his own,
101–105
vizier's daughter and bandit in
sheep's clothing, 98–101
—Lang / Wilkins
Fairer-than-a-Fairy, 274–281
grateful prince: girl helps hero escape old man, 394–414
prince saved from fates: crocodile, serpent, dog, 485–496
wounded lion (prince), 385–
393
—Lester / Leopard *

healing leaves for blind king, 59–
68
—Lore of Love
ill-starred mating of earth and
sea, 87–95
—Manning / Cats *
Little Wonder; witch-stepmother
turns boy into dog, drives his
sister out, 65–74
—Manning / Cauldron *
prince and retinue turned into
trees; girl breaks spell, 39–45
—Nesbit / Fairy *
Bellamant; ugly each Sunday,
101–122
Melisande, or Long/Short Division, 59–78
—Nielsen / Old Tales *
wife accused of murdering children, [5–15]
—Old Wives / Carter
battle of the birds, 76–85
Nourie Hadig cares for sleeping
prince, seven years, 192–199
—Rockwell / Puss *
fisherman, his wife, and the flounder, 42–52
Il'ya saves city; captures Nightingale (monster), 76–80
Kate Crackernuts breaks evil
spells, 19–26
Mikula (peasant) and Vol'ga
(prince), 21–22
Sukhman kills 40,000 Tartars,
41–42
—Scriven / Full Color *
Cinderella, 69–73
—Shah / Central Asia
charcoal burner and enchanted
bear, 92–102
seven divs for brothers, 13–18
—Strauss / Trail
Rapunzel: soliloquy (poem), 11–
13

—Trolls / Asbjornsen
  goose-girl: "meant" to marry
  Prince of England, 60–63
  seven foals (princes under
  spells); task: watch, report, behead, 53–59
  spell: East of the sun . . . (poor
  man's daughter given to white
  bear), 26–35
—Turkey / Walker, 307 (index)
—Turkish (Art I) / Walker
  to win beautiful mute, prince must
  make her speak, 34–41
—Victorian / Hearn
  Little lame prince and his travelling-cloak, 132–191
PRINCE(-s) and PRINCESS(-es)
  see also Sleeping Beauty (Briar
  Rose)
—Arabian / Lewis
  Moorish sorcerer vs. king, 60–64
  prince detests women; princess
  disgusted by men, 66–80
  Princess Dunja: all men are faithless, 52–59
  princess elopes on wedding day
  (to another), 217–221
  princess loved by cousins (three
  brothers), 174–183
  sea rose of Princess Brow of Lilies, 212–216
  test for succession: prince marries tortoise, 43–51
—Arabian / McCaughrean
  Moorish sorcerer vs. king, 133–
  141
  test for succession: prince marries tortoise, 142–149
—Arabian / Riordan
  prince detests women; princess
  disgusted by men, 66–77
—Bomans / Wily *
  spoiled prince, perfectionist, is reformed by witch, 126–131

—Brooke / Telling *
  Sleeping Beauty: event after
  awakening, 3–33
—Douglas / Magic *
  Ahmad: bring back the most marvelous, 3–11
  white cat (enchanted princess),
  69–83
—Dulac / Fairy *
  blue bird (prince transformed),
  77–90
  fire bird: princess, heart of prince,
  153–164
  hind of the wood: crayfish fairy,
  43–59
  serpent-prince: marries, regains
  human form, 29–42
—Frog Rider (Chinese)
  Wooden horse; castle in the sky,
  24–46
—Grimm / Complete *
  Faithful John: quest for princess
  of Golden Dwelling, 43–51
  Iron Hans, 612–620
  iron stove: princess frees prince;
  breaks taboo, 571–577
  Lady and lion [man by night],
  398–404
  riddle: raven poisoned by witch,
  128–131
  six servants help prince win
  daughter of sorceress, 600–
  607
—Grimm / Legends (Ward), II:438 (index)
—Grimm / Sixty *
  Iron Hans, 317–325
  Lady and lion [man by night],
  235–240
—Hepburn / World *
  Tattercoats: gooseherd plays
  flute; prince falls in love, 90–
  109
—Lang / Wilkins

heart of ice (Caylus), 190–219
prince's mother would eat princess and children, 14–17
—Manning / Cats *
kind witch raises foundling to be knight; bewitched Cat-Johann his aide, 111–117
—Muddleheads / Harris
haughty princess rejects arranged marriage, 115–130
—Nesbit / Fairy *
charmed life, or Princess and Liftman, 25–42
last dragon; pet of princess, 161–171
—O'Brien / Tales *
giant Trencross abducts princess; white cat helps rescue, 92–105
—Old Wives / Carter
Juleidah: princess disguised as lowly kitchen-worker, 39–46
—Rockwell / Puss *
Briar Rose; gifts of the Wise Women, 53–59
Frog prince (princess makes rash promise), 66–74
—Russian Hero / Warner *
Dunai: archery contest ends in death, 37–41
three princes/brides, one a frog-princess, 101–106
—Scriven / Full Color *
Frog prince, 57–59
Rapunzel, 9–12
—Shah / Central Asia
Feroz-Shah and the mechanical flying horse, 131–145
Gushtasp and the Princess of Roum, 78–81
prince who married a peri (fairy), 49–55
princess imprisoned in mountain of jade, 19–24

Rustam and the iron fortress, 25–30
three wishes granted by genie, 31–44
—Turkish / Walker
princess marries pig (prince under spell), 114–117
—Turkish (Art I) / Walker
prince disguised as gooseherd to win proud wife's love, 138–144
—Unicorn / Coville *
princess, cat/prince, and conceited unicorn, 120–134
—Wilde / Lynch *
remarkable rocket: fireworks at wedding, 55–72
Prince Desir and Princess Mignone (Beaumont)
—Zipes / Beauties * 233–245
PRINCESS(-es)
—Arabian / Lewis
king trades daughter for flying ebony horse, 106–116
—Arabian / McCaughrean
king trades daughter . . . , 225–242
Man with three wives; jinni of well, 185–193
—Arabian / Riordan
king trades daughter . . . , 56–65
—Bomans / Wily *
cobbler's three wishes from gnome; learns money's limitations, 53–61
curse: lock of hair; king's cruelty to "bird witch," 165–173
three riddles; win princess; fearless woodcutter, 202–204
—Cambodian / Carrison
Princess Amaradevi: husband accused of treachery, 23–30
—Carter / Sleeping *
Ricky and twin princesses:

beauty but stupid; ugly but clever, 93–102

—Clarkson / World *

Boots discovers how to do tasks; wins princess, 277–281

—Corrin / Eight-Year *

attempts to prevent princess wanting the moon, 91–101

princess: save magic fishbone until needed, 147–160

—Crane / Beauty *

Yellow Dwarf and proud princess, [34–47]

—Douglas / Magic *

rescue: Jack the Giant Killer, 131–139

—Dramatized / Kamerman

king promises marriage: make princess speak, 47–60

magic cloak; princesses wear out shoes, 435–446

Peach tree kingdom; imposter; bride test, 288–305

Quick-witted Jack; suitor tests, 400–412

servant tells princess stories, in exchange for clothes, 10–14

—Dulac / Fairy *

Bashtchelik (real steel), 91–113

green serpent: one twin princess cursed, ugly, 124–138

suitor test: Ivan and the chestnut horse, 60–68

Urashima Taro; Dragon Sea-King's palace, 140–152

—Grimm / Complete *

blue light summons tiny servant, 530–534

cat (princess) gives horse to miller's apprentice, 482–485

cunning tailor: riddle, bear, princess, 525–528

devil with the three golden hairs, 151–158

Drummer rescues princess from glass mountain, 781–791

Four clever brothers, 580–584

goose-girl at well; princess weeps pearls, 725–734

Goosegirl: servant's imposture revealed by horse-head, 404–411

griffin: suitor's tasks to win princess, 681–688

Hans the hedgehog: princess promised, 497–502

hero must hold crystal ball before enchantress to free princess, 798–801

huntsman takes deceitful captain to abduct princess, 508–514

King Thrushbeard; haughty princess, 244–248

king's son who feared nothing (Grimm), 545–550

queen dies; king would marry their daughter, 326–331

Raven; spell broken by persistence of young man, 431–436

sea-hare: suitor must conceal self from princess, 769–772

tailor overcomes evil shoemaker, 386–496

three black princesses, 620–621

youngest huntsman rescues princesses from dragon, 420–424

Youth who could not shudder, 29–39

—Grimm / Sixty *

blue light summons tiny servant, 244–249

Four clever brothers, 220–234

Goosegirl, 67–73

King Thrushbeard, 312–316

Raven; spell broken . . . , 250–256

Water of life, The, 264–270

PRINCESS (continued)
Youth who could not shudder, 300–311
—Hamilton / Dark *
One-Inch boy, the demon Oni, and the princess, 23–26
Yama, his son dissuades edict of her death, 137–142
—Hamilton / People *
Beautiful girl of the moon tower, 53–59
Manuel's riddle; fills sack with lies; fortune, 65–75
—Jaffrey / Seasons
Savitri nags underworld king; husband restored, 10–15
—Jewish / Frankel
princess to God: restore my lover or take my life, 360–365
ruby/serpent: Solomon's daughter shut in tower; power of love, 254–257
scorpion in goblet: virtuous rabbi rewarded, 437–446
—Jewish / Sadeh
Blackface: merchant's son in love with princess, 117–121
brothers' widow-mother marries lion, 92–95
eagle takes rabbi's son to Christian palace, 273–275
lost princess: king's curse, to Evil One's kingdom, 386–389
marriage: princess to donkey's head, 4–8
Pearlneck: coveted by foe's daughter, 143–146
princess who refused to talk, 106–111
smitten: baker's apprentice and gold-spewing cup, 268–271
task: make princess talk, 111–112
young man and princess/lawyer, 277–279

—Lang / Wilkins
Charming wins Goldilocks, 31–43
enchantment: princess must stay in tower . . . , 415–431
gnome king Rubezahl captures princess, 497–512
Princess Mayblossom (good vs. evil fairies), 137–153
sent to check on fairy gifts, 186–189
—Lester / Leopard *
illness; body parts argue: which is most important, 45–51
—Lewis / Proud
Eliduc: knight unfaithful; wife enters convent, 88–100
Two Lovers Mountain: carry princess to top, 48–52
—Lines / Magical *
Raja's son seeks Princess Labam, 56–66
—Lore of Love
King Nala and Princess Damayanti, 110–119
lovers forced apart; rendezvous in dreams, 37–49
—Manning / Cats *
able to call twelve sailors at will, Vasily saves Leeshy Cat, 37–50
—Manning / Cauldron *
amber witch: common man, loved by princess, sent to get amber, 18–31
crusader beaten, robbed by comrades; witches reveal secrets, = reversal, 46–57
donkey, gift of troll-child, helps hunter rescue princess, 9–17
gives Jack ring (can change self to any size); rescues princess from giant, 78–89
—Muddleheads / Harris

Copper Canoeman weds human princess, 75–93
Mink Being wants to marry human princess, 5–25
—Nesbit / Fairy *
Belinda and Bellamant; beauty only on Sunday, 101–122
princesses transformed to golden apples, 141–158
—Nielsen / Old Tales *
blue belt (mother conspires with troll to kill son), [37–62]
widow's son, [16–36]
—O'Brien / Tales *
fairies take Gilly for ride to France; abduct princess; strike her dumb, 106–117
goatskin-clad Eamonn: task to make princess laugh (succeeds), 38–43
—Quayle / Shining *
Shining Princess (from Moon People) and deceptive suitors, 13–23
—Reeves / Shadow
White doe: curse put on Valdemar, 131–153
—Russian Hero / Warner *
Dobrynya spares abductor/ dragon, 69–70
—Scriven / Full Color *
betrothed to poor minstrel: King Grizzly Beard, 89–92
Golden goose [task: make princess laugh], 61–63
—Shah / Central Asia
(div; chaos) princess and the donkey, 82–86
dream of Habeeb, 56–61
nobleman and slave (later king), 103–108
three wishes granted by genie, 31–44
—Spring / Philip

golden fish rewards kindness, 103–113
king "never heard of this before," 134–139
princess's veil; father demands many tests, 75–81
Tibetan envoy wins princess, 42–49
—Trolls / Asbjornsen
boy who became lion, falcon, ant, 64–70
—Turkish / Walker
saved by mirror (spyglass), carpet (travel), lemon (cure), 132–134
—Turkish (Art I) / Walker
overhears secrets: how to win princess, escape spell, 123–136
—Unicorn / Coville *
king would own unicorns; princess: they must be free, 24–37
stealing water touched by unicorn horn, to cure sick friend, 7–22
untypical: plain, good stepmother and sisters! 120–134
—Victorian / Hearn
Necklace of Princess Fiorimonde, 210–227
—Vietnam / Terada *
mountain/water gods rivals for princess, 50–53
—Williams-Ellis / Tales *
The Laidly Worm, 134–141
—Yolen / Faery Flag
queen's face in the cloth; three witches, 87–100
—Zipes / Beauties *
Princess Camion (Lubert), 261–293
Princess Minute and King Floridor (Caylus), 253–257
Princess Rosette (d'Aulnoy), 501–514

Princess Zeineb and King Leopard (Bignon), 145–150
Ricky and twin princesses: beauty but stupid; ugly but clever, 52–57, 95–100
Ricky with Tuft; man not ugly to princess who loves him, 52–57, 95–100
Princess and the goatherd
—Turkish / Walker, 118–122
Princess and [on] the pea
—Andersen / Raverat * 52–55
—Corrin / Favourite * 59–60
Princess Belle-Etoile
—Crane / Beauty * [21–33]
—Crane / McLean * 16–27
Princess in the chest; faithful guard
—Lang / Wilkins, 369–384
Princess Mayblossom
—Lang / Wilkins, 137–153
PRINCIPLES
—Bomans / Wily *
Princess Steppie and King's rigid "principles," 20–27
PRISON
—Jewish / Frankel
ruby/serpent: Solomon's daughter shut in tower; power of love, 254–257
PRIVACY
—Jones / Tales *
invasion: Goldilocks and the three bears, 8–15
PROBLEM SOLVING
—Aesop / Reeves-Wilson *
thirsty "Crow and pitcher," 99–100
—Allison / I'll Tell *
crow finds way to get to water in pitcher, 109
—Bomans / Wily *
donkeys and camels: brothers help others, foolishly can't help selves, 147–151

—Jewish / Sadeh
man who went to the "dickens," 146–149
—Paxton / Belling *
belling the cat (Aesop; a verse version), [6–9]
crow and the pitcher (Aesop), [22–23]
—Shannon / More *
fifteen folktales, 1–64
PRODIGIES
—Legends / Cavendish, 399–400 (index)
PRODUCTIVITY (marvelous)
—Yep / Rainbow *
Virtue goes to town, 118–123
PROFESSOR
—Pellowski / Family *
handkerchief story, 63
PROFLIGATE
—Jewish / Sadeh
young man and princess/lawyer, 277–279
PROHIBITIONS AND COMPULSIONS, UNIQUE
—Arabian / Lewis
Hasan, the alchemist, and the Jinn princess, 138–143
prohibitions disregarded; evils, 10–16
tale of the one-eyed beggar, 10–16
—Corrin / Imagine *
Chura ("Simba"); his love returns from underworld; can marry only Simba, 142–150
—Dulac / Fairy *
Bashtchelik (real steel), 91–113
—Grimm / Complete *
Virgin Mary, the woodcutter; forbidden room, 23–29
wizard captures three sisters; Fitcher's bird, 216–220
—Jewish / Frankel

demon princess/wife and the broken oath, 432–437
—Jewish / Sadeh
Blackface: no lights in stores on Thursdays, 117–121
—Lang / Wilkins
Blue Beard (murderous husband), 110–115
Little King Loc, 441–459
Water of life (brothers fail; sister succeeds), 362–368
—Lester / Leopard *
town where snoring was not allowed, 27–30
—Lewis / Proud
Lanval: knight boasts, nearly loses his lady, 26–47
—Old Wives / Carter
girl forbidden to pound in the mortar, 33–38
—Russian / Ivanits, 250 (index)
—Turkish (Art I) / Walker
Cihansah enters forbidden room; sees girl-fairy-pigeons, 207–217

PROMETHEUS
—D'Aulaire / Greek * 72
—Fahs / Old *
brings fire to mankind, 145–147
—Gods / Schwab, 761 (index)
—Greek / Osborne
rash; chariot of the sun god, 1–6
—Hamilton / In the Beginning *
brings fire to mankind, 132–137
—Hoke / Giants
Hercules and the pygmies, 130–132

PROMISE(-s) (*often foolish; often broken*)
see also AGREEMENT(-s); BARGAIN, FOOLISH; Rumpelstiltskin
—Arabian / Lewis

king trades daughter for flying ebony horse, 106–116
king's quest: secure seventh diamond girl, 144–152
Moorish sorcerer vs. king, 60–64
—Arabian / McCaughrean
king trades daughter . . . (as above), 225–242
Moorish sorcerer vs. king, 133–141
—Arabian / Riordan
king trades daughter . . . (as above), 56–65
—Caduto / Keepers *
how Raven made the tides, 103
—Cambodian / Carrison
lost, king tells child how to recognize a king, 86–89
—Celts / Hodges *
Cuchulain: The champion of Ireland, 17–31
—Chaucer / Cohen *
franklin's tale: will love when stones are gone, 67–84
—Corrin / Imagine *
goldsmith steals woodcarver-friend's gold; woodcarver "turns" goldsmith's children into bears, 23–46
—Coyote / Bierhorst
sickness: promises come easy in time of need, [18]
—Douglas / Magic *
fisherman and the genie, 13–19
Rapunzel: her daughter promised to witch, 27–33
—Dramatized / Kamerman
Frost Giant: builder of the wall, 422–434
ogre; guess name; carpenter's ear, 278–287
—Fahs / Old *
hunter in Walumbe's country of Death, 181–184

Niyak, Umak, and the eagle, 71–80
—Grimm / Complete *
  cock and hen, in cart pulled by duck, trick innkeeper, 65–66
  frog; princess' promise; kissed, reverts to prince, 17–20
  Hans the hedgehog: princess promised, 497–502
  King of the golden mountain, 425–430
  Lady and the lion, 398–404
  rose given to child helping another gather wood, 819
  twelve huntsmen; prince forgets his betrothed, 334–336
—Grimm / Sixty *
  King of the golden mountain, 274–280
  Lady and the lion, 235–240
  twelve huntsmen, 271–273
—Hall / Treasury *
  Little Black Sambo, 68–76
—Hamilton / People *
  Manuel's riddle; fills sack with lies; fortune, 65–75
—Hodges / Celts *
  Dermot in the Land-under-Wave, 57–73
—Jewish / Sadeh
  bread cast upon the water [unwise], 28–31
—Lang / Wilkins
  queen poisons stepdaughter's suitor, 460–473
—Lore of Love
  foolish promise; enchanter's snare, 121
—Maori / Kanawa *
  Maui nets sun; frees on promise to go more slowly, 24–26
—Old Wives / Carter
  for her fidelity, king-robber-ogre

  absolve woman of promise(s), 13–15
  magic bag opened; giant forgives in exchange for son at age seven, 76–85
  promise kept; honor satisfied, 13–15
  suitor cures (goomer-dust) mighty breaking of wind problem, 73–75
—Rockwell / Puss *
  Frog prince (princess makes rash promise), 66–74
—Scriven / Full Color *
  Frog prince, 57–59
—Shah / Central Asia
  three wishes granted by genie, 31–44
—Spring / Philip
  princess's veil; father demands many tests, 75–81
—Turkish / Walker
  princess marries pig (prince under spell), 114–117
—Turkish (Art I) / Walker
  promise to Allah: donkey, carrying child, will climb minaret, 176–177
—Williams-Ellis / Tales *
  frog-prince; Well of the World's End, 55–61
  Tom-Tit-Tot spins skeins for girl, 185–195
—Yolen / Faery Flag
  face in the cloth; princess and witches, 87–100

PRONUNCIATION
—Jewish / Sadeh
  pious rabbi punished for faulty vowel sounds, 211–213

PROPER PLACE
—Leonardo / Fables *
  Spider in the keyhole, 22–23

PROPER ROLE
—Grimm / Complete *
    mouse, bird, sausage [trade du-
    ties = disaster], 131–133
—Grimm / Sixty *
    mouse, bird, sausage [as above],
    108–110
—Water Buffalo (Chinese)
    inanimate objects take over; per-
    ish, 21–22
PROPERTY (*ownership*)
    see also POSSESSIONS
—Fahs / Old *
    stolen drum to dance by, 86–90
—Jones / Tales *
    destruction: Goldilocks and the
    three bears, 8–15
—Leete / Golden *
    Goldilocks and the three bears,
    74–78
PROPERTY: PUNISHMENT FOR
MISDEEDS REGARDING
—Egyptian / Harris
    clever thief: treasure of
    Rhumpsinitus, 114–116
—Fahs / Old *
    drought: lizard keeps others from
    well, 91–95
—Jaffrey / Seasons
    king beaten with magic stick for
    taking magic bowl from old
    man, 103–109
—Water Buffalo (Chinese)
    innkeeper steals magic donkey,
    table cloth, stick, 103–110
PROPHECY (-cies) (*often threaten-*
    ing; escape sought)
—Bell / Classical Dict, 191–194 @
—Celts / Hodges *
    how Finn Mac Cool got his wis-
    dom tooth, 34–52
—Chaucer / Cohen *
    nun's tale: ignoring prophetic
    dreams, 19–31

    wife of Bath: what do women
    want most, 55–63
—Crossley / Dead *
    Pedlar of Swaffham: dream dis-
    closes treasure, 27–37
—Douglas / Magic *
    Sleeping Beauty, 55–61
—Dulac / Fairy *
    fire bird: princess, heart of prince,
    153–164
—Egyptian / Harris
    Anpu and Bata, 77–83
    doomed prince: fate foretold by
    Seven Hatitors, 71–76
—Erdoes / Sound *
    coming of the white man (wa-
    sicum), 74–81
—Fahs / Old *
    Maui in bird-shape, to Under-
    world; parents, 37–43
—Grimm / Legends (Ward), II:438 (in-
    dex)
—Hamilton / People *
    Most useful slave [can prophesy],
    160–164
—Jaffrey / Seasons
    birth of Krishna: wicked king Kans
    tries to kill him, 22–25
    king unbearably arrogant when
    told how he cannot be killed,
    87–91
—Jewish / Frankel, 650 (index)
—Lang / Wilkins
    fate of king's son: marry a slave,
    513–527
    prince saved from fates: croco-
    dile, serpent, dog, 485–496
—Legends / Cavendish, 408 (index)
—Lines / Magical *
    Joseph (in Egypt) prophecies
    good/lean years, 149–169
—Lore of Love
    groom for the sea-lord's daugh-
    ter, 8–15

maiden's question: my future
husband? 24–25
—Reeves / Shadow
shape-change knight as lover;
their child will avenge, 1–48
—Turkish (Art I) / Walker
cock killed, cooked, eaten; still
continues to deride prince, 80–
81
magic hen, and fate of two broth-
ers, 61–69
Prose Edda
—Hamilton / In the Beginning *
Imir: The frost giant, 68–71
—Mercatante / Encyclopedia, 789 (in-
dex)
PROSERPINE
—Wolkstein / Love, 251 @
PROSPERITY
—Jewish / Frankel
Elijah: gift of seven years of pros-
perity, 585–586
—Jewish / Sadeh
banished queen, source of hus-
band's success, 279–281
PROTECTIVE DEITIES
—Lurker / Dict Gods, 408 (index)
Proud-humbled, see PRIDE-
BROUGHT-LOW.
PROVENCAL TALES
—Provencal / De Larrabeiti, 1–222
PROVERBS
—Mex-Am / West, 39–45, 257–
264
—Plants / Dyer, 128–144
—Women / Dyer
women in, 249–253 (index)
PROVIDENCE, DIVINE
—Grimm / Complete *
aged mother blames God for
death of sons, 826–827
sparrow and his four children,
657–660
—Jewish / Frankel

God works in mysterious ways,
594–596
—Jewish / Sadeh
hurt leg: whatever happens is for
our good, 285
water carrier in the wilderness,
351
Prowess, see SHAM PROWESS.
PRUDENCE
see also DISCRETION; FORE-
SIGHT
—Aesop / Reeves-Wilson *
Dog and dog's reflection, 36–37
Monkey and fisherman [false
self-confidence], 43
Zorian the star-gazer, 101–102
—Animal Legends / Kerven *
friends ask too much: guinea's
crest feathers; lizard's skin,
[24–25]
—Bierhorst / Monkey *
toad hides/rides in hawk's bag;
tries to float; crashes, 136–137
—Bruchac / Iroquois *
Hodadenon: last one left, 169–
182
—Coyote / Bierhorst
coyote eats all his animals; peo-
ple discreetly leave, [8]
—Jewish / Sadeh
wisdom vs. gold: Solomon and
the three brothers, 54–56
—Leonardo / Fables *
imprudence: vine clings to old
tree, 86
—Paxton / Aesop *
grasshopper and the ants, [36–39]
—Shah / Central Asia
Wali and the magic saddle-bag,
69–77
—Turkish / Walker
Hoca: tax collector keeps records
on pastries, 45–46
—Water Buffalo (Chinese)

cat teaches tiger, but not how to
climb trees, 78–81
—Yep / Rainbow *
bedtime snacks, 4–10
PRYDERI
—Lines / Magical *
birth of Pryderi; Queen unjustly
punished, 116–122
PSYCHE
—Douglas / Magic *
Venus, Cupid and Psyche, 151–
165
—Greek / Osborne
Cupid and Psyche: the four tasks,
57–65
Psyche and Eros
—Wolkstein / Love, 111–146, 265 @
PSYCHIC MEDIUM
—Floyd / Gr Am Myst
Leonore Piper (of Boston), 83–86
PSYCHICAL RESEARCH
—Occult & Parapsych / Shepard, 1–
1617 @
PSYCHOLOGICAL . . .
see also EXISTENTIAL TALES
—Strauss / Trail, 1–35
PTAH
—Egyptian / Harris, 131 (index)
—Egyptian / Ions, 144 (index)
Pueblo Indians, see INDIANS:
PUEBLO.
PUMA
—Bierhorst / Monkey *
rabbit repeatedly dupes puma,
77–80
—Coyote / Bierhorst
wolf slanders coyote; coyote
turns tables, [34]
PUMPKIN
—Hamilton / People *
tall tale: fast-growing, 76–80
—Leonardo / Fables *
willow, magpie and pumpkin, 92–
95

—Turkish / Walker
magic pumpkin (provides food)
stolen and recovered, 62–
66
—Turkish (Art I) / Walker
(holds sticks that beat), simpleton
gives to padishah-thief, 195–
198
PUN
—Scary / Young *
coffin follows boy; takes cough
drops to "stop the coughin',"
33
Rap! Shylock Bones finds
"ghost" to be "wrapping" paper, 31–32
PUNISHMENT
see also CLEVER MEANS . . . ;
DEAD: RETURN; DECEP-
TION PUNISHED; DIVINE
PUNISHMENT; MEDDLING
PUNISHED; REWARDS . . . ;
etc.
—Cambodian / Carrison
guards propose punishment for
treacherous prince, 73–76
—Egyptian / Harris
Ra's anger over rebellious mankind, 34–35
—Fahs / Old *
Deucalion's flood; cruel greed of
human race, 58–63
—Grimm / Complete *
devil with the three golden hairs,
151–158
—Hamilton / Dark *
John (brother) kills Little Tom,
takes credit for his feat, 132–
136
—Jaffrey / Seasons
how "unkillable" king is killed,
87–91
—Jewish / Frankel, 650 (index)
—Jewish / Sadeh

Ashmodai rules in Solomon's
   place, 58–61
man who ran after two (Elijah and
   Elisha), 136–137
miser-innkeeper tells what happened after death, 172–176
misers locked out from their
   wealth, 169–172
pious rabbi punished for faulty
   vowel sounds, 211–213
—Lang / Wilkins
   Charming wins Goldilocks, 31–43
—Mex-Am / West
   motif index, 300
—Nielsen / Old Tales *
   beautiful but dumb (speechless),
   [5–15]
—Palestinian / Speak (Muhawi)
   motif-index, 399
—Water Buffalo (Chinese)
   fish-seller; guard asks one-half of
   reward, 5–8
**PUNISHMENT for BREAKING
   TABOO**
—Caduto / Keepers *
   Manabozho and the maple trees,
   145
—Clarkson / World *
   Cherry of Zennor: banished from
   fairyland, 129–134
—Corrin / Favourite *
   must wed troll-princess: East of
   the sun . . . , 1–15
—Grimm / Complete *
   Iron Hans, 612–620
   King of the golden mountain,
   425–430
—Grimm / Sixty *
   Iron Hans, 317–325
   King of the golden mountain,
   274–280
—Lang / Wilkins
   Blue Beard (murderous hus-
   band), 110–115

—Lore of Love
   King Nala and Princess Damayanti, 110–119
—Maori / Kanawa *
   wife carries food before husband;
   enchanted lake disappears,
   82
—Old Wives / Carter
   girl must share food with cat; forgets, 160–165
   kissed by dog (taboo), prince forgets his new wife, 76–85
   wash water, not thrown out, lets
   wool spinners in, 211–212
—Water Buffalo (Chinese)
   crow-messenger disobeys God
   of Heaven, 23–29
PUNISHMENT, CRUEL
—Old Wives / Carter
   Parsley-Girl: woman steals from
   nuns' (i.e., witches') garden,
   86–88
—Spanish-Am / Van Etten *
   lizard demands daughter after father chops down tree, 19–24
PUNISHMENT: DEEDS PUNISHED
—Arabian / Lewis
   treachery: good barber and evil
   dyer, 123–130
—Carter / Sleeping *
   Sweetheart (Leprince de
   Beaumont), 113–124
—Egyptian / Harris
   brothers (Lies and Truth personified), 84–85
—Erdoes / Sound *
   mockery: Iktome ridicules hawk,
   60–61
—Grimm / Complete *
   dog and the sparrow, 280–282
   ear of corn used to clean dress,
   791–792
   soldier can reduce others to immobility, 808–811

tailor and goldsmith see little folk dancing, 742–745

three sisters encounter St. Joseph, 815–818

ungrateful son, 636

—Grimm / Sixty *

dog and the sparrow, 36–40

—Hamilton / People *

Little Eight John breaks six tabus, 121–125

wolf insults birds; borrowed feathers; walrus, 43–48

—Journey Sun (Chinese)

cruel stepmother, false wife, ghost, 6–23

—Lewis / Proud

Bisclavret: wife keeps husband in wolf-form, 29–35

—Muddleheads / Harris

Robin Woman and Sawbill Duck Woman, 44–59

sea hunters swallowed by whirlpool, 26–43

—Quayle / Shining *

white hare tricks crocodiles; revenge; kind prince heals hare, 24–32

—Spring / Philip

brothers: one honest, one greedy, 94–97

—Turkish / Walker

duck as judge: rabbit removed stone from wolf's back, 15

—Turkish (Art I) / Walker

golden pears: dervish punishes selfish farmer, 53–57

magic hen, and fate of two brothers, 61–69

—Vietnam / Terada *

Tam kills stepsister Cam; takes her place as king's wife, 23–34

PUNISHMENT FITTED TO CRIME

—Beat / Bryan *

call cat: frog threatens hen; hawk gets frog, 3–13

—Chinese / Chin *

finding wife for River God, 17–26

—Crossley / British FT *

fairies give bad-tempered hunchback a second hump, 145–152

—Dramatized / Kamerman

A most special dragon, 79–87

—Egyptian / Harris

challenge: read letter without breaking seal, 108–113

—Jewish / Frankel

Yahweh: ten plagues punish Egyptians, 109–113

—Scriven / Full Color *

organ grinder's monkey; spider; forced dance, 29–33

PUNISHMENT: HELL

—Egyptian / Harris

judgment by King of the Dead, 103–107

PUNISHMENT, HUMILIATING

—Dramatized / Kamerman

Midas; anything touched, turns to gold, 177–190

—Grimm / Complete *

soldier can reduce others to immobility, 808–811

three sisters encounter St. Joseph, 815–818

—Old Wives / Carter

wives cure boastfulness: vulture fights pigeons, 211–212

PUNISHMENT, MIRACULOUS

—Arabian / Riordan

merchant's life saved by storytelling, 100–107

PUNISHMENT and REMISSION

—Jewish / Frankel

man who breaks betrothal vow punished by childlessness, 523–527

—Lang / Wilkins

Sylvain and Jocosa (befriended
by fairy), 178–185
PUNS
—Kessler / Turtle Knock * 1–48
—Kessler / Turtle Riddle * 1–48
PUPPETS
—Bosma / Classroom, 59
PURGATORY
—Baring-Gould / Curious
St. Patrick's Purgatory, 84–87 @
—Christian / Every, 116–121
—Hamilton / Dark *
priest denies afterworld, until vis-
ited by angel of death, 119–125
PURIFICATION
—Bell / Classical Dict, 195 @
PURIM
—Aleichem / Holiday *
goldspinners: family makes
money on activities; play, mes-
senger service, 86–108
—Jewish / Frankel
Good Purim, Good Purim! 528–
530
PURITAN(-s)
—American / Read Dgst, 444 (index)
—Gobble / Graham-Barber *
Thanksgiving Day words; etymol-
ogy, 122 (index)
PURITY
—Turkish (Art I) / Walker
stonecutter: dervish-thieves re-
vealed in court of discernment,
72–80
PURSE
—Clouston / Popular
inexhaustible, I.72–122
lost purse; amount of money
overstated, II.367–371
Pursuits, see ESCAPE(-s) AND
PURSUIT(-s).
PURVIS, Will
—Southern [legends] / Floyd
man who wouldn't die, 96–98

Puss in Boots
—Bedtime / Padoan & Smith * 81–83
—Carter / Sleeping * 26–32 Pursuit(s)
—Corrin / Favourite * 197–203
—Crossley / British FT * 190–211
—Douglas / Magic * 99–107
—Lang / Wilkins, 1–7
—Rockwell / Puss, 80–88
—Zipes / Beauties * 21–24
Puss in Boots [in verse] (Kauffman)
—Hall / Treasury * 94–97
PWYLL
—Celtic / MacCana, 143 (index)
PYGMIES
—Hoke / Giants
Hercules and the golden apples,
130–132
—Vanishing / Mercer *
help Lightning (personified) kill
marauding elephants, 71–73
pygmy befriended by monkeys,
steals fire, 68–70
Pyle, Howard
—Lines / Magical *
Apple of contentment, The, 15–23
PYRAMUS
—Lore of Love
doomed trysts: Apollo; Pyramus,
77

QILIN
—Chinese / Christie
justice by ordeal, 130–136
QINGKE
—Journey Sun (Chinese)
qingke (barley) seed stolen from
snake king by Achu, 24–46
QUARREL
—Aesop / Reeves-Wilson *
the cock and the maids, 64
—Caduto / Keepers *
Loo-Wit, the fire-keeper, 41–43

QUAT
—Hamilton / In the Beginning *
   creation myth: Finding night, 8–
   13
QUATGORO
—Hamilton / In the Beginning *
   Melanesian creation myth (stone-
   mother), 8–9
QUEEN(-s)
—Arabian / Lewis
   abandoned children (grown) re-
   stored, 166–173
—Arabian / Riordan
   abandoned children . . . , 78–87
—Douglas / Magic *
   Queen Igraine, Merlin and Arthur,
   141–149
—Dramatized / Kamerman
   Queen of Hearts: The stolen
   tarts, 98–105
—Dulac / Fairy *
   Finn, and Queen of many-colored
   bedchamber, 69–76
—Grimm / Legends (Ward), II:439 (in-
   dex)
—Jewish / Sadeh
   banished queen moves in with
   poor woodseller, 279–281
—King Arthur / Senior
   Queen Beale Isoud, 318 (index)
—Lester / Leopard *
   healing leaves for blind king, 59–
   68
—Lewis / Proud
   Chevrefoil (hazel and honey-
   suckle); Tristram, lover, 79–81
—Nesbit / Fairy *
   Billy the King [hired to be eaten
   by dragon], 1–22
—Williams-Ellis / Tales *
   stepdaughter: The Laidly Worm,
   134–141
QUEEN BEALE ISOUD
—King Arthur / Senior, 318 (index)

Queen bee
—Grimm / Complete * 317–319
—Grimm / Sixty * 206–208
**Queen of the island of flowers
   (Mailly)**
—Zipes / Beauties * 121–127
QUEEN of the MISSISSIPPI
—Dulac / Fairy *
   boy gathers six helpers: the
   seven conquerors, 22–28
QUEENLINESS
—Tibet / Timpanelli *
   girl who was already queen, 43–51
QUEST(-s)
   see also MARVELOUS
   OBJECT . . .
—Arabian / Lewis
   king's quest: secure seventh dia-
   mond girl, 144–152
—Bruchac / Iroquois *
   Hodadenon: last one left; chest-
   nuts, 169–182
—Celts / Hodges *
   Dermot in the Land-under-Wave,
   57–73
—Cotterell / Encyclopedia, 257 (index)
—Dulac / Fairy *
   Bashtchelik (real steel), 91–113
   fire bird: princess, heart of prince,
   153–164
—Erdoes / Sound *
   vision quest [spirits can't be
   forced], 63–67
—Fahs / Old *
   healing waters for plague-
   stricken wife, 52–56
   struggle: boy half-good, half-bad,
   1–6
—Fairies / Briggs
   Sword of Light; king of Esaidh
   Ruadh, 356–359
—Frog Rider (Chinese)
   seeks husband, working on con-
   struction of Great Wall, 83–91

—Ghosts / Starkey
    Draiglin' Hogney defeated by
      youngest brother, 80–87
—Greek / Osborne
    Orpheus and Eurydice: quest in
      underworld, 45–48
—Grimm / Complete *
    devil with the three golden hairs,
      151–158
—Jewish / Frankel
    angry king: daughter taken cap-
      tive because of his curse, 531–
      536
    mouse seeks a wife (fable: run-
      ning after power), 463–465
    student marries ugly girl; leaves
      her; son seeks father, 588–
      594
—Jewish / Sadeh
    lost princess: king's curse, to Evil
      One's kingdom, 386–389
    nightingale and shroud wearers;
      queen gives birth to animals,
      25–28
—Journey Sun (Chinese)
    drink from Red Spring, under
      power of Red Devil, 125–140
—Journeys / Norris *
    city of ultimate beauty and happi-
      ness, [29–32]
—Lewis / Proud
    Guigemar: woman to endure an-
      guish and lift curse, 10–19
    Milun/lover wait 20 years to be
      wed, 65–75
—Russian Hero / Warner *
    Ivan son of Mare kills his treach-
      erous brothers, 120–124
    Koshchei the Deathless; "death"
      hidden in egg, 96–99
    Sukhman kills 40,000 Tartars,
      41–42
    three kingdoms: copper, silver,
      gold, 53–56

—Shah / Central Asia
    Rustam and Tahmina; woman to
      animal, 87–91
—Sioux / Standing Bear *
    Horse Dreamer and Singing Colt,
      51–54
—Strauss / Trail
    Rapunzel: soliloquy (poem), 11–
      13
—Turkey / Walker, 307 (index)
—Turkish (Art I) / Walker
    Cihansah pursues/finds pigeon-
      girl, 207–217
    sons seek Hazaran nightingale
      for padishah's mosque, 230–
      239
—Vanishing / Mercer *
    Eskimo wife abducted by giant
      bird, 42–49
—Yolen / Faery Flag
    words of power: Late Blossoming
      Flower, 21–39

QUICHE MAYA
—Hamilton / In the Beginning *
    Popul Vuh, 86–99

QUICK THINKING
—High John / Sanfield *
    caught killing sheep, pretends
      self-defense, 19–22
    John verifies: Master killed deer
      with "one shot," 63–68
    slaves forbidden to catch catfish,
      34–39
—Turkish / Walker
    boast re archery prowess; the
      third shot, 43–44

QUILL
—Greaves / Hippo *
    rhino borrows porcupine's quill to
      treat wound, 64–65

QUILLO (toymaker)
—Hoke / Giants
    defeat of tyrannical giant Hundar,
      41–64

QUILT
—Pellowski / Family *
  grandmother's aprons, 113–117
QUOTATIONS
—Demons / Gettings, 197–206

RA (creator/sun-god) (sometimes RE)
—Egyptian / Harris, 132 (index)
—Egyptian / Ions, 35–45 @; 144 (index)
  secret name of, 24–25
—Egyptian / Mercatante, 129–130
—Hamilton / In the Beginning *
  Apophis; creation myth, 110–115
  eyes, 112, 114
—Man Myth & Magic, 3164 (index)
—Wolkstein / Love, 252 @
RA-HARAKHTE
—Egyptian / Ions, 144 (index)
RABBI
—Geras / Grandmother *
  tablecloth: rabbi determines owner, 31–40
—Jewish / Frankel
  imposter rebbe: healing the hasid, 519–520
  Rabbi Amnon of Mayence, 398–400
—Jewish / Sadeh
  Abraham ben Ezra and the bishop, 220–221 Adam Baal Shem: bequest of mystical writings, 341–343
  Adam Baal Shem: magical transport of palace, 340–341
  apprentice baker's blessing, 112–117
  king saved by rabbi's wife (Rabbi Levi in Prague), 232–233
  Leib Sorehs and the matchmaker, 370–373
  pious rabbi punished for faulty vowel sounds, 211–213
  Rabbi Isaac Abrabanel and king's shoe, 222–223
  rabbi scolds poor man offering bread to God, 238–239
  Rabbi Yehiel and King of France, 223–224
  repentance; the poisonous snake, 266–268
  valuable ring given by mistake, 374
—Schwartz / Gates, 810 (index)
RABBIT(-s)
  see also BRER RABBIT TALES; HARE
—Animals / Rowland, 189 (index)
—Arabian / Riordan
  Amina's tale: evil sisters turn rabbit (jinn in disguise) into dog, 116–119
—Beat / Bryan *
  gets last (very small) tail from creator, 53–70
—Bierhorst / Monkey *
  gets caught; dupes coyote to take his place, 72–76
  rabbit marries coyote's daughter, 81–83
  rabbit repeatedly dupes puma, 77–80
—Bruchac / Iroquois *
  origin: legs, tail, lip, 65–67
  origin of small nose, 74–78
  rabbit and the willow tree, 65–67
  rabbit outwits fox (trying to eat him), 74–78
—Carle / Treasury *
  Winners [rabbit races snail] (Andersen), 61–63
—Childcraft 1 / Once *
  foolish, timid rabbit: "earth breaking up," 166–168

Potter: Tale of Peter Rabbit, 192–196

Velveteen Rabbit becomes real when loved, 175–181

—Clarkson / World *
safe in burrow; in unsuitable houses, eaten by fox, 159–161

—Corrin / Six-Year *
Tim Rabbit uses mushroom as umbrella, 161–165

—Dramatized / Kamerman
Quick-witted Jack; suitor test, 400–412

—Erdoes / Sound *
Rabbit Boy (good) vs. Iktome (evil), 98–102

—Georgia Coast / Jones
twenty-two Afro-American, Georgia-coast tales; in dialect, 1–171 *passim*

—Haboo / Hilbert
grizzly and rabbit play on ice-covered lake, 155–157

—Hamilton / Dark *
free spirits: Bouki and Malice, 102–107

—Hamilton / People *
Bruh Alligator meets trouble, 35–41

Bruh Fox makes Tar Baby; rabbit gets stuck, 13–19

He lion, Bruh bear, Bruh rabbit, 5–12

how stop stolen magic hoe? 31–34

Manuel's riddle; fills sack with lies; fortune, 65–75

—Hopi Coyote / Malotki
coyote learns sorcery; transformed; eaten by his children, 166–177

—Lester / Brer Rabbit *
Brer Wolf steals Brer Rabbit's lucky rabbit foot, 145–151

—Lester / Leopard *
contest: how many spots does leopard have? 53–57

—Navajo Coyote / Haile
rabbit tricks, and escapes from, coyote, 12, 38–39

—Pellowski / Family *
Buddhist tale: The hungry stranger, 126–129

handkerchief story, 67–68

—Scary / Young *
bunny disobeys mother; is nearly eaten by snake, 34–36

—Tall Tales / Downs: Bear
how Mr. Rabbit fooled Mr. Possum / W.H. Vann, 99–102

—Turkish / Walker
duck as judge: rabbit removed stone from wolf's back, 15

—Vanishing / Mercer *
sun: origin of brown spot between shoulders, 115–117

—Water Buffalo (Chinese)
rabbit get revenge on lion, 33–35

white rabbit: origin of long ears, pink eyes, 93–102

RACCOON

—Bruchac / Iroquois *
raccoon tricks the crayfish, 69–72

—Tall Tales / Downs: Bear
Major Brown's coon story / R. Dorson, 3–4

RACE(-s) (*athletic competition*)
see also Aesop: Hare . . .

—Bruchac / Iroquois *
clever turtle beats beaver, 47–49

—Carle / Treasury *
Winners [rabbit races snail] (Andersen), 61–63

—Chinese / Chin *
year of the rat [etc., Chinese calendar], 157–167

—Clouston / Popular
hare and tortoise, I.266–273

—Curry / Beforetime *

with help of lookalike relatives,
frog wins race with coyote, 57–
59

—Dramatized / Kamerman
Hans Brinker: skates for poor
children, 200–211

—Greaves / Hippo *
how cheetah got his speed, 28–29
tortoise tricks hare in race, 114–
118

—Greek / Osborne
Atalanta and Hippomenes:
golden apples, 51–54

—Harris-Parks / Jump *
Brer Terrapin "wins" race with
Brer Rabbit, 19–24

—Jewish / Sadeh
riddle: owner of horse coming in
last will inherit kingdom, 168

—Lester / Brer Rabbit *
Brer Turtle beats Brer Rabbit, 31–
34

—Paxton / Aesop *
race: tortoise and the hare, [22–
27]

—Tall Tales / Downs: Bear
Harold Peavey's fast cow (G.
Cronyn), 229–248

—Vanishing / Mercer *
hedgehog (cheating) wins race
with ostrich, 102–105

RACE (people): origin
—Hamilton / In the Beginning *
Blacks and Whites: Kono crea-
tion myth, 14–19

**RACE-CHANGE TRANSFORMA-
TION**
—Hoke / Giants
Finlay, the giant killer, 142–149

RACE PREJUDICE
—Jewish / Frankel
anti-semitism, 648 (index)
Elijah: soft like reed, not hard like
cedar, 583–584

RAGING HORDE
—Grimm / Legends (Ward), II:439 (index)

RAILROADERS
—American / Read Dgst
Casey Jones, John Henry, etc.,
360–362

RAIN
—Caduto / Keepers *
Hero Twins and Swallower of
Clouds, 79–81

—Cotterell / Encyclopedia, 257 (index)

—Gullible Coyote / Malotki
coyote on prayer mission for rain,
105–117
maxim: rain when sun is shining
means coyote is mating, 58

—Hamilton / Dark *
Wanjiru girl swallowed by the
earth, 108–112

—Leonardo / Fables *
arrogant water falls as rain, 72

—Southern [legends] / Floyd
rains of snakes, etc., 74–77

RAIN (GOD or SPIRIT)
—Greaves / Hippo *
elephant vs. Rain Spirit: who is
greater, 53–58

—Mercatante / Encyclopedia, 791 (index)

RAINBOW
—Earthmaker / Mayo *
double rainbow = mother and
child (Quileute tale), 38–40
hunter and Rainbow Woman;
husband lost (Hoh tale), 38–
40

—Hopi / Talashoma-Malotki
hide and seek with life at stake,
50–69

—Lang / Wilkins
Fairer-than-a-Fairy, 274–281

—Man Myth & Magic, 3164 (index)

RAINMAKING
—Chorao / Child's FTB *
  ants push sky; rescue Indian from
  tree top, 43–50
—Greaves / Hippo *
  elephant vs. Rain Spirit: who is
  greater, 53–58
—Hopi Coyote / Malotki
  coyote and the Korowiste kachi-
  nas, 195–227, 303, 307 @
RAIN STORM
—Earthmaker / Mayo *
  origins, 27 @
RAKSHASA
—McGowen / Encyclopedia * 46–
  47
RAM
—Bell / Classical Dict, 197–198 @
RAM (Indic hero)
—Jaffrey / Seasons
  how Ram, son of Dashrat, de-
  feated demon king Ravan, 48–
  69
**Ram [a King Lear type, by
  d'Aulnoy]**
—Zipes / Beauties * 389–399
RAMACHANDRA
—Indic / Ions, 144 (index)
RAMAZAN
—Turkey / Walker, 307 (index)
RAMESSES II
—Egyptian / Harris, 132 (index)
  princess, healing by Kohns the
  Determiner, 88–91
—Egyptian / Ions, 144 (index)
RAMMAN
—Babylonia / Spence, 404 (index)
RANGI-POTIKI
—Polynesians / Andersen, 501 (in-
  dex)
RAPE
—Hopi / Talashoma-Malotki
  old wizard plots to seduce beauti-
  ful girl, 70–91

**Rapunzel (Grimm) (daughter prom-
  ised to witch)**
—Allison / I'll Tell * 58–60
—Chorao / Child's FTB * 33–40
—Corrin / Favourite * 87–92
—Douglas / Magic *
—Grimm / Complete * 73–76
—Grimm / Sixty * 80–83
—Lang / Wilkins, 128–131
—Strauss / Trail
  prince's soliloquy (poem), 11–13
Rapunzel (existential retelling)
—Switzer / Existential, 71–78
RAS SHAMRA
—Gray / Near East, 144(index)
RASH ACT(-s)
—Allison / I'll Tell *
  gingerbread boy; chase; the fox,
  22–23
Rashomon: ogre loses arm
—Quayle / Shining * 103–111
RAT (-s)
—Animals / Rowland, 189 (index)
—Baring-Gould / Curious
  Bishop Hatto: famine and rats,
  122–126 @
—Chinese / Chin *
  year of the rat (Chinese calen-
  dar), 157–167
—Chorao / Child's *
  Pied Piper (agreement broken),
  51–55
—Clarkson / World *
  rats jump from ship, endlessly,
  247–248
—Quayle / Shining *
  mother's mirror warns Sachiko of
  stepmother in rat-form, 90–96
—Tall Tales / Downs: Bear
  red rats of Plum Fork (Jesse Stuart), 45–56
—Vanishing / Mercer *
  abduction: little duck and big water-rat, 54–57

Rattlesnake, see under SNAKE.
RAVAN (demon)
—Jaffrey / Seasons
how Ram, son of Dashrat, de-
feated demon king Ravan, 48–
69
RAVANA
—Indic / Ions, 144 (index)
Raven, see BIRD: RAVEN.
Raven, The
—Grimm / Complete * 431–436
—Grimm / Sixty * 250–256
RAZOR
—Leonardo / Fables *
razor: escapes, loafs, rusts, 54
Re (god), see RA.
REALITY
—Aesop / Reeves-Wilson *
Dog and dog's reflection, 36–
37
—Bomans / Wily *
wings: "madman" wants to go to
heaven without dying, 152–
155
—Childcraft 1 / Once *
Velveteen Rabbit becomes real
when loved, 175–181
Rebbe, see RABBI.
Rebirth, see REINCARNATION.
Receiving, see GIVING AND RE-
CEIVING.
RECIPES
—Lore of Love, 58–59
RECITATIONS
—Oral Trad / Cunningham
recitations, 1–264
**RECOGNITION BY PERSONAL
CHARACTERISTICS**
—Arabian / Lewis
Anklet [magic pot; magic pins]
49–51
—Corrin / Favourite *
true wife can wash shirt (East of
the sun), 1–15

—Crossley / British FT *
Mossycoat to ball; leaves slipper,
which fits only her, 86–99
—Grimm / Complete *
goose-girl at well; princess weeps
pearls, 725–734
Iron Hans, 612–620
—Grimm / Sixty *
Iron Hans, 317–325
—Old Wives / Carter
kissed by dog (taboo), prince for-
gets his new wife, 76–85
—Vietnam / Terada *
Tam kills stepsister Cam; takes
her place as king's wife, 23–34
Red Riding Hood, see Little Red Rid-
ing Hood.
REDEEMING THE TIME
—Jewish / Frankel
lion, man, pit, and snake (fable),
466–467
REDEMPTION
—Jewish / Frankel
rabbi's son: the Lesser Light,
536–538
—Jewish / Sadeh
father punished: reborn as dog,
361–362
REDFERN, Paul
—Southern [legends] / Floyd
final flight, 83–87
Reed, A.W. and Inez Hames
—Hoke / Giants
The giant and his swing, 130–
132
REENACTMENT
—Turkish / Walker
duck as judge: rabbit removed
stone from wolf's back, 15
Reeves, James
—Corrin / Imagine *
Two greedy bears, 23–46
—Witches / Iosa *
Old Moll (poem), 10

REFERENCE BOOKS
see also BIBLIOGRAPHY; DIC-
TIONARIES
—Ashliman / Guide, 1–368
—Gillespie / Best Books
folk literature; annotated list,
275–309
—Hearne / [Bibliog.]
Choosing books for children, 1–
228 *
For reading out loud! 1–266
—Lipson / Best Books
New York Times guide, 1–421 *
—Lynn / Fantasy *
annotated bibliography, 1–771
—Norwegian / Hodne, 1–400
REFLECTION
—Aesop / Alley *
dog, carrying meat, and his re-
flection, 24–25
—Hopi Coyote / Malotki
foolish fear of reflection in water,
105–111
—MacDonald / Sourcebook *
motif index, 688
—Paxton / Belling *
dog in river: greed: foolish loss of
meat, (Aesop), [38–39]
REFLECTION (meditative)
—Demi / Reflective *
a Chinese mirror, [28]
REFUGEES
—Corrin / Imagine *
Pari hides in golden candelabra;
prince buys, falls in love, 151–
160
—Old Wives / Carter
two battered wives find refuge in
dead whale, 225–226
—Scary / Young *
witch would chop down tree sheltering children, 47–51
REGENERATION
—Hamilton / Dark *

tiny thing: Anishinaba and Boshk-
wadosh, 54–59
REGRET
—Fahs / Old *
wish of Midas: all touched turns to
gold, 115–117
—Leonardo / Fables *
flea leaves dog; looks for better
life on sheep, 71
REHUA
—Polynesians / Andersen, 501 (index)
REINCARNATION
—Egyptian / Harris
Anpu and Bata; betrayed, 77–
83
challenge: read letter without
breaking seal, 108–113
—Floyd / Gr Am Myst
Bridey Murphy, 136–141
—Indic / Ions, 144 (index)
—Jewish / Frankel
return of rich man's soul, 504–
506
—Jewish / Sadeh
atone for sin: reincarnated bride,
243
father punished: reborn as dog,
361–362
Gehazi, for punishment, is reincarnated as dog, 134–136
—Muddleheads / Harris
pieces of cut-out heart become
wolverines, 75–93
—Spring / Philip
lovers reincarnated as butterflies,
35–41
—Vietnam / Terada *
chess player dies; enters body of
newly dead butcher, 75–77
Prime Minister, in former life a tea
server, 83–87
—Witch Encyc / Guiley, 418 (index)
—Yolen / Faery Flag

minstrel killed: plant growing from grave, 41–46
—Yolen / Werewolves
White Wolf: boy's initiation to manhood, 45–69

REINCARNATION AS MUSICAL INSTRUMENT
—Grimm / Complete *
singing bone: murder revealed, 148–150

REINCARNATION AS PLANT
—Fahs / Old *
maize spirit: origin of corn, 148–151
—Old Wives / Carter
Beauty, murdered, returns as bamboo; made into bed, 200–204
—Russian Hero / Warner *
little simpleton: silver saucer and juicy apple, 106–108
—Vietnam / Terada *
Tam kills stepsister Cam; takes her place as king's wife, 23–34
—Yolen / Faery Flag
reincarnation: plant growing from grave, 41–46

REINCARNATION: BOY TO BIRD
—Grimm / Complete *
juniper tree: murder exposed by singing bird, 220–229
—Old Wives / Carter
Beauty, murdered by Pock Face, returns as sparrow, 200–204
—Scary / Young *
boy reincarnated as bird; sings tale of murder; revenge, 78–83
—Vietnam / Terada *
Tam kills stepsister Cam; takes her place as king's wife, 23–34

REJUVENATION
—Bell / Classical Dict, 199 @
—Grimm / Complete *

old man made young again, 640–642
—Hamilton / In the Beginning *
Maidu creation myth, 34–41
—Igloo / Metayer
woman a walking skeleton: magic drum, 13–18
—Jaffrey / Seasons
Shravan Kumar: wife asks; banyan tree gives shade and healing milk, 16–20
—Jewish / Frankel
stepmother sends Miriam to be killed in forest, 579–583
—Leonardo / Fables *
testament of the eagle, 118
—Old Wives / Carter
attempt to disfigure stepdaughter (Cinderella-type), 171–177
—Russian Hero / Warner *
turning old folk into young: smith and devil, 19–20
witch (blood sister) and sun's sister, 60–61
—Williams-Ellis / Tales *
King O'Toole's goose made young by St. Kevin, 37–43

RELATIVES (often cruel, treacherous)
—Clarkson / World *
Indian Cinderella: Strong Wind will marry truthful girl, 43–45
—Grimm / Complete *
snake-leaves revive treacherous wife, 94–96
—Jaffrey / Seasons
King Kans sends demon-nurse to kill Krishna, 22–25
wrestling, Krishna defeats elephant and two giants; kills Kans, 32–36
—Lang / Wilkins
queen poisons stepdaughter's suitor, 460–473

—Lewis / Proud
Bisclavret: wife keeps husband in wolf-form, 29–35
—Lines / Magical *
sisters set trap for Finist the Falcon, 31–45
—Old Wives / Carter
Pock Face drowns Beauty; tells husband she has smallpox, 200–204
—Rockwell / Puss *
Kate Crackernuts (gets head of sheep), 19–26
—Turkish / Walker
Karacor and the giants, 52–61
—Vietnam / Terada *
look-alike brothers love the same girl, 109–113
magic crossbow used to kill king, 120–125

RELIGION(-s)
see also particular religions, e.g., CHRISTIANITY; HINDU; INDIAN RELIGION; JEWS; etc.
—Babylonia / Spence, 405 (index)
—Christian / Every
sources; bibliography, 130–141
—Man Myth & Magic, 3165 (index)
Eastern, 3193–94 (index)
Western, 3190–93 (index)
—Mex-Am / West
motif index, 301
—Navajo Coyote / Haile
roaming among gods, 3–7 @
—Norwegian / Hodne, 163–177
—Polynesians / Andersen, 452–468
—Spanish-Am / Van Etten *
mistaken communication: God is lost, 32
—Unnatural / Cohen, 147 (index)

RELIGIOUS BELIEFS
—Bomans / Wily *

Christmas: travelers turned away, 174–175
worldly wisdom of eleven kings; need twelfth King (Christ), 185–192
—Fahs / Old *
being: can't see or feel; still real, 20–23
—Grimm / Complete *
sparrow and his four children, 657–660
Virgin Mary, the woodcutter; forbidden room, 23–29
—Yolen / Werewolves
Wolf's flock, 201–223

RELIGIOUS FEASTS/FASTS
see also particular feasts, e.g., CHRISTMAS; EASTER; PASSOVER; etc.
—Geras / Grandmother *
overcrowded house (move animals in/out; seems larger), 77–85

RELIGIOUS REWARDS
—Egyptian / Harris
judgment by King of the Dead, 103–107
—Erdoes / Sound *
vision quest [spirits can't be forced], 63–67
—Fahs / Old *
Capilano sisters bring peace and brotherhood, 104–107
—Grimm / Complete *
rich and poor men enter heaven, 695–696
—Wilde / Happy *
selfish giant (repents; led to Paradise by Christchild), 59–69

RELIGIOUS TALES
—Ashliman / Guide
titles arranged in Aarne-Thompson system, 150–169 @

**Reluctant dragon, The
(K. Grahame)**
—Victorian / Hearn, 326–344
Remarkable persons, see EX-
TRAORDINARY PERSONS.
Remarkable rocket, The
—Wilde / Happy * 105–133
—Wilde / Lynch * 55–72
REMARRIAGE
—Jewish / Sadeh
woman whose husband disap-
peared, 81–83
REMEDY WORSE THAN DISEASE
—Grimm / Complete *
fear of owl, people burn down
barn to kill it, 711–713
REMUS
—Roman / Usher, 132 (index)
Repartee, see RETORT . . .
REPENTANCE
see also ATONEMENT
—Grimm / Complete *
three green twigs: hermit must do
penance, 823–825
—Jewish / Frankel, 650 (index)
—Jewish / Sadeh
merchant buys dead partner's sin
and guilt, 83–86
rabbi and the poisonous snake,
266–268
—Journey Sun (Chinese)
drink from Red Spring, under
power of Red Devil, 125–140
—Vietnam / Terada *
Prime Minister, in former life a tea
server, 83–87
REPETITION (technique)
—Turkish (Art I) / Walker, xxxiv-
xxxv @
REPETITIVE (RHYMES, etc.)
—Allison / I'll Tell *
little red hen (industrious), 16–17
—Bierhorst / Monkey *
bad compadre oft exploits Juan;

animals perform his impossible
tasks, 94–106
—Bomans / Wily *
chimney sweep's curse (personified) captured by curate, 93–96
—Bryan / Lion *
hide and seek: Jackal's favorite
game, 40–59
Jumoke ("Foolish Boy") outwits
Ananse, 60–86
—Childcraft 1 / Once *
the little red hen, 98–99
—Clarkson / World *
gold in chimney; witch: "have you
seen a maid o mine?" 26–29
mouse tries to regain bitten-off
tail, 237–241
—Corrin / Imagine *
prince unwittingly marries Sorfarina four times, 11–22
—Erdoes / Sound *
coming of the white man (wasicum), 74–81
—Fahs / Old *
drought: lizard keeps others from
well, 91–95
—Grimm / Complete *
Snowdrop [=Snow White and the
seven dwarfs], 249–258
—Grimm / Sixty *
Snowdrop (as above), 161–170
—Hamilton / People *
give me back my "tailypo," 116–
120
Little Daughter sings, and escapes from wolf, 60–63
—Manning / Cats *
crocodile would eat Soafara; she
escapes with help of Roller
Bird, 51–57
old couple: repeated tries to cut
down tree; bird supplies needs,
101–106
—O'Brien / Tales *

Amada defeats giants (who daily return to life) and series of monsters, 21–30

—Old Wives / Carter
mother foils attempt to abduct daughter, 33–38
Mr. Fox: his betrothed dreams of him mutilating woman for ring, 8–10
orphan twins visit mother: market of the dead, 166–169

—Scary / Young *
boy reincarnated as bird; sings tale of murder; revenge, 78–83
Hobbyahs: master dismembers barking dog (tragicomedy), 26–30

—Spanish-Am / Van Etten *
coyote disrupts farm's animals, 11–18

—Turkish / Walker
just say Hic! [don't say that!] 76–79
magpie spills milk; loses/regains tail, 11–13

—Turkish (Art I) / Walker
Coral Lady: the cutworm and the mouse, 20–22

—Water Buffalo (Chinese)
plop! spread of unquestioned danger, 30–32
woman's coin keeps rice-jar full; tiger would steal, 55–61

—Witches / Iosa *
old witch (Jacobs); kind girl and her selfish sister, 34–39

—Yep / Rainbow *
Wong I, II and III: The boasting contest, 96–105

REPORTER

—Brooke / Telling *
John Henry wins tunnel-digging race, 77–110

REPTILE(-s)

—Beasts / McHargue
imaginary, 47–49 @

—Tall Tales / Downs: Bear
surest thing in show business (J.H. Ford), 74–83

REQUEST

—Navajo Coyote / Haile
repeated four times, best to grant, 68 @

RESCUE(-s) [bravery and cleverness in]
see also CAPTIVE(-s)

—Bierhorst / Naked *
boy who learned the songs of the birds, 60–66

—Bryan / Lion *
lion steals ostrich chicks, 3–23

—Caduto / Keepers *
Sedna, woman under the sea, 95–97

—Carter / Sleeping *
Hop o' my Thumb, abandoned, leaves trail to find home, 69–80

—Celts / Hodges *
Gareth of Orkney wins his spurs, 133–154

—Chinese / Chin *
finding wife for cruel River God, 17–26
monkey: on road to fetch scriptures, 95–110

—Corrin / Imagine *
prince abducted; Volkh uses his six, prince's three wishes, 124–135

—Crane / Beauty *
Yellow Dwarf and proud princess, [34–47]

—Crossley / Dead *
Yallery Brown (rescued from imprisonment under stone), 79–85

446

—Erdoes / Sound *
  girl saves brother; battle of the
    Rosebud, 10–15
—Ghosts / Starkey
  moon (personified) captured/
    rescued (bogles), 96–101
—Greaves / Hippo *
  bushfire: giraffe saves oxpecker's
    nest, 84–86
—Grimm / Complete *
  brothers: one rescues princess;
    is rescued by other, 290–
    311
  drummer rescues princess from
    glass mountain, 781–791
—Hamilton / Dark *
  elf king, Childe Rowland and
    Burd Ellen, 65–72
—Indian Myth / Burland
  lazy boy with supernatural
    strength, 49–50
—Jewish / Frankel, 650 (index)
—Jewish / Sadeh
  lost princess: king's curse, to Evil
    One's kingdom, 386–389
—Lang / Wilkins
  lute player: wife rescues husband
    from prison, 528–533
  magic ring: happiness and power
    if . . . , 220–227
—Lore of Love
  loved one in the lower world,
    108
—Manning / Cats *
  man marries bird-wife; his mother
    drives her out, 75–82
  water-pool: boy, hare, fox, wolf,
    bear vs. Baba Yaga, 58–64
—Manning / Cauldron *
  amber witch: common man, loved
    by princess, sent to get amber,
    18–31
  donkey, gift of troll-child, helps
    hunter rescue princess, 9–17

  gives Jack ring (can change self
    to any size); rescues princess
    from giant, 78–89
  Whirlwind abducts queen and
    (evil) son; rescue by youngest
    son, 106–117
—Maori / Kanawa *
  Putawai: rescued, married to un-
    derworld spirit, 92–100
  Putawai: returned from under-
    world; her underworld child,
    92–100
—Russian Hero / Warner *
  Dobrynya spares abductor/
    dragon, 69–70
  how Sadko angered the sea tsar,
    45–48
  Koshchei the Deathless; Bulat
    the Brave; Vasilisa, 96–99
  three kingdoms: copper, silver,
    gold, 53–56
  Vasilisa (Golden Braid) and Ivan
    the Pea, 63–68
—Scary / Young *
  dogs kill witch who would chop
    down tree sheltering children,
    47–51
—Shah / Central Asia
  Feroz-Shah and the mechanical
    flying horse, 131–145
  Iskandar's seven sisters and the
    emerald ring, 118–125
  princess imprisoned in mountain
    of jade, 19–24
  Rustam and the iron fortress, 25–
    30
—Sioux / Standing Bear *
  hunter on ledge, saved by young
    eagles, 20–25
—Yep / Rainbow *
  protector of sailors: Dream Flier,
    144–151
RESEARCH
—Clarkson / World *

analyses of ten tools (indexes, etc.), 5–13
folktales in the college classroom, 399–412 @

RESOURCEFULNESS
see also CLEVERNESS
—Turkey / Walker, 307 (index)

RESPECT
—Jewish / Frankel
chief sage's golden shoes, 566

RESPONSIBILITY
—Hamilton / People *
Bruh Rabbit: how stop stolen magic hoe? 31–34
—Jewish / Sadeh
singing donkey and dancing camel, 167

RESTITUTION
—Ghosts / Starkey
buggane, Broder Menine, the tailor, 16–23

RESURRECTION
—Bell / Classical Dict, 200 @
—Jewish / Sadeh
eagle takes rabbi's son to Christian palace, 273–275
rabbi and the Graf, 301
—Mercatante / Encyclopedia, 791 (index)

RESUSCITATION
see also LIFE RESTORED
—Baring-Gould / Curious
Seven Sleepers of Ephesus, 44–49
—Bruchac / Iroquois *
Hodadenon's family, 169–182
—Childcraft 3 / Stories *
cow-tail switch (sons contribute to father's return from death), 32–37
—Clarkson / World *
killed children restored in exchange for coffin-lid, 197–198

—Clouston / Popular, 407–412, 497–499
—Coyote / Ramsey
arrow-point maker and tobacco-hunter, 76–78
—Dulac / Fairy *
Bashtchelik (real steel), 91–113
—Egyptian / Harris
Anpu and Bata, 77–83
—Grimm / Complete *
Brother Lustig and St. Peter, 367–377
brothers: one rescues princess; is rescued by other, 290–311
snake-leaves revive treacherous wife, 94–96
wizard captures three sisters; Fitcher's bird, 216–220
—Grimm / Legends (Ward), II:440 (index)
—Jaffrey / Seasons
how Ganesh got his elephant head, 121–123
Karvachauth: wife clings to demon until husband is restored, 75–79
Savitri nags underworld king; husband restored, 10–15
—Jewish / Frankel
princess to God: restore my lover or take my life, 360–365
scorpion in goblet: virtuous rabbi rewarded, 437–446
—Lang / Wilkins
Princess in the chest; faithful guard, 369–384
—Maori / Kanawa *
Hutu trick "game": with Pare, catapulted out of underworld, 106–110
—Navajo Coyote / Haile
tingling maiden: coyote as suitor-seducer, 15, 69–77
—Old Wives / Carter

Beauty, murdered, returns as bamboo; made into bed; restored, 200–204

ghoul's fingernail kills girl; nail removed, girl revives, 160–165

RETORTS (including repartee with ruler, judge, etc.)

—Cambodian / Carrison
Siva believes eagle's dreams; owl asks equal treatment, 67–72

—Frog Rider (Chinese)
short tales (29) of Nasrdin Avanti, 111–135

—Geras / Grandmother *
faces of Czar: clever repartee, 14–20

—Grimm / Complete *
shepherd boy adopted by king, 651–652

—Grimm / Sixty *
Fox [100 tricks] and the cat, 227–228

—Hamilton / People *
better "wait till Martin [ghost] comes," 133–137

—Old Wives / Carter
escaping slowly: goat and kids in Lion's house, 221

—Turkish / Walker
lion asks: how does my den smell? 16

—Turkish (Art I) / Walker
hoca mistakenly mounts donkey backward, 98–99

REVENANT(-s)
see also GHOST; DEAD: RETURN . . .

—Bruchac / Iroquois *
husband: vampire skeleton, 129–133

—Clarkson / World *
corpse seen leaving coffin; kills two children, 197–198

—Ghosts / Starkey
Treasure ghost of Fife, 88–95
Tregeagle's ghost, 58–65

—Hamilton / People *
Little Eight John and Old Raw Head Bloody Bones, 121–125

—Jewish / Sadeh
dybbuk: haunt of man who killed Zechariah, 159–160
Menashe dies to atone for past sin, 162–163
mourner's prayer for the dead, 139–140
Yishma'el reincarnated to atone for murder, 160–162

—Lore of Love
stone statue drags Don Juan to hell, 61–63

—Scandinavian / Kvideland, x, 421, 427 (index)

—Scary / Young *
ghost sucks blood from Indian mother and child, 87–88

REVENGE

—Allison / I'll Tell *
fox and stork; dinner invitations; victim of joke, 110

—Coyote / Bierhorst *
enemies in sinking boat; revenge-minded forget all else, [20]

—Curry / Beforetime *
gopher kills hagfish, causer of parents' death, 52–56

—Grimm / Complete *
bewitched: straw believed to be a beam, 645
carter runs over/kills dog; sparrow seeks revenge, 280–282

—Grimm / Sixty *
carter . . . (as above), 36–40

—Hopi / Talashoma-Malotki
girls (one turned to bull-snake; killed) love same boy, 118–135

old wizard plots to seduce beautiful girl, 70–91
—Igloo / Metayer
ball players [losers die], 32–34
—Jewish / Sadeh
Maimonides: king's ring found in
fish, 215–217
vizier's daughter and bandit in
sheep's clothing, 98–101
—Lewis / Proud
Yonec: true father killed by jealous husband's trap, 53–60
—Lore of Love
stone statue drags Don Juan to
hell, 61–63
—Pirate Ghosts / McSherry
red swimmer: father and daughter murdered by Luke Treach,
45–68
treasure: digging at Pistol Key,
166–181
—Scary / Young *
boy reincarnated as bird; sings
tale of murder, 78–83
ghost of murdered Oiwa haunts
samurai husband to death, 21–
25

REVERSAL of FORTUNE
—Arabian / Lewis
treachery: good barber and evil
dyer, 123–130
—Bierhorst / Monkey *
bad compadre oft exploits Juan;
animals perform his impossible
tasks, 94–106
youngest son, lazy Tup, gets ants
to clear/plant/harvest cornfield,
44–51
—Childcraft 3 / Stories *
Chin has three questions for the
Living Kuan-yin, 93–99
—Chinese / Chin *
palace plot: rival concubines, 77–
92

—Clouston / Popular
king's favorite envied and plotted
against, II.444–457
—Demi / Reflective *
by wits, turn bad times to good,
[6]
—Igloo / Metayer
Kautaluk: Great Spirit grants marvelous strength, 35–39
—Jewish / Sadeh
desperate man and prophet
Jonah, 154–158
man who went to the "dickens,"
146–149
nightingale; queen gives birth to
animals, 25–28
poor brother and three beasts,
140–143
rich man will pay to say: I don't
believe in God, 324–326
woman who was almost stoned to
death, 18–20
—Manning / Cats *
when heads are cut off, mouse-
queen spell broken, 83–91
—Manning / Cauldron *
crusader beaten, robbed by comrades; witches reveal secrets,
46–57
—Mex-Am / West
motif index, 300
—Oral Trad / Cunningham
Big Klaus and Little Klaus, 72–
76
—Palestinian / Speak (Muhawi)
motif-index, 397
—Spanish-Am / Van Etten *
rich neighbor deceived re source
of poor man's wealth, 25–28
—Turkish (Art I) / Walker
apprentice shoe merchant dismissed for request to Allah,
116–122
good to the good, and damnation

to the evil: poor man and grand vizier, 204–207

shah spares lustful pilgrim; favor later returned, 93–98

Revivication, see LIFE RESTORED; RESUSCITATION.

REVOLUTION (U.S. history)

—American / Read Dgst

myths to make men fight, 90–97

REVULSION

—Strauss / Trail

princess revolted by frog before it turns (poem), 24–26

REWARD(-s) (usually magic, or marvelous)

[see also good qualities such as "kindness"; all usually rewarded; these tales may include the correlative topic "punishment"]

—Allison / I'll Tell *

crane's long beak; bone in wolf's throat (fable), 101

—Arabian / McCaughrean

Pearl-Harvest, 36–50

—Bomans / Wily *

hunter spares deer, swan, raven; saves man accused of theft, 16–19

—Childcraft 3 / Stories *

cow-tail switch (sons contribute to father's return from death), 32–37

—Frog Rider (Chinese)

magic gourd; 120 monsters burned up, 71–82

—Grimm / Complete *

devil with the three golden hairs, 151–158

by eating white snake, servant understands animal language, 98–101

failing vs. non-failing in feeding animals, 698–704

girl shares bread with three little men, 78–83

Mother Hulda, 133–136

three sisters encounter St. Joseph, 815–818

Turnip, The, 637–640

white bride and black bride, 608–612

—Grimm / Sixty *

by eating white snake . . . (as above), 197–201

Mother Hulda, 111–115

Turnip, The, 213–216

Water of life, The, 264–270

—Jaffrey / Seasons

queen's necklace; washerwoman's reward: light lamp, 81–84

—Jewish / Frankel, xiii, 651 (index)

crane removes bone from wolf's throat (fable), 459–460

death: good man, bad man: temporal honor, eternal reward, 578–579

Moshele's gift: poor water-carrier prays for 1,000 rubles, 554–556

—Lang / Wilkins

Toads and diamonds, 106–109

—MacDonald / Sourcebook *

motif index, 342–349

—Mex-Am / West

motif index, 300

—Old Wives / Carter

battle of birds: prince given magic bag, 76–85

—Palestinian / Speak (Muhawi)

motif-index, 399

—Spring / Philip

brothers: one honest, one greedy, 94–97

—Russian Hero / Warner *

witch (blood sister) and sun's sister, 60–61

—Scriven / Full Color *
   Ali Baba and the forty thieves,
      20–25
—Trolls / Asbjornsen
   stepsisters: one kind, one cruel;
      escape service of witch, 42–50
—Turkish / Walker
   Deli feigns death, frightens
      thieves, gets reward, 80–84
—Water Buffalo (Chinese)
   fish-seller and the one-eyed yak,
      5–8
—Yep / Rainbow *
   beggar woman: child of calamity,
      46–52
   mouse: The superior pet, 80–85

RHINOCEROS
—Greaves / Hippo * 65–66 @
   borrows porcupine's quill to treat
      wound, 64–65
   tug-of-war: hare vs. hippo and
      rhinoceros, 118–120
   why giraffe has a long neck, 86–
      88
   why rhino scatters his dung, 60–
      64

RHYMES (*including magic*)
   see also POETRY; REPETITIVE
—Allison / I'll Tell *
   Mother Goose, etc. (forty-one se-
      lections), 71–94
—Am Child / Bronner
   rhymes of play, 51–82
—Bomans / Wily *
   children escape from witch with
      help of top, kite, doll, 88–93
—Dulac / Fairy *
   boy-suitor gathers six helpers:
      the seven conquerors, 22–28
—Folk-rhymes / Northall
   England, 1–565
—Hall / Treasury *
   Little Brown Bear afraid of the
      dark, 22–25

—Manning / Cats *
   rhyming water-nick fries fish; bear
      and monkeys feast, 97–100
—Mex-Am / West, 53–64, 267
—Old Wives / Carter
   she-ghoul: wife and children flee;
      man does not believe danger;
      is eaten, 216–220
—Quayle / Cornish *
   Cherry Winbroome in service of
      little people, 91–102
—Scary / Young *
   Bloody Mary (a tale in rhyme),
      58–60
—Talk / Goss
   thirteen tales, and commentary,
      435–493
—Turkish (Art I) / Walker
   tyrant Bolu Bey blinds man; son
      gets revenge, 99–109
—Williams-Ellis / Tales *
   Well of the World's End, 55–61

RIBBON
—Scary / Young *
   bride always wears ribbon around
      neck; husband removes; her
      head falls off, 61–63

RICE
—Old Wives / Carter
   wife gives rice to lover; tricks hus-
      band to accept chaff for grain,
      72
—Vanishing / Mercer *
   Nagas myth: food for men and
      mice; origin, 89–90

RICH and POOR
   see also POOR
—Bierhorst / Monkey *
   bad compadre oft exploits Juan;
      animals perform his impossible
      tasks, 94–106
—Bomans / Wily *
   return: rich man tries to restore
      his childhood home, 76–78

—Dramatized / Kamerman
Plum Blossom and the dragon,
38–46
—Fahs / Old *
rich young man: sell all, give to
poor, 118–120
—Frog Rider (Chinese)
magic brush: things painted become real, 47–59
—Grimm / Complete *
God's food: rich sister refuses
aid, 822
rich and poor men enter heaven,
695–696
—Jaffrey / Seasons
Doda and Dodi: rich woman does
not feed poor sister-in-law, 38–
46
—Jewish / Frankel
let them eat stones, 506
—Jewish / Sadeh
brothers; man who went to the
"dickens," 146–149
poor brother and three beasts,
140–143
rich man prepared for rainy day,
178–179
—Spanish-Am / Van Etten *
rich neighbor deceived re source
of poor man's wealth, 25–28
—Wilde / Lynch *
young king dreams: the poor suffer to provide grandeur, 73–
94
Ricky [or Riquet] with the Tuft
—Carter / Sleeping * 93–102
—Zipes / Beauties * 52–57
alternate version: Ricky does not
become handsome, 95–100
RIDDLES
—Am Child / Bronner, 113–142
—Bomans / Wily *
woodcutter solves riddles; wins
princess, 202–205

—Campbell / West Highlands
Ridere of riddles, II.36–46
—Childcraft 2 / Time *
Morris and Boris (Wiseman), 76–
91
—Childcraft 3 / Stories *
Clever Manka [riddle re swiftest
. . .], 120–127
—Chinese / Chin *
clever daughter-in-law, 3–14
—Clarkson / World *
clever Manka (solves riddles;
problem-tasks), 93–95
—Dramatized / Kamerman
bee rewards King Solomon's
kindness, 250–257
—German-American / Barrick, 47–66
—Grimm / Complete *
cunning tailor: riddle, bear, princess, 525–528
devil's grandmother solves riddle
for hero, 563–566
peasant's wise daughter, 439–
440
riddle: princess listens to sleeping prince, 128–131
riddling tale, 663
—Hamilton / People *
Manuel's riddle; fills sack with
lies; fortune, 65–75
Riddle tale of freedom, 156–159
—Jewish / Sadeh
Abraham ben Ezra and the
bishop, 220–221
daughter wiser than her father,
289–291
mother sells son for human sacrifice, 330–331
owner of horse coming in last will
inherit kingdom, 168
riding/walking, laughing/crying
(all at same time), 297
—Kessler / Turtle Knock * 1–48
—Kessler / Turtle Riddle * 1–47

—Lester / Brer Rabbit *
  bee hive in gum tree, 91–95
—Mex-Am / West, 47–52, 264
—Old Wives / Carter
  fool would buy brains from wise
    woman; good wife supplies
    need, 96–100
  wise little girl solves czar's rid-
    dles, 28–30
—Pellowski / Story * 99–101
—Russian / Afanasev, 660 (index)
—Shannon / More *
  never seen, never heard: king vs.
    Aesop, 35–38
—Tibet / Timpanelli *
  evil helper takes real daughter's
    place; exposed, 15–27
—Turkey / Walker, 307 (index)
—Turkish / Walker
  porter solves three riddles, wins
    sultan's daughter, 91–96
—Turkish (Art I) / Walker
  to win beautiful mute, prince must
    make her speak, 34–41
Riddle, The
—Grimm / Complete * 128–131
Riddler, The (poem)
—Crossley / British FT, 309–312
Riddling tale
—Grimm / Complete * 663
RIDICULE
—Igloo / Metayer
  owl, ridiculed, kills wolf, 55–
    57
RIGHT AND WRONG
—Caduto / Keepers *
  Four Worlds: the Dine story of
    creation, 31–34
RIGHT VS MIGHT
—Egyptian / Harris
  throne of Egypt: Horus vs. Seth,
    41–47
Rikki-Tikki-Tavi
—Corrin / Eight-Year * 173–191

RING(-s) (often magic)
—Arabian / Lewis
  treachery: good barber and evil
    dyer, 123–130
—Clouston / Popular
  ring and fish legends, I.398–403
—Corrin / Imagine *
  Pari hides in golden candelabra;
    prince buys, falls in love, 151–
    160
—Dulac / Fairy *
  blue bird (prince transformed),
    77–90
—Grimm / Complete *
  girl lost in wood; witch, ring, and
    dove/prince, 558–560
  King of the golden mountain
    [wishing ring], 425–430
—Grimm / Legends (Ward), II:441 (in-
    dex)
—Grimm / Sixty *
  King . . . [as above], 274–280
—Jewish / Frankel, 647 (index)
  rabbi's magic ring: rabbi to were-
    wolf; wife to donkey, 450–455
  Solomon: this too shall pass,
    257–260
—Jewish / Sadeh
  Maimonides: king's ring found in
    fish, 215–217
  secret name of God: Ashmodai
    rules in Solomon's place, 58–
    61
—Lang / Wilkins
  King Solomon's ring; Dragon of
    the North, 285–297
  magic ring: happiness and power
    if . . . , 220–227
—Lester / Leopard *
  healing leaves for blind king, 59–
    68
—Lewis / Proud
  Yonec: lover forgotten by jealous
    husband, 53–60

—Lore of Love
  curse causes husband to forget
    wife, 26–31
—MacDonald / Sourcebook *
  motif index, 689
—Manning / Cats *
  witch abducts king's two children;
    Katchen the cat helps escape,
    9–15
—Manning / Cauldron *
  gives Jack ring (can change self
    to any size); rescues princess
    from giant, 78–89
  prince and retinue turned into
    trees; girl breaks spell, 39–
    45
—O'Brien / Tales *
  adventures of Marteen: grateful
    beggar gives magic gold-
    producing ring, 31–37
—Reeves / Shadow
  hawk (knight) as lover; protection
    from cruel husband, 1–48
  twin girls parted at birth; reunited
    at wedding of one, 113–128
—Shah / Central Asia
  Iskandar and the emerald ring
    (calls jinn), 118–125
RIO (a person)
—Hamilton / Dark *
  Rolling Rio, gray man, and Death,
    5–13
RIO GRANDE
—Speck / New World, 528 (index)
RISK
—Allison / I'll Tell *
  mice in council: belling the cat,
    121
RITES OF PASSAGE
—Man Myth & Magic
  analytics, 3188 (index)
RITUAL
—Persian / Hinnells 120–133, 143 (in-
    dex)

RIVALS
—Chorao / Child's FTB *
  ants push sky; rescue Indian from
    tree top, 43–50
—Corrin / Imagine *
  Pari hides in golden candelabra;
    prince buys, falls in love, 151–
    160
—Earth / Hadley *
  Beebyeebyee marries water god
    (fish-man), [25–26]
—Erdoes / Sound *
  treachery: two warriors love same
    girl, 25–30
—Grimm / Complete *
  youngest huntsman rescues
    princesses from dragon, 420–
    424
—Yep / Rainbow *
  cats and dogs as "Natural ene-
    mies," 12–18
RIVER(-s)
—American / Read Dgst
  life and legends (U.S.), 136–157
—Curry / Beforetime *
  Klamath: witches steal all
    salmon; coyote destroys secret
    dam, 42–47
—Demi / Reflective *
  river god/ocean god: exhalted im-
    age deflated, [26]
—Glooskap / Norman *
  rapids: secluded home found by
    wolves, 51–60
—Grimm / Legends (Ward), II:441 (in-
    dex)
—Igloo / Metayer
  Coppermine River legend:
    feigned death, 78–81
—Jewish / Frankel, 647 (index)
—Jewish / Sadeh
  Baal Shem Tov and the imps,
    352–353
—Journeys / Norris *

great chase: Mirragen the Cat-
man vs. Gurangatch, [10–12]
—Leonardo / Fables *
river in fury to possess lily, 34
—Russian Hero / Warner *
Black Stream (personified); dam
removed, 43
Sukhman kills 40,000 Tartars,
41–42
—Yep / Rainbow *
Breaker's bridge, 118–123
RIVER-MAN
—Spanish-Am / Van Etten *
proper/improper use of river:
good/bad life, 37–41
ROAD(-s)
—Hoke / Giants
Paul Bunyan and Babe straighten
crooked trail (tall tale), 27–29
—Journeys / Norris *
road to death: old man takes form
of bullock, [16–18]
**ROANOKE COLONY (North Caro-
lina)**
—Southern [legends] / Floyd, 10–13
ROAST BEEF
—Bomans / Wily *
famine: innkeeper roasts his own
leg to satisfy guests, 111–115
ROBBER(-s)
see also THIEF; also individual
tales: Ali Baba . . . ; Bremen
Town musicians; etc.
—Arabian / McCaughrean
woman marries (a) robber (b)
pickpocket; mutton, 218–224
—Bell / Classical Dict, 202–203 @
—Dramatized / Kamerman
grants three wishes; capture bandit, 324–333
—Egyptian / Harris
clever thief: treasure of
Rhumpsinitus, 114–116
—Grimm / Complete *

crafty peasant cheats devil, 767–
768
God creates animals; devil creates goats with long tails, 642–
644
soldier can reduce others to immobility, 808–811
Wolf and the seven [goat] kids,
39–42
—Grimm / Legends (Ward), II:441 (index)
—Grimm / Sixty *
Wolf and the seven [goat] kids,
202–205
—Jewish / Frankel
dim-witted boy buys box of bones
(etc., chain tale), 414–418
—Jewish / Sadeh
vizier's daughter and bandit in
sheep's clothing, 98–101
—Lore of Love
French soldier and Saracen
maid, 98–106
—Pirate Ghosts / McSherry
Terrible Old Man and three
would-be robbers, 69–72
—Pourrat / French
seven tales, 157–196
—Russian / Afanasev, 660 (index)
—Spanish-Am / Van Etten *
postman cons robber to shoot
holes in uniform (until gun is
empty), 83–87
—Tibet / Timpanelli *
girl who was already queen, 43–
51
—Water Buffalo (Chinese)
cat teaches tiger, but not how to
climb trees, 78–81
Robber bridegroom
—Grimm / Complete * 200–204
—Grimm / Sixty * 120–124
Roberson, Jennifer
—Unicorn / Coville *

Court of the summer king, 136–155

Roberts, Helen
—Dramatized / Kamerman
Builder of the wall, 422–434
Musicians of Bremen Town, 155–161
Test for William Tell, 493–503

Roberts, Theodore Goodridge (1877–1953)
—Pendragon / Ashley
For to achieve your adventure, 101–119

ROBIN HOOD
—Childcraft 3 / Stories *
shooting match at Nottingham Town (Pyle), 279–295
—Dramatized / Kamerman
Robin Hood outwits the sheriff, 61–78
—Legends / Cavendish, 275–277
—Rovin / Superheroes
mass media, 243

Roc, *see* BIRDS, MYTHICAL: ROC.

ROCK(-s)
see also STONE(-s)
—Bell / Classical Dict, 203–205 @
—Hoke / Giants
Bulai's Bones (Fiji tale), 130–132
origin of rocks and stones, 130–132
—Jewish / Frankel, 647 (index)
—Jonsen / Trolls *
stone cheese [troll tricked by youngest son], 24–32
—MacDonald / Sourcebook *
motif index, 708–709
—Vanishing / Mercer *
bears' tower: rock "grows," to protect girls, 118–120
—Williams-Ellis / Tales *
youngest sister saves her two bewitched sisters, 125–130

ROCK-CRYSTAL
—Precious Stones / Kunz, 403 (index)

Rocking-horse land (Housman)
—Victorian / Hearn, 318–324

ROGUE(-s)
—Clouston / Popular
Little Fairly, et al.; versions, II.229–288, 489–491
sharpers and the simpleton, II.27–42
—Dramatized / Kamerman
Merry Tyll and the three rogues, 162–176
—Grimm / Complete *
rogue and old beggar-woman; clothes catch fire, 646

ROKITA
—Corrin / Imagine *
huntsman's pact with forest-demon to produce unknown bird, 70–79

ROLAND
—Knights / Heller-Headon, 74–83

ROMANTIC TALES
—Ashliman / Guide
titles arranged in Aarne-Thompson system, 170–203 @
—Norwegian / Hodne, 188–206

ROME, ANCIENT (Roman myth and legend)
—Allison / I'll Tell *
Androcles and lion (with thorn in paw), 119
—Christian / Every, 144(index)
—Clouston / Popular, II.512 (index)
—Cotterell / Encyclopedia, 257 (index)
—Dictionary / Leach, 1228 (index)
—Douglas / Magic *
Androcles and the lion, 167–175
—Grimal / Dictionary, 597 (index)
—Hamilton / Dark *

Perseus' task: behead Medusa, 43–48
—Jewish / Frankel, 658 (index)
—King Arthur / Senior
expedition to Rome, 61–71
—Legends / Cavendish
foundation, 164–166
—Limburg / Weird , 122 (index)
—Man Myth & Magic, 3165 (index)
—Medicine-Plants / Read Dgst
ancient lore, 16
—Mercatante / Encyclopedia, 738–739 (index)
—Roman / Perowne, 1–144 @
Christianity, 128–141 @
Cyble (the Great Mother), 62 @
Egyptian influence, 88–97 @
Epicureans and Stoics, 72–77 @
gods, 12–23 @
Mosaic and Persian influence, 100–109 @
state cult, 35–46 @
worship, 24–34 @
—Roman / Usher, 1–132 @
Camillus: rise of Rome, 111–114 @
conqueror of the world, 11–13 @
early republic, 105–110 @
gods from the east, 27–30 @
heroes and emperors, 116–122 @
Kings Numa and Tarquin, 93–104 @
ROMULUS
—Roman / Usher, 80–86, 132 (index)
RONGO
—Polynesians / Andersen, 502 (index)
ROOM, FORBIDDEN TO ENTER
—Clouston / Popular, I.198–205
—Grimm / Complete *
Virgin Mary, the woodcutter, 23–29
—Muddleheads / Harris

room; Copper Canoeman weds
human princess, 75–93
—Nielsen / Old Tales *
godmother keeps baby, [5–15]
widow's son, [16–36]
ROOSTER(-s) (and cocks)
see also Bremen Town musicians
—Aesop / Holder
cock and the jewel, 20–21
—Bird Symbol / Rowland
under "cock," 202 (index)
—Cambodian / Carrison
rooster foils polecat's plan to eat
him, 49–51
—Coyote / Bierhorst *
pays to be clever when you're the
weaker one, [14]
—Demi / Reflective *
know/treasure the more valuable,
[24]
—Grimm / Complete *
cock and hen, in cart pulled by
duck, trick innkeeper, 65–66
—Grimm / Sixty *
Adventures of Chanticleer and
Partlet, 74–79
—Jewish / Sadeh
singing rooster; princess who refused to talk, 106–111
—Leonardo / Fables *
happiness, 106
—Man Myth & Magic, 3122 (index)
—Russian / Afanasev, 657 (index)
—Russian Hero / Warner *
cock and the corn mill, 52–53
—Turkish (Art I) / Walker
killed, cooked, eaten; still continues to deride prince, 80–81
—Witch Encyc / Guiley, 411 (index)
ROSAMUND
—Reeves / Shadow
Launfal: secret love for Rosamund, 49–83

ROSE(-s)
—Plants / Dyer, 326 (index)
—Wilde / Lynch *
  nightingale gives life to produce
  red rose for student-in-love,
  14–23
Rose, The
—Grimm / Complete * 819
Rose and the ring, The (Thackeray)
—Victorian / Hearn, 36–105
Rossetti, Christina (1830–1894)
—Victorian / Hearn
  Goblin market [poem], 192–208
ROUND TABLE
  see also ARTHURIAN RO-
  MANCES
—Celts / Hodges *
  symbol, 134
—King Arthur / Ashe, 191 (index)
—King Arthur / Senior, 321 (index)
—Knights / Heller-Headon, 1–190
ROUNDS
—Clarkson / World *
  a dark and stormy night; endless
  tale, 249–250
ROYAL MINISTERS
—Arabian / McCaughrean
  two wazirs: who will succeed the
  king, 203–207
RU
—Earth / Hadley *
  lifting the sky (Ru; blue stone),
  [13–14]
RUBY
—Jewish / Frankel
  ruby/serpent: Solomon's daugh-
  ter shut in tower; power of love,
  254–257
—Precious Stones / Kunz, 403 (in-
  dex)
RULERS
—Egyptian / Harris
  throne of Egypt: Horus vs. Seth,
  41–47

—Grimm / Complete *
  shepherd boy adopted by king,
  651–652
—Shannon / More *
  last request saves life of ruler's
  wife, 43–46
RUMANIA
—Dictionary / Leach, 1228 (index)
Rumble-Mumble Goose-Egg
—Trolls / Asbjornsen, 71–82
Rumplestiltskin
—Clarkson / World * 103–105
—Corrin / Favourite * 165–169
—Grimm / Complete * 264–268
—Grimm / Sixty * 133–137
—Lang / Wilkins, 27–30
—Leete / Golden * 48–57
—Scriven / Full Color * 13–15
—Strauss / Trail
  reflections of mother on child
  (poem), 28–29
Rumpelstiltskin (existential retelling)
—Switzer / Existential, 17–23
RUNAWAY
—Dramatized / Kamerman
  Johnny Appleseed rescues runa-
  way girl, 537–548
RUNE
—Scandinavian / Davidson, 143 (in-
  dex)
Rusalka, see WATER-SPIRIT.
RUSE(-s)
—Legends / Cavendish, 399 (index)
—Spanish-Am / Van Etten *
  postman cons robber to shoot
  holes in uniform (until gun is
  empty), 83–87
Ruskin, John (1819–1900)
—Victorian / Hearn
  King of the Golden River
  (Ruskin), 3–23
RUSSIA / RUSSIAN TALES
—Clouston / Popular, II.512 (index)
—Corrin / Imagine *

Volkh's journey to the east, 124–135
—Dictionary / Leach, 1228 (index)
—Dramatized / Kamerman
  gold found in the forest, 388–399
  Peter and the wolf, 375–380
  Stone soup, 381–387
—Dulac / Fairy *
  fire bird: princess, heart of prince, 153–164
  Ivan and the chestnut horse, 60–68
  Snegorotchka, 1–6
—Hamilton / In the Beginning *
  Ulgen: Altaic creation myth, 28–33
—Legends / Cavendish, 7, 290–297
—Manning / Cauldron *
  Elsa, abducted by witch to tend her baby, escapes aided by goat, 90–98
—Mercatante / Encyclopedia, 739 (index)
—Russian / Afanasev, 1–661
—Russian / Ivanits
  folk beliefs, 1–257
—Russian Hero / Warner * 1–132
  history: Old Russia, 11–13 @
  Nightingale (half-man, half-bird) captured, 76–80
  prodigy: Volkh leads invasion of India, 92–94
  Sukhman kills 40,000 Tartars, 41–42
—Williams-Ellis / Tales *
  Baba Yaga; Marusia's kindness helps escape, 113–124

RUSTLER
—Old Coot / Christian *
  Old Coot and (as?) rustler: crow envies hawk, 17–26
RUSTUM (variant endings: -am, -em, -om)
—Legends / Cavendish, 132–134

—Shah / Central Asia
  iron fortress, 25–30
  warrior-hero leaves wife (Tahmina), 87–91

SABBAT
—Witch Encyc / Guiley, 287–290
SABBATH
—Jewish / Frankel, 651 (index)
  disturbance: Baal Shem Tov's heavenly portion restored, 489–491
  gold buttons provide money for needs, 493–495
  pious man (Ariel) and the lion, 343–344
—Jewish / Sadeh
  golem of Prague, 228–230
  rabbi Alfasi and the lion, 252–253
—Schwartz / Gates, 811 (index)
SABINE WOMEN
—Roman / Usher, 87–92 @
SACAJAWEA
—American / Read Dgst, 176–177
SACRED PERSONS
—Chinese / Chin *
  monkey: on road to fetch scriptures, 95–110
SACRIFICE
  see also HUMAN SACRIFICE; SELF-SACRIFICE
—Caduto / Keepers *
  buzzard's red skin; stealing the sun, 49–50
  sacrifice brings life; turtle's back, 25–26
—Chinese / Chin *
  finding wife for cruel River God, 17–26
—Jewish / Frankel, 651 (index)
—Persian / Hinnells, 143 (index)
—Man Myth & Magic, 3166 (index)

—Mercatante / Encyclopedia, 793 (index)
—Mesoamerican / Leon-P, 293 and 298 (index)
—Witch Encyc / Guiley, 418 (index)
SACRIFICE, CRUEL
—Celts / Hodges *
   Merlin: life and magic powers, 117–132
—Chinese / Chin *
   finding wife for River God, 17–26
   palace plot: cat put in place of baby, 77–92
—Grimm / Complete *
   Faithful John: quest for princess of Golden Dwelling, 43–51
—Starkey / Ghosts
   Whuppity Stoorie, 44–51
—Wilde / Happy *
   nightingale gives heart's blood to stain rose red, 41–56
SADDLE-BAG
—Shah / Central Asia
   Wali and the magic saddle-bag, 69–77
SADNESS
—Bomans / Wily *
   Joshua: frog/poet has an unreasoning deep sorrow, 116–118
SAFED
—Schwartz / Gates, 811 (index)
SAGAS
—Lycanthropy / Otten, 334 (index)
SAGES
—Mesoamerican / Leon-P, 293 (index)
SAHARA TALE
—Vanishing / Mercer *
   hedgehog, by cheating, wins race with ostrich, 102–105
   hedgehog tricks fox; makes him his "saddle-horse," 99–101
SAILOR(-s)
   see also SEA STORIES

—American / Read Dgst
   Old Stormalong, 240–243
   villains and victims, 248–255
—Yep / Rainbow *
   protector of sailors: Dream Flier, 144–151
—Yolen / Shape Shift
   Dinesen: sailor-boy's tale, 52–60
SAINT(-s)
   see also HIDDEN SAINTS
—Animals / Rowland, 190 (index)
—Beasts / McHargue, 118 (index)
—British / Briggs *
   eight tales, 251–260
—Celtic / MacCana, 143 (index)
—Christian / Every, 89–105
—Grimm / Legends (Ward), II:443, 450 (index)
—Hope / Holy Wells
   England; antiquities, 1–222
—Irish / Glassie
   nine tales, 49–66
—Jewish / Sadeh
   not in Paradise: Paradise is in the saints, 378
—Legends / Cavendish, 430–431 (index)
—Man Myth & Magic, 3166 (index)
—Mercatante / Good/Evil, 240 (index)
—Plants / Dyer, 326–327 (index)
—Russian / Ivanits, 250 (index)
SAINT AUGUSTINE
—Lycanthropy / Otten, 325 (index)
—Plants / Dyer, 326–327 (index)
SAINT BRENDAN
—Floyd / Gr Am Myst
   pre-Columbus voyagers in the New World, 142–145
SAINT CHRISTOPHER
—Grimm / Complete *
   kings' daughters aid hero in tasks: win girl or die, 515–524
SAINT COLLEN
—Fairies / Briggs, 345–346

SAINT FRANCIS of Assisi
—Wolves / Lopez
the Wolf of Gubbio, 212–214 @
SAINT GEORGE
—Baring-Gould / Curious
martyr, his legend in Greek, Latin,
Muslim, Syrian, Oriental, the
Legenda Auria, early sources,
92–101 @
—Dragons / Baskin * [40–41]
—Knights / Heller-Headon, 174–175
—Monsters / Hall, 8–9
—Saint George / Fox, 1–187
dragon legend, 23–38
Perseus connection, 39–58
SAINT IGNATIUS of Sardinia
—Fahs / Old *
blood of defrauded poor, 125–
126
SAINT IOANN the Long Suffering
—Russian Hero / Warner * 62 @
SAINT JOSEPH
—Grimm / Complete *
three sisters encounter St. Jo-
seph, 815–818
Saint Joseph in the forest
—Grimm / Complete * 815–818
SAINT KEVIN
—Williams-Ellis / Tales *
King O'Toole's goose made
young by St. Kevin, 37–43
SAINT NICHOLAS
—Russian / Ivanits, 250 (index)
SAINT NIKOLAI OF MOZHAISK
—Russian Hero / Warner *
how Sadko angered the sea tsar,
45–48
SAINT OLAF
—Scandinavian / Kvideland, xvii, 427
(index)
SAINT PATRICK
—Celts / Hodges *
swan children restored by St. Pat-
rick's coming, 5–14

SAINT PATRICK'S PURGATORY
—Baring-Gould / Curious, 84–87 @
SAINT PETER
—Grimm / Complete *
Brother Lustig and St. Peter,
367–377
Hansel gambles in heaven and in
hell, 378–380
moon stolen by four men; St. Pe-
ter, 713–715
SAINT PETROC
—Ghosts / Starkey
Tregeagle's ghost, 58–65
SAINT THOMAS AQUINAS
—Lycanthropy / Otten, 335 (index)
SAINT THOMAS (West Indies)
—Pirate Ghosts / McSherry
hangman's rope: Saul Macartney
and Capt. Fawcett, 84–144
SAINT TRINIAN
—Ghosts / Starkey
buggane, Broder Menine, the tai-
lor, 16–23
SAINT URSULA
—Baring-Gould / Curious
myth sources, 102–105 @
Salad, The [fed to witch]
—Grimm / Complete * 551–558
—Grimm / Sixty * 292–293
SALAMANDER
—Beasts / McHargue, 56 @
Sale of worthless objects, *see*
SWINDLERS;
see also under ANIMAL(-s)
SALEM WITCHES
—Witch Encyc / Guiley, 291–300,
418 (index)
Salmon, *see* FISH: SALMON.
SALT
—Aesop / Reeves-Wilson *
trickery backfires: donkey carry-
ing salt, 92–94
—Chinese / Christie
discovery, 101

—Clarkson / World *
  magic mill: why sea is salt, 336–
  339
—Fahs / Old *
  analogy: can't see or feel; still
  real, 20–23
—Hopi Coyote / Malotki
  coyote on salt expedition, 127–
  139
—Spring / Philip
  girl sheepherder finds water and
  salt, 98–102
—Turkish / Walker
  son "loves father like salt," 108–
  113
—Williams-Ellis / Tales *
  Cap o' Rushes (loves father "like
  salt"), 8–16
SAMAEL
—Schwartz / Gates, 811 (index)
SAMBO
—Hall / Treasury *
  Little Black Sambo [trades
  clothes for life], 68–76
SAMHAIN
—Witch Encyc / Guiley, 418 (index)
SAMOA
—Polynesians / Andersen, 504 (in-
  dex)
SAMSON
—Jewish / Frankel, 185–189
—Rovin / Superheroes
  mass media, 249
SAMURAI
—Dramatized / Kamerman
  Great samurai sword, 306–316
SAND STORIES
—Pellowski / Story * 60–74
SANDPAINTINGS
—Navajo / Klah
  creation myths, 25–35, 173–203
Sangrail, see GRAIL.
SANTA CLAUS
—Scarry's Best *

Trouble at Santa's workshop,
  [17–20]
SANTA FE, NM
—Spanish-Am / Van Etten *
  soldier buys love [unrequited] po-
  tion from witch, 33–36
SANTERIA
—Witch Encyc / Guiley, 303–307
SAPPHIRE
—Precious Stones / Kunz, 404 (in-
  dex)
SARARUMA (evil spirit)
—Earth / Hadley *
  fire destroys all but one couple,
  [21–22]
SARASWATI (Sanskrit)
—Wolkstein / Love, 252 @
SARGON
—Babylonia / Spence, 406 (index)
SATAN(-ism)
  see also DEVIL
—Christian / Every, 144 (index)
—Cotterell / Encyclopedia, 257 (in-
  dex)
—Davidson / Dictionary, 261
—Gray / Near East. 132–133
—Jewish / Frankel, 651, 658 (index)
—Mercatante / Good/Evil 241 (index)
—Witch Encyc / Guiley, 307–311,
  419 (index)
SATI
—Wolkstein / Love
  Shiva and Sati, 73–89, 264 @
SATIRE
  see also POLITICAL SATIRE
—Wilde / Lynch *
  devoted friend: Little Hans and
  the miller, 24–40
  remarkable rocket: fireworks at
  prince's wedding, 55–72
SATYR
—Aesop / Zwerger *
  man (blows on hands; on hot por-
  ridge) and satyr, 7

—Animals / Rowland, 190 (index)
—South / Mythical
sources; bibliographical essay,
207–223 (P. Grootkerk), 389
(index)
SAUSAGE
—Clarkson / World *
ridiculous [foolish; three] wishes,
305–307
—Grimm / Complete *
Mouse, bird, sausage [trade du-
ties = disaster], 131–133
—Grimm / Sixty *
Mouse, bird . . . (as above), 108–
110
—Zipes / Beauties *
foolish wishes [sausage on wife's
nose], 64–66
SAVING
—Geras / Grandmother *
Chelm couple make plan; each
leaves it to other; wheels on
chest, 49–56
SAVIORS
—Cotterell / Encyclopedia, 257 (in-
dex)
—Lurker / Dict Gods, 409 (index)
Savitri and Satyavan
—Jaffrey / Seasons, 10–15
SAXONS
—Grimm / Legends (Ward), II:443 (in-
dex)
SCANDINAVIA (-ian tales)
—Dictionary / Leach 1229 (index)
—Dramatized / Kamerman
Simple Olaf, 413–421
—Hoke / Giants
giant, no heart in his body, 93–
102
—Man Myth & Magic, 3167 (index)
—Scandinavian / Davidson
Christianity and paganism, 124–
140
—Scandinavian / Kvideland, 1–429

SCANDINAVIANS (people)
—Humor / Midwest, 93–111
SCARAB BEETLE
—Egyptian / Ions, 144 (index)
Scarborough, Elizabeth
—Yolen / Werewolves
Wolf from the door, 119–126
Scare, see FEAR.
SCHAMIR (stone-cutting)
—Baring-Gould / Curious, 112–115 @
Scheherazod
—Arabian / Lewis
escapes execution by story-
telling, 6–9
storyteller's life spared, 222–224
—Arabian / McCaughrean
escapes . . . (as above), 1–9
storyteller's life spared, 243–249
—Arabian / Riordan
escapes . . . (as above), 8–11
—Douglas / Magic *
Ahmad: bring back the most mar-
velous, 3–11
SCHOLAR(s)
—Chinese / Chin *
customs: marriage; scholarship
(Ju Yingtai), 61–73
—Jewish / Frankel, 644 (index)
—Vietnam / Terada *
Do Be offends temple god, 42–49
SCHOOL
—Nesbit / Fairy *
princesses transformed to golden
apples, 141–158
SCHOOLMASTER
—Corrin / Six-Year *
snow-man, a bully, tricked; melts
at stove, 19–23
SCHWARTZ, Howard
—Schwartz / Gates, 811 (index)
Schwartz, Susan
—Yolen / Werewolves
Wolf's flock, 201–223
Schweitzer, Darrell

—Pendragon / Ashley
midnight, moonlight, and secret
of the sea, 385–401

SCIENCE
—Lycanthropy / Otten, 334 (index)

SCIENTIFIC THEORIES
—Cambodian / Carrison
absurdity: woman tricked, endanger baby, then robbed, 31–35

SCOLOG
—O'Brien / Tales *
swan bride: king's son's quest for Scolog's daughter, 82–95

SCORPION
—Jewish / Frankel
scorpion in goblet: virtuous rabbi rewarded, 437–446

SCOTLAND / SCOTTISH TALES
—Campbell / West Highlands, v.I-IV
—Celts / Hodges *
Lad of Luck and monster of the loch, 89–103
Tam Lin freed from evil spell by love, 76–83
—Dramatized / Kamerman
King Horn, 447–457
—Ghosts / Starkey
Jack Mackintosh: treasure ghost of Fife, 88–95
—Ghosts / Time-Life
ghost stories, 1–143
harp: strings from hair of murdered sister, 32–37
phantom battle (Killiecrankie, 1689), 70–74
phantom tenants of Castle Glamis, 85–91
—Hoke / Giants
Finlay, the giant killer, 142–149
—Legends / Cavendish, 202–206
—Lore of Love
warlock tricked: hair from heifer, 84

—Lynn / Fantasy * 766 (index)
—Old Wives / Carter
Maol a Chliobain repeatedly gets better of giant, 24–27
—Unicorn / Hathaway
Knight of the Lion / Lady of the Unicorn, 96–99 @

SCRIBE
—Jewish / Sadeh
page watcher: troll and scribe, 255–256

SCRYING
—Witch Encyc / Guiley, 419 (index)

SCULPTOR
—Lore of Love
sculptor carves palace (solid rock) for princess, 79–83

SEA
see also OCEAN
—Bell / Classical Dict, 209–211 @
—Campbell / West Highlands, IV.440 (index)
—Celts / Hodges *
Bells of Ys, 104–114
—Clarkson / World *
magic mill: why sea is salt, 336–339
—Cotterell / Encyclopedia, 257 (index)
—Creatures (illus) / Huber * 155 (index)
—Glooskap / Norman *
giant bird, Wuchowsen, makes storms rage, 21–28
—Greek / Osborne
death: lost at sea: Ceyx and Alcyone, 13–16
—Nesbit / Fairy *
Billy the King [treacle and toffee; dragon], 1–22

SEA DEITIES/GODS/SPIRITS
—Fairies / Briggs
shony, 362–363
—Lore of Love

Toyotama: ill-starred mating of earth and sea, 87–95
—Lurker / Dict Gods, 409–410 (index)
—Mercatante / Encyclopedia, 794 (index)
—Muddleheads / Harris
sea hunters swallowed by whirlpool, 26–43
—Scandinavian / Kvideland, xv (index)
Seafood, see FOOD: SEAFOOD.
Sea-hare, The
—Grimm / Complete * 769–772
SEA-MAIDEN
—Campbell / West Highlands, I.72–104
SEA MONSTER
—Beasts / McHargue, 88–101 @
—Creatures (illus) / Huber * 39–43
—Monsters / Cohen, 147–188 @
—Monsters / Hall, 42–61
—Werewolves / Aylesworth, 84–103, 111–116
SEA SERPENT(-s)
—Beasts / McHargue, 93–101 @
—Floyd / Gr Am Myst
Gloucester (Mass.) monster, 94–97
—Gould / Mythical, 260–337 @
—McGowen / Encyclopedia * 49–50
—Monsters / Cohen, 178–184 @
—Southern [legends] / Floyd
monsters of the deep (Florida coast), 141–147
—Tall Tales / Downs: Bear
Spoonville Beach (H. Helfer), 8–15
—Vietnam / Terada *
sea snake captures mandarin's wife, 88–94
SEA STORIES
—American / Read Dgst, 230–255
whalers' tales, 232–235
—Pellowski / Family *

paper-cutting story: captain from Krakow, 92–101
—Pirate Ghosts / McSherry, 1–206
—Vietnam / Terada *
lady of stone: man unknowingly marries his sister, 115–118
SEA TSAR
—Russian Hero / Warner *
how Sadko angered the sea tsar, 45–48
Sadko of Novgorod: musician becomes rich merchant, 44
SEA WOLF
—Wolves / Lopez
origin, 92
SEAL(-s)
—Caduto / Keepers *
origin: Sedna, woman under the sea, 95–97
—Coyote / Ramsey
Wasco boy chooses to live with seals, 73–74
—Haboo / Hilbert
seal-hunting brothers, 73–86
—McGowen / Encyclopedia
seal-people * 49
—Monsters / Hall
seal maiden, 31
—Muddleheads / Harris
recovered from Big Raven, 60–74
Seal-wife
—Animal Legends / Kerven * [10–11]
Seal woman [fisherman hides her skin]
—Crossley / British FT * 11–16
SEASON(-s)
—Bruchac / Iroquois *
hunting of the Great Bear (Big Dipper), 189–195
—Caduto / Keepers *
fisher to Skyland: origin of Big Dipper, 117–120
—Constellations / Gallant * 202 (index)

—Earthmaker / Mayo *
  Snowmaker torments the people
    (Micmac tale), 48–52
  Wahconda makes the earth
    shake (Oto tale), 54–56
—Greek / Osborne
  origin: kidnapping: Ceres and
    Proserpina, 35–39
—Haboo / Hilbert, 23–32, 111–117
—Scriven / Full Color *
  children find cowslips: Keys of
    summer, 41–42
  Persephone: winter and summer,
    75–78
—Water Buffalo (Chinese)
  crow-messenger disobeys God
    of Heaven, 23–29
SECRET(-s)
—Bryan / Lion *
  son of Mother Wind [name a se-
    cret], 24–39
—Clouston / Popular, II.513 (index)
  lucky imposter: pretence to
    knowledge, II.413–431
  secrets learned from birds, I.242–
    248
—Giant / Harrison *
  boy tells secret to giant-captur-
    ers: he's getting measles, 7–
    17
—Hamilton / Dark *
  marriage to boar/man; secret
    must be kept, 113–118
—Jewish / Frankel
  Yossele the holy miser gives se-
    cretly, as God gives, 557–560
—Jewish / Sadeh
  king's horn: secrets can't be kept
    forever, 323–324
—Leonardo / Fables *
  indiscretion: oyster in love with
    the moon, 30
—Old Wives / Carter
  girl escapes marriage to hyena in

human form; transforms to se-
    cret thing, 64–65
—Reeves / Shadow
  Launfal: secret love for Ro-
    samund, 49–83
—Trolls / Asbjornsen
  goose-girl: "meant" to marry
    Prince of England, 60–63
—Turkish (Art I) / Walker
  death, if shepherd does not keep
    secret his knowing language of
    animals, 190–194
SECRET COMMAND
—Turkish / Walker
  magic pumpkin (provides food)
    stolen and recovered, 62–66
SECRETS LEARNED
  see also Ali Baba and the forty
    thieves
—Dramatized / Kamerman
  ogre; guess name; carpenter's
    ear, 278–287
—Dulac / Fairy *
  serpent-prince: marries, regains
    human form, 29–42
—Grimm / Complete *
  Faithful John: quest for princess
    of Golden Dwelling, 43–51
  goldfish gives magic castle to
    fisherman, 388–393
  Simeli Mountain: treasure secret
    overheard, 627–630
  two travellers: tailor and shoe-
    maker, 386–496
—Scriven / Full Color *
  Rumpelstiltskin, 13–15
—Turkish / Walker
  Keloglan overhears jinns' se-
    crets, 23–28
—Turkish (Art I) / Walker
  overhears secrets: how to win
    princess, escape spell, 123–136
  patience stone: gypsy girl usurps
    lady's position, 111–116

—Water Buffalo (Chinese)
  enormous candy-man; magic
  drum; long nose, 70–77
SEDER
—Jewish / Frankel
  Gentile's impatience at *seder*
  meal, 562–563
SEDNA
—Caduto / Keepers *
  Sedna: woman under the sea,
  95–97
SEDUCTION
—Bell / Classical Dict, 212 @
—Bierhorst / Monkey *
  rabbit marries coyote's daughter,
  81–83
—Gullible Coyote / Malotki
  coyote lusts for seductress; is
  killed, 105–117
—Hoke / Giants
  man (ogre) tricked by Molly, 65–
  70
—Jewish / Frankel
  Rabbi's mirror allows king to see
  treachery in his bedroom, 405–
  409
—Jewish / Sadeh
  dress: charm causes lewdness,
  20–21
—Lore of Love
  warlock tricked: hair from heifer,
  84
—Old Wives / Carter
  hare seduces woman, 47
  teacher's wife seduces pupil,
  60
—Scriven / Full Color *
  Snow Queen [girl rescues friend],
  35–36
—Turkish (Art I) / Walker
  Haci's daughter marries, is repeatedly assaulted, 24–33
  shah spares lustful pilgrim; favor
  later returned, 93–98

SEED(-s)
—Fahs / Old *
  analogy: can't see or feel; still
  real, 20–23
  what kind of life: seed analogy,
  185–188
—Leonardo / Fables *
  ant's pact with grain of wheat,
  58–59
—Yolen / Faery Flag
  killed minstrel's song: plant growing from grave, 41–46
SEER(-s)
  see also FUTURE; PROPHECY
—Bell / Classical Dict, 212–214 @
—Cotterell / Encyclopedia, 257 (index)
—Jewish / Sadeh
  king and forty crows; dream, 31–
  34
—Tibet / Timpanelli *
  test of "seer": reputation made by
  luck/coincidence, 29–41
—Turkish / Walker
  stargazer to the sultan, 98–107
SELENE
—D'Aulaire / Greek * 86
SELF
—Aesop / Reeves-Wilson *
  laughing at oneself: The bald
  knight, 86–87
—Demi / Reflective *
  can't move away from; owl and
  turtledove, [8]
SELF-AGGRANDIZEMENT
—Wilde / Lynch *
  remarkable rocket: fireworks at
  prince's wedding, 55–72
SELF-CONFIDENCE
—Greek / Osborne
  (excess) chariot of the sun god,
  1–6
SELF-DECEIT
—Allison / I'll Tell *

fox and grapes: contempt for
what one can't obtain, 131
SELF-DEPENDENCE
—Corrin / Eight-Year *
princess: save magic fish-
bone until needed, 147–
160
SELF-IMAGE
—Cambodian / Carrison
father/son ride/carry donkey to
market, 102–106
—Demi / Reflective *
crab thinks of self as beautiful,
[14]
river god/ocean god: exhalted im-
age deflated, [26]
SELF-IMMOLATION
—Jewish / Sadeh
Jewish pope; bastard converts to
Catholicism, 195–197
SELF-IMPORTANCE
—Aesop / Reeves-Wilson *
mice and weasels fight for leader-
ship, 30–31
—Carle / Treasury *
frog wishes to be big as ox
(Aesop), 70–71
SELF-IMPROVEMENT
—Vietnam / Terada *
training and meditation: snake
princess, 14–17
Self-injury, *see* DECEPTION into
SELF-INJURY.
SELF-INTEREST
—Aesop / Reeves-Wilson *
The two travellers, 103–104
Selfish giant, The (O. Wilde)
—Victorian / Hearn, 254–258
—Wilde / Happy * 59–69
—Wilde / Lynch * 6–13
SELFISHNESS
—Allison / I'll Tell *
fox uses goat (escape from well),
120

—Bruchac / Iroquois *
husband; vampire skeleton, 129–
133
—Greaves / Hippo *
why leopard hides his food in
tree, 26
—Jewish / Frankel
miser: mirror and the glass, 552–
553
—Paxton / Aesop *
dog in the manger: keeping what
we can't use, [28–30]
—Turkish (Art I) / Walker
golden pears: dervish punishes
selfish farmer, 53–57
—Wilde / Lynch *
selfish giant: always winter, children not allowed in garden, 6–
13
SELF-KNOWLEDGE
—Coyote / Bierhorst *
while coyote gabs, wolf raids his
house, [16]
SELFLESSNESS
—Wilde / Lynch *
devoted friend: Little Hans and
the miller, 24–40
SELF LOVE
—Greek / Osborne
face in the pool: Echo and Narcissus, 29–32
—Lore of Love
vanity's reflection: Echo and Narcissus, 74
SELF-MUTILATION
—Muddleheads / Harris
princess rejects arranged marriage, 115–130
SELF-PRESERVATION
—Coyote / Bierhorst *
coyote, puma and donkey divide
catch unequally, [36]
SELF-RELIANCE
—Bomans / Wily *

marriage proposal: shy frog, 109–111

SELF-REVELATION
—Strauss / Trail, 1–35

SELF-SACRIFICE
—Bruchac / Iroquois *
dogs who saved their master, 85–91
—Celts / Hodges *
Dermot in the Land-under-Wave, 57–73
how Finn MacCool got his wisdom tooth, 34–52
—Jewish / Frankel
Rashi's companion-to-be in Paradise, 388–392
Moshele's gift: poor water-carrier prays for 1,000 rubles, 554–556
—Jewish / Sadeh
Gehazi, for punishment, is reincarnated as dog, 134–136
giving life for one's friend, 121–122
—Leonardo / Fables *
mother pelican's blood restores babies to life, 56
—Spring / Philip
Akui frees water; turns to stone, 87–93
—Wilde / Lynch *
happy prince: statue persuades swallow to help aid the poor, 41–54
nightingale gives life to produce red rose for student-in-love, 14–23
—Williams-Ellis / Tales *
Sister Long-Hair steals stream from mountain god, 161–171

SELF-SEEKING
—Leonardo / Fables *
fig tree: barren, then loaded, then regret, 32

SELF-VICTIMIZATION
—Paxton / Aesop *
goose that laid golden eggs, [16–18]

SELF-WORTH
—Coyote / Bierhorst *
crocodile brags; coyote says: look at self, not ancestors, [40]

SELKIES
—Fairies / Briggs, 353–355
Roane, the, 340–341
—Lynn / Fantasy * 766 (index)

SEMITES
—Babylonia / Spence, 406 (index)

SENSITIVENESS
—Turkey / Walker, 308 (index)

SENTINEL (guard)
—Lang / Wilkins
princess in the chest; faithful guard, 369–384

SEPTUAGINT
—Jewish / Frankel
the legend, 282–284

SERMON
—Turkish (Art I) / Walker
Nasreddin Hoca cleverly avoids preaching, 22–23

SERPENT(-s)
see also SEA SERPENT; SNAKE(-s); WATER SERPENT
—Bell / Classical Dict, 214–217 @
—Cotterell / Encyclopedia, 258 (index)
—Creatures (illus) / Huber * 155 (index)
—Dulac / Fairy *
green serpent: one twin princess cursed, ugly, 124–138
serpent-prince: marries, regains human form, 29–42
—Egyptian / Ions, 144 (index)
shipwrecked sailor and the huge serpent, 64–65
—Egyptian / Mercatante
prince doomed to three fates:

crocodile, serpent, dog, 36–38
serpent bestows wealth on shipwrecked sailor, 155–158
—Grimm / Complete *
King of the golden mountain, 425–430
—Grimm / Legends (Ward), II:445 (index)
—Grimm / Sixty *
King of the golden mountain, 274–280
—Jaffrey / Seasons
serpent-king: Krishna defeats evil, five-headed Kaliya, 30–31
—Jewish / Frankel
ruby/serpent: Solomon's daughter shut in tower; power of love, 254–257
serpent (prince at night); wife burns skin; spell broken, 446–449
—Man Myth & Magic, 3168 (index)
—Mercatante / Encyclopedia, 794 (index)
—Russian / Ivanits, 250 (index)
—Russian Hero / Warner *
Russian folk tales, 62–63 @
—Scandinavian / Davidson
world serpent, 144 (index)
—Turkish (Art I) / Walker
dead mother advises stepdaughter: nurse, teach, wed serpent-prince, 183–188
—Woman's Ency / Walker, 903–909 @

SERVANT(-s)
—Bierhorst / Monkey *
boy-servant of Chac (rain-god); repeated disobedience, 66–69
—Grimm / Complete *
faithful; Mother Hulda, 133–136
Goosegirl: imposture of princess revealed, 404–411

mistreated servant in grave; master's fate, 749–752
six servants help prince win daughter of sorceress, 600–607
snake-leaves revive treacherous wife, 94–96
twelve idle servants, 648–650
—Grimm / Legends (Ward), II:445 (index)
—Grimm / Sixty *
Goosegirl: imposture of princess revealed, 67–73
Mother Hulda, 111–115
—Jewish / Sadeh
Rabbi Adam Baal Shem: bequest of mystical writings, 341–343
servant of Baal Shem Tov forgets all stories save one, 357–361

SERVANTS: HUMOR
—Grimm / Complete *
wise servant; sarcasm, 671–672
—Turkish (Art I) / Walker
foolish servant checks on fly in water glass, 91–92
—Vietnam / Terada *
servant fans his sweating master, 126

SERVANTS: TREACHEROUS
—Dulac / Fairy *
hind of the wood: crayfish fairy, 43–59
—Egyptian / Harris
Ra's anger over rebellious mankind, 34–35
—Greaves / Hippo *
hare kills leopard's cubs; blames men, 22–26
—Jewish / Frankel
rabbi's mirror allows king to see treachery in his bedroom, 405–409
—Old Wives / Carter

servant forces girl and maid to change places, 160–165

SETH (or Set) (Egyptian myth)
—Egyptian / Harris, 132 (index)
throne of Egypt: Horus vs. Seth, 41–47
—Egyptian / Ions, 144 (index)
—Egyptian / Mercatante
god of evil and darkness, 143–145
Horus and Set contend for kingship, 57–68
—Wolkstein / Love
Isis and Osiris, 1–36, 253 @

SETNA
—Egyptian / Harris
Setna and the Book of Thoth, 92–102
—Egyptian / Mercatante
Setna and the magic book, 145–153

SEVEN
—Man Myth & Magic, 3168 (index)

SEVEN AGAINST THEBES
—Gods / Schwab, 251–272

SEVEN AXEMEN
—Hoke / Giants
Paul Bunyan and Babe, 11–29

SEVEN DEADLY SINS
—Animals / Rowland, 190 (index)

Seven ravens, The
—Grimm / Complete * 137–139
—Grimm / Sixty * 284–287

Seven Swabians (Grimm)
—Carle / Treasury * 99–103
—Grimm / Complete * 538–542

Seven wise masters
—Clouston / Popular, II.513 (index)

SEX
—Gullible Coyote / Malotki
mate dies; Coyote Woman grinds his penis to enjoy sex, 55–67
—Jewish / Frankel, 651 (index)

—MacDonald / Sourcebook *
motif index, 360–364
—Mesoamerican / Leon-P, 298 (index)
—Mex-Am / West
motif index, 301
—Palestinian / Speak (Muhawi)
motif-index, 401–402

SEX CHANGE
—Old Wives / Carter
Eskimo grandmother as "male" hunter; impregnates granddaughter, 181–182

SEX, ILLICIT
—Douglas / Magic *
Merlin and Arthur: illicit sex, 141–149
—Erdoes / Sound *
flute entices girls to "ghostly lover," 95–97
—Old Wives / Carter
teacher's wife seduces pupil, 60
—Shah / Central Asia
bead-seller and the jinn's sister, 62–68

SEX PERVERSIONS
—Old Wives / Carter
Eskimo woman married her son's wife, 170

SEX ROLE
—Fahs / Old *
Navajo First Man/Woman quarrel, 128–132
—Old Wives / Carter
isolated princess makes male form; God gives soul, 222–224

SEXUAL HARASSMENT
—Turkish (Art I) / Walker
Haci's daughter marries, is repeatedly assaulted, 24–33

SEXUAL SINS PUNISHED
—Lore of Love
cursed embrace: Liba and Guntram, 32–35

SHADOW
—Aesop / Reeves-Wilson *
    quarrel over "rental" of shadow,
    64
—Maori / Kanawa *
    Patupaiarehe (fairies) steal shad-
    ows of jewels, 62–66
—Spanish-Am / Van Etten *
    river-man: proper/improper use
    of river: good/bad life, 37–41
Shadow of the hawk
—Reeves / Shadow, 1–48
SHAGGY DOG STORY
—Clarkson / World *
    definition; example, 231 @
Shahrazad, see Scheherazod.
**SHAKESPEARE, William (1564–
    1616)**
—Limburg / Weird , 122 (index)
—Mercatante / Encyclopedia, 794 (in-
    dex)
SHALLOWNESS
—Paxton / Belling *
    hare's "friends" exposed by dan-
    ger (Aesop), [16–21]
SHALMANESER (king)
—Babylonia / Spence, 407 (index)
SHAM MIRACLES
—Arabian / McCaughrean
    thief pretends to be ass under
    spell, 150–152
—Corrin / Imagine *
    goldsmith steals woodcarver-
    friend's gold; woodcarver
    "turns" goldsmith's children
    into bears, 23–46
SHAM PROWESS
—Clarkson / World *
    Brave Kong (frightened "hero")
    routs army; kills crocodile,
    356–359
    Strong-Man-Jack killed seven
    [butterflies] at a whack, 264–
    271

—Grimm / Complete *
    skillful huntsman, 508–514
    Valiant tailor, 112–120
—Grimm / Sixty *
    Valiant tailor, 88–97
—Jewish / Frankel
    king's counselor pretends shep-
    herd's wisdom is his own, 422–
    424
—Turkish / Walker
    Kazan kills forty flies, becomes
    "hero," 67–74
SHAMAN(-ism)
—Bierhorst / Naked *
    Two Feathers: skills test, 11–
    18
—Igloo / Metayer
    child-killer escapes as shooting
    star, 70–72
    forced marriage: huntress, 99–
    107
    seal hunters on ice floe: Lost at
    sea, 49–54
    Taligvak: ostracized shaman
    saves village from famine, 61–
    69
—Indian Myth / Burland, 143(index)
—Man Myth & Magic, 3169 (index)
—Northern / Norman
    eleven tales, 171–202
—Witch Encyc / Guiley, 419 (index)
—Yolen / Werewolves
    White Wolf: boy's initiation to
    manhood, 45–69
SHAME
—Muddleheads / Harris
    wives: Robin Woman and Sawbill
    Duck Woman, 44–59
**SHAPE-SHIFTER(-s) / SHAPE-
    CHANGER(-s)**
    see also IKTOME; TRANSFOR-
    MATION(-s)
—Chorao / Child's *
    teakettle turns into badger, 21–27

—Erdoes / Sound *
Iktome's misadventures, 16–22
—Fahs / Old *
Maui in bird-shape, to Under-
world; parents, 37–43
—Fairies / Briggs, 360–362, 442
—Glooskap / Norman *
Ice Giants outwitted by Glooskap,
11–19
—Hopi / Talashoma-Malotki
hide and seek with life at stake;
girl to tadpole, 50–69
—Imaginary / Nigg
raven, 125–127
—Lang / Wilkins
magic ring: happiness and power
if . . . , 220–227
—Lewis / Proud
Yonec to hawk: lover killed by
jealous husband's trap, 53–60
—Lycanthropy / Otten
Norse sagas (Davidson), 142–
158 @
—Man Myth & Magic, 3169 (index)
—Manning / Cauldron *
gives Jack ring (can change self
to any size); rescues princess
from giant, 78–89
—Muddleheads / Harris
Robin Woman and Sawbill Duck
Woman, 44–59
seal of Mouse Children recovered
from Big Raven, 60–74
—Quayle / Cornish *
borne by tidal wave, mermaid
meets/mates carpenter-singer,
51–63
Cherry Winbroome in service of
little people, 91–102
—Russian Hero / Warner * 100 @
Ivan son of Mare; herons change
to women, 120–124
prodigy Volkh Vseslav'evich, 92–
94

turning old folk into young: smith
and devil, 19–20
White Wolf: boy's initiation to
manhood, 45–69
wolf helps quest; warnings ignored, 112–116
—Spring / Philip
golden fish rewards kindness,
103–113
—Strauss / Trail
woman reflects on her fox-life
(poem), 22–23
—Yolen / Shape Shift
boy who would be wolf (R. Curtis), 6–21
dog-husband (variations), 37
Gabriel-Ernest (Saki), 24–35
imaginary: magic circus horse (P.
Maclennan), 62–67
into anything, 5
sailor-boy's tale [rescue by
wer-falcon] (I. Dinesen), 52–
60
twelve tales, with commentary,
1–182
wer-cat: Moon change (A.W.
Turner), 38–41
wer-fox: attaining ability, 51
wer-fox: The stranger (S. Oppenheim), 52–60
SHARECROPPER
—High John / Sanfield *
Old Boss "de-ducks" John the
sharecropper, 80–83
tops or bottoms; outwits owner
three times, 89–96
SHARING
—Bomans / Wily *
chest (casket symbol) and the
student, 193–196
—Bruchac / Iroquois *
Hodadenon: last one left, 169–
182
—Dramatized / Kamerman

rich woman; poor woman, 191–
199
—Grimm / Complete *
rewards: three sisters encounter
St. Joseph, 815–818
—Spanish-Am / Van Etten *
beggar-woman turned away:
curse for not sharing, 50–51
Sharing joy and sorrow
—Grimm / Complete * 704–705
SHAWL
—Quayle / Cornish *
ghost: old woman dies, leaves
shawl to little girl, 88–90
SHEEP
—Animals / Rowland, 190 (index)
—Bell / Classical Dict, 218 @
—Childcraft 1 / Once *
lie or "story": sheep with wooden
collar, 147–157
—High John / Sanfield *
caught killing sheep, pretends
self-defense, 19–22
—Hopi Coyote / Malotki
coyote sheep-killer, duped into
taking sweatbath; dies, 119–
125
—Paxton / Aesop *
boy who cried wolf, [33–35]
—Yolen / Baby Bear *
sheep can't count themselves
(10 add up to "90"), [22–
23]
Sheepherder, see SHEPHERD(-s)
SHEEPSKIN-GIRL
—Turkish (Art I) / Walker
using disguise and bracelet, girl
seeks bride for her widowerfather, 224–230
Sheer [share] crops
—Clarkson / World * 272–274
SHEIK
—Arabian / McCaughrean
Keys of destiny; Iram, 65–82

SHEKHINAH
—Schwartz / Gates, 812 (index)
SHEPHERD(-s)
—Aesop / Alley *
Shepherd boy and the wolf, 4–
9
—Arabian / Lewis
princess elopes on wedding day
(to another), 217–221
—Bell / Classical Dict, 219–220 @
—Campbell / West Highlands
two shepherds, II.94–112
—Crossley / British FT *
shepherd visits fairyland; breaks
taboo (drinks from well), 248–
250
—Grimm / Legends (Ward), II:446 (index)
—Jewish / Frankel
king's counselor pretends shepherd's wisdom is his own, 422–
424
—Paxton / Aesop *
boy who cried wolf, [33–35]
—Spanish-Am / Van Etten *
ant, etc., tell suitor what drum is
made of (flea hide), 65–72
doctor, rancher, sheepherder
(winner) try to drive out skunk,
101–105
—Turkish (Art I) / Walker
death, if shepherd does not keep
secret his knowing language of
animals, 190–194
Shepherd boy
—Grimm / Complete * 651–652
SHEPHERDESS
—Spring / Philip
girl sheepherder finds water and
salt, 98–102
**Shepherd's boy and the wolf [cry
"wolf"]**
—Aesop / Zwerger * 9
Shepherd's pipe

—Jewish / Sadeh, 396; commentary, 413–421 @

Sherlock, Philip M.
—Childcraft 3 / Stories *
    Anansi and the plantains, 108–113

SHIELD
—Bell / Classical Dict, 221 @

Shifty Lad
—Campbell / West Highlands, I.330–354

Shining Princess
—Quayle / Shining * 13–23

SHINNY
—Hopi / Talashoma-Malotki, 207 @

SHIP(-s)
—Bell / Classical Dict, 222 @
—Clouston / Popular
    magic barks, I.218–222
—Reeves / Shadow
    white doe: knotted garment; pledge, 131–153

SHIP-BURIAL(-s)
—Scandinavian / Davidson, 143 (index)

SHIPWRECK(-s)
    see also Sinbad . . .
—Coyote / Bierhorst *
    ocean advises coyote to become merchant; ship's date cargo lost, [38]
—Douglas / Magic *
    roc, its egg eaten, gets vengeance on Sinbad, 21–25
—Egyptian / Mercatante
    serpent bestows wealth on shipwrecked sailor, 155–158
—Yep / Rainbow *
    protector of sailors: Dream Flier, 144–151

SHIRT
—Grimm / Legends (Ward), II:446 (index)

SHIVA
—Cotterell / Encyclopedia, 258 (index)
—Indic / Ions, 144 (index)
—Jaffrey / Seasons
    how Ganesh got his elephant head, 121–123
—Man Myth & Magic, 3169 (index)
—Mercatante / Encyclopedia, 795 (index)
—Wolkstein / Love
    Shiva and Sati, 73–89, 253, 264 @

SHOE(-s)
    see also Cinderella; Twelve dancing princesses
—Arabian / McCaughrean
    miser's everlasting shoes, 58–64
—Bomans / Wily *
    cobbler's three wishes from gnome; learns money's limitations, 53–61
—Chinese / Chin *
    golden carp (slipper; Cinderella-type), 47–57
—Clouston / Popular
    of swiftness, I.72–122
—Crossley / British FT *
    piper cuts off feet of frozen corpse, to steal shoes, 283–286
—Geras / Grandmother *
    golden shoes (worn on hands to keep them clean), 21–29
—Grimm / Legends (Ward), II:446 (index)
—Jewish / Sadeh
    Rabbi Isaac Abrabanel and king's shoe, 222–223
—MacDonald / Sourcebook *
    motif index, 698
—Manning / Cauldron *
    Whirlwind abducts queen and

(evil) son; magic shoes take him away, 106–117

—Scary / Young *
fear! who's following me? [flapping sole of shoe], 57

—Turkish (Art I) / Walker
apprentice shoe merchant dismissed for request to Allah, 116–122

—Yep / Rainbow *
slippers: comfort for immigrants, 162–168

SHOEMAKER(-s)

—Bomans / Wily *
three wishes from gnome; learns money's limitations, 53–61

—Dramatized / Kamerman
Leprechaun shoemakers, 239–249

—Grimm / Complete *
tailor overcomes evil shoemaker, 386–496

—Russian Hero / Warner *
three kingdoms (task): copper, silver, gold, 53–56

Shoemaker and the elves (Grimm)

—Childcraft I / Once * 107–109

—Hall / Treasury * 104–107

Shoemaker and the elves (*existential retelling*)

—Switzer / Existential, 54–62

Shoes that were danced to pieces, The

—Grimm / Complete * 596–600

Shooting star, see STAR.

SHORT SIGHTEDNESS

—Childcraft 1 / Once *
Pooh; too fat to get out of door (Milne), 201–207

—Grimm / Complete *
Fred and Kate [repeated foolish acts], 283–289
merchant, in a hurry, does not replace horseshoe nail, 748

—Grimm / Sixty *
Fred and Kate, 144–155

—Old Wives / Carter
three sillies: man tries to jump into trousers, 104–107

—Rockwell / Puss *
Mr. Vinegar (makes series of bad trades), 60–65

—Scary / Young *
stone golem brought to life; rabbi can't keep him busy, 17–20

—Turkish / Walker
boast re archery prowess, 43–44

—Turkish (Art I) / Walker
donkey and camel: irresistible urges, 44–45

Shroud: the unquiet grave

—Grimm / Complete * 502–503

SHU

—Egyptian / Ions, 144 (index)

SHYLOCK

—Jewish / Frankel
pound of flesh: Shylock and Pope Sixtus IV, 400–403

SHYSTER

—Coyote / Bierhorst *
doc always says "you're doing fine," [30]

SIBERIAN MYTH

—Mercatante / Good/Evil, 101–105 @

SIBYL

—Roman / Usher, 132 (index)
golden bough: Aeneas in the Underworld, 51–57 @

SICILIAN TALES

—Clouston / Popular, II.513 (index)

SICK (-ness)

—Bierhorst / Sacred
Indian prayers, 77–91

—Coyote / Bierhorst *
promises come easy in time of need, [18]

—Fahs / Old *

animals vs. human enemy; plants
give medicine, 71–80
—Leonardo / Fables *
woodlark: key to life or death,
18–19
—Russian / Ivanits, 248 (index)
SIEGE
—Egyptian / Harris
capture of Joppa; cunning of
Djhuty, 69–70
—Grimm / Legends (Ward)
besieged, II:390 (index)
—Turkish (Art I) / Walker
seven-year siege lifted by
woman's cleverness, 144–146
SIEGFRIED
—Knights / Heller-Headon, 24–37
SIGHT-SEEING
—Gullible Coyote / Malotki
dancing skeleton; eyes pop out,
go sight-seeing, 77–82
SIGN(-s)
—Dramatized / Kamerman
King Horn; chamberlain deceives
queen, 447–457
—Harris-Parks / Again
Brer Rabbit's courtship: wins
Miss Molly Cottontail, 30–39
—Jewish / Frankel, 651 (index)
SIGN LANGUAGE
—Turkey / Walker, 308 (index)
Sign of the cross, *see* CROSS.
SILENCE
—Clouston / Popular
wager: who will speak first, II.15–
26
—Douglas / Magic *
six swans (enchanted princes
saved by their sister), 35–41
—Turkish (Art I) / Walker
brothers quarrel, don't speak;
one sends blank letter, 69–70
SILVER
—Witch Encyc / Guiley, 419 (index)

Simeli Mountain
—Grimm / Complete * 627–630
SIMPLE LIFE
see also Aesop: Town mouse . . .
—Allison / I'll Tell *
city mouse and country mouse,
124–125
—Bruchac / Iroquois *
girl not satisfied with simple
things, 123–127
SIMPLETON (good-hearted fool)
—American / Read Dgst
Foolish John gets dollar for each
hair in cow's hide, 52
—Bomans / Wily *
simple blackberry-picker has
riches in beauties of nature,
47–53
—Bryan / Lion *
Jumoke ("Foolish Boy") outwits
Ananse, 60–86
—Childcraft 1 / Once *
Lazy Jack (follows suggestions
foolishly), 110–114
—Clarkson / World *
Koshalki-Opalki (how simpleton
became king), 19–22
—Clouston / Popular
sharpers and the simpleton,
II.27–42
—Crossley / Animal (Grimm) *
cat/mouse partnership, 21–25
—German-American / Barrick
numskull tales, 111–116
—Grimm / Complete *
Hans in luck; series of foolish
tradings, 381–386
three feathers: youngest prince
marries toad, 319–322
—Grimm / Sixty *
Hans in luck, 10–16
—Jewish / Frankel
thinks he's in Warsaw, really at
home in Chelm, 567–570

two husbands: which is greater
fool? 418–420
Yom Kippur flute carries synagogue prayers to heaven, 475–
477
—Old Wives / Carter
fool would buy brains from wise
woman; good wife supplies
need, 96–100
—Turkish / Walker
just say Hic! [repetitive] 76–79
SIMPLICITY
—Cambodian / Carrison
lost, king tells child how to recognize a king, 86–89
—Jewish / Frankel
king and: contented simple man,
dissatisfied clever man, 538–
544
—Jewish / Sadeh
rabbi scolds poor man offering
bread to God, 238–239
SIN
see also SEVEN DEADLY SINS
—Jewish / Frankel, 651 (index)
sinners, 644 (index)
—Jewish / Sadeh
Aaron's bull: supports world but
sin adds to load, 163–164
fly and spider; incense: knowledge
and understanding, 389–392
merchant buys dead partner's sin
and guilt, 83–86
SIN (moon-god)
—Babylonia / Spence, 407 (index)
SINBAD
—Arabian / Lewis
Sinbad's first and last voyage,
94–105
—Arabian / McCaughrean
Sinbad's first and last voyage,
16–21
Sinbad's second voyage, 22–28
Voyage of Sinbad, 10–15

—Arabian / Riordan
Sinbad makes wine in pumpkin,
51–55
Sinbad's first and last voyage,
38–55
—Douglas / Magic *
roc, its egg eaten, gets vengeance, 21–25
SING(-er; -ing)
see also SONG(-s)
—Arabian / Lewis
court singer, slave girl, beggar-
singer, 91–93
—Corrin / Imagine *
Arion wins prize; is thrown overboard; saved by dolphin, 161–
163
—Grimm / Complete *
magic results: One-eye, Two-
eyes, and Three-eyes, 585–592
—Hamilton / People *
Little Daughter sings, and escapes from wolf, 60–63
—Hopi Coyote / Malotki
Bird Girls, grinding corn, give
feathers to Coyote Girl, 91–97
—Lang / Wilkins
charm protects betrothed from
yara (fairies), 474–484
—MacDonald / Sourcebook *
motif index, 699
—Old Wives / Carter
wicked stepmother: fruit tree low-
ers branches when boy sings,
178–180
—Yolen / Faery Flag
reincarnation: plant growing from
grave, 41–46
Sing a song of sixpence
—Allison / I'll Tell * 93
SINGER, Isaac Bashevis
—Lynn / Fantasy *
bibliography (about the author),
601–603

Singing bone, The
—Grimm / Complete * 148–150
Singing, soaring lark, The
—Grimm / Complete * 398–404
SINNERS
—Jewish / Frankel, 644 (index)
SINUHE
—Egyptian / Mercatante, 159–167
SINULU
—Hoke / Giants
    hummingbird directs slaying of
      stone giant, 71–78
Sir Gawain, see GAWAIN, Sir.
Sir John Barleycorn (poem)
—Crossley / British FT * 132–134
SIREN(-s)
—Animals / Rowland, 190 (index)
—Bird Symbol / Rowland, 211 (index)
—McGowen / Encyclopedia * 50
—South / Mythical
    sources; bibliographical essay,
      147–153 (R. Berman), 390 (in-
      dex)
SISTER(-s)
    see also BROTHER(-s) and
      SISTER(-s)
—Bruchac / Iroquois *
    two daughters: wise obedience,
      foolish disobedience, 116–
      121
—Haboo / Hilbert
    legend of the Three Sisters
      (mountains), 123–126
—Jewish / Sadeh
    nightingale and shroud wearers;
      jealousy, 25–28
—Turkey / Walker, 308 (index)
Sister Aimee
—Floyd / Gr Am Myst, 123–126
SISYPHUS
—D'Aulaire / Greek * 126
SITA
—Jaffrey / Seasons
    how Ram, son of Dashrat, de-

    feated demon king Ravan, 48–
    69
SITTING BULL
—Erdoes / Sound *
    his dancing horse, his death,
      103–107
Six servants (Grimm)
—Corrin / Six-Year * 173–181
—Grimm / Complete * 600–607
Six swans, The (Grimm)
—Grimm / Complete * 232–237
—Lang / Wilkins, 260–264
—Witches / Iosa * 2–9
SIZE
    see also BUNYAN, Paul;
      GIANT(-s); THUMB-SIZED
—Allison / I'll Tell *
    frog (tries to be big as ox) ex-
      plodes, 108
—Coyote / Ramsey
    small overcomes large: wren kills
      elk, 60–63
—Curry / Beforetime *
    mountain lion "defeated" by mos-
      quito (cricket's aide), 70–73
—Dramatized / Kamerman
    Big Paul Bunyan; Babe, the blue
      ox, 514–525
—Giant / Harrison *
    witch's spell: giant sees/fears
      butterflies, etc., 19–30
—Hall / Treasury *
    Teeny-tiny, 13–16
—Hoke / Giants
    Hercules and the golden apples,
      130–132
—Manning / Cats *
    small-small cat seeks advice on
      growing large, 126–127
—Russian Hero / Warner *
    last of the giants: Svyatogor,
      125–128
SKELETON
—Bierhorst / Naked *

Cannibal Island; skeleton gives advice, 44–51

—Bruchac / Iroquois *
vampire skeleton, 129–133

—Coyote / Ramsey
Skeleton-Man: arrow-point maker and tobacco-hunter, 76–78

—Gullible Coyote / Malotki
dancing skeleton; eyes pop out, go sight-seeing, 77–82

—Scary / Young *
Indian maid, married in Land of the Dead, returns with child, 69–72

—Spanish-Am / Van Etten *
skeleton gives treasure to brave boy, 109–114

SKILLED PERSONS

—Arabian / Lewis
court singer, slave girl, beggar-singer, 91–93

—Childcraft 1 / Once *
five Chinese brothers (swallow sea, etc), 115–121

—Grimm / Complete *
brothers: barber, blacksmith, fencing master (most skilled?), 561–62
Four clever brothers, 580–584
skillful huntsman, 508–514

—Grimm / Sixty *
Four clever brothers, 220–234

Skillful huntsman

—Grimm / Complete * 508–514

SKIN

—Hamilton / Dark *
witch takes off skin; as cat, rides Big Henry, 143–148

SKULL

—Erdoes / Sound *
mice powwow in elk skull, 68–70

—Ghosts / Cohen, 235–241

—Ghosts / Time-Life
screaming skulls, 56–60

—Man Myth & Magic, 3170 (index)

—Pellowski / Family *
who lives in this little house? (storytelling on fingers), 58–61

—Russian Hero / Warner *
magic doll helps Vasilisa escape Baba-Yaga, 86–92

—Turkey / Walker, 308 (index)

SKUNK(-s)

—Bierhorst / Naked *
Turtle's war party vs. Seven Sisters, 31–36

—Bruchac / Iroquois *
turtle makes war on men, 55–59

—Gullible Coyote / Malotki
witch-coyote and skunk; skunk deceives rabbits, 131–148

—Haboo / Hilbert
skunk's spu, 159–163

—Navajo Coyote / Haile
coyote: great kill; race; skunk tricks coyote, 10, 31–32

—Spanish-Am / Van Etten *
doctor, rancher, sheepherder (winner) try to drive out skunk, 101–105

Skunnee Wundee [Indian boy] and the stone giant

—Scary / Young * 14–16

SKY

see also HEAVENS

—Bruchac / Iroquois *
sky-world: creation of Earth, 15–17

—Caduto / Keepers *
skyland: origin of Big Dipper, 117–120

—Earth / Hadley *
lifting the sky (Ru; blue stone), [13–14]

—Haboo / Hilbert
journey to sky and back down to earth, 3–5

—Jones / Tales *
   falling: Chicken Licken, 16–20
—Man Myth & Magic, 3170 (index)
—Manning / Cats *
   Istvan climbs pea-plant into heav-
     ens; finds seven-eyed goat;
     falls into swamp, 107–110

SKYFALLS
—Floyd / Gr Am Myst
   raining snakes and steaks, 61–
     63
—Southern [legends] / Floyd
   rains of snakes, etc., 74–77

SKY GODS/DEITIES
—Cotterell / Encyclopedia, 258 (in-
   dex)
—Hamilton / In the Beginning *
   Mawu and Lisa (Fon myth), 42–
     45
   Olorun: Owner of the sky, 72–77
   Sedi and Melo (gods), 116–121
—Lurker / Dict Gods, 410–411 (index)
—Mercatante / Encyclopedia, 796 (in-
   dex)
—Scandinavian / Davidson, 51–71,
   143 (index)

SLANDER
—Baring-Gould / Curious
   priest (6th cent.) slandered, de-
     posed, restored, 156–159 @
—Coyote / Bierhorst *
   wolf slanders coyote; coyote
     turns tables, [34]
—Jewish / Frankel
   anecdote: slays three, 382

SLAVE(-ery) / SLAVE TALES
   see also BRER RABBIT; HIGH
     JOHN . . .
—Afro-American / Abrahams, 263–
   295
—Allison / I'll Tell *
   Androcles and lion (with thorn in
     paw), 119
—American / Read Dgst, 445 (index)

   trickster: John and the Master,
     272–273
   underground railroad, 274–278
—Arabian / Lewis
   slave girl (Sweet-Friend) and Ali
     Nur, 25–34
—Arabian / McCaughrean
   Keys of destiny; Iram, 65–82
—Bell / Classical Dict, 225 @
—Bruchac / Iroquois *
   Hodadenon: slaves not in crea-
     tor's plan, 169–182
—Corrin / Imagine *
   Chura ("Simba"); his love returns
     from underworld; can marry
     only Simba, 142–150
—Crossley / Animal (Grimm) *
   wolf (master) outsmarted by fox,
     45–48
—Douglas / Magic *
   Roman slave: Androcles and the
     lion, 167–175
—Hamilton / Dark *
   free spirits: Bouki and Malice,
     102–107
—Hamilton / People * 48 @
   carrying the running-always,
     141–146 @
   Gullah (Angolan), 172 @
   How Nehemiah got free;
     Juneteenth, 147–150 @
   Most useful slave [can prophesy],
     160–164
   People could fly [to freedom],
     166–172
   Riddle tale of freedom, 156–
     159
   Talking cooter [mud turtle]; mas-
     ter frees slave, 151–155
—High John / Sanfield *
   body of song and story devel-
     oped in, 3–7 @
   conditions of slaves,
     13,23,40,50,62,79,84,97 @

freedom, on bet he can make mean Master laugh, 73–78

origin of term "coons," 23 @

—Jewish / Frankel
Elijah appears as slave; sold to help poor man, 584–585

—Jewish / Sadeh
Abraham ben Ezra and the bishop, 220–221
Elijah sold as slave to help poor man, 124–126

—Lang / Wilkins
fate of king's son: marry a slave, 513–527

—Shah / Central Asia
nobleman and slave (later king), 103–108

—Southern [legends] / Floyd
voodoo practices since days of slavery, 104–108

SLAVIC MYTH

—Mercatante / Encyclopedia, 739 (index)

—Mercatante / Good/Evil, 93–99 @

—Russian Hero / Warner * 1–132

SLEEP(-ers; -ing) / SLEEPING SPELL

see also Sleeping Beauty

—Baring-Gould / Curious
Seven Sleepers of Ephesus, 44–49

—Bell / Classical Dict, 225–226 @

—Dulac / Fairy *
Finn, and Queen of many-colored bedchamber, 69–76

—Fairies / Briggs
sleeping warriors, 370–373

—Grimm / Complete *
Twelve Apostles (sleep 300 years, awaiting Redeemer), 818–819

—Jewish / Frankel
angry king: daughter taken captive because of his curse, 531–536

—Jewish / Sadeh
king, "sleep" and "slumber," 208–210

—Lang / Wilkins
Fairer-than-a-Fairy, 274–281
The little soldier (Deulin), 243–259

—Lester / Leopard *
town where sleeping was not allowed, 27–30

—Muddleheads / Harris
seal of Mouse Children recovered from Big Raven, 60–74

—Old Wives / Carter
Nourie Hadig: magic sleep caused by ring sent by mother, 192–199

—Quayle / Shining *
Urashima: lives under-sea for three [i.e., 300] years, 57–68

—Turkish (Art I) / Walker
stepmother's ring causes girl to appear dead, 82–88

Sleeping Beauty (Little Briar Rose)

—Allison / I'll Tell * 46–48

—Bedtime / Padoan & Smith * 65–67

—Brooke / Telling *
event after awakening: prince and dragon, 3–33

—Carter / Sleeping * 9–20

—Corrin / Favourite *
Thorn Rose, 138–140

—Corrin / Six-Year *
Perrault's version, 108–112

—Douglas / Magic * 55–61

—Grimm / Complete * 237–241

—Grimm / Sixty * 31–35

—Hall / Treasury * 62–65

—Lang / Wilkins, 8–13

—Leete / Golden * 94–107

—Rockwell / Puss *

Briar Rose: gifts of the Wise
Women, 53–59
—Scriven / Full Color * 48–51
—Strauss / Trail
reflections during 100 years of
waiting (poem), 33–35
—Zipes / Beauties * 44–51
Sleeping Beauty (*existential retelling*)
—Switzer / Existential, 38–45
Slipper, *see* SHOE.
SMALL-MINDED
—Manning / Cats *
small-small cat seeks advice on
growing large, 126–127
Small persons, *see* THUMB-
SIZED . . . .
SMAUG
—Dragons / Baskin * [18–19]
SMELL
—Yep / Rainbow *
pretense: Professor of smells,
20–35
Smith, Clark Ashton
—Pirate Ghosts / McSherry
A vintage from Atlantis, 158–
165
Smith, Gladys V.
—Dramatized / Kamerman
Tiger, brahman, and jackal, 212–
217
Smith, Lady Eleanor
—Pirate Ghosts / McSherry
No ships pass, 13–39
Smith, Sherwood
—Yolen / Werewolves
Monster mash, 127–150
SMITH(-s; blacksmith; smithy)
—Cotterell / Encyclopedia, 258 (index)
—Lang / Wilkins
Princess in the chest; faithful
guard, 369–384
—Russian Hero / Warner * 18 @

tsar's son flees, to escape
dragon, 18–19
turning old folk into young: smith
and devil, 19–20
SMOKING
see also PIPE (smoking)
—Hopi Coyote / Malotki, 325 @
coyote foolishly tries to cut pocket
in his skin; dies, 113–117
SMUGGLER
—Fairies / Briggs
fairies on the eastern green, 132–
134
SNAIL
—Bierhorst / Monkey *
Christ chased; birds help/hinder
his flight, 133–135
—Carle / Treasury *
Winners [rabbit races snail] (Andersen), 61–63
—Vietnam / Terada *
worm and snail are born to two
sisters, 59–63
SNAKE(-s)
see also SERPENT
—Aesop / Holder *
dove and the snake, 2–3
—American / Read Dgst
Iroquois friend-turned-snake and
monster serpent woman, 49–
50
White Corn introduces Snake Order to Pueblos, 62–65
—Animals / Rowland, 190 (index)
—Beat / Bryan *
frog/snake children play until told:
snakes eat frogs, 41–52
—Bierhorst / Monkey *
earthquake: witch escapes from
great-horned-snake, 118–
120
—Bruchac / Iroquois *
Djisdaah, chief of all snakes, 93–
95

girl not satisfied with simple
things, 123–127
monstrous, two-headed snake a
traitor, 97–102
snakes make war of revenge, 93–
95
—Childcraft 3 / Stories *
Chin has three questions for
the Living Kuan-yin, 93–
99
—Chinese / Chin *
white snake (in woman form), 29–
44
—Cotterell / Encyclopedia, 258 (index)
—Egyptian / Harris
doomed prince: fate foretold by
Seven Hatitors, 71–76
—Grimm / Complete *
by eating white snake, servant
understands animal language,
98–101
hazel-branch protects against
snakes, etc., 830
snake-leaves revive treacherous
wife, 94–96
—Grimm / Legends (Ward), II:447 (index)
—Grimm / Sixty *
by eating white snake (as above),
197–201
—Hopi / Talashoma-Malotki
Kokosori and his witch wife, 23–
41
—Japanese / Tyler, 339 (index)
—Jewish / Frankel
have mercy on animals, not men,
376–378
—Jewish / Sadeh
marriage of man and snake-
woman, 79–80
—Journey Sun (Chinese)
Dragon King of Langqiong; five
tales, 61–80

—Leonardo / Fables *
snake and the birds, 113
—Lester / Brer Rabbit *
task/test: capture Mr. Snake,
149–150
—Lore of Love
demigod Karkotaka, 117–118
—Lurker / Dict Gods, 439–440 (index)
—MacDonald / Sourcebook *
motif index, 701–702
—Old Wives / Carter
governor marries "Chinese princess" (snake-woman), 142–
148
—Pellowski / Story *
sand story, 64–69
string-story, 22–30
—Scary / Young *
bunny disobeys mother; is nearly
eaten by snake, 34–36
—Southern [legends] / Floyd
handling poisonous snakes in
churches, 133–140
—Tall Tales / Downs: Bear
musical snake / R. Scudday,
154–156
—Turkish / Walker
jackal shows crow: destroy
cheater by trick, 17–19
—Turkish (Art I) / Walker
Camesap befriended by
Sahmeran, padishah of
snakes, 218–224
to cure ruler, Camesap eats part
of Sahmeran, learns language
of plants, 218–224
death, if shepherd does not keep
secret his knowing language of
animals, 190–194
—Vietnam / Terada *
Da Trang crab: grateful snake
gives magic pearl, 37–41
snake princess; man saves life; it
returns in human form, 14–17

—Water Buffalo (Chinese)
 rescued by lad, gives him magic
 gifts, 103–110
SNAKEBITE
—Clarkson / World *
 man who knew how to cure
 (Cambodian), 309–312
SNAKE: BOA
—Davy Crockett / Dewey * 32–33
SNAKE: COBRA
—Chorao / Child's FTB *
 girl given to the Ranee's pet fish
 Muchie Lal, 21–31
—Corrin / Eight-Year *
 Rikki-Tikki-Tavi (mongoose) kills
 cobras, 173–191
SNAKE-MAN
—Journeys / Norris *
 road to death: old man takes form
 of bullock, [16–18]
SNAKE: PYTHON
—Frog Rider (Chinese)
 Shigar saves birds from python;
 shoots down six suns, 60–70
SNAKE: RATTLESNAKE
—Bierhorst / Naked *
 Turtle's war party vs. Seven Sis-
 ters, 31–36
—Davy Crockett / Dewey * 34–35
—Erdoes / Sound *
 three brothers transformed to rat-
 tlers; remain friendly, 37–42
—Gullible Coyote / Malotki
 coyote deceives beautiful maid:
 devil's-claw as rattlesnake,
 119–129
—Southern [legends] / Floyd
 behold the fanged serpent: snake
 lore, 122–126
—Wildlife / Gillespie, 247 (index)
SNAKE-WOMAN
—Lang / Wilkins
 The little soldier (Deulin), 243–259
Snegorotchka

—Dulac / Fairy *
 snow-child lives one winter, melts
 in spring, 1–6
SNOOP
—Caduto / Keepers *
 How Coyote was the Moon, 111
SNORING
—Lester / Leopard *
 town where snoring was not al-
 lowed, 27–30
Snorri, see STURLUSON, Snorri.
SNOW
—Bruchac / Iroquois *
 rabbit and the willow tree, 65–67
—Coyote / Ramsey
 Kalapuya boy and seven-headed
 snake, 112–117
—Earthmaker / Mayo *
 origins, 47 @
—Leonardo / Fables *
 snowflake becomes avalanche,
 20
—Yep / Rainbow *
 boy in power of: "Snake-spoke,"
 86–95
SNOW CHILD
—Dulac / Fairy *
 Snegorotchka: lives one winter,
 melts in spring, 1–6
**Snow maiden [child made of snow;
 melts]**
—Corrin / Imagine * 112–115
SNOW-MAN
—Corrin / Six-Year *
 a bully, takes people's clothes;
 melts at schoolmaster's stove,
 19–23
—Shannon / More *
 problem: how to handle huge
 balls, 8–10
**Snow Queen [seduces boy; girl
 rescues],**
—Lang / Wilkins, 336–361
—Scriven / Full Color * 35–36

Snow-White and Rose-Red
—Allison / I'll Tell * 38–39
—Grimm / Complete * 664–671
—Hall / Treasury * 88–93
—Lang / Wilkins, 99–105
—Leete / Golden * 16–31
**Snow White and the seven dwarfs
    (Grimm)** (*also* "Snowdrop")
—Allison / I'll Tell * 64–66
—Bedtime / Padoan & Smith * 17–
    19
—Chorao / Child's FTB * 7–19
—Corrin / Favourite * 125–136
—Grimm / Complete * 249–258
—Grimm / Sixty * 161–170
—Lang / Wilkins, 167–177
—Strauss / Trail
    dwarf's/witch's soliloquy (poem),
        5–7
Snow White (*existential retelling*)
—Switzer / Existential, 119–125
Snowdrop *see* Snow White and the
    seven dwarfs.
SOCIAL CLASSES
—Grimm / Complete *
    Eve's various children: God be-
        stows blessings unequally,
        734–736
SOCIAL JUSTICE
—Frog Rider (Chinese)
    Frog rider (man under spell); wife
        fails task; frog dies, 1–23
SOCIAL ROLE
—Fahs / Old *
    weeping of the birch tree; harp,
        15–18
Social solidarity, *see* SOLIDARITY.
SOLAR BARQUE
—Egyptian / Ions, 144 (index)
SOLDIER(s)
—Bomans / Wily *
    wager with King; traps ghost; be-
        comes king, 37–43
—Grimm / Complete *

blue light summons tiny servant,
    530–534
devil's grandmother solves riddle
    for hero, 563–566
discharged soldier serves Devil
    for seven years, 463–466
soldier can reduce others to im-
    mobility, 808–811
—Grimm / Legends (Ward), II:447 (in-
    dex)
—Grimm / Sixty *
    blue light summons tiny servant,
        244–249
—Lang / Wilkins
    how six men travelled the wide
        world, 299–304
    little soldier (Deulin), 243–259
—Manning / Cats *
    king loses sight; cure if washed in
        Katchka's blood, 118–123
—Nesbit / Fairy *
    toys; town in the library, 81–98
—Spanish-Am / Van Etten *
    head severed by witch; it rolls
        down Santa Fe street, 33–36
Sole, The
—Grimm / Complete * 709
SOLIDARITY (social; human)
—Aesop / Reeves-Wilson *
    trees: handle for woodcutter's
        axe, 112–113
—Allison / I'll Tell *
    bundle of sticks: strength in stick-
        ing together, 114
—Jewish / Frankel
    bird's nest: human ladder to
        God's love, 495
—Leonardo / Fables *
    cedar and many other trees,
        81
—Paxton / Aesop *
    gratitude: lion spares mouse;
        mouse frees lion from net, [19–
        21]

—Yep / Rainbow *
  "We are all one," 72–78
SOLITUDE
—Leonardo / Fables *
  stone leaves, for the road; regret,
  80
SOLOMON, KING
—Dramatized / Kamerman
  bee rewards King Solomon's
  kindness, 250–257
—Geras / Grandmother *
  Bavsi's feast: wisdom from walking in another's shoes, 6–13
—Imaginary / Nigg
  seal of Solomon: wizard and the
  chonchon, 117–119
—Jewish / Frankel, x, 195–260, 659
  (index)
  ruby/serpent: Solomon's daughter shut in tower; power of love,
  254–257
  Solomon visits deserted palace;
  learns "vanities," 251–254
—Jewish / Sadeh
  jars of honey; first judgment by
  Solomon, 47–49
  man with two heads, 56–58
  punishment: Ashmodai rules in
  his place, 58–61
  tin sword; ruthless woman, 52–
  54
  wager: poor man naked on cold
  mountain top, 50–51
  wisdom vs. gold: the three brothers, 54–56
—Legends / Cavendish, 431 (index)
Son and father, see FATHER AND
  SON.
SONG(-s)
  see also FOLKSONG; INDIAN
  SONG; SING . . .
—Allison / I'll Tell * 135–154
  motion songs and finger plays,
  161–181

—Am Child / Bronner
  parodies, 95–111
—Arabian / McCaughrean
  Pearl-Harvest, 36–50
—Erdoes / Sound *
  Iktome's misadventures, 16–22
—Glooskap / Norman *
  secluded home found by wolves,
  51–60
—Grimm / Legends (Ward), II:447 (in-
  dex)
—Hamilton / Dark *
  free spirits: Bouki and Malice,
  102–107
—MacDonald / Sourcebook *
  motif index, 704
—Spanish-Am / Van Etten *
  father kills meadowlark, dies;
  need "spirit of song" to live,
  54–56
Song of Songs, The
—Wolkstein / Love, 91–109, 265 @
SORCERER(-s) (-ery)
  see also WIZARD
—Arabian / Lewis
  Hasan, the alchemist, and the
  Jinn princess, 138–143
  Moor vs. king; claims prince, 60–
  64
—Arabian / McCaughrean
  Moor vs. king; claims prince,
  133–141
—Bierhorst / Naked *
  Mother of ghosts; life-restored,
  37–43
—Chinese / Chin *
  white snake (in woman form), 29–
  44
—Egyptian / Harris
  challenge: read letter without
  breaking seal, 108–113
—Glooskap / Norman *
  plot to kill Glooskap, 29–37
—Grimm / Complete *

bewitched: straw believed to be a beam, 645
—Grimm / Legends (Ward), II:448 (index)
—Gullible Coyote / Malotki, 176 @
—Hopi / Talashoma-Malotki
old wizard plots to seduce beautiful girl, 70–91
—Hopi Coyote / Malotki, 329 @
—Jewish / Sadeh
dress: charm causes lewdness, 20–21
sorcerer vs. the Baal Shem Tov; magic duel, 348–350
—Lycanthropy / Otten, 335 (index)
—Lynn / Fantasy *
annotated bibliography, 344–367
—Quayle / Cornish *
Lord Pengerswick and the witch of Fraddam, 103–108
—Russian / Ivanits, 251 (index)
—Shah / Central Asia
abducts Iskandar's seven sisters, 118–125

SORCERESS
—Chinese / Chin *
punishment: finding wife for River God, 17–26
—Russian Hero / Warner *
Sister Alenushka and Brother Ivanushka, 108–109

SORFARINA
—Corrin / Imagine *
prince unwittingly marries Sorfarina four times, 11–22

SORROW
see also SADNESS
—Bomans / Wily *
wind-man controls four winds: happiness to one is sorrow to another, 76–78
—Clouston / Popular
irrational excesses, II.322–326

SOUL
see also BODY AND SOUL; REINCARNATION
—Baring-Gould / Curious
Piper of Hamelin: souls of children in the wind, 116–120 @
—Cotterell / Encyclopedia, 258 (index)
—Grimm / Complete *
grave-mound: devil and grave-watchers, 792–796
—Grimm / Legends (Ward), II:448 (index)
—Hamilton / Dark *
origin of butterflies: souls of the once-alive, 119–125
—Jewish / Sadeh
pony's IOU: soul of departed one, working off debt, 354
—Man Myth & Magic, 3171 (index)
analytics, 3200 (index)
—Scandinavian / Kvideland, 422 (index)
—Scary / Young *
Ki'in spirits eat souls, take over bodies; boy outwits Ki'in, 52–56
—Tree / Kerven *
parallel lives: brother shares soul with mango tree, [20–21]

SOUL, EXTERNAL or SEPARABLE
—Celts / Hodges *
Lad of Luck and monster, 89–103
—Crossley / British FT *
butterfly soul flutters, goes into horse skull, 365–367
—Dulac / Fairy *
Bashtchelik (real steel), 91–113
—Egyptian / Harris
Anpu and Bata; betrayed, 77–83
—Fairies / Briggs, 355–359
the green mist, 201–202
young king of Esaidh Ruadh, 356–359

—Hamilton / People *
    Beautiful girl of the moon tower,
      53–59
—Jaffrey / Seasons
    brother and mango tree share
      common soul; unwatered,
      nearly die, 94–95
—Nesbit / Fairy *
    Charmed life, or Princess and
      Lift-man, 25–42
—Palestinian / Speak (Muhawi)
    motif-index, 390
—Russian Hero / Warner *
    Koshchei the Deathless; "death"
      hidden in egg, 96–99

SOUND(-s)
—Corrin / Six-Year *
    Little Red Engine: talks with
      animals; ill (needs oil), 24–
      27
—Southern [legends] / Floyd
    mysterious sounds, Rabun
      County, GA, 91–95

SOUP
—Dramatized / Kamerman
    Stone soup, 381–387
—Rockwell / Puss *
    Nail Soup, 12–18

"SOUR GRAPES"
—Aesop / Holder *
    fox and the grapes, 14–15

SOUTH AFRICA
—Vanishing / Mercer *
    how Bushmen came to be hunt-
      ers and gatherers, 74–75

SOUTH AMERICA (-an tales)
—Bierhorst / So Am
    Indian religion and mythology, 1–
      269
—Hoke / Giants
    hummingbird directs slaying of gi-
      ant Sinulu, 71–78
—Mercatante / Encyclopedia, 740 (in-
    dex)

SOUTH CAROLINA
—Southern [legends] / Floyd
    healing springs, 88–90
    Scape Ore Swamp: the "Lizard-
      Man," 127–132
SOUTH DAKOTA
—Erdoes / Sound *
    thunderbirds: Black Hills; Bad
      Lands, 33–36
SOUTHERN STATES (U.S.)
—Ghost (South) / McNeil, 1–170
—Southern [legends] / Floyd, 1–
    177
Southey, Robert (1774–1843)
—Corrin / Six-Year *
    Three bears, 70–73
SOUTHWEST
—Jameson / Buried
    legendary lost mines, gold, etc.,
      1–220
SOVIET UNION
    see also RUSSIA
—Lynn / Fantasy * 767 (index)
SOW
—Aesop / Zwerger *
    dog and sow [argue: whose ba-
      bies are better], 21
SO'YOKO
—Hopi / Talashoma-Malotki, 207 @
—Hopi Coyote / Malotki, 325 @
SPAIN
—Dictionary / Leach, 1232 (index)
—Speck / New World, 529 (index)
SPAIN: Seville
—Lore of Love
    stone avenger drags Don Juan to
      hell, 61–63
SPANIELS
—Lang / Wilkins
    Heart of ice (Caylus), 190–219
Sparrow and his four children
—Grimm / Complete * 657–660
Speaking animals, see TALKING
    ANIMALS.

SPEAKING TABOO
—Grimm / Complete *
  iron stove: princess frees prince;
    breaks taboo, 571–577
—Williams-Ellis / Tales *
  Anansi (death for saying "five"),
    143–150
SPEAR
—Bell / Classical Dict, 228 @
SPECIES
—Gould / Mythical
  extinction of fabulous animals,
    42–77 @
—Sioux / Standing Bear *
  large tree moves itself to be with
    its own kind, 65–67
Spectacles, see EYEGLASSES.
SPEECH
—Am Child / Bronner
  words to tease, insult, etc., 37–49
SPELL(-s) (usually broken)
  see also DISENCHANTMENT
—Arabian / Riordan
  genie removes curses on porter,
    Amina, Safia, Zubaida, 124–
    125
—Bomans / Wily *
  grandmother's spell begets "Sun-
    day child"; gigantic, leaves
    earth for sun, 169–173
  spell-book: each year witch takes
    two naughtiest children, 27–36
—Clouston / Popular
  petrifying victims, I.168
—Corrin / Imagine *
  Black Thief tells story of three
    enchanted maidens, 101–105
—Crane / McLean *
  Princess Belle-Etoile; evil Queen,
    16–27
—Dramatized / Kamerman
  Bridge to Killybog Fair, 227–238
  A most special dragon, 79–87
—Dulac / Fairy *
  serpent-prince: marries, regains
    human form, 29–42
—Fairies / Briggs
  to obtain power over fairies, 376–
    378
—Folk-rhymes / Northall
  England, 125–159
—Grimm / Complete *
  Jorinda and Joringel, 339–342
—Grimm / Sixty *
  Jorinda and Joringel, 17–20
—Hamilton / Dark *
  marriage to boar/man; secret
    must be kept, 113–118
—Jewish / Frankel
  serpent (prince at night); wife
    burns skin; spell broken, 446–
    449
—Lang / Wilkins
  Dwarf Long Nose (boy under
    spell), 534–556
—Manning / Cats *
  juniper bush: when heads are cut
    off, mouse-queen spell broken,
    83–91
  kind witch raises foundling to be
    knight; bewitched Cat-Johann
    his aide, 111–117
—Manning / Cauldron *
  Martin kills witch; lions freed of
    enchantment, 66–77
—O'Brien / Tales *
  fairies take Gilly, abduct princess;
    strike her dumb; Gilly learns of
    curing herb, 106–117
—Rockwell / Puss *
  Frog prince (princess makes rash
    promise), 66–74
—Russian Hero / Warner *
  three princes/brides, one a frog-
    princess, 101–106
—Scriven / Full Color *
  Snow Queen [girl's tears melt ici-
    cle in boy's heart], 35–36

—Tree / Kerven *
bamboo-princess freed from spell, [28–29]
—Trolls / Asbjornsen
seven foals (princes under spells); task: watch, report, behead, 53–59
—Victorian / Hearn
Melilot (H. Morley), 117–127
—Williams-Ellis / Tales *
bewitched sisters turned to stone, 125–130
Tamlane (knight) rescued from elfland, 151–159
—Witch Hndbk / Bird * 42–49
—Yep / Rainbow *
sickness or disability: "The ghost's bride," 54–59

SPHINX
—Animals / Rowland, 190 (index)
—Creatures (illus) / Huber * 155 (index)
—Egyptian / Harris
Great Sphinx of Gaza, 66–68
—McGowen / Encyclopedia * 51
—South / Mythical
sources; bibliographical essay, 179–191 (F. Scafella), 390(index)

SPIDER(-s)
see also ANANSI TALES
—Beat / Bryan *
how animals, birds, fish got tails, 53–70
—Caduto / Keepers *
Grandmother Spider and Swallower of Clouds, 79–81
How Grandmother Spider stole the Sun, 49–50
—Greek / Osborne
weaving contest: Arachne made first spider, 19–21
—Hamilton / In the Beginning *

Nyambi: creation of mankind, 64–67
—Hopi / Talashoma-Malotki
Hopi boy and his two pet eagles, 150–199
—Hopi Coyote / Malotki, 331 @
—Jewish / Frankel
saves David from Saul, 199
—Leonardo / Fables *
Spider in the keyhole, 22–23
—MacDonald / Sourcebook *
motif index, 705–706
—Scriven / Full Color *
organ grinder's monkey; spider; forced dance, 29–33
—Spanish-Am / Van Etten *
ant and (begging) grasshopper visit spider's home, 95–96

Spider-man, see IKTOME.
SPIDER PEOPLE
—Navajo Coyote / Haile
how people killed coyote, 15, 78–81
SPIDER WOMAN
—Fahs / Old *
how Tewas came to live at Turtle Mountain, 7–14
—Hopi / Talashoma-Malotki, 208 @
hide and seek with life at stake, 50–69, 208 @
Hopi boy and his two pet eagles, 150–199
—Hopi Coyote / Malotki
coyote and spider families entertain; coyote's lust, 43–55
Spindle, shuttle, and needle
—Grimm / Complete * 764–767
SPINNING
see also Rumpelstiltskin
—Douglas / Magic *
prophecy; Sleeping Beauty, 55–61
—Grimm / Complete *

three spinners help attain bride's mother's boast, 83–86
—Quayle / Cornish *
Duffy's pact: devil will do her work; guess name for release, 75–87

SPIRIT(-s) / SPIRIT-BEINGS
see also ELEMENTALS; FAMILIAR(-s); GHOST(-s); GREAT SPIRIT; GUARDIAN SPIRITS; HOUSE-SPIRITS; WATER SPIRIT(-s)
—Bomans / Wily *
naked soul of King Pim, 121–125
—Bruchac / Iroquois *
(monster snake) wife of Thunderer, 146–154
—Coyote / Ramsey
"stick" Indians, 85
—Crossley / British FT *
piper and pooka; carried to mountain top to play for weeping woman, 17–23
—Erdoes / Sound *
found in all movement; good and evil, 98–102
—Fahs / Old *
maize spirit: origin of corn, 148–151
—Fairies / Briggs
Denham tracts, 93–94
—Floyd / Gr Am Myst
house of Sarah L. Winchester, 156–159
—Grimm / Legends (Ward), II:449 (index)
—Hamilton / Dark *
horned women: twelve witches vs. Spirit of the Well, 32–37
—Hoke / Giants
tree spirit: Indian boy kills giants; then falls, 112–118
—Hopi / Talashoma-Malotki

game animals made hard to catch, 50–69
—Journeys / Norris *
visit to spirits of Mt. Katahdin, [19–21]
—Lore of Love
butterfly-spirit; loved one in lower world, 108
evil spirit: demon-bride's marriage to mortal, 68–73
—Lycanthropy / Otten, 335 (index)
—Man Myth & Magic, 3171 (index)
—Muddleheads / Harris
sea hunters swallowed by whirlpool, 26–43
Volcano Woman/Frog Woman, 94–114
—Northern / Norman
eighteen tales, 203–244
—Polynesians / Andersen, 288–348
—Russian / Ivanits, 251 (index)
—Russian Hero / Warner *
domovoi, living in stove, 29–30
spirits of forest, stream, home: leshii, 24–25 @
—Scary / Young *
Ki'in spirits eat souls, take over bodies; boy outwits Ki'in, 52–56
Pele, Spirit of Fire, vs. Na-Maka; Kilauea, 84–86
—Vanishing / Mercer *
bears' tower: rock "grows," to protect girls, 118–120
—Vietnam / Terada *
chess player dies; enters body of newly dead butcher, 75–77
spirits ask man to die and be their leader (general), 78–80

Spirit in the bottle
—Grimm / Complete * 458–462

SPIRIT PHOTOGRAPHY
—Ghosts / Cohen, 241–251

SPIRITUALISM
—Floyd / Gr Am Myst
    Fox Sisters: Leah, Kate, Margaret, 70–73
—Occult & Parapsych / Shepard, 1557–63 (index)
SPIRITUALITY
—Mesoamerican / Leon-P, 293 (index)
SPOILED . . .
—Bomans / Wily *
    Lady of the lake: prince loved/ saved by young girl, 9–16
SPONGER
—Coyote / Bierhorst *
    wolf and puma fight; coyote steals the kill, [22]
—Jewish / Sadeh
    guest stays till food runs out, 321
SPONTANEOUS HUMAN COMBUSTION
—Floyd / Gr Am Myst
    Jack Angel, 110–113
—Southern [legends] / Floyd
    fire from heaven? 78–82
SPOONFULS
—Beat / Bryan *
    husband counts spoonfuls; loses wives, 30–40
SPRIGGANS
—Fairies / Briggs, 380–381
—Quayle / Cornish *
    (to) buy a house, old woman seizes their plunder, 72–74
    magic ointment put on eye makes one invisible, 13–20
    miser would steal gold from fairy Gump; foiled, 64–71
SPRING (season)
—Caduto / Keepers *
    Spring defeats Winter, 129–131
SPRING(-s) (water)
—Earthmaker / Mayo *
    hot springs, 41 @

    Smoking Waters; Indian wars (Ute tale), 42–46
—Fahs / Old *
    quest: healing for plague-stricken wife, 52–56
—Southern [legends] / Floyd
    South Carolina's healing springs, 88–90
Sprite, see WATER SPRITE.
SPUNKIES
—Fairies / Briggs, 381–382
SQUASH
—Vietnam / Terada *
    squash seeds: origin of Dao People, 54–58
SQUID
—Yolen / Shape Shift
    Judas fish (T.N. Scortia), 98–117
SQUIRE
—Knights / Heller-Headon, 40–41, 54–55
SQUIRREL
—Greaves / Hippo *
    eating contest: elephant vs. squirrel, 52–53
—Lester / Brer Rabbit *
    task/test: capture Brer Squirrel, 148–149
Stag and the hounds
—Aesop / Holder * 24–25
STALLION
—Manning / Cats *
    boy Altin's golden knucklebone, water cat, and stallion, 29–36
STAR(-s)
    see also CREATION OF HEAVENLY BODIES
—Amer Ind / Erdoes, 125–175
—American / Read Dgst
    Shawnee star lore, 132–133
—Babylonia / Spence, 408 (index)
—Bell / Classical Dict, 231–234 @
—Bruchac / Iroquois *

hunting of the Great Bear (Big Dipper), 189–195

—Caduto / Keepers *
fisher to Skyland: origin of Big Dipper, 117–120

—Chinese / Chin *
cowherd's marriage to fairy weaving maid, 113–125

—Constellations / Gallant * 1–203
Arab names, 199
Aries, 199
Big Dipper, 199
double star, 200
Pisces, 202
Pleides, 202

—Coyote / Ramsey
coyote in love; origin of Crater Lake, 210–211

—Curry / Beforetime *
why coyote is thin: falls "ten snows," riding Evening Star, 48–51

—Greaves / Hippo *
Southern Cross: giraffe watches over sun; rewarded by Creator, 89

—Greek / Osborne
Great Bear and Little Bear: origin, 41–43

—Jewish / Frankel
origin: moon punished for wanting to be brighter than sun, 7–9

—Journey Sun (Chinese)
Yangang saves village incinerated by shooting star, 47–60

—MacDonald / Sourcebook *
motif index, 707

—Polynesians / Andersen, 504 (index)

—Unicorn / Hathaway
celestial unicorn, 171–183 @

STARFRUIT

—Vietnam / Terada *
elder brother inherits all but starfruit tree, 3–6

STARGAZER

—Turkish / Walker
stargazer (seer) to the sultan, 98–107

Star-money

—Grimm / Complete * 652–654

STARVATION

—Grimm / Complete *
God's food: rich sister refuses aid, 822

—Hopi Coyote / Malotki
coyote and the Korowiste kachinas, 195–227, 303, 307 @

—Sioux / Standing Bear *
Standing Bear's horse; facing starvation, 32–36

STATUE

—Bell / Classical Dict, 234–236 @

—Coyote / Bierhorst *
coyote mistakes statue for (brainless) live person, [42]

—Grimm / Legends (Ward), II:450 (index)

—Wilde / Happy *
happy prince [statue sends swallow with jewels for poor], 15–38

—Wilde / Lynch *
happy prince . . . [as above], 41–54

Stealing, *see* THIEF.

Steinbeck, John (1902-1968)

—Pendragon / Ashley
The knight with the two swords, 49–69

Stenbock, Eric

—Lycanthropy / Otten
The other side, 269–280

STEPDAUGHTER

—Turkish (Art I) / Walker
dead mother advises stepdaughter: nurse, teach, wed serpent-prince, 183–188

STEPFATHER

—Bierhorst / Naked *

Porcupine's grandson [abandoned boy], 93–100
—Manning / Cats *
able to call twelve sailors at will, Vasily saves Leeshy Cat, 37–50

Stephens, James
—Hoke / Giants
In the orchard, 156

STEPMOTHER (usually cruel)
see also Cinderella; Snow White . . . ; Vasilisa
—Celts / Hodges *
swan children restored by St. Patrick's coming, 5–14
—Chinese / Chin *
golden carp killed; its bones do magic for friend, 47–57
—Dulac / Fairy *
magic pipe makes all dance, 114–123
White Caroline, Black Caroline, 15–21
—Ghosts / Starkey
Black Annis (witch) defeated, 52–57
Joe Reardon and the three sister-ghosts, 102–109
—Grimm / Complete *
brother transformed to fawn; sister faithful, 67–73
girl shares bread with three little men, 78–83
true bride; prince forgets betrothal, 752–760
—Hamilton / Dark *
reward/punishment by Father Frost, 49–53
—Old Wives / Carter
little red fish and clog of gold (Cinderella-type), 171–177
many wives: each considered mother of all children, 178–180
—Quayle / Shining *

mother's mirror warns Sachiko of stepmother in rat-form, 90–96
—Rockwell / Puss *
Kate Crackernuts breaks evil spells, 19–26
—Russian / Afanasev, 661 (index)
—Russian Hero / Warner *
magic doll helps Vasilisa escape Baba-Yaga, 86–92
Morozko the frost demon, and his bride, 33–37
—Scary / Young *
beheads boy; makes his sister think she killed him; cooks boy, 78–83
—Shah / Central Asia
prince who married a peri (fairy), 49–55
Wali and the magic saddle-bag, 69–77
—Williams-Ellis / Tales *
Baba Yaga; Marusia's kindness helps escape, 113–124 QS
—Witches / Iosa *
wicked stepmother sends twins to giant witch, 18–22

STEPSISTERS
—O'Brien / Tales *
magic apples: red produce horns on eater; golden apples remove, 31–37
—Trolls / Asbjornsen
one kind, one cruel; serving in house of witch, 42–50

STICK (magic)
—Coyote / Ramsey
Kalapuya boy and seven-headed snake, 112–117
—Water Buffalo (Chinese)
innkeeper steals magic donkey, table cloth, stick, 103–110

STINGINESS
—Jaffrey / Seasons
Doda and Dodi: rich woman does

not feed poor sister-in-law, 38–
46
—Jewish / Frankel
more mud, the better, 550
Stith Thompson Motif Index, see
MOTIF.
STOKER, Bram (1847–1912)
—Dracula / McNally,
19–33, 161ff @
Stolen child, The [poem by Yeats]
—Victorian / Hearn, 252–253
Stolen farthings
—Grimm / Complete * 654–655
STOMACH
—Lester / Leopard *
body-parts argue: which is most
important, 45–51
—Paxton / Belling *
feet and stomach: who's helping
whom (Aesop), [32–33]
STONE(-s) (often magic) see also
ROCK(-s)
—Bell / Classical Dict, 238–239 @
—Chaucer / Cohen *
the franklin's tale: will love when
stones are gone, 67–84
—Earth / Hadley *
stone tells story of stories (to Se-
neca Indian), [29–31]
—Grimm / Legends (Ward), II:451 (in-
dex)
—Leonardo / Fables *
leaves solitude for the road; re-
gret, 80
—Scary / Young *
Indian boy (with turtle) vs. Stone
Giant; rock-skipping, 14–16
—Spanish-Am / Van Etten *
angry reply: clearing field to
"grow more stones," 52–53
—Spring / Philip
Akui frees water; turns to stone,
87–93
—Trolls / Asbjornsen

goose-girl: "meant" to marry
Prince of England, 60–63
—Water Buffalo (Chinese)
no "difference of seasons" for,
23–29
—Witch Encyc / Guiley, 419 (index)
STONE COATS
—Bierhorst / Naked *
Lodge Boy and Thrown Away
[chipmunk-sized boy], 79–86
Whirlwinds vs. man-eating gi-
ants, 19–23
—Bruchac / Iroquois *
Stone Coat Woman aids hunters,
135–144
STONE GIANT(-s)
—American / Read Dgst
disease; Iroquois False Face So-
ciety, 51
—Bruchac / Iroquois *
Skunny-Wundy defeats the
Stone Giants, 161–167
—Scary / Young *
Indian boy (with turtle): rock-
skipping contest, 14–16
STONEHENGE
—Celts / Hodges *
Merlin: life and magic powers,
117–132
—King Arthur / Ashe, 191 (index)
STONERIBS
—Indian Myth / Burland
hero/son of Volcano Woman, 45–
49
Stone soup
—Allison / I'll Tell * 8–9
STORK
—Aesop / Reeves-Wilson *
guest's food in plate/bottle: Fox
and stork, 95–96
—Corrin / Imagine *
Caliph and Vizier into storks; for-
get magic word; marriage to
(enchanted) owl, 164–76

STORM(-s)
  see also BLIZZARD; RAIN
    STORM
—Earthmaker / Mayo *
  Brave Girl and the storm monster
    (Seneca tale), 28–32
—Glooskap / Norman *
  giant bird, Wuchowsen, strength
    of sea winds, 21–28
—Grimm / Legends (Ward), II:451 (in-
    dex)
—Sioux / Standing Bear *
  Thunder Dreamer, the medicine
    man, 41–43
—Southern [legends] / Floyd
  Last Island's last day (Louisiana
    coast), 56–60
STORY MAPPING (analysis)
—Bosma / Classroom, 116 (index)
Story of Schlauraffen land
—Grimm / Complete * 660
STORYTELLER(-s; -ing)
  see also Scheherazod
—African / Abrahams, 1–29 @
—Afro-American / Abrahams,   3–
    35 @
—Allison / I'll Tell * xiii-xvii, 103, 112,
    122, 126 @
  keep plots straight, 43 @
  lighting a story, 13 @
  pauses in telling, 53 @
  reading aloud, 61 @
  well-told tale: ten steps, 18–19 @
—Bierhorst / Monkey * 14–17 @
—Bomans / Wily *
  storyteller wants to see a gnome
    before he dies, 141–142
—Brooke / Telling *
  retelling "Jack and the Bean-
    stalk," 113–132
—Bruchac / Iroquois *
  origin of legends, 12–13
—Caduto / Keepers *
  how to . . . , 7–15

origin: Great Stone (a standing
    rock) tales, 3–4
—Crossley / British FT *
  abductee must tell tale to receive
    hospitality, 77–85
—Douglas / Magic *
  Shahrazad: bring back the most
    marvelous, 3–11
—Dramatized / Kamerman
  King who was bored; endless
    tale; execution, 334–345
  servant tells stories, in exchange
    for clothes, 10–14
—Earth / Hadley *
  stone tells story of stories (to Se-
    neca Indian), [29–31]
—MacDonald / Sourcebook *
  motif index, 709
—Old Coot / Christian *
  Coyote promises "gold" (i.e.,
    tales) to Old Coot, 3–13
  Old Coot and (as?) rustler: crow
    envies hawk, 17–26
  wager: gambler won't say
    "enough"; story of tracking
    coyote, 29–38
—Old Wives / Carter
  how husband weaned wife from
    fairy tales, 227–228
—Oral Trad / Cunningham
  recitations, 1–264
—Pellowski / Family * 1–150
  annotated bibliography, 134–
    142 @
  directory of events, worldwide,
    143–150 @
  drawing in sand, snow, or mud,
    119–125
  foreign languages: finger stories
    when traveling, 102–106 @
  handkerchief stories, 62–73 @
  how to tell, 48–52 @
  kinds of stories, 27–47 @
  origami, 74–84 @

paper cutting/tearing stories, 85–101 @

when to tell, 7–26 @

why tell stories, 1–6 @

—Pellowski / Story * 1–116

finger-play stories, 92–98

picture-drawing stories, 47–76

riddling, 99–101

sand stories, 60–74

stories using musical instruments, 102–112

stories with dolls, 77–91

string stories, 3–46

—Scary / Young *

children and scary stories, 95–100 @

—Yep / Rainbow *

Wong I, II and III: boasting contest, 96–105

Strange musician, The

—Grimm / Complete * 56–58

STRANGER

—Jewish / Frankel

tramp (Elijah), stranger to be treated kindly, 604–605

STRATEGY

—Aesop / Reeves-Wilson *

contest: who is stronger? "Wind and sun," 88–91

STRAW . . .

—Grimm / Complete *

bewitched: straw believed to be a beam, 645

personification: straw, coal, and bean, 102–103

—Grimm / Sixty *

personification . . . (as above), 29–30

STRAWBERRIES

—Coyote / Ramsey

swallowing match: coyote/bear, 118

—Grimm / Complete *

girl shares bread with three little men, 78–83

STRENGTH (fabulous; marvelous)

—Aesop / Alley *

Wind and the sun, 20–23

—Aesop / Holder *

laden ass and a horse, 10–13

—Allison / I'll Tell *

bundle of sticks: strength in sticking together, 114

—Bell / Classical Dict, 241 @

—Corrin / Eight-Year *

Bash Tshelik, man of steel, 120–133

—Hamilton / Dark *

very large son: landowner tries to exploit giant, 97–101

—Igloo / Metayer

Kautaluk: Great Spirit grants marvelous strength, 35–39

—Indian Myth / Burland

lazy boy with supernatural strength, 49–50

—Jewish / Frankel

sun, wind, and man: which is strongest? 465

—Legends / Cavendish, 397 (index)

—Nielsen / Old Tales *

blue belt (magic strength), [37–62]

—Paxton / Aesop *

gratitude: lion spares mouse; mouse frees lion from net, [19–21]

—Russian Hero / Warner *

gypsy cons dragon: he's stronger, 71–72

last of the giants: Svyatogor, 125–128

Mikula (peasant) and Vol'ga (prince), 21–22

Vasilisa (Golden Braid) and Ivan the Pea, 63–68

—Trolls / Asbjornsen

Rumble-Mumble Goose-Egg,
71–82
**STRENGTH: CONTESTS WON BY
DECEPTION**
—Grimm / Complete *
Valiant tailor, 112–120
—Grimm / Sixty *
Valiant tailor, 88–97
STRING STORIES
—Pellowski / Story * 3–46
Strong Hans
—Grimm / Complete * 688–695
STRONG MAN
see also BUNYAN, Paul
—Crossley / British FT *
old Pict snaps iron pipe with fin-
gers, 142–144
—Crossley / Dead *
Tom Hickathrift [remarkable
strength], 11–19
—Dulac / Fairy *
boy gathers six helpers: the
seven conquerors, 22–28
Finn, and Queen of many-colored
bedchamber, 69–76
—Grimm / Complete *
thumbling nursed by giant ac-
quires fabulous strength, 412–
420
—Hoke / Giants
remarkably strong man, 103–
111, 119–129
—Russian Hero / Warner *
Vasilisa (Golden Braid) and Ivan
the Pea, 63–68
STUBBORN
—Corrin / Imagine *
Sorfarina not sorry for slapping
prince, as child, 11–22
STUDENT(-s)
see also COLLEGE STUDENTS
—Vietnam / Terada *
student enamored of two women
(spirits), 95–98

—Wilde / Lynch *
nightingale gives life to produce
red rose for student-in-love,
14–23
STUDY
—Jewish / Frankel, 651 (index)
STUPIDITY
—Clarkson / World *
humor: not recognizing selves in
mirror, 367–369
—Grimm / Complete *
will not beat wife if he finds some-
one more stupid, 476–480
STURLUSON, Snorri (1173–1241)
—Hamilton / In the Beginning *
Prose Edda, 68–71
—Scandinavian / Davidson, 143 (in-
dex)
STUTTERING
—Bomans / Wily *
echo well: misshapen people not/
aware of defects, 97–100
SUBSTITUTION
see also CHANGELING(-s); ES-
CAPE BY SUBSTITUTION
—Grimm / Complete *
maiden escapes marriage to
hare, 332–334
—Hamilton / People *
Wiley triumphs over Hairy Man,
90–103
—Jaffrey / Seasons
Doda and Dodi: rich woman
sends snakes to sister-in-law;
sweets to mother, 38–46
—Lang / Wilkins
fate of king's son: marry a slave,
513–527
—Lines / Magical *
North Wind gifts, meal-producing
cloth; gold-producing ram, stolen, 66–70
—Old Wives / Carter
rich farmer covets young girl; she

substitutes mare for wedding, 61–63

sons of servants substituted for prince (promised to giant), 76–85

—Quayle / Shining *
Shining Princess (from Moon People) and deceptive suitors, 13–23

—Spring / Philip
woman chosen to be "king" "marries" her husband, 58–74

—Williams-Ellis / Tales *
Sister Long-Hair steals stream from mountain god, 161–171

—Yep / Rainbow *
ghost girl for human-live girl, 54–59

SUCCESS
see also UNPROMISING ONE SUCCEEDS

—Bryan / Lion *
Jumoke ("Foolish Boy") outwits Ananse, 60–86

—Coyote / Ramsey
unpromising suitor: Kalapuya boy and seven-headed snake, 112–117

—Dramatized / Kamerman
Simple Olaf becomes king's advisor, 413–421

—Hoke / Giants
defeat of tyrannical giant Hundar, 41–64

—Jewish / Frankel
Good Purim, Good Purim! 528–530

—Lang / Wilkins
accidental: Charming wins Goldilocks, 31–43

—Paxton / Aesop *
race: tortoise and the hare, [22–27]

SUFFERING
—Arabian / McCaughrean
Keys of destiny; Iram, 65–82

—Hamilton / In the Beginning *
origin: cosmic egg; creation myth, 20–23

—Jewish / Sadeh
good suffer along with the evil, 3

—Lewis / Proud
Guigemar: woman to endure anguish and lift curse, 10–19

—Reeves / Shadow
White doe: cured by special love, 131–153

—Wilde / Lynch *
happy prince: statue persuades swallow to help the poor, 41–54

SUICIDE
—American / Read Dgst
Rainbow Woman and cottonwood-tree husband, 204

—Bell / Classical Dict, 242–245 @

—Chinese / Chin *
marriage not allowed (Ju Yingtai), 61–73

—Maori / Kanawa *
Hutu accused of killing girl (a suicide), 106–110

SUITOR(-s) (usually tested . . .)
—Arabian / Lewis
king trades daughter for flying ebony horse, 106–116

—Arabian / McCaughrean
king trades (as above), 225–242

—Arabian / Riordan
king trades (as above), 56–65
Princess Dunja: all men are faithless, 52–59
princess loved by cousins (three brothers), 174–183

—Bell / Classical Dict, 245–256 @

—Bierhorst / Naked *

rejected; Turtle, his sister, and
Great Wind, 110–115
Two Feathers: skills test, 11–18
—Bomans / Wily *
woodcutter solves riddles; wins
princess, 202–205
—Clarkson / World *
Boots outperforms brothers;
magic ax, shovel, walnut, 277–
281
—Clouston / Popular
test: virtuous wife, importunate
suitors, II.289–316
—Coyote / Ramsey
Kalapuya boy and seven-headed
snake, 112–117
—Douglas / Magic *
Ahmad: bring back the most mar-
velous, 3–11
—Dramatized / Kamerman
Quick-witted Jack, 400–412
—Dulac / Fairy *
Bashtchelik (real steel), 91–113
boy gathers six helpers: Queen of
the Mississippi, 22–28
Ivan and the chestnut horse, 60–
68
serpent-prince: marries, regains
human form, 29–42
—Egyptian / Harris
doomed prince: fate foretold by
Seven Hatitors, 71–76
—Grimm / Complete *
griffin: suitor's tasks to win prin-
cess, 681–688
Hans married: uncle deceives
bride's father, 387–388
Iron Hans, 612–620
King Thrushbeard; haughty princess, 244–248
kings' daughters aid hero in
tasks: win girl or die, 515–524
Marriage of Mrs. Reynard [Fox],
193–196

Queen bee, The, 317–319
riddle: princess listens to sleep-
ing prince, 128–131
sea-hare: suitor must conceal
self from princess, 769–772
White snake, The, 98–101
—Grimm / Sixty *
Iron Hans, 317–325
King Thrushbeard, 312–316
Marriage of Mrs. Reynard, 288–
291
Queen bee, The, 206–208
White snake, The, 197–201
—Harris-Parks / Again
Miss Wolf (Brer Wolf's niece) and
mosquitoes, 22–29
—Igloo / Metayer
owl-suitor rejected by ptarmigan,
40–41
—Imaginary / Nigg
Hans kills basilisk, wins baker's
daughter, 29–31
—Jewish / Sadeh
prince: multiple "impossible"
tests, 101–105
princess who refused to talk,
106–111
—Lang / Wilkins
Charming wins Goldilocks, 31–43
Heart of ice (Caylus), 190–219
prince saved from fates: croco-
dile, serpent, dog, 485–496
queen poisons stepdaughter's
suitor, 460–473
—Lewis / Proud
Two Lovers Mountain: carry princess to top, 48–52
—Lines / Magical *
Princess Labam, suitor test:
Raja's son helped by ants; ti-
ger, 56–66
—Lore of Love
gods rejected; King Nala and
Princess Damayanti, 110–119

Sir Eglamour and Lady Chrystobel, 128–139
test: bravest wins Ixtaccihuatl,
52–57
—Muddleheads / Harris
Mink Being wants to marry human princess, 5–25
princess rejects arranged marriage, 115–130
—Norwegian / Hodne, 255–267
—Old Wives / Carter
Aunt Kate's goomer-dust causes
mighty breaking of wind, 73–75
giant's daughter aids hero in
tasks required to win her, 76–
85
—Quayle / Shining *
Shining Princess (from Moon
People) and deceptive suitors,
13–23
—Rockwell / Puss *
Dummling: The Golden Goose,
30–39
—Scriven / Full Color *
Golden goose, 61–63
—Spanish-Am / Van Etten *
magician flea: finding three
nights' secret sleeping place,
29–31
must guess what drum is made of
(flea hide), 65–72
—Spring / Philip
king "never heard of this before,"
134–139
princess's veil; father demands
many tests, 75–81
Tibetan envoy wins princess, 42–
49
woman's love: wife rejects series
of suitors, 58–74
—Turkey / Walker, 308 (index)
—Turkish / Walker
porter solves three riddles, wins
sultan's daughter, 91–96

—Turkish (Art I) / Walker
to win beautiful mute, prince must
make her speak, 34–41
—Williams-Ellis / Tales *
master thief: perform three thefts,
win girl, 77–95
SUKKOS (harvest festival)
—Aleichem / Holiday *
boy ruins esrog (citrus) by break-
ing stem; another blamed, 69–
85
incompetent handyman builds
shed; it collapses, 3–16
SULTAN
—Arabian / Lewis
slave girl (Sweet-Friend) and Ali
Nur, 25–34
—Douglas / Magic *
Shahrazad: bring back the most
marvelous, 3–11
—Turkey / Walker, 308 (index)
SUMER
—Dictionary / Leach, 1232 (index)
SUMERIAN TALES
—Wolkstein / Love
Inanna and Dumuzi, 37–71,
264 @
SUMMER
—Fahs / Old *
grizzly vs. coyote on day/season
lengths, 96–99
—Scriven / Full Color *
children find cowslips: Keys of
summer, 41–42
—Unicorn / Coville *
quest for unicorn horn: cure of
winter sickness, 136–155
SUN (*includes origin; often personi-
fied*)
see also CREATION OF HEAV-
ENLY BODIES
—Aesop / Alley *
wind vs. sun: which is stronger?
20–23

—Aesop / Holder *
marriage of the sun, 16–19
—Aesop / Reeves-Wilson *
contest: who is stronger? "Wind
and sun," 88–91
—Allison / I'll Tell *
too much heat—if sun marries
and has children, 113
—Amer Ind / Erdoes, 125–175
—Bell / Classical Dict, 246 @
—Bierhorst / Mexico
religion and mythology, 236 (index)
—Bierhorst / Monkey *
Blue Sun: beheads younger
brother every day; various origins, 107–112
Lord Sun courts woman; succeeds over father's objections,
84–91
—Bierhorst / So Am
Indian religion and mythology,
268 (index)
—Bomans / Wily *
grandmother's spell begets "Sunday child"; gigantic, leaves
earth for sun, 169–173
—Bruchac / Iroquois *
chipmunk ridicules bear, and
pays, 37–39
—Bullchild / Sun
honoring Creator Sun, 325–390
—Caduto / Keepers *
How Grandmother Spider stole
the Sun, 49–50
—Celts / Hodges *
traditional Scottish folk prayer, 84
—Constellations / Gallant * 203 (index)
—Cotterell / Encyclopedia, 258 (index)
—Coyote / Ramsey
brothers become sun and moon,
78–81

sun-box: crows free sun held by
eagle, 71–72
—Curry / Beforetime *
because it's easier, sun rolls on
ground; with help, mole replaces, 89
coyote rides sun (why his back
and tail are dark), 100–106
coyote steals sun and sets it on
course, 10–21
—Dramatized / Kamerman
hare steals sun and foils pursuers, 7–9
—Earthmaker / Mayo * 53 @
Black Elk digs up the mountains
(Apache tale), 18–22
Wahconda makes the earth
shake (Oto tale), 54–56
—Egyptian / Harris, 144 (index)
Hathor: Eye of the sun, 26–33
—Fahs / Old *
Zoroaster: Mazda vs. Manyu,
140–147
—Greaves / Hippo *
giraffe watches over sun; rewarded by Creator, 89
—Greek / Osborne
chariot of the sun god, 1–6
—Hamilton / In the Beginning *
Ananse creation myth, 52–57
Lowa: creation myth, 104–
109
Mawu and Lisa (Fon myth), 42–
45
—Hopi / Talashoma-Malotki
hide and seek with life at stake,
50–69
—Indian Myth / Burland, 143(index)
twins: Nagenatzoni and
Thobadestchin, 97–100
—Jewish / Frankel, 647 (index)
God made sun/moon equal in
brightness; moon wants more,
7–9

sun, wind, and man: which is strongest? 465
—Journey Sun (Chinese)
woman (and newborn son) on 99-year trip to restore sun, 1–5
—Lester / Leopard *
why sun and moon [personified] are in sky, 1–4
—Lurker / Dict Gods, 442 (index)
sun deities/gods, 412 (index)
—MacDonald / Sourcebook *
motif index, 711
—Man Myth & Magic, 3172 (index)
—Maori / Kanawa *
Maui nets sun; frees on promise to go more slowly, 24–26
—Mercatante / Encyclopedia
sun deities/gods, 797 (index)
—Mesoamerican / Leon-P, 293, 298 (index)
—Navajo / Klah creation myths, 77–89
—Old Wives / Carter
woman seeks Golden Sun for information on egg-thief, 4–7
—Polynesians / Andersen, 504 (index)
—Russian / Ivanits, 251 (index)
—Russian Hero / Warner *
foolish man exchanges daughter for help, 57–60
Russian wonder tales, 56 @
sun, frost, wind: honor most powerful, 32
traveler meets sun in her mother's house, 56–57
witch (blood sister) and sun's sister, 60–61
—Shannon / More *
frog wins bet; tho facing west he still sees dawn-rays first, 51–52
—Spring / Philip
wonderful brocade picture: sun-maiden/sun-mountain, 23–34
—Vanishing / Mercer *
how Rabbit (Omaha Indian) caught the sun, 115–117
Juruna people: origin of present order; personification, 22–27
lazy Indian boy and colors in the sun, 112–114
SUNDAY CHILD
—Bomans / Wily *
grandmother's spell begets child; so gigantic, leaves earth for sun, 169–173
SUNJATA
—Legends / Cavendish, 310–312
SUNNIVA
—Yolen / Shape Shift
Dinesen: The sailor-boy's tale, 52–60
Superhuman tasks, see TASKS.
SUPERIORITY COMPLEX
—Grimm / Sixty *
Fox [100 tricks] and the cat, 227–228
SUPERMAN (TV program)
—Rovin / Superheroes, 294–297
SUPERNATURAL, The ("supernaturals")
—Arabian / McCaughrean
Man with three wives, 185–193
—British / Briggs *
eleven tales, 261–273
—Erdoes / Sound *
thunderbirds: four; egg "bigger than S. Dakota," 33–36
—Folk Ballads / McNeil
folk ballads, II.115–159
—Grimm / Complete *
nixie (mill-pond) captures young man; wife rescues, 736–742
Our Lady's Little Glass, 825–826
true bride; prince forgets betrothal, 752–760
—Muddleheads / Harris

Robin Woman and Sawbill Duck Woman, 44–59

sea hunters swallowed by whirl-pool, 26–43

—Navajo Coyote / Haile

chart: the seventeen tales, 11 @

coyote: creator of the Ute people, 14, 59–62

signs of warning: noise in the tra-chea, 14, 55–58

Youngest Brother, 16, 22–24 @, 85–88

—Scandinavian / Kvideland, xix (in-dex); 422 (index)

SUPERSTITION

—American / Read Dgst, 446 (in-dex)

Bayou wisdom, 53

—German-American / Barrick, 168–177

—Limburg / Weird , 92–94

—Plants / Dyer, 262–280

—Precious Stones / Kunz, 1–18 @

—Occult & Parapsych / Shepard, 1–1617 @

SUPERVISION

—Dramatized / Kamerman

wise woman helps man be good overseer, 265–277

SUPREME DEITIES/GODS

—Cotterell / Encyclopedia, 258 (in-dex)

—Mercatante / Encyclopedia, 797 (in-dex)

SURGEON

—Grimm / Complete *

body parts removed; cat eats; other parts substituted; effects, 535–538

SURVIVAL

—Aesop / Reeves-Wilson *

cooperation: Lion, goat, and vul-ture, 74–75

—Allison / I'll Tell *

lion, fox, ass: dividing spoils "equally," 116

—Caduto / Keepers *

diversity of peoples and life forms, 93–95

folly: trap all animals in magic bag, 165–167

—Crossley / Animal (Grimm) *

Bremen Town musicians [natural actions], 54–59

SURYA

—Indic / Ions, 144 (index)

SUTTON HOO

—Scandinavian / Davidson, 143 (in-dex)

SWAHILI TALE

—Lang / Wilkins

Nunda, eater of people, 602–614

SWALLOWED-ALIVE

—Bierhorst / Naked *

Whirlwinds vs. Stone Coats, 19–23

—Clouston / Popular

men swallowed by monster fish, I.403–411

—Coyote / Ramsey

coyote vs. monster, 9–12

—Greaves / Hippo *

elephant vs. Rain Spirit: who is greater, 53–58

—Grimm / Complete *

Tom Thumb, 187–193

Wolf and the seven [goat] kids, 39–42

—Grimm / Sixty *

Tom Thumb, 125–132

Wolf and the seven kids, 202–205

—Gullible Coyote / Malotki

eating watermelons; coyote swal-lows horned lizard, 149–154

—Hamilton / Dark *

Manabozo: manitou hare swal-lowed by king of fishes, 27–31

—Lester / Leopard *
  monster swallows three villages,
  13–15
—Turkish / Walker
  bear tricks (goat) kids; goat gets
  even, 4–7
—Williams-Ellis / Tales *
  great greedy beast eats everything, 177–184
SWALLOWING
—Childcraft 2 / Time *
  old lady who swallowed a fly (folksong) 206–211
—Clarkson / World *
  cat eats enormous quantity: animals, people, etc.; all escape,
  223–225
SWAMP FOX (Francis Marion)
—American / Read Dgst, 95
**SWAN(-s) (-children; -knight;
  -maiden)**
  see also Ugly duckling, The
—Baring-Gould / Curious
  Helias: Knight of the Swan, 146–
  150
  swan-children; Helias: Knight of
  the Swan, 146–150
  swan-maidens: hearts of seven
  Samoyeds, 140–144
—Bell / Classical Dict, 248 @
—Bird Symbol / Rowland, 211 (index)
—Carle / Treasury *
  Wild swans (Andersen), 42–60
—Celts / Hodges *
  swan children restored by St, Pat-
  rick's coming, 5–14
—Douglas / Magic *
  six swans (enchanted princes
  saved by their sister), 35–41
—Dulac / Fairy *
  White Caroline, Black Caroline,
  15–21
—Fairies / Briggs
  swan-maidens, 386–387

—Grimm / Legends (Ward)
  swan-knight, II:452 (index)
—Igloo / Metayer
  contest: swan vs. crane; dancing;
  neck-wrestling, 43–45
—Lore of Love
  King Nala and Princess Damay-
  anti, 110–119
—McGowen / Encyclopedia
  swan-maidens * 52
—O'Brien / Tales *
  swan bride: king's son's quest for
  Scolog's daughter, 82–95
SWARGA
—Indic / Ions, 144 (index)
SWEATBATH
—Hopi Coyote / Malotki
  coyote sheep-killer, duped into
  taking sweatbath; dies, 119–
  125
SWEDEN
—Dictionary / Leach, 1232 (index)
SWEDISH TALES
—Manning / Cauldron *
  donkey, gift of troll-child, helps
  hunter rescue princess, 9–
  17
SWEET-FRIEND
—Arabian / Lewis
  slave girl (Sweet-Friend) and Ali
  Nur, 25–34
Sweet porridge
—Grimm / Complete * 475–476
**Sweetheart (Leprince de
  Beaumont)**
—Carter / Sleeping * 113–124
Sweetheart Roland
—Grimm / Complete * 268–271
—Grimm / Sixty * 156–160
SWIFTNESS
—Bell / Classical Dict, 249 @
Swinburne, Algernon
—Barber / Anthology
  Tristram of Lyonesse, 195–203

SWINDLER(-s)
—Clarkson / World *
    Pedro de Urdemalas sells ever-
    boiling pot, and the like, 293–
    295
—Turkish (Art I) / Walker
    swindlers swindled: sold flute be-
    lieved to restore life, 147–153
SWISS TALE
—Dramatized / Kamerman
    Test for William Tell, 493–503
SWORD(-s)(often magic)
—Bell / Classical Dict, 250–251 @
—Celts / Hodges *
    Excalibur, 156 *
    Merlin: life and magic powers,
    117–132
—Douglas / Magic *
    Merlin and Arthur: the sword,
    141–149
—Grimm / Legends (Ward), II:453 (in-
    dex)
—Hamilton / People *
    Bruh Rabbit: how stop stolen
    hoe? 31–34
—Jewish / Frankel
    Shah, in disguise, tests cobbler's
    faith (wooden sword), 344–346
—Knights / Gross *
    sword in the stone, 7–25
—Knights / Heller-Headon
    description; parts, 22–23
—Legends / Cavendish, 403 (index)
—Lurker / Dict Gods, 442 (index)
—Man Myth & Magic, 3173 (index)
SWORD OF LIGHT
—Fairies / Briggs
    quest: king of Esaidh Ruadh,
    356–359
SWORDSMITH
—Knights / Heller-Headon, 20–21
**Sylvain and Jocosa (befriended by
    fairy)**
—Lang / Wilkins, 178–185

SYMBOL (-ism)
—Hamilton / People *
    He lion, Bruh bear, Bruh rabbit,
    5–12
—Man Myth & Magic
    analytics, 3188–89 (index)
—Persian / Hinnells, 143 (index)
—Schwartz / Gates, 813 (index)
SYNAGOGUE
—Schwartz / Gates, 813 (index)
SYRIA /SYRIAN DEITIES
—Dictionary / Leach, 1232 (index)
—Roman / Perowne, 98 @
SYRINX
—D'Aulaire / Greek * 94

TABLE, MAGIC
—Grimm / Complete *
    magic: wishing-table, gold-ass,
    cudgel in sack, 177–187
—Turkish (Art I) / Walker
    given to simpleton, stolen by
    padishah, recovered, 195–
    198
TABLECLOTH
—Geras / Grandmother *
    rabbi determines owner, 31–40
—Water Buffalo (Chinese)
    innkeeper steals magic donkey,
    tablecloth, stick, 103–110
TABLETS
—Babylonia / Spence, 408 (index)
TABOO (tabu)
    see also:
    DEATH: for BREAKING TABOO
    DRINKING TABOO
    EATING TABOO
    LOOKING TABOO
    NAME TABOO
    OBEDIENCE
    PUNISHMENT for BREAKING
    TABOO

ROOM FORBIDDEN TO ENTER
SECRETS
SPEAKING TABOO
TIME TABOO
TOILET TABOO
TOUCHING TABOO
TRANSFORMATION: for break-
ing taboo
—Baring-Gould / Curious
Melusina: total privacy on Satur-
days, 129–133 @
—Caduto / Keepers *
Awi Usdi: deer and excessive
hunting, 173–174
breaking causes sickness, 173–
174
—Chinese / Chin *
conscripted husband of Meng-
Jiang Nyu, 128–139
—Clarkson / World *
Cherry of Zennor: offending fair-
ies, 129–134
dancing after midnight on Shrove
Tuesday, 214–219
looking into traveling fox's bag,
251–253
Selena Moor: eating in fairyland,
109–111
—Crossley / British FT *
shepherd visits fairyland; breaks
taboo (drinks from well), 248–
250
—Fahs / Old *
Niyak, Umak, and the eagle, 71–
80
—Grimm / Legends (Ward), II:453 (index)
—Igloo / Metayer
punishment: The ghost hunter,
82–91
—Jaffrey / Seasons
Karvachauth: husband dies when
wife breaks taboo; Nine Earth
Mothers, 75–79

—MacDonald / Sourcebook *
motif index, 88–92
—Maori / Kanawa *
woman looks into spring; drowns
village, 85–86
—Muddleheads / Harris
hunter given fortune, must not kill
fish, 26–43
—Old Wives / Carter
wash water, not thrown out, lets
wool spinners in, 211–212
—Palestinian / Speak (Muhawi)
motif-index, 388
—Russian Hero / Warner *
domovoi, living in stove, 29–30
TAHITI
—Hamilton / In the Beginning *
creation myth, 100–103
—Tree / Kerven *
one banyon tree covers moon,
[4–5]
TAIL(-s)
—Baring-Gould / Curious
Tailed men, 62–66 @
—Beat / Bryan *
Raluvhimba: how animals, birds,
fish got tails, 53–70
—Clarkson / World *
how manx cat lost her tail, 329–
331
mouse tries to regain bitten-off
tail, 237–241
—Coyote / Bierhorst *
coyote loses tail, tries to get others to cut tails off, [12]
—Greaves / Hippo *
why dassie has no tail, 122–
124
—Hamilton / People *
give me back my "tailypo," 116–
120
—Hopi Coyote / Malotki
water serpent: coyote fashions
long tail as ruse, 9–21

—MacDonald / Sourcebook *
  motif index, 713
—Russian / Ivanits, 251 (index)
—Turkish / Walker
  magpie spills milk; loses/regains
    tail, 11–13
—Vanishing / Mercer *
  pygmy befriended by monkeys,
    steals fire, 68–70
TAILOR(-s)
—Clouston / Popular
  tailor's dream; cheat; versions,
    II.79–85
—Crossley / British FT *
  Billy: crippled tailor flees ghosts in
    graveyard, 244–246
—Grimm / Complete *
  cunning tailor: riddle, bear, prin-
    cess, 525–528
  four clever brothers, 580–584
  glass coffin; bewitched maid,
    672–678
  stupid giant conned by boastful
    tailor's "power," 745–747
  tailor overcomes evil shoemaker,
    386–496
  tailor throws footstool from
    heaven, 175–177
  valiant tailor (seven at one blow),
    112–120
—Grimm / Sixty *
  four clever brothers, 220–234
  valiant tailor, 88–97
—Jewish / Frankel
  tailor's sleeve: divorce, 521–523
—Jewish / Sadeh
  impious tailor trades clothes with
    pauper, 337
  two tailors and wonderful photo-
    graph, 204–208
—MacDonald / Sourcebook *
  motif index, 713
—Russian Hero / Warner *
  leshii as assistant, 25

Tailor in heaven
—Grimm / Complete * 175–177
TALE TITLE INDEX
—MacDonald / Sourcebook *
  motif index, 393–555
TALEBEARER
—Caduto / Keepers *
  how Coyote was the Moon, 111
TALENT(-s)
—Aesop / Holder *
  hare vs. tortoise: compensating,
    with perseverance, 22–23
—Grimm / Complete *
  Eve's various children: God be-
    stows blessings unequally,
    734–736
—Grimm / Sixty *
  Fox [100 tricks] and the cat, 227–
    228
—Leonardo / Fables *
  razor: escapes, loafs, rusts, 54
—Paxton / Aesop *
  gratitude: lion spares mouse;
    mouse frees lion from net, [19–
    21]
TALES: bibliographies, etc.
see BIBLIOGRAPHY; REFERENCE
  BOOKS.
Tales of the paddock
—Grimm / Complete * 480–482
TALISMAN
—Precious Stones / Kunz, 19–
    114 @
  engraved/carved gems, 115–
    142 @
—Witch Encyc / Guiley, 420 (index)
Talk (by yam, dog, tree, stone, etc.)
—Clarkson / World * 229–232
TALK(-ing)
  see also TONGUE
—Old Coot / Christian *
  the auguring match (talking con-
    test), 41–56
—Turkish (Art I) / Walker

510

to win beautiful mute, prince must make her speak, 34–41

TALKING ANIMAL(-s)

see also ANIMAL-HUMAN COMMUNICATION

—Arabian / McCaughrean
donkey advises ox to feign illness, 104–107

—Bryan / Lion *
Jackal's favorite game, 40–59
lion steals ostrich chicks, 3–23

—Celts / Hodges *
swan children of Lir, 5–14

—Chaucer / Cohen *
nun's tale: Chauntecleer and Pertelote, 19–31

—Chinese / Chin *
cowherd's marriage to fairy weaving maid, 113–125

—Clarkson / World *
talk (by yam, dog, tree, stone, etc.), 229–232

—Crossley / Animal (Grimm) *
fox and cat; arrogance and modesty, 8–10

—Grimm / Complete *
Good bargain: peasant thinks frog and dog are speaking, 51–55
Three languages, The, 169–171
Three sluggards, 647
White snake, The, 98–101

—Grimm / Sixty *
Three languages, The, 223–226
White snake, The, 197–201

—Hamilton / People *
cooter refuses to talk; master frees slave, 155–155
He lion, Bruh bear, Bruh rabbit, 5–12

—Jones / Tales *
Chicken Licken, 16–20

—Lynn / Fantasy *
annotated bibliography, 67–103

—Quayle / Shining *
white hare tricks crocodiles; revenge; kind prince heals hare, 24–32

—Scriven / Full Color *
organ grinder's monkey; spider; forced dance, 29–33

—Vietnam / Terada *
unusual food: rice cakes for New Year, 105–108

—Yolen / Faery Flag
wolves retell three tales, 103–119

TALL TALES

see also BUNYAN, Paul; FINN Mac COOL; PECOS BILL; etc.

—American / Read Dgst, 446 (index)
mountain men (U.S.), 178–180

—Brown / Amer Folklore, 1–168 @
bibliography, 153–163
colloquial style, 122–127 @
contexts and functions, 31–38 @
definition, 11 @
Sut Lovingood, 74–88 @
the texts, the telling, 17–31 @
written; varieties, 39–73 @

—Bruchac / Iroquois *
four Iroquois hunters; contest, 156–159

—Childcraft 3 / Stories *
Tony Beaver: how it snowed fur and rained fry cakes, 199–201

—Coyote / Ramsey
Tillamook man lives with Thunderer, 140–144

—Crockett Almanacs
facsimile ed., including fifty-three tales, 1–116

—Davy Crockett / Dewey * 1–48

—Dramatized / Kamerman
Big Paul Bunyan; Babe, the blue ox, 514–525

—Erdoes / Sound *
man outruns bullet, 71

—Grimm / Complete *
thumbling nursed by giant acquires fabulous strength, 412–420
—Hamilton / People *
fast horse; fast-growing pumpkin/turnip, 76–80
other terms for, 80 @
—Irish / Glassie
eight tales, 103–114
—Mex-Am / West, 111–115
Don Gregorio dives into bull to escape Apaches, 113–115
—Norwegian / Hodne
tales of lying, 298–314
—Pecos Bill / Dewey * 1–56
—Pecos Bill / Kellogg * 1–40
—Shannon / More *
stranger wins bet on "believing" tall tales, 53–56
—Tall Tales / Downs: Bear
American animals, 1–358
turkey-buzzard flies off with mule, 40–44
—Turkey / Walker, 308 (index)
—Turkish (Art I) / Walker
Tekerleme; how field came to be, and was harvested, 11
—Williams-Ellis / Tales *
monkeys steal forty-nine nightcaps, 173–174
—Yep / Rainbow *
Wong I, II and III: The boasting contest, 96–105

TALMUD
—Clouston / Popular, II.514 (index)
—Jewish / Frankel, xi-xii (index)
—Schwartz / Gates, 813 (index)

TAM LIN
—Celts / Hodges *
freed from evil spell by love, 76–83

Tam Lin (poem)
—Crossley / British FT * 270–282

TAMA (god)
—Maori / Kanawa *
birth; found on shore, wrapped in mother's hair, 12–16

TAMERLANE (Emperor)
—Turkish / Walker
Nasreddin Hoca; two tales, 37–47

TAMLANE
—Fairies / Briggs, 449–453

TAMMUZ
—Babylonia / Spence, 409 (index)

TANE-MAHUTA
—Polynesians / Andersen, 506 (index)

TANGAROA (deity)
—Polynesians / Andersen, 506 (index)
creation myths, 349–402
Taniwah (dragon) of Rotorua trapped/killed, 52–60

TANNHAUSER
—Baring-Gould / Curious
Mountain of Venus, 78–82 @

TANUKI
—Hamilton / Dark *
Bumbuku, the tanuki magic tea-kettle, 76–81

TAOISM
—Dictionary / Leach, 1233 (index)

Tappin, *see* TERRAPIN.

TAR BABY
—Hamilton / People *
Bruh Fox makes Tar Baby; rabbit gets stuck, 13–19
tale variants (some 300), 19 @
—Harris-Parks / Again, 6–13
—Lester / Brer Rabbit * 10–16

TARA
—Ellis / Dict Irish Myth, 217–219
—Celtic / MacCana, 143 (index)

TARAHUMARA
—Dictionary / Leach, 1217 (index)

TARASQUE
—Dragons / Baskin * [34–35]
—McGowen / Encyclopedia * 53

TAROT
—Man Myth & Magic, 3173 (index)
—Witch Encyc / Guiley, 420 (index)
—Woman's Ency / Walker, 976–
 983 @
TARQUIN the Proud
—Roman / Usher, 96–104 @
TARTAR TALES
—Clouston / Popular, II.514 (index)
TARZAN
—Rovin / Superheroes
 mass media, 305–308
**TASK(-s) (often "impossi-
 ble")(many done with
 "help")**
 see also individual tales, e.g.,
 Rumpelstiltskin
—Arabian / Lewis
 arrows shot; princess loved by
 cousins (three brothers), 174–
 183
 test for succession: prince marries tortoise, 43–51
 well's magic objects do "impossible" tasks, 117–122
—Arabian / McCaughrean
 test for succession, 142–149
—Bierhorst / Monkey *
 bad compadre oft exploits Juan;
 animals perform his impossible
 tasks, 94–106
 bird bride: toad helps youngest
 son re oft-ruined cornfield, 25–
 31
 with help of giant's daughter,
 young man does four impossible tasks, 56–65
 youngest son, lazy Tup, gets ants
 to clear/plant/harvest cornfield,
 44–51
—Bomans / Wily *
 balloon message; with godmother's help, knight kills
 dragon, 197–202

 three riddles; win princess;
 fearless woodcutter, 202–
 204
—Celts / Hodges *
 Cuchulain: champion of Ireland,
 17–31
 Gareth of Orkney wins his spurs,
 133–154
—Chaucer / Cohen *
 wife of Bath: what do women
 want most, 55–63
—Chinese / Chin *
 clever daughter-in-law, 3–14
—Clarkson / World *
 clever Manka (solves riddles;
 problem-tasks), 93–95
—Clouston / Popular
 Beryn in Falsetown, II.99–114,
 478–480
—Corrin / Eight-Year *
 Bash Tshelik, man of steel, 120–
 133
—Corrin / Favourite *
 true wife "buys" three nights with
 husband (East of the sun), 1–
 15
—Corrin / Imagine *
 Black Thief: quest for King
 Conal's horses, 97–111
—Corrin / Six-Year *
 Silly Simon (foolishly carries donkey; makes girl laugh), 120–
 124
—Coyote / Ramsey
 Kalapuya boy and seven-headed
 snake, 112–117
—Crossley / Animal (Grimm) *
 fox helps old horse, 34–38
—Crossley / British FT *
 fool and mule follow gold/tur-
 quoise bird, 295–303
 giant's daughter helps prince escape death, 313–330
—Douglas / Magic *

Ahmad: bring back the most marvelous, 3–11

golden apples of immortality, 177–179

help in tasks: Cupid and Psyche, 151–165

white cat; find the best: dog, cloth, princess, 69–83

—Dulac / Fairy *

boy-suitor gathers six helpers: the seven conquerors, 22–28

—Egyptian / Harris

Hathor: return to Eye of the sun, 26–33

Wenamon: build sacred boat for Amon-Ra, 117–125

—Ghosts / Starkey

Dauntless girl; ghost reveals treasure, 72–79

Jack Mackintosh: no cock crows, no horns, 88–95

pact with devil; hammer curly hair straight, 8–15

—Greek / Osborne

Cupid and Psyche: the four tasks, 57–65

—Grimm / Complete *

animals help youngest brother: Queen bee, The, 317–319

cat (princess) gives horse to miller's apprentice, 482–485

catch Golden Bird, apple thief, 272–279

drummer rescues princess from glass mountain, 781–791

fox helps horse trick lion, 595–596

griffin: suitor's tasks to win princess, 681–688

iron stove: princess frees prince; breaks tabu, 571–577

kings' daughters aid hero in tasks: win girl or die, 515–524

master-thief given three tasks, 773–780

tailor overcomes evil shoemaker, 386–396

three spinners help attain bride's mother's boast, 83–86

two travellers: tailor and shoemaker, 386–496

youth who could not shudder, 29–39

—Grimm / Sixty *

animals help youngest brother: Queen bee, The, 206–208

catch Golden Bird, apple thief, 1–9

fox helps horse trick lion, 241–243

youth who could not shudder, 300–311

—Hamilton / Dark *

Baba Yaga, Vasilisa, and her doll, 14–22

horned women: twelve witches vs. Spirit of the Well, 32–37

Perseus' task: behead Medusa, 43–48

—Hamilton / People *

Devil's daughter helps John de Conquer, 107–114

Manuel's riddle; fills sack with lies; fortune, 65–75

—Hoke / Giants

giant, no heart in his body, 93–102

Hercules and the golden apples, 130–132

Strong Gottlieb, 103–111

—Imaginary / Nigg

bring elixir of the gods; the garuda, 73–75

Hans kills basilisk, wins baker's daughter, 29–31

—Jewish / Frankel

missing ruble: man sent for jew-

els brings deserting husband,
509–514

scorpion in goblet: virtuous rabbi
rewarded, 437–446

—Jewish / Sadeh
king must empty well with bottom-
less bucket, or else, 239–241

make princess talk, 111–112

nightingale; queen gives birth to
animals, 25–28

—Journey Sun (Chinese)
cruel stepmother, false wife,
ghost, 6–23

Yangang saves village incinerated by shooting star, 47–60

—Lang / Wilkins
Charming wins Goldilocks, 31–43

Grateful prince: girl helps hero
escape old man, 394–414

Princess in the chest; faithful
guard, 369–384

—Lester / Brer Rabbit *
capture Brer Squirrel, 148–149

capture Mr. Snake, 149–150

—Lester / Leopard *
body parts argue: which is most
important, 45–51

—Lines / Magical *
Ian Direach to bring the blue falcon, 45–55

—Lore of Love
sculptor carves palace (solid
rock) for princess, 79–83

Sir Eglamour: ogre Maroc, giant
boar, dragon, 128–139

—Manning / Cauldron *
amber witch: common man, loved
by princess, sent to get amber,
18–31

crusader beaten, robbed by comrades; witches reveal secrets,
= reversal, 46–57

donkey, gift of troll-child, helps
hunter rescue princess, 9–17

—Nesbit / Fairy *
Belinda: find bell not made to
ring, 101–122

Bellamant: stay underwater for
five minutes, 101–122

—O'Brien / Tales *
Amada defeats giants (who daily
return to life) and a series of
monsters, 21–30

Eamonn: bring flail (keeps Danes
away) from hell, 38–43

goatskin-clad Eamonn: make
princess laugh (succeeds), 38–
43

Lord Mount Dhraggin: weaver
"kills" three-score and ten, 72–
81

swan bride: king's son's quest for
Scolog's daughter, 82–95

—Oral Trad / Cunningham
small boy (Willy) traps wild hog,
kills bull and three giants, 65–
68

—Russian / Afanasev, 661 (index)

—Russian Hero / Warner *
magic doll helps Vasilisa escape
Baba-Yaga, 86–92

three princes/brides, one a frog-
princess, 101–106

wolf helps quest; warnings ignored, 112–116

—Scriven / Full Color *
Rumpelstiltskin, 13–15

—Shah / Central Asia
bead-seller and the jinn's sister,
62–68

kill lion: cobbler's son and serpent
(enchanted princess), 109–
117

seven-day-old baby, story to
king, 62–68

—Shannon / More *
buy one thing and fill four different needs [watermelon], 15–18

—Spanish-Am / Van Etten *
 doctor, rancher, sheepherder
  (winner) try to drive out skunk,
  101–105
—Spring / Philip
 golden fish rewards kindness,
  103–113
 princess's veil; father demands
  many tests, 75–81
—Starkey / Ghosts
 Tregeagle's ghost, 58–65
—Tibet / Timpanelli *
 evil helper takes real daughter's
  place, 15–27
—Trolls / Asbjornsen
 Askelad and the silverducks, 11–
  16
 boy who became lion, falcon, ant,
  64–70
 cut oak; provide year-around water well, 36–40
 Rumble-Mumble Goose-Egg,
  71–82
 seven foals (princes under
  spells); task: watch, report, behead, 53–59
 stepsisters: one kind, one cruel;
  escape service of witch, 42–50
—Turkey / Walker, 308 (index)
—Turkish / Walker
 Karacor and the giants, 52–61
 princess marries pig (prince under spell), 114–117
—Turkish (Art I) / Walker
 Cengidilaver: hero aided by jinn,
  1–10
 father (lusting for son's wife)
  gives him three "impossible"
  tasks, 172–176
 to cure ruler, Camesap eats part
  of Sahmeran, learns language
  of plants, 218–224
 to win beautiful mute, prince must
  make her speak, 34–41

 youngest son aided in quest by
  nine-headed female giant,
  230–239
—Vietnam / Terada *
 unusual food: rice cakes for New
  Year, 105–108
—Williams-Ellis / Tales *
 carry water in sieve; Well of the
  World's End, 55–61
 Tom-Tit-Tot spins skeins for girl,
  185–195
—Witches / Iosa *
 animals help kind children escape giant witch, 18–22
 brothers envious of Pinkel's favor
  with king, 23–31
—Yep / Rainbow *
 building "Breaker's bridge," 118–
  123

TATA JUAN PESCADOR
—Mex-Am / West, 104–105
TATTERCOATS
—Hepburn / World *
 gooseherd plays flute; prince falls
  in love, 90–109
TATTLETALE
—Lester / Brer Rabbit *
 Mr. Jack Sparrow meets his end,
  35–37
TATTOO
—Hamilton / In the Beginning *
 Lowa: creation myth, 108
—Maori / Kanawa *
 Mataora, warrior chief, meets un-
  derworld Turehu, 68–80
—Polynesians / Andersen, 507 (in-
  dex)
Tawhaki cycle
—Polynesians / Andersen, 157–191
TAX COLLECTOR
—Turkish / Walker
 Hoca: tax collector keeps records
  on pastries, 45–46
Taylor, Keith

—Pendragon / Ashley
Buried silver, 227–259
Te . . . [Polynesian names: *see* word
after "Te" . . .]
TEACH, Edward (d.1718)
—Southern [legends] / Floyd
Blackbeard the Pirate, 154–161
TEACHER AND PUPIL
—Erdoes / Sound *
White Buffalo Woman (Lakota),
117–123
TEAKETTLE
—Chorao / Child's *
teakettle turns into badger, 21–27
—Hamilton / Dark *
Bumbuku, the tanuki magic tea-
kettle, 76–81
TEAMWORK
—Yep / Rainbow *
Virtue goes to town, 118–123
TEARS
—Grimm / Complete *
goose-girl at well; princess weeps
pearls, 725–734
TEED, Cyrus Read
—Southern [legends] / Floyd
theory: Earth a concave sphere,
21–23
Teeny-tiny
—Corrin / Six-Year * 42–44
—Hall / Treasury * 13–16
—Turkish / Walker
Teeny-Tiny and Witch-Woman,
49–51
TEFNUT (Egyptian)
—Wolkstein / Love, 255 @
Tekerleme
—Turkish (Art I) / Walker, 11
TELL, William
—Baring-Gould / Curious
versions and variations, 50–54
—Dramatized / Kamerman
Test: shoot apple off son's head,
493–503

TEMPER
—Maori / Kanawa *
Rona screams at moon, is
snatched up to moon's surface,
102–104
TEMPLE
—Babylonia / Spence, 409 (index)
—Jewish / Frankel, 651 (index)
—Schwartz / Gates, 813 (index)
TEMPTATION
—Vietnam / Terada *
scholar (Do Be) offends temple
god, 42–49
TENGU
—Japanese / Tyler, 340 (index)
—McGowen / Encyclopedia * 53–54
TENNESSEE
—Southern [legends] / Floyd
lost sea, 64–67
Rugby colony: Thomas Hughes,
50–54
Tennyson, Alfred (1809–1892)
—Barber / Anthology
Idylls of the King, 169–184
TEOTIHUACAN
—Mesoamerican / Leon-P, 294 (in-
dex)
TERRAPIN
see also TORTOISE; TURTLE
—Hamilton / People *
Tappin: how turtle got marks on
back, 20–25
—Harris-Parks / Jump *
Brer Terrapin "wins" race with
Brer Rabbit, 19–24
moon in millpond: Brers Rabbit
and Terrapin play trick, 35–38
TERRITORIAL CLAIM
—Bruchac / Iroquois *
turtle's race with beaver, 47–49
TERRYTOP
—Quayle / Cornish *
Duffy's pact: devil to do her spin-
ning, 75–87

TEST(-s)
see also BRIDE; CONTEST;
MARRIAGE; SUITOR;
VIGILANCE; WIFE [tests]
—Celts / Hodges *
prowess: Cuchulain, champion of
Ireland, 17–31
—Crossley / Animal (Grimm) *
endurance: Hedge-King [choos-
ing king of birds], 15–20
—Douglas / Magic *
Merlin and Arthur: the sword,
141–149
—Dramatized / Kamerman
shoot apple off son's head, 493–
503
—Ghosts / Starkey
bugganes; stay in frightful place,
16–23
—Jewish / Frankel, 651 (index)
—Jewish / Sadeh
master thief, 291–295
—Lester / Leopard *
contest: how many spots does
leopard have? 53–57
—MacDonald / Sourcebook *
motif index, 172–206
—Mex-Am / West
motif index, 299
—Palestinian / Speak (Muhawi)
motif-index, 393–394
—Paxton / Belling *
honesty is the best policy
(Aesop's "lost ax"), [24–27]
—Shah / Central Asia
loyalty: nobleman and slave (later
king), 103–108
—Shannon / More *
cock crow in kettle: clean hand
reveals thief, 31–34
—Tibet / Timpanelli *
unwilling "seer": reputation made
by luck/coincidence, 29–41
—Turkish (Art I) / Walker

stonecutter: dervish-thieves re-
vealed in court of discernment,
72–80
—Williams-Ellis / Tales *
master thief: perform three thefts
to win girl, 77–95
—Yep / Rainbow *
courage: stay in haunted house:
boasting contest, 96–105
TET
—Vietnam / Terada *
unusual food: rice cakes for New
Year, 105–108
TETRAGAMMETON
—Jewish / Sadeh
Rabbi Joseph de la Reina; fight
against Samael, 233–237
TEUTONS
—Dictionary / Leach, 1233 (index)
TEXAS
—American / Read Dgst, 167–173
—Jameson / Buried
legendary lost mines, gold, etc.,
157–216
—Southern [legends] / Floyd
Virgin Mary in Lubbock (1988),
100–103
—Tall Tales / Downs: Bear
six tales, 145–178
TEZCATLIPOCA
—Hamilton / Dark *
pretender: sacrificed, after year
of high living, 60–64
**Thackeray, William Makepeace
(1811–1863)**
—Victorian / Hearn
Rose and the ring, The, 36–105
Thane, Adele
—Dramatized / Kamerman
Baker's neighbor, 471–480
Big Paul Bunyan; Babe, the blue
ox, 514–525
A gift for Hans Brinker, 200–211
King who was bored, 334–345

Merry Tyll and the three rogues, 162–176

"THANKS BE TO GOD" (expression)
—Spanish-Am / Van Etten *
start/stop monastery mare; farmer starts, at edge of cliff, 44–47

THANKSGIVING DAY
—Gobble / Graham-Barber *
related words; etymology, 1–122

THEBES
—Egyptian / Harris, 132 (index)
—Egyptian / Ions, 144 (index)

Theft, *see* THIEF . . .

THEOPHILUS
—Baring-Gould / Curious
priest (6th cent.) slandered, deposed, restored, 156–159 @

THESEUS
—Gods / Schwab, 206–230
—Greek / Switzer, 207 (index)
—Grimal / Dictionary, 601 (index)

THETIS
—Lore of Love
A Groom for the sea-lord's daughter, 8–15

THIEF (incl. theft; thievery)
see also RESTITUTION
also individual tales,
e.g. Ali Baba . . . ; Jack and the beanstalk
—Arabian / McCaughrean
thief pretends to be ass under spell, 150–152
—Bomans / Wily *
hunter spares deer, swan, raven; saves man accused of theft, 16–19
—Cambodian / Carrison
Princess Amaradevi: husband accused of treachery, 23–30
series of thefts; cheater cheated, 58–64

woman tricked, endanger baby, then robbed, 31–35
—Campbell / West Highlands
Shifty Lad, I.330–354
—Clarkson / World *
cat, etc., attack thieves in dark, drive them away, 154–156
golden arm: return from dead to punish husband-thief, 194–195
ogre: Molly Whuppie steals sword, purse, ring, 54–56
stolen pig disguised as baby in crib, 286–288
—Clouston / Popular
clever thief tales: cobbler and calf, etc., II.43–52
robbery of king's treasury; versions, II.115–165, 480–488
—Corrin / Imagine *
Black Thief: quest for King Conal's horses, 97–111
goldsmith steals woodcarver-friend's gold; woodcarver "turns" goldsmith's children into bears, 23–46
—Coyote / Bierhorst *
blind woman cured, but coyote steals all her possessions, [28]
—Crane / Beauty *
fairy: Yellow Dwarf and proud princess, [34–47]
—Crossley / Animal (Grimm) *
cat/mouse partnership, 21–25
—Crossley / British FT *
piper cuts off feet of frozen corpse, to steal shoes, 283–286
—Dramatized / Kamerman
covetous councilman tricked; returns gold, 504–513
olive jar; steals gold, 360–374
Lady Moon and the thief, 23–31
—Egyptian / Harris

clever thief: treasure of
Rhumpsinitus, 114–116
—Erdoes / Sound *
ghost (Indian foils would-be rob-
bers of dead man), 82–85
—Fahs / Old *
stolen drum to dance by, 86–90
—Grimm / Complete *
Four clever brothers, 580–584
master thief: boy deceives/kills
his teacher, 337–338
master-thief given three tasks,
773–780
tailor throws footstool from
heaven, 175–177
—Grimm / Sixty *
Doctor Know-All [discovers
thieves], 281–283
Four clever brothers, 220–234
—Hamilton / People *
Bruh Rabbit: how stop stolen
magic hoe? 31–34
—Harris-Parks / Again
Brers Mink-Possum-Coon-Fox-
Bear guard butter, 14–21
—High John / Sanfield *
caught killing sheep, pretends
self-defense, 19–22
John in court ("owned wagon
since it was wheelbarrow"),
85–88
overhears the Lord and Devil "dividing up souls," 44–49
stolen piglet, "just possum," 14–
18
—Japanese / Tyler, 340 (index)
—Jewish / Frankel
dim-witted boy buys box of bones
(etc., chain tale), 414–418
—Jewish / Sadeh
detected by magic, 22–25
exposed by psychology, 318
learning wisdom from (seven
ways), 363

master thief, 291–295
pious thief saves king's life, 262–
263
poor man and thieving ministers,
264–266
rich man will pay to say: I don't
believe in God, 324–326
—Lang / Wilkins
Nunda, eater of people, 602–614
—Lines / Magical *
North Wind gifts: innkeeper
steals stick, which beats him,
66–70
—MacDonald / Sourcebook *
motif index, 271–280, 716
—Manning / Cauldron *
her cat advises witch: make self
invisible to steal farmer's eggs,
32–38
—Old Wives / Carter
Maol a Chliobain repeatedly gets
better of giant, 24–27
—Pellowski / Story *
string-story: farmer and yams, 9–
15
—Russian Hero / Warner *
cock and the corn mill, 52–53
no bigger than a finger, 128–129
—Scandinavian / Kvideland, xviii, 427
(index)
—Shannon / More *
banker denies having received
money Brahman entrusted to
him, 39–42
cock crow in kettle: clean hand
reveals thief, 31–34
students outwit king's ruse for ex-
posing thief, 47–50
—Spring / Philip
wise king exposes gold thief, 50–
57
—Tibet / Timpanelli *
unwilling "seer": reputation made
by luck/coincidence, 29–41

—Tree / Kerven *
    Elder Tree Witch steals milk;
      burnt by Granny, [14–15]
—Trolls / Asbjornsen
    cleverness: Askelad and the sil-
      verducks, 11–16
—Turkish / Walker
    boys steal hoca (teacher) saddle-
      bags, 36
    Deli feigns death, frightens
      thieves, gets reward, 80–84
    foolish parents give con man gifts
      for dead son, 85–87
    Hasan, the heroic mouse-child,
      8–10
    pretense: three tricksters "steal"
      pot of butter, 88–90
—Turkish (Art I) / Walker
    simpleton recovers three magic
      objects from padishah-thief,
      195–198
    stonecutter: dervish-thieves re-
      vealed in court of discernment,
      72–80
—Unicorn / Coville *
    stealing water touched by uni-
      corn horn, to cure sick friend,
      7–22
—Water Buffalo (Chinese)
    innkeeper steals magic donkey,
      table cloth, stick, 103–110
—Williams-Ellis / Tales *
    master thief: perform three thefts,
      win girl, 77–95
Thief and his master
—Grimm / Complete * 337–338
THISBE
—Lore of Love
    doomed trysts: Apollo; Pyramus,
      77
THOMAS, Vivia (d. 1870)
—Classic / Downer, 178–180
THOMAS the Rhymer
—Fairies / Briggs, 394–395

THOR
—Hoke / Giants
    battle with King of the Giants,
      119–129
—Norse / Crossley, 275 (index)
—Scandinavian / Davidson
    sky god, 59–71, 144 (index)
THORNBUSH
—Jewish / Frankel
    Moses and the burning bush,
      107–109
THORNS
—Grimm / Complete *
    magic fiddle makes everyone
      dance, 503–508
—Grimm / Sixty *
    magic fiddle . . . , 182–189
THOTH (deity)
—Egyptian / Harris, 132 (index)
    Hathor: transformed to baboon,
      26–33
—Egyptian / Ions, 144 (index)
—Egyptian / Mercatante, 189–190
—Wolkstein / Love, 255 @
THOUGHT
—Bomans / Wily *
    personification: chest (casket
      symbol) and the student, 193–
      196
—Scandinavian / Kvideland
    changing someone's mind, vii (in-
      dex)
    powers of, vii (index)
THREAT
—Beat / Bryan *
    call cat: frog threatens hen; hawk
      gets frog, 3–13
THREE (number)
—Man Myth & Magic, 3174 (index)
Three apprentices, The
—Grimm / Complete * 542–545
Three army surgeons, The
—Grimm / Complete * 535–538
Three bears, see Goldilocks . . .

Three bears (Southey)
—Corrin / Six-Year * 70–73
Three billy goats Gruff, The
—Allison / I'll Tell * 12–13
—Childcraft 1 / Once * 87–88
—Douglas / Magic * 119–121
—Hall / Treasury * 66–67
—Jones / Tales * 42–44
Three black princesses, The
—Grimm / Complete * 620–621
Three brothers (Grimm)
—Corrin / Six-Year * 45–48
Three brothers: barber, black-smith, fencing master
—Grimm / Complete * 561–62
Three feathers
—Grimm / Complete * 319–322
Three green twigs
—Grimm / Complete * 823–825
Three heads of the well
—Crossley / British FT * 28–35
Three languages, The
—Grimm / Complete * 169–171
—Grimm / Sixty * 223–226
Three little birds (Grimm)
—Grimm / Complete * 445–449
Three little kittens
—Allison / I'll Tell * 85
Three little men in the wood
—Grimm / Complete * 78–83
Three little pigs
—Allison / I'll Tell * 20–21
—Yolen / Faery Flag
  retelling in "old wolves' home,"
  103–119
Three little pigs (*existential retelling*)
—Switzer / Existential, 93–101
Three measures of salt
—Old Wives / Carter, 66–71
Three sillies [foolish worry]
—Corrin / Favourite * 192–196
Three sluggards
—Grimm / Complete * 647
Three snake-leaves

—Grimm / Complete * 94–96
Three sons of fortune (trade for gold)
—Grimm / Complete * 342–344
Three spinners
—Grimm / Complete * 83–86
Three wishes [pudding, or sausage, on nose]
—Corrin / Favourite * 122–124
—Corrin / Six-Year * 59–61
THRESHER
—Quayle / Cornish *
  piskie threshers; leave after gift of
  suits of clothes, 45–50
THRIFT
—Hoke / Giants
  Managing-Molly outwits courting
  ogre, 65–70
Thumb, Tom, *see* Tom Thumb.
Thumbelina
—Allison / I'll Tell * 54–56
—Corrin / Favourite * 107–121
—Douglas / Magic * 43–53
—Lang / Wilkins, 305–316
THUMBLING (thumb-sized person)
—Grimm / Complete *
  thumbling nursed by giant ac-
  quires fabulous strength, 412–
  420
—MacDonald / Sourcebook *
  motif index, 144–145
THUMB-PIANO STORIES
—Pellowski / Story * 103–110
THUMB-SIZED . . .
  see also Tom Thumb.
—Bierhorst / Naked *
  Lodge Boy and Thrown Away
  [chipmunk-sized boy], 79–86
—Grimm / Complete *
  blue light summons tiny servant,
  530–534
—Grimm / Sixty *
  blue light summons tiny servant,
  244–249

—Hall / Treasury *
 Teeny-tiny, 13–16
—Hamilton / Dark *
 One-Inch boy, the demon oni,
 and the princess, 23–26
—Russian Hero / Warner *
 No Bigger than a Finger, 128–
 129
—Turkish / Walker
 Hasan, the heroic mouse-child,
 8–10
THUNDER
—Bruchac / Iroquois *
 Heno, the Thunderer (grandfa-
 ther rescuer), 123–127
 wife of Thunderer, 146–154
—Caduto / Keepers *
 how Thunder and Earthquake
 made Ocean, 93–95
—Coyote / Ramsey
 defeated (wrestling) by boy; ban-
 ished, 195–200
—Earthmaker / Mayo *
 how thunder and lightning came
 (Puget Sound tale), 34–36
 origins, 33 @
—Indian Myth / Burland, 143(in-
 dex)
 earth and sky spirits, 69–71
—Man Myth & Magic, 3175 (index)
—Mercatante / Encyclopedia, 800 (index)
—Russian / Ivanits, 251 (index)
—Sioux / Standing Bear *
 Thunder Dreamer, the medicine
 man, 41–43
 Thunder Horse leaves hoofprint
 in rock, 75–76
THUNDER GODS
—Mercatante / Encyclopedia, 800 (index)
—Vietnam / Terada *
 squash seeds: origin of Dao Peo-
 ple, 54–58

Thunderbird, *see under* BIRDS:
 MYTHICAL.
THUNDERERS
—Bierhorst / Naked *
 Lodge Boy and Thrown Away
 [chipmunk-sized boy], 79–86
Thurber, James (1894–1961)
—Hoke / Giants
 The great quillow, 41–64
TIAMAT
—Dragons / Baskin * [8–9]
—Hamilton / In the Beginning *
 Marduk, god of gods, 78–85
TIAWATH
—Babylonia / Spence, 409 (index)
TIBER RIVER
—Roman / Usher, 132 (index)
TIBET(-an) (-an tales)
—Creatures (illus) / Huber * 100–108
—Dictionary / Leach, 1233 (index)
—Legends / Cavendish, 5 (index)
—Lore of Love
 trees with interwoven branches:
 tragic love, 122–127
—Tibet / Timpanelli * 1–53
TIDDY MUN
—Fairies / Briggs, 395–398
Tiddy Mun, marsh spirit
—Crossley / Dead * 65–70
TIDE
—Caduto / Keepers *
 how Raven made the tides, 103
—Lore of Love
 ill-starred mating of earth and
 sea, 87–95
TIGER(-s)
—Animal Legends / Kerven *
 Anansi: how tiger and monkey
 both escaped, [28–29]
—Animals / Rowland, 191 (index)
—Clarkson / World *
 judge: tiger cured of snakebite
 threatens to eat man, 309–312
—Dramatized / Kamerman

deception: Tiger, brahman, and jackal, 212–217
tiger does work of ox he killed, 32–37
—Hall / Treasury *
Little Black Sambo, 68–76
—Journeys / Norris *
tiger-servant: journey to hell/heaven and back, [26–28]
—Lester / Brer Rabbit *
with Brer Elephant's help, causes Brer Tiger to leave area, 62–65
—Lines / Magical *
Princess Labam, suitor test: Raja's son helped by ants; tiger, 56–66
—MacDonald / Sourcebook *
motif index, 718
—Manning / Cats *
baby wrens lie; father wren "scares off" King Tiger, 124–125
—Scary / Young *
tiger's eyes: it eats man, puts on his clothes, eats wife, 73–77
—Vietnam / Terada *
Mister Thirty: tiger remorseful after killing man, 18–22
rope burns: how tiger got its stripes, 7–9
—Water Buffalo (Chinese)
cat teaches tiger, but not how to climb trees, 78–81
water-buffalo vs. tiger, 85–88
woman's coin keeps rice-jar full; tiger would steal, 55–61
—Yolen / Baby Bear *
tiger meets other animals (in this book), looking for name, [26–31]

TIIKUYWUUTI
—Hopi / Talashoma-Malotki
hide and seek with life at stake, 50–69, 208 @

Till Eulenspiegel, *see* EULENSPIEGEL, Till.
TIME (*incl. magic passage of*)
—Arabian / McCaughrean
old fox and crow as hunting partner, 198–202
—Dulac / Fairy *
Urashima Taro; Dragon Sea-King's palace, 140–152
—Fairies / Briggs
fairyland, 398–400
—Grimm / Complete *
elves: magic aging; servant at christening, 199
—Jewish / Frankel
pursuit of gazelle; "60 days" [1 hour] learning common life, 410–414
—Jewish / Sadeh
tailor and Haman: "years" really only 15 minutes, 201–204
—Journeys / Norris *
visit to spirits of Mt. Katahdin, [19–21]
—Nesbit / Fairy *
magic apples: age with each wish, 125–138
—Quayle / Shining *
Urashima lives under-sea for three [really 300] years, 57–68
—Yep / Rainbow *
after thousands of years: homecoming, 144–151
TIME TABOO
—Douglas / Magic *
Cinderella; time deadline, 109–117
—Lang / Wilkins
Princess in the chest; faithful guard, 369–384
TIME TRAVEL
—Lynn / Fantasy *
annotated bibliography, 311–332

TIMING (opportune)
—Coyote / Bierhorst *
    dead: the help comes too late,
      [32]
**Tinder-box, The (alt= The Blue
    light)**
—Andersen / Raverat * 1–19
—Lang / Wilkins, 327–335
TINKER
—Chorao / Child's *
    teakettle turns into badger, 21–27
TINTAGEL
—King Arthur / Ashe, 191 (index)
TITANIC (ship)
—Floyd / Gr Am Myst
    premonitions of the sinking, 164–
      168
TIU (god)
—Hamilton / Dark *
    Fenris, wolf-child of Loki, 82–86
TOAD
    see also FROG
—Bierhorst / Monkey *
    bird bride: toad helps youngest
      son re oft-ruined cornfield, 25–
      31
    hides/rides in hawk's bag;
      crashes; whence is flattened
      out, 136–137
—Dramatized / Kamerman
    grants three wishes; capture ban-
      dit, 324–333
—Grimm / Complete *
    iron stove: princess frees prince;
      breaks taboo, 571–577
    three feathers: youngest prince
      marries toad, 319–322
—Lang / Wilkins
    Toads and diamonds (kind girl
      and proud sister speak), 106–
      109
—Pirate Ghosts / McSherry
    witch's familiar: Pedro goes to
      sea, 182–200

—Witch Encyc / Guiley, 420 (index)
Toad bridegroom
—Clarkson / World * 59–61
Toads and diamonds [the fairies]
—Carter / Sleeping * 63–68
—Lang / Wilkins, 106–109
Toad's escape (Grahame)
—Childcraft 3 / Stories * 6–21
TOBACCO
—Coyote / Ramsey
    arrow-point maker and tobacco-
      hunter, 76–78
—Indian Myth / Burland
    origin, 111
TOFFEE
—Nesbit / Fairy *
    Billy the King [hired to be eaten
      by dragon], 1–22
TOILET TABOO
—Grimm / Complete *
    bearskin: devil gives money-
      providing cloak, 467–472
    discharged soldier serves Devil
      for seven years, 463–466
TOLKIEN, J.R.R.
—Lynn / Fantasy *
    bibliography (about the author),
      614–625
Tom Hickathrift
—Crossley / Dead * 11–19
Tom Thumb (Grimm)
—Allison / I'll Tell * 62–63
—Carle / Treasury * 9–20
—Crossley / British FT * 155–174
—Fairies / Briggs, 402–404
—Grimm / Complete * 187–193
—Grimm / Sixty * 125–132
Tom Thumb (*existential retelling*)
—Switzer / Existential, 126–133
**Tom Thumb (Thumbling's travels
    [variant])**
—Grimm / Complete * 212–216
Tom-Tit-Tot
—Corrin / Six-Year * 166–178

—Crossley / British FT * 47–54
—Fairies / Briggs, 404–409
—Old Wives / Carter, 113–117
—Williams-Ellis / Tales *
    spins skeins for girl, 185–195
TOMBSTONE
—Vietnam / Terada *
    tombstone grateful: soldier (practice shooting) never hit, 130
TONGUE
—Jewish / Frankel
    life and death in power of, 229–231
—Leonardo / Fables *
    liar: the tongue and the teeth, 40
—Lester / Leopard *
    body parts argue: which is most important, 45–51
—Women / Dyer, 63–76 @
Tongue-cut sparrow, The
—Quayle / Shining * 44–56
Tongue meat
—Old Wives / Carter
    conversation as nutritious, 215
TONTLAWALD
—Lang / Wilkins
    mistreated girl lives with fairies, 557–570
TOOTH
—Leonardo / Fables *
    liar: the tongue and the teeth, 40
TOP
—Bomans / Wily *
    children escape from witch with help of top, kite, doll, 88–93
TOPAZ
—Precious Stones / Kunz, 405 (index)
TOPS OR BOTTOMS
—High John / Sanfield *
    sharecropper outwits owner three times, 89–96
TORAH
—Jewish / Frankel, 651 (index)

Moses and angels wrestle, 130–132
readings, 642 (index)
—Jewish / Sadeh
    eagle takes rabbi's son to Christian palace, 273–275
    page watcher: troll and scribe, 255–256
—Schwartz / Gates, 814 (index)
TORAH: SCHOLAR/STUDY
—Jewish / Sadeh
    apprentice baker's blessing, 112–117
    Baal Shem Tov and the transmuted frog, 344–345
    Jewish maid weds old Torah scholar, to escape Graf's son, 368–369
    Rabbi Adam Baal Shem: bequest of mystical writings, 341–343
    study overpowers she-demon, 66–69
TORCH
—Bell / Classical Dict, 255 @
TORNADO
—Earthmaker / Mayo *
    making of whirlwind [horse: Red Wind; Kiowa tale], 24–26
TORTOISE
see also TERRAPIN; TURTLE;
also Aesop: Hare and the tortoise
—Arabian / Lewis
    test for succession: prince marries tortoise, 43–51
—Arabian / McCaughrean
    test for succession [as above], 142–149
—Clouston / Popular
    race: hare and tortoise, I.266–273
—Dulac / Fairy *
    Urashima Taro; Dragon Sea-King's palace, 140–152
—Fahs / Old *

hoarded knowledge shared with all, 29–31
—Greaves / Hippo * 136–138 @
elephant vs. Rain Spirit: who is greater, 53–58
how "living stones" eggs are cared for, 134–136
tortoise tricks hare in race, 114–118
—Paxton / Aesop *
race: tortoise and the hare, [22–27]
—Vanishing / Mercer *
Jaboti plays his flute, 13–15
—Water Buffalo (Chinese)
carried, opens mouth, falls to earth, 9–12
TORTURE
—Jewish / Sadeh
eating much (glutton), can bear much torture, 338
TOUCHING TABOO
—Scary / Young *
bride always wears ribbon around neck; husband removes; her head falls off, 61–63
TOURNAMENT(-s)
—Knights / Heller-Headon, 120–121
TOWER OF LONDON
—Ghosts / Cohen, 126–131
TOWN
—Nesbit / Fairy *
town in the library, 81–98
Town mouse . . . see under Aesop.
TOY(-s)
—Am Child / Bronner,
constructions by children, 199–236
—Bomans / Wily *
children escape from witch with help of top, kite, doll, 88–93
—Childcraft 1 / Once *
Velveteen Rabbit becomes real when loved, 175–181

—Lynn / Fantasy *
annotated bibliography, 333–343
TRADING
—Grimm / Complete *
Hans in luck; series of foolish tradings, 381–386
—Grimm / Sixty *
Hans in luck, 10–16
TRAGEDY
—Folk Ballads / McNeil
folk ballads, II.91–113
—Lewis / Proud
Two Lovers Mountain: carry princess to top, 48–52
TRAITOR(-s)
see also TREACHERY
—Aesop / Reeves-Wilson *
birdcatcher and partridge, 50
—Bruchac / Iroquois *
monstrous, two-headed snake a traitor, 97–102
snakes make war of revenge, 93–95
—Cambodian / Carrison
Princess Amaradevi: husband accused of treachery, 23–30
—Childcraft 3 / Stories *
good and evil: Glooscap vs. Malsum [and Lox], 143–151
—Crossley / Animal (Grimm) *
cat/mouse partnership, 21–25
—Grimm / Complete *
Strong Hans escapes from robber den, 688–695
TRAMP
—Rockwell / Puss *
Nail Soup, 12–18
TRANSFORMATION(-s):
see also SHAPE-CHANGER; WEREWOLF; WITCH(-es)
see also particular stories, e.g. Cinderella
—Arabian / Lewis

flock of white birds; the Jinn princess, 138–143
king into "ass" (slave for five years), 184–87
—Arabian / McCaughrean
king into "ass" (as above), 208–217
—Baring-Gould / Curious
Helias: Knight of the Swan, 146–150
—Bierhorst / Naked *
Chestnut pudding: getting inside mole's body, 3–10
humans to fleas: Quilt of men's eyes, 101–109
Last Remaining [man to cloud; witch to bear], 87–92
—Bruchac / Iroquois *
heads of eaten children to fish, 97–102
—Caduto / Keepers *
Loo-Wit (Indian maid) to Mt. St. Helens, 41–43
—Clouston / Popular, I.413–460 @
fairy hind, I.215–218
—Coyote / Ramsey
coyote takes self apart to get through hole, 133–134
—Douglas / Magic *
Europa and Zeus (bull), 181–184
—Dramatized / Kamerman
Bridge to Killybog Fair, 227–238
Sleeping mountains: Ixtlaccihuatl and Popocatepetl, 346–359
—Dulac / Fairy *
green serpent: one twin princess cursed, ugly, 124–138
—Earth / Hadley *
Beebyeebyee marries water god (fish-man), [25–26]
—Egyptian / Harris
Hathor: Eye of the sun, 26–33
—Erdoes / Sound *

stone-boy, his mother, his ten lost uncles, 108–116
—Fahs / Old *
Niyak and Umak; swansdown to swan, 71–80
—Ghosts / Starkey
Joe Reardon and the three sister-ghosts, 102–109
McGregor and the kelpy, 66–71
—Glooskap / Norman *
Ice Giants outwitted by Glooskap, 11–19
—Greek / Osborne
birds: Ceyx and Alcyone, 13–16
weaving contest: Arachne made first spider, 19–21
—Grimm / Complete *
Hans the hedgehog: princess promised, 497–502
juniper tree: murder exposed by singing bird, 220–229
Lady and lion [man by night], 398–404
nixie (mill-pond) captures young man; wife rescues, 736–742
Salad; fed to witch, 551–558
Sweetheart Roland; girl flees murderous stepmother, 268–271
three feathers: youngest prince marries toad, 319–322
white bride and black bride, 608–612
—Grimm / Sixty *
Lady and lion [man by night], 235–240
Seven ravens [transformed brothers], 284–287
Sweetheart Roland . . . , 156–160
—Hamilton / Dark *
marriage to boar/man; secret not kept; woman to frog, 113–118
—Hamilton / People *
wicked man not wanted in heaven or hell, 126–132

Wiley triumphs over Hairy Man, 90–103

—Hoke / Giants
giant to beautiful woman; White Feather falls, 112–118
ogre to man; Finlay, the giant killer, 142–149

—Hopi / Talashoma-Malotki
hide and seek with life at stake, 50–69
Kokosori and his witch wife, 23–41

—Hopi Coyote / Malotki
Coyote Woman and Turkey Woman roast their children, 77–81

—Igloo / Metayer
The eagle and the hunter, 108–111
The orphan and the bears [bearmen], 24–31
white foxes, 108–111
woman a walking skeleton: The magic drum, 13–18

—Jewish / Frankel
rabbi's magic ring: rabbi to werewolf; wife to donkey, 450–455

—Jewish / Sadeh
Baal Shem Tov and the frog (Torah scholar), 344–345
Blackface: merchant's son in love with princess, 117–121
fish released, becomes boy's adviser, 95–97
marriage of man and snake-woman, 79–80
marriage: princess to donkey's head, 4–8
pony's IOU: soul of departed one, working off debt, 354
prince, to escape capture, 101–105

—Journey Sun (Chinese)
Green Peony: Wives in the mirror, 109–124

—Lore of Love
demon-bride's (snake) marriage to mortal, 68–73
ill-starred mating of earth and sea, 87–95

—Lycanthropy / Otten, 336 (index)

—Manning / Cats *
boy Altin's golden knucklebone, water cat, and stallion, 29–36
imp becomes gigantic when threatened; shifts shape to cat, 16–18
juniper bush: when heads are cut off, mouse-queen spell broken, 83–91
man marries bird-wife; his mother drives her out, 75–82
witch abducts king's two children; Katchen the cat helps escape, 9–15

—Manning / Cauldron *
donkey, gift of troll-child, helps hunter rescue princess, 9–17

—Navajo Coyote / Haile
chickadee and coyote (pluck out eyes) 12, 35

—O'Brien / Tales *
Hookedy Crookedy: to serve king, transformed as knight, marries king's daughter, 53–71
swan bride: king's son's quest for Scolog's daughter, 82–95

—Old Wives / Carter
governor marries "Chinese princess" (snake-woman), 142–148

—Quayle / Shining *
mother's mirror warns Sachiko of stepmother in rat-form, 90–96

—Rockwell / Puss *
Kate Crackernuts (gets head of sheep), 19–26

—Roman / Usher
tales from ancient Rome, 124–129 @

—Spanish-Am / Van Etten *
  Pedro and priest's mule trade
    places; bad for both, 90–94
—Tree / Kerven *
  drums: unfaithful bride reverts to
    thorn tree, [16–19]
  thorn tree to beautiful bride of
    poor man, [16–19]
—Turkish (Art I) / Walker
  brothers eat hen's head, neck;
    one padishah, other vizier, 61–
    69
  Cihansah enters forbidden room;
    sees girl-fairy-pigeons, 207–
    217
  dead mother advises stepdaugh-
    ter: nurse, teach, wed serpent-
    prince, 183–188
  overhears secrets: how to win
    princess, escape spell, 123–
    136
—Turkey / Walker, 309 (index)
—Unicorn / Coville *
  princess, cat/prince, and con-
    ceited unicorn, 120–134
—Williams-Ellis / Tales *
  The Laidly Worm of Spindlestone
    Heugh, 134–141
  Tamlane rescued from elfland,
    151–159
—Yep / Rainbow *
  dog-spirit in form of human, 96–
    105
  dragon to wizard's slave: The
    rainbow people, 162–168
  snake to form of drowned brother,
    118–123
—Yolen / Faery Flag
  words of power: Late Blossoming
    Flower, 21–39
—Yolen / Shape Shift, 6–21, 44–
    50
  monster, as punishment, 147
  underwater; squid, 97

TRANSFORMATION: *animal to another animal*
—Bierhorst / Naked *
  torture: dog to larger dog, 60–66
—Coyote / Ramsey
  coyote to buffalo, 20–22
—Erdoes / Sound *
  contest with birds; for deception,
    bat turned into mouse, 90
  mice (made tiny by medicine
    man) powwow in elk skull, 68–
    70
—Grimm / Complete *
  ungrateful son; chicken turns to
    toad, 636
—Hopi Coyote / Malotki
  coyote learns sorcery; trans-
    formed to cottontail; eaten by
    children, 166–177
—Old Wives / Carter
  Eskimo turns lice into sled dogs,
    181–182
TRANSFORMATION: *animal to ob-
  ject*
—Vietnam / Terada *
  worm and snail are born to two
    sisters, 59–63
—Yep / Rainbow *
  parrot to whirlwind: "Snake-
    spoke," 86–95
TRANSFORMATION: *animal to per-
  son*
—Aesop / Reeves-Wilson *
  cat to woman [per Venus], 61
—Bruchac / Iroquois *
  girl not satisfied; snake to man,
    123–127
—Chinese / Chin *
  marriage to white snake (in
    woman form), 29–44
—Clarkson / World *
  seal's skin: seal to woman, 136–
    137
—Dulac / Fairy *

blue bird (prince transformed),
77–90
Urashima Taro; Dragon Sea-
King's palace, 140–152
—Earthmaker / Mayo *
Rainbow Woman; duck to giant
woman (Hoh tale), 38–40
—Grimm / Complete *
cat (princess) gives horse to
miller's apprentice, 482–485
—Hepburn / World *
Tattercoats: gooseherd plays
flute; prince falls in love, 90–
109
—Igloo / Metayer
wolves into men: child kidnapped
by wolf-men, 73–77
—Quayle / Shining *
Lord Bag-o'-Rice aids serpent
(Dragon King); kills giant centi-
pede, 33–43
—Vietnam / Terada *
snake princess, 14–17
—Yep / Rainbow *
The rainbow people, 162–168
—Yolen / Shape Shift, 52–60, 78–
96
TRANSFORMATION: *for breaking ta-
boo*
—Grimm / Complete *
Faithful John: quest for princess
of Golden Dwelling, 43–51
—Lang / Wilkins
Water of life (brothers fail; sister
succeeds), 362–368
—Turkish (Art I) / Walker
will turn to stone; quest for arro-
gant princess, 123–136
TRANSFORMATION: *by eating/
drinking*
—Grimm / Complete *
Salad, The, 551–558
—Grimm / Sixty *
Salad, The, 292–293

TRANSFORMATION: *human to animal*
—Grimm / Complete *
hero must hold crystal ball before
enchantress to free princess,
798–801
sea-hare: suitor must conceal
self from princess, 769–772
—Hoke / Giants, 150–155
—Lore of Love
groom for the sea-lord's daugh-
ter, 8–15
—Old Wives / Carter
Parsley-Girl: magic wand turns
nuns (*i.e.*, witches) to frogs,
86–88
—Russian Hero / Warner *
prodigy Volkh turns soldiers to
ants, 93
—Shah / Central Asia
Rustam and Tahmina; woman to
animal, 87–91
—Unicorn / Coville *
boy/unicorn: being of power and
light, 63–77
—Unicorn / Hathaway
Severe: man becomes unicorn
(Pulci), 107–110 @
—Yolen / Shape Shift, 70–75
TRANSFORMATION: *human to bird*
—Arabian / Lewis
Anklet [magic pins; girl turns into
dove], 49–51
—Bierhorst / Monkey *
lazy farmer trades places with
buzzard; dies foolishly, 37–43
—Celts / Hodges *
children of Lir to swans, 5–14
—Corrin / Imagine *
Caliph and Vizier into storks; for-
get magic word; marriage to
(enchanted) owl, 164–76
—Crossley / British FT *
baker's daughter turned into owl;

refuses bread to fairy/old
woman, 331–333
midwife uses eye ointment; can
see fairies, 287–292
—Douglas / Magic *
six swans (enchanted princes
saved by their sister), 35
—Dulac / Fairy *
serpent-prince: marries, regains
human form, 29–42
White Caroline, Black Caroline,
15–21
—Grimm / Complete *
father vows to kill twelve brothers
if daughter is born, 59–64
girl lost in wood; witch, ring, and
dove/prince, 558–560
Godfather Death, 209–212
Jorinda and Joringel, 339–342
Seven ravens [transformed broth-
ers], 137–139
—Grimm / Sixty *
Jorinda and Joringel, 17–20
Seven ravens . . . , 284–287
—Hoke / Giants, 150–155
—Igloo / Metayer
man into bird: The ghost hunter,
82–91
—Journey Sun (Chinese)
turned to dog; qingke (barley)
seed stolen, 24–46
—Lang / Wilkins
enchantment: princess must stay
in tower . . . , 415–431
mistreated Tontlawald girl lives
with fairies, 557–570
Sylvain and Jocosa (yellow bird),
178–185
—Lewis / Proud
Yonec: lover killed by jealous
husband's trap, 53–60
—Turkish (Art I) / Walker
young wife turned into bird by
stepmother, 82–88

—Yep / Rainbow *
cats and dogs as "natural enemies," 12–18
TRANSFORMATION: *human to different human*
—Lang / Wilkins
Dwarf Long Nose (boy under
spell), 534–556
—Vietnam / Terada *
ugly man changes self to test
wife's fidelity, 64–68
TRANSFORMATION: *human to do-
mestic animal*
—Arabian / McCaughrean
thief pretends to be ass under
spell, 150–152
—Arabian / Riordan
Amina's tale: evil sisters turned to
dogs, 116–119
into hounds; life saved by storytelling, 100–107
—Bomans / Wily *
Maraboe, Morsegat [children to
black cats] and cannibal-witch,
27–36
—Grimm / Complete *
lambkin and the little fish, 625–
627
Salad, The, 551–558
—Grimm / Sixty *
Salad, The, 292–293
—Jewish / Sadeh
to dog; princess who refused to
talk, 106–111
—Journeys / Norris *
road to death: old man takes form
of bullock, [16–18]
—Lang / Wilkins
Heart of ice (Caylus), 190–219
—Manning / Cats *
Little Wonder; witch-stepmother
turns boy into dog, drives his
sister out, 65–74
—Russian Hero / Warner *

Sister Alenushka and Brother
Ivanushka, 108–109
—Shah / Central Asia
enchanted horse (man) understands, obeys, 31–44
enchanted horse, really a man;
Jade Mountain, 19–24
princess imprisoned in mountain
of jade, 19–24
—Turkish (Art I) / Walker magic hen,
and fate of two brothers, 61–69
—Yolen / Shape Shift, 44–50
TRANSFORMATION: *human to fish*
—Coyote / Ramsey
man to fish; woman married to
merman, 150–152
—Grimm / Complete *
lambkin and the little fish, 625–
627
TRANSFORMATION: *human to ob-
ject*
—Arabian / Riordan
Amina's tale: evil sisters turned to
dogs, 116–119
—Grimm / Complete *
brothers: one rescues princess; is
rescued by other, 290–311
Frau Trude; change to block of
firewood, 208–209
—Hamilton / People *
Little Eight John turned into
grease spot, 121–125
—Hoke / Giants, 150–155
—Hopi / Talashoma-Malotki
how the Poqangwhoyas turned
two girls to stone, 92–107
—Igloo / Metayer
child-killer escapes as shooting
star, 70–72
—Lang / Wilkins
Fairer-than-a-Fairy, 274–281
—Nesbit / Fairy *
princesses to golden apples,
141–158

—Russian Hero / Warner *
Dunai: archery contest ends in
death, 37–41
—Spring / Philip
Akui frees water; turns to stone,
87–93
—Vietnam / Terada *
look-alike brothers love the same
girl, 109–113
TRANSFORMATION: *human to plant*
—Greek / Osborne
Baucis and Philemon: oak and
linden (1 trunk), 67–70
Cupid's arrows: Daphne into laurel tree, 23–26
—Lore of Love
lovers become trees; branches
join, 122–127
—Manning / Cauldron *
prince and retinue turned into
trees; girl breaks spell, 39–
45
—Vietnam / Terada *
look-alike brothers love the same
girl, 109–113
TRANSFORMATION: *human to rep-
tile*
—Erdoes / Sound *
three brothers transformed to rattlers; remain friendly, 37–42
—Grimm / Complete *
frog; princess' promise; kissed,
reverts to prince, 17–20
—Journey Sun (Chinese)
small yellow dragon defeats big
black dragon, 81–89
—Rockwell / Puss *
Frog prince (princess makes rash
promise), 66–74
—Russian Hero / Warner *
three princes/brides, one a frog-
princess, 101–106
—Scriven / Full Color *
Frog prince, 57–59

TRANSFORMATION: *human to wild beast*

—Corrin / Imagine *
   goldsmith steals woodcarver-friend's gold; woodcarver "turns" goldsmith's children into bears, 23–46
—Dulac / Fairy *
   hind of the wood: crayfish fairy, 43–59
—Greek / Osborne
   Atalanta and Hippomenes: into lions, 51–54
—Grimm / Complete *
   brother transformed to fawn; sister faithful, 67–73
   Golden Bird; fox, formerly a prince, 272–279
   kings' daughters aid hero in tasks: win girl or die, 515–524
—Hopi / Talashoma-Malotki
   two girls (one turned to coyote) in love with same boy, 118–135
—Lang / Wilkins
   Snow White and Rose Red (befriend bear), 99–105
—Lines / Magical *
   Oisin's mother transformed into Fawn, 169–174
—Navajo Coyote / Haile
   Changing Bear Maiden (widow) transformed to monster bear, 16, 82–84
—Russian Hero / Warner *
   witch (blood sister) and sun's sister, 60–61
—Yep / Rainbow *
   changeling: man to wild beast, 162–168
—Yolen / Shape Shift, 6–21, 24–35
—Yolen / Werewolves
   Bad blood, 3–34
   Met by moonlight, 224–237
   Monster mash, 127–150

   Night calls (nuclear holocaust), 95–118
   Passing of the pack (son replaces father as leader), 151–171
   White Wolf: boy's initiation to manhood, 45–69
   Wolf from the door, 119–126

TRANSFORMATION: *object to animal*

—Caduto / Keepers *
   Loo-Wit, the fire-keeper, 41–43
—Chinese / Chin *
   shoes to guide-birds, 128–139
—Erdoes / Sound *
   how Sioux Nation came into being, 72–73
—Spring / Philip
   wonderful brocade picture, 23–34
—Vietnam / Terada *
   squash seeds: origin of Dao People, 54–58

TRANSFORMATION: *object to another object*

—Arabian / Lewis
   test for succession: prince marries tortoise, 43–51
—Arabian / McCaughrean
   test for succession . . . , 142–149
—Bierhorst / Naked *
   torture: tears become wampum, 60–66
—Bruchac / Iroquois *
   Stone Coat Woman aids hunters, 135–144
—Dulac / Fairy *
   serpent-prince: marries, regains human form, 29–42
—Greaves / Hippo *
   why giraffe has a long neck, 86–88
—Grimm / Complete *
   glass coffin; bewitched maid, 672–678

tailor and goldsmith see little folk dancing, 742–745

water-nixie, The, 364–365

—Muddleheads / Harris
blubber to boulders, 44–59

—Tibet / Timpanelli *
horse speaks: kill me; skin becomes palace, 1–13

TRANSFORMATION: *object to person*

—Childcraft 1 / Once *
Pinocchio: puppet becomes alive, 212–226

Velveteen Rabbit—becomes real when loved, 175–181

—Dulac / Fairy *
buried moon (captured by evil bog creatures), 7–14

Snegorotchka, 1–6

—Grimm / Complete *
Pink [carnation], The, 355–360

—Grimm / Sixty *
Pink [carnation], The, 171–176

—Jewish / Frankel
rabbi fashions golem to thwart evil priest of Prague, 455–458

—Lang / Wilkins
gnome king Rubezahl captures princess, 497–512

—Old Wives / Carter
isolated princess makes male form; God gives soul, 222–224

TRANSFORMATION: *by putting on skin/clothing*

—Fahs / Old *
Maui in bird-shape, to Underworld; parents, 37–43

—Grimm / Complete *
princess marries donkey; it removes animal skin at night, 632–635

Six swans: sister faithful to transformed brothers, 232–237

—Jewish / Frankel

serpent (prince at night); wife burns skin; spell broken, 446–449

—Lewis / Proud
Bisclavret: wife keeps husband in wolf-form, 29–35

—Russian Hero / Warner *
Ivan son of Mare kills his treacherous brothers, 120–124

—Yolen / Werewolves
Flesh and blood, 172–188

Wolfskin, 84–94

TRANSFORMATION: *repeated/multiple*

—Arabian / Lewis
Moorish sorcerer vs. king, 60–64

—Arabian / McCaughrean
Moorish sorcerer vs. king, 133–141

—Bruchac / Iroquois *
rabbit outwits fox, 74–78

—Carter / Sleeping *
Sweetheart (to monster, lion, bull, etc.), 113–124

—Celts / Hodges *
freed from evil spell by love, 76–83

—Coyote / Ramsey
twig to boy to elk, 153–156

—Dramatized / Kamerman
mythical reptiles, 79–87

—Egyptian / Harris
Anpu and Bata, 77–83

—Grimm / Sixty *
Fundevogel: rosebush, church, duck, 84–87

—Hamilton / People *
Beautiful girl of the moon tower, 53–59

—Hoke / Giants
giant vs. Indian Chief, 150–155

—Lines / Magical *
Ian Direach: fox changes to sword, horse, boat, etc., 45–55

—Lore of Love
  nymph to animal, etc., 8–15
—Manning / Cauldron *
  hero Tow-how: magic disk helps
    foil hideous old witch, 58–65
—Spring / Philip
  dragon seen by unprotected
    men, 119–133
—Trolls / Asbjornsen
  boy who became lion, falcon, ant,
    64–70
—Water Buffalo (Chinese)
  stone-mason never satisfied, 89–
    92
—Yep / Rainbow *
  snake to worm to snake: "Snake-
    spoke," 86–95
—Yolen / Werewolves
  Not all wolves, 70–83
TRANSFORMATION: *at will*
—Chinese / Chin *
  monkey: on road to fetch scrip-
    tures, 95–110
—Crossley / British FT *
  Gruagach transforms self into
    mare; fights griffin, 228–243
—Grimm / Complete *
  Fundevogel, 241–244
  kings' daughters aid hero in
    tasks: win girl or die, 515–524
  master thief: boy deceives/kills
    his teacher, 337–338
—Grimm / Sixty *
  Fundevogel, 84–87
—Hamilton / People *
  Beautiful girl of the moon tower,
    53–59
—Old Wives / Carter
  girl marries crab; it takes human
    form from banyan tree, 19–21
  girl marries hyena in human form;
    she changes to tree, etc., 64–
    65
—Russian Hero / Warner *

  prodigy Volkh leads invasion of
    India, 92–94
—Starkey / Ghosts
  McGregor and the kelpy, 66–71
TRANSSEXUALISM
—Bell / Classical Dict, 257 @
TRANSVESTISM
—Bell / Classical Dict, 257–258 @
TRANSYLVANIA
—Dracula / McNally
  map (1566), 16–17 @
—Vanishing / Mercer *
  Gypsy girl gives parents/brothers
    to devil, 50–53
TRAP
  see also VICTIM TRAPPED
—Bierhorst / Monkey *
  rabbit gets caught; dupes coyote
    to take his place, 72–76
—Carle / Treasury *
  monkey chosen king; foolishly
    falls into trap (Aesop), 40–41
—Jewish / Sadeh
  Rabbi Yehiel and King of France,
    223–224
—Lester / Brer Rabbit *
  cons Brer Wolf into trap built for
    himself, 106–109
  trapped in hollow log; burns up
    Brer Wolf, 117–122
TRAPPERS
—American / Read Dgst, 174–189
TRASH
—Fahs / Old *
  people cooperate to "kill" pollu-
    tion dragon, 169–171
TRAVEL(-ler)
—Bierhorst / Sacred
  Indian travelers, 63–75
—Jewish / Frankel
  numskull thinks he's in Warsaw,
    really at home in Chelm, 567–
    570
—Legends / Cavendish, 397 (index)

—Lynn / Fantasy *
to otherworlds; annotated bibliography, 210–234
Traveling companion (Andersen)
—Carle / Treasury * 131–146
TREACH, Luke
—Pirate Ghosts / McSherry
red swimmer: father and daughter murdered, 45–68
TREACHERY
see also SERVANTS: TREACHEROUS
—Arabian / Lewis
good barber and evil dyer, 123–130
slave girl (Sweet-Friend) and Ali Nur, 25–34
—Cambodian / Carrison
Princess Amaradevi: husband accused of treachery, 23–30
—Chinese / Chin *
palace plot: rival concubines, 77–92
—Corrin / Imagine *
Arion wins prize; is thrown overboard; saved by dolphin, 161–163
—Coyote / Bierhorst *
ocean advises coyote to become merchant; ship's date cargo lost, [38]
—Crossley / Animal (Grimm) *
cat/mouse partnership, 21–25
—Douglas / Magic *
evil sisters: Beauty and the Beast, 85–97
—Dramatized / Kamerman
King Horn; chamberlain deceives queen, 447–457
—Erdoes / Sound *
treachery: two warriors love same girl, 25–30
—Gullible Coyote / Malotki
Coyote Woman kills Antelope Woman; tries to get her children, 27–36
—Hoke / Giants
Strong Gottlieb, 103–111
—Imaginary / Nigg
fisherman and the kaha, 77–79
—Jewish / Frankel
have mercy on animals, not men, 376–378
Rabbi's mirror allows king to see treachery in his bedroom, 405–409
—Jewish / Sadeh
nightingale; queen gives birth to animals, 25–28
pious thief saves king's life, 262–263
poor man and thieving ministers, 264–266
Rabbi Isaac Abrabanel and king's shoe, 222–223
vizier; princess who refused to talk, 106–111
—Lewis / Proud
Bisclavret: wife keeps husband in wolf-form, 29–35
—Manning / Cauldron *
crusader beaten, robbed by comrades; witches reveal secrets, = reversal, 46–57
Whirlwind abducts queen and (evil) son; rescue by youngest son, 106–117
—Russian Hero / Warner *
little simpleton: silver saucer and juicy apple, 106–108
son of Mare kills his treacherous brothers, 120–124
three kingdoms: copper, silver, gold, 53–56
wolf helps quest; warnings ignored, 112–116
—Shah / Central Asia

Feroz-Shah and the mechanical flying horse, 131–145
—Tibet / Timpanelli *
   evil helper takes real daughter's place, 15–27
—Turkish / Walker
   Muslim preacher sells wisdom to king, 37–42
—Turkish (Art I) / Walker
   good to the good, and damnation to the evil: poor man and grand vizier, 204–207
   patience stone: gypsy girl usurps lady's position, 111–116
   sons seek Hazaran nightingale for padishah's mosque, 230–239
—Yep / Rainbow *
   cats and dogs as "natural enemies," 12–18

TREASON
—Bell / Classical Dict, 259 @

TREASURE (- trove)
—Arabian / Lewis
   Ali Baba and the forty thieves, 188–198
   changing luck: destiny or capital, 17–24
   inexhaustibility; commoner made king, 81–90
   princess loved by cousins (three brothers), 174–183
—Arabian / McCaughrean
   Ali Baba and the forty thieves, 108–121
   Keys of destiny; Iram, 65–82
—Arabian / Riordan
   Ali Baba and the forty thieves, 88–99
—Clarkson / World *
   Cluricaune shows hiding place of treasure, 115–117
—Classic / Downer

Lost Cave with the Iron Door (Wichita Mountains), 85–92
—Crossley / British FT *
   Welsh boy tries to take gold; King Arthur's sleeping army, 38–44
—Crossley / Dead *
   Pedlar of Swaffham: dream discloses treasure, 27–37
—Egyptian / Mercatante
   Rhampsiniths (Herodotus), 192–195
—Ghost (South) / McNeil
   ghosts and hidden treasure, 79–87
—Ghosts / Starkey
   Dauntless girl; ghost reveals treasure, 72–79
   Jack Mackintosh: Treasure ghost of Fife, 88–95
   Joe Reardon and the three sister-ghosts, 102–109
—Grimm / Complete *
   Simeli Mountain: treasure secret overheard, 627–630
—Grimm / Legends (Ward), II:455 (index)
—Jameson / Appalachians
   caches, mines, Civil War loot, 1–207
—Jameson / Buried
   legendary southwest lost mines, gold, etc., 1–220
—Jewish / Frankel, 647 (index)
—Jewish / Sadeh
   dream: beneath the bridge, 383
   poor brother and three beasts, 140–143
—Lang / Wilkins
   how six men travelled the wide world, 299–304
   Snow White and Rose Red (befriend bear), 99–105
—MacDonald / Sourcebook *
   motif index, 720

538

—Pirate Ghosts / McSherry
 digging at Pistol Key, 166–181
—Quayle / Shining *
 old man makes dead trees
 bloom; dog unearths treasure,
 69–76
—Rockwell / Puss *
 Jack and the Beanstalk, 1–11
—Scandinavian / Kvideland
 buried, xvi (index)
—Schwartz / Gold
 cities, 114 @
 codes, maps and signs, 51–70,
 115 @
 haunts, 105–110
 legends and true stories, 1–128
 pirate ships, Spanish galleons,
 25–37, 122
 retrieval equipment, 71–85,
 116 @
—Scriven / Full Color *
 Ali Baba and the forty thieves,
 20–25
—Spanish-Am / Van Etten *
 skeleton gives treasure to brave
 boy, 109–114
—Starkey / Ghosts
 Joe Reardon and the three sister-
 ghosts, 102–109
—Turkish / Walker
 Keloglan overhears jinns' secrets, 23–28
—Turkish (Art I) / Walker
 death, if shepherd does not keep
 secret his knowing language of
 animals, 190–194
—Yep / Rainbow *
 unearthed by pet mouse, 80–
 85

TREASURE: *accidently found*
—Arabian / Lewis
 treachery: good barber and evil
 dyer, 123–130
—Corrin / Six-Year *

 by mistake, crossing-sweeper
 takes magic broom, 87–92
—Jaffrey / Seasons
 crow drops queen's necklace on
 washerwoman's doorstep, 81–
 84

TREASURE-PRODUCING ANIMAL
—Chinese / Chin *
 golden carp (Cinderella-type),
 47–57
—Grimm / Complete *
 brothers: one rescues princess; is
 rescued by other, 290–311
—Turkish (Art I) / Walker
 magic hen, and fate of two brothers, 61–69

TREE(-s) (*often magic, marvelous . . .*
)
—Aesop / Reeves-Wilson *
 handle for woodcutter's axe,
 112–113
—Bell / Classical Dict, 260 @
—Bomans / Wily *
 prince plants tree so he can be
 above clouds, 131–134
—Brooke / Telling *
 acquire wisdom by being taught;
 Johnny Appleseed, 37–48
—Caduto / Keepers *
 earth's origin; primal water; turtle's back, 25–26
 seasonal sap, 145
—Chorao / Child's FTB *
 ants push sky; rescue Indian from
 tree top, 43–50
—Fairies / Briggs, 159–161
—Grimm / Complete *
 One-eye, Two-eyes, and Three-
 eyes, 585–592
—Jewish / Frankel, 647 (index)
—Leonardo / Fables *
 chestnut or fig: which is better
 treated by man? 48
 peach tree envies walnut tree, 26

—Lines / Magical *
    Cormac Mac Art: branch removes
      memory of woe, 141–149
    tree produces apple of content-
      ment (Pyle), 15–23
—Lore of Love
    trees with interwoven branches:
      tragic love, 122–127
—Lurker / Dict Gods, 444 (index)
—MacDonald / Sourcebook *
    motif index, 720–721
—Man Myth & Magic, 3175 (index)
—Manning / Cats *
    boy Altin's golden knucklebone,
      water cat, and stallion, 29–36
    old couple: repeated tries to cut
      down tree; bird, instead, sup-
      plies needs, 101–106
—Manning / Cauldron *
    prince and retinue turned into
      trees; girl breaks spell, 39–45
—Norse / Crossley
    world tree: Yggdrasill, 276 (index)
—Old Wives / Carter
    wicked stepmother: fruit tree low-
      ers branches when boy sings,
      178–180
—Paxton / Aesop *
    patience: fox eats lunch found in
      hollow tree, [6–9]
—Quayle / Shining *
    old man makes dead trees bloom
      (with ashes of pet dog), 69–
      76
—Russian / Ivanits, 251 (index)
—Russian Hero / Warner *
    magic tree: cock and corn mill,
      52–53
—Scandinavian / Davidson
    world tree, 144 (index)
—Tree / Kerven *
    coal given to willows and birches;
      rub them, make fire, [8–9]
—Turkish (Art I) / Walker

    golden pears: dervish punishes
      selfish farmer, 53–57
—Vanishing / Mercer *
    animal-life and forest spirits re-
      store cut-down tree, 34–35
    Ona myth: "die" in fall; "reborn"
      in spring, 80–83
—Water Buffalo (Chinese)
    bear fruit without resowing, 23–
      29

TREE: APPLE
—Celts / Hodges *
    other world, 75
—Plants / Dyer, 321 (index)
—Witches / Iosa *
    Old witch (Jacobs); kind girl and
      her selfish sister, 34–39

TREE: BANYON
—Jaffrey / Seasons
    roots to the underworld; ghosts,
      9 @
    Shravan Kumar: wife asks; ban-
      yan tree gives shade and heal-
      ing milk, 16–20
—Tree / Kerven *
    one banyon tree covers moon,
      [4–5]

TREE: BIRCH
—Fahs / Old *
    weeping: gifts to mankind are so
      small, 15–18

TREE: CHESTNUT
—Bruchac / Iroquois *
    Hodadenon: last one left, 169–
      182

TREE: COTTONWOOD
—American / Read Dgst
    Rainbow Woman and cotton-
      wood-tree husband, 204
—Sioux / Standing Bear *
    large tree moves itself to be with
      its own kind, 65–67

TREE: ELDER
—Plants / Dyer, 323 (index)

—Tree / Kerven *
  Elder-Tree-Witch steals milk;
    burnt by Granny, [14–15]
TREE: FIG
—Leonardo / Fables *
  berates elm because it has no
    fruit, 95
TREE: GINGKO
—Water Buffalo (Chinese)
  wolf pretends to be grandmother,
    62–69
TREE: HAWTHORN
—Tree / Kerven *
  fairies' revenge for cutting down
    hawthorn bush, [26–27]
TREE: JUNIPER
—Grimm / Complete *
  murder exposed by singing bird,
    220–229
TREE of KNOWLEDGE
—Schwartz / Gates, 814 (index)
TREE: LAUREL
—Greek / Osborne
  Cupid's arrows: Daphne into lau-
    rel tree, 23–26
TREE of LIFE
—Plants / Dyer, 22–24
—Gray / Near East, 144 (index)
TREE: MANGO
—Jaffrey / Seasons
  brother and mango tree share
    common soul; unwatered,
    nearly die, 94–95
—Tree / Kerven *
  parallel lives: brother shares soul
    with tree, [20–21]
TREE: MAPLE
—Caduto / Keepers *
  Manabozho and the maple trees,
    145
—Journey Sun (Chinese)
  drink from Red Spring, under
    power of Red Devil, 125–
    140

TREE: OAK
—Man Myth & Magic, 3157 (index)
TREE: OLIVE
—Geras / Grandmother *
  talking plants' contest: which is
    most beautiful? 57–65
TREE: PEACH
—Dramatized / Kamerman
  Peach tree kingdom; imposter;
    bride test, 288–305
TREE: PINYON
—Curry / Beforetime *
  origin: coyote and pine-nut
    thieves, 90–99
TREE: SYCAMORE
—Lester / Leopard *
  woman and the tree children, 37–
    39
TREE: THORN
—Tree / Kerven *
  transformed to beautiful bride of
    poor man, [16–19]
TREE: TOTARA
—Maori / Kanawa *
  boasts it can reach sky father,
    83
TREE: WALNUT
—Leonardo / Fables *
  fall of the bell tower, 78
TREE: WILLOW
—Leonardo / Fables *
  willow, magpie,and pumpkin, 92–
    95
Tregeagle's ghost
—Ghosts / Starkey, 58–65
TRIAL (*legal*)
—Lewis / Proud
  Lanval: Queen Guinivere claims
    seduction attempt, 26–47
—Lycanthropy / Otten, 336 (index)
TRIALS (*ritual*)
—Hamilton / Dark *
  tiny thing: Anishinaba and Boshk-
    wadosh, 54–59

TRICK OR TREAT
—Limburg / Weird , 10–12
TRICKER-TRICKED
—Aesop / Reeves-Wilson *
  donkey carrying salt, 92–94
  guest's food in plate/bottle: Fox
    and stork, 95–96
—Bierhorst / Monkey *
  three would-be buyers of jar mur-
    dered; fool "buries" one thrice,
    32–36
—Harris-Parks / Again
  Tar-Baby story, 6–13
—Lester / Brer Rabbit *
  Wiley Wolf and Riley Rabbit: play
    Riding/Tying the Bag, 101–104
—Williams-Ellis / Tales *
  Anansi (death for saying "five"),
    143–150
TRICKERY (*by humans or human-like*
  animals)
  see also SWINDLER(-s); TRICK-
    STER
—Bierhorst / Naked *
  turtle and partridge hide bagged
    elk from wolves, 67–71
—Chorao / Child's *
  Hansel and Gretel; witch killed,
    29–40
  hare repeatedly tricks lion, 43–
    49
—Clarkson / World *
  Hodja stories, 289–292
—Corrin / Six-Year *
  little jackal tricks alligator into re-
    vealing self, 93–97
—Coyote / Bierhorst *
  wolf slanders coyote; coyote
    turns tables, [34]
—Coyote / Ramsey
  coyote takes self apart to get
    through hole,133–134
  coyote the eye-juggler, 245–247
—Crossley / Animal (Grimm) *

  wolf [foiled] and seven young
    goats, 29–34
  wolf (master) outsmarted by fox,
    45–48
—Crossley / British FT *
  farmer and boggart [trick: crop
    above/below ground], 224–227
—Curry / Beforetime *
  coyote: many tricks trying to get
    deer meat from badger; fails,
    78–88
—Douglas / Magic *
  Puss in Boots; ogre becomes
    mouse, 99–107
—Grimm / Complete *
  cock and hen, in cart pulled by
    duck, trick innkeeper, 65–66
  man tied in sack; Turnip, The,
    637–640
  riddle: princess listens to sleep-
    ing prince, 128–131
  spirit in the bottle, 458–462
  Tom Thumb, 187–193
—Grimm / Sixty *
  man tied in sack; Turnip, The,
    213–216
  Tom Thumb, 125–132
—Gullible Coyote / Malotki
  baby turtle left behind; coyote
    tricked to carry it home, 69–75
  witch-coyote and skunk; skunk
    deceives rabbits; tricks coyote,
    131–148
—Hamilton / People *
  Wiley triumphs over Hairy Man,
    90–103
—Harris-Parks / Again
  Brer Rabbit "fishing" in a well,
    2–5
—Harris-Parks / Jump *
  Brer Fox hunts, Brer Rabbit gets
    the game, 11–16
  Brer Rabbit uses Brer Fox as rid-
    ing horse, 27–32

moon in millpond: Brers Rabbit and Turtle play trick, 35–38

—High John / Sanfield *
John eats George's possum while George sleeps, 58–61
John tricks house-slave George; George gets even, 51–57

—Hoke / Giants
three giants tricked to death by boy's wits, 34–40

—Hopi Coyote / Malotki
coyote on salt expedition, 127–139

—Imaginary / Nigg
tengu, 101–103

—Jewish / Sadeh
human donkey, 307
master thief, 291–295

—Jones / Tales *
The Gingerbread Boy, 35–41

—Jonsen / Trolls *
The stone cheese [troll tricked by youngest son], 24–32

—Lester / Brer Rabbit *
Brer Fox feigns death; Brer Rabbit tricks him, 29–31
Brer Fox tricked; gets beaten by Mr. Man, 75–78
[with] Brer Wolf kills a cow; pretends to be poisoned, 115–117
lettuce patch; Mr. Man's daughter, 78–81
steals Brer Fox's peanuts; puts blame on Brer Bear, 71–74
tricks Brer Fox: "Hold'im [horse] down," 6–8
tricks Sister Cow (horns stuck in tree), 23–26
tries to trick Brer Buzzard out of his share of garden, 69–71

—Manning / Cats *
Pussy Cat Twinkle sells fur (life) to wizard; saved by female cat, 19–28

—Manning / Cauldron *
boy to be eaten by Water Witch; "hidden" by schoolmates all dressing alike, 118–127

—Maori / Kanawa *
Hutu trick "game": with Pare, catapulted out of underworld, 106–110

—Muddleheads / Harris
Mink Being wants to marry human princess, 5–25
seal of Mouse Children recovered from Big Raven, 60–74

—O'Brien / Tales *
fairy-cobbler can lead to gold; Bridget tricked with red garters, 17–20

—Paxton / Aesop *
boy who cried wolf, [33–35]

—Russian Hero / Warner *
Alesha (priest's son) battles Tugarin, 72–76
captive Mashen'ka tricks bear, 116–117
witch (blood sister) and sun's sister, 60–61

—Trolls / Asbjornsen
boy tricks devil into nut; smith smashes it, 41

—Turkish / Walker
jackal shows crow: destroy cheater by trick, 17–19

—Vanishing / Mercer *
hedgehog tricks fox; makes him his "saddle-horse," 99–101

—Water Buffalo (Chinese)
hare, crow, and greedy merchant, 18–20
monkey trick: tie tails, eat horse's rump, 82–84

—Williams-Ellis / Tales *
boy's series of trades: feather to village chief, 102–112

master thief: perform three thefts, win girl, 77–95

TRICKSTER(-s) (*usually animal, or animal-form*)
see also ANANSI STORIES; BIRD(-s): RAVEN; BRER RABBIT TALES; COYOTE; MOUSE WOMAN
—African / Abrahams, 153–229
—Afro-American / Abrahams, 177–217
—Amer Ind / Erdoes
twenty-four tales, 333–386
—American / Read Dgst
Nihausan eats family of bears, 204–205
—Bierhorst / So Am
Indian religion and mythology, 268 (index)
—Clarkson / World *
coyote gulls white man into giving up clothes, etc., 283–285
eight tales, 257–297
—Cotterell / Encyclopedia, 259 (index)
—Erdoes / Sound *
Iktome: hawk gets even for being ridiculed, 60–61
Iktome's misadventures, 16–22
Veeho: abused wife gets revenge, 68–70
Veeho: doing a trick with eyeballs, 86–89
—Hamilton / Dark *
Bumbuku, the tanuki magic teakettle, 76–81
—Hamilton / People *
Bruh Fox makes Tar Baby; rabbit gets stuck, 13–19
—High John / Sanfield *
High John the Conqueror; sixteen tales, 1–113
—Hopi Coyote / Malotki
Coyote Woman and Turkey Woman roast their children, 77–81
—Imaginary / Nigg
raven, 125–127
—Indian Myth / Burland, 144 (index)
—Mercatante / Encyclopedia, 801 (index)
—Mercatante / Good/Evil 242 (index)
—Navajo Coyote / Haile
chart: the seventeen tales, 11 @
coyote and skunk: great kill; race; skunk tricks coyote, 10, 31–32
coyote robe: coyote as both hero and evil trickster, 14, 65–68
rabbit tricks, and escapes from, coyote, 12, 38–39
tingling maiden: coyote as suitor-seducer, 15, 69–77
—Northern / Norman, 99–138
—Scandinavian / Kvideland, 428 (index)
—Turkey / Walker, 309 (index)
—Yep / Rainbow *
avoiding becoming "Bedtime snacks," 4–10

TRIFLE
—Water Buffalo (Chinese)
trifles may cause disasters, 13–17

TRINITY
—Babylonia / Spence, 410 (index)
—Grimm / Complete *
Virgin Mary, the woodcutter; forbidden room, 23–29

Tristan and Iseult
—Wolkstein / Love, 181–233, 266 @

TRISTRAM, Sir (*also* TRISTAN)
—King Arthur / Senior, 321 (index)
—Knights / Heller-Headon, 124–135
—Lacy / Arth Ency, 567–579
—Lewis / Proud
Chevrefoil (hazel and honeysuckle); lover, 79–81

TROJAN (- horse; - tales; - war)
—Bell / Classical Dict, 281–282 @
—Dictionary / Leach, 1234 (index)
—Gods / Schwab, 299–571
—Mercatante / Encyclopedia, 801 (index)
—Roman / Usher, 132 (index)
    great battle; end of the war, 69–79 @
    siege: Turnus, 64–68 @
TROLL(-s)
—Clouston / Popular, I.133–154
—Douglas / Magic *
    three billy goats Gruff, 119–121
—Ghosts / Starkey
    Tammy escapes from Lucky Minnie (troll), 110–115
—Jewish / Sadeh
    page watcher: troll and scribe, 255–256
—Jones / Tales *
    The three billy goats Gruff, 42–44
—Jonsen / Trolls *
    illustration, [8]
    three billy goats Gruff, [4–14]
    trolls and the pussy cat [a white bear], 15–23
—Lynn / Fantasy * 768 (index)
—MacDonald / Sourcebook *
    motif index, 721
—McGowen / Encyclopedia * 55–56
—Manning / Cauldron *
    donkey, gift of troll-child, helps hunter rescue princess, 9–17
—Nielsen / Old Tales *
    blue belt (magic strength), [37–62]
    widow's son joins trolls, [16–36]
—Rockwell / Puss *
    cat (white bear) on the dovrefell, 71–79
—Scandinavian / Kvideland, xii, xvi, 428 (indexes)
—Trolls / Asbjornsen
    Askelad and the silverducks, 11–16
    boy who became lion, falcon, ant, 64–70
    East of the sun . . . (poor man's daughter given to white bear), 26–35
    Rumble-Mumble Goose-Egg, 71–82
    the three Billikin Whiskers vs. troll under bridge, 17–18
    trolls invade each Christmas Eve; mistake white bear for cat, 51–52
—Williams-Ellis / Tales *
    trolls driven away by bear ("great white cat"), 17–23
TROUBLE(-s)
    see also SWALLOWED-ALIVE
—Grimm / Complete *
    absurd anticipations: Clever Elsa, 171–174
—Grimm / Sixty *
    Clever Elsa, 177–181
—Hamilton / People *
    Bruh Alligator meets trouble, 35–41
—Jewish / Sadeh
    fly and spider; incense: knowledge and understanding, 389–392
—Yep / Rainbow *
    cause, on earth: Trouble-snake, 118–123
TROUSERS
—Turkish / Walker
    man asks wife, mother, daughter to shorten pants, 135–138
TROWS
—Fairies / Briggs, 413–415
Troy, *see* TROJAN . . .
True bride, The
—Grimm / Complete * 752–760
True story of Little Golden Hood

—Lang / Wilkins, 132–136
True Thomas (ballad of)
—Fairies / Briggs, 415–417
TRUITONNE
—Dulac / Fairy *
    blue bird (prince transformed),
      77–90
TRUST
—Lines / Magical *
    girl requests red flower; must
      marry Finist the Falcon, 31–45
—Russian Hero / Warner *
    Sukhman kills 40,000 Tartars,
      41–42
TRUST IN GOD
—Jewish / Frankel
    Elijah's cup to be sold to provide
      needs for seder, 605–606
    Shah, in disguise, tests cobbler's
      faith (wooden sword), 344–346
TRUTH(-fulness)
    see also CLEVER DETECTION
      OF TRUTH; HONESTY
—Dramatized / Kamerman
    Quick-witted Jack; suitor test;
      tub, 400–412
—Egyptian / Harris
    brothers (Lies and Truth personi-
      fied), false accusation, 84–
      85
—Jewish / Frankel
    strongest thing in the world, 272–
      273
—Old Wives / Carter
    test: Nourie Hadig tells her tragic
      story to Stone of Patience,
      192–199
—Paxton / Belling *
    honesty is the best policy
      (Aesop's "lost ax"), [24–27]
—Turkish / Walker
    lion asks dog: how does my den
      smell? 16
Tsar, *see* CZAR.

TSESSEBE
—Greaves / Hippo * 104–106 @
    how tsessebe got his horns, 104–
      106
TUATHA DE DANANN
—Celtic / MacCana, 143 (index)
TUG-OF-WAR
—Greaves / Hippo *
    hare vs. hippo and rhino, 118–
      120
—Lester / Leopard *
    turtle cons elephant and hippo,
      17–20
TULA
—Mesoamerican / Leon-P, 299 (in-
    dex)
TUNNEL
—Brooke / Telling *
    John Henry wins digging race
      with steam hammer, 77–110
Turkey (country), *see* TURKISH
    TALES.
TURKEY (fowl)
—High John / Sanfield *
    Christmas: "what you do to it,
      we'll do to you," (John kisses
      its butt), 99–102
—Hopi Coyote / Malotki
    Coyote Woman and Turkey
      Woman roast their children,
      77–81
—Wildlife / Gillespie, 249 (index)
TURKISH TALES
—Clouston / Popular, II.514 (index)
—Dictionary / Leach, 1234 (index)
—Dramatized / Kamerman
    Covetous councilman (tricked; re-
      turns gold), 504–513
—Restless / Cohen *
    horse-back ride: girl ten-years-
      dead, 24–30
—Turkey / Walker, 1–310
—Turkish / Walker, 1–155
    glossary, 149–153 @

—Turkish (Art I) / Walker, 1–250
   elements; analysis, xxi–xxxvii [@]
   glossary; folk elements, 241–
      248 [@]
   historical survey, ix–xv [@]

TURNIP
—Hamilton / People *
   tall tale: fast-growing, 76–80

Turnip, The
—Grimm / Complete * 637–640
—Grimm / Sixty * 213–216

TURQUOISE
—Precious Stones / Kunz, 405 (index)

TURTLE(-s)
   see also HARE; TERRAPIN;
      TORTOISE
—Animal Legends / Kerven *
   how turtle got her shell, [15–17]
—Bierhorst / Naked *
   turtle and partridge hide bagged
      elk from wolves, 67–71
   Turtle, his sister, and Great Wind,
      110–115
   Turtle's war party vs. Seven Sis-
      ters, 31–36
—Bruchac / Iroquois *
   makes war on men, 55–59
   origin of cracked shell, 55–59
   race with bear, 51–53
   race with beaver, 47–49
—Caduto / Keepers *
   cracked shell: Turtle flew south
      for winter, 157–158
   earth's origin; primal water; tur-
      tle's back, 25–26
—Childcraft 1 / Once *
   turtle "killed" by being thrown into
      water, 172–173
—Clarkson / World *
   origin of cracks on shell, 342–347
—Coyote / Ramsey
   wins swimming race with buffalo,
      22–23

—Curry / Beforetime *
   coyote steals sun, guarded by
      turtle, 10–21
—Earthmaker / Mayo *
   Earth is on Big Turtle's back
      (Wyandot tale), 2–4
—Erdoes / Sound *
   remaking of the (third) world,
      126–129
—Fahs / Old *
   sign: Spider Woman's web-
      pattern on back, 13–14
—Gullible Coyote / Malotki, 179 [@]
   baby turtle left behind; coyote
      tricked to carry it home, 69–
      75
—Hamilton / In the Beginning *
   earth created on back of (Huron
      myth), 58–63
   Maidu creation myth, 34–41
—Hamilton / People *
   Talking cooter; master frees
      slave, 151–155
—Lester / Brer Rabbit *
   Brer Turtle as traveler, 26–29
   Brer Turtle put in sack; replaced
      with hornet's nest, 110–112
   race: Brer Turtle beats Brer Rab-
      bit, 31–34
—Lester / Leopard *
   tug-of-war: turtle cons elephant
      and hippo, 17–20
—MacDonald / Sourcebook *
   motif index, 722–723
—Quayle / Shining *
   Urashima rewarded for kindness,
      57–68
—Scary / Young *
   Indian boy (with turtle) vs. Stone
      Giant; rock-skipping, 14–16
—Spanish-Am / Van Etten *
   beggar-woman turned away:
      curse: chicken turns to turtle,
      50–51

—Vanishing / Mercer *
   origin, in Aussie creeks, 61–64
Turtle Mountain
—Fahs / Old *
   how Tewas came to live at Turtle
      Mountain, 7–14
Turtledove, Harry
—Yolen / Werewolves
   Not all wolves, 70–83
TWAIN, Mark (1835–1910)
—Brown / Amer Folklore
   autobiography: a tall tale, 108–
      121 @, 165 (index)
   frontier, 89–107 @
TWELVE
—Man Myth & Magic, 3176 (index)
Twelve apostles, The
—Grimm / Complete * 818–819
Twelve brothers
—Grimm / Complete * 59–64
**Twelve dancing princesses
   (Grimm)**
—Corrin / Favourite * 212–218
—Dramatized / Kamerman, 435
—Grimm / Complete * 596–600
—Grimm / Sixty * 41–46
—Turkish / Walker, 29–34
Twelve huntsmen, The
—Grimm / Complete * 334–336
—Grimm / Sixty * 271–273
Twelve idle servants
—Grimm / Complete * 648–650
TWINS / TWIN MYTHS
—Bierhorst / Sacred
   Indian prayers, 17, 158
—Bierhorst / So Am
   Indian religion and mythology,
      268 (index)
—Dulac / Fairy *
   green serpent: one twin princess
      cursed, ugly, 124–138
—Hamilton / In the Beginning *
   Fon creation myth: Mawu and
      Lisa, 42–45

—Lewis / Proud
   Le Fresne: twin "found" at sister's
      wedding, 20–28
—Reeves / Shadow
   twin girls parted at birth; reunited
      at wedding of one, 113–128
Two brothers
—Grimm / Complete * 290–311
Two kings' children
—Grimm / Complete * 515–524
**Two travellers: tailor and shoe-
   maker**
—Grimm / Complete * 386–496
TYR
—Scandinavian / Davidson
   sky god, 51–54, 143 (index)
TYRANNY / TYRANTS
   see also GIANT(-s)
—Chinese / Chin *
   finding wife for River God, 17–26
—Coyote / Bierhorst *
   coyote, puma and donkey divide
      catch unequally, [36]
—Fahs / Old *
   drought: lizard keeps others from
      well, 91–95
—Glooskap / Norman *
   panther-witch and her scissorbill
      birds, 39–49
TYROLIAN TALES
—Dictionary / Leach, 1234 (index)
—Manning / Cauldron *
   Martin kills witch; lions freed of
      enchantment, 66–77
TZADDIK
—Schwartz / Gates, 814 (index)

Uchida, Yoshiko
—Childcraft 3 / Stories *
   Old man with the bump, 58–65
Uenuku
—Polynesians / Andersen, 93–114

UFO(-s)
—Floyd / Gr Am Myst
    Maurice Jessup and the Phila-
    delphia experiment, 117–
    119
    nightflyers (1897); Robert Lowen,
    174–177
—Occult & Parapsych / Shepard,
    1568–69 (index)
—Southern [legends] / Floyd
    restless skies: early times to the
    present, 44–50
UGARRI
—Tree / Kerven *
    forest spirit imprisons boys in
    tree, [6–7]
UGLY (*ugliness*)
—Carter / Sleeping *
    Ricky with Tuft; man not ugly to
    princess who loves him, 93–
    102
—Corrin / Imagine *
    popplesnitch ("bird"): hunter's
    pact with demon; marry and
    ugly woman will save, 70–79
—Demi / Reflective *
    crab thinks of self as beautiful,
    [14]
—Dulac / Fairy *
    green serpent: one twin princess
    cursed, ugly, 124–138
    White Caroline, Black Caroline,
    15–21
—Earth / Hadley *
    hideous Kanya, god of fire, tries
    in vain to get a wife, [17–18]
—Grimm / Complete *
    Maid Maleen, in menial disguise,
    at lover's court, 801–807
—Jewish / Frankel
    student marries ugly girl; leaves
    her; Elijah makes her beautiful,
    588–594
—Lore of Love

    King Nala and Princess Damay-
    anti, 110–119
—O'Brien / Tales *
    Hookedy Crookedy frees mare
    and bear from giant, 53–71
—Vietnam / Terada *
    ugly man changes self to test
    wife's fidelity, 64–68
—Zipes / Beauties *
    Ricky with Tuft; man not ugly to
    princess who loves him, 52–
    57, 95–100
Ugly duckling, The (Andersen)
—Allison / I'll Tell * 34–35
—Bedtime / Padoan & Smith * 97–99
—Chorao / Child's * 57–63
—Corrin / Favourite * 16–29
—Hall / Treasury * 109–114
—Leete / Golden * 58–73
Ugly duckling, The (*existential retell-
    ing*)
—Switzer / Existential, 150–157
ULGEN (*god***)**
—Hamilton / In the Beginning *
    Russian creation myth, 28–33
UMAK
—Fahs / Old *
    Niyak and the eagle, 71–80
UMBRELLA
—Corrin / Six-Year *
    Tim Rabbit uses mushroom as
    umbrella, 161–165
UNCLE REMUS
    see also BRER RABBIT
—Lester / Brer Rabbit *
    Harris/Lester versions, xiii-xxi @
UNDERGROUND
—Bierhorst / Monkey *
    earthquake: witch escapes from
    great-horned-snake, 118–120
—Corrin / Imagine *
    Chura ("Simba"); his love re-
    turns; can marry only Simba,
    142–150

UNDERGROUND SEA
—Southern [legends] / Floyd
    lost sea (Tennessee), 64–67
UNDERSEA LIFE
—Arabian / Lewis
    merman trades jewels for fruit,
    131–137
—Arabian / McCaughrean
    merman trades jewels for fruit,
    83–96
—Dulac / Fairy *
    Urashima Taro; Dragon Sea-
    King's palace, 140–152
—Lore of Love
    Toyotama: ill-starred mating of
    earth and sea, 87–95
—Southern [legends] / Floyd, 24–
    30
—Vietnam / Terada *
    husband accuses faithful wife of
    infidelity, 10–13
    sea snake captures mandarin's
    wife, 88–94
UNDERWORLD
    see also HADES; HELL
—Bell / Classical Dict, 262–264 @
—Cotterell / Encyclopedia, 259 (in-
    dex)
—Coyote / Ramsey
    land of the dead: coyote and ea-
    gle, 81–84
    spirit of dead wife, 33–37
—Egyptian / Harris
    judgment by King of the Dead
    (Osiris), 103–107
—Egyptian / Ions, 144 (index)
—Fahs / Old *
    hunter in Walumbe's country of
    Death, 181–184
    Maui in bird-shape, seeks par-
    ents, 37–43
—Greek / Osborne
    Cupid and Psyche: the four tasks,
    57–65

    kidnapping: Ceres and Proser-
    pina, 35–39
    Orpheus and Eurydice: quest in
    underworld, 45–48
—Hamilton / People *
    Tappin: how turtle got marks on
    back, 20–25
—Hopi Coyote / Malotki, 333 @
—Jaffrey / Seasons
    Savitri nags underworld king;
    husband restored, 10–15
—Lore of Love
    rescue of loved one, 108
—Lurker / Dict Gods
    gods of, 414 (index)
—Maori / Kanawa *
    Hutu trick "game": with Pare, cat-
    apulted out of underworld,
    106–110
    Mataora, warrior chief, meets
    underworld Turehu, 68–
    80
    Putawai: evil wairua carries girl to
    underworld, 92–100
—Mercatante / Encyclopedia, 802 (in-
    dex)
—Roman / Usher, 132 (index)
    golden bough: Aeneas in the Un-
    derworld, 51–57 @
    souls after death, 25–26 @
—Russian Hero / Warner *
    Ivan son of Mare; search for
    wives, 120–124
—Scriven / Full Color *
    Persephone: winter and summer,
    75–78
UNDINES
—Lang / Wilkins
    captured children; Little King Loc,
    441–459
Ungrateful son
—Grimm / Complete * 636
UNICORN
—Animals / Rowland, 191 (index)

—Beasts / McHargue, 61–75 @, 118 (index)

—Creatures (illus) / Huber * 28, 155 (index)

—Dragons / Johnsgard, 79–163
ancient, 104–121
medieval, 121–132

—Gould / Mythical, 338–365 @

—Leonardo / Fables * 117

—Lynn / Fantasy * 768 (index)

—Man Myth & Magic, 3177 (index)

—Monsters / Cohen, 266–270 @

—Monsters / Hall, 36–41

—South / Mythical
sources; bibliographical essay, 5–26 ; 391 (index)

—Unicorn / Bradley
chiefly illustrated in color [unpaged]

—Unicorn / Coville * 1–166
hunting season: children try to save unicorn, 79–89
king would own unicorns; princess: they must be free, 24–37
pierced by horn, boy becomes a unicorn, 63–77
poems: eight in this collection . . . *passim*
princess, cat/prince, and conceited unicorn, 120–134
quest for unicorn horn: cure of winter sickness, 136–155
task: help young girl regain will to live, 92–104
Unicorn in the maze (Lindholm), 7–22
valley of the unicorns (L'Engle), 41–60
what news the eagle brought (C.S.Lewis), 105–117

—Unicorn / Hathaway
ancient China, 41–51 @
annotated bibliography, 186–187 @

celestial unicorn, 171–183 @
centuries [13th-15th] of search, 127–139 @
false unicorn, 140–149 @
first animal named; Old Testament, 29–39 @
hunt of the unicorn, 77–87 @
karkadann, 52–62 @
Knight of the Lion / Lady of the Unicorn, 88–99 @
magical horn [healing; poison; river impurities], 113–123 @
myth and mass culture, 150–169 @
Noah's Ark, 38–39 @
Severe: poem by Luca Pulci, 107–110 @
Vibhandaka: unicorn-boy of India, 65–73 @
wild people and wood nymphs, 100–111 @

—Yolen / Faery Flag
dumb child draws unicorns; is healed, 48–57

Unidentified underwater objects (UUOs)

—Floyd / Gr Am Myst, 178–182

UNIQUE EXCEPTIONS

—Chinese / Chin *
golden carp (Cinderella-type), 47–57

—Douglas / Magic *
Merlin and Arthur: the sword, 141–149

—Lines / Magical *
apple of contentment: only true owner can pick; weds king, 15–23

—Switzer / Existential
Cinderella (*existential retelling*), 38–45

UNIQUE, QUEST FOR THE

—Lines / Magical *

Little Fool Ivan and princess who lives at end of world, 70–85
—Turkish (Art I) / Walker
Cengidilaver: quest for rosebush, nightingale, gardener, 1–10

UNITED STATES
see also AMERICA; CIVIL WAR; REVOLUTION
—American / Read Dgst, 1–448
—Dictionary / Leach 1234–35 (index)
—Legends / Cavendish, 329–336
—Lynn / Fantasy * 768–770 (index)

UNITY OF MANKIND
see also SOLIDARITY
—Caduto / Keepers *
How Grandmother Spider stole the Sun, 49–50
White Buffalo Calf Woman and sacred pipe, 187–188

UNIVERSE
see also WORLD
—Hamilton / In the Beginning *
Phan Ku: Chinese creation myth, 20–23
—Persian / Hinnells
Persian mythology, 22–23

UNKINDNESS (usually punished)
see also KINDNESS
—Bruchac / Iroquois *
snakes make war of revenge, 93–95
—Clarkson / World *
gold in chimney; animals deliver unkind girl to witch, 26–29
—Crossley / British FT *
baker's daughter turned into owl; refuses bread to fairy/old woman, 331–333
fairy-wife lost when husband strikes her third time, 353–364
—Grimm / Complete *
mistreated servant in grave; master's fate, 749–752

white bride and black bride, 608–612
—Lang / Wilkins
enchantment: princess must stay in tower . . . , 415–431
—Muddleheads / Harris
rejection of arranged marriages: evil result, 115–130
—Russian Hero / Warner *
bear bites off head of woman who cut off its leg, 117–120
—Turkish (Art I) / Walker
unkind stepsister gets chest of snakes, 46–51

UNMARRIED MOTHERS
—Vietnam / Terada *
shame, 63 @

UNMARRIED WOMEN
—Women / Dyer
old/young maids, 175–182 @

UNNATURAL ALLIANCES
—Crossley / Animal (Grimm) *
cat/mouse partnership, 21–25

UNPROMISING ONE SUCCEEDS
see also HERO, UNLIKELY; YOUNGEST . . .
—Bryan / Lion *
Jumoke ("Foolish Boy") outwits Ananse, 60–86
—Cambodian / Carrison
Phnong family murdered; one child is saved, 78–85
—Celts / Hodges *
Gareth of Orkney wins his spurs, 133–154
—Childcraft 1 / Once *
homely cat chosen over millions . . . , 258–263
—Chorao / Child's *
ugly duckling (Andersen), 57–63
—Crossley / Animal (Grimm) *
hare and hedgehog race, 39–44
hedge-king (bird) defeats bear, 49–53

—Crossley / British FT *
 illegitimate girl cared for by her
 mother; marries laird's son,
 218–223
—Douglas / Magic *
 unpromising hero: Jack the Giant
 Killer, 131–139
—Grimm / Complete *
 cat (princess) gives horse to
 miller's apprentice, 482–485
 good bargain: peasant thinks frog
 and dog are speaking, 51–55
 three feathers: youngest prince
 marries toad, 319–322
—Hepburn / World *
 Tattercoats: gooseherd plays
 flute; prince falls in love, 90–
 109
—Hoke / Giants
 success of unpromising hero,
 34–40, 41–64
—Jewish / Frankel
 king and: contented simple man,
 dissatisfied clever man, 538–
 544
—Lang / Wilkins
 Nunda, eater of people, 602–
 614
—Lines / Magical *
 Joseph (in Egypt) advisor to
 Pharaoh, 149–169
—Russian Hero / Warner *
 little simpleton: silver saucer and
 juicy apple, 106–108
—Switzer / Existential
 ugly duckling (first woman in major league baseball), 150–157
—Turkish / Walker
 lazy, bald Keloglan wins sultan's
 daughter, 20–22
—Turkish (Art I) / Walker
 apprentice shoe merchant dismissed for request to Allah,
 116–122
—Vietnam / Terada *
 elder brother inherits all but starfruit tree, 3–6
Unreality, *see* DAYDREAMS; REAL-
 ITY.
Unwise act, *see* FOOL . . .
UPPER WORLD
 see also HEAVENS; Jack and the
 beanstalk; SKY
—Chinese / Chin *
 cowherd's marriage to fairy weaving maid, 113–125
—Lang / Wilkins
 gnome king Rubezahl captures
 princess, 497–512
—Quayle / Shining *
 Shining Princess (from Moon
 People) and deceptive suitors,
 13–23
UPPER WORLD, JOURNEY TO
 see also VOYAGE TO THE
 MOON
—Animal Legends / Kerven *
 reward for saving eagle chicks:
 journey to sky, [22–23]
—Corrin / Six-Year *
 by mistake, crossing-sweeper
 takes magic broom, 87–92
—Curry / Beforetime *
 coyote rides the sun, 100–106
—Grimm / Complete *
 flail from heaven, 514–515
—Journey Sun (Chinese)
 woman (and newborn son) on 99-
 yr trip to restore sun, 1–5
—Russian Hero / Warner *
 cock and the corn mill, 52–53
UPPSALA
—Scandinavian / Davidson, 144 (in-
 dex)
UR
—Babylonia / Spence, 410 (index)
URAEUS
—Egyptian / Ions, 144 (index)

Urashima Taro; Dragon Sea-King's palace
—Dulac / Fairy * 140–152
URBAN LEGENDS
—Scandinavian / Kvideland, 428 (index)
URIEL
—Davidson / Dictionary, 298–299
URSA MAJOR
—Constellations / Gallant * 203 (index)
URUK
—Wolkstein / Love, 256 @
USEFULNESS
—Aesop / Holder *
    antlers as utility or ornament; stag and the hounds, 24–25
—Aesop / Reeves-Wilson *
    stag: proud of antlers; ashamed of legs, 29
UTENSILS, MAGIC
—Arabian / Lewis
    Anklet [magic pot; magic pins] 49–51
—Chorao / Child's *
    teakettle turns into badger, 21–27
—Clarkson / World *
    do-all ax chops wood, plows, etc., on command, 49–51
—Corrin / Six-Year *
    by mistake, crossing-sweeper takes magic broom, 87–92
—Frog Rider (Chinese)
    magic brush: things painted become real, 47–59
—Grimm / Complete *
    magic pot produces porridge, 475–476
    spindle, shuttle, and needle help girl marry prince, 764–767
—Hamilton / People *
    Bruh Rabbit: how stop stolen magic hoe? 31–34

—Russian Hero / Warner *
    cock and the corn mill, 52–53
UTHER PENDRAGON, King
—Celts / Hodges *
    Merlin: life and magic powers, 117–132
—Douglas / Magic *
    Merlin and Arthur: birth, childhood, the sword, 141–149
—King Arthur / Senior, 321 (index)
UTILITY
—Allison / I'll Tell *
    value: stag's legs vs. antlers, 100
UTOPIAN
—Southern [legends] / Floyd
    Rugby colony: Thomas Hughes in Tennessee, 50–54
—Water Buffalo (Chinese)
    five wishes: crow-messenger disobeys God, 23–29
UTU
—Wolkstein / Love, 257 @

Vahl, Rod
—Dramatized / Kamerman
    Indian boy without a name, 526–536
VAINAMOINEN
—Fahs / Old *
    weeping of the birch tree; harp, 15–18
VALHALLA
—Norse / Crossley, 275 (index)
Valiant tailor (seven at one blow)
—Grimm / Complete * 112–120
—Grimm / Sixty * 88–97
—Lang / Wilkins, 64–72
VALUES (choice, relativity, etc.)
—Aesop / Holder
    cock and the jewel, 20–21
—Bomans / Wily *
    cobbler's three wishes from

gnome; learns money's limitations, 53–61

—Corrin / Imagine *
clever peasant girl [riddle: most valued], 116–123

—Crossley / British FT *
John Chapman, pedlar of Swaffham, 251–264

—Demi / Reflective *
know/treasure the more valuable, [24]

—Douglas / Magic *
Beauty and the Beast, 85–97

—Geras / Grandmother *
talking plants' beauty contest: olive tree the winner, 57–65

—Grimm / Complete *
poverty and humility lead to heaven, 820–821

—Jewish / Frankel
Solomon visits deserted palace; learns "vanities," 251–254
three friends: what counts at time of death, 379

—Lang / Wilkins
princess sent to check on fairy gifts, 186–189

—Lines / Magical *
magic apple of contentment: highest value, 15–23

—Manning / Cats *
small-small cat seeks advice on growing large, 126–127

—Rockwell / Puss *
Mr. Vinegar (makes series of bad trades), 60–65

—Turkish (Art I) / Walker, xxviii @

—Yep / Rainbow *
prudent/foolish brothers: butterfly man, 60–68

—Yolen / Faery Flag animal vs. human; mother's teaching; multiple transformations, 21–39

VAMPIRE
—Dracula / McNally
Old World folklore, 142–159 @
—Limburg / Weird, 66–69
—Man Myth & Magic
analytics, 3200 (index)
—McGowen / Encyclopedia * 56–57
—McNally / Clutch
twenty-five selections from literature and history: ancient, medieval, modern, contemporary, 1–255
—Monsters / Cohen, 271–275 @
—South / Mythical
sources; bibliographical essay, 243–264; 392 (index)
—Unnatural / Cohen, 53–70, 148 (index)
vampire bat; 19th cent. engraving, 55

VANIR
—Scandinavian / Davidson, 144 (index)

VANISHING
—Southern [legends] / Floyd
Paul Redfern's final flight, 83–87

Vanity, *see* PRIDE.

VARUNA
—Indic / Ions, 144 (index)

VASILISA
—Hamilton / Dark *
Baba Yaga, Vasilisa, and her doll, 14–22
—Russian Hero / Warner *
magic doll helps Vasilisa escape Baba-Yaga, 86–92
three princes/brides, one a frog-princess, 101–106

Vasilisa, the priest's daughter
—Old Wives / Carter, 57–59

VAYU
—Indic / Ions, 144 (index)

VEGETATION
—Babylonia / Spence, 411 (index)

VENUS
—Baring-Gould / Curious
   Mountain of Venus, 78–82 @
—Douglas / Magic *
   Cupid and Psyche, 151–165
—Greek / Osborne
   Atalanta and Hippomenes:
      golden apples, 51–54
   Cupid and Psyche: the four tasks,
      57–65
—Man Myth & Magic, 3177 (index)
—Roman / Usher, 132 (index)
—Room / Classical Dict
   by-names (list), 319–322 @
VERACRUZ
—Dictionary / Leach, 1218 (index)
Vergil, *see* Virgil.
VERNAL EQUINOX
—Constellations / Gallant * 203 (in-
   dex)
Verse, *see* POETRY.
VICEROY
—Jewish / Sadeh
   lost princess: king's curse, to
      Evil One's kingdom, 386–389
VICTIM TRAPPED
   see also TRAP
—Clarkson / World *
   Anansi captured by gum-man
      (tarbaby), 259–261
—Hamilton / People *
   Bruh Fox makes Tar Baby; rabbit
      gets stuck, 13–19
—Turkish / Walker
   Karacor and the giants, 52–61
VICTORY
—Bell / Classical Dict, 266 @
VIETNAMESE TALES
—Vietnam / Terada * 1–136
VIGIL(-s)
—Knights / Heller-Headon, 56–57
VIGILANCE TEST
—Lines / Magical *
   girl buys three nights from be-

trothed of Finist the Falcon,
   31–45
VIKING PERIOD
—Scandinavian / Davidson, 144 (in-
   dex)
Village of fools (Gotham)
—Crossley / British FT * 36–37
Villeneuve, G.S. de
—Lang / Wilkins
   Beauty and the beast, 44–63
—Zipes / Beauties *
   Beauty and the beast, 153–245
VINE
—Leonardo / Fables *
   imprudent vine clings to old tree,
      86
VIOLENCE
—Aesop / Alley *
   wind vs. sun: which is stronger?
      20–23
—Aesop / Reeves-Wilson *
   who is stronger? Wind and sun,
      88–91
VIPER
—Animals / Rowland, 192 (index)
**VIRGIL (Vergilius Maro)(70–19
   b.c.)**
—Grimal / Dictionary, 602 (index)
—Mercatante / Encyclopedia, 802 (in-
   dex)
—Roman / Perowne, 122–126 @
—Roman / Usher, 132 (index)
VIRGINITY
—Bell / Classical Dict, 267 @
VIRTUE(-s)
—Fairies / Briggs
   esteemed by fairies, 420–421
—Jewish / Frankel
   Moshele's gift: water-carrier
      prays for 1,000 rubles, 554–
      556
—Leonardo / Fables *
   woodlark: love; home, the noble
      heart, 18–19

VIRTUE (man's name)
—Yep / Rainbow *
    Virtue goes to town, 118–123
VISHNU (*sometimes* VISHNA)
—Cotterell / Encyclopedia, 259 (index)
—Imaginary / Nigg
    the garuda, 74
—Indic / Ions, 144 (index)
—Jaffrey / Seasons
    heavenly nectar of immortality:
      Vishnu, Moon, demon Rahu,
      71–72
—Man Myth & Magic, 3178 (index)
—Wolkstein / Love, 257 @
VISION (sight)
—Erdoes / Sound *
    vision quest [spirits can't be
      forced], 63–67
VISIONS
—Arabian / Lewis
    holy man sent to make king
      aware of his gifts, 184–87
—Arabian / McCaughrean
    holy man . . . [as above], 208–
      217
—Christian / Every, 144 (index)
—Jewish / Frankel
    tailor's sleeve: divorce, 521–
      523
VOCATION
—Journeys / Norris *
    hell: prayers of good person
      make evils disappear, [26–28]
**VODIANOI (VODYANOI) (spirit of
    water)**
—McGowen / Encyclopedia * 57–58
—Russian / Ivanits, 251 (index)
VOLCANO
—Earthmaker / Mayo *
    monster overeats and erupts,
      65 @
    mountain roars! (overeats;
      erupts; Nisqually tale) 66–70

—Lore of Love
    couple's reunion in flames:
      Popocatepetl, 52–57
—Scary / Young *
    Pele, Spirit of Fire, vs. Na-Maka;
      Kilauea, 84–86
VOLCANO WOMAN
—Indian Myth / Burland, 45–49
—Muddleheads / Harris
    Asdilda desecrates Cormorant
      Hat, 94–114
VOODOO (VODOUN)
—American / Read Dgst
    New Orleans, rites, prescriptions,
      56–57
—Man Myth & Magic, 3178 (index)
—Medicine-Plants / Read Dgst
    ancient lore, 23
—Mercatante / Good/Evil, 173–179 @
—Pirate Ghosts / McSherry
    hangman's rope: Macartney and
      Fawcett, 84–144
—Southern [legends] / Floyd
    practices since days of slavery,
      104–108
—Witch Encyc / Guiley, 349–353,
    420 (index)
Voragine, Jacques de
—Baring-Gould / Curious
    Seven Sleepers of Ephesus, 44–
    49
VORTIGERN
—King Arthur / Ashe, 191 (index)
VOW
—Celts / Hodgess *
    Cuchulain: champion of Ireland,
      17–31
—Jewish / Frankel, 651 (index)
    demon princess/wife and the bro-
      ken oath, 432–437
VOYAGE TO THE MOON
—Corrin / Six-Year *
    by mistake, crossing-sweeper
      takes magic broom, 87–92

WADJET (serpent goddess)
—Wolkstein / Love, 245 @
Wadsworth, Wallace
—Hoke / Giants
    Paul Bunyan and his Great Blue
      Ox, 11–29
WAGER(-s) (bets)
    see also GAMBLER(-ing)
—Bomans / Wily *
    soldier's wager with King; traps
      ghost; becomes king, 37–43
—Clarkson / World *
    Gudbrand on Hill-side: bets wife
      will not complain, 75–78
—Crossley / Animal (Grimm) *
    hare and hedgehog race, 39–
      44
—Crossley / British FT *
    prince bets head in card game
      with giant, 313–330
—Curry / Beforetime *
    animal-people wager fire-stones,
      and lose, 33–41
—Grimm / Complete *
    Hansel gambles in heaven and in
      hell, 378–380
—Hamilton / People *
    most useful slave [can prophesy],
      160–164
—High John / Sanfield *
    bet on eating 40-pound water-
      melon (eats one for practice),
      41–43
    freedom, on bet he can make
      mean Master laugh, 73–78
    master bets on slave's foreknowl-
      edge, 24–33
    master's walking stick: "three
      ends" (bet), 9–12
—Old Coot / Christian *
    wager: gambler won't say
      "enough" to Old Coot's stories,
      29–38
—Russian Hero / Warner *

    Sadko of Novgorod: musician be-
      comes rich merchant, 44
—Shannon / More *
    frog wins bet; though facing west
      he still sees dawn-rays first,
      51–52
    slave (John) "loses" bet, but wins
      money (how?), 57–60
    stranger wins bet on "believing"
      tall tales, 53–56
—Turkish / Walker
    survive cold night; candle 100
      meters away, 47–48
—Yep / Rainbow *
    Wong I, II and III: The boasting
      contest, 96–105
WAGES
—Corrin / Six-Year *
    Silly Simon (follows suggestions
      foolishly), 120–124
—Grimm / Complete *
    thumbling nursed by giant ac-
      quires fabulous strength, 412–
      420
—Hoke / Giants
    Strong Gottlieb, 103–111
Wagner, Jenny
—Childcraft 1 / Once *
    bunyip of Berkeley's Creek, 231–
      235
WAGNER, Richard (1813–1883)
—Lacy / Arth Ency, 616–622
WAHCONDA
—Earthmaker / Mayo * 43 @
    makes the earth shake; takes
      Sun-Flower (Oto tale), 54–56
WAKONYINGO
—McGowen / Encyclopedia * 58
WALES
—Dictionary / Leach, 1235 (index)
—Lynn / Fantasy * 770 (index)
WALKING STICK
—High John / Sanfield *
    "three ends" (bet), 9–12

WALL
—Dramatized / Kamerman
   Frost Giant: builder of the wall,
      422–434
WALRUS
—Hamilton / People *
   wolf insults birds; tries to kill help-
      ful walrus, 43–48
WAND, MAGIC
—Starkey / Ghosts
   Draiglin' Hogney defeated by
      youngest brother, 80–87
—Yep / Rainbow *
   cats and dogs as "Natural ene-
      mies," 12–18
WANJIRU
—Hamilton / Dark *
   girl swallowed by the earth, 108–
      112
WAQIYASMA (chief)
—Journeys / Norris *
   scatter throughout the land; tribal
      origins, [13–15]
WAR(-s)
   see also ANIMAL WARFARE;
      BATTLE(-s); INDIAN WARS
—Aesop / Reeves-Wilson *
   birds, beasts, and bat, 55–56
—Bell / Classical Dict, 270 @
—Cotterell / Encyclopedia, 259 (in-
      dex)
—Crossley / Animal (Grimm) *
   hedge-king (bird) defeats bear,
      49–53
—Curry / Beforetime *
   war between beasts and birds;
      fickle bat, 68–69
—Fahs / Old *
   morality: Krishna helps good king
      win over evil, 108–113
   two kings dispute over land, 101–
      103
—Folk Ballads / McNeil
   folk ballads, I.33–46
—Irish / Glassie
   five tales, 210–215
—Jewish / Frankel, 651 (index)
—Mercatante / Encyclopedia, 804 (in-
      dex)
—Mesoamerican / Leon-P, 300 (in-
      dex)
—Nielsen / Old Tales *
   widow's son brings about victory,
      [16–36]
—Scandinavian / Kvideland, xviii, 428
      (index)
—Vietnam / Terada *
   magic crossbow: China and Viet-
      nam, 125 @
WAR DEITIES
—Lurker / Dict Gods, 415 (index)
WARLOCK
—Lore of Love
   tricked: hair from heifer, 84
WARNING(-s; attention to)
—Bierhorst / Naked *
   Mother Swan's daughters, 72–
      78
—Grimm / Complete *
   Wolf killed by man [fox's warning
      ignored], 350–351
—Grimm / Sixty *
   Wolf killed by man, 211–212
—Navajo Coyote / Haile
   signs of warning: noise in the tra-
      chea, 14, 55–58
—Turkish (Art I) / Walker
   laborer purchases four pieces of
      advice, to his good fortune,
      179–183
WARRIORS
—Legends / Cavendish, 394 (index)
—Quayle / Shining *
   Isle of Demons; Momotaro's sam-
      urai: dog, pheasant, monkey,
      77–89
—Turkish (Art I) / Walker
   woodcutter's wife, once a mighty

warrior disguised as man, 200–
204
WART HOG
—Greaves / Hippo * 113 @
why he goes on his knees, 108
why he is so ugly, 109–112
WASHER AT THE FORD
—McGowen / Encyclopedia * 58–59
WASHERWOMAN
—Jaffrey / Seasons
crow drops queen's necklace on
washerwoman's doorstep, 81–
84
WASP
—Bierhorst / Monkey *
Lord Sun courts woman; she be-
comes moon; origin of wasps,
flies, 84–91
WASTREL
—Jewish / Sadeh
young man and princess/lawyer,
277–279
WATER (sometimes magic)
see also DRINK; FLOOD;
OCEAN; RAIN; SEA; WELL(-s)
—Grimm / Complete *
Youth who could not shudder;
cold water, 29–39
—Grimm / Legends (Ward), II:458 (in-
dex)
—Grimm / Sixty *
Youth who could not shudder,
300–311
—Jewish / Frankel, 647 (index)
—Lang / Wilkins
Fairy of the Dawn; magic well
water, 571–601
—Lester / Leopard *
visit: why sun and moon [personi-
fied] are in sky, 1–4
—MacDonald / Sourcebook *
motif index, 727–728
—Man Myth & Magic, 3178 (index)
—Manning / Cats *

chain-tale: boy, hare, fox, wolf,
bear vs. Baba Yaga, 58–64
—Mercatante / Encyclopedia, 804 (in-
dex)
—Russian / Ivanits
holy, 251 (index)
—Russian Hero / Warner * 37 @
—Williams-Ellis / Tales *
Sister Long-Hair steals stream
from mountain god, 161–171
—Witch Encyc / Guiley, 420 (index)
WATERBUCK
—Greaves / Hippo * 95–96 @
how waterbuck got white circle on
rump, 92–95
waterbuck runs into swamp; es-
capes lion, 91–92
WATER BUFFALO
—Vietnam / Terada *
how tiger got its stripes, 7–9
—Water Buffalo (Chinese)
water-buffalo vs. tiger, 85–88
WATER CAT
—Manning / Cats *
boy Altin's golden knuckle-
bone, water cat, and stallion,
29–36
WATER DEMON
—Russian Hero / Warner *
Vodyanoi, 48–49 @
water sprites, 48 @
WATERFALL
—Williams-Ellis / Tales *
Sister Long-Hair steals stream
from mountain god, 161–171
WATER HOLE
—Greaves / Hippo *
elephant vs. Rain Spirit: who is
greater, 53–58
fight with baboon: how zebra got
stripes, 99–102
Water-horse, see KELPIE.
Water-horse and water-bull
—Fairies / Briggs, 427–428

WATER JAR
—Jewish / Sadeh
two shopkeepers, eagle, mountain of gold, 271–273
WATER of LIFE
—Russian / Afanasev, 661 (index)
—Russian Hero / Warner *
Vasilisa (Golden Braid) and Ivan the Pea, 63–68
wolf helps quest; warnings ignored, 112–116
Water of life (Grimm)
—Grimm / Complete * 449–455
—Grimm / Sixty * 264–270
—Lang / Wilkins, 362–368
WATERMELON
—Gullible Coyote / Malotki
coyote and horned lizard eat watermelons; coyote swallows horned lizard alive, 149–154
—Shannon / More *
task: buy one thing that will fill four different needs, 15–18
Water monster, see MONSTER(-s).
Water-nixie, The
—Grimm / Complete * 364–365
WATER SERPENT
see also SEA SERPENT
—Hopi Coyote / Malotki, 335 @
coyote fashions long tail as ruse, 9–21
WATER SPIRIT(-s)
see also KELPIE; NIXIE
—Celts / Hodges *
Lad of Luck and monster, 89–103
—Crossley / British FT *
Hughbo works for farmer, until wife makes clothes for him, 265–269
—Earth / Hadley *
storm: Lin maiden (ghost) guides lost seamen to safety, [27–28]
—Grimm / Complete *
nixie (mill-pond) captures young man; wife rescues, 736–742

—Lang / Wilkins
Little King Loc, 441–459
—Lore of Love
demon-bride's marriage to mortal, 68–73
—Muddleheads / Harris
sea hunters swallowed by whirlpool, 26–43
—Russian Hero / Warner *
Rusalka and the seal-hunter, 28–29
Sadko of Novgorod: musician becomes rich merchant, 44
—Scandinavian / Kvideland, xv, 428 (index)
—Spanish-Am / Van Etten *
river-man: steals (later returns) people's money, shadows, 37–41
—Starkey / Ghosts
McGregor and the kelpy, 66–71
WATER-SPRITE
—Baring-Gould / Curious
Melusina: mortal wed to water-sprite, 129–133 @
—McGowen / Encyclopedia *
Rusalka, 48
—Russian / Ivanits
Rusalka, 250 (index)
—Russian Hero / Warner *
Kapsirko outwits demon, 49–50
WATER of STRENGTH/WEAKNESS
—Russian / Afanasev, 661 (index)
WATERS: ORIGIN OF CHARACTERISTICS
—Caduto / Keepers *
Four Worlds (Dine); origin of water features, 31–34
how Raven made the tides, 103
how Thunder and Earthquake made Ocean, 93–95
Sedna, woman under the sea, 95–97
—Earthmaker / Mayo *

mysterious; whirlpools, 71 @
why Great Spirit made waters like
  mirrors (Iroquois), 72–74
—Erdoes / Sound *
  remaking of the (third) world,
  126–129
—Russian Hero / Warner *
  Sukhman kills 40,000 Tartars,
  41–42
—Yep / Rainbow *
  Trouble-snake, 118–123
Watts, Frances B.
—Dramatized / Kamerman
  Bridge to Killybog Fair, 227–238
  Leprechaun shoemakers, 239–
  249
WAZIR
—Arabian / McCaughrean
  two wazirs: who will succeed the
  king, 203–207
WEAK (*the weaker one as hero; win-
  ner over the stronger . . .* **)**
—Aesop / Alley *
  Lion and the mouse, 16–19
—Aesop / Holder *
  laden ass and a horse, 10–13
—Aesop / Reeves-Wilson *
  Oak and reed [survives storm], 27
  race: Hare and Tortoise, 68–73
—Arabian / Riordan
  misfortune: porter; three ladies of
  Baghdad, 108–125
—Bierhorst / Naked *
  Lodge Boy and Thrown Away
  [chipmunk-sized boy], 79–86
—Coyote / Bierhorst *
  pays to be clever when you're the
  weaker one, [14]
—Coyote / Ramsey
  boy steals Thunder's wife, 18–20
—Curry / Beforetime *
  mountain lion "defeated" by mos-
  quito (cricket's aide), 70–73
—Fahs / Old *

Glooskap ignored by baby, 153–
  155
—Grimm / Complete *
  Tom Thumb, 187–193
—Hamilton / People *
  Wiley triumphs over Hairy Man,
  90–103
—Harris-Parks / Jump *
  Brer Rabbit tricks Brer Wolf into
  trunk, 3–8
—Hoke / Giants
  triumph of weak (but clever) over
  strong, 71–78
—Turkish / Walker
  Hasan, the heroic mouse-child,
  8–10
  Karacor and the giants, 52–61
WEALTH
  see also MONEY; POOR; RICH;
  TREASURE
—Arabian / Lewis
  changing luck: destiny or capital,
  17–24
—Arabian / McCaughrean
  Keys of destiny; Iram, 65–82
—Bomans / Wily *
  cobbler's three wishes from
  gnome; learns money's limitations, 53–61
  simple blackberry-picker has
  riches in beauties of nature,
  47–53
—Caduto / Keepers *
  Awi Usdi: fortune lost for breaking
  hunting taboo, 173–174
—Chorao / Child's *
  tinker's teakettle turns into
  badger, 21–27
—Clouston / Popular
  advantages of speaking to a king,
  II.360–366
  counting chickens before
  hatched [opulence], II.432–
  443

—Coyote / Bierhorst *
   hidden, hoarded gold might as
     well be stone, [10]
—Egyptian / Mercatante
   serpent bestows wealth on ship-
     wrecked sailor, 155–158
—Fahs / Old *
   blood of defrauded poor, 125–
     126
   magic pillow: dream projects van-
     ity, 121–124
—Jaffrey / Seasons
   Parvati provides palace to cover
     Queen's well-intentioned lie,
     115–119
—Jewish / Frankel, 651 (index)
   Elijah, three sons, three wishes,
     587–588
   two brothers (rich/poor) granted
     wish ("enough"), 602–604
—Jewish / Sadeh
   apprentice baker's blessing,
     112–117
   piece of copper makes junk man
     rich, 183–186
   Pinchas and the dead monkey,
     189–190
   servant of Baal Shem Tov forgets
     all stories save one, 357–361
   seven good years: now or later,
     187–189
   Solomon's wager with fate, 64–
     65
—Mercatante / Encyclopedia, 805 (in-
   dex)
—O'Brien / Tales *
   poor farmer trades cow for magic
     bottle, 46–52
—Russian Hero / Warner *
   Sadko of Novgorod: musician be-
     comes rich merchant, 44
—Turkish / Walker
   ruler gives daughter to poor man
     as punishment, 139–147

WEAPONS, MAGIC
—Coyote / Ramsey
   Cry-Because-He-Have-No-Wife,
     29–30
—Crane / Beauty *
   Yellow Dwarf and proud princess,
     [34–47]
—Grimm / Complete *
   brothers: one rescues princess; is
     rescued by other, 290–311
   skillful huntsman, 508–514
WEASEL
—Animals / Rowland, 192 (index)
—Curry / Beforetime *
   mink and bluejay retrieve Little
     Weasel, stolen by lizard, 60–67
   weasel opens weather-bundles,
     in roadrunner's pack, 5–9
—Harris-Parks / Again
   Brers Mink-Possum-Coon-Fox-
     Bear guard butter, 14–21
WEATHER
   see also RAIN; SEASONS; etc.
—Bierhorst / Sacred
   Indians, 93–107
—Bomans / Wily *
   wind-man controls four winds:
     happiness to one is sorrow to
     another, 76–78
—Caduto / Keepers *
   Spring defeats Winter, 129–131
—Coyote / Ramsey
   Chetco: monster swept out to
     sea, 146–147
   Frost and Thunder, 193–195
—Curry / Beforetime *
   origin: bundles, in roadrunner's
     pack, 5–9
—Earthmaker / Mayo *
   phenomena; origins; Indian leg-
     ends, 1–89
—Folk-rhymes / Northall
   England, 459–478
—Giant / Harrison *

giant's tantrums cause earth-
quakes, etc., 33–42
—Man Myth & Magic, 3178 (index)
—Plants / Dyer, 114–127
—Turkish / Walker
boasting mouse misunderstands
natural phenomena, 1–3
WEATHER DEITIES
—Lurker / Dict Gods, 416 (index)
**WEATHER: ORIGIN OF PRESENT
ORDER**
—Caduto / Keepers *
Spring/ Winter, 129–131
—Curry / Beforetime *
weasel opens weather-bundles,
in roadrunner's pack, 5–9
—Erdoes / Sound *
thunderbirds: weather phenom-
ena, 33–36
WEAVING
—Greek / Osborne
weaving contest: Arachne and
Minerva, 19–21
WEDDING(-s)
see also BRIDE; MARRIAGE
—Grimm / Complete *
Robber bridegroom, 200–204
—Grimm / Sixty *
Robber bridegroom, 120–124
—Jewish / Sadeh
finger: she-demon claims bride-
groom as her husband, 241–
242
—Reeves / Shadow
twin girls parted at birth; reunited
at wedding of one, 113–128
—Russian / Ivanits, 251 (index)
—Turkey / Walker, 310 (index)
WEDDING FEAST
—Grimm / Complete *
Robber bridegroom [witness to
murder], 200–204
—Grimm / Sixty *
Robber bridegroom . . . , 120–124

Wedding of Mrs. Fox, see Marriage
of . . .
WEESACK-KACHAK
—Earth / Hadley *
muskrat rebuilding earth, [6–7]
WELL(-s)
—Arabian / Lewis
well's magic objects do "impossi-
ble" tasks, 117–122
—Arabian / McCaughrean
Man with three wives; jinni, 185–
193
—Bell / Classical Dict, 272–273 @
—Bomans / Wily *
echo well: misshapen people not/
aware of defects, 97–100
—Campbell / West Highlands, IV.442
(index)
—Fahs / Old *
drought: lizard keeps others from
well, 91–95
—Harris-Parks / Again
Brer Rabbit "fishing" in a well,
2–5
—Hope / Holy Wells
England; antiquities, 1–222
—Jewish / Frankel, 647 (index)
—Lester / Brer Rabbit *
in the well: Brer Rabbit tricks Brer
Fox, 44–46
—MacDonald / Sourcebook *
motif index, 729
—Turkish (Art I) / Walker
grateful fairy-padishah teaches
farmer (with termagant wife) to
cure the sick, 188–190
**WELSH in NORTH AMERICA (12th
cent.)**
—Southern [legends] / Floyd
Prince Madoc, 38–43
WELSH TALE
—Dramatized / Kamerman
Baron Barnaby's box, 549–
558

WENAMON
—Egyptian / Harris
  voyage: build sacred boat for
    Amon-Ra, 117–125
WER-BEASTS / WER-CREATURES
—Werewolves / Aylesworth
  other than wolves, 64–75, 125–
    126 (index)
—Yolen / Shape Shift, 4
WERE-FOX
—Strauss / Trail
  woman reflects on her fox-life
    (poem), 22–23
—Yolen / Faery Flag
  foxwife, 12–20
WEREWOLF
—Clarkson / World *
  child transformed by old woman's
    curse, 202–206
—Classic / Downer
  Talbot County (Georgia), 63–65
—Grimm / Legends (Ward), II:459 (in-
    dex)
—Jewish / Frankel
  Baal Shem Tov and the devil-
    hearted werewolf, 473–475
  rabbi's magic ring: rabbi to were-
    wolf; wife to donkey, 450–455
—Lewis / Proud
  Bisclavret: wife keeps husband in
    wolf-form, 29–35
—Lycanthropy / Otten, 336 (index)
  aetiology (Illis), 195–199 @
  allegory: Clemence Housman,
    281–320
  converse with priest (Giraldus
    Cambrensis), 57–61
  Eugene Field: The werewolf,
    262–268
  Jean Grenier, 62–68
  King Arthur and Gorlagon, 234–
    255
  Marie de France: Lay of the were-
    wolf, 256–261

  medical descriptions; history, 19–
    47 @
  myths and legends (six), 221–
    280
  Ovid: Lycaon and Jupiter, 227–
    230
  Petronius Arbiter: Satyricon,
    231–233
  Stenbock: The other side, 269–
    280
  Stubbe Peeter, 69–76
  trial records; historical accounts,
    49–98
—Man Myth & Magic, 3179 (index)
—McGowen / Encyclopedia * 59–
    60
—Monsters / Cohen, 276–280 @
—Reeves / Shadow
  betrayed husband; becomes at-
    tached to king; curse removed,
    99–110
  husband becomes "Garwal,"
    three days each week, 99–
    110
—Russian Hero / Warner * 100 @
—Scandinavian / Kvideland, ix (in-
    dex)
—South / Mythical
  sources; bibliographical essay,
    265–289 (by M. Cheilik); 392
    (index)
—Unnatural / Cohen, 33–52, 148 (in-
    dex)
—Werewolves / Aylesworth
  European history, 32–47
  ritual for becoming a werewolf,
    21–25
  theories of origin, 76–83
  trials, 48–63
—Wolves / Lopez, 307 (index)
—Woman's Ency / Walker, 1068–
    1072 @
—Yolen / Shape Shift
  commentary on, 23

Curtis, R.: The boy who would be wolf, 6–21
Saki: Gabriel-Ernest, 24–35
—Yolen / Werewolves
  Bad blood (faculty adviser and teen-ager), 3–34
  Flesh and blood (becomes werewolf when putting on dress), 172–188
  Green messiah (genetic engineering), 189–200
  gypsy werewolf, Nazi soldiers, Jewish children, 238–253
  how to become a werewolf, ix-xi @
  Jew shelters werewolf, 70–83
  Met by moonlight (protected by wolfgirl), 224–237
  Monster mash (band contest on night of full moon), 127–150
  Night calls (nuclear holocaust), 95–118
  Passing of the pack (son replaces father as leader), 151–171
  ridding self of the curse, 35–44
  unhappy children find key to otherworld, 254–267
  werewolf adopts human child, 35–44
  White Wolf: boy's initiation to manhood, 45–69
  Wolf's flock (finds redemption in Children's Crusade), 201–223
  Wolfskin (boy rents, and becomes werewolf), 84–94
  woman student interviews wolves, 119–126
WEST (U.S.)
—American / Read Dgst, 305–331
—Oral Trad / Cunningham
  recitations, 1–264
WEST INDIES
—Dictionary / Leach, 1219, 1136 (index)

WHALE(-s)
—Animals / Rowland
  aspidochelone, 17–20 @
—Arabian / McCaughrean
  Voyage of Sinbad, 10–15
—Caduto / Keepers *
  origin: Sedna, woman under the sea, 95–97
—Indian Myth / Burland
  killer whales, 44–45
WHEAT
—Leonardo / Fables *
  ant's pact with grain of wheat, 58–59
WHEEL OF FORTUNE
—Jewish / Frankel
  ibn Ezra's bad luck, 394–395
WHERE THERE'S A WILL . . .
—Allison / I'll Tell *
  crow finds way to get to water in pitcher, 109
  White Caroline, Black Caroline
—Dulac / Fairy * 15–21
WHIRLPOOL(-s)
—Earthmaker / Mayo *
  mysterious, 71 @
—Indian Myth / Burland
  lady Hanging Hair, 40–41
—Muddleheads / Harris
  sea hunters swallowed by whirlpool, 26–43
WHIRLWIND
—Bierhorst / Naked *
  Whirlwind vs. Stone Coats (man-eating giants), 19–23
—Earthmaker / Mayo *
  origin, 23 @
—Russian Hero / Warner *
  man and the elements, 31 @
  three kingdoms: copper, silver, gold, 53–56
WHISTLE(-ling)
—Bomans / Wily *
  cobbler's three wishes from

gnome; learns money's limitations, 53–61
—Giant / Harrison *
  giant who threw tantrums, 33–42
—Hamilton / People *
  Manuel's riddle; fills sack with lies; fortune, 65–75
WHITE, E.B. (1899–1985)
—Lynn / Fantasy *
  bibliography (about the author), 635–638
White, T.H. (1906–1964)
—Barber / Anthology
  The once and future king, 213–220
WHITE (color)
—Man Myth & Magic, 3179 (index)
White bride and black bride
—Grimm / Complete * 608–612
White cat, The (d'Aulnoy)
—Lang / Wilkins, 73–90
White doe: curse put on Valdemar
—Reeves / Shadow, 131–153
WHITE FELL
—Lycanthropy / Otten
  Housman: The were-wolf (allegory), 281–320
White snake, The
—Grimm / Complete * 98–101
—Grimm / Sixty * 197–201
—Lang / Wilkins, 238–242
WHITE WOMAN
—Grimm / Legends (Ward), II:459 (index)
Whitehead, Henry S.
—Pirate Ghosts / McSherry
  Seven turns in a hangman's rope, 84–144
Whittaker, Helene
—Dramatized / Kamerman
  Gift from Johnny Appleseed, 537–548
WHITTINGTON, Dick
  see also Puss in Boots

—Clouston / Popular
  his cat; six versions, II.65–78
Whittington, Mary K.
—Yolen / Werewolves
  Wolfskin, 84–94
Whitworth, Virginia Payne
—Dramatized / Kamerman
  The king and the bee, 250–257
  Magic cloak, 435–446
Who lives in this little house?
—Pellowski / Family * 58–61
WHOWIE
—McGowen / Encyclopedia * 60–61
Whuppity Stoorie
—Fairies / Briggs, 430–431
—Ghosts / Starkey, 44–51
WICCA
—Witch Encyc / Guiley, 421 (index)
WICKED RULER
—Fahs / Old *
  girl chooses death over unfaithfulness, 44–51
WICKEDNESS
  see also EVIL . . .
—Allison / I'll Tell *
  lax conscience: wolf needs excuse to eat lamb, 111
—Grimm / Complete *
  mistreated servant in grave; master's fate, 749–752
—Jewish / Sadeh
  chickens and glassware; diagnosis reveals evil, 356–357
—Lang / Wilkins
  Little good mouse (fairy helps imprisoned queen), 116–127
—Strauss / Trail
  Red Riding Hood; soliloquy of "waiting wolf" (poem), 14–16
WIDOW
—Campbell / West Highlands
  Barra widow's son, II.121–132
  three widows, II.232–252
—Jewish / Frankel

vengeful widow: bride brought back to life, 484–485

—Jewish / Sadeh
mourner's prayer for the dead, 139–140

—Women / Dyer, 183–190 @

WIFE (wives)
see also ABDUCTION; HUSBAND . . . ; QUEEN; WOMEN

—Arabian / Lewis
Attaf's hospitality; Jafar's misfortunes, 199–209
well's magic objects do "impossible" tasks, 117–122

—Arabian / McCaughrean
man puts nagging wife in well, 185–193

—Beat / Bryan *
husband counts spoonfuls; loses wives, 30–40

—Clarkson / World *
becomes obedient on seeing husband kill recalcitrant horse, 86–91
Gudbrand on Hill-side wins bet: wife will not complain, 75–78

—Clouston / Popular
divorce averted by wife's devotion, II.327–331
murdering would-be lovers, II.332–359
test: virtuous wife, importunate suitors, II.289–316

—Corrin / Eight-Year *
feigns illness: monkey's heart will cure, 102–109

—Corrin / Six-Year *
boy-mouse seeks wife (moon, cloud, wind, etc.), 125–131

—Coyote / Ramsey
Cottontail Boy steals Thunder's wife, 18–20
Cry-Because-He-Have-No-Wife, 29–30

—Egyptian / Harris
treachery; Anpu and Bata, 77–83

—Fairies / Briggs
Wife of Bath's tale (Chaucer), 432–434

—Frog Rider (Chinese)
seeks husband, at Great Wall; changes to a fish, 83–91

—Geras / Grandmother *
rabbi deemed clever (due to wife's quick thinking), 31–40

—Ghosts / Time-Life
O'Iwa (Japanese) murdered ghost-wife's revenge, 51–55

—Grimm / Complete *
Fred and Kate [repeated foolish acts], 283–289
snake-leaves revive treacherous wife, 94–96
test: marriage of Mrs. Reynard [Fox], 193–196
will not beat wife if he finds someone more stupid, 476–480

—Grimm / Legends (Ward), II:459 (index)

—Grimm / Sixty *
Fred and Kate, 144–155
marriage of Mrs. Reynard [Fox], 288–291

—Hopi / Talashoma-Malotki
Kokosori and his witch wife, 23–41

—Jewish / Frankel
Elijah, three sons, three wishes, 587–588
rabbi's magic ring: mean-spirited wife to donkey, 450–455
Solomon: craftsman's wife and the glass vial, 245–248
unpaid pledge: man wants wife to die, 520–521

—Jewish / Sadeh
balances husband's bad luck, 285–287

banished queen, source of husband's success, 279–281

charity saves peddler's wife from foreordained death, 335–336

woman who was almost stoned to death, 18–20

—Lang / Wilkins

prince saved from fates: crocodile, serpent, dog, 485–496

—Legends / Cavendish

faithful, 405 (index)

—Lewis / Proud

Eliduc: married-knight unfaithful; wife enters convent, 88–100

—MacDonald / Sourcebook *

motif index, 730

—Muddleheads / Harris

chief mistreats his two supernatural beings, 44–59

—Restless / Cohen *

snow-ghost wife bears ten children, 16–23

—Russian / Afanasev, 661 (index)

—Shannon / More *

last request saves life of ruler's wife, 43–46

witch asks: you love wife more than child? 48–49

—Spring / Philip

woman's love: wife rejects series of suitors, 58–74

—Turkey / Walker, 310 (index)

—Turkish (Art I) / Walker

grateful fairy-padishah teaches farmer (with termagant wife) to cure the sick, 188–190

—Vanishing / Mercer *

quest for wife abducted by giant bird, 42–49

—Vietnam / Terada *

husband accuses faithful wife of infidelity, 10–13

sea snake captures mandarin's wife, 88–94

WIFE ABUSE

—Erdoes / Sound *

Veeho: abused wife gets revenge, 68–70

—Grimm / Complete

sharing joy and sorrow * 704–705

—Maori / Kanawa *

Mataora; husbands must not beat wives, 68–80

—Old Wives / Carter

two battered wives find refuge in dead whale, 225–226

Wife of Bath's tale (Chaucer)

—Fairies / Briggs, 432–434

WIFE: TESTS

—Grimm / Complete *

King Thrushbeard, 244–248

—Grimm / Sixty *

King Thrushbeard, 312–316

—Old Wives / Carter

Beauty survives tests; Pock Face (murderess) dies, 200–204

—Vietnam / Terada *

ugly man changes self to test wife's fidelity, 64–68

WILD . . . (hunt, man, woman, etc.)

—Grimm / Complete *

Iron Hans, 612–620

—Grimm / Legends (Ward), II:460 (index)

—Grimm / Sixty *

Iron Hans, 317–325

—Legends / Cavendish, 407 (index)

—Unicorn / Hathaway

unicorn and wood nymphs, 100–111 @

Wild Edric

—Fairies / Briggs, 432–434

WILD HOG

—Hamilton / Dark *

John (brother) kills Little Tom, takes credit for his feat, 132–136

WILDCAT
—Davy Crockett / Dewey * 26–31
—Greaves / Hippo *
    jackal boast: can outrun dogs,
    45–47
Wilde, Oscar (1854–1900)
—Victorian / Hearn
    Selfish giant, The, 254–258
—Wilde / Happy *
    The devoted friend, 73–101
    The happy prince, 15–38
    The nightingale and the rose, 41–
    56
    The remarkable rocket, 105–133
    The selfish giant, 59–69
—Wilde / Lynch *
    The devoted friend, 24–40
    The happy prince, 41–54
    The nightingale and the rose, 14–
    23
    The remarkable rocket, 55–72
    The selfish giant, 6–13
    The young king, 73–94
Willful child, The
—Grimm / Complete * 534–535
Williams, Margery
—Childcraft 1 / Once *
    Velveteen Rabbit (becomes real
    when loved), 175–181
WILL-O'-THE-WISP
—Crossley / Dead *
    dead moon [boggles; marsh folk],
    1–9
—Hamilton / People *
    dead soul; marsh light, 132 @
    WILL-O'-THE-WYKES
Willow-wren, The
—Grimm / Complete * 705–708
**WIND(-s) (including origins of pres-
    ent order)**
    see also WHIRLWIND
—Aesop / Alley *
    wind vs. sun: which is stronger?
    20–23

—Aesop / Reeves-Wilson *
    contest: who is stronger? Wind
    and sun, 88–91
—Animal Legends / Kerven *
    kangaroo's first human encoun-
    ter: comes in windstorm, [12–
    14]
—Baring-Gould / Curious
    Piper of Hamelin: souls of chil-
    dren in the wind, 116–120 @
—Bell / Classical Dict, 274 @
—Bierhorst / Naked *
    Turtle, his sister, and Great Wind,
    110–115
—Bomans / Wily *
    wind-man controls four winds:
    happiness to one is sorrow to
    another, 76–78
—Bryan / Lion *
    son of Mother Wind [name a se-
    cret], 24–39
—Caduto / Keepers *
    benefits; Gluscabi and Wind Ea-
    gle, 67–71
    pipe/breath/wind carry prayers to
    Creator, 187–188
    Spring defeats Winter [North and
    South winds], 129–131
—Coyote / Ramsey
    South Wind marries ocean's
    daughter, 129–130
—Earth / Hadley *
    Iroquois creator has animals help
    control the four winds, [11–12]
    North Wind (lady) wishes to marry
    Zephyr, [15–16]
—Haboo / Hilbert
    work of the winds, 122
—Hamilton / In the Beginning *
    Lowa: creation myth, 104–109
—Jewish / Frankel, 647 (index)
    sun, wind, and man: which is
    strongest? 465
—Jewish / Sadeh

lost princess: king's curse, to Evil One's kingdom, 386–389
—Lurker / Dict Gods, 445 (index)
    wind deities, 416 (index)
—MacDonald / Sourcebook *
    motif index, 731
—Mercatante / Encyclopedia, 805 (index)
—Polynesians / Andersen, 513 (index)
—Russian / Ivanits, 252 (index)
—Russian Hero / Warner *
    old woman honors wind (personified), 31
    sun, frost, wind: honor most powerful, 32
—Trolls / Asbjornsen
    East of the sun . . . (poor man's daughter given to white bear), 26–35

WINE
—Bell / Classical Dict, 275–277 @
—Jewish / Frankel, 647 (index)
—Leonardo / Fables *
    Wine of Mahomet, 88
—Pirate Ghosts / McSherry
    vintage from Atlantis, 158–165

WING(-s)
—Arabian / McCaughrean
    Keys of destiny; Iram, 65–82
—Bell / Classical Dict, 277–278 @
—Bomans / Wily *
    "madman" wants to go to heaven without dying, 152–155
—Lurker / Dict Gods, 445–446 (index)

WINGED HORSES
—Lynn / Fantasy * 771 (index)

WINGED SERPENT
—Gould / Mythical, 182–192 @

Winning, see CONTEST; RACE; TASK; WEAK.

WINTER
    see also COLD
—Caduto / Keepers *

    Spring defeats Winter, 129–131
—Fahs / Old *
    grizzly vs. coyote on day/season lengths, 96–99
—Greek / Osborne
    kidnapping: Ceres and Proserpina, 35–39
—Wilde / Lynch *
    selfish giant: always winter, children not allowed in garden, 6–13

Winther, Barbara
—Dramatized / Kamerman
    Great samurai sword, 306–316
    Sleeping mountains, 346–359

WISDOM (including wise/foolish persons)
    see also FOOL
—Bomans / Wily *
    love more important than wealth, 53–61
    origin of laughwort (plant), 62–70
—Brooke / Telling *
    acquire by being taught; Paul Bunyan, 37–48
—Bryan / Lion *
    acquired by experience/mistakes: four African tales, 1–86
—Caduto / Keepers *
    folly: trap all animals in magic bag, 165–167
—Celts / Hodges *
    How Finn Mac Cool got his wisdom tooth, 34–52
    Merlin: life and magic powers, 117–132
—Clarkson / World *
    hares safe in burrow; in unsuitable houses, eaten by fox, 159–161
—Clouston / Popular
    old lady entices Death to climb prune tree, I.389–390

—Coyote / Bierhorst *
  while coyote gabs, wolf raids his
    house, [16]
—Fahs / Old *
  Midas: all touched turns to gold,
    115–117
—Grimm / Complete *
  peasant's wise daughter, 439–440
—Hamilton / In the Beginning * 135
—Jewish / Frankel, 652 (index)
  king's counselor pretends shep-
    herd's wisdom is his own, 422–
    424
  Solomon visits deserted palace;
    learns "vanities," 251–254
  Solomon's gift, 214–216
  three brothers go to Solomon to
    learn, 221–224
—Jewish / Sadeh
  daughter wiser than her father,
    289–291
  fly and spider; incense: knowl-
    edge and understanding, 389–
    392
  girl who had a cow's mouth, 275–
    276
  learning from child; and from
    thief, 363
  wisdom vs. gold: Solomon and
    the three brothers, 54–56
—Lurker / Dict Gods, 417 (index)
—MacDonald / Sourcebook *
  motif index, 207–219
—Mex-Am / West
  motif index, 299
—Rockwell / Puss *
  Briar Rose; gifts of the Wise
    Women, 53–59
—Shah / Central Asia
  wise man and apprentice, 45–48
—Spanish-Am / Van Etten *
  asks three sisters: why do you
    clear your field? 52–53
—Tree / Kerven *

  up Oobi-Oobi mountain to land of
    flowers, [22–25]
—Turkish / Walker
  Muslim preacher sells wisdom to
    king, 37–42
—Yep / Rainbow *
  experience: Snake-spoke, 86–
    95
WISDOM ACQUIRED
—Dramatized / Kamerman
  Great samurai sword, 306–316
  The magic box, 265–277
—Old Wives / Carter
  fool would buy brains from wise
    woman; good wife supplies
    need, 96–100
WISDOM LEARNED from ANIMALS
  see also ANIMAL(-s), WISE
—Celts / Hodges *
  how Finn MacCool got his wis-
    dom tooth, 34–52
**WISDOM LEARNED from CHIL-
DREN**
—Grimm / Complete *
  Old man and his grandson, 363–
    364
—Grimm / Sixty *
  Old man and his grandson, 141
—Unicorn / Coville *
  king would own unicorns; prin-
    cess: they must be free, 24–37
**WISDOM LEARNED by EDUCA-
TION**
—Bruchac / Iroquois *
  wisdom: gifts of the Little People,
    41–44
—Brooke / Telling *
  acquire wisdom by being taught,
    37–48
—Caduto / Keepers *
  folly: Gluscabi hunting; bag never
    fills, 165–167
—Grimm / Complete *
  Four clever brothers, 580–584

—Grimm / Sixty *
 Four clever brothers, 220–234
—Shah / Central Asia
 wise man and apprentice, 45–48
**WISDOM LEARNED from EXPERI-
 ENCE**
—Bierhorst / Naked *
 Turtle's war party vs. Seven Sis-
 ters, 31–36
—Bomans / Wily *
 berry picker rich with beauties of
 nature, 47–53
 bored king discovers pleasure of
 work, 101–103
 prince learns to accept imperfec-
 tions: girl's freckles, 126–131
—Bryan / Lion *
 Jackal's favorite game, 40–59
 Jumoke ("Foolish Boy") outwits
 Ananse, 60–86
—Corrin / Six-Year *
 discontented pig: some unpleas-
 antness in all work, 116–119
—Geras / Grandmother *
 Bavsi's feast: wisdom from walk-
 ing in another's shoes, 6–13
 overcrowded house (move animals in/out; seems larger), 77–
 85
—Jewish / Frankel
 Solomon visits deserted palace;
 learns "vanities," 251–254
—Journey Sun (Chinese)
 Fanjiangshan secures justice;
 three episodes, 90–108
—Scriven / Full Color *
 Goldilocks and the three bears,
 27–28
 King Grizzly Beard, 89–92
—Water Buffalo (Chinese)
 little camel tests mother's advice,
 39–43
—Yep / Rainbow *
 "Snake-spoke," 86–95

Wisdome of Dr. Dodypol
—Fairies / Briggs, 438–440
Wise folks
—Grimm / Complete * 476–480
Wise servant, The
—Grimm / Complete * 671–672
**WISH(-es) (-granted) (includes "ab-
 surd" wishes)**
—Clarkson / World *
 transferred wishes used un-
 wisely, 305–308
—Corrin / Eight-Year *
 princess: save magic fishbone
 until needed, 147–160
—Dramatized / Kamerman
 grants three wishes; capture bandit, 324–333
 happy adults: children at wishing
 well, 15–22
 Midas; anything touched, turns to
 gold, 177–190
—Dulac / Fairy *
 blue bird (prince transformed),
 77–90
 magic pipe makes all dance,
 114–123
 White Caroline, Black Caroline,
 15–21
—Fahs / Old *
 wish of Midas: all touched turns to
 gold, 115–117
—Frog Rider (Chinese)
 God of the West; wishing pearl,
 92–99
—Greek / Osborne
 golden touch: Bacchus grants
 King Midas' wish, 9–11
—Grimm / Complete *
 hospitality: poor man rewarded;
 rich man punished, 394–
 398
 magic fiddle makes everyone
 dance, 503–508
 Pink [carnation], The, 355–360

white bride and black bride, 608–612

wishing cloak: Salad; fed to witch, 551–558

—Grimm / Sixty *
    magic fiddle makes everyone dance, 182–189
    prince; Pink [carnation], The, 171–176
    Salad [as above], 292–293

—Jewish / Frankel
    Elijah, three sons, three wishes, 587–588
    two brothers (rich/poor) granted wish ("enough"), 602–604

—Jewish / Sadeh
    anything touched turns to gold, 181–182
    Moses (prophet) and the monkey woman, 304–305

—Leete / Golden *
    foolish wishes: the Little fir tree, 80–93

—Manning / Cats *
    small-small cat seeks advice on growing large, 126–127

—Navajo Coyote / Haile
    coyote and skunk: great kill; race; skunk tricks coyote, 10, 31–32

—Nesbit / Fairy *
    magic apples; age with each wish, 125–138

—Rockwell / Puss *
    fisherman, his wife, and the flounder, 42–52

—Scriven / Full Color *
    how to catch a leprechaun, 85–87

—Shah / Central Asia
    Wali and the magic saddle-bag, 69–77
    wishes (three) granted by genie, 31–44

—Vietnam / Terada *
    hunter given one wish; origin of the gecko, 69–71

—Water Buffalo (Chinese)
    five wishes: crow-messenger disobeys God, 23–29

Wishing-table, gold-ass, cudgel in sack

—Grimm / Complete * 177–187

WITCH(-es)
    see also COVEN; SALEM WITCHES
    see also individual tales, e.g. Hansel and Gretel

—American / Read Dgst, 448 (index)

—Bierhorst / Monkey *
    underground: witch escapes from great-horned-snake; earthquake, 118–120

—Bierhorst / Naked *
    Chestnut pudding: magic food supply, 3–10
    Last Remaining [escape; after plague], 87–92
    theft: Quilt of men's eyes, 101–109

—Bomans / Wily *
    balloon message; with godmother's help, knight kills dragon, 197–202
    children escape from witch with help of top, kite, doll, 88–93
    city hires wizard to destroy "wily witch"; stalemate: they marry, 3–9
    curse: lock of princess' hair; king's cruelty to "bird witch," 165–173
    each year witch takes two naughtiest children in Finland, 27–36
    spoiled prince, perfectionist, is reformed by witch, 126–131

—British / Briggs *
    fifteen tales, 275–304

—Chorao / Child's *
Hansel and Gretel, 29–40
—Clarkson / World *
toad-witch causes cows to dry up,
185–187
witches' ride: recite charm to
make broom fly, 173–175
wolf-child: charms to ward off
witches, 202–206
—Classic / Downer
witch stump (Lake Drummond,
Va.), 66–67
—Corrin / Six-Year *
by mistake, crossing-sweeper
takes magic broom; to moon,
87–92
—Curry / Beforetime *
Ixkareya: witches steal all
salmon; coyote destroys secret
dam, 42–47
—Dulac / Fairy *
Finn, and Queen of many-colored
bedchamber, 69–76
—Ghosts / Cohen
the Bell (Tennessee) witch, 157–
163
—Ghosts / Starkey
Black Annis defeated, 52–57
—Giant / Harrison *
witch's spell: giant sees/fears
butterflies, etc., 19–30
—Glooskap / Norman *
panther-witch and her scissorbill
birds, 39–49
—Grimm / Complete *
blue light summons tiny servant,
530–534
Fundevogel, 241–244
Jorinda and Joringel, 339–
342
Salad; fed to witch, 551–558
Sweetheart Roland; girl flees
murderous stepmother, 268–
271
—Grimm / Legends (Ward), II:461 (index)
—Grimm / Sixty *
blue light summons tiny servant,
244–249
Fundevogel, 84–87
Jorinda and Joringel, 17–20
Salad; fed to witch, 292–293
Sweetheart Roland . . . , 156–
160
—Halloween ABC / Merriam * [26]
—Hamilton / Dark *
control, capture, kill, 148 @
horned women: twelve witches
vs. Spirit of the Well, 32–37
marriage to boar/man; secret
must be kept, 113–118
witch takes off skin; as cat, rides
Big Henry, 143–148
—Hamilton / People *
helpful witch and John de Conquer, 107–114
Manuel's riddle; fills sack with
lies; fortune, 65–75
—Hartland / English *
seven tales, 183–203
—Hopi / Talashoma-Malotki, 209 @
Kokosori and his witch wife, 23–
41
old wizard plots to seduce beautiful girl, 70–91
—Jewish / Sadeh
Baal Shem Tov and the witch,
343
old woman; princess who refused
to talk, 106–111
—Lang / Wilkins
Dwarf Long Nose (boy under
spell), 534–556
—Legends / Cavendish, 396 (index)
—Limburg / Weird, 70–75, 122
—Lore of Love
cursed embrace: Liba and Guntram, 32–35

—MacDonald / Sourcebook *
   motif index, 732–733
—Man Myth & Magic, 3179 (index)
   analytics, 3183 (index)
   European, 3131 (index)
   modern, 3153 (index)
—Manning / Cats *
   abducts king's two children;
      Katchen the cat helps escape,
      9–15
   able to call twelve sailors at will,
      Vasily saves Leeshy Cat, 37–
      50
   kind witch raises foundling to be
      knight; bewitched Cat-Johann
      his aide, 111–117
   Little Wonder; stepmother turns
      boy into dog, drives his sister
      out, 65–74
—Manning / Cauldron *
   amber witch: common man, loved
      by princess, sent to get amber,
      18–31
   crusader beaten, robbed by com-
      rades; witches reveal secrets,
      = reversal, 46–57
   donkey, gift of troll-child, helps
      hunter rescue princess, 9–17
   Elsa, abducted by witch to tend
      her baby, escapes aided by
      goat, 90–98
   gives Jack ring (can change self
      to any size); rescues princess
      from giant, 78–89
   her cat advises witch who makes
      self invisible, to steal farmer's
      eggs, 32–38
   hero Tow-how: magic disk helps
      foil hideous old witch, 58–65
   Martin kills witch; lions freed of
      enchantment, 66–77
   mother takes water from Water
      Witch's lake; son to die, 118–
      127
   prince and retinue turned into
      trees; girl breaks spell, 39–
      45
   twelve tales, 1–127
   Whirlwind abducts queen and
      (evil) son; magic shoes take
      him away, 106–117
—Medicine-Plants / Read Dgst
   herbs; ancient lore, 20–21
—Old Wives / Carter
   cat-witch: foot cut off becomes
      hand with ring on finger, 149–
      150
   Parsley-Girl: woman steals from
      nuns' (i.e., witches') garden,
      86–88
—Pirate Ghosts / McSherry
   toad (familiar): Pedro goes to
      sea, 182–200
—Quayle / Cornish *
   Duffy's pact: devil will do spin-
      ning; guess name for release,
      75–87
   good dog Devil; annual delivery
      of maid to phantom cats, 37–
      44
   Lord Pengerswick and the witch
      of Fraddam, 103–108
   magic ointment put on eye makes
      one invisible, 13–20
   Piggin: care and conditions of
      changelings, 29–36
—Russian / Afanasev, 662 (index)
—Russian / Ivanits, 252 (index)
—Russian Hero / Warner *
   captive tricks witch's daughter;
      geese help escape, 82–85
   old Russia, 81–82 @
   witch (blood sister) and sun's sis-
      ter, 60–61
—Scandinavian / Kvideland, 428 (in-
   dex)
—Scary / Young *
   children escape by changing

sheets with granny-witch's children, 47–51

girl jabs stick in witch's grave; "She's got me!", 37–39

Old Raw Head: hillbilly steals/ butchers witch's hog, 11–13

—Scriven / Full Color *
Hansel and Gretel, 43–47

—Spanish-Am / Van Etten *
owl wishes: to lie to a witch means death, 48–49

Santa Fe soldier buys love [unrequited] potion, 33–36

—Spring / Philip
golden fish rewards kindness, 103–113

—Strauss / Trail
Snow White . . . ; soliloquy (poem), 5–7

—Talk / Goss
fourteen tales, and commentary, 299–359

—Tree / Kerven *
Elder Tree Witch steals milk; burnt by Granny, [14–15]

—Trolls / Asbjornsen
stepsisters: one kind, one cruel; escape service of witch, 42–50

—Turkish / Walker
Teeny-Tiny and Witch-Woman, 49–51

—Turkish (Art I) / Walker
Haci's daughter marries, is repeatedly assaulted, 24–33

stepmother "kills" stepdaughter, takes her place as bride, 82–88

witches' gifts: tears to pearls, laugh to roses, water to gold, 159–168

—Unicorn / Coville *
quest for unicorn horn: cure of winter sickness, 136–155

—Unnatural / Cohen, 148 (index)
change shape and fly; illus., 19

—Williams-Ellis / Tales *
Baba Yaga; Marusia's kindness helps escape, 113–124

—Witch Encyc / Guiley, 1–419

—Witch Hndbk / Bird * 1–96
beauty secrets, 56–61

casting spells, 42–49

choosing/furnishing homes, 6–13

fashion hints, 62–69

festivals, 78–89

fortune-telling, 36–41

garden, 26–35

hobbies and crafts, 70–77

kitchen/cookery, 14–25

modern witches, 90–93

old wives' tales, 50–55

zodiac, 38–39

—Witches / Iosa *
brothers envious of Pinkel's favor with king, 23–31

Halloween song (poem), 1

Old Moll (poem, by Reeves), 10

Old witch (Jacobs), 34–39

wicked stepmother sends twins to giant witch, 18–22

Witch of Willowby Wood (poem, by Bennett), 16–17

—Yolen / Faery Flag
face in the cloth; princess and witches, 87–100

minstrel killed: plant growing from grave, 41–46

WITCH: APPEARANCE and HABITS

—Bomans / Wily *
bird-witch, 165–167

witch and wizard try to best each other; stalemate; marry, 3–8

wizards: successive generations become less evil, 71–75

—Grimm / Complete *
disobedient child visits Frau Trude, 208–209

—Old Wives / Carter

cat-witch steals wool; slave
blamed, 149–150
—Starkey / Ghosts
form of witch: Black Annis, 52–
57
witch's bleeding, 52–57
WITCH DOCTOR
—Greaves / Hippo *
why giraffe has a long neck, 86–
88
—Witch Encyc / Guiley, 421 (index)
WITCH: EVIL DEEDS
—Clarkson / World *
witches' ride: bobo (fool) misuses
charm; dumped, 173–175
—Grimm / Complete *
brothers: one rescues princess; is
rescued by other, 290–311
—Old Wives / Carter
innkeeper (witch) uses magic
buckwheat to turn men into
asses, 155–157
WITCH HUNTS
—Lycanthropy / Otten, 337 (index)
WITCH-MAIDEN
—Lang / Wilkins
King Solomon's ring; Dragon of
the North, 285–297
**WITCH: OVERCOME/ESCAPED
FROM**
—Bierhorst / Naked *
Last Remaining [escape, after
plague], 87–92
—Erdoes / Sound *
Iyan Hokshi, the stone boy, 108–
116
—Grimm / Complete *
blue light summons tiny servant,
530–534
Fundevogel, 241–244
Jorinda and Joringel, 339–342
—Grimm / Sixty *
blue light summons tiny servant,
244–249

Fundevogel, 84–87
Jorinda and Joringel, 17–20
—Old Wives / Carter
innkeeper (witch) turned into ass
by guest; punished four years,
155–157
—Russian Hero / Warner *
captive tricks witch's daughter;
geese help escape, 82–85
Sister Alenushka and Brother
Ivanushka, 108–109
—Scary / Young *
children escape by changing
sheets with granny-witch's chil-
dren, 47–51
—Starkey / Ghosts
Black Annis (witch) defeated, 52–
57
WITCH: RECOGNITION
—Clarkson / World *
toad-witch recognized by missing
(cut off) hand, 185–187
—Manning / Cauldron *
Witch Longnose and her cat Peri-
winkle, 32–38
WITCH TRIALS
—Lycanthropy / Otten, 337 (index)
WITCHCRAFT
see also LYCANTHROPY
—Floyd / Gr Am Myst
Salem, Mass. (1692), 12–16
—Irish / Glassie
illness and; seven tales, 185–
203
—Lycanthropy / Otten, 336 (index)
discoverie (Reginald Scot), 115–
126 @
medical origins of European
craze, 200–219 @
—Lynn / Fantasy *
annotated bibliography, 344–367
—Occult & Parapsych / Shepard,
1449–56 @; 1572–73 (index)
—Plants / Dyer, 55–70

—Polynesians / Andersen, 514 (index)
—Scandinavian / Kvideland, xii, 423 (index)
—Unnatural / Cohen, 1–32
—Witch Encyc / Guiley, 369–379
   churches, 61–65
—Woman's Ency / Walker, 1081–1091 @

WITNESS
—Ghosts / Starkey
   Tregeagle's ghost, 58–65
—Ghosts / Time-Life
   Jim Tregeagle case; ghost of dead man testifies, 126–131

Wives, see WIFE.

WIZARD(-s)
   see also SORCERER; WARLOCK
—Bomans / Wily *
   city hires wizard to destroy "wily witch," 3–8
   evil wanted by 4 generations of wizards; people turn it to good, 71–75
   three riddles; wizard can read future in his magic book, 202–204
—Bruchac / Iroquois *
   husband; vampire skeleton, 129–133
—Celts / Hodges *
   Curoi and Cuchulain, 17–31
—Fairies / Briggs, 440–442
   green sleeves, 202–204
—Glooskap / Norman *
   Ice Giants outwitted by Glooskap, 11–19
—Grimm / Complete *
   wizard captures three sisters; Fitcher's bird, 216–220
—Imaginary / Nigg
   wizard and the chonchon, 117–119
—Manning / Cats *

Pussy Cat Twinkle sells fur (life) to wizard; saved by female cat, 19–28
—Russian Hero / Warner *
   Old Russia, 81–82 @
—Spring / Philip
   golden fish rewards kindness, 103–113
—Unicorn / Coville *
   boy/unicorn: being of power and light, 63–77
—Witch Encyc / Guiley, 421 (index)
—Yep / Rainbow *
   landlord: The rainbow people, 162–168

WOLF (wolves)
   see also Aesop: Boy who cried "wolf."
—Aesop / Reeves-Wilson *
   trust: Wolf and goat, 114
   Wolf in sheep's clothing, 20–21
—Aesop / Zwerger *
   Shepherd's boy and the wolf, 9
—Allison / I'll Tell *
   crane's long beak; bone in wolf's throat (fable), 101
   wolf and [goat's] kid, 130
—Animals / Rowland, 192 (index)
—Bedtime / Padoan & Smith *
   Peter and the wolf, 49–51
—Bell / Classical Dict, 279–280 @
—Bierhorst / Naked *
   turtle and partridge hide bagged elk from wolves, 67–71
—Carle / Treasury *
   wolf and dog: rather be hungry than a slave (Aesop), 104–105
—Clarkson / World *
   fool carries complaints to God, who gives him gift of luck, 319–323
—Coyote / Bierhorst *
   pays to be clever when you're the weaker one, [14]

wolf slanders coyote; coyote
turns tables, [34]
—Crossley / Animal (Grimm) *
wolf [foiled] and seven young
goats, 29–34
wolf (master) outsmarted by fox,
45–48
—Dramatized / Kamerman
Peter and the wolf, 375–380
—Glooskap / Norman *
secluded home found by wolves,
51–60
—Grimm / Complete *
gossip wolf and the fox, 353–354
Wolf and the man [fox's warning],
350–351
Wolf and the seven [goat] kids,
39–42
—Grimm / Legends (Ward), II:461 (index)
—Grimm / Sixty *
Wolf and the man [fox's warning],
211–212
Wolf and the seven [goat] kids,
202–205
—Haboo / Hilbert
moose, wolf, and mole, 145–149
wolf brothers kill elk and beaver,
10–13
—Hamilton / Dark *
Fenris, wolf-child of Loki, 82–86
Manabozo: manitou hare swallowed by king of fishes, 27–31
—Hamilton / People *
insults birds; borrowed feathers;
walrus, 43–48
Little Daughter sings, and es-
capes from wolf, 60–63
—Harris-Parks / Again
Miss Wolf (Brer Wolf's niece) and
mosquitoes, 22–29
—Harris-Parks / Jump *
Brer Rabbit tricks Brer Wolf into
trunk, 3–8

—Hoke / Giants
giant, no heart in his body, 93–
102
—Igloo / Metayer
Kajortoq: bears and wolf become
fox's food, 19–23
owl, ridiculed, kills wolf, 55–57
—Jewish / Frankel
crane removes bone from wolf's
throat (fable), 459–460
—Lang / Wilkins
True story of Little Golden Hood,
132–136
—Lester / Brer Rabbit *
animals with horns vs. animals
with claws; Brer Wolf exposed,
122–124
Brer Rabbit repays with cow, but
Brer Wolf ends only with the
tail, 51–53
[with] Brer Wolf kills a cow; pretends to be poisoned, 115–117
caught by Brer Wolf; tricks him
into saying grace, 37–40
cons Brer Wolf into trap built for
himself, 106–109
mosquitoes, and Brer Wolf's
daughter, 124–127
says that molasses is "fox blood,"
141–144
steals Brer Rabbit's lucky rabbit
foot, 145–151
talking house: tricks Brer Wolf to
reveal himself, 68–69
trapped in hollow log; burns up
Brer Wolf, 117–122
tricks Brer Wolf into trunk; kills
him with boiling water, 40–42
Wiley Wolf and Riley Rabbit: play
Riding/Tying the Bag, 101–104
—Lycanthropy / Otten, 337 (index)
—MacDonald / Sourcebook *
motif index, 733–734
—Man Myth & Magic, 3180 (index)

—Manning / Cats *
  chain-tale: boy, hare, fox, wolf,
    bear vs. Baba Yaga, 58–64
  Istvan climbs pea-plant into heav-
    ens; finds seven-eyed goat;
    falls into swamp, 107–110
—O'Brien / Tales *
  goatskin-clad Eamonn: fife forces
    dancing (wolf and jealous rival
    Fiac), 38–43
—Paxton / Aesop *
  boy who cried wolf, [33–35]
—Russian / Afanasev, 662 (index)
—Russian / Ivanits, 252 (index)
—Russian Hero / Warner *
  helps quest for firebird; warnings
    ignored, 112–116
  No Bigger than a Finger (swal-
    lowed-alive), 128–129
  wolf tricked: tail frozen in ice,
    111
—Scandinavian / Davidson, 144 (in-
    dex)
—Scary / Young *
  white wolf, eventually thought to
    be boy's ghost, 40–42
—Scriven / Full Color *
  Little Red Riding Hood, 37–39
—Sioux / Standing Bear *
  wolves save woman caught in
    blizzard, 3–9
—Spanish-Am / Van Etten *
  cat/rooster/sheep/ox escape
    from wolves/coyote, 97–100
—Strauss / Trail
  Red Riding Hood; soliloquy of
    "waiting wolf" (poem), 14–16
—Turkish / Walker
  duck as judge: rabbit removed
    stone from wolf's back, 15
—Water Buffalo (Chinese)
  wolf pretends to be grandmother,
    62–69
—Wolves / Lopez, 1–309

curse victim: Last Rites given to
  "wolf" woman, 236
eight Aesop fables (texts), 254–
  256
female, 301 (index)
in literature, 203–270 @
social structure, 306 (index)
St. Ailbe (6th century), 246
St. Francis and the Wolf of Gub-
  bio, 212–214 @
which has better life: wolf or In-
  dian dog, 110–111
Woman Who Lived With Wolves
  (Sioux legend), 121–122
—Yolen / Faery Flag
  wolf/child: she-wolf and the colo-
    nel, 61–78
  wolves retell three tales, 103–
    119
Wolf and the dog
—Carle / Treasury * 104–105
Wolf and the fox
—Crossley / Animals (Grimm) * 45
—Grimm / Complete * 351–353
Wolf and the lamb
—Carle / Treasury * 108–109
Wolf and the man [fox's warning]
—Grimm / Complete * 350–351
—Grimm / Sixty * 211–212
Wolf and the seven [goat] kids
—Crossley / Animals (Grimm) * 29
—Grimm / Complete * 39–42
—Grimm / Sixty * 202–205
**Wolfram von Eschenbach (13th
  century)**
—Barber / Anthology
  Parzival, 93–111
Wolkstein, Diane
—Wolkstein / Love
  Inanna and Dumuzi, 37–71,
    264 @
  Isis and Osiris, 1–36, 261 @
  Layla and Majnun, 147–180,
    266 @

Psyche and Eros, 111–146, 265 @
Shiva and Sati, 73–89,
    264 @
Song of Songs, The, 91–109,
    265 @
Tristan and Iseult, 181–233,
    266 @
WOLVERINE WOMAN
—Muddleheads / Harris
    Copper Canoeman weds human
    princess, 75–93
WOMANIZER
—Jewish / Sadeh
    father's advice on carousing, etc.
    averts evil, 333–334
—Pirate Ghosts / McSherry
    blue spectacles: user not wholly
    good, 73–83
WOMEN
    see also ABDUCTION; HERO-
        INE; INDIAN WOMEN; OLD
        WOMAN; PRINCESS;
        QUEEN; SUITOR(-s);
        WIDOW; WIFE
—African / Abrahams, 297–298 @
—Bruchac / Iroquois *
    creation of Earth; first woman,
    15–17
—Caduto / Keepers *
    last word: origin of death, 181–
    182
—Cambodian / Carrison, 30 @
—Celts / Hodges *
    loathly lady, 58
—Chaucer / Cohen *
    wife of Bath: what do women
    want most, 55–63
—Chinese / Chin *
    customs: marriage; scholarship
    (Ju Yingtai), 61–73
—Clouston / Popular
    women whose love is slighted,
    II.499–502
—Crockett Almanacs

nine "she-male" tales, xlvii (in-
    dex)
—Hamilton / In the Beginning *
    Hina negates curses of creator,
    100–103
    origin: Erlik (devil) vs. Ulgen, 28–
    33
    Pandora: a "new creation" by
    Zeus, 136–137
—Hoke / Giants
    the Wise One; Finlay, the giant
    killer, 142–149
—Jewish / Sadeh
    devotion and love: Solomon and
    Queen Keshira, 61–62
    Solomon, the tin sword; ruthless
    woman, 52–54
—Legends / Cavendish
    captured or won, 407 (index)
    family, 405 (index)
    feminine villainy, 406 (index)
—Lycanthropy / Otten, 337 (index)
—MacDonald / Sourcebook *
    motif index, 734
—Man Myth & Magic, 3180 (index)
—Mesoamerican / Leon-P, 294, 300
    (index)
—Old Wives / Carter, 1–242
    Sermerssuaq: remarkably strong
    Eskimo, 1
—Polynesians / Andersen, 514 (in-
    dex)
—Reeves / Shadow
    beauty: Launfal's secret love for
    Rosamund, 49–83
—Switzer / Existential
    ugly duckling (first woman in ma-
    jor league baseball), 150–157
—Turkey / Walker, 310 (index)
—Turkish (Art I) / Walker
    padishah would kill them all;
    saved by woodcutter's story,
    200–204
—Woman's Ency / Walker, 1–1124 @

—Women / Dyer, 1–253 @
  bad women, 84–91 @
  beauty, 15–33 @
  curiosity, 191–198 @
  dress, 34–47 @
  eyes, 48–62 @
  fickleness, 120–124 @
  goodness, 77–83 @
  hate, 99–100 @
  local allusions, 125–137 @
  love; love tests, 92–98, 101–107 @
  marriage, 144–157 @
  red-haired, 113–119 @
  secrets, 108–112 @
  sister legends, 199–205 @
  superstitions about, 216–227 @
  tears and blushes, 228–234 @
  tongue, 63–76 @
  will, 138–143 @
  wives, 158–174 @

WONDER
—Trolls / Asbjornsen
  task: cut oak; provide year-around water well, 36–40

WONDER MOUNTAIN
—Grimm / Legends (Ward), II:461 (index)

WONDER-TALES
—African / Abrahams, 35–105

WOOD NYMPHS
—Unicorn / Hathaway unicorn and wild people, 100–111 @

WOODCARVER
—Corrin / Imagine *
  goldsmith steals woodcarver-friend's gold; woodcarver "turns" goldsmith's children into bears, 23–46
—Quayle / Cornish *
  borne by tidal wave, mermaid meets/mates carpenter-singer, 51–63
—Spanish-Am / Van Etten *

poor boy desires a real horse, 57–61

WOODCUTTER(-s)
—Aesop / Reeves-Wilson *
  trees: handle for axe, 112–113
—Yep / Rainbow *
  after thousands of years: homecoming, 144–151

Woodcutter's wealthy sister (She-Ghoul)
—Old Wives / Carter, 216–220

Wooden bowl (worn to hide girl's beauty)
—Quayle / Shining * 97–102

WOODEN HORSE
—Frog Rider (Chinese)
  castle in the sky; prince/princess, 24–46

WOODWOSE
—Fairies / Briggs, 442–445

Wooing, see COURTSHIP.

WORD(-s)
—Bierhorst / Sacred
  power, 3
—Gobble / Graham-Barber *
  Thanksgiving-Day-related; etymology, 1–122
—Hamilton / People *
  People could fly [to freedom], 166–172
—Jewish / Sadeh
  princess who refused to talk, 106–111
—Williams-Ellis / Tales *
  white-faced simini (forced to use foolish words), 142–144

WORK
—Aesop / Reeves-Wilson *
  prosper by hard work: Farmer and sons, 108–109
—Allison / I'll Tell *
  bequest: working hard is a treasure, 99
  little red hen (industrious), 16–17

—Bomans / Wily *
king totally bored; has all, = nothing; learns work, 101–103
—Brooke / Telling *
John Henry wins tunnel-digging
race, 77–110
—Corrin / Six-Year *
discontented pig: some unpleasantness in all work, 116–119
—Coyote / Bierhorst *
field (estate); gold assumed; real
legacy is hard work, [46]
—Crossley / Dead *
Yallery Brown (malevolent being), 79–85
—Earth / Hadley *
to heaven on a pole [contest won
by deception], [8–9]
—Paxton / Aesop *
grasshopper and the ants, [36–
39]
—Spanish-Am / Van Etten *
wise woman asks three sisters:
why do you clear your field?
52–53
WORKERS
—Jewish / Frankel, 644 (index)
WORLD
see also ALTERNATE WORLDS;
CREATION MYTHS; END OF
THE WORLD
—Jewish / Sadeh
Aaron's bull: supports world but
sin adds to load, 163–164
—Russian Hero / Warner *
lower, middle, upper, 51 @
—Tree / Kerven *
pre-people, ruled by animals and
trees, [8–9]
WORLD WAR I
—American / Read Dgst
the Lost Battalion, 380–381
WORM(-s)
—Crossley / British FT *

burnt to ashes, Samuel's ghost
must walk until he finds all his
parts, 73–76
—Indian Myth / Burland
pet of chief's daughter, 42, 44
—Jewish / Sadeh
worms' complaint: men are too
skinny, 167–168
—Vietnam / Terada *
worm and snail are born to two
sisters, 59–63
WORSHIP
see also ANCESTOR WOR-
SHIP
—Babylonia / Spence, 411 (index)
—Plants / Dyer, 28–40
WOUND
—Lewis / Proud
Guigemar: woman to endure an-
guish and lift curse, 10–19
Wounded lion, The
—Lang / Wilkins, 385–393
Wrede, Patricia C.
—Unicorn / Coville *
princess, cat, and unicorn, 120–
134
Wren and the bear
—Grimm / Complete * 472–474
—Grimm / Sixty * 57–59
WRESTLING
—American / Read Dgst
ghost-wrestler weakens when
close to fire, 205
—Coyote / Ramsey
boy defeats Thunder, 195–200
—Fahs / Old *
maize spirit: origin of corn, 148–
151
struggle: boy half-good, half-bad,
1–6
—Igloo / Metayer
contest: swan vs. crane; dancing;
neck-wrestling, 43–45
—Jaffrey / Seasons

Krishna defeats elephant and two giants; kills Kans, 32–36

WRITING
—Babylonia / Spence, 411 (index)
—Leonardo / Fables *
  guardian of man's thoughts, 17

WRONGDOING
—Corrin / Eight-Year *
  Atri: ring bell if wrongly dealt with, 75–78
—Coyote / Ramsey
  Little Raccoon and Grandmother, 58–60

WUCHOWSEN
—Glooskap / Norman *
  giant bird, strength of sea winds, 21–28

WULBARI (god)
—Hamilton / In the Beginning *
  Krachi creation myth, 52–57

Wylie and the hairy man
—Young / Scary * 64–68

Wynken, Blynken, and Nod
—Childcraft 1 / Once * 298–299

WYVERN
—Beasts / McHargue, 48 @

YAHWEH
—Hamilton / In the Beginning *
  Genesis; the creation, 120–125
—Jewish / Frankel
  Moses and the burning bush, 107–109
—Jewish / Sadeh
  Rabbi Joseph de la Reina; fight against Samael, 233–237
—Man Myth & Magic, 3180 (index)
—Mercatante / Encyclopedia, 806 (index)

YALE (heraldic beast)
—Beasts / McHargue, 51 @

YALLERY BROWN
—Fairies / Briggs, 446–447
—Crossley / Dead * 79–85

YAMA
—Hamilton / Dark *
  Yama, god of Death, marries mortal (shrew; leaves), 137–142
—Indic / Ions, 144 (index)

YAMS
—Pellowski / Story *
  string-story: farmer and yams, 9–15

YAQUI
—Dictionary / Leach, 1217 (index)

YARA
—Lang / Wilkins
  charm protects betrothed from fairies, 474–484

YEAR
—Pellowski / Story *
  why named (Buddhist) for animals, 87–89

Yeats, William Butler (1865–1939)
—Victorian / Hearn
  Stolen child, The, 252–253

Yellow dwarf (d'Aulnoy)
—Zipes / Beauties * 459–476

YELLOW FEVER
—Floyd / Gr Am Myst
  Gulf Coast, 19th century, 120–122

YELLOWJACKET [people]
—Curry / Beforetime *
  coyote steals fire; origin of stripes, 33–41

YESHIVAH
—Schwartz / Gates, 815 (index)

YETI
—McGowen / Encyclopedia * 7–8
—Monsters / Hall, 100–115

YIDDISH TALES
—Yiddish / Weinreich, 1–413

YIMA
—Persian / Hinnells, 34–38, 143 (index)
YIN-YANG
—Chinese / Christie, 144 (index)
—Japanese / Tyler, [341] (index)
Yolen, Jane (author)
—Pendragon / Ashley
  Dragon's boy, The, 32–48
—Unicorn / Coville *
  The boy who drew unicorns, 157–166
  The transfigured hart [excerpt], 79–89
—Yolen / Werewolves
  Green messiah, 189–200
YORUBAS
—Dictionary / Leach, 1200 (index)
—Hamilton / In the Beginning *
  Olorun: Owner of the sky, 72–77
Young giant, The
—Grimm / Complete * 412–420
Young king, The
—Wilde / Lynch * 73–94
Young Tam Lin
—Fairies / Briggs, 449–453
YOUNGEST
—Trolls / Asbjornsen
  task: cut oak; provide year-around water well, 36–40
YOUNGEST BROTHER
—Arabian / Lewis
  princess loved by cousins (three brothers), 174–183
—Clarkson / World *
  Boots discovers how to do tasks; wins princess, 277–281
—Dulac / Fairy *
  Bashtchelik (real steel), 91–113
—Ghosts / Starkey
  Draiglin' Hogney defeated by youngest brother, 80–87
—Grimm / Complete *
  Queen bee, The, 317–319

  singing bone: murder revealed, 148–150
  task: catch Golden Bird, apple thief, 272–279
—Grimm / Sixty *
  Queen bee, The, 206–208
  task: catch Golden Bird, apple thief, 1–9
—Trolls / Asbjornsen
  Askelad and the silverducks, 11–16
  seven foals (princes under spells); task: watch, report, behead, 53–59
—Witches / Iosa *
  brothers envious of Pinkel's favor with king, 23–31
YOUNGEST CHILD
—Jewish / Sadeh
  nightingale; queen gives birth to animals, 25–28
YOUNGEST DAUGHTER (surpasses . . .)
—Douglas / Magic *
  Cinderella; the youngest is victorious, 109–117
—Old Wives / Carter
  Maol a Chliobain repeatedly gets better of giant, 24–27
YOUNGEST SON (surpasses . . .)
—Arabian / Lewis
  test for succession: prince marries tortoise, 43–51
—Arabian / McCaughrean
  test for succession . . . , 142–149
—Bierhorst / Monkey *
  bird bride: toad helps youngest son re oft-ruined cornfield, 25–31
  lazy Tup gets ants to clear/plant/harvest cornfield, 44–51
—Bierhorst / Naked *
  Animal-Foot hitter kills sorcerer, 24–30

—Grimm / Complete *
  wishing-table, gold-ass, cudgel in
    sack, 177–187
—Grimm / Sixty *
  Water of life, The, 264–270
—Hoke / Giants
  Agnar: giant, no heart in his body,
    93–102
—Jewish / Sadeh
  princess who refused to talk,
    106–111
—Lang / Wilkins
  Fairy of the Dawn; magic well
    water, 571–601
  Nunda, eater of people, 602–614
—Manning / Cauldron *
  Whirlwind abducts queen and
    (evil) son, 106–117
—Rockwell / Puss *
  Dummling: The Golden Goose,
    30–39
  Puss in Boots, 80–88
—Russian Hero / Warner *
  three princes/brides, one a frog-
    princess, 101–106
  wolf helps quest for firebird; warn-
    ings ignored, 112–116
—Spring / Philip
  wonderful brocade picture, 23–34

YOUTH
—Bell / Classical Dict, 284 @
Youth who could not shudder
—Grimm / Complete * 29–39
—Grimm / Sixty * 300–311
**Youth who went forth to learn what
  fear was**
—Grimm / Complete * 29–39
**YU (the Great, founder of Xia dy-
  nasty)**
—Chinese / Christie, 144(index)
YUGOSLAVIA
—Dictionary / Leach, 1236 (index)
YULETIDE
—Russian / Ivanits, 252 (index)

YURUKS
—Turkey / Walker, 310 (index)

ZAMBIA
—Hamilton / In the Beginning *
  Lozi people: creation myth, 64–
    67
ZEBRA
—Greaves / Hippo * 102–103 @
  how zebra got stripes, 99–102
  special prey of wild dogs, 35–38
  zebra's only choice: striped coat,
    97–99
ZECHARIAH
—Jewish / Sadeh
  dybbuk: haunt of man who killed
    Zechariah, 159–160
ZEUGLODON
—Monsters / Cohen, 187–188 @
ZEUS
—Cotterell / Encyclopedia, 259 (in-
    dex)
—D'Aulaire / Greek * 192 (index)
—Douglas / Magic *
  Europa and Zeus, 181–184
—Fahs / Old *
  Deucalion's flood; cruel greed
    punished, 58–63
  Prometheus brings fire to man-
    kind, 145–147
—Gods / Schwab, 764 (index)
—Greek / Switzer, 208 (index)
—Grimal / Dictionary, 603 (index)
  genealogical tables, 526–527 @
—Hamilton / In the Beginning *
  Kronos; Pandora, 132–137, 138–
    147
—Legends / Cavendish, 433 (index)
—Lore of Love
  A Groom for the sea-lord's
    daughter, 8–15
—Man Myth & Magic, 3181 (index)

—Mercatante / Encyclopedia, 807 (index)
—Room / Classical Dict
by-names (list), 330–335 @
ZODIAC
—Babylonia / Spence, 412 (index)
—Constellations / Gallant * 203 (index)
—Davidson / Dictionary
angelic governors, 342
—Pellowski / Story *
why years are named (Buddhist)
for animals, 87–89
—Precious Stones / Kunz, 406 (index)
—Witch Hndbk / Bird * 38–39
ZOHAR
—Schwartz / Gates, 815 (index)
ZOMBIE
—McGowen / Encyclopedia * 62
—Monsters / Cohen, 281–283 @
—Restless / Cohen *

Haiti: deadly dinner: Matthieu
Toussel, 60–72
—Unnatural / Cohen, 119–129
ZOO
—Dramatized / Kamerman
Peter and the wolf, 375–380
ZOOLATRY
—Egyptian / Mercatante, 215 @
ZOROASTER (-tian)
—Dictionary / Leach, 1236 (index)
—Fahs / Old *
Zoroaster: Mazda vs. Manyu,
140–147
—Legends / Cavendish, 134–
135
—Persian / Hinnells, 143 (index)
ZU (storm-god)
—Babylonia / Spence, 412 (index)
Zuni Indians, see INDIANS: ZUNI.
ZURVANISM
—Persian / Hinnells, 74–90, 143 (index)

ABOUT THE AUTHOR

JOSEPH SPRUG has master's degrees in philosophy and library science, both from The Catholic University of America, and both of which he has taught. Since 1947 he has had full-time administrative positions in college/university, public, and special libraries. In addition, he has reviewed hundreds of books, made indexes for more than 500 books, edited a periodical index, had ten books (all indexes) published, and served on national, professional library associations. He organized the Gimbel Aeronautical History Collection at the U.S. Air Force Academy. At present he continues to do freelance indexing and is cataloging the Richard McKeon philosophy collection at Mount Angel Abbey in Oregon.

Comments on this Index, and suggestions for the next compilation of *Index to Fairy Tales* (in preparation), are invited.

Joseph Sprug
Mount Angel Abbey Library
Mount Angel, Oregon 97373